The
INCREDIBLE
UMBRELLA
Tetralogy

The Incredible Umbrella

The Incredible Umbrella in Oz

The Amorous Umbrella

The Cosmic Umbrella

Also by Marvin Kaye

Ghosts of Night & Morning

Fantastique

The Last Christmas of Ebenezer Scrooge

The Passion of Frankenstein

The

INCREDIBLE
UMBRELLA

Tetralogy

MARVIN KAYE

WILDSIDE PRESS

CONTENTS

INTRODUCTION

Writing the Incredible Umbrella stories came naturally to me. I grew up loving literature in all the incarnations that appear in the first three books: namely and in order the worlds of (1) Gilbert and Sullivan; (2) Charles Dickens and Arthur Conan Doyle; (3) the world of horror, notably Bram Stoker's *Dracula*, Mary Shelley's *Frankenstein* and the short ghostly stories of E. F. Benson; (4) Henry Fielding's *Jonathan Wild*; (5) the Arabian Nights; (6) Edwin Abbott's *Flatland*; (7) Fairyland; (8) the world of American daytime dramas—soap operas; (9) the worlds of Shakespeare; and finally, L. Frank Baum's Oz.

My first literary agent was William B. R. Reiss of the Paul Reynolds Agency, later the John Hawkins Agency. Bill sold my first Hilary Quayle mysteries and my first non-fiction books. One day he suggested that he could probably sell a novel based on one of Dr. Watson's stories not yet told in Arthur Conan Doyle's Sherlock Holmes series. I thought of one at once and immediately began to write *The Incredible Umbrella*, which was published in 1979 by Doubleday after the first parts appeared in *Fantastic* magazine. My editor Pat LoBrutto wanted me to start right away on a sequel, which I was unprepared to do, but he told me that if I did he'd also buy a book of my short stories; well, short story collections are hard to sell, so of course I said and started on *The Amorous Umbrella* (when my colleagure Jane Yolen heard the title she laughed loud and long). Though written second, "Amorous" was meant to be third in the series. Doubleday published it in 1981.

When my late friend Parke Godwin read my first Umbrella book he said, "This is you writing with your shoes off."

Reviews were universally favorable for the first Umbrella book. It was sometimes remarked that I was obviously influenced by L. Sprague deCamp & Fletcher Pratt's "Incompleat Enchanter" series and to some extent this is true. But a much greater influence was John Myers Myers's wonderful fantasy novel *Silverlock*.

Pat contracted for the third title in the series, but I was going through a difficult period and just couldn't write comedy at that time, so Doubleday voided my contract, though they were so generous they did not ask for the advance to be repaid.

A long time passed. Then in 2014, I began a long period of quick and enjoyable writing, including several plays, the final volume of *The Masters of Solitude* trilogy and the remaining Umbrella stories, *The Incredible Umbrella in Oz* and *The Cosmic Umbrella*. The Oz story turned out to be much shorter, a novella, while "Cosmic" is a short story.

I'm glad to see them finally assembled and as of this writing with illustrations by my friend the cartoonist and writer Marc Bilgrey. The order that they should be read in is as they appear in this volume: *The Incredible Umbrella, The Incredible Umbrella in Oz, The Amorous Umbrella* and *The Cosmic Umbrella*.

—Marvin Kaye
Manhattan, New York
January 2016

THE INCREDIBLE UMBRELLA

*To Dick Wexelblat with love for a lifelong friendship
and for introducing me to most of these characters;
to William B.R. Reiss for conceiving the original idea
and then representing it. And thanks to Ted White,
Sol Cohen and Pat Lo Brutto for having such devilishly
intelligent senses of humor.*

PART I

EPILOGUE

"We've a first-rate assortment of magic," ["We've a first-rate assortment" etc. is a quote from Wells's first act patter song] said the dapper little merchant. He swept his manicured hand in a vague gesture, indicating the cabalistic paraphernalia cluttering the room's niches and nooks. "Some of my stock, in fact, is so odd that even *I* haven't begun to explore its possibilities. You have no idea, therefore, how happy I am to make your acquaintance, Mr...?" He twirled his finger in an embarrassed gesture. "Forgive my absentmindedness. When you've got one foot in this world and the other in the next, it's difficult to remember where one's head is!"

"Perhaps," said his companion, "I'd better give you my card."

"Ah, quite," said the merchant, "and I must let you have one of mine. Bit of a commercial puff, you know, but you'll find all the necessaries thereon..." The two rummaged in their pockets, withdrew billfolds, extracted and proffered to one another neat white identificatory pasteboards.

The little merchant examined his visitor's calling-card with unexpressed disapproval. It *was* so dry, so lacking in showmanship...

J. ADRIAN FILLMORE

38 C Pugh Street
College Hills, Penna.
377-0725

"I presume this is the seat of some institution of higher learning?" he asked.

Fillmore nodded. "My alma mater, as well as my current...or, rather, recent locus of employment is Parker College. I teach—taught?—English literature, American drama, Shakespeare. You've heard of him?"

"Yes, yes," the other said. "He is often quoted, or at least paraphrased. In fact, we have a court of Elsinore, don't you know?"

The pedagogue puzzled for a moment, leaning his stocky frame back in the overstuffed morris chair that occupied a corner of the magician's back-room. Then his brows unknitted. "Of course," he ventured, "there was a one-act play, was there not? *Rosencrantz*—"

"Don't tell me!" the magician interrupted. "I had rather not inquire too deeply into the literature of your time; I might grow curious as to my own fate and you, no doubt, would be rash enough to tell me! However, if I may venture to alter the topic—?" Fillmore nodded.

"I am rather curious to hear your tale."

"But I thought—" began the other, pointing in the direction of the fireplace.

The magician rose, walked to the side of the grate where he had propped the umbrella. He picked it up and examined it. It was a curiously large instrument and had evidently seen much usage: the handle was tarnished and the grip was frayed; the once-vibrant colors, though still startling, had faded and the material itself was worn. Holding it, he twirled it in his hands.

"Yes, yes," he said to Fillmore, "I know perfectly well your mode of passage. This instrument is one of mine, without doubt—one of my earliest models, in fact. It also happens to be the very first to make its way back to me and the circumstance fills me with delight! I've wondered how effective some of my spells are. This makes me so happy I'm rather inclined to sing about it—"

"No, no!" his guest protested. "I've had quite enough of that sort of thing for some time, thank you. I should prefer my arias confined within the context of a recital or operatic production."

"As you will," the magician replied, somewhat vexed. "However, if you insist on prose, let me prevail on you to supply it. For I really cannot restrain myself in these climes..." With that, he began clearing his throat in a sort of intoned warning which might have become a full-fledged *arpeggio* if Fillmore hadn't hastened to speak.

"Very well, then. I suppose you would like the details of my trip?"

"Oh, quite," said the magician. "Begin if you will with the finding of this trinket. And, for heaven's sake, catch me up to date on your adventures here: the mixture of customs must be most amusing."

Fillmore frowned. "*That* is certainly relative to one's vantage-point. However—"

Holding up his hand, the magician kept the resultant silence long enough to replace the umbrella by the fireside. Then he scurried back to his seat. But on the way, he passed the piano; pausing briefly there, he struck up a pompous fanfare, then plumped himself back down on the sofa.

"I couldn't resist," he giggled, wiggling into a comfortable listening posture.

Fillmore cleared his throat.

CHAPTER ONE

The first semester following a seventh-year sabbatical is bound to be a let-down, but in Fillmore's case, it was disastrous. To begin with, the research grant had not come through, so he'd been forced to venture to London on his own meager nest-egg. Once there, he learned, to his dismay, that no amount of pleading, cajoling or upbraiding would enable him to study the original promptscript for *The Yeomen of the Guard*. Thus, the entire excursion had no point at all; even the opportunity to see, in person, the locality of the Boar's-Head Tavern and the monetary establishment that occupied the portion of Baker Street once tenanted by more illustrious men could not assuage the young man's bitter disappointment.

There was so little time left and he had postponed the dissertation so long that he stood in danger of losing his position. To make matters infinitely worse, Dover had been promoted, in his absence, to dean of the arts and letters college and that meant Fillmore would have to work with a new thesis adviser: either Cable, a total incompetent, or Quintana, with whom he simply could not get along.

The worst of it was that Fillmore couldn't care less. The planning of his sabbatical research had been so long in the formulation and the initial correspondence had been so encouraging that the ultimate result was all the more crushing. If the trustees hadn't been sick or on vacation, he might have been successful; but the only one he'd gotten to see was a business manager who'd dismissed the quest—and his letters of introduction—with the sort of offhand rudeness that one might seek in vain to find a twin to in any other business but the theatre.

So he really didn't care if this meant the loss of his teaching position or not. He was in one of those moods in which nothing suited him—neither his name, which he'd always more or less detested; his too-stocky frame, too short to impress anyone but a Welshman; his native reticence, which consigned him to dateless nights and losing debates. He hated his job, his insufficient salary, his cramped apartment and his equally unspacious VW, which stood in its usual disrepair in the back of the apartment building...unwashed, untuned, uncomfortable.

* * * *

It was an autumn afternoon when he walked across the leafy mall past the administration building and into the cheerless concrete shell that housed the literature college. The sun slanted obliquely through shedding treetops and flickered off the glassy particles embedded in the walkway that branched out of the mall. A girl in slacks, hair tied in a ponytail, brushed past Fillmore, teasing his nose with the overdose of perfume she'd doused upon her wrists. Somewhere a bell chimed the hour of three. As he mounted the steps to the side door of Mallin Hall, he could just catch the reflection of his unsmiling face in the glass of the door: his penetrating eyes looked past his too-familiar features and studied the departing contours of the scented coed on the path behind him.

Sighing, Fillmore opened the door and entered the gloom of the stairwell.

"Well, well, young man, it looks like we'll be working together," rumbled Quintana without the least hint of pleasure at the idea. "We'll have to shape up, now won't we? *Won't we?*"

Standing by the triple bank of windows giving on the flank of classroom seats, Fillmore allowed his attention to wander. The autumn sun was shedding a cozy glow over the rolling landscape and he would give much to be anywhere else than in the predictable world of the Parker department of English literature, listening to the predictable admonitions of the gross department head, Quintana.

"You know, of course, that you have one scant semester to polish off that dissertation, do you not? And that means beginning all over again, choosing an entirely new topic...which I must approve. If not—well, you certainly must be aware that I will have no recourse—Damn it, Fillmore, *are* you listening?"

Turning abruptly around, Fillmore had to waste a second refocusing his eyes to the unlighted interior of the classroom. Quintana was sitting up straight in the wooden seat behind the nicked old desk, his jowly face hard to discern in the gloom. Behind him, the green slateboard helped further weary the eyes; it was a mass of notes and diagrams pertaining to the birth dates of various Victorian writers.

"When," Quintana rasped, "will you stop woolgathering? *When?*"

"Can't say," Fillmore yawned, with no attempt to cover his mouth. "Perhaps never."

And he walked out, paying no attention to the other's raving.

* * * *

Of course, it was an immature action; he was well aware how childish it must appear, how strongly it must reinforce Quintana's prejudices against him. But the oppressive midday demon of apathy had taken possession of Fillmore, buffering him from any consideration of his action's probable aftermath. At worst, he would be let go and what matter whether that transpired now or thirteen weeks hence?

Outside, Fillmore drew in a revitalizing breath of September air. It was the kind of day when, if he were still an undergraduate, he would have gone wandering in the russet-and-green hills, writing sonnets to dark ladies he had yet to meet. Undergraduates sat about upon the campus lawns, some with books cracked, others merely enjoying one another's company. The steps of the library beckoned upward to the selfless pleasures within, but Fillmore resisted, preferring the expansiveness of the unbounded afternoon.

Walking towards the town's main street (some hundred yards down the sloping mall), he loitered here and there, watching birds pecking residues of bread from sidewalk-cracks, gazing at squirrels seeking acorns in the autumn grass. Out on the front lawn facing Old Main a company of ROTC students waited out the cadences of a military march performed by a student band. An airplane droned above; had Fillmore cared to look up and risk scorching his corneas, he would have seen the ship's silhouette partially blotting out the sun's shining round.

On such an afternoon, Fillmore decided, there was only one thing he could possibly enjoy doing. So he passed through the vaulting gate that arched the lower end of the mall and walked down Allen Avenue to the spot where he'd parked the VW. Climbing in, he nosed into the sparse traffic, made a U-turn and drove off to Interstate 15A-S.

* * * *

Like a ghost keeping a vigil, ["Like a ghost keeping a vigil" paraphrases a duet from G&S's *The Yeomen of the Guard*.] Fillmore haunted all the book-and-curio shops in every burg and village within a fifty-mile radius of College Heights. Almost any Saturday, after eating a modest breakfast, he would hop into the VW and pick some likely direction: for the next several hours, he would lose himself in myriads of junk shops, antique stores, Salvation Army rescue mission centers—anywhere he could snuffle around like a foraging animal rummaging for tidbits.

Old books, antiques, 78rpm recordings, side-tables, stereopticons, Edison thick-discs, comic books and calendars: all were interesting to him; it was Fillmore's principal amusement and (fortunately for his reduced post-sabbatical budget) still remained within the reach of his pocketbook.

His favorite browsing spot was a converted garage halfway up an unpaved driveway in Bellavista Falls, ten miles south of Parker College. Nameless, it was a linoleumed place run by a woman named Rose. A perimeter of bookshelves (unfinished pine nailed together in random fashion) around the shop walls enclosed a few tables of oddities.

The selection, though limited, was frequently renewed and the white-haired proprietress kept her prices modest...not that she was unaware of the value of every treasure in her stock, far from it. But Rose plain refused to profiteer, as she put it, from a pastime of her "dotage."

"Besides," she once told Fillmore, "the prices I charge keeps *my* suppliers from getting suspicious.

And sometimes that means I can get my hands on a goodie that *I* want!"

He had never been able to figure out what the specializations of the skinny little shopkeeper were, but neither did he care, since they never seemed to conflict with his greatest interests.

A third reason for being partial to Rose's place was the fact that few fellow-collectors knew of it. It was just out of the way enough to prevent hordes of knowledgeable antiquarians and scholars from stripping it bare of its treasures...which would have equally displeased Rose and J. Adrian Fillmore. (Gad, how he hated that name!)

That afternoon he made a delightful haul—as he was wont to call the results of any particularly weighty collectorial trip. First, there was the Benziger edition of Benson's *A Mirror of Shallot*—only the second copy he had ever seen and the first he could afford. (Rose, in her paradoxical fashion, had penciled "weird tales—very scarce" in the flyleaf, then charged him $4.00 for it.) Then, he also found a hardback edition of Carr's *The Nine Wrong Answers*: though less illustrious than the Benson unearthing, it was a scarce title nonetheless, especially since the paperback editions were all abridged; at any rate, it was a bargain at 19¢. (Where did she come up with her figures?)

From the record rack, he actually plucked a mint condition of "Dipper Mouth Blues," which he'd long decided was apocryphal, and—though he rarely bought second-hand LPs—took a chance on the venerable "*Mikado*" which had Robert Rounseville in the role of Nanki-Poo; it was the last remaining album of that brilliant but woefully under-recorded tenor that Fillmore lacked to make his Rounseville collection complete...

"Is that all, young man?" Rose asked, as she tallied up the tab.

"I think so, Rose. I seem to have gotten something—uh—interesting from most of the tables and racks today."

"Curios," she sniffed, resettling the rimless glasses on her thin-bridged nose. "You hardly look at them."

"Yes," said Fillmore, "but I can scarcely afford everything in the shop and—"

"Now," she interrupted, taking him by the sleeve and pulling him back to the centre of the shop, where the antique table stood, "if you don't like what's here, you don't have to buy. But I'd think, if I were going to drive all the way in from College Heights, I'd take a bare minute to inspect every last little goodie."

With a resigned shrug—but with a perfectly good will—Fillmore examined with greater care the table of odds and ends he'd casually noted earlier on his path to the books.

As he browsed, Rose stood looking off into space, no particular expression—or, at least, no interpretable one—on her puckered face. Leaning against a bookcase, she kept her hands dug deep in the large pocket of her rose-print cotton dress. ("Don't care how cold it is," she would say. "I don't change to wool until the calendar tells me it's winter!")

The only sound disturbing the late autumn afternoon was the muted ticking of the ship's-clock upon the reinforced soapbox where Rose kept her cigarbox of change and bills. Several minutes passed by, but—save for Fillmore's gently sentient inspection—nothing stirred in the garage-shop.

But at last, the collector looked up from the table and sought the businesswoman's attention. He had an odd object in his hand: a long, heavy pole that ended in a large flounce of some silky material emblazoned with orange-and-yellow stripes on which various cabalistic symbols seemed to dance in pastel figurations.

It was clearly an umbrella, but its size was rather impractical: too large for everyday use, too small for beach-basking. The grip, made of blackest leather, was somewhat worn away; it seemed to turn slightly. The cloth shade was frayed and the colors, though startling enough, were yet faded from what must have been their initial brilliance.

Fillmore couldn't place the period or design: it seemed too ludicrous for serious commercial distribution. And yet, if it were a toy, it could not possibly be lifted by even the most sinewy urchin. Perhaps it was a theatrical prop of some sort?

"Oh, that," sneered Rose. "Pretty, ain't it? It's no good—don't work worth a damn."

"How doesn't it work?"

"Won't open."

"Oh." Fillmore, disappointed, started to lay the instrument back down. As he did, he spied some inscription on the inside; pushing up the cloth a little ways, he peered to make out the words half-obliterated by frequent handling.

Along the length of the pole were three letters: NGT. Opposite them, halfway around the circumference was another line, but time also had worn it down to near-illegibility. The only thing discernible was a number and the beginnings of another word: 70 SIM—Fillmore replaced the umbrella on the table.

"Oh, I really thought you might be interested in that one," Rose sighed.

"Well," said Fillmore, "I *might* fancy it, if I only knew a little more about it. Where it comes from, for instance. But not only is it nondescript...according to you, it doesn't even function. How much did you want for it, anyway?"

"It's cluttering up perfectly good table space," the woman grumbled, then waved her hand in disgust. "Give me a quarter and take it away."

* * * *

"A pittance for my masterpiece?" raged the magician. "And my latest models fetch seven-and-six! And that's without those tatty astrologic symbols rimed all over the cloth!" Popping a pill in his mouth, he held his pulse and waited until it slowed. "Well, never mind, lad," he said, "I pray you please resume." He delivered the latter request in recitative.

CHAPTER TWO

It was raining the following morning and Fillmore watched the streaks of water trace interminable tears down the cold faces of his bedroom windows. He had no classes to teach that day and he was so lethargic that he might have been content to stay in bed and stare at the patterns upon the panes.

But at length he forced himself to rise, wash his face and teeth and shave. His attention wandered during the latter process, but the tiny wounds he kept inflicting on himself called him back repeatedly. When he'd finished with the ritual, Fillmore ruefully surveyed his face: the skin, once he'd daubed it with styptic, was clear and it showed few wrinkles; of course there was the merest trace of crow's-feet about the eyes, but that was not entirely due to age. There was once a time when Fillmore toyed with the notion of becoming an actor: daily he would emote before mirrors, working with grimace and greasepaint to cultivate a pair of Byronic eyes...like a "demon's that is dreaming"; brooding; introspective. The result, now that Fillmore had abandoned histrionic presumptions and now that he was a staid teacher-cum-doctoral candidate, was that his eyes always felt strained and pained: tired mirrors of a weary spirit.

He dressed slowly, choosing one of the lusterless gray wool suits that served as unofficial uniforms for Parker College pedants. His only flight of personal taste was reserved for the neckwear he looped about his throat: a loud silk ascot. Many were the stuffy afternoons when he'd throttled his 16½ neck with a sober Windsor-knot tie. At last, he protested the fitless shirts at his clothier's—only to find that there was no way short of customizing to fit his broad-shouldered frame and thick throat into the same garment. Having no choice but to buy medium shirts with collars too small for him, he elected to breathe freely: leaving the top shirt-button always open, he affected the ascot, much to the tacit horror of the hidebound Quintana.

Fillmore supposed he ought to do his best to avoid offending the department head on this of all days, yet he could not bring himself to choke off his windpipe with a tie, even under the present desperate circumstances.

He had already decided he would have to kowtow to Quintana. Upon waking that morning with the damp chill of autumn thunderstorm penetrating the bedroom, Fillmore immediately recalled his rude exit from the previous day's session. There would be no alternative, he realized: he must humble himself, beg forgiveness on the grounds, perhaps, that his sour sabbatical had left him temporarily witless.

Yet he took plenty of time getting ready for the distasteful ceremony. After dressing, he spent the better part of an hour idling through the morning papers while dawdling over a glass of reconstituted orange juice, a half-burned piece of toast with margarine and instant coffee with powdered cream substitute—none of which, fortunately, he bothered to taste. The postman shoved a few letters under the door; he perused them without interest...a subscription renewal form for the *Journal of Aesthetics*, an envelope full of discount coupons for popular-brand cereals and detergents and the telephone bill.

After washing the dishes and after he'd doused them with boiling water, Fillmore entered the living-room, where he began to fleck the dust from the tops of the furniture. But, as usual when there were books about, his attention wandered within five minutes.

At first he leafed through his new acquisitions of the day before. Then, noting one of the stories in the Benson volume, he rooted about among his anthologies trying to find where he'd first come across the tale. Successful in that quest, he went to something else; so, by further tangencies too convoluted to record, Fillmore lost himself for the better part of an hour in the solacing solitude of his library.

Just before he remembered his obligatory ordeal-to-come, he was browsing through *Studies of Literature* when he came across an article on Gilbert and Sullivan by Arthur Quiller-Couch. One passage in particular caught Fillmore's eye:

> What disgusts one in Gilbert from the beginning to the end, is his insistence on the physical odiousness of any woman growing old. As though, Great Heaven! they themselves did not find it tragic enough—the very and necessary tragedy of their lives!

Gilbert shouts it, mocks it, apes with it, spits upon it. He opens with this dirty trump card in *Trial by Jury*...

"What in all good hell is he talking about?" Fillmore asked aloud. "There aren't any old ladies in *Trial by Jury*. Except for the elderly, ugly daughter of the rich attorney in the judge's song. How does that go?...

> '...But I soon got tired of third-class journeys,
> And dinners of bread and water;
> So I fell in love with a rich attorney's
> Elderly ugly daughter.'

"And the judge becomes rich because of all the business the grateful attorney sends his way and—

> 'At length I became as rich as Gurneys—
> An incubus then I thought her,
> So I threw over that rich attorney's
> Elderly ugly daughter...'"

"Good Gad, is that what Quiller-Couch was complaining about? The only person the song mocks is the cad of a judge himself. Hmmm! I'll have to nickname him Quiller-Grouch from now on..."

Just then Fillmore spied the kitchen clock through the living-room portal. It was just after eleven; he simply couldn't postpone the distasteful appointment with Quintana any longer. He must seek him out and, if needs be, grovel.

* * * *

As he wrapped his scarf about his throat and struggled with the heavy rubber rain-slicker, Fillmore continued to wrestle with the problem of W. S. Gilbert's old ladies.

It was a cliché of Gilbertian scholarship that the librettist-dramatist treated his old women cavalierly. Yet, thought Fillmore, I can hardly call any cogent examples to mind: Katisha, I suppose, in *The Mikado* and Ruth in *The Pirates of Penzance*...

The thought was abruptly cut off as he opened the apartment-house door and was nearly drenched. In his preoccupation with the scholastic problem, he'd neglected to don overshoes or take an umbrella out of the coat-closet.

Like Shelley's Frankenstein, Fillmore loved to slosh through a wild thundershower, untrammeled natural forces singeing his gray-tinged locks; but there were limits to transcendental pleasures and this downpour, he told himself, was one of them. If it meant his hairline would be plastered upon his brow in strings and if it meant the sacrifice of his trousers-crease, then it was high time to consider prudent covering from the storm.

Nodding absently to a neighbor, Fillmore returned to his apartment to fetch overshoes and bumbershoot.

* * * *

While laboring to pull the recalcitrant galoshes over his black Bostonians, Fillmore had two thoughts, only one of which was laudable.

"Why not pursue this problem of the old ladies?" he asked himself. "The research I've done won't be wasted: I can find a good basis here, I should imagine, for a new dissertation topic."

Having at last stretched the rubbers over his shoes, he reached into the closet again for his austere black umbrella. Then he had his second thought and withdrew his hand.

"Well, of course she said it wouldn't work, but let's see, all the same..." Entering his bedroom, he opened up the extra closet where he kept his curios and took out the peculiar object of his musings. It looked larger than he remembered and its garish colors and devices, faded though they were, practically glowed in the drab, chilly bedroom.

Was there a catch along the pole to release the hood? Yes, there was and Fillmore pressed it. But nothing happened.

"Rose must have been right," he sighed. "The button's stuck. How Quintana's eyes would have popped!" Now that the decision was out of his hands, Fillmore told himself he never would have *really* walked into the department head's office carrying the outlandish rain-guard. Yet it would have been a noble gesture, a vestigial symbol of dignity.

Even as he thought it, Fillmore laughed. Imagine this gaudy oddment being construed as dignified! Staring at himself in the mirror, he made a comical face and twirled the umbrella once around by the handle in Chaplinesque fashion.

There was a sudden snap. The release button popped out an eighth of an inch farther from the pole.

* * * *

"Precisely so," said the magician. "The handle was never loose; it's a safety catch. Prevents the fool thing from slipping open by accident. Of course, it's not necessary on the later models. We've worked out all the bugs by now—"

* * * *

Fillmore pressed the release and the umbrella snapped open. My

God, he thought, it's bigger than I imagined, even considering how bulky it is...

The hood stretched out to the furthest corners of the room, blocking off the ceiling. It grew and grew, blotting from sight the entire room, the street below, the town. It hid the world.

Yet through the translucent material, Fillmore could still see the pale sunlight creeping through the rain-laved windowpane. But even as he watched, he saw the sunbeams grow stronger and commence to beat and glow as if the pulse of the universe were behind and the umbrella-hood was the heart-wall of the cosmos.

The perimeter of the cloth was a single, seamless circle. But Fillmore, astonished, suddenly realized that, like a wing, it was fluctuating in the wind.

Wind?!

Gravity shifted: his stomach executed an Immelman turn. The umbrella was no longer above him. He was streaming head-first after its downward flight and the wind plucked fiercely at him, trying to rip him away from the incredible instrument.

Then it reversed once more and he soared into cacophonous night, alive with vague glints of color. Whether he was hurtling over some plain or through some void, he did not know, for he dared not look down. He clung with both hands to the umbrella-grip and his arms began to ache. Fillmore fastened his gaze upon the bizarre shapes and colors emblazoned on the hood above, but he suddenly closed his eyes tight.

"I'm going mad," he thought, "or else the whole world's turned topsy-turvy!"

For the suddenly-sinister cabalistic symbols seemed as possessed by the elemental fury of flight as the umbrella itself.

To his vast surprise, all sensation of rising and falling ceased as soon as he closed his eyes. Above him, the umbrella folded up. His feet touched grass and summer sun shone upon his wind-chapped cheeks.

Fillmore opened his eyes. As he did, a fanfare sounded from somewhere nearby. It was like the beginning of an overture.

CHAPTER THREE

It *was* an overture.

The merry strains of some sprightly gigue or hornpipe seemed to shimmer on the sunny air: as Fillmore listened, amazed, entranced, the music passed through a transitory passage into a sweetly doleful refrain. Then, before his spirit could be more than minimally mellowed by the gentle melancholy of the subject, the music was off again in a sprightly run of violins and violas, overlarded with scampering trills of piccolo, flute and clarinet.

The only trouble with the delightful serenade was that it seemed to have no point of origin. It pervaded the air, rang about the teacher's ears, swelled up from the ground...but proceeded from no discernible source. Yet it was so gracious and pleasing to his ears that, for the first time in many dreary, disappointing months, Fillmore felt refreshed, at rest. The fact that he had just undergone some undefinable transference did not, for the moment, disturb him; he enjoyed the cool breezes and warm sun bathing his upturned face. He remained still until the last melodic strains died away into the whispered sibilance of the nearby zephyr and a not-too-distant seaside.

Fillmore was standing on a grassy knoll overlooking a rocky seacoast. In the distance, a calm sea bore up an anchored schooner. Along the horizon, a network of rock-faces, wattled with caves, described a jagged skyline; from some point directly in front of the nether cave-mouth, smoke ascended, but the roll of the grassy mound on which he stood cut off the source of the haze from his vision.

In the other direction, as far as Fillmore could see, a gentle meadowland rolled parallel to the stony abutments of the coast. The landscape was deserted and the only movement was the bending of the grass-field under the caress of the breeze that carried warm summer smells to his nose. Overhead, a seagull wheeled lazily a moment, then dove towards the sea. At the perimeter of the water, the surf broke smoothly in places, while in others, the rocks sticking out into the sea kicked up spume that glinted like a shower of gems in the sunlight. The sky was pastel blue, noon-bright and cloudless.

Lowering the now-shut umbrella so that its point rested against the ground, Fillmore found himself surprisingly apathetic to the fact that he had just undergone an impossible polarity of physical circumstance: where he had been indoors, he was now in an unpopulated expanse; where it was raining, it was now sunny; where it had been autumn, it was now late spring or early summer. And Parker College was land-locked and hemmed in by the ancient Appalachians; but this unfamiliar seascape thrilled with the tang and promises of ocean voyages and far lands. He had always loved the sea, detested the claustrophobic mountains that enclosed him in with the petty systems and niggling tyrannies of his parochial life.

Thus, he experienced a curious emotional tranquility in the face of a circumstance that would have thoroughly disoriented another mortal. But Fillmore, nurtured on the fantasies and utopias of the imaginative fiction that he loved, was well prepared for magical transposition: unconsciously, he had longed for it so long that it rather seemed tardy, having come.

As he stood upon the bluff taking in unpolluted ocean air, he was aware, rationally at least, that he may have lost his faculties. But even in thought, he scoffed at the possibility of experiencing sensory impressions while simultaneously doubting their very existence. He was too much of a post-Nietzschean to negate himself in an Oriental wash of cosmic solipsism. "No," he told himself, "I've actually been propelled elsewhere." The umbrella clearly was the mode of transit...but what sort of propulsion might it represent? Spatial, temporal or dimensional?

He examined the device once more, seeking evidence of some recognizable mechanical principle employed in the intricacies of the instrument. But his scrutiny was unsuccessful. Fillmore decided to try it again, this time studying the mode of operation. He turned the handle, watched the catch pop out once more. He pressed it with his finger.

Nothing happened. Fillmore fiddled with the release, shoved the movable shaft forward up the pole, plucked at the folds of the hood. But the umbrella would not open again.

* * * *

"I didn't engineer it that way," the magician remarked. "But apparently there are physical laws governing it. I've seen it myself. You've got to finish a sequence..."

* * * *

Just as a graduate student pigeonholes interesting bits of information that crop up on tangents to the main thrust of his research, so Fillmore set aside for later musings the murky issue of his transposition and whether it was the product of superior technology, sinister sorcery or a deranged mentality.

The day was too lovely to let gloomy thoughts dominate him. Slipping off rubbers, slicker and scarf, he carelessly dropped them on the ground and began walking in the direction of the cave-pocked cliff-side, swinging his umbrella as he spryly sprang over the resilient earth of the green knoll. Overhead, the seagull, sated, circled lazily. The surf plashed with the predictability of a pre-classical passacaglia.

Walking, Fillmore began to hum light-heartedly to himself...a rare practice for the pedant. After some minutes, the hum grew into a kind of wordless caroling. He stopped, amazed, delighted; the corners of his mouth crinkled up. How long had it been since he'd sung to himself out loud?

Imagine what one of his sober-faced colleagues would think of such unorthodox behavior! He laughed, considering the notion and resolved what he might do should he come on some dour-visaged professorial type upon his balmy seafront.

Fitting notion to action, he warbled in improvised recitative: "Good gentleman, I pray you tell me what clime this is? I prithee speak, oh speak, I pray you!"

"Why?" intoned a basso nearby. "Who are you who asks this question?"

Fillmore started. All blithe resolve collapsed miserably with the knowledge that he'd been heard and evidently mocked. He blushed mightily.

By that time, Fillmore was standing on a sandy plain at the foot of the low bluff. The seaside was directly off and to his right. In the distance, he could see the fire that produced the smoke wafting above the cliff-wall. A group of people were huddled about it, but they were too far away to distinguish.

The person who'd spoken—or rather chanted—was much nearer, some twenty-five feet away and just rounding a small out-cropping between the spot where Fillmore stood and the sea.

The scholar gaped at the newcomer's outlandish appearance. A tall, portly man in his middle ages, he walked in a curious swaggering manner that was almost a dance-step. He had flaming red hair, an immense bristling mustache jutting out several inches on either side of his face and a Mephistophelean goatee just above the rugged jawline. But his barb was what astounded Fillmore: treading in calf-high hard-leather black boots, the stranger wore purple, satiny slacks partially obscured by a yellow vest, over which had been draped a long purple coat (of a different shade than the trousers) with huge brass buttons and reinforced cuffs. A lace ruffle encircled the bull-neck and on the man's head was perched a flat black hat with the lateral curve of a boomerang. Above his waist, there was a leather belt fully four inches wide, buckled in front; in it was thrust a pair of single-shot pistols of so antique a design that Fillmore recognized them at once. Yet they gleamed, both barrel and wood, as if new-purchased.

When the other approached near enough for normal converse, Fillmore spoke. "I beg your pardon, but I seem to be lost. Where am I?"

"Cornwall," the other lilted, still chanting. "And who are you?"

Fillmore was mildly annoyed. He'd gotten the point; was there any necessity for the stranger to further mock his recent outburst of musical high spirits?

However, choosing to ignore the affront, he satisfied the stranger's curiosity by briefly identifying himself by name and occupation.

"If you will come with me," the other said, still intoning, "I will deem it a pleasure. Permit me to introduce myself: Samuel is my name." His voice fell on the last phrase and the invisible strings described a two-note cadence.

Fillmore wasn't certain he wanted to accompany the odd stranger, but before he could express any objection, the fantastical Samuel had a pistol in each hand. With the merriest of smiles, he repeated his request. The scholar tried to put up his hands, but only succeeded with one, the umbrella being too heavy to loft single-limbed.

Stepping off in the direction Samuel indicated, they walked in silence. As they slogged along, Fillmore took occasional glances back at the bizarre figure. He certainly knew little enough about the customs of the Cornish (somewhere on the south coast of Britain, wasn't it?), but he doubted that they included the flamboyant costuming of his captor.

Before long, they came to a small precipice of rock just landward of the ring of people earlier spied. The various stone mounds cut them off from sight during the latter portion of his enforced walk.

At the foot of the precipice, Samuel bowed in courtly fashion, told Fillmore to be patient a moment, and—to the scholar's astonishment—rounded the rock and disappeared from view, leaving his captive unguarded.

Fillmore's initial impulse was to run. But not being an athlete, he doubted his chances in protracted pursuit across the havenless lea. So he did the next best thing: he hid. Climbing halfway up the face of the rock, he pressed himself as deep as he could into a shallow niche and awaited the development of events.

He hadn't long to wait. Presently, Samuel returned, followed by a small group of men dressed in similar fashion. One young man, obviously a person of some rank, was beardless and hatless; he wore a long face and walked arm-in-arm with a stout woman in her mid-forties. She was wearing long skirts, impractical for the country and time of year and had an ample corseted bodice and puffed shoulders.

"Well, Samuel?" the sad-faced youth asked. "Where is your prisoner?"

"Well, I left him here and requested that he wait," the other replied in a hurt voice. For once, he did not sing.

"Samuel," the woman asked, "did you ask him politely enough?"

"I was the embodiment of gentility!"

"But *did* you ask politely?" she persisted.

"Indeed, I did! Am I to blame because the chap hadn't the manners to wait? I took him most fair by the rocks below the bluff. You'd think he would have realized he was honor-bound to stay our coming." Shaking his head dolefully, Samuel looked away, scanning the skies with a vacant expression. He had the air of one grievously wronged. As his gaze passed near Fillmore's eyrie, the scholar squirmed as far back into the depression as the ungainly umbrella would permit. He had it behind his back, for fear its gaudiness would serve as telltale.

"I ask ye, Master Frederic," Samuel said, "is there aught for which I can be faulted?"

Frederic, the sad-faced youth, shook his head and in a rich tenor voice, intoned, unaccompanied: "By your lights, there is no crime. Nor should I have wished any other outcome to the happenstance adventure. But, Samuel, I fear I must tell you..."

"Aye?"

The young man hesitated. In the brief silence, Fillmore , upon his perch, heard the strains of a rum-tiddly-tum kind of music strike up from some invisible source.

"No," said Frederic, "I cannot fail in my duty to tell you, Samuel. Though it hurt your sensibilities, I must point out that no truly professional buccaneer would be as trusting or as kind hearted as you or the rest of our band appear to be!"

With that, the music swelled and Frederic continued his discourse in song:

> *The man would a pirate be,*
> *And ply his craft upon the sea*
> *Must learn to play a villainous part,*
> *With stiff upper lip and an ossified heart.*
> *Though lasses crave quarter with wailing and sighs,*
> *And maidens assail you with tears in their eyes,*
> *No mercy afford them—for oft I've heard say*
> *That women are pirates and steal hearts away.*

He broke into the refrain:

To be a buccaneer—

which the rest of the group echoed with

"—aneer—"

Frederic continued the chorus.

To be a buccaneer—
You must plunder and thunder
And send some ships under
And fill all your messmates with fear!

The other pirates—for it was by now apparent the kind of peril Fillmore faced—joined in with Frederic to repeat the chorus. Then the long-faced young man sang a second verse to Samuel.

The man who would a pirate be,
And quest for gold upon the sea
Must wear a scowl instead of a grin,
And never wait by till his prey ask him in.
And once you've elected to follow our trade—
Be cunning and daring and never afraid;
But should you be lacking in ruthless éclat,
* Just pick some attorney and pattern on that*
To be a buccaneer—

CHORUS:

—'aneer.

FREDERIC:

To be a buccaneer—
You must plunder and thunder
And send some ships under
And fill all your messmates with fear!

Joining in on the repeat of the chorus, the entire band copied Samuel's rolling gait and hornpiped their way around the rock and off to their camp, voices fading in the distance. The last *pizzicatti* plunked invisibly after them and the seaside again was silent and deserted.

Fillmore climbed down with some difficulty, the umbrella hindering the likelihood of a safe descent. When he reached the ground at last, he slumped against the pile, panting, as much winded as he was nonplussed.

For what he had just seen, there was nothing in Fillmore's philosophy to offer up a sensible explanation. Lacking the objective proof for determining whether he had gone mad, he had to content himself with the supposition that the things he'd seen and heard really existed.

Could the whole group be mad? But then, where did the music come from? A loudspeaker? Yet the perfect accord with which the pirates echoed Frederic's ostensibly spontaneous song was uncanny!

Fillmore laughed suddenly. Could it be that there was nothing more peculiar about the business than that he'd stumbled on some vacationing repertory company rehearsing at seaside, staying in character and, in true ensemble fashion, expanding and improvising on the dramatic material in which they were professionally involved?

If so, Fillmore was well aware of the show they were rehearsing. But he set the thought aside, not wishing to be reminded of a personally depressing subject.

He determined on a course of action: he would creep carefully round the stone and seek some safe vantage-point where he could study at greater leisure the comings and goings of this odd company.

* * * *

Five minutes later, he lay in a V-notched cut in the loam overhanging the pirate's camp. Below, Samuel stood in front of the assemblage of thieves, telling his story to the leader of the band: a large, shovelhatted individual seated on an ornate throne in the middle of the clearing. Over one eye, he wore a black patch and a skull-and-crossbones grinned gauntly from the standard clutched in his knuckly right hand.

As Samuel unfolded his tale, Fillmore noted once again the pistols thrust into the buccaneers belt; he began to question his theatrical-company theory.

Looking over the group, one by one, Fillmore noted that the sad-faced young man was absent. No sooner had he thought it than someone tapped him on the shoulder and he almost jumped out of the niche where he lay.

Whirling around and pushing himself to his feet with the aid of the umbrella-staff, Fillmore edged away from the ledge until he was out of sight of the pirates. He stared directly into the mournful eyes of young Frederic.

"Wh-what do you want?" he asked, clutching the umbrella for possible use as a weapon.

"Quick," Frederic replied, "there is no time! You must hurry away from here. Men who stick at no offenses—

Scarcely had he uttered "offenses" than *he* jumped and whirled. Behind him was the stout woman Fillmore had seen upon the path.

"Ruth! What are you doing here?"

"I followed you, master," said the formidable woman. "I see you've caught the scamp our dunderheaded Samuel let go."

"Ruth, I intend to let him fly from here."

"Indeed?" Ruth asked, then stepped in front of Frederic and scrutinized Fillmore with calculating feminine eyes. "Are you married, man?" she asked.

"No."

"Frederic," Ruth told her companion, "I feel I am required to point out that you are a pirate until next week and have a duty to serve the band to whom you are indentured."

"Thanks to you!" Frederic said bitterly. "You were supposed to apprentice me to a pilot, not a pirate!"

"Well," she whined, "I did not catch the word aright—"

"Through being hard of hearing," he finished, bored. "I note your affliction was remarkably short-lived. And pray do not sing me *that* song again of how you made the mistake! I've heard it more times than my stomach can take!" He emphasized the rhyme.

"Oh, is that so?" Ruth snarled. "Well, it just so happens that my deafness cleared up in the sea-air, Mr. Smarty! And as for my singing—"

"Please, please," Fillmore interrupted, clearing his throat, "haven't you forgotten about me?" He was beginning to enjoy his ridiculous predicament. A new theory had occurred to him, hardly original: but what if the entire experience really were a dream? In that case, he would just as soon have as much of it as possible before waking.

"Oh, terribly sorry," Frederic said. "Well, I suppose I *must* take you back down with us. Sorry for the inconvenience and all that—

> *But I really must plunder*
> *And thunder and blunder*
> *And act like a true buccaneer.*

He sang it unaccompanied, reaching high A on "true," after which he sniffed disdainfully at Ruth. Then, pointing to the descending, path, he waited for Fillmore to begin downwards, before following with Ruth upon his arm.

CHAPTER FOUR

The pirate king, who introduced himself as Richard, demanded that Fillmore give over all his money. The aftermath of that action turned the teacher's suspicion concerning the buccaneers into absolute certainty in his mind.

Placing the contents of his pocket upon the flat stone directly in front of the chief pirate's throne, Fillmore leaned against his umbrella-shaft and shrugged.

"That's the lot of it: $34 and a few odd coins. You might have picked some more prosperous prey."

"Here, here," the pirate king rumbled, pulling at the waxy black mustache that curled up impressively almost to his hairline. "What kind of trumpery do ye seek to foist off on us, young man?" He reached out and wadded up a chunk of bills in his fist, surveying it with suspicion. "I've never seen the likes of such currency!"

"Why, it's solid American legal tender," Fillmore protested.

The other stood up and glowered down on him from his one good eye. But Fillmore stared back, suppressing a smile. It was certainly a vivid dream! "Hear me, stranger," the pirate commanded, "I spent me earliest maiden voyage in the New World and I remember naught like this counterfeit ye've flaunted! Surely—"

"Here, here, Dick," Samuel rumbled, standing to the right of Fillmore, "the lad's right enough, even if he did insult me mightily. There's nothing else resembling money in his pockets."

"Indeed?" the king asked. "I should like to know how, then, he intended to get about in Cornwall? Or anyplace else in England for that matter!"

Fillmore held up a finger tentatively. "Your majesty, if you will permit me, I think I can explain my peculiar predicament" The scholar had, in fact, been doing some quick thinking and had come up with an idea which he proposed to put to the test: a method for gaining sympathy.

"Well," said the pirate, "we are a bit short for entertainment. Perhaps you might begin at the beginning and tell us your entire story."

"Very well," said Fillmore, "I am a professor—"

"No, no!" the king protested. "Begin when you were born and work forward!"

"I was going to allude to my birth," Fillmore said, "but if you wish it the long way around..."

"We do!" the pirates chorused in one voice.

"All right, then...I was born...And Fillmore was off, covering all the chief details of his life: his boyhood in Philadelphia, the early demise of both parents in an accident, his eventual supervision by a disinterested aunt whose only redeeming feature was the immense library she kept and let him roam in. He passed on to his friendless, though scholastically distinguished adolescence, touched upon his cheerless college days, followed by graduate work and his most recent position—he already regarded it as a closed epoch of his life—as doctoral candidate and literary instructor. Finally, he described the purchase of the umbrella and his strange journey to the Cornish coast.

When he was done, Fillmore noted with satisfaction that, except for Ruth and Frederic, there wasn't a dry eye among the pirates. He asked innocently what had touched them about his tale.

The pirate king, sniffing, answered in an andante baritonic passage, "Although our dark career sometimes involves the crime of stealing, we rather think that were not altogether void of feeling."

"The story that you've told," Samuel sang in continuation, "has robbed our hearts of joy—"

ALL: We pity you, poor fellow—

KING: For you are an o-o-orphan boy!

"Yes," said Fillmore, nodding gleefully, "I am an orphan boy."

The king looked at him oddly. The music ceased. "Well, I know you are, lad—but why didn't you sing it!"

Fillmore shrugged, chuckling to himself. He was right: these were physical embodiments of W.S. Gilbert's *Pirates of Penzance*! In the operetta, all the pirates, being orphans, were merciful to fellow unfortunates—and this outlandish throng followed suit, even to the extent of using a similar melodic response.

"Here, lad," said the king, waving a hand at Fillmore's pocket contents on the stone shelf, "take back your goods. And, as an orphan, you are automatically elected—"

"An honorary member of the band?" Fillmore asked smugly.

"That's right! How d'ye know?"

"Fey quality, I suppose," he replied, refraining from exposing a full rehearsal of the plot of *The Pirates of Penzance*. Cassandras, he recalled, are rarely believed and certainly never popular...

"Look here, Richard," Frederic addressed the chief of pirates from the door of an adjacent hut, "we can't allow the poor bloke to roam about without money, now can we?"

The other was vigorously shaking his head. "No, no, Frederic, I was coming to that. What do ye say, men, to staking this unfortunate fellow from our coffers?"

The rest of the pirates cheered the suggestion mightily and within a matter of moments, Fillmore found himself laden down with gems and trinkets, rolls of pounds sterling and clinking handfuls of crowns and shillings.

The untypical piratical business attended to, the dazed scholar found himself the centre of attention. On all sides, pirates young and old, tender and toothless, vied for his autograph. They deafened him with questions, shook his hand, bent his ear with sea tales, made him tipsy with bottles of grog passed hand to hand.

The day wore on and someone scared up meat for a stew-pot The scholar, finding himself curiosity-of-the-day, was easily pressed into staying for dinner, which promised to be a feast.

The firelight flickered gently and the sounds of a guitar clung upon the evening air like clusters of musical grapes. This time, the source of music was apparent: an elderly pirate in golden pantaloons, gypsy bandana and wine-scarlet coat serenaded the drowsy •company ringed about the slowly dying flames. Along the circle of faces the alternating lights and darks of fire and night played hide-and-seek. Here a crew member tipped a bottle up to his mouth, the glass catching the glint of reflected light. There a chubby buccaneer snored off a tipsy sleep, his many chins pillowed on his capacious breast as he leaned against a pile of stolen carpeting. Everywhere the celebrants talked to one another in whispering groups of twos and threes.

Fillmore was on the pirate chieftain's left hand and, at the moment, held earnest converse with the maid-of-all-work, Ruth. Frederic was on her extreme side, brooding in his cups.

"But why did you do it?" the scholar asked with great intensity.

Ruth shrugged, clasping her hands in front of her broad midriff. "I was a member of this band myself for many years. It was Samuel's idea—he's my uncle—to seek employ in town where I could snatch some little cherub. But it...well, it didn't quite work out like that. Frederic was going to be apprenticed, anyway. I missed the carefree life of a pirate's helper. So I simply combined the two projects. Alas...it slipped my mind that we wanted to ransom off the youth." She sighed profoundly, then swallowed half-a-tankard of ale. Wiping her lips, she cast a wary eye on Frederic, to see whether he was paying attention. But he seemed to be off in some world of his own.

Fillmore could not resist pursuing the line of his contention. Lowering his voice and bending his head closer to Ruth's ear, he asked whether she were truly in love with her charge, young Frederic.

"Hardly," she shrugged. "He's a child, for heaven's sake! I like maturer men," Ruth explained, pinching Fillmore playfully on the cheek.

Hardly noticing, he persisted: "Yet I understand the two of you are betrothed?"

"So you may have heard. But the truth is, I've at last wearied of this hardy existence. I'm fully forty-seven years old, though you wouldn't believe it to look at me." She paused, waiting for corroboration. Getting none, she proceeded, a little testy. "Anyway, this stripling by my side is the sole ticket I've got back to town, to a life of idle leisure. I'll tolerate him, I will, if I can get what I want."

"Exactly what I suspected!" Fillmore exclaimed happily. "I knew your affection for him disappeared much too swiftly at the end of Act One—"

"What the deuce are you talking about?" Ruth asked, mystified.

"Never mind!" the scholar happily replied. "The important thing is that you don't love him at all!"

Ruth studied him shrewdly. "Does it mean all that much to you, then?"

"Why, you cannot imagine how that news pleases me! It's uplifted my spirits tremendously!" Perhaps Fillmore would have been a trifle less enthusiastic had he been a trifle more sober. But he was and he wasn't— so he opened the way for what was to follow.

Which was Ruth: without warning, the massive woman flung herself into his arms, knocking the wind from his chest like a pair of bellows squashed by a falling rock.

"Adrian, my love!" she exclaimed. "Say no more! I am yours!"

Sputtering, the professor would have protested the hasty dedication Ruth made of herself...but the matter was wrested from his control with alarming rapidity.

"Friends!" Frederic shouted lustily, waking even the chubby pirate. "Good news!" The young man, in a flash, had come out of his introspective trance; he leaped to his feet and called out in a heartier manner than he'd displayed up to that time. "Good news, messmates! Our honorary brother has become betrothed!"

Pirates rushed upon the pair—Fillmore and Ruth—pummeling them on the back, shaking hands, expressing vociferous good wishes. So great was the din, that two sounds were entirely drowned out.

The first was Fillmore's thin, protesting voice. "Nor he cried, "this is a dreadful mistake! I don't want to marry anybody!"

The second sound lost in the bustle and brouhaha was the whine of a bullet ricocheting off the surrounding cliff-face.

CHAPTER FIVE

It was a most peculiar fight.

The assailants, concealed behind every looming precipice and stone-pile, opened fire without warning (though they seemed to take pains not to injure anyone). The noise was deafening, as each bullet echoed amongst the crags and crevices.

The pirates, taken unawares, were panic-stricken—facing, as they were, unseen foes protected by the night and a superior position. The brigands, forgetting all about Fillmore and Ruth, streamed off, dove, ran in circles, all the while grabbing loot and weapons. Everyone shouted imprecations, warnings, instructions; no-one heeded the pirate-king standing in the center of the clearing waving his arms wildly and shouting for obedience.

Over the whole confused scene roared the prestissimo clamor of brass and galloping strings, shrieking woodwinds and pulse-quickening tympani—a blustering tone-poem to the spirit of strife. It tore at Fillmore's eardrums.

At his sleeve, Ruth—a knife in her left hand and a pistol in the other—plucked insistently. She pointed at the largest tent across the clearing from the spot where she and Fillmore were standing. "Quick! Over there!" she cried. "The tent behind the throne—quick, beloved! There is additional weaponry inside. Get yourself firearms, dirks and life-preservers...you may want to hit!" She howled the command with the delirious joy of one long deprived of a favorite sport. Pushing him with all her might, the blood-thirsty Ruth nearly sent her hapless prey sprawling.

Fillmore wasted no time in following her orders—inasmuch as they provided him an opportunity to escape her proprietary grasp. He ran across the clearing, keeping far away from the illuminating flames. Confusing shapes loomed out of darkness and were swallowed up again; someone bumped into his shoulder with a sharp instrument and scratched him slightly. Samuel, somewhere behind him, bellowed out disregarded commands.

The music's din suddenly paused on a tense tremolo just as Fillmore reached the tent. Looking back, he saw the pirate-king standing erect by his throne, the Jolly Roger defiantly aloft in his fist-grasp. Samuel stood next to him, broadsword in one hand, a pistol in the other. Across the nearly extinguished fire stood Frederic, arms akimbo, looking very bored. Ruth, next to him and armed to the teeth, was chiding the lad for his indifference. No one else was in the clearing—but in the shadows and behind each tent-flap, Fillmore could espy the terrified gaze of the cowed band of brigands.

The bullets ceased. Except for the anxious sawing of the invisible strings, all was silent. Fillmore held his breath.

Then a supercilious voice sneered at them from some elevated, night-cloaked vantage-point. "Lay down your arms, pirates! We charge you yield in the name of Her Majesty's Navy!"

"Who are you?" the pirate shouted.

"Sir Joseph Porter, K.C.B.!" the other sneered. "And if you do not do as you are told, I have a crewful of man-o'-war's-men available to enforce my will! Surrender, pirates!"

His words produced an extraordinary effect. Throwing down their arms, the pirate chieftain and Samuel shouted to their men to scatter; then the pair rushed pell-mell off to the safety of the hillside. The concealed pirates followed suit, swarming like ants into the many cave-mouths riddling the rock-face. Frederic followed at a lope, still rather bored by the entire proceedings. The only animation he showed, even momentarily, was a brief, longing glance that he cast back in the direction of the unseen naval company. Bullets began to fly once more.

Ruth rounded the fireside and confronted Fillmore. "Well, aren't you coming?"

"Why is everyone running? Isn't anyone going to fight?"

"Bah!" she sneered. "They're cowards all! Afraid to be captured by Sir Joseph."

"Why?"

"Don't you know?" she asked, eyebrows raised. "No, I suppose you wouldn't, being a stranger. Sir Joseph's got the longest and dullest tale of how he got to be ruler of the queen's navy and he sings it at every possible opportunity. Besides, he never goes anywhere without his entire family—the distaff portion, at any rate! One's own relatives are quite boring enough: someone else's are positively intolerable!"

The situation was more complicated than Fillmore imagined possible and he had little leisure to reflect on it. The important thing at the moment was to escape from the domineering Ruth.

"Well?" she barked at him, oblivious to the bullets whizzing about her head. "Are you coming with me, lad?" Her tone left little doubt about his fate if he refused.

"Yes, certainly...ah...love," he replied. "But I haven't had an opportunity to arm myself as you suggested."

"Well, then, be quick about it!" she snapped, pistol raised in his direction. Around them, the cacophonous battle-music was raging once more.

"I'll be just a second," said Fillmore, entering the weapons-tent. Moving with great rapidity, he snatched up the sharpest-looking dagger and made a long, noiseless lateral cut in the back wall of the canvas enclosure. Withdrawing the point, he thrust again some inches above the center of the slit and cut downward, stopping by necessity at the juncture. Next he jabbed the dagger-point into the bottom of the flap.

"What's taking you so long?" Ruth yelped. "Don't pick and choose—grab the first thing you can lay your hands on!"

"I...I'm loading up!" he retorted. "I'll just be another ten seconds!"

"We'll see!" she snarled. "One...two...three...four..."

Fillmore sliced upward along the canvas, until the blade met the lateral cut.

"Five...six...seven...eight...

"No fair!" he thought, plunging through the opening. She should be adding "a-thousand" after each number to make them equivalent to a full sec—

"Nine...ten!" shouted Ruth, storming into the tent—just in time to see the scholar withdraw his right leg and light out for the hillside.

With a bellow of rage, she fired at his silhouette, etched dark against a blacker night. But the shot went wild.

Fillmore ran faster than he'd done in years. Even when he was sure that Ruth no longer pursued him, he continued to flee, paying no attention whatsoever to direction. Suddenly, he collided into something hard and rebounded backwards; the dagger went flying off into the night. Groaning, he rubbed his injured nose and inched forward.'

The obstruction he'd encountered was a tree-trunk. Fillmore slumped down on the grass and leaned against the bole, waiting for the pain to subside. Once the ache in his head abated to the level of a dull throb, he began to assess his situation. It wasn't too bad, all things considered: the pirates were concealed and perhaps by now Ruth had joined them. As for the navy, they wouldn't even be aware of his exis—

A thought hit him like a slap across the face: where was the umbrella?! He leapt to his feet, horrified; it was gone.

With an awful pang, he realized it must still be on the ground by the fire where he'd put it down. He'd forgotten all about it ever since the business with Ruth began.

It was a desperate idea to return for it, but the fugitive had no alternative. The umbrella was the only conceivable chance he had to escape from this rapidly-palling world, the only possible bridge back to his own place and time.

Creeping back the way he came, Fillmore attempted to retrace his steps. The music had stopped and the only sound was the distant susurration of the waves. He ran into another tree, gently enough this time. He became thoroughly disoriented. Which way should he go? Was the camp in that direction? Or was it the other way? Why couldn't he see the glowing embers of the fire? How far could he have run, anyway...?

Then, a disconcerting thought occurred to him. All that afternoon, he'd noticed no hint of woodland on the open meadow. Yet he was now hiding behind a tree-bole, one of many in the immediate vicinity. His frantic run in the dark must have taken him further landward than he'd calculated. How would he find his way back without a light?

As if in answer to his thoughts, the blinding spill of an open lantern cut across the night, dazzling him momentarily. A familiar tenor voice rang out.

"Hold, rascal! Just put those hands high in the air, if you will!"

Fillmore complied, waiting for the newcomer to advance. The lantern swung in a slow arc and the other drew near enough for the scholar to make out his face...as well as the firearm leveled at his own breast.

"Frederic," he said, surprised, "what are you doing in that outfit?"

"I beg your pardon, sir!" said the other, affronted. "My name ain't Fred and this is my proper uniform as an able-bodied seaman!"

In the lantern-glow, Fillmore studied the other. It was impossible: he looked exactly like the young pirate and spoke in the same light upper register. But the sailor was clad in the simple shirt and bell-bottoms of a humble foremast hand; on his head was stuck a white cap with blue horizontal stripe and a tongue of ribbon protruding from in back. Around the base of the cap, superimposed in white upon the lateral stripe was a neat legend: *H.M.S. Pinafore.*

"What's your name, sailor?" Fillmore asked.

"Rackstraw's the name. Ralph Rackstraw." But he pronounced it 'Rafe.' "A.B.S., Her Majesty's Navy. Now identify yourself!"

Fillmore calculated his chances quickly. This seaman, evidently part of a search-party, must have been told off to round up the pirates: it was likely he believed Fillmore to be part of the brigand-band. How could he discourage that notion?

Fillmore briefly told his story, but Rackstraw listened with obvious disbelief. He looked especially dubious when the scholar asserted that he'd been captured by the pirates. "And they've stolen a valuable piece of my property which I simply have to get back!"

"Pray tell," Rackstraw said, a little too politely. "Now if you'll just come with me, I'll take you to my captain who is, even now, at the pirate's lair. You can tell him your story. This way—here, I'll just take your wrist and guide you..."

It was clear the seaman didn't credit a word he'd said. Following unwillingly, Fillmore desperately tried to think of a way to gain the sailor's confidence. Rackstraw...Rafe Rackstraw...what was he like in *H.M.S. Pinafore*?

Of course! the scholar thought, snapping his fingers. In the operetta, Rafe is in love with the captain's daughter. But he's afraid to court her because of the disparity in their social stations...

"I can give you good advice," he told the sailor abruptly.

"About what?" Rackstraw asked unenthusiastically.

"About love."

"What are you talking about?"

"About you," Fillmore winked, though it went unnoticed in the darkness. "I know a secret concerning you and a certain young lady."

The sailor stopped, eyed his captive suspiciously. "Indeed? And how d'ye know anything about me, since we're strangers?"

"Bit of a fey quality, I fancy."

"Well, well," the sailor grumbled, "and just what do you know?"

"Let's say this much," Fillmore told Rackstraw. "You are in love with a lovely young girl of high rank and position."

"Ay? What else?" the other asked, surprised.

"Have no fear, I won't divulge your secret." Privately, Fillmore wondered what would happen if he did tip off Rafe's love for his captain's daughter too soon? Would the very underpinnings of this mad universe crumble? "What I want to do is advise you to keep up your hopes. Things are not so black as they seem."

"They're not?" Rackstraw asked ardently. "These are the first encouraging words I've heard since this affair grew too hot for me to bear! But how can you prophesy thus? The lady doesn't even know that I exist."

"You're wrong there," Fillmore answered. "She loves you with a passion equal to your own for her."

The sailor whirled around in a merry figure, the lantern flickering in a sudden flare-up as he did. Fillmore felt obliged to warn him about it, simultaneously requesting that he moderate his whoopings.

Checking his enthusiasm, Rafe began walking briskly forward once more, practically dragging Fillmore by the wrist.

In the distance, the scholar could see the newly-lit fire of the campsite; in its glow, he made out blue-coated and white-shirted officers and tars. The battle music had long since climaxed and died.

At his side, Rafe mumbled happily to himself. "Ah, if I might only believe these tidings, how glad I would be! But what could I do to advance my case?"

"Take my advice," Fillmore answered, unsolicited. "Speak to her at your earliest opportunity."

"But if she spurns me?"

"Well," said Fillmore, smiling at the notion of putting words into Rackstraw's mouth, "all I can say is that your love is as good as any other's! Is not your heart as true as another's? Have you not hands and eyes and ears and limbs like another?" He got the little speech from *Pinafore* almost letter-perfect, having himself played the part of Rafe—woeful miscasting!—once many years before in junior high school.

"Aye, aye!" the sailor shouted. "What you say is true, friend! I'll speak to her at the first opportunity! Friend, your hand." He held out his weather-tanned right arm, sinewy and bare to the elbow and shook Fillmore's heartily.

There, that's done! thought the scholar. No more nonsense about my status with this Rackstraw...

The two drew up short, having reached the campsite. Stepping forward briskly, Rackstraw smartly saluted a gold-epauleted figure in captain's hat and dress blues.

"Captain Corcoran, sir?"

"Aye, Rafe?"

"Rackstraw reporting!"

"So I see," said the captain, peering over the seaman's shoulder at the oddly-dressed personage just behind. "Have you captured one of the blighters?"

"Aye, aye, sir! The queer-looking pirate we saw grappling with the fat woman."

The captain strode up to the dumbfounded Fillmore. "Sir," he said, "I arrest you in the name of Queen Victoria! Clap him in irons!"

Several sailors appeared and grabbed the scholar firmly by the arms.

The captive protested volubly, glancing about wildly for his umbrella. It was nowhere in sight.

"Here, here, my good fellow," Corcoran admonished. "It's quite obvious that you are a pirate, don't try to deny it!"

"Prove it!" Fillmore challenged.

"Very well," said the captain, sticking his hand inside the other's jacket pocket and withdrawing a large quantity of notes and gems. "Why, man, your pockets all are fair bulging with loot! If you want to pass for innocent, you must do better than this."

* * * *

Fillmore looked down at the riches, horrified: he'd forgotten the probably-stolen goods and monies pressed upon him earlier by the tender-hearted pirates. The evidence was most incriminating.

His guards pulled at him roughly, impelling him in the direction of the seaside, where several dinghies were beached.

As he passed Rackstraw, Fillmore glowered. The sailor shrugged, holding up his hands in a "what-can-I-tell-you" attitude.

"Duty's duty," the sailor said. "But thanks for the advice, all the same."

CHAPTER SIX

It was a rare morning, even for July. The sea-breeze gently fanned the sailors's cheeks. The sun, already bright, shed just enough warmth to take the chill out of the early air. The sea was calm and the surface of the water rippled gently in a wind strong enough to waft the ship on her homeward journey, yet sufficiently mild to caress, rather than buffet the crewmen working on deck.

The *Pinafore* was a-bustle with activity, as Captain Corcoran plotted out the trip back to Portsmouth and the sailors hurried to meet the tide. As they went about their nautical duties, they sang a slow but lusty a cappella oceanic hymn:

> *Up merry mates, the anchor weigh!*
> *Unfurl the sheets and spare no toil.*
> *This is the sailor s happiest day—*
> *Homeward we turn from foreign soil!*

Down below, one of the ship's passengers failed to appreciate the musicale.

"Foreign soil, indeed!" Fillmore sniffed, sitting on his hard bunk in the brig. "These insular British...they've only sailed from Portsmouth to Penzance, hardly an ocean voyage! Bah!"

Oblivious to their enforced guest's displeasure, the sailors took up the refrain again:

> *Back to the homes so far away—*
> *Back to the girls who for us sighed—*
> *Homeward we sail and home we'll stay*
> *...Until the turning of the tide!*

"Blah-blah blah blah-blah-blah blah blah blah!" yelled Fillmore through the one porthole. But his mockery went unheeded.

Any thought of enjoying his adventure had left him during the night: he was sore and stiff from trying to rest on the unyielding cot chained to the brig's bulkhead. The rocking of the ship did not sit well on his stomach, either, and the provender afforded him was fit only to dump through the porthole—causing, no doubt, the demise of any hapless fish near enough to partake of the slop.

As near as Fillmore could tell, the captain of the *Pinafore* intended sailing back to Portsmouth, where the captive would be handed over to the authorities to be transported to London. There, he would be tried for piracy.

It was apparent by the contiguity—within the space of one day—of characters both from *Pinafore* and *Pirates of Penzance* that he'd gotten himself stuck in a Gilbert & Sullivan world. All ideas of madness or dreaming had been scuttled: his joints ached too powerfully to question the objective reality of his whereabouts. Why he should be in such a world was another issue entirely; he could easily accept a dimensional transfer via the missing umbrella into many sorcerous, idyllic or even familiarly mechanistic societies. But a musical world patterned on fourteen theatrical operettas? It was absurd to the *nth*!

Under other conditions, the opportunity to investigate the Gilbertian cosmos might be charming enough. But Fillmore was finding himself too put-upon a figure in the melodramatic churnings of the plot he'd gotten stuck inside: first threatened by pirates, then by marriage; now confined to horrendously filthy quarters with no future prospects but trial for piracy and likely enough, subsequent hanging.

Any inclination to regard the entire business as too silly for notice was fast quelled whenever the ship rode an occasional swell and the brig lurched sickeningly. Too, Fillmore remembered an admonition that had been given to the hero of a science-fiction book he'd once read. In it, the protagonist found himself unexplainably in an alien world; asking a supercomputer to assist him, the metal brain warned, "Do not underestimate the danger of your position. If you die here, you will stay dead!"

* * * *

He must get off the ship somehow, that much he knew. How to do it was another matter. Afterwards! Well, that he had figured out...wasn't the inscription on the umbrella 70 SIM—? During the night, Fillmore deciphered what it probably meant.

He must reach London and seek professional advice. But first, he had to work his way out of the present predicament. And that meant some serious thought.

The key must lie in the workings of this topsy-turvy universe, the scholar told himself for the fiftieth time in the past hour. If music can start up from no determinate source and if individuals can blend their thoughts in perfect harmony, then there must be other peculiarities that, once grasped, could be wrested to his purpose.

* * * *

"Peculiarities!" the sorcerer asked with surprise. "But my good man, our people study music from very babyhood. It is expected of them. To speak without an occasional chorus or solo is as unthinkable as to imagine that God did not put his Holy Orchestra above to manifest His Will to us! The music is Holy Tone, my lad, showing us the way to interpret His Intentions!" His face took on the fixed expression of one who dare not be contradicted on an axiom of faith.

* * * *

The single victory Fillmore had enjoyed—that of the pirates's good will and ill-sequeled generosity—was based upon the artifice of mentioning his orphancy: it was a device that employed the very über-knowledge that the scholar possessed concerning the G&S world he was in. It took advantage of one of its topsy-turvy values: that black-hearted pirates might be emotionally-tender little children within.

Hold on! That concept bore further examination. If, indeed, the pirates were gentle fellows, what might that mean in terms of the entire complex of laws governing G&S-land?

Fillmore thought of all the villains he could bring to mind: there was Sir Despard Murgatroyd in *Ruddigore*: a noble, principled gentleman. What about Don Alhambra in *The Gondoliers*? Hardly a villain. Neither was the loutish Wilfred in *The Yeomen of the Guard*. In fact, Fillmore realized with some surprise, there were scarcely any real villains at all in the Gilbert & Sullivan operettas.

Heroes? Ah, that was another matter...the lot of them were shallow, vain and spiteful: from the defendant in Trial by Jury through the abominable Colonel Fairfax in *The Yeomen*—

Good God! Fillmore mused, I'm beginning to sound like Quiller-Grouch. Yet there was considerable truth in what he'd asserted: look at his own brief experiences on this side of the umbrella—so to speak. The pirates themselves had treated him nicely enough. But the noble Frederic got him into the mess with Ruth by shouting out the nuptial news with suspicious alacrity.

And that two-faced Rafe Rackstraw was responsible for his present predicament. It was pretty obvious, was it not, that Fillmore had made a grave tactical error in trusting the "heroic" seaman?

Better if he'd cast his lot with a villain...

And the idea Fillmore had been chasing around inside his brain finally held still long enough to apprehend it.

Dashing over to the barred door of the brig, Fillmore shouted until the watch came back to see what he wanted.

"'ere now," said the tar, "you'll do well to keep down the din."

"I'd like some company," Fillmore confided.

"Oh, is 'at so? And who, pray tell, would you like me to summon? Perhaps Sir Joseph himself? I'll call a special party to row to his yacht and fetch him over straight!"

Not at all, not at all," the scholar demurred. "But if I'm not mistaken you have a sailor aboard, do you not, who answers to the name of Dead-eye?"

The sailor shuddered. "Is it Dick Deadeye ye're wanting? Faith and you'll be welcome to him, right enough! I'll fetch 'im straightaway."

"And see we're not disturbed!" Fillmore shouted.

"That you won't be," the sailor called over his shoulder. "Not with him about!"

* * * *

"It's a beast of a name, ain't it?" Dick Deadeye said, squinting at Fillmore with his one good eye.

The scholar, bored, repeated the expected response for the third time in half as many hours. "It's not a nice name, no."

"I'm ugly, too, ain't I?" he snarled, wiping his hairy hand across an unshaven chin.

"You are certainly plain."

"And I'm three-cornered too, ain't I?"

Fillmore nodded, idly wondering just what it meant to be "three-cornered." Perhaps it alluded to Deadeye's habit of walking in a crouching manner, his elbows and knees presenting sharp angles with the bend of his back.

"I said I'm three-cornered, ain't I?"

"You certainly are triangular."

"Ha-ha," the villain laughed. "That's it. I'm ugly and you hate me for it, don't you?"

"I do not hate you," said the scholar for the umpteenth time. "Where I come from, physical beauty is not a necessary attribute to popularity!" He shuddered as he said it and kept his fingers crossed.

"So you did, so you did," the other answered, "but what of it? You want a favor of me, do you not?"

"Now that you mention it—"

The sailor sniffed angrily. "I thought as much! I'll say good-bye!" He began to gesture toward the distant guard. Before he could get his attention, Fillmore yanked down his arm.

"See here!" he said. "It's not so awful. Simply find me my umbrella and help me escape!"

"Ha! Ye call that simple."

"I have it all planned...arrange to take the watch down here in the brig. Do it just outside of Portsmouth. Slip in and take the valuables they confiscated from me. Keep them for your own. All I want is a few odd pound-notes and the umbrella. Especially the umbrella."

"How will I explain your disappearance?" Deadeye asked dubiously. "There's no chance you could get the keys and overpower me."

Fillmore shook his head. "Not necessary. Claim you saw me vanish before your very eyes. Impute it to magic. No-one will doubt your word, if you give it with sufficient malevolence..."

"Naah, naah," the other said vehemently, pacing from side to side in the narrow brig. "It's too great a risk. And I get nothing from it."

"I said you could keep the money and jewels." Sneering, the seaman turned a twisted, baleful expression upon Fillmore. "Money!" he spat. "What good would that do me, eh? Would it fix my face, mend my halting walk?"

The questions were unanswerable. Fillmore said nothing for some time; instead, he watched the bitter tar stride back and forth, back and forth, two paces one way, two paces the other—

"Think of it this way," Fillmore said at last. "Helping me escape will be a blow against a callous society which scorns you and keeps you type-cast as a blackguard."

The sailor stopped pacing. Saying nothing, he stared for a long time through the porthole at the face of the afternoon sky. The minutes passed, but Dick Deadeye said nothing. Fillmore became fidgety and, at last, decided he had better break the silence. But just as he cleared his throat to speak, the other finally addressed him, without turning.

"There's truth in what you say, friend." Deadeye's voice was a little higher in pitch than normal, but otherwise he had himself in full control. "I've considered your plan and I'll help you in it."

Fillmore caught his breath, rose from the bunk. "How soon will we be in Portsmouth?"

"If we catch the tide," said Deadeye, turning, "we should weigh anchor there this very evening, or tomorrow morning at the latest."

"Then it must be tonight," said Fillmore, expressing the obvious. "Can you get watch?"

"Aye—it's my regular round this night," said Deadeye. "Be prepared for my coming and I'll be brisk to prepare your going."

A whining bass-line slithered through the gloom of the brig. My

God, Fillmore thought, the damned music even extends down here!

Deadeye sang in a sly, insinuating fashion:

> *Good fellow, I'll assist you in your leaving;*
>> *Sing hey, the mystic fellow that you are!*
>>> *I'll fetch you your umbrella late this evening.*
>> *Sing hey, the mystic fellow and the tar!*
>>> *The mystic, mystic fellow,*
>>> *The mystic, mystic fellow,*
>> *Sing hey, the mystic fellow and the tar!*

He looked at Fillmore a little sourly and the teacher supposed he should have joined in on the chorus. But it had been too many years since he'd been involved in amateur theatricals and he wasn't about to start now—"Well?" Deadeye grunted. "Ain't you gonna sing your verse?"

Fillmore groaned inwardly. For the love of God, he thought, the song is in response-and-reply form: it takes a minimum of two verses to complete it. Though the scholar was completely unenthusiastic about joining in on the fun-and-games, he worried that 1) Deadeye might refuse after all if Fillmore didn't return the expected polite answer and 2) his refusal to sing might somehow damage the very fabric of this strange universe into which he'd been tumbled.

Gesturing with resigned good will, he did his best to think up a few appropriate rhymes. It was easier than he imagined possible. But Fillmore held on to some shred of individuality by talking his verse in a kind of singspiel:

> *Kind sailor, I appreciate your daring—*
>> *Sing hey, the doughty sailor that you are!*
> *Be sure you snatch it when there's no-one staring...*
>> *Sing hey, the mystic fellow and the tar!*
>>> *The mystic, mystic fellow,*
>> *The mystic, mystic fellow,*
>>> *Sing hey, the mystic fellow and the tar!*

Dick Deadeye joined him in the chorus this time. At the end, the sinister bass rounded out the musical thought and the duo solemnly shook hands like a pair of soloists at the end of a conceit.

"Just out of curiosity," Deadeye asked, "what will you do once you've escaped?"

"Head towards London," Fillmore replied. "There's a sorcerer there, I've heard, who'll help me quit this strange sphere, I hope."

"I see," the sailor said. "Then—"

The bass accompaniment, which had not quite died away, swelled up afresh. Deadeye went into a quick finale, which Fillmore instantly recognized. He had no choice but to join right in.

DEADEYE: *This very night*
With bated breath—

FILLMORE:—*And muffled oar—*

DEADEYE: *Without a light,*
As still as death—

FILLMORE :—*I'll steal ashore!*
I'll flee from here
And seek to find—

DEADEYE:—*The proper one—*

FILLMORE: *A sorcerer*
Who'll ease my mind—

DEADEYE:—*And get ye gone*!

They repeated it thrice, gathering speed as they sang (or, in Fillmore's case, declaimed) until they reached the final line once more. They uttered it in unison and, in Fillmore's version, it came out "And get me gone!" It sounded just like a first-act finale.

The bright flourishes that rushed to a final tonic-dominant alternation were so loud and bombastic that Fillmore feared they would attract the attention of the guard or, for that matter, anyone above them on deck.

* * * *

"Impossible!" the sorcerer exclaimed. "We value our privacy! Listen in on someone else's musical statements? Not done, my lad! As soon imagine some nightmare society whose police listened in unannounced at a gentleman's own home! You see what I mean? It's simply not done!" The little merchant-magician shook his head from side to side in utter disbelief. "Simply isn't done," he repeated.

CHAPTER SEVEN

How he got on the gondola, Fillmore had no idea, but it was a picturesque trip. The twin gondoliers sang out the attractions as they glided past in no discernibly logical order: "Castle Adamant...Tower of London...Site of the Statutory Duel...Utopia...Mount Olympus (!)...Castle Bunthorne..."

And then the scenery shimmered and shifted and he was walking through a quaint fishing village. He spied another castle in the distance. It played a coquette's game. As he approached, it retreated. He veered toward the coastline and suddenly the place planted itself squarely in his path.

A bevy of maidens in flowery array scattered rose-petals where he walked. They sang:

> *Oh, happy the lily when kissed by the bee,*
> *And, sipping tranquilly, quite happy is he!*

Fillmore could not imagine how he reached the village. Somehow he was certain it was in Cornwall, yet he could not recall jumping ship. For that matter, the *Pinafore* was already some distance away from...

From?

His thoughts were thoroughly muddled.

At least the castle was over its bout of diffidence. Suddenly...

SCENE.—Picture Gallery in Ruddigore Castle. The walls are covered with full-length portrait frames, but where the pictures should be are only blank spaces reminiscent of the famous uncompleted painting of George Washington. A single portrait stands completed, that of a bishop...Sir Desmond Murgatroyd, Sixteenth Baronet of that accursed line of noblemen.

SIR DESMOND *(popping his head momentarily out of the canvas)*: It's a wretched likeness!

A slim, medium-sized gentleman with graying hair and grandiloquent airs, entered. He was clad in the respectable at-home-wear of a British country squire.

"Let me guess," Fillmore murmured. "You are Sir Ruthven Murgatroyd, the latest Lord of the line?"

By way of reply, there was a tremendous orchestral crash and the other began to sing melodramatically. Fillmore recognized the melody as the duet which begins Act II of *Ruddigore*, Gilbert's spoof on nineteenth-century melodrama.

RUTHVEN:

> *I once was a thoroughly wicked young Bart.*
> *Because I was accursed!*

A crime every day I had to commit
And so I did my worst!

My turn, Fillmore thought with resignation. He sang.

FILLMORE:

For if you refused, in horrible pain
You'd die—I know the tale!
This curse was enforced by all of the ghosts
Of every Murgatroyd male!

(Suddenly Fillmore felt strange. If he could have described the sensation in a word, he might have chosen *fixed*.)

Murgatroyd stopped singing momentarily to eye the professor with surprise and suspicion. "How did ye know about my spectral ancestors?"

Fillmore shrugged. "Bit of a fey quality, I fancy."

"It's true," Murgatroyd nodded, leaning against the bishop's portrait-frame. "The curse temporarily separated me from my true love, Rose Maybud. But then it occurred to me that sooner or later, every Murgatroyd vows to sin no more. On the day he says that say, he dies. Or used to."

"Yes, I know," said Fillmore. "You reasoned that deciding not to commit one's daily crime was tantamount to suicide, but suicide is itself a crime, so no Murgatroyd should ever have died at all."

"Quite. And as a result, all my forefathers immediately returned to life—"

Sir Desmond, the bishop, again stuck his astral noggin out of his frame. "All but one! Bishops don't commit suicide!"

His descendant ignored him. "And now the castle is full of Murgatroyds, eating me into ruin, swearing and gaming and hunting all the foxes in the country! It's a dreadful bore!"

"Well," Fillmore philosophically observed, "at least you and Rose Maybud were united in matrimony."

The same thundering *tutti* sounded.

"Not so," said Murgatroyd, with a heart-felt yet rather exaggerated sigh...

RUTHVEN:

I once was a happily-married Lord
I'm now lovelorn and glum
My wife went and left me, totally bereft me,
And now my word is Mum!

Fillmore winced. Typical Gilbertian trick: when nothing else rhymes, stick anything in at all. And then he realized it was his turn again. What should I sing? The theme this set is personal misfortune...

FILLMORE:

And I who was once a modest scholar
Am totally unemployed,
Extremely befuddled and thoroughly muddled
And more than a bit annoyed!

(As he sang, he felt odder and odder. He almost sensed himself condensed, notated on a two-dimensional plane. "Shades of *Flatland*" he mused.)

RUTHVEN (speaking):

Well, we *were* married, Rose and I. But then she grew restless and took to studying at an adjacent woman's university. Eventually her study of old lore and metaphysics led her to consult a sorcerer who sold her— (*He stops suddenly.*)

FILLMORE:

Sold her what?

RUTHVEN (pale with rage):

AH-HA! SIRRAH! I HAVE YOU NOW! MARRIAGE-DESTROY-ER!

FILLMORE:

What the deuce are you talking about?

Murgatroyd points to Fillmore's umbrella.

"Odd," the professor thought to himself, "I didn't have it a moment ago...

RUTHVEN:

It is the very instrument which stole her from me! I shall punish thee, knave!

FILLMORE:

You already are! Dreadful over-acting!

RUTHVEN:

Revenge!

Sir Ruthven Murgatroyd ties Fillmore to a post with a good stout rope...and then makes hideous faces at him. After a moment of this, he stops and unties the professor, gleefully chortling all the while.

RUTHVEN:

I'll wager you've been taught a lesson you shan't forget, rascal! (Anxiously) I trust you did not find me too over-bearingly rude?

* * * *

Fillmore was just about to answer when someone shook him. He woke with a start.

He was on the cot of the *Pinafore* brig. Dick Deadeye stood over him, gently nudging his shoulder.

"'Tis time, mate! Heave to and prepare to disembark!"

The teacher arose and gratefully took the umbrella which Deadeye, good as his word, snatched when no one above deck was staring.

"Bit of a strange dream," J. Adrian Fillmore murmured. "I wonder what it meant?"

* * * *

"I should say," the sorcerer reflected, *"that it was not so much a dream as a warning...*

CHAPTER EIGHT

The diminutive executioner bowed low and, smiling graciously, indicated a grillwork bench overlooking the placid pool. Satisfied that the stranger with the preposterous parasol was at ease, he picked up his gleaming, untarnished headsman's axe and, toddling back over the delicate arch spanning the pond, nodded to a bevy of pale-skinned, tittering maidens whose lovely faces were hidden by delicate fans. Then, rounding the circular perimeter of a ruby-hued pagoda, the peculiar Japanese disappeared from sight.

Fillmore, heaving a profound sigh, felt comfortable for the first time in days. He rested his eyes on the odd-shaped vegetation that lent a somewhat theatrical aura to the pleasant Oriental hideaway.

His escape from the *Pinafore* came off without a hitch. But hiking sixty miles in just under two days—sleeping in fields, keeping out of sight of the constabulary—sapped his strength and wore holes in his shoes. Only once, though, did he draw a suspicious stare: on a meadow just south of London, his garish umbrella got a squint-eyed glance from a crimson-coated Grenadier who, fortunately, was busy marching with his fellows at the time. They, in turn, were in the van of a magnificent procession of peers busily stomping all over the greensward, singing and sneering and trampling down the wildflowers. It was the only close shave; otherwise, the flight had been quite uneventful.

Now it was sheerest luxury to rest his aching joints in this quaint reproduction of a Japanese village that he'd found below Hyde Park on Knightsbridge. Some sort of ethnic exposition, it was a nicely secluded place for Fillmore to revitalize himself.

He'd stopped the headsman for directions to St. Mary's Axe, guessing who the little hatchet man must be—surely there could be no more perfect individual to ask. Ko-Ko, the Lord High Executioner of *The Mikado*, was the meekest of men (he'd never beheaded a soul). Furthermore, it would be extremely unlikely for the little Japanese to be the least bit concerned or aware about fugitive Occidental "pirates."

Ko-Ko returned. "So sorry not to be able to assist you personally. I am totally unaware of London geography. However, my wife is coming to answer your question. I think you'd better kneel."

His wife? Fillmore wondered. But Ko-Ko, in the operetta, wasn't married. No...wait a minute...at the very end...

Just then, a ferocious Oriental woman of huge proportions stormed across the bridge over the pool, heading in the scholar's direction. The reinforced customs of a lifetime die hard, so he rose to his feet, gaping with dismay at the formidable female. Like her husband, she was dressed primarily in black; her kimono, cinched at the waist with a blood-red belt, was capacious. Black, beetling brows lowered above a thin, cruel mouth and her hair, stuck all over with knitting needles, looked like some infernal spiky cactus.

Good God! the professor thought, his sense of security instantly evanescing, it's Katisha, the one real villain in all the G&S operettas! She's the one that Ko-Ko marries at the very end of the show. But that meant that the two of them here were living beyond the final scene that Gilbert wrote! What—

"Down on your knees, swine!" she bellowed, approaching him and Ko-Ko. Quailing, Fillmore instantly complied. "How dare you stand in my presence?" she roared. "Do you not know who I am?!"

"I think so," the scholar muttered. "You're Katisha, daughter-in-law elect to the Mikado."

"Not any more," the frightful apparition howled, gnashing her teeth.

"Just when I was conditioning the Mikado's son to love me—"

"It's a lengthy process," Ko-Ko remarked.

"Silence, worm!" she snarled, kicking at him. Ko-Ko dodged with practiced agility. "Well," she continued, "just as Nanki-Poo was in my pow—in my arms, a shameless hussy stole him. So I went mad and married this insignificant termite instead!"

Making fun of an old lady in love, indeed! Fillmore shuddered, recalling Quiller-Couch's accusation. As soon make sport of a tornado!

A nervous orchestral figure struck up and Katisha continued her complaint in song:

> *My life at court*
> *Has been cut short*
> *Because I'm wed*
> *To this dunderhead!*
> *This conjugal pest*
> *Has filled my breast*
> *With flames of hate*
> *For my marital state.*
> *So if I'm rude*
> *And tend to brood,*
> *It would be shrewd*
> *Not to intrude,*
> *Not to intrude—*

Ko-Ko attempted to intervene:

> *Beloved wife,*
> *No need for strife*
> *Or quarrel, dear,*
> *Is needed here,*
> *Is needed here!*
> *This passer-by*
> *Did catch my eye*
> *And asked a way*
> *I could not say:*
> *He doth entreat*
> *Of us, my sweet,*
> *Directions meet*
> *To find a street.*

"*What*?!" shrieked Katisha. "You dared disturb my rest because some vagabond wishes to inquire directions?"

"Yes," Fillmore replied fearfully. "Trying to find 70 St. Mary's Axe. Some of the residents elide it—70 Simmery Axe...?"

The virago glowered at him, but said nothing. Ko-Ko leaned against his official chopper, staring at Fillmore with perplexed anticipation.

Here we go again! the scholar groaned inwardly. The verses they sang are part of a patter trio. If I don't respond, they'll just stand there gawping at me.

Then it occurred to him: how many adolescent parties had he spent, tipsy, trying to find a third voice for an impromptu rendition of this very trio? And here was a chance to sing along with one of the original characters...how could he resist?

* * * *

"I wish you had, all the same ," said the sorcerer, shaking his head. "As long as you confined yourself to rhythmic declamation, you were in comparatively little danger. But once you started singing...well, well, how could you know?"

* * * *

FILLMORE:

If you'll excuse
The time that you'll lose,
I'm desperate to know
Which way to go
To find the shop
Where I must stop:
A store a djinn,
A djinn
Is said to live in.
A place of spells
And witches and knells.
A man named Wells
Presides there and sells.

"There! I've finally played their silly game," the scholar thought, mightily pleased with himself.

But his recital created an unexpected effect on his auditors. Katisha, snatching up the skirts of her kimono, ran along to the main archway of the replicatory village. Clapping her hands, she bellowed out something in Japanese.

"What's wrong?" Fillmore asked Ko-Ko, who was staling at him in great dismay.

"I'm afraid," said the executioner, pale face turning even whiter, "you've run afoul of one of our Mikado's innumerable laws. Anyone who practices magic, or seeks to practice magic, or even thinks about practicing it is a criminal, according to our ruler's stem decree!" Glancing in Katisha's direction, Ko-Ko continued the patter trio:

> *Oh, dear,*
> *I fear*
> *There's danger near!*
> *Our emper-or*
> *Had decreed war*
> *On magic lore.*
> *I fear, what's more,*
> *Bad luck's in store*
> *For you, Fillmore!*

This was the worst predicament yet, the scholar realized with horror. The dire threats of torture and death that run beneath the surface gaiety of *The Mikado* give that operetta, joyous though it is, an underlying somberness of tone unique in the series. What might the Mikado's punishment be for seeking to consort with a sorcerer? The penalty, of course, would fit the crime—would it be something lingering, perhaps with a wizard's-kettle filled with boiling oil a necessary ingredient?

"Well," the professor told himself, "I'm not about to find out." Snatching up his umbrella, he raced around the corner of a purple pagoda...but the way was cut off by a huge company of fierce samurai who, in answer to Katisha's shouted commands, were running towards him, whirling their giant swords menacingly.

Spinning, Fillmore lit out in another direction. But it was no use: more warriors clad in black togas were coming at him that way as well. He turned this way and that: everywhere, hordes of samurai with hideous expressions on their faces and hair tied in severe back-knots swarmed forth from every nook and alleyway. Their bloodthirsty cries startled women, set children to weeping. Many bystanders hurried indoors, heads ducked low as they dashed for sanctuary.

Fillmore halted in his tracks. It was clearly a case of stand fast, or be snipped by snickersnees. Breathing hard, he faced the terrible Katisha who was striding toward him with a cruel smile on her face.

The music, which had mocked his abortive flight with a programmatic episode depicting pursuit, returned to the familiar strains of the patter trio and Katisha sneered her second refrain.

KATISHA:

And so
Although
You're ready to go
Upon your quest,
I must protest
(It is no jest):
For your crime confessed,
As you may have guessed,
I now arrest—

FILLMORE (defiantly):

I'll go
And show
Both friend and foe
How much I dare.
I'm well aware
You don't much care—
—It's my affair—
Yet I declare
I'll take my share
Although ill I'll fare.

He wasn't really feeling all that courageous, but the sentiments were easy to express in the obligatory trio part for which he was responsible.

The entire Japanese village immediately joined in for the coda. Samurai, geishas, water-carriers, rickshaw-runners, sushi-shop chefs, Katisha and Ko-Ko all roared out an ominous prediction of Fillmore's potential punishment:

To sit in solemn silence in a dull dark dock,
In a pestilential prison with a life-long lock,
Awaiting the sensation of a short, sharp shock
From a cheap and chippy chopper on a big black block.

The mixed chorus was so loud that the noise could be heard all the way across the length and breadth of Hyde Park.

CHAPTER NINE

So, for the second time in as many days, J. Adrian Fillmore found himself shut up in a prison cell.

The new one, at least, was more comfortable than the space-starved brig, but otherwise the conditions were just as bad and the food equally unpalatable. Being on dry land, of course, was an improvement over the queasy movement of the anchored ship, but the Fleet more than offset the advantage by the uncleanly squalor in which it was allowed to be maintained.

Luckily for him, the Mikado's jurisdiction did not extend to England, a fact which might not have helped much if Katisha's will had prevailed. But the conscientious Ko-Ko brought the matter before Commons and Fillmore—as a vaguely American citizen (in the eyes of the G&S world's citizenry)—was released from the shrewish woman's custody. However, he was immediately rearrested for piracy; it was for that alleged crime that he now languished in jail, awaiting the time of his trial.

Several weeks elapsed in the interim. As near as he could reckon (for no one kept him informed about the time), his day in court should be almost at hand. In the meantime, much must have transpired in the topsy-turvy kingdom on the other side of Fillmore's cell-window. He imagined paragraphs got into all the papers about his supposed crimes, capture and forthcoming trial, but the matter failed to interest him.

What was more intriguing to his scholar's mind was that the familiar plots of at least three Gilbert & Sullivan operettas had run their course since he'd first come over with the umbrella (now one of the prosecutor's exhibits). In fact, in the case of *The Mikado*, the story as Fillmore remembered it had already ended.

What about *H.M.S. Pinafore*? The ship docked at Portsmouth weeks ago, with Rafe Rackstraw preparing even then to speak to the captain's daughter. Thus, by now, the scholar realized, the couple must be married and Rafe and Captain Corcoran—as in the operetta—would have changed places with each other. But it made little difference which one testified against him: the captain-turned-seaman who honestly believed he was guilty, or the sailor-turned-captain whose personal gratitude towards Fillmore would certainly not stand in the way of Rackstraw condemning the accused.

As for *The Pirates of Penzance*, their destinies would also have been worked out long before Fillmore stood trial.

Evidently, the conclusion of storylines as Fillmore knew them had no negative effect whatsoever on the world he was stuck in. But there was one plot, if ended, that mightily worried him: what if the story of *The Sorcerer* terminated? In that case, whether the scholar won his freedom or no, he was still in prison, albeit a larger one...

He could not ignore the irony of the notion. Life at Parker College— reclusive, unchallenging, emotionally and physically frustrating—was itself an incarceration for Fillmore. Yet escape, for which he'd so long pined, was decidedly worse—at least in the Gilbertian cosmos, where he'd been shot at, smothered with unsolicited ardor, forced to turn fugitive and, at the last, threatened with loss of life as well as liberty.

In all those picaresque romances he'd devoured with unexpressed longing, high adventure was supposed to be one exhilarating round of ample bosoms, intrepid treks over enemy territory, duels of wits and swords in which virtue ultimately triumphed. But in fact, he bitterly recalled, there had been few enough wits to challenge and the distaff opportunities had been non-existent. (For that matter, in the Gilbertian scheme of things, the heroines Fillmore might meet would only turn out to be vain, empty-headed little egotists.) As for the cross-country trip, there simply was nothing charming in snatching bits of food on the run and sleeping out-of-doors in the same underwear.

The real disappointment about his plight was the absence of joy in the grotesque world he'd landed in. It was characteristically paradoxical that he'd undergone such turmoil and discomfort in a milieu which had, in his own time, provided such delicious enjoyment during leisure hours. The answer, though, was obvious on reflection (for which he had ample time in his present state). Once, at a faculty supper for a visiting G&S star, Fillmore heard the thespian vigorously emphasize the secret of playing Gilbert & Sullivan: "You must never, never play for laughs! Gilbert's characters are quite serious in what they say, do and sing— that's what makes them so funny. If you 'camp' up Gilbert, you sacrifice the wit and fun for cheap college-frat inanities."

Then what could the scholar expect in a world conforming to the G&S system of logic? No doubt some impartial observer might find a degree of drollery in his troubles, just as Fillmore might chuckle at the observer if their positions were reversed. But there was no bright side to being cast as victim.

Victim... that was the word to hold onto, he mused. Up till now, Fillmore had played too passive a role in events involving himself. Even when engineering the escape from the *Pinafore* brig, he'd experienced a curious detachment from circumstances...

And look where it had gotten him! No, he must review his strategy and plan to react more directly, more emotionally in his future trial. Having broken the singing barrier with Katisha and Ko-Ko, he had no intention of letting up when—

With a croaking groan and muffled clang, the door to his cell suddenly burst open, dispelling a dense dust-fog that made him cough and choke. An elderly, gnarled turn-key stood in the entrance.

"Up, lad," he rasped in a tone harmonically attuned to the protestations of the door hinges, "it's time to go to trial."

"What? Just like *that*? Without warning—at this hour of the morning and without breakfast?"

"I'll keep it warm for ye. Shouldn't take long to toss you back."

Sliding off the bunk and into his shoes, the prisoner dryly thanked the jailer for his vote of confidence. Lacing up, Fillmore stood and walked stiffly through the cell-door, blinking at the unaccustomed brightness of the prison corridor.

CHAPTER TEN

On this day of the month, the 25th
in the year 1875,
in the City and County of London
Shall be tried at 10 a.m. in Old Bailey
The criminal action of

VICTORIA REGINA

vs.

J. ADRIAN FILLMORE

on the charges of piracy and eluding justice.

FOR THE STATE: *The Hon. Samuel T. Cellier.*
FOR THE DEFENSE: *Defendant will be self-represented.*
THE RT. HON. RICHARD D. CARTE PRESIDING.

SCENE.—A Court of Justice.

Barristers, Attorneys and Jurymen discovered.

CHORUS

Hark, the hour of ten is sounding:
Heart with anxious fear is bounding,
Hall of justice crowds surrounding,
Breathing hope and fear—
For today in this arena,
Summoned by a stern subpoena,
Fillmore, sued by V. Regina,
Shortly will appear.

He was, in fact, already there, but that did not for a moment interfere with their caroling. He looked around with great interest at the bustling courtroom, which had already taken up a modified opening chorus from *Trial by Jury*, Gilbert's only one-act operetta. Studying the assemblage,

Fillmore was reminded of the equally-preposterous trial scene in Dickens's *Pickwick Papers*. He recalled a little of one descriptive passage: "There were already a pretty large sprinkling of spectators in the gallery and a numerous muster of gentlemen in wigs, in the barristers's seats: who presented, as a body, all that pleasing and extensive variety of nose and whisker for which the bar of England is so justly celebrated...The whole, to the great wonderment of Mr. Pickwick, were divided into little groups, who were chatting and discussing the news of the day in the most unfeeling manner possible—just as if no trial at all were coming on."

Fillmore's seat was to the left and in front of the judge's bench—as yet unoccupied. He was grateful to be allowed, in his capacity as counsel for the defense, to sit there, avoiding the dock. He was relieved that he would not have to spend the entire morning under the collective scrutiny of the tatty onlookers who jammed the place.

Counsel for the Crown entered. Fillmore, rising to his feet, gasped when he saw the tall, portly figure in black legal robes stride up to the right-hand anterior table and drop a pile of musty old lawbooks upon it.

There was no mistaking the flaming red hair and jutting mustache—the prosecutor was Samuel, the lieutenant of the Penzance pirates! Crossing the brief distance between the two tables, the brigand smiled brightly at Fillmore and stretched out his hand.

"Delightful to see you again, my good fellow!" he told the flabbergasted scholar. "Hope you won't take umbrage at anything I say later on, you know. Just doing a job and all that."

"But...but..." Stammering, Fillmore could not express his thought. He gestured in wild circles with both hands.

Samuel laughed. "Daresay you're wondering what I'm doing here, eh? Long story, my lad! Let the judge tell it. Here he is now—"

Fillmore turned, following Samuel's pointing finger. A majestic entrance hymn was struck up by the members of the jury and in came the presiding judge.

It was the pirate king.

Draped in flowing judicatory attire, he looked the soul of respectability—although the black patch over his eye still seemed slightly sinister. On his head, instead of his jolly-roger bonnet, the judge wore a frizzy white wig.

"What the devil?" cried Fillmore. "How can they possibly have assigned you to judge my case?"

The ex-pirate sat and beamed a paternal smile at the defendant. "Why, lad, it's a jolly day! Never expected to see ye again!"

"I repeat...*how can you be my judge?*"

His honor looked a little hurt at the question. "Why, young man, someone has to do it. Why not me? If you'd like to know the manner of my ascendancy, then lend an ear."

Before the defendant could protest, the invisible orchestra struck up a lively introduction and the pirate-cum-judge commenced to sing:

> *When Fred'ric turnèd twenty-and-one*
> *He embraced the tenets of justice;*
> *He swore his piratical doings were done*
> *And he'd seek out our band just to bust us—*
> *So he headed a handful of laddies in blue,*
> *And he sent forth these constabulary*
> *To the Cornwallish coast and the lair of my crew*
> *Whom they promptly proceeded to harry.*

(The jurors and spectators echoed the last couplet).

> *We fought strong and hard, but scarce did we win,*
> *When events took a turn unexpected—*
> *For the bobbies cried, 'Yield! To the queen, give in!'*
> *And my men promptly genu-u-flected.*
> *But the tide soon turned when we told them the news*
> *That once we'd been Peers of this Nation—*
> *So our crimes, they said, they'd politely excuse*
> *If we'd only resume our station.*

JURORS & SPECTATORS: So their crimes, they said, they'd politely excuse

If they'd only resume their station.

JUDGE: So now I'm a judge!

ALL: And a good judge, too!

JUDGE: Yes, now I'm a judge!

ALL: And a good judge, too!

JUDGE: Though homeward as you trudge,

My sinecure you grudge—

Yet I'll live and die a judge!

ALL: And a good judge, too!

SAMUEL rises.

RECIT—SAMUEL

Swear thou the jury!

AN USHER: Kneel, jurymen, oh, kneel!

(All the jury kneel in the jury-box and so are hidden from the audience.)

While the swearing-in took its course, Fillmore slumped down in his seat, frantically trying to assess the ridiculous situation. He supposed nothing more truly Gilbertian could have transpired than that he be prosecuted and judged by the very criminals who'd pressed the incriminating money and jewels on him in the first place.

The only encouraging thing he noted was the absence of that same evidence upon the exhibit table just beneath the judge's elevated bench. Good old Dick Deadeye surely must have remained steadfast by getting rid of the gems and specie found on Fillmore. The only object on the prosecutor's table, the scholar saw with some relief, was his umbrella.

Samuel rose. After a few brief remarks concerning the two charges leveled against the defendant, he pointed out 1) the absence of any pirated property, save for one peculiar parasol—a filched fashion accessory, no doubt. The loot, of course, must have been hidden away during accused's flight. As for 2), the red-haired counsel explained that the *Pinafore* was off at sea once more, but various documents in his possession attested to accused's being taken in Cornwall with the stolen goods.

As he concluded his latter point, a restrained little air sneaked under as he spoke. Without changing rhythm or timbre, he passed from prose to lyric...

> *With a sense of deep emotion,*
> *I approach this heinous case;*
> *For I hadn't any notion*
> *Any thief could be so base!*
> *He was caught with pockets swollen,*
> *Stuffed with jewelry and cash he'd stolen.*

ALL: He was caught, & c.

(Fillmore was beginning to feel decidedly strange. If he could have described the sensation in a single word, he might have chosen *fixed*.)

COUNSEL:

Picture now his crime denying,
Though he's guilty as can be—
This the charge we now are trying:
Fillmore for high piracee!
Doubly criminal, this raptor,
For he broke away from capture!

ALL:

Doubly criminal, & c.

(*All the jury rise as one man.*)

JURY (shaking their fists at Fillmore):

Monster! Monster! Dread our ire!
Quail thou, thief! Thou criminal and liar!
Come! Substantial punishment!
Substantial pun—

FILLMORE (leaping up):

Silence in court!

(*The defendant controls himself with great difficulty.*)

SONG—DEFENDANT

Oh, gentlemen, listen, I pray,
Though I own that my temper is flaming.
No vestige of truth ever lay
In what learned counsel is claiming.
And it's every prisoner's right
When falsely arrested with booty
To do what he can to take flight—
In fact, I would call it a duty!
Ah!
And as for the jewelry and pelf
They claim that they found in my pocket—
They came from our good Judge himself:
'Tis he that should be on the docket!

ALL:

Ah!
And as for the—

Swept up in the forward thrust of the trial, feeling very odd indeed, J. Adrian Fillmore would have plunged ahead in a second verse of his accusatory defense, but just then someone nudged him from behind. While the rest of the courtroom parroted his refrain, he turned to see what was wanted.

A big policeman pushed a small neatly-folded piece of paper at him and whispered, "Little gentleman in the back insisted I get this to you immediately."

Thanking the policeman, Fillmore took the note and scanned the crowd in vain for its author. He unfolded it hurriedly, since it was almost time for his second verse. But what he saw written thereon stopped him in mid-syllable. The music died away and judge, counsel, jury and the rest of those assembled in the courtroom stared at him in vast puzzlement.

The note was written in a big, flamboyant flourish. It said:

> If you ever want the umbrella to operate for you again, restrict yourself to speech—or, at worst, declamation to music!
> But, for heaven's sake, *don't sing*!

At the bottom was scrawled the initials: JWW.

So the sorcerer himself had sought him out! Hearing of the trial, or reading about it in the papers, the merchant magician must have instantly recognized the umbrella as an instrument of his own manufacture.

What could the note mean? Evidently, Fillmore stood in some kind of danger of which he was unaware. But if it was connected with the operation of the umbrella, then he would do well to heed its manufacturer's warning...

Turning to face the bench, the scholar begged to be excused from continuing his defense in song.

The judge looked genuinely puzzled. "It's your privilege, of course," he explained, "but I can't imagine why you chose to stop. You were doing so well..."

There was a murmur of assent from the jury and Fillmore noted with satisfaction that even Samuel slyly winked at him. But he stood fast.

"Many thanks for these kind words," he told the judge, "but I feel I will be more in my element if I carry on in prose, Your Honor. Now, the case as I understand it is this: I am accused of piracy, a charge which I flatly deny. Secondly, I am guilty of escaping from the custody of—"

"Oh, I think perhaps we may forget about that," the judge said. "Your point is well taken: duty of the captured to try to make a bolt for it and all that. What d'ye think?" he added, looking in the direction of the jury. They all nodded their heads vigorously.

"But, m'boy," His Honor continued, "I'm afraid we can't forget about this piracy business. The gold and jewels and monies given you were all taken on the High Seas...and you were an honorary member of our band (pardon, hem!: our former band) of pirates."

"Yes," Fillmore protested, "but I didn't take the loot! It was all stolen long before I saw it."

"It was stolen all the same," Samuel remarked.

"Oh, ay," the foreman of the jury grumbled, but the judge held his finger up to his lips. Then, looking down with benevolence at the defendant, the arbiter clasped his hands across his breast and rocked for a moment in meditation.

"The point, you see," he said at last, "is not who stole the goods, but rather, who finally profited by them. We pirates all reformed and would have returned our ill-got gains. But there was a substantial cache that you'd taken with you and since you never were a peer, there is no legal recourse but to prosecute you for receiving stolen goods and using them to your ends."

That, thought Fillmore is already a different charge than the legal definition of piracy—but the brand of justice meted out in a Gilbertian courtroom is too unorthodox to waste precious time haggling over such a point. What he must do, instead, is confront the court with the same sort of chop-logic it was wielding against him...

"Is it quite certain, then," Fillmore asked slyly, "that you are absolutely resolved that possession of loot is tantamount to piracy?"

"Quite certain," the judge said.

"We are so resolved?" Samuel replied, almost simultaneously. The members of the jury vigorously nodded their collective heads.

"Will nothing shake you?" Fillmore inquired.

"Nothing," was the unanimous answer. "We are adamant."

"Very good, then. In that case, I must demand that my accomplices in this offense be apprehended and tried along with me."

A murmur filled the courtroom. The judge rapped for silence, then stared at Fillmore with knitted brows. "How's this, lad, how's this? Are ye confessing?"

"Only within the rigid limits of your definition of the crime."

"Come now, laddie. I know right well ye'd no partners in this mishap."

The scholar, enjoying the confusion he'd implanted, rounded the table and paused to pour himself a glass of water. Taking his time swallowing it, he let his long-dormant theatrical predilection come forward. He sensed the moment when suspense amongst the jurors had built to an optimum level. Setting down the water-glass carefully, Fillmore glowered at the jury, then—suddenly whirling on the judge—dramatically pointed a finger skyward.

"I put it to the court," he said in ringing tones: "Are not those who take possession of stolen property and bear it off culpable under the very principle of justice which condemns me?!"

"Yes, yes, I suppose so," said the presiding official, leaning so far over his lofty perch that his wig slid down over his eyes. "But who do ye accuse of such conspiracy?"

Drawing in a deep breath, Fillmore said, "The captain and crew of the *Pinafore!*"

A mighty burst of babbling, shouts and exclamations swelled up and rode an angry crest. Samuel, hopping to his feet, protested volubly. The spectators in the gallery above and behind Fillmore were divided between titterers and hissers.

His Honor adjusted his top-knot so that he could direct his single-eyed glare full upon the prisoner. "That is an extremely serious accusation!" he fumed. "Consider! Where is the remnant of the piratical plunder? Do I have it? No! Do you have it any longer! No! But who took it from me? Captain—now able-bodied seaman—Corcoran!"

"The loot vanished when you did!" Samuel snapped.

"That's what *they* tell you! But where am I? In prison! And where is the *Pinafore*? Far off in some foreign sea, that's where!"

"It's true!" shouted a voice from the back of the hall. "Why didn't the blighters show up to testify?"

A chorus of voices hushed the objector, but the point was made. An undertone of murmuring dissent swept the court.

"Damme," cried the judge, rapping for order. "I simply cannot arrest the entire ship! Especially when they ain't even here..."

"Nothing simpler," said Fillmore, who'd been waiting for the moment to thrust home. "The subtleties of the legal mind should be equal to the emergency. Here we have established a precedent—"

"We have?" the judge asked, perplexed.

"Yes! You pirates, being absolved from your crimes, have resumed your former station, leaving the burden of guilt to rest on my shoulders. Thus, all you have to do is quit me of blame and affix responsibility on the *Pinafore* company."

"But we cannot promulgate such a scandal!"

"You wont have to," Fillmore explained. "When they come back to Portsmouth, find out what disposition was made of the treasure...ask a sailor by the name of Dick Deadeye for the particulars...then simply absolve the lot of them and try to convict whoever has the cache by then. You can go on indefinitely!"

"Well, well," the ex-pirate mused, toying with his gavel, "that seems a workable proposition. I don't like it, mind—but..." Looking at the jury, he shrugged. "Well, Mr. Foreman, I think we'll have to accept defendant's solution, won't we?"

The twelve good men and true wrangled among themselves for a moment, then the foreman rose and said they could not agree on a decision.

The judge, seized by a sudden fit of pique, ripped off his bothersome wig and flung it in their direction. Glancing at Fillmore, he asked sarcastically whether defendant would mind if the bench sang? Getting no opposition, His Honor swept off the papers and lawbooks from his desk in a rage and embarked upon a musical tirade:

> *All these legal tangles tease me!*
> *His proposal doesn't please me!*
> *Yet I'm stumped for things to say*
> *To explain his point away!*
> *Barristers and you attorneys,*
> *Set out on your homeward journeys;*
> *Gentle, simple-minded jury—*
> *Get ye gone and check your fury.*
> *Put your briefs upon the shelf—*
> *   I will free the man myself!*

A triumphal chord sounded; the jurors all applauded and came out of the box, thronging Fillmore to shake his hand. Samuel slapped him on the back and exclaimed how glad he was that justice had been done.

Remembering the admonition of the note, Fillmore restricted himself to speaking as the inevitable finale was stuck up by the omnipresent invisible orchestra:

> *Oh, joy unsated!*
> *I'm vindicated.*
> *I'm quite elated*
> *   And in the clear!*

Suddenly, there was a commotion at the back of the court. The doors burst open and a large, dowdy woman in billowing, multi-pleated dress and an imposing hat rushed up the aisle. Pushing through the milling crowd, she made her way to the newly-freed scholar who was at the exhibit table gathering up his umbrella.

With horror, he saw it was Ruth. She threw her arms around him and crushed him to her breast.

Singing, she took up the finale:

> *At last I've found you;*
> *With love I will surround you.*
> *My arms impound you*
> *And clutch you near.*

SAMUEL:

I wonder whether
They'll live together
In marriage tether
In manner true?

The judge, descending, thoughtfully grasped Fillmore by the arm and yanked him away from the importunate female. Pushing him up the aisle, he offered advice that the other had every intention of heeding.

JUDGE:

I would not stay, sir!
You'll rue the day, sir.
I'd run away, sir,
If I were you!

Though I am a Judge.

ALL:

And a good judge, too!

JUDGE:

Though I am a judge—

ALL:

And a good judge, too!

JUDGE:

I'll tell you all the truth:
If I had to marry Ruth—
I would sooner lose a tooth!

ALL:

And a good tooth, too!

Dashing into the outside corridor, Fillmore saw the judge push the courtroom door shut behind him—not altogether unlike the closing of a curtain at a play. As the portal slammed tight, the scholar could hear the final dominant chord sustained by the universal accompaniment.

Fillmore spared no time in quitting the building. Outside, a dapper little monocled man in striped trousers, cutaway morning coat and brushed top-hat stepped up to him, bowed low and held out his wallet for inspection.

In it was the ornately-drawn business card which Fillmore later would receive a copy of:

JOHN WELLINGTON WELLS
President,
J. W. Wells & Co., Family Sorcerers.
If anyone anything lacks,
He'll find it already in stacks at
70 ST. MARY'S AXE, LONDON
("SIMMERY AXE")

PROLOGUE

"The biggest danger you faced was subsumption," Wells told his guest. "You were beginning to accept the axioms and tenets upon which my world is formulated. A little more singing and you could have found yourself permanently stuck here."

"But why," Fillmore asked, "did you engineer such a danger into your umbrella?"

"I didn't. The instrument—which I must admit is far beyond my comprehension—operates on principles and universal dictums that I've never been able to completely pin down in the limited uses I've made of the umbrella."

"Oh? So you've been elsewhere? In other dimensions?"

"Whatever you call them," the magician replied, nodding his head sagely. "I've found worlds parallel to this one, but with many intriguing variations in living-style. In point of fact, the umbrella actually comes from one of them—"

"Impossible," the scholar scoffed, rising to stretch after his long sedentary session. "How could you have reached another dimension without the umbrella?" John Wellington Wells giggled. "You forget I'm a sorcerer, lad! One time I wafted myself into an alien universe, spied upon a master mathematician explaining the principles of this very device to an associate. But when I heard what purpose the inventor had in mind for his cosmic-travel engine (so to speak), I stole it away. Then it was a relatively simple matter to analyze its working parts and manufacture more of them. Of course, I've been most discreet in seeing that only the right people get possession of them..." Fillmore looked thoughtfully at the frayed and faded instrument propped up in a corner of the room. "I wonder how that one found its way to Rose's junk-shop?"

The little man shrugged. "It's anyone's guess. Perhaps its owner allowed himself to be subsumed in your own world."

"Who would do a thing like that?"

"Someone tone-deaf, perhaps. Such people are our 'handicappeds.' But we are disgressing, are we not? I was discussing the properties and peculiarities of my traveling-wands. Normally, I furnish customers with adequate printed instructions. Since you have had no such briefing, I had better explain a most important factor in use of the instrument."

"Which is?" asked Fillmore.

"There is a very fine line between participation and subsumption. For some reason, when you make a dimensional hop with the umbrella, you must complete a sequence. You have to participate in some basic block of activity..."

The scholar nodded. "My adventures followed the developing logic of an operetta. I had to solve the chief plot dilemma before the finale could be attained and the umbrella would work again."

"Yes," said Wells, "and you must now hurry in your departure, before a new sequence involving you gets under way." Rising and strolling to the piano, he played a few random notes while he collected his thoughts. "What I am trying to say," he continued, "is that the participation in other climes will be vastly different from this world. It won't always be so obvious as to what may ensnare you permanently..."

"Then how can I protect myself?"

"By doing what you did here: try to figure out the underlying postulates of the world you're in and manipulate them without accepting them. Do you understand?"

The professor nodded, then walked over to the umbrella and picked it up. "The only thing that bothers me is the degree to which I was put-upon here, even when I wasn't singing."

"Ah, yes," said Wells, nodding sagely. "You yourself sensed the cheat. Man tends to remain stable in whatever dimension he inhabits. You must really try not to allow yourself to be victimized, you know!"

"But what can I do about it?"

"Don't know exactly. You'll think of something. It's a matter of identity, more than anything, I believe. If you really accept yourself in a certain kind of role, the chances are you'll be it."

Fillmore shrugged. "Well, I'll have to think it over." He held the umbrella aloft, point towards the ceiling. "How do you make this thing go where you want it, anyhow?"

Wells put a finger in the air in an instructory attitude. "It is absolutely essential to fix the kind of place in mind where you want to travel."

"But I wasn't thinking of anything in particular when I opened it!"

"Then it just picked up whatever you were musing about at the time. Do you recall what it was?"

The scholar slapped his forehead with an open palm. "Of course! Gilbert and Sullivan! The old ladies in love and all that!"

"What is this gilbertandsullivan, anyway?" the sorcerer asked. "You mentioned it many times in your narrative."

"They wrote the operettas which certain events in this world echo. But you mean to tell me you've never even heard of them?"

"No, but why should I? You must remember that in our own world, we have our own objective realities. Your world is the only one I've heard of, up to now, that bears any relationship to mine—but it's so prosaic-sounding, I don't think I shall ever visit it. But..." The dapper little merchant paused, a worried frown creasing the corners of his eyes.

"Yes?" Fillmore prompted, putting his umbrella back down.

"Well...I said I wouldn't ask this sort of thing, but...well, dash it, you so much as hinted to me that my fate is rather dreary, according to the operetta that you know."

Fillmore fidgeted. "Well...ah, what happens in *The Sorcerer* is that you sell a love-philtre to a young man who will use it indiscriminately on his entire village. And then, in order to straighten out the mess, you—in the operetta—sacrifice yourself to Ahrimanes to break the spell."

"Oh, is *that* all?" laughed the sorcerer, relieved. "*That* happened to me some time ago. I made up that whole silly business of sacrificing myself! Fact is, it was an easy spell to remove—but I didn't want to get involved in any lawsuits."

It was the scholar's turn to laugh. "Thank heavens—it is the one really unsatisfactory ending in the whole G&S series..."

* * * *

"Well," Wells asked, "are you ready to take flight?"

"Ready!" said the other, holding up the umbrella again and releasing the catch.

"Do you know where you want to go?"

"Well, I'm a little torn between home or seeking out the one man who could unriddle the mystery of this umbrella."

"Which mystery are you talking about?" asked the sorcerer.

"Why it takes the user to literary, rather than actual, dimensions."

"Well," said Wells, "as I've said, all the places I've been to have been actual enough. But what enlightened genius are you referring to? What man could possibly unravel the enigma of my marvelous umbrella?"

But the little magician never learned the answer. There was a sudden rap at the front door of the shop, which Wells had locked so he could hear his guest's tale undisturbed.

Looking through the entryway to the back room, the two men saw who was knocking. Fillmore paled. Crying out a hurried farewell, he pressed the button of the dimensional-transfer machine...

"Wait!" the magician shouted. But J. Adrian Fillmore was no longer there. Both he and the umbrella, Wells knew, were sweeping the stars away from some heavenly threshold in the precipitate fury of their flight.

* * * *

There were two people at the front door: Ruth and a small, bald-headed civil servant, dry in manner and parched of spirit.

"Where is he?" the shrew demanded, but the wizened functionary hushed her.

"By law," he said, "you should not even be here while I deliver this, madam."

"Deliver what?" asked Wells.

"Subpoena for one J. Adrian Fillmore."

"On what charges?"

"What else?" Ruth snapped. "Breach of promise of marriage!"

"Oh, dear," the sorcerer mumbled to himself, "another sequence! I do hope he got away in time..."

* * * *

But Fillmore's thoughts were confused when he pressed the umbrella catch. Vivid memories of Ruth throwing herself upon him at the conclusion of his trial in Old Bailey crowded his brain and muddled the process of selection.

And what was worse, he knew nothing then of the principle of universal economy...

PART II

CHAPTER ONE

All afternoon, the equinoctial gales whipped London with elemental violence. The wan October sun, obscured by hueless clouds, shed pallid light but little warmth. Winds screamed down avenues and alleys, while at the window-panes, a driving rain beat a merciless tattoo. It was as if all the destructive forces of Nature had foregathered, penned beasts, to howl at and threaten mankind through the protecting bars of his cage, civilization.

As evening drew in, the storm waned, though the wind still moaned and sobbed in the eaves like a child-ghost whimpering in a spectral schoolroom. From the Thames, great curlings of fog billowed forth, obscuring the green aits and meadows, creeping up alleys and mews, blanketing the city in an impenetrable miasma. Amber streetlamps glowed feebly in the mist-shroud like the eyes of corpses. Few foot travelers ventured out in the mud and the only sound heard on some streets was the occasional rhythmic clip-clop and simultaneous metallic squeal of a passing Hansom.

Newman Street was deserted and smothered by the river-vapor. The mud was so thick and the appurtenances of inhabitation so difficult to discern that one might well believe a Stegosaurus could wander along its morass-like reaches. But at precisely ten past nine, a less impressive figure suddenly appeared on the empty thoroughfare: a smallish, somewhat stocky man.

His footsteps echoed down the street and he stalked along for a time before assaying a cross-street. He was inadequately dressed in a gray woolen suit with ascot tucked in at the throat. He was hatless and wore no topcoat. Though he carried an umbrella in one hand, he made no effort to use it as a shield from the steady drizzle.

Up one alley, down another, past shadowy blocks of homes, tenements, commercial establishments, the solitary pedestrian walked, his collar turned up and his head bowed. He hunched his shoulders, but the rain soaked into the material he wore on his back, ran down and squelched soddenly in his shoes, making the toes of his socks into sopping sponges. Once he stepped into a puddle deep enough to drown a cat. Shivering, he extricated his foot and forlornly tried to wring the excess moisture from his trouser-leg.

Turning into Lombard Street, he spied the lights of a distant tavern. He huddled into a covered entranceway and fished in his pocket for his wallet. Finding it, he counted over the meager currency therein: roughly thirty-four dollars in U.S. dollars that had been generously converted to pounds sterling by his benefactor, John Wellington Wells. But would it be usable in this cosmos? And did he, in fact, reach the very place he'd been meaning to visit?

Fillmore meditated briefly, made a 'decision, then stepped off in the direction of the far-off inn.

After a few moments more of slogging through mud and rain, he drew near to the place. A sign suspended from an iron scrolled arm set at right, angles to the bricks above the tavern-door proclaimed the name of the establishment:

THE GEORGE AND VULTURE

That disturbed him. But he wiped off his shoes on the small bracket for that purpose set next to the steps and went inside, grateful to get out of the wetness.

* * * *

The tap-room was sparsely populated that evening. A trio of gamesters took turns at the dart-board and an elderly, kindly-looking gentleman with a bit of a paunch sat at a corner table taking supper with a young, dandyish companion. The only other individual in the room when the drenched itinerant entered was the bartender.

Fillmore's bedraggled condition drew quizzical glances from the dart throwers, but said nothing. Approaching the bar, he held out a pound-note and ascertained from the bewildered tapster that it was, indeed, acceptable tender. The newcomer then ordered a pint of ale.

"Bit of a foul night for a stroll," observed the bartender as he set the libation on the polished counter-top before his customer.

The stranger nodded, downing a quarter of the brew at one gulp. Wiping his mouth, he eyed the bartender quizzically, then motioned to him.

"I say, would you mind very much if I asked you a question?"

"Of course not."

"Even if it seems a trifle peculiar?"

The tapster grinned, placed his hands flat on the counter-top and leaned over to his customer. "If," he said in a low voice, "you think aught can surprise me after twenty-year of tavern-tending, ye've much to learn. Ask away."

"Well...this is London, isn't it?"

"George Yard, right enough."

"Well and good but—" Fillmore shrugged. "Well, what I want to know is this: what year is this?"

"Why, 'ninety-five," the other replied, a bit nonplussed in spite of his assurances.

"Yes, yes," Fillmore nodded impatiently, "But—do you mean eighteen ninety-five?"

The bartender swallowed, wet his lips and took a breath before trusting himself to affirm the century. Then he found a reason to busy himself at the opposite end of the tavern.

Fillmore slowly sipped his ale, oblivious to the muted buzz that rose when the tapster began to talk to the dart-players. He ignored their collective gaze and busied himself moistening his interior and wondering how to dry off his exterior.

A tap on his shoulder. The dandyish gentleman stood by his side.

"Allow me to introduce myself. My name is Snodgrass—"

(Fillmore's ill-defined fears began to take shape.) "I beg to be forgiven for invading your privacy but my companion and I, you see, could not help but notice your somewhat uncomfortable condition. My friend is the most compassionate of men and wishes to make your acquaintance and perhaps assist you in your putative predicament."

The stranger thanked Snodgrass and followed him back to the table at the rear of the room, where the elderly, portly gentleman' in cutaway, gaiters and ruffled shirt rose to take his hand in greeting. With his other hand, he adjusted the rimless pince-nez upon the broad bridge of his nose and smiled.

"Pleased to meet a fellow scholar," he said, upon perusing Fillmore's Parker College business card. "Eh? What? Bless me, yes, quite right, you heard correctly, that is my name. I daresay what little reputation I may have established is not the least bit tainted with the calumnies of false report. But sit you down, sir, sit you down and dry off as you may. Won't you share some of this excellent cold beef? And allow me to refill your tankard?"

Fillmore thanked him mightily and set to with a will, not to mention a hearty appetite. His last meal had been in prison, awaiting trial at Old Bailey. The meat and ale were so excellent that he did not permit the trifle of a possible mislocation of cosmoses to upset him.

After he'd made a clean sweep of a quarter of the beef and had his glass refilled twice, Fillmore apologized for interrupting the dinner colloquy of his host.

"Bless my soul," said the old gentleman, "this is in no way an interruption, my good sir. Mr. Snodgrass here, who is, by the way—"

"A poet," observed Fillmore.

The old man's eyebrows raised. "Goodness, does his reputation, too, precede him? How did you know his occupation? I had thought he'd yet to be published!"

The scholar shrugged. "Oh, it's a bit of a fey quality that I have, I fancy."

"Well, well," the other chuckled. "I am suitably impressed. But, as I say, Mr. Snodgrass here is a capital poet—"

"My blushes," the other simpered.

"Now, Augustus, modesty ill becomes a man of true genius. You are a servant of the Muse and there is glory there! At any rate," said the host, turning to his guest, "my friend here is somewhat concerned with an affair of the heart and I thought to give him proper advice...which, indeed, I did. As I completed my statement, my attention was drawn to note your extremely dampish plight. And how, if I may be so bold, do you manage to be out on such a night as this without adequate protection? I presume your umbrella must be damaged; else it should have shielded you more efficiently from the elemental deluge."

"Well," Fillmore said, somewhat reluctantly, "I do not know whether I should repay your generosity with a rehearsal of my predicament. It is so wild a tale you would doubtless judge me madder than King Lear." The consequence of this remark was for Fillmore's host and the poet to positively entreat his adventures. So the stranger at length embarked upon his lengthy personal history, ending with his arrival on Newman Street and his subsequent trek to the George and Vulture.

When he had done at last, the others sat back, their mouths agape.

"Bless my soul," said the elderly gentleman. "That is certainly the strangest romance I have ever had the privilege to audit! No mind if it be true or no—it is an history worthy of the Arabian Nights. What do you say of it, Snodgrass?"

The poet had a dreamy look in his eyes. "I see," he sighed, "a major epic, a heroic narrative. I shall apply myself this very night while the fit is still upon me!" Suddenly leaping up, he excused himself and rushed from the room.

His companion laughed heartily, then apologized for the poet's precipitate departure. "When Inspiration descends unto his noble rhymer's brow, it ill beseemeth him to let her wait admittance until he pay the check." Still chuckling, the rotund little gentleman rose. "No matter, though, I am better conditioned than he, I can well afford it and had, indeed, meant to persuade him so." He graciously waved Fillmore to follow him.

In the lobby of the inn, he retrieved his room key, then, turning to his guest, said, "I keep rooms in this establishment Pray let me loan you some fitting—ho, ho!—apparel, for you cannot hope to go about unnoticed in your present state. No, no! I shall hear of no polite declinings. I am very handsomely off, my good fellow and it shall vastly please me to make a present of some necessaries with which you may better shield yourself from the raging elements...

* * * *

An hour later, the two descended the stairs to the lobby. Fillmore, dry and warm in slightly loose-fitting apparel, carried an oilskin bag beneath his arm. In it was his sopping clothing. Over his arm, the inoperable umbrella dangled.

As they neared the front door, the scholar whispered to his host, but that person vigorously shook his head.

"I repeat, positively not, sir! Your entertaining tale is ample payment enow for these scraps of cloth you've accepted. I urge you to keep your monies for a more pressing use. Why, if your story be true, you have but a few odd pound-notes on your person!" His eyes twinkled as he "humored" his guest.

At the door, Fillmore asked directions to his ultimate destination and feared it did not exist. But the old man's answer allayed his doubts.

"Why, indeed, that street is no great ride away, but see here, you cannot walk there on this foul night! I insist you let me fee a Hansom for your transport."

The scholar protested vigorously, but to no avail. His host, apologizing for a temporary absence of his man-servant on a family matter, himself stepped into the drizzle and smoke to hail a cab. It was no simple matter on such a night to find one, let alone flag one down in the limited visibility the fog afforded. But after much assiduous labor and much raising of the voice, the portly benefactor finally arranged for his friend's transportation.

As he entered the cab, Fillmore thanked his host repeatedly and the other as often belittled the charity as privilege and necessary duty. Closing the cab-door, the elderly gentleman stepped around to the front of the vehicle and told the driver the proper destination. He paid him in advance.

"The address wanted," said Mr. Pickwick, "is 221 Baker Street. Just out of Marylebone Road..."

CHAPTER TWO

Inside the cab, J. Adrian Fillmore tried to collect his thoughts. It was not easy because of the unaccustomed joggling and jostling his bones were receiving, but he did what he could to resolve the nagging doubts as to his whereabouts.

London it was and the year was correct, but was it the time and situation—in short, was it the universe—of Sherlock Holmes?

His thoughts, confused and harried by the sight of Ruth through the front door-pane of Wells's shop, rushed past in a chaotic jumble as he pressed the button to open the umbrella's hood. After that, all was a disordered kaleidoscope of colors and voids as he flew through uncomputed curvings of space. His hurried departure allowed no time to consider personal comfort. When he found himself in the middle of a dark, rainy street, Fillmore cursed the enforced celerity of his flight. "And, damn it," he muttered in the dark interior of the lurching cab, "what stupidity made me abandon my raincoat and galoshes back on the Cornwall seacoast?"

At least, Pickwick saw to it that he would be able to survive the weather until such time as he might expand his wardrobe. But the thought of the old gentleman brought fresh dismay. He was in London all right—but it appeared to be that of Charles Dickens! The benign heroes of the *Pickwick Papers* were pleasant enough, but they hardly qualified to assist Fillmore in his cerebral quest. Besides, memories of the grimmer aspects of some of the "Boz" narratives haunted him and made him most uneasy. His umbrella, ruled by cosmic quirk, would not permit him egress from this milieu until he completed a sequence of action—and Dickens's plots sometimes covered entire lifetimes. And in the meantime, what might he do inadvertently to mire himself permanently in the world of Dickens?

Was there a possibility that by some principle of universal economy, the London of Dickens was also the same world as that of Watson and Holmes? To learn the answer, the scholar was headed towards Baker Street.

"Sherlock Holmes," he mused, with a thrill of anticipation. "If anyone in the multiplicity of worlds that seem to coexist with the earth I know can analyze the umbrella, then—"

The sentiment was interrupted by the abrupt stoppage of the cab and the simultaneous hurling-forward of the passenger. He bruised his head against the edge of the opposite seat.

The driver shouted, "221 Baker." Fillmore dismounted, offering, as he did, an epithet to the cabbie in lieu of a tip.

Picking up the oilskin container of clothing, Fillmore crossed the road just as the disgruntled Hansom driver pulled away. A bit of mud spattered up from the wheels of the cab, but the scholar ignored the inconvenience in his excitement as he spied the large brass plate on the house opposite. His hopes were high as he scanned the inscription:

221
S. HOLMES, CONSULTANT

Apply at Suite B

Dashing up the steps to the front door, he pushed it open and mounted one flight. The interior was cheery, just as he'd always imagined it. Green wallpaper paralleled the staircase and the flickering of gas-lamps set in staggered sconces brightened the hall considerably.

He stopped in front of the B apartment and knocked. Almost immediately, a powerfully-built, moustached man in dressing-gown opened the door and invited him to enter.

Stepping inside, Fillmore asked, "You are the good doctor, I presume?"

"Why, yes," the other chuckled, "at least I hope to merit the appellation. But I imagine you have come to see Holmes, have you not?"

"I have, indeed," the scholar replied, his heart beating rapidly, like that of a school-boy who sees his first love approaching.

"Sit down, my good man," the doctor invited, meanwhile pulling on a bell-rope in the corner of the cozy sitting-room where he'd ushered his caller. "The fact is, I'm afraid Holmes is off tending to that dreadful business in Cloisterham. Chap missing, you may have read about it in the papers: Drood. But it's a close undercover game Sherrinford is playing and my presence there would only have confused things, so—" The doctor stopped, peering at his visitor with concern. "Pray tell me, sir, are you troubled by some indisposition?"

Fillmore, pale, could barely speak. "What," he whispered, "what did you call Mr. Holmes?"

"Why, Sherrinford, of course! All the world knows Sherrinford Holmes, do they not? Not the least (I fancy I may compliment myself) because of the narratives which I have penned concerning his exploits."

"And what," the scholar asked, still hoarse, "and what is your name?"

The doctor chuckled. "The fickleness of fortune and all that, eh? I'd thought my little publications might have added some touch of notoriety to the name of Ormond Sacker, but apparently—"

Fillmore rose in agitation and paced the room, thinking feverishly. Why were the names the doctor used so nightmarishly different from the ones he'd expected to hear? Sherrinford, not Sherlock. Ormond Sacker, instead of John H. Watson, M.D.

On the other hand, why did they also sound so familiar?

"Here, here, my good fellow," said Sacker worriedly, "I can see you are in considerable agitation. Pray be seated. Perhaps, in the absence of Holmes, I can shed some light on your problem. Meantime, I notice that the storm has not left you untainted. Be seated, be seated, man. I have rung for Mrs. Bardell and she will be up directly with tea and perhaps—"

Fillmore interrupted, even paler than before. "Mrs.—*whom*?"

80 | **MARVIN KAYE**

"Why—Bardell, Mrs. Bardell, our landlady!" the doctor said, great-ly amazed.

"*Not Mrs. Hudson!*"

"Hudson? I should think not. There used to be a Mrs. Warren taking care of this building, but she sold to a Mrs. Martha Bardell and that is who...but see, the knob is turning now. This is the very woman."

The door opened and a plump woman entered, bearing an ornate silver tea-service in her arms. But when she saw Fillmore, the woman screamed and dropped the tray. The hot liquid splashed upon the rug.

"What the devil!" Sacker exclaimed. "Mrs. Bardell! Have you taken leave of your senses?"

"It's him," the woman wailed, "*it's him*!"

"What *are* you speaking about, madam?"

"Him!" she howled, pointing an accusatory finger at J. Adrian Fill-more.

He, in turn, stared in flabbergasted dismay at the landlady. She was dressed in a green housecoat with flounce sleeves of a lighter shade with vertical stripes. On her head she wore a white, lace-trimmed domestic's cap, tied in a bow beneath her chin. But despite the disparity of apparel, Fillmore recognized her immediately.

It was Ruth.

CHAPTER THREE

Prison. A home away from home, Fillmore mused bitterly. First, the *Pinafore* brig. Then the Fleet. Now the Fleet again. Three times incar-cerated since buying the blasted umbrella. Before then, never a serious brush with the law. (He didn't count the abortive undergraduate party. At 8 P.M., no one had shown, so he glumly went out to get himself a steak sandwich. When he got back, the place was teeming with uninvited guests and a coterie of irate campus cops who, fortunately, had no idea who the host was.)

He huddled in a corner for warmth but did his best to avoid bodily contact with the lice-ridden sot next to him. In a far corner, a man with a broken nose and a piercing stare watched Fillmore every second.

At least, they'd let him keep the umbrella for the time being. After the trial, the authorities might well confiscate his property and then the scholar would be stuck here for good.

Stuck where? It was obviously Dickensian London, but it took Fill-more quite a few hours to figure out the weirdly-altered names of Holmes and Watson. When the answer came, it naturally disturbed him, but at least he began dimly to perceive the principle of universal economy.

Sherrinford Holmes. Ormond Sacker. These were names Arthur Conan Doyle toyed with before settling on "Sherlock" and "John H. Watson." Fillmore had landed himself smack in the middle of an incomplete *draft* of *A Study in Scarlet*. An *incomplete* draft. After all, what had Sacker said Holmes was busy doing? Investigating the Edwin Drood mystery—a notoriously unfinished masterpiece...

"That damned Ruth," the scholar muttered, clutching his umbrella close and trying to ignore the fixed gaze of the man with the broken nose. "Must have been trying to bring charges against me for breach-of-promise."

Nothing else made sense. It was apparent he'd inherited the "sequence" from the earlier cosmos, because he was in The Fleet awaiting such a trial. Mrs. Bardell, though astonishingly similar in face and form to Ruth, was really Sacker-and-Holmes's landlady...the very same Mrs. Bardell who sued Mr. Samuel Pickwick and landed him in prison in *The Pickwick Papers*.

"Well, at least the old boy did me a favor and now, it appears I'm doing him one, whether he ever learns it or no." It worried the scholar. The outrageously comic trial of Bardell vs. Pickwick is the dramatic focal point of that Dickens tome. But some bounder that resembled Fillmore apparently once jilted Mrs. B. and as a result, the hapless alien seemed to be usurping the breach-of-promise trial that ought to—

"There I go again!" Fillmore grumbled to himself. "Confusing fictional events with what takes place in these strange places I end up in. Do they follow the stories I read on 'normal earth?' Do they branch off wherever they wish? Maybe this is just an earlier trial and Pickwick's is yet to come here. *Or* maybe this is also a *draft* stage of the *Pickwick Papers* Ms. Then how do I—?"

He could not even finish the thought. It was too complicated. As hard to define as the identical looks of Mrs. Bardell and Ruth. Perhaps, he pondered, the entire cosmic system is a network of interlinking puzzle boxes, one heartwall economically doubling, tripling in alternative dimensions and each soul, in sleep, shares identities across the gaps of space and relative times.

"Bah," he murmured. "Einstein notwithstanding. Time is a concurrency."

But his philosophic gum-chewing was disturbed by a sharp poke in the ribs. It was the shifty-eyed ferret seated by him in the corner of the cell. "'Ere now," he whispered to Fillmore, "that's a peculiar thing ye've got there. Where'd ye fetch it?"

Fillmore tried to ignore him, but the ferret exchanged the poke for a pinch. "Owl" the scholar yelped. "Stop that!"

"I asked ye a question," the ferret whispered. "And keep yer voice low, if ye value living!"

The scholar faced his tormentor squarely, an angry retort on his lips, but the impulse stopped when he beheld the other's expression. The ferret's face was strained, each muscle tensed to the stretching-point. His eyes rolled independent of the fixed head and they moved in the direction of the sinister individual on the other side of the cell. The man with the broken nose.

Fillmore did not look at him. He regarded the ferret anxiously and replied as quietly as his questioner.

"I bought my umbrella far from here. What matter is it?"

"'im. Don't ye see how he stares at it. I never saw one to covet something so much. Never takes 'is eyes off it."

"I thought he was staring at me."

The ferret shook his head. "Last night, when ye slumbered, 'e crept near to examine it. Mutterin' to 'isself. Thought he'd snatch it then." The ferret shrugged. "But then, where'd 'e go with it?" The beady eyes narrowed, glinting with an eager urgency. "Ye want advice, man? If he asks for it, don't argue. Sell it, or make it a gift. Don't cross 'im!"

Fillmore shook his head. "Impossible. I can't part with my umbrella!"

"I tell ye, man, 'e's half-mad! Don't cross 'im! They'll 'ave 'im out in a day or two and then 'e'll wait for ye and 'e'll 'ave 'is cane."

What in all good hell is he babbling about? Fillmore wondered. The man has no cane. In fact, he walks perfectly well. Look at him—

The man with the broken nose was standing. He turned his gaze briefly on the little ferret and that person shrank away from Fillmore and cowered in a corner of the cell.

What kind of a crazy sequence is this, anyway? If this is the Bardell trial, why should I worry about strange men with umbrella fixations? Even if he is dangerous and even if he gets out of prison and tries to wait for me, my trial will keep me here indefinitely. And then? Damn, I may never escape!

"Permit me to introduce myself." The tall, sinister man proffered his card.

Fillmore stood. He was startled at the meek civility of the other's mien. From a distance, he appeared so menacing. But now, he must rectify his mistake. A toff, doubtless, confined for some minor infraction of the peace. He was well dressed, dark suit, ruffled shirt, a thin tie which might have passed muster a century later on campus.

The card told him nothing. It bore nothing but a name, "A. I. Persano."

"I trust my reputation is not unknown to you?" he asked. His face was smiling in a way that might suggest a double meaning to the question. But Fillmore knew no one intimately in this peculiar world of confused beginnings, so he could certainly not identify the stranger by reputation.

"I have been admiring that odd instrument which you have over your arm," Persano remarked. "May I examine it more closely?"

Fillmore found it hard to deny the reasonable request, so mildly was it made and yet, something warned him to refuse. From the corner of his eye, he saw the ferret urgently motioning him to comply. With considerable reluctance, the scholar relinquished the instrument.

The tall man minutely inspected the umbrella, turning it this way and that, pausing to push back the cloth folds and read the partially-obliterated inscription on the handle. As he did, Fillmore studied the lean, hard face. The eyes never blinked. The mouth was set in a half-grin that could easily be assessed as cruel. The nose, too, at close scrutiny, was even more disturbing than it first appeared. It was not broken after all. Rather it had been *sliced*, as if by some sharp edge. A deep lateral furrow creased the bridge, so that it resembled an ill-set fracture. But Persano was not the kind to indulge in violent roughhouse, Fillmore was sure. He was too contained, too deceptively calm. He might deal in rapier, never in bludgeon.

Persano returned the umbrella without comment.

Then, apparently satisfied, he asked what Fillmore was doing in jail. The scholar outlined the details of his case and the other clucked in doleful sympathy.

"Who defends you?" the tall man asked.

"Myself."

"And who represents the Bardell interests?"

Fillmore shuddered. He knew who Martha Bardell's barristers must be. "Messrs. Dodson and Fogg, I do presume."

"What? Then you're a fool, man. You have no choice but to raise capital sufficient to fee attorneys as crooked as those pettifoggers!"

"I haven't the money," Fillmore demurred. He refused to petition Pickwick. That might be an action which would mire him in the mishmosh-world he'd stumbled into. The best course was to maintain a detached air from the circumstances afflicting him...

"Since you are destitute," Persano said, smiling, "I have a suggestion."

Silence.

Fillmore knew what the other was about to say.

"Sell me your umbrella. I will pay handsomely for it."

"Why?"

"It...amuses me."

Fillmore shook his head. To his relief, the other did not press his request. Persano merely smiled more broadly. "Very well," he murmured. "There are other ways."

The following day, A. I. Persano was released from prison.

Two days later, a warder unlocked the door of the cell.

"Fillmore." He jerked his thumb to the door. "Out."

"Is it time for my trial?"

The warder shook his head. "Won't be one. Ye're free."

"Free?'

The ferret clucked in warning. "I told ye."

"How can I be free?" the scholar demanded, amazed, puzzled, overjoyed—and simultaneously uneasy.

"Plaintiff's counsel dropped charges. No estate worth speaking of to cover the expense."

"Estate? What are you talking about?"

The warder drew one finger across his throat in a gesture as meaningful in one world as another. "Bardell," he said. "Last night. Someone cut 'er throat."

CHAPTER FOUR

For once, he was not anxious to get out of prison. He dragged his footsteps along the last corridor before the outside gate and cudgeled his brains to make out what sort of dreadful sequence he'd landed in.

It could be the grimmer side of Dickens, he thought. Perhaps the only way to terminate one's existence here is to die. He shuddered.

At the front gate, he entreated the constable accompanying him to protect him, but the other merely grunted, "Oh, ye'll be noted, right enough," then turned and left Fillmore to the mercy of the streets.

What did he mean by that? the scholar wondered. Then, with a shock of dismay, he realized that he must be considered gravely suspect in the eyes of the police. "Bah!" he snapped, loud enough to be heard. "If I couldn't hire an attorney, what makes them think I could afford an assassin to murder Mrs. Bardell?"

He peered about nervously, but there was no trace of the sinister Persano anywhere. It was early, but the sickly pall of London mist obscured the sun. Few foot-passengers traversed the section of thoroughfares near The Fleet.

Fillmore walked aimlessly for a time, trying to work out the problem of the cosmic block of action he was expected to participate in. Since the breach-of-promise trial had come to naught, he could only presume that the uncompleted sequence with Ruth in G&S-land had finally run its course. But a new situation appears to have taken up, the scholar mused, worriedly. A dreadful situation, very like.

He was just crossing Bentinck Street at the corner of Oxford when he heard a sudden clatter of hooves and the rumble of a large vehicle. He swerved in his tracks and paled. A two-horse van, apparently parked at a nearby curb, was in furious motion, bearing directly down on him. Fillmore uttered a lusty yell and leaped a good six or seven feet onto the curb. Without stopping, he ducked down behind a lamp-post and did not rise until the carriage rolled into the distance and was lost to sight and sound.

He rose, puffing mightily. The jump was the heartiest exercise he'd undergone since trying to run away from Katisha weeks earlier. His heart pounded against his rib-cage. Fillmore glanced right and left, but the few pedestrians in view went about their business, oblivious to the near-accident which had just occurred.

But was it an accident?

He continued his journey, but did not allow himself the luxury of abstracted thought. Instead, Fillmore looked right and left, backwards and forwards, fearful of another attack. And yet the street seemed deserted. He was practically the only pedestrian on the avenue.

His very solitariness made him even more anxious. He was an easy target for anyone who might be following just beyond the curtain of the fog. At the next corner, he looked down the cross street and decided to take it, in hopes of coming to a more populous quarter of town.

There was a constable in the middle of the block.

Fillmore breathed a sigh of relief. At least he was safe for a few steps...

The constable turned and regarded him. The man's face became ash-white. He stuck his whistle to his lips and blasted it, at the same time thrusting an arm directly at the professor. Fillmore, astonished, hopped back a step and wondered whether he ought to run.

At the same instant, a huge brick smashed with tremendous impact upon the pavement directly in front of him. One more step and the brick would have crushed his skull.

Fillmore and the officer regarded each other for a second or two, too relieved to speak. Then Fillmore stepped far out into the street—looking carefully both ways—and walked over to the other, thanking him with great earnestness.

"I pride myself," said the constable, "on a quick reaction time. Fortunate for you, right enough."

"Yes...but who dropped that deuced brick?" Fillmore squawked.

The other's eyes widened. "Never occurred to me it wasn't an accident! Come, then! Better be brisk!"

Without another word, the constable dashed into the doorway of the large, cold tenement house from which the missile had apparently been impelled. Fillmore accompanied him, preferring to be in the company of the law at that moment than to be left waiting defenseless in the street.

They climbed dark, interminable stairs, redolent of cabbage and other less tolerable reeks. At length they found the skylight, which was reachable only by means of an iron ladder stapled with great brackets against the wall. It was a sheer vertical climb and Fillmore did not relish it.

At last they stood upon the roof, a good four or five stories above the street (Fillmore lost count of how many flights they'd taken in the ascent). There was a large chimney-stack off to one side and the remnants of a clothesline, evidently blown down by a gust of wind. By the street edge of the roof lay a pile of shingles, slate and brick, the flotsam of some antique building venture.

"There's your accident," the officer said, jerking his head towards the pile of construction leavings. "Wind must've worked one loose. Bit of a hazard, I'd best move 'em."

Fillmore, after thanking the policeman once more, left him laboring on the roof. He doubted it was an accident and if it was not, then he was in danger from the assailant who must still be in the neighborhood. He wanted to cling to the protection of the law, but his conscience would not permit him to endanger the officer who saved his life—and proximity to J. Adrian (what a beastly name!) Fillmore might do just that.

On the stairwell, he tried the catch of the umbrella, but it would not open. The sequence was far from finished.

Just as he was turning the corner of the last landing leading to the street level and the doorway out, he thought he heard a slight noise below, in the corner of the corridor alongside the first approach of the stairwell. He peered down the side of the banister but it was dark and he could see nothing.

He paused, unsure of what to do, whether to go back or forward. To rejoin the policeman would only prolong the danger. With a sudden burst of nerve, Fillmore leaped the railing and, umbrella pointed downward, dropped to the floor below.

A thud and a moan. A burly body broke his fall. He lugged the lurker into the moted dustlight and saw a feral visage, rich in scars and whiskers. A life-preserver—the British equivalent of a blackjack—was still clutched in the assailant's hand, but the man was unconscious.

Fillmore slumped against the wall, almost nauseous with fear. In the past half-hour, his life had been attempted three times, and, what may have been worse, he'd met the dangers with expedition and a physical courage all unsuspected in his makeup. It worried him as much as the danger.

Maybe *that's* what's got me stuck in this damned place! Fillmore shook his head to clear it of the vertigo that the fall brought about. No time for cosmic trepidations. Probably more danger, any moment, any second...

He quickly turned out the pockets of the man on the floor, but found nothing incriminating or enlightening. The life-preserver he stuck into his own back pocket.

Slowly, fearfully, Fillmore cracked open the front door. The street was no longer sparse of population. A knot of people milled about, shouting, giving unobeyed orders; one person was busily engaged in retching on the sidewalk.

The professor hurried down the front steps and peered through the press of people. There was a body smeared along the street, a bloody rag of flesh and dislocated bone.

It was the policeman. Someone must have shoved him from the roof, Fillmore realized, horrified.

"The chimney! The bastard must have been behind it!"

Angry for the first time since the game of stalk-and-attack started, Fillmore wanted to punish the killer who destroyed a man who'd saved his own life. He trotted to the middle of the street, shielding his eyes from the glare of hidden sun shining through blanched clouds. Was there someone still on the roof? Could he take him, too, like the thug in the stairwell?

For answer, a fierce face suddenly appeared at the edge of the building-top. An odd weapon quickly swiveled into position and pointed straight at the scholar.

He ran zigzag, hoping to evade the inevitable shot. But the other was a crack marksman. Even with the difficulty of hitting a moving target, the villain managed to lodge one shot in Fillmore's shoulder.

The professor staggered. What did that character say in the Fredric Brown novel? "If you are killed here, you will be dead...in every world." Fillmore stumbled to his feet. The strange weapon—which made no noise—was already in position for another shot.

My God! It's an air rifle!

The horrible universe suddenly fell into place. Terror overcame Fillmore and gave him the strength of mad desperation. He shot out across the street, waving the umbrella in huge, confusing arcs, changing direction every few seconds. He headed for the juncture of streets again and as he did, shouted and screamed for help. Some of the denizens of the neighborhood huddled about the constable's body stared at the crazy fellow and decided instantly that it was he who must have murdered the officer. No one advanced to Fillmore's aid.

Oddly enough, there was no second bullet. Fillmore reached the intersection safely. He saw a Hansom slowly rumbling down the middle of the avenue. "I must look a fearful sight," he thought, "shoulder bleeding, weird umbrella waving about like a Floradora girl's prop...

Fillmore took no chances. He ran straight into the path of the Hansom, shouting for it to stop. At the last instant, remembering the dreadful attempt of the two-horse van to run him down, he experienced an awful qualm. But the cab pulled to a stop.

"Baker Street," Fillmore gasped, jumping in and slamming the door. "Number 221."

The cab rattled off slowly. The scholar gasped for sufficient breath, then pounded the sides and shouted for the driver to make haste, but to no avail. The Hansom lumbered sluggishly along, neither creeping nor hurrying. Fillmore stuck his head out of the window and surveyed the street behind. There were no vehicles in pursuit.

He leaned back against the wall of the cab and panted. "Safe for a time, at least," he murmured. "I just hope that Sherringford—"

Before he could even complete the thought, the cab lurched to a stop. Fillmore stuck his head out the window. "Here, what is this? This isn't Baker Street!"

"No, sir," the cabbie said, dismounting. He walked to Fillmore's door and stood by it, preventing it from opening. "Taking on another passenger, we are, sir." Fillmore regarded him blankly. Then he swung around in his seat, hoping to get out the other way. But that door was already opening.

The new passenger rested his cane against the seat and closed the door behind himself. He settled comfortably into the place opposite Fillmore.

"You've caused us a deal of trouble this morning," A. I. Persano remarked mildly.

CHAPTER FIVE

The cabbie whipped the horse to a froth. The Hansom rattled along at breakneck speed. Fillmore braced himself to keep from bouncing straight through the flimsy ceiling. He gritted his teeth at the ache in his shoulder.

Persano, riding as skillfully as if mounted on a thoroughbred, was quite amiable. He regarded the other's persecution as a tiresome necessity, to be managed with swift expedition, but utterly without malice. Not to be discussed in polite company. The Code, by all means!

"Had you been reasonable," he stated mildly, "all this pother might have been eclipsed."

"Meaning I should have given you the umbrella?"

Persano gravely inclined his head.

"Rubbish!" Fillmore said with great asperity. "You are in a frenzy to get this instrument. Therefore, you must know its function. It follows, then, that you know I couldn't part with it at any price."

Persano clucked disapprovingly. "I could tell the authorities that the umbrella was stolen from my employer."

"You are blathering nonsense! Anyone with a shred of sense must deduce your employer has no desire to see this instrument's astonishing properties made public. You could have reported it stolen in prison. Instead, two people are dead because of it and I have a bullet in my shoulder."

"An unfortunately staged episode," Persano agreed, stifling a yawn. "The Colonel has no idea of how to achieve maximum effect with minimal effort. His aggression grows in inverse proportion to his waning manhood."

Suddenly, the puzzle, nearly solved, all clicked into place. The ferocious Colonel Sebastian Moran! ("The second most dangerous man in London, Watson!") And the kindly sorcerer, John Wellington Wells, admitted to spying on a master mathematician, from whom he stole the umbrella. The instrument must be the brainchild of the brilliantly evil kingpin of London crime, Professor Moriarty! And then, another thought: Holmes once spoke of two especially dangerous members of the Moriarty gang. One was Moran. Persano must be the other.

Fillmore, shuddering, commented on Persano's remark. "You are, of course, referring to Colonel Moran."

For a split-second, the mask of indifference dropped and the other subjected Fillmore to a deadly scrutiny. Then his eyes clouded over again and Persano propped his cane by his chin and chuckled.

"Cards on the table, eh?" He nodded approvingly. "Very well, then, an end to games-playing: you, sir, are either an agent or a fool."

"What do you mean?" Fillmore stanched the wound in his throbbing shoulder with a handkerchief.

"It cannot be that you are with the Yard," Persano mused. "A *provocateur* would not allow a fellow-constable to blindly face an unseen foe without ample warning. Nor, for that matter, would Sherrinford Holmes stick someone else's neck on the chopping-block. No. You did not lure me into an imminent trap. You are engaged in a lone game against the greatest organization of its type in the world. You are, therefore, a colossal fool."

"In a word, you refer to Professor Moriarty's organization."

"*Who*?" Persano asked, pretending perplexity.

There was a lengthy silence.

"I do not know to whom you refer," Persano said, "but I might amend what I said before. I called you a fool. I suspect you are worse: a veritable lunatic. But the tense soon shall alter..."

Fillmore clutched the umbrella tight, his thoughts racing. His life was in great danger. In whichever world he blundered, he ended up a victim. In this clime, he might well end his sequence permanently.

"This needs no further discussion, I think," Fillmore said airily, attempting an ease of manner which he hoped might match his opponent's. He shifted in the uncomfortable carriage seat. "You will steal the umbrella and there's an end of it."

Persano shook his head, an earnest expression on his face. "Really, that is not possible. Don't you see? You, an independent agent, are somehow privy to details that my employer would not like bruited about. You are able to set my face and name to several recent incidents of dubious merit. You carry a pellet in you from an air-gun and there are many unsolved crimes connected with such a weapon. What is worse, you know the Colonel's last name. No, no, it's quite impossible, surely you see my position?"

His eyebrows raised quizzically. He really seemed concerned lest Fillmore fail to comprehend and sanction the deplorable step that must be taken.

It did not fool Fillmore. Persano had never taken pains to cover his involvement in the "incidents." What was worse, he freely volunteered information about Moran's association with other atrocities. Persano evidently never at all intended to let the scholar survive.

"Look," he blurted, "I have a different suggestion. Come with me someplace else so that I am no longer in this world. I'll go back to my own cosmos! Then you can take the damned umbrella and return here!"

Persano shook his head again. "I can't do that. How do I know how long it will take before that thing decides to work again? If it could work now, you wouldn't be here at this moment. But even if you could waft us elsewhere immediately, you know I could not use the umbrella for long afterwards and I have no time to wait."

"Why couldn't you use it?" Fillmore asked.

Persano eyed him curiously. "I think you actually don't know."

"Know *what*?" His shoulder still hurt. The carriage decelerated to a more bearable rate, but he still was unable to sit comfortably.

Persano reached over and took the umbrella. Fillmore tried to hold tight, but the other easily plucked it from his grasp. Persano pushed aside the hood-folds and put his thumb on the catch.

"Observe." He pushed the button.

Nothing happened.

"It is imprinted with your brain-pattern. It will take it a long time to readjust. Unless..."

He let the thought dangle in the air, drumming his fingertips on the central pole of the bumbershoot.

A long while passed. They stared at one another without speaking.

Then the horse slowed to a walk.

"We are almost there," Persano said in a low voice.

"Where?"

"A warehouse. Prepare to disembark."

Persano looked out the window. As he did, Fillmore suddenly realized why he was having so much trouble sitting comfortably. There was something in his back-pocket—

The life-preserver!

Carefully, carefully, he reached his hand around to get the sapping tool. His fingers crept. Persano stared out the window.

Good! Teeth clenched, a cold perspiration bespangling his brow, the pedant strained for the ersatz blackjack. *Another quarter-inch...*

It snagged in a fold of his pocket and he could not yank it free. Fillmore tugged, but his arm was in an awkward position and he hadn't ample leverage to twist out the thing cleanly.

The carriage shuddered to a stop.

"End of the line," Persano announced, turning. His eyes narrowed. "What are you doing?" he asked, his tone suggesting the indulgent displeasure of a kindly schoolteacher towards a wayward urchin.

Fillmore frantically pulled at the cosh. The whole back-pocket of his pants ripped off. At last, he had it in his hand!

But the quick movement triggered Persano. Swiftly, soundlessly, he shot forward and clutched Fillmore's throat in a steel grip. He was not angry, only methodical. Whatever Fillmore was trying to do, Persano immediately recognized it as a last-ditch effort and knew he must bring it to naught. Though the business was clearly beneath him—throttling was the preserve of brutal underlings—he squeezed Fillmore's windpipe quite efficiently, nonetheless.

The scholar once read that it only takes a professional killer seven seconds to choke someone to death. Already the lights of life danced dimly and dwindled. He knew he only had strength in his arm for a single assault—

He cracked the preserver against the base of Persano's neck. (Gesture derived from countless spy and war films.) Persano slumped for a second, only a second; the quick mind analyzed the extent of damage with incredible celerity and marshaled strength for a new attack.

But Fillmore only needed the one respite. He heaved Persano off and simultaneously raked one hand upwards over the other's face from jaw to nose (a trick out of *Shane*) while the other hand slammed the life-preserver into the throat thus presented for the blow (*Bad Day at Black Rock*).

Persano gagged and doubled up.

Dropping the cosh, Fillmore wrested free the umbrella and jumped out the opposite side of the carnage from whence he'd entered. Just then, the driver pulled the other door open; seeing he was gone, he cursed at Fillmore, slammed the door and started after him. Fillmore threw his weight against the Hansom, hoping to tip it over onto the driver, but the effort drew fresh pain from his shoulder-wound and only earned him a good jarring butt.

He saw the feet of the driver rounding the carriage, so he started the other way. An idea struck him and he vaulted onto the driver's seat. ("Thanks to Gene Autry!") and slapped the reins.

The horse ambled forward two inches and stopped.

"Damn! It always looks so *easy*!"

The driver came up on him. A sinewy, saturnine thug he was, with a dagger in his hand. He hauled himself onto the seat, slashing at Fillmore, but the professor administered a stunning blow to the chest with the whip-handle ("courtesy Lash LaRue") and the rascal landed on his back in the street, roaring.

The horse, mistaking the bellow for an order, reared up.

"*Whoa*!" Fillmore yelled. The animal, unfamiliar with the western idiom, interpreted the word as a seconding motion and immediately adopted the measure by dashing forth. The cab careened to one side, righted itself and lurched behind the crazed beast.

The jolt pitched Fillmore backwards. He nearly lost his grip on the umbrella, but clutched frantically, regained his hold and simultaneously squirmed onto his face so he could embrace the cab-roof with arms spread wide.

The horse stormed down the cobbled thoroughfare, which was a road that directly paralleled the river. Warehouses sped past; a confusion of disappearing dry-docks. Cursing dockwallopers sprang out of the path of the runaway.

Fillmore hugged the roof, too winded and frightened to move. But suddenly, the blade of a sword swiftly emerged from the roof one-sixteenth of an inch in front of his nose. He decided to budge after all.

While the blade was withdrawing for another thrust, he scrambled into the driver's seat and fished for the reins. No use; they hung over the lip and jounced in the roadbed; he strained but could not reach them. Next thing he knew, the furious pitch of the ride bumped his teeth together so he bit his tongue and shoved him straight back against the cab housing. He instantly pushed forward, narrowly avoiding the sword-point which emerged at the place where his body made impact.

He ran his hand down the umbrella and tried to snap it open. *No go!* Then he saw a new danger up ahead. About two blocks in the distance, the street curved sharply; where it turned, the embankment terminated and there was a sheer unprotected drop into the river.

Two thoughts, born of desperation and an acquaintanceship with Hopalong Cassidy and screen versions of *The Three Musketeers*, popped into his head. He peered ahead—yes! Just before the turn there was a custom-house with empty flagpole jutting from the second-story...

He sprang forward onto the traces and grabbed the link-pin with the handle of the umbrella. Fillmore seized the shaft of the bumbershoot and hauled up until the pin was almost free. He stood up, balancing wobbly, squinting to gauge the correct angle and distance, waiting for the vital precise second.

"*Now!*"

Jumping as high as he could, he latched onto the flagpole with one hand, at the same time tugging on the umbrella so the link-pin disengaged. The carriage-top smartly smacked his ankle and, with a tremendous effort, Fillmore hooked the umbrella over his other arm and got a second purchase on the pole with his left hand. The carriage rumbled past beneath him. A bolt of pain struck his shoulder, but he endured it, watching with grim approval the event happening in the street below.

The cab lost speed and the steed, no longer shackled to it, pulled on ahead. It negotiated the bend, but the carriage lumbered straight to the edge, teetered for a fraction of a second, then plummeted into the icy Thames with a colossal splash.

"And that," Fillmore observed with satisfaction, "is the last anyone will see of Mr. A. I. Persano!"

His pleasure was short lived. Now that the immediate danger was over, it occurred to him that he hadn't the foggiest idea of how to get down from the flagpole without breaking his neck (He'd never caught up with any Harold Lloyd films.) But it didn't take him long to devise a course of action.

"*Help!*" Fillmore shouted. "*Get me the hell off of here.*"

CHAPTER SIX

Sacker shook his head incredulously. "That is the strangest story I have ever heard, sir. Either you are up to something nefarious, or you are mad."

"I tell you that I am not lying!" Fillmore protested. "Would I mention Professor Moriarty if I were part of his gang?"

The argument had been going on for several minutes and the professor was beginning to despair of ever convincing the good doctor that he was anything but a raving lunatic. Had it not been for his shoulder wound, Sacker probably would not have permitted him entry into Sherrinford Holmes's flat, half convinced as he was that Fillmore was indirectly responsible for Mrs. Bardell's murder.

The doctor shook his head slowly. "You come to me with wild tales about dimensional transfers—whatever that means—and worlds where I only exist in an unpublished manuscript and Holmes is not Holmes! The least marvelous portion of your romance is that which you claim happened this morning: runaway Hansoms, customs-clerks hauling you off flagpoles, brickbats and dead policemen! Surely, sir, you do not find it marvelous that I have some difficulty swallowing all this?"

Fillmore nodded wearily. It had been a most exhausting day and his bandaged shoulder still throbbed dully. The night was drawing on and he wanted nothing more dramatic than sleep. But duty was duty, in whatever world he inhabited. If the Moriarty gang were so bent on attaining the umbrella, it could only follow that the infamous professor had some awful scheme in mind.

But Sacker was adamant. "Holmes only mentioned this pedagogue of yours once and that recently. Whatever he did, I do not know. For Holmes only alluded to him on that one occasion at the time of his disappearance."

"*His disappearance?!*"

Sacker nodded. "Yes. I do recall Holmes's relief. And his perplexity. One day, he said, Moriarty was in London, the next he was nowhere on the face of the earth. 'And good riddance, Sacker!' he remarked and there was an end of the conversation. I never heard Moriarty's name again until you brought it up tonight."

"Well, well," Fillmore said impatiently, "whatever may be the status of the professor, he has a strong and wicked organization which still carries on his works. It must be quashed. And since its lieutenants know about my umbrella, it is imperative that I speak to Sherrinford Holmes immediately!"

"Well, as for that," Sacker suggested, "I suppose you could come along with me tonight. Holmes has communicated from Cloisterham, where that business is all but wrapped up. He needs some final service pertaining to one Mr. Sapsea and I am to perform it." Sacker chuckled. "Holmes rarely asks me to tackle anything histrionic. It must be a goose, indeed, to whom I must play the poker!"

Fillmore's brows knit. It sounded familiar...ah, yes, the "Sapsea" fragment found in Dickens's study after his death, an enigmatic portion of the *Edwin Drood* manuscript that remained unpublished for many years. The rough-draft aspect of the present world still held. It occurred to the scholar that in a place comprised of unfinished or half-polished literary concepts, it might not be *possible* to complete a sequence and get free. He nervously tapped his finger against the curved grip of the umbrella and tried to follow the thought, but Sacker spoke again.

"I must ask you not to interfere with the progress of the case, or attempt to communicate with Holmes until he gives me leave to bring you forward. If you can agree to that, then you may accompany me on the 10:40 out of Charing Cross."

"Very well," Fillmore replied reluctantly. "But perhaps I might be able to give you a note to pass on to Holmes when we arrive. Time *may* be of the essence!"

The doctor nodded. "And now, since we can do nothing until it is time to entrain, I suggest we follow my friend's habit of tabling all talk of hypothetical crises until we have detabled. I will send round for an amiable Bordeaux and ask Mrs. Raddle, our new landlady, to set out supper. Does that seem agreeable?"

"Oh, of course," Fillmore concurred, dimly wondering where he'd heard of Mrs. Raddle before. "I take it you have decided not to regard me as an imminent threat."

"Well, sir," Sacker chuckled, "I must admit that is an odd angle for a man to shoot himself as a piece of corroborative evidence. I still cannot accept the wild history you related, but if you are mad, sir, at least it is an engaging malady. Besides, I detect a man of learning in you and a scholar is by no means the worst of dinner companions."

Fillmore thanked the doctor for his courtesy and mentally noted that Sacker/Watson certainly matched the old Holmesian observation (was it first made by Christopher Morley?) that a man might be honored to meet the Great Detective, but it would be Watson with whom a wintry evening, a cold supper and brandy would be most enjoyed.

While the good physician stepped downstairs to talk to Mrs. Raddle (she's in *Pickwick Papers*, too, isn't she?), Fillmore busied himself looking about the drawingroom/library. It was easy to tell which portion of the bookshelves belonged to Holmes and which to Sacker. One half, or better, was crammed full of standard references and albums of clippings of criminous activity. The other side of the room was devoted to a broad assortment of escape literature—tales of early English battles, ghost stories, high romance on the seas, an occasional sampler of sentimental poetry and (perhaps in deference to Holmes's profession) a tattered copy of the lurid *Newgate Calendar*, a volume destined for ignominy in another world.

Sacker had one book open on a table by his easy-chair and the professor walked over to inspect what it was. "Ah! A man of similar tastes in fantasy," he murmured. "Benson's *The Room in the Tower* and other ghastly tales." He turned the book around and flipped through it, holding Sacker's place. The doctor evidently had just begun reading a short story, "Caterpillars." Fillmore remembered it with a shudder.

The doctor reentered the room and made a courteous remark concerning escapist literature, the likes of which Fillmore held in his hand. "Yes, yes, the Bensons are rather a dynasty," Sacker agreed. "I have another one, by Edward's brother, Robert Hugh. *The Mirror of Shallot*. Odd. Excellent."

Fillmore checked himself. He had been about to comment on the finding of the identical volume years later on the day he purchased the umbrella, but it occurred to him that the doctor would regard the assertion as further evidence that his wits weren't all in working order.

Supper was sumptuous, if simple fare. A roast beef, rare and huge. A brace of game. Trifle, coffee and brandy. The only disappointment was the Bordeaux, which was temporarily out of stock. In apology, Mrs. Raddle sent up a cherished tawny port, which Sacker set aside for post-dessert, if the professor so desired. The doctor clearly had no enthusiasm for the stuff. Fillmore, however, had not dined well since sharing supper with Mr. Pickwick and he availed himself of all there was to be had, including the landlady's prize port, the effect of which was to lull him into a much-needed sleep.

He awoke with a start. It was dark in the room and there wasn't a sound. He reached out, encountered a night-stand with a box of matches on it. He fumbled for one, lit it, noted the box to be one of those cheap cardboard pillboxes into which matches had been crammed. Perhaps it belonged to Holmes; it sounded like his brand of freeform adaptation, Persian slippers used to hold shag tobacco, knives stuck to the mantel to fix correspondence in place...

There was a lamp nearby. Fillmore lit it and turned up the key so he could better determine what surroundings he had. It was a small bedchamber, plain, with a wardrobe and a low table with mirror behind it where Holmes assuredly put on his disguises. There was a piece of paper affixed to the mirror in a place where Fillmore could not help but notice. He rose and took the lamp with him so he could read what was written thereon.

"My dear Fillmore," it said, "I had no idea your injury so exhausted you. It was impossible to rouse you and considering this as a physician, I am not so sure it will be wise for you to spend the better part of the night on a drafty railway train. Your resistance is low and you may do yourself an injury by coming, susceptible as you may be to sundry ills and fevers. I have put you in Holmes's bed, mine being uncharacteristically untidy and his having had the benefits of Mrs. Raddle's ministrations and am off to catch the 10:40. If you do not sleep the night, you may wish to read; I will leave the drawing-room lights on for you. You are, of course, welcome to whatever fare you can find and you may also use my toilet articles, shaving brush, etc. We shall return in a few days. If you feel the urgent need to see Holmes as soon as possible, you may, of course, join us in Cloisterham. The decision is yours. But, pertaining to the dangers you rehearsed, I must say, on your behalf, that a hasty perusal of Holmes's files shows that there is indeed in London one "Is. Persano," an athlete, duelist and singlestick competitor of awesome accomplishment. His card is checked in red ink, which Holmes employs for particularly dangerous criminals. If this is the same individual whom you claim to have dogged you, it may be wisest to stay at Baker Street and do not set foot out-of-doors until we get back. But I must not miss the train.

Farewell. O.S."

Fillmore was too drowsy to clear his head and recall the reference that was bumping about in the back of his brain. He still felt logy. Rubbing his eyes, yawning, he walked to the door connecting with the drawingroom/library. At least sleep had refreshed his memory on the matter of Mrs. Raddle. She was Bob Sawyer s landlady in Dickens and a contributory vexation to Mr. Pickwick. A low, spiteful shrew who might do anything for money.

Roused from sleep, Fillmore's appetite had also returned. He wondered whether any of the beef was still left, or if it was all put away.

And what about the umbrella?

Certainly Sacker would have left it behind, yet Fillmore experienced a few qualms until he opened the door and saw the instrument propped in the same corner where he'd left it. That was reassuring; even more so was the sight of the unconsumed food still waiting, covered, on the table.

"The benevolent Dr. Sacker-alias-Watson," Fillmore beamed, stepping forward to lift the cover on the plate of beef. And then his warm sense of well-being plummeted and died.

There was a man seated in the doctor's easy chair by the fireside, a book on his lap; he was reading intently.

"By all means, sit and eat," Persano invited. "I have a few pages yet to go."

The man with the sliced nose did not even deign to look at Fillmore. He seemed possessed by the Benson volume in his hands.

Fillmore dashed over to the umbrella and got a grip on it. He pushed aside the drapery that encloaked the left front window. The street outside was empty.

Should I smash through the glass, make a bit of a vault into the street? But a thought occurred to him concerning air-guns. He peered at the dark edifice directly opposite. A sudden glint of reflected light shone and was instantly gone, but it was enough to inform Fillmore that someone lurked behind one of the windows of Camden House, which must be the empty home across Baker Street from 221. (It was in Camden House that Colonel Moran lurked when he attempted to assassinate Sherlock in "The Adventure of the Empty House.")

There was no point in trying a dash for it. Unless there was a back way, Fillmore was trapped with Persano.

"In case you are in a gymnastic mood," Persano remarked, "allow me to advise you that the house is entirely surrounded. Now pray wait a moment longer. I have but a single page to complete."

Fillmore stood rooted to the spot, his appetite gone, waiting for the villainous Persano to come to the end of the tale in which he was engrossed.

Persano perceptibly shuddered as he closed the book. "That was indeed a horror!" he remarked. "I have always been a devotee of the fantastic. Are you familiar with the genre?"

Fillmore said nothing.

"Oh, come," said the other, "the mere matter of the umbrella and your inevitable demise can surely wait. There is nothing more soothing in this world than to contemplate something truly dreadful, such as Benson's 'Caterpillars,' and then come safely back to this mundane world where the only atrocities are the humdrum stuff of daily business. The tale is not up to 'The Room in the Tower,' but then, what is? Still, the idea of ghastly crab-like caterpillars, giant ghostly creatures and their miniature daylight counterparts that scuttle about with their excrescent bodies and infect those that they bite with cancer—such is no ordinary *cauchemar*. It almost makes the idea of ordinary death-by-violence drab and comfortable."

Persano flashed his mirthless smile at Fillmore. Then, in a leisurely fashion, he extracted a thin cigar, bit off the end, spat it and requested a light from the scholar. Numbly, Fillmore tossed the pillbox to the other, who caught it, took out a match, struck it and lit the cigar.

Persano regarded the matchbox momentarily. "A box like this figures in the tale. Do you know it? An artist captures a miniature crab-like caterpillar and keeps it in the box until he changes his mind and treads on the insect, which seals his doom." His shoulders went up and he shivered in fear. "I believe if I found such a creature in this box, my mind would snap. I have seen the ravages of the disease." He regarded his cigar with melancholy dissatisfaction. "That is the curse of all earthly endeavor, is it not? We bargain and bully and bludgeon for our own ends, but in no wise can we crush the microbes that infest us from within. I should *hope* I should go mad and do terminal injury to myself rather than undergo such a horror as I once witnessed and have just read about." He regarded the professor darkly, then his wicked smile reappeared. "But I wax melancholy. Shall we proceed to brighter matters?"

"How did you get in?" Fillmore asked hoarsely.

"All, that's the spirit! Ask questions, buy time, my friend. Since you ask, The Raddle's holdings were recently purchased by our interests and we set her up here after the death of Mrs. Bardell. She was instructed to inform us if anyone of your description and peculiar appurtenances—(he indicated the umbrella)—should appear to Dr. Sacker. I presume that you are an agent of Holmes, after all, in which case the dear boy is grown uncommon careless."

"I thought you'd drowned," Fillmore accused sullenly.

"Sorry for the disappointment. But be assured, sir, I hold no grudge for your maneuver. It was cleverly executed. But I am no mean swimmer. And as for tracking you down again, our system of surveillance is so thorough that you would have been found out in any event within a mere matter of hours. I confess, though, I did suspect this is where you would probably go. The only thing that at all bothered me was the possibility that the umbrella might function once more. But it does not appear to be in any hurry to remove you from this unlucky world, does it?"

"One must finish a sequence," Fillmore grumbled. "I beg your pardon?"

The scholar briefly explained the necessity of participating in some basic block of action correspondent to the base literary form of the cosmos in which one was deposited by the parasol.

Persano nodded. "I see. That explains why the Professor has not yet returned. But what a deuced unpleasant condition! Imagine, for instance, ending up in Stoker's Hungaria and having no other way out but to combat Count Dracula. A horror, this umbrella, if one were carried by it into a world of night."

"Yes," Fillmore observed, stalling for time, "but no one who knows how it works would deliberately choose such a place."

"Well, no matter," Persano said, extinguishing his cigar, "the time has come to terminate this disagreeable matter. You will give me the umbrella."

"I will not!"

Weariness etched lines on Persano's face as he contemplated a struggle. "Come, come, man, bow to the inevitable. You cannot escape and you know it perfectly well. Moran has a bead drawn on the front of the house and there are thugs in front and back." He consulted a pocket-watch. "It lacks two or three minutes of midnight. My men have been told to wait until twelve. If I haven't returned by then with the umbrella, they are to forcibly enter and destroy you on sight. I'm afraid they would be rather messy about it." Persano rose, picked up his cane, which had been resting on the floor and withdrew the sword from its innermost depths. "Permit me to dispatch you swiftly and mercifully, while there is still time. It is the least I can do for so innovative and tenacious an opponent."

"*Have at you, then*!" Fillmore shouted, suddenly lofting the umbrella. Swinging it in both hands, he swept it at Persano in the manner of an antique broad-sword.

Persano appeared rather disappointed in Fillmore as he dodged the blow. "As a gentleman, I waited until you woke. Perhaps, after all, I should have slain you in your sleep." He parried an umbrella-swash with a neat turn of the wrist. "Didn't you read Sacker's message? I am expert at this. Your form is barely passable academy and rusty at that."

Fillmore, not wasting energy replying, panted and puffed as he tried to hack Persano to pieces. But the other met each attack with easy indifference, not deigning to attempt to get under Fillmore's guard with his own stroke.

When, at last, the scholar collapsed, breathless, back against the wall, Persano clucked dolefully. "You expend precious time needlessly. There is but a scant minute ere the clock chimes twelve and then there will be tedious butchery. For the love of order, sir, I entreat you to accept an easy death!"

Fillmore lowered the umbrella. "Well, then," he gasped, still winded, "I suppose I must recognize the inevitability of my mortality. But it's hard." He nodded for the stroke that would end his life.

Persano reached across the table and, seizing the tawny port, poured a measure into a wine-glass. He approached Fillmore, sword in one hand, the glass in the other. He held out the wine for the professor to take. "Drink this. It contains a potent sleeping-draught. When the doctor called for Bordeaux, The Raddle, following my instructions, brought this instead. It works quickly. I will withhold the *coup de grâce* until you slumber."

Fillmore took the wine. The clock began to chime midnight as he raised the glass to his lips...

No!

The instinct for survival was too strong. He tried to dash the liquor into Persano's eyes, but the villain, half-expecting the gesture, ducked; the wine spattered his shirt. Persano's hand shot out. He grabbed the umbrella and wrenched it around, but Fillmore desperately resisted.

The two struggled fiercely, silently. But the exertions of the day were too much for Fillmore and he finally collapsed beneath the weight and superior strength of the other. Persano, pulled off balance, toppled onto his opponent, but even as he did, he jammed his elbow against Fillmore's throat.

"You *do* believe in last-minute heroics! You can't say I didn't try to bring you a painless death."

He stood up, planting a foot hard against Fillmore's chest, pinioning him. A pounding noise at the street door. The landlady shot the bolt. Coarse voices, the sound of many feet pounding up the stairs.

"My men," said Persano, mildly regretful. "Farewell." He poised the sword in the air, ready to plunge it into Fillmore's throat.

The scholar braced himself. A wave of hatred for Persano supplanted what fear he might have felt. He clutched the umbrella, wishing he could wield it one more time. His thumb brushed against the release-catch.

The tip of the sword started down for Fillmore's jugular. But as it did, something unexpected happened.

The umbrella snapped open with a click.

CHAPTER SEVEN

There were dark, rolling clouds overhead and in the air the heavy, oppressive sense of thunder. Slowly the darkness fell and as it did, Fillmore felt a strange chill overtake him and a lonely feeling.

Of Persano, there was no trace. He'd fallen off somewhere during the flight of the umbrella, his sword flailing wildly as he fell, screaming, to whichever earth Fillmore's distracted imagination dictated.

A dog began to howl in a farmhouse somewhere far down the road—a long, agonized wailing, as if from fear. The sound was taken up by another dog and then another and another, till, borne on the wind which sighed along the dark and lonely mountain road, a cacophony of howling tormented his ears. In the sound, too, there was a deeper chuckling menace—that of wolves.

An arch of trees hemmed in the road, which became a kind of tunnel leading somewhere that he dreaded to contemplate. But there was no use trying to avoid a sequence, that was one fact he'd finally learned. The professor trudged on in the darkness, shivering at the icy air of the heights. The trees were soon replaced by great frowning rocks on both sides; the rising wind moaned and whistled through them and it grew colder and colder still. Fine powdery snow began to fall, driving against his pinched face, settling in his eyebrows and on the rims of his ears.

The baying of the wolves sounded nearer and nearer. Off a ways to the left, Fillmore thought he could discern faint flickering blue flames, ghost-lights that beckoned to him, but he fearfully ignored them.

How long he trod the awful lightless road, he could not tell. The rolling clouds obscured the moon and he could not read the crystal of his watch, nor could he strike a match. Persano had never returned them.

The path kept ascending, with occasional short downward respites. Suddenly the road emerged from the rock-tunnel and led across a broad, high expanse into the courtyard of a vast ruined castle, from whose tall black casements no light shone. Against the moonlit sky, Fillmore studied the jagged line of broken battlements and knew instinctively where he was.

A bit worse than Persano, he mused, approaching the great main door, old and studded with large iron nails, set in a projecting arch of massive stone. There was no bell or knocker, but he had no doubt that soon the tenant would sense his presence and admit him.

Perhaps it would be better to flee. But he did not relish the thought of another minute on the freezing road with the wolves constantly drawing nearer. True, he'd heard them to be much maligned animals, gentle and shy, but somehow he found it hard to believe at that moment.

The occupant of the castle was fiercer than wolves, but Fillmore guessed it was his destiny to meet him and if so, it would be better to do so face to face rather than hide and wait for him to seek Fillmore out.

The matter was settled when he heard a heavy step approaching behind the door. A gleam of light appeared through the chinks. Chains rattled, huge bolts clanged back, a key turned in a seldom-used lock and the rusty metal noisily protested. But at last, the portal swung wide.

An old man stood there, clean shaven but for a white mustache, dressed in black from head to toe. He held an old silver lamp in his hand; it threw flickering shadows everywhere. He spoke in excellent English, tinged, however, with the dark coloration of a middle-European accent.

"I bid you welcome. Enter freely and of your own will." He did not move. But neither did Fillmore. A frown creased the old man's brow. He spoke again. "Welcome to my house. Come freely. Go safely; and leave something of the happiness you bring!"

A bit better, Fillmore thought, stepping across the threshold. As he did, the host grasped his hand in a cold grip strong enough to make him wince.

Fillmore started to speak, but the tall nobleman held up his hand for silence until the howling of the wolves died away.

"Listen to them," he beamed. "Children of the night! What music they make!"

Damn Persano! Fillmore swore to himself. *I'm right! He would have to put such a notion into my head just before the umbrella opened!*

He followed his host upstairs. En route, he had to tear a passage through a gigantic spider-web.

The tall man smiled and Fillmore knew what he was about to say. "The spider—" he began, but the professor finished it for him.

"—spinning his web for the unwary fly. For the blood is the life, eh?"

The Count frowned. "How did you know what was in my mind?"

Fillmore shrugged. "Bit of a fey quality, I fancy."

* * * *

Some five hundred miles distant from the castle is a town, Sestri di Levante, situated on the Italian Riviera. Near it stands the Villa Cascana on a high promontory overlooking the iridescent blue of the Ligurian Sea.

It was the latter part of a glorious afternoon in spring. The sun sparkled on the water, dazzling the eye so the place where the chestnut forest above the villa gave way to pines could not easily be discerned.

A loggia ran about the pleasant house and outside a gravel path threaded past a fountain of Cupid through a riot of magnolias and roses. In the middle of the garden there suddenly appeared a stranger, walking with a cane. He seemed bewildered.

"I've lost him temporarily," Persano murmured. "But he must be in this world and if he is, I'll find him and finish him at last. Then I'll take the umbrella and go home. Meantime, there are far less pleasant places where I might have ended up."

He gazed about, noting with pleasure the marble fountain playing merrily nearby. He drank in the salty freshness of the sea-wind and decided it would be a good place to sit and devise a scheme of action. Persano strolled the gravel-path and stopped at a bench near the Cupid fountain. He sat down and lit a cigar with the last match remaining in the pillbox he'd secured from Fillmore. He tossed away the empty box. It arced high and landed in the fountain.

Overhead, a bird twitted in the chestnuts. Someone seated in the villa—spying Persano and wondering who he was—hailed the stranger, but the shouted greeting received no answer. Persano was staring at the pillbox bobbing on the surface of the water. An awful presentiment overtook him and the blood drained from his face.

Slowly, reluctantly, step by step, he dragged himself to the fountain and stared, horrified, at the floating pillbox, which had landed open, like a miniature boat braving the crests of the fountain freshet.

A small caterpillar crawled into the cardboard box and scuttled this way and that. It was most unusual in color and loathsome in appearance: gray-yellow with lumps and excrescences on its rings and an opening on one end that aspirated like a mouth. Its feet resembled the claws of a crab.

Persano's eyes bulged as the creature, sensing his presence, began to wriggle out of the box and swim in his direction...

* * * *

"I admit you are an unusual visitor," said Dracula. "An interesting fellow, if that is the slang these days. Try some of this wine. It is very old."

"No, thank you," Fillmore demurred, having had his fill of soporif-ics-in-disguise. "I must say that you are an excellent host. The chicken was excellent, if thirsty."

"Perhaps you would prefer beer?" the vampire asked, anxious to please.

"If I can open the bottle myself."

Dracula shook his head. "You do me wrong. There are ancient customs which no host may defy, even if he be—how do the peasants call it?—*nosferatu*!"

"Yes, but I seem to recall the case of one Jonathan Harker—"

"Harker?" Dracula echoed surprised "How do you know him? He is at this moment on the way from England to conduct some business for me."

"And you have no intention of letting him leave here *not* undead," Fillmore accused Dracula.

"You wrong me, young sir. When the formula I repeated below is stated by a host and a nobleman, it dare not be violated. *I* will do nothing to prevent Harker's departure."

"Except lock the doors and ring the castle with wolves," Fillmore countered sarcastically.

The vampire shrugged. "If I did not lock the doors, the wolves might get in..."

"Well, at any rate, you can see why I do not trust your wine."

"Yes," Dracula nodded, "you seem totally cognizant of my identity, nature and intentions. But knowing all this, why would you enter here of your own free will?"

"Well, it's a long story."

Dracula smiled icily. "I have until sun-up."

So Fillmore told the story of the umbrella yet again, omitting only the references to Mrs. Bardell's cut throat and the near-skewering of his own jugular by Persano...details that he was afraid might disagreeably excite the Count.

"Hah! Can such things be?" the vampire mused once the tale was done. His piercing eyes shone with an unholy crimson light. "Long ago, what arcane researches I carried on, seeking things beyond the mundane world in which I felt trapped. And the things I discovered only proved a far worse incarceration for me. But this—this umbrella—what opportunity lies within its mystic compass!"

Fillmore began to grow uneasy. He'd spun out the history till close to daybreak, figuring that the coming dawn would enable him to escape while Dracula slept. Even more to the point, he mentally punned, he might be able to rid the place of the vampire with a stroke of the point of his umbrella and, in such wise, complete the sequence and get out of this world of horror into which his fight with Persano unluckily plunged him.

It escaped him until that moment that Dracula might look on the parasol as a far greater tool for spreading the brood of the devil than the original plan he'd devised to purchase Carfax Abbey from John Harker and move to England and its teeming millions. But how could London compare with the available necks of countless billions in worlds without number?

Fillmore stole a nervous glance towards the casement, hoping that dawn might shine through it soon. By no means could he allow the umbrella to fall into Dracula's hands!

"The night is nearly ended," the caped nobleman said, rising. His eyes fixed Fillmore's in an hypnotic stare. "I must sleep the day. Let me show you your room."

"The octagonal one, I know. Never mind, I'll find it." Fillmore strode across the large chamber and opened the door to his bed-chamber. It was just where Stoker said it would be. At the door, he paused and fixed the vampire with a stem gaze that he hoped would command respect.

"I depend on you, Count, to be as good as your word. A vampire may lie—but a nobleman, never."

"We understand each other perfectly well," Dracula smiled, bowing his head gravely. "I have given my word and I will repeat it. No harm to you shall come from me."

And he strode from the room, slamming the door shut behind him. Fillmore hurried to the portal and tried it, but it was securely locked.

The professor was worried. Dracula could not be trusted and yet he had given his word as a patrician. Could he go against it, evil though he was? Fillmore did not think so.

He walked back to his room and stretched out on the bed, exhausted from the perils of the umbrella's flight and the terrible walk through the Carpathian forest. He began to sink into a delicious lassitude.

No, no, no, no, no, no! his mind repeated over and over, a still, small voice protesting a fact out of joint, a snag in logic, an unforeseen menace...

"I have given my word and I will repeat it. No harm to you shall come from me."

Dracula did not say Fillmore would be unharmed. He said he would not *personally* hurt him.

Fillmore tried to get up, but his limbs were leaden. Above him, not far away, a dancing swirl of dust-motes pirouetted in a beam of moonlight. In the middle of the mist shone two mocking golden eyes, like those of an animal.

He tried to groan, but no sound emerged. He had forgotten Dracula's three undead mistresses who lived (?) with him in the vaults beneath the castle.

The fairest and most favored of the three was in the coffin-shaped room with Fillmore, baring her teeth for the inevitable bite.

He fell into a merciful swoon.

CHAPTER EIGHT

Some days, it is nigh onto impossible to get out of bed. The body, filled with a not altogether unpleasant lassitude, refuses to function. Too weak to protest, the mind feebly struggles to rouse the limbs, but to no avail, so weak is the will, so sapped the corporeal being. Easier to capitulate, to drift in that half-state between slumber and waking.

And so Fillmore remained in a condition of wan enthrallment for the greater part of the day. Only as the autumnal gloom began to draw in, signaling the approach of evening, did his torpid brain make an effort to gather in those wandering fantasies which possessed it and pack them away. Very deep within, clawing at the prison-door of consciousness, a voice urged him to wake.

He pushed himself up unwillingly and sat on the edge of the soft bed, head dangling, trying to recollect where he was.

A wolf greeted the oncoming sunset.

With a start, he sat bolt upright, remembering everything. He peered across the room with nervous dread, but to his surprise, the umbrella was still there. Getting to his feet, swaying from unexpected weakness, he lurched over to it and tried pressing the catch, but, as he anticipated, it did not open. He turned this way and that, seeking a mirror, finally recalling that Dracula did not keep any such reminders of his vampiric status about the house.

When Fillmore put a hand to his neck, he knew he needed no glass to confirm what his fingers felt. He winced at the two tender spots, the tiny punctures that still felt tacky.

Luckily, according to Bram Stoker, vampires rarely finish off a victim in one night. But Fillmore felt so enervated that he very much doubted whether he could survive a second attack.

And the sun was going down.

He ran to the large casement in the dining-room and stared out. The castle was built on a rocky precipice. The valley, spread out far below and threaded with raging torrents, was such a great distance straight down that if he fell, only a parachute could save him.

But how did Harker escape in Dracula? He emulated the Count, creeping from rugged stone to stone, crawling down the side of the castle like a great lizard to the courtyard underneath. But the drop was sheer, with no apparent footholds or niches for the hands to grasp. Nor was there a courtyard; only cruel and jagged rocks...

He ran to his room and pushed open the narrow aperture. The same vista—exit was impossible from either window!

Then how did Harker scale the walls? He beat his fists against his temples, thinking, thinking. He remembered that, in the novel, the solicitor walked out the dining-room door into the corridor and explored the vast pile. Somewhere on the castle's south side must be the window that permitted access to the lower floors and the courtyard.

But the door to the corridor was locked.

Fillmore tore about like a madman, trying the door at the end opposite the octagonal room, but it, too, was locked. He set his back to the main door and bumped it, but the only thing that gave was his back.

Darting to the window a second time, he watched in fascinated horror as the sun dipped beneath the ridges and crests of the mountains. Only a thin slice of the golden rim remained on the horizon.

Figure another five or six minutes worth of sunlight and perhaps an equal time of after-light. Another minute for the vampires to rouse themselves and come up here. Then, at the most generous estimate, I have an unlucky thirteen minutes to—

"Well, say it!" he snapped at himself, aloud. "To save myself from a fate worse than death. Literally."

The teacher sat upon the edge of his bed and applied his mind to his predicament. Panic would accomplish nothing, he realized, so he might as well employ the residue of time in seeing whether there were any way out at all.

A chorus of wolves shivered on the rising wind.

He shuddered.

"There's enough of that, damn it!" he told himself. "It's about time I stopped behaving like a victim everywhere I fly to. Let's see now: can't get out the doors, windows are too high up, no way to safely climb down the wall. I'd probably dash my brains out, anyway, even if I tried it."

And then a new and startling notion flashed into his mind. He jumped to his feet and nervously paced the room.

"No time to follow it all up," he declaimed aloud like the actor he once aspired to be, "but some of it must be scanned! Is there an alternative reason? Quick—work out a chain of logic!"

He ticked off propositions on his fingertips. "*One*: a sequence has to be completed wherever one goes with the umbrella. *Two*: I am no longer in the Holmesian rough-draft world. *Hence*: I completed the sequence there. But how? Some of the literary works on which that place is based were unfinished in *my* original earth. Could it be that my adventure with Persano stopped just because it isn't over?!"

Fillmore shook his head. "Too many paradoxes. *The Pickwick Papers* was completed by Dickens and that was—is—a part of Persano's world. So events cannot be dictated by literature that I know, at least not entirely. Which is confusing, but forget philosophy for now; ask Holmes, if I live to meet him!" He put the issue behind him with a flourish of one hand, a gesture he often used when confronting an adamantly incorrect student. "The vital question now is—*why did the umbrella open?*"

Only one answer fit. When Persano aimed his sword at Fillmore's throat, the scholar's life in that world was, for all practical purposes, terminated. Therefore, the sequence had to be at an end and the umbrella finally worked.

Therefore, in a world of horror, where there are victims galore, all one must do to escape is...die.

He certainly hoped he was right.

Picking up the umbrella, Fillmore strode purposefully to the window and tried opening it. But the rusty latch would not budge. He spied an immense pewter candelabra, seized it and hurled the thing forcibly. It bumped the glass and clattered to the floor.

"*Hell*!" Exasperated, he stuck his face against the window and saw that it was doubly thick. He also perceived that the last sliver of sun was gone and the after-light was fading swiftly.

Then, from far below in the very bowels of the castle, he heard a metallic grating noise, followed by an iron thunderous clang, like a great door slammed open. Desperately he wrestled with one of the Count's chairs. It was incredibly heavy and took a tremendous effort of the will for him to loft it at all, let alone swing it. But swing it he did and the window shattered most gratifyingly. The massive piece of furniture tumbled after the raining shards down, down into the depths of the valley.

Fillmore scrambled onto the window-seat, umbrella in hand, thumb on the catch. Gazing out at the panoramic vista, he felt queasy. Heights terrified him. If he were wrong and the umbrella did not open, he would be crushed on the rocks and then—since he had been bitten by the vampire-woman—he might have to join the legions of the undead.

There was the sound of a heavy tread in the corridor outside. Screwing up his courage, Fillmore forced himself to look out at the landscape and conquer his fear of falling. He saw the valley cloaked in shadow and very far off, the glint of rushing water, a distant cataract.

The cataract strong then—

"NO!" he admonished himself. "No other literature this time, just Sherlock Holmes!"

—cataract strong then plunges along—

"Sherlock Holmes!"

—striking and raging as if a war waging—

"Sherlock Holmes, Sherlock Holmes, Sherlock Holmes!"

—its caverns and rocks among—

"SHERLOCK HOLMES!" Fillmore shouted, jumping out the window.

Behind him, in the room, the doors flung wide. The blond fiend raced to the window, snarling.

"Gone!" she howled, turning to accuse her mate. "How did you dare permit this? You might have taken the umbrella while he slept!"

The Count, entering with a swirl of his cape, coldly replied, "I pledged my word I would not harm him. I may be a vampire, but I am a Nobleman first and a *boyar* does not break his word." In truth, Dracula had realized that transporting fifty boxes of native soil across the dimensions would be a grueling project. London was quite good enough...

The woman told him precisely what she thought of his aristocratic airs. "Your precious blue blood," she snapped spitefully, "is tainted with the plasma of the lowest village peasants."

"And yours isn't?" he sneered, staring haughtily down his long aquiline nose at her.

"The least you could have done would have been to hide the thing so I could have supped again!"

"As for that," said Dracula, waving his hand with grand disdain, "you are already more plump than is seemly."

"*Plump*?!" she screamed. "You told me that's the way you like me best!"

The matter proceeded through a great many more exchanges and retorts, but it is perhaps indelicate to dwell at length on the secrets of patrician domestic life and so it were good to draw the present chapter to a close.

CHAPTER NINE

Fillmore wanted to throw up, but he was too terrified to move. Below, the ferocious cataract raged. A needle-spritz of foam slashed up through the curtain of mist created by the falls, occasionally spattering droplets on his face. The long sweep of green water whirled and clamored, producing a kind of half-human shout which boomed out of the abyss with the spray.

"Miserable damned umbrella!" he grumbled. "I said 'Sherlock Holmes time and again—NOT *The Cataract of Lodore*!"

The shelf on which the umbrella deposited him was barely big enough for his posterior. Fortunately, it (the shelf) was cut high and deep enough so he could arch his back against the black stone. There was just enough space to stand the umbrella upright next to him along the vertical axis of the niche, but otherwise there was no room to move or turn. Eventually, he supposed, he would either fall into the chasm or else figure a way to get down safely.

His feet dangled precariously over the edge. Below them, the cliff bellied out so he could not see straight down. But to the right, he spied a footpath that looked as if it ought to pass directly beneath his perch. Yet to the left there was a sheer drop into the torrent, so he could not be certain that the path extended all the way to the point just south of where he sat. If it did, he might be able to slide down the cliff-side and land on the narrow walkway. It looked about a yard wide, surely large enough to break the momentum of his fall.

But what if the path stopped before it got to where he was sitting? Then he'd plummet right down the mountain.

Well, sooner or later I'll have to risk it. Unless—

Unless the umbrella had whisked him back to his own world, where Southey's cataract was situated. Sequence-rules did not seem to apply to one's home cosmos (or else the bumbershoot could not have operated in the first place, or so Fillmore reasoned).

He pushed the button half-heartedly. Nothing happened. He was still stuck on the meager rocky mantel.

He glanced above him and saw, too far to reach, a bigger niche, covered with soft green moss. He looked down and was seized by vertigo. He shut his eyes and shoved his back against the eroded cliff-wall, wishing he could sink inside it.

"Get hold of yourself! If you have to drop, you'd better be in full control of your muscles!" he told himself, wishing that he could somehow find a way to shut off the sound of the cascading flood—a strange, melancholy noise like lost souls lamenting in the deep recess of the pool into which the churning streams poured.

He tried to reestablish his equilibrium by turning his attention to the expanse of blue sky above him. The weather was mild and there was a pleasant breeze that he wished, all the same, would stop tugging and flapping his sleeve like insistent child-fingers begging him to come play in the rapids below.

There were few clouds and none obscured the sun which shone high and bright.

Gazing nervously into the heavens, squinting to minimize the glare, Fillmore suddenly opened his eyes wide in surprise. A fact popped into his head, something he'd read in the rubric to *The Cataract of Lodore* in the textbook he used to teach English Romantic Fiction.

"Tourists who make special jaunts to view the site which inspired Southey's famous exercise in onomatopoeia are generally disappointed because—"

Because why? How did the rest of the rubric read?

Before the thought could be brought to mind, Fillmore was distracted by the sound of approaching footsteps...a rapid, yet heavy tread.

He sighed with relief. *Maybe it'll be someone who can help me get down from here!*

The footsteps neared. Fillmore stared down at the footpath curving around the mountainside to his right. A long moment passed, during which the footfalls grew louder, but slowed to a walk. And then a man rounded the bend and emerged into the professor's angle of vision.

The newcomer was extremely tall and thin. Clean-shaven, with a great dome of forehead and eyes sunk deep in his skull, the stranger was pale and ascetic in cast. Chalk-dust clung to his sleeves; his shoulders were rounded and his head protruded forward as if he had spent too much time in closet study of abstruse intellectual problems.

Stopping in the middle of the narrow path, he peered with puckered, angry eyes at a place some steps in front of him. He spoke in an ironical tone of voice.

"Well, sir," he said, "as you are wont to quote, 'Journeys end in lovers meeting.'"

For a brief, disoriented second, Fillmore thought he himself was being addressed. Then there was a murmur from a spot directly beneath the ledge where he was dizzily balanced and he realized that someone had been waiting all the while right under him, hidden by the bellying rock-swell that the mountainside described just below his feet.

"I warned you I would never stand in the dock," the tall man said in a dry, reprimanding voice. "Yet you have persevered in your attempts to bring justice upon my head."

The unseen man murmured a laconic reply.

"In truth," the other continued, "I doubted that you could so effectively quash the network of crime it took me so long to build up. But you have outstripped your potential and I underestimated you, to my cost." As he spoke, his head was never still, but moved in a slow, oscillating pattern from side to side, like some cold-blooded reptile. "However," he went on, "you have also underestimated me. I said if you were clever enough to bring destruction on me, I would do the same for you. I do not make idle threats."

Another murmur Fillmore could not hear—more protracted this time—and then the tall one grimly nodded. "Yes, I will wait that long. He who stands on the brink of world's-end rarely objects to the delay of a second or two before time stops."

Crossing his arms patiently, he waited silently, staring fixedly at the person Fillmore could not see.

But by then, of course, the teacher knew the identity of both antagonists, seen and unseen. With the knowledge came the recollection of the forgotten detail pertaining to the cataract of Lodore.

"Tourists who make special jaunts to view the site which inspired Southey's famous exercise in onomatopoeia," said the rubric, "are generally disappointed because the falls dry up by the time they visit in summer. The Lodore falls are best seen in colder weather."

The sky and sun and the breeze told Fillmore it must be late spring. Therefore, the cascading waters below could not be Lodore.

It had to be Reichenbach Falls, instead.

Reichenbach Falls...scene of the dramatic final meeting between Sherlock Holmes and his archenemy, Professor Moriarty...perfectly logical, considering that Fillmore simultaneously thought of Holmes and a waterfall. The umbrella took him precisely where it had been told.

All the same, he mused grumpily, *it might have picked a less disagreeable ringside seat!*

And yet, for all his fearful giddiness, Fillmore felt a bit like an Olympian looking down on the petty squabbling of puny mortals. The analogy was furthered by the fact that he knew both what was taking place and that which was about to happen.

Right now, he thought, *Holmes is writing a farewell message to Watson. When he finishes it, he'll put it on top of a boulder close by and anchor the paper by placing his silver cigarette-case upon it.*

Fillmore had read "The Final Problem" several times. It was a bitter tale, the one in which Arthur Conan Doyle tried to kill off his famous detective; Fillmore often wondered what it must have been like to read it when it first appeared in print, not knowing that Holmes would be resurrected ten years later in "The Adventure of the Empty House." (Fillmore grinned to himself, thinking of the heresy his mind had just committed: referring to Conan Doyle as the author of the Holmes tales. "Are ye mad, man?" his pals at the local branch of the Baker Street Irregulars would say. "Watson wrote those *factual* accounts. Doyle was just the good Doctor's literary agent!")

Fillmore finally knew what he was going to do: simply wait until the adventure ran its course. Holmes would finish the message, rise and walk to the edge of the footpath. Moriarty, disdaining weaponry, would fling himself upon his enemy and the pair would struggle and tussle on the very edge of the falls. At the last, Holmes's superior knowledge of baritsu ("the Japanese system of wrestling, which has more than once been very useful to me") would win the day and Moriarty would take the horrible, fatal plunge alone. Then Fillmore could hail Holmes, who would surely help him to get down.

After that, I'll warn him that Colonel Moran is skulking about here someplace and—

And?

There was no point in making any other plans just yet. If Holmes were unable to rescue him from the awful ledge, there would be no future for J. Adrian (Blah!) Fillmore!

At that moment, Moriarty unfolded his arms.

"If the message is done, sir," he said, "then I presume we may proceed with this matter?"

A murmur and then footsteps.

He's walking to the end of the path. Now Moriarty will follow him and suddenly try to push Holmes off balance.

Moriarty did not move. A mirthless trace of humor tilted up the corner of his mouth.

Fillmore was suddenly seized by the chill premonition that something extremely unpleasant was about to take place.

"You surprise me at the last," the evil Professor remarked. "Had you expected some gentleman's Code of Honor, sir? My foolish lieutenant Persano might subscribe to such nonsense, but then again, he would be better suited physically to grapple with a man thoroughly skilled in singlestick. And baritsu."

"What!" It was the first time Fillmore heard the crisp voice beneath him.

"Come, come," said Moriarty, drawing a revolver out of his coat, "I keep files on my enemies, too, you know."

No! *This is wrong*! Fillmore was stunned. *This isn't how the story turns out*!

"I am vexed," Moriarty stated. "You have twice underestimated me, sir." He raised the pistol and aimed.

Fillmore had no time to wonder whether direct interference might change the texture of the world he was in—it was already different. He did not concern himself, either, with the dangers of subsumption or, for that matter, the more immediate risk that he might break his neck.

Transferring the umbrella to his right hand, he shoved himself off the perch with a yell to warn the detective below. As he descended, he flailed the umbrella in Moriarty's direction.

The Professor immediately raised his arm and snapped off a shot at Fillmore, but he was aiming at a moving target and the bullet ricocheted harmlessly off a boulder. Before he could fire a second time, Holmes grasped his arm in an iron grip and instantly afterwards, Fillmore landed on the path in a heap.

The arch-antagonists struggled violently scant inches from the end of the walkway. Fillmore did his best to get out from underfoot, but elbows poked his ribs and feet trod his toes. He was an integral part of the *mêlée*.

The detective grunted. The criminal cursed. They swayed on the very lip of the precipice. Then Holmes unexpectedly and slickly slipped out of Moriarty's grip. The movement set the Professor off balance. With a cry of fear, he flailed, both hands clawing the air. One touched the grip of the umbrella and, instinctively, Moriarty clutched at it, wrenching it from Fillmore's grasp.

Forgetting all danger, Fillmore lurched forward and tried to get the umbrella back, but Moriarty, uttering one long terrified scream, pitched over backwards into the abyss.

Fillmore scrambled on his hands and knees to the edge and, with Holmes, watched the Napoleon of Crime falling, falling, the umbrella wildly waving. He vanished from view in the scintillating curtain of spray.

For a long while they watched, but they could not discern any movement in the maelstrom. Fillmore thought he could hear Moriarty's cry of terror eternally intermingled with the half-human roar of the falls.

Rousing themselves, they walked down the path a ways. Then the tall, thin man with the well-remembered face addressed Fillmore good-humoredly.

"In the past," he chuckled, "I have been skeptical of the workings of Providence, but nevermore shall I doubt the efficacy of a *deus ex machina*, no matter what guise it descends in!"

Fillmore would have replied but they were all at once interrupted by a barrage of rocks from above.

"That would be Colonel Moran," Fillmore remarked. "He's just about on schedule."

Holmes looked at him curiously but decided to forestall all questions until after they escaped from the assiduous administrations of Moriarty's sole surviving lieutenant.

CHAPTER TEN

Late that evening, two men sat drinking ale in a pothouse in Rosen-laui. For a long while, only one of them spoke, but at last, he ended his narrative.

"That is certainly the most singular history I have ever heard," said the other, taller one, signaling to the waiter for more brew. "It is more surprising to me than that awful business at Baskerville and, at least to you, quite as harrowing."

"And now," said Fillmore, "I suppose you are going to suggest I consult a specialist in obscure nervous diseases?"

"Not at all, old chap," the lean detective grinned. "There is an internal cohesion that I should be prompted to trust in, to begin with. But knowing all that I do about the late Professor Moriarty, your tale makes considerable sense."

"It *does*?"

"Moriarty himself prefigured the possibility of a dimensional-transfer engine in his brilliant paper on *The Dynamics of an Asteroid*. Not in so many words, you understand, but the concept was buried within if one had the comprehension and the philosophical tools to prize it forth. The Professor certainly foresaw the ramifications of his theory, at least in this interesting—and rather distressing—side-channel of his research. I shudder to think what might have happened had he manufactured enough of them to arm his entire army of villains! Criminal justice in England (perhaps in the entire cosmos, eventually) would be totally unworkable." Holmes tapped his fingers against the frosted stein which the waiter set down before him. "Of course, I suppose it would have then been up to me to devise a similar engine and make it available to society at large." He shook his head, smiling ruefully. "I wish you could have held onto it. I should have been most interested in examining it."

"I'm extremely disappointed myself," Fillmore said. "I came here specifically to ask you about the umbrella and now it's gone!"

"You wanted to find out how it worked?"

"No," he replied, shaking his head. "I wanted to learn why it works so strangely."

Holmes laughed. "Oh, you are referring, I suppose, to the business of its taking you to so-called literary dimensions?"

Fillmore nodded. He had a sudden inkling of what Holmes was about to say.

"That, my dear Fillmore, is quite elementary! The physics and mathematics of space strongly imply the co-existence of many worlds in other dimensions. What are these places like? Surely, space is so infinite that there must be an objective reality to planets of every conceivable kind, variances and patterns mundane and fantastic."

"Yes, yes, but why *literary* permutations?"

"You have been going about the problem backwards," said Holmes. "These places do not exist because people on your earth dreamed them up. I should say rather the reverse was more likely."

"Meaning?"

"Meaning the 'fiction' of your prosaic earth must be borrowed, in greater or lesser degree, from notions and conceptions that occur across the barriers of the dimensions. Have you not heard writers (though surely not Watson) protest that they do not know from what heaven their inspirations descend? Even my good friend the doctor's agent, Conan Doyle, has sometimes told me that he invents characters in his historical romances that 'write themselves.' Does this not suggest that these artists may be unwittingly tapping the logical premises of other parallel worlds?"

"Then, in my case—" Fillmore began, but Holmes already knew.

"Of course! You are an instructor in literature and drama. Your mind is evidently psychically attuned to the alternative earths which the literature of your world has told you of—and succeeded in captivating your imagination with."

Fillmore nodded and sipped his ale. They sat in silence for a few moments before he spoke again.

"Your theory makes a great deal of sense and yet—"

"And yet?"

"It does not totally explain why it has been necessary for me to complete a sequence of action in each world I visit."

Holmes nodded. "That, I should say, is a three-pipe problem. But it will have to be left for a time when we can breathe more freely. Colonel Moran will surely pick up our trail before the night is over. We must proceed swiftly and you must stay close by. Since he may have observed your role in the death of his chief, you may well be marked for extermination."

"I don't mind at all sticking with you," Fillmore admitted as they rose from the table, "especially since I have no recourse now but to be subsumed."

"I am not positive that subsumption is an inevitable function of the umbrella," said Holmes, insisting on taking the check, "but you are right to the extent that the instrument is now out of reach of our human resources."

They walked out of the tavern and inhaled the clear, cold air of evening.

"I suppose you do not intend to get in touch with Watson, under the circumstances?"

"No," Holmes shook his head, "it would involve him in too great a risk. The dear boy is an innocent when it comes to dissembling. Moran will reason my path lies homeward, but if I do go to London, there will be danger for all and sundry. Moran might kidnap Watson to flush me out. No, I must stay away from England for a time."

"And therefore you will change your name to Sigerson and—"

"How the devil did you know that?!" Holmes snapped, his brows beetling. Then his face cleared and he nodded merrily. "Of course! You have a contemporaneous awareness of certain likely events in this world. But I pray, sir, if we are to travel companions, please refrain from casting yourself too often in the role of a Nostradamus. There is a piquancy to quotidian unawareness of one's Fate."

Fillmore agreed and they walked on for a time in silence. Then Holmes suggested that the professor ought to consider what role he might want to assume in the present world.

"Why, no one knows me here," the other said in some amazement. "Why should I need to be anyone but myself?"

"Because you will bring us into rather risky focus during our travels abroad if you insist on remaining a man without a background and point of origin. First thing we must do is purchase a good set of false papers. You will need a well-worked-out history—"

"And a new name!" Fillmore said, suddenly and decisively.

"What on earth for? What's wrong with the one you have?"

"I thoroughly detest it!"

"Yes, yes, but you are apt to slip up if you stray too far from your original nomenclature. If you must pick a new name, choose one close enough to the present one so it won't take long to get used to it."

"Very well," Fillmore agreed, lapsing into thoughtful silence.

I'll get rid of that hateful middle name and call myself by my original first one, the one my aunt didn't like because it belonged to my father. A bitter memory crossed his mind and he determined to be done entirely with the painful past. The hell with the surname, too! I'll go back to the old spelling.

They stumped along for another quarter-hour and at last Holmes suggested they take shelter in the barn he saw upon the rise and stay there until the morning came. Fillmore agreed.

A few minutes later, they stretched out in straw and prepared to slumber. A peculiar idea occurred to the scholar at that moment and he smiled.

"Something amusing?" Holmes asked.

Fillmore nodded. "It just crossed my mind...if your theory is correct and artists in my world really do unwittingly borrow from the events of alternative earths, then it is possible that I am already figuring in some work of literature back where I came from!"

Holmes chuckled. "I do not think I am going to dwell on that thought just now. My poor tired brain has had enough of metaphysics for one day!"

With that, the Great Detective said good night and went to sleep.

His companion lay there for a long time, thinking about the morrow when he would take on his new name and identity and start a new and exciting life. The professor gazed into the darkness and pondered the perilous perplexities of the stars.

* * * *

In his cozy Victorian study, the doctor gazed down on the new manuscript. The thing was more fun, he thought, if he could think of the perfect name.

There was already evidence that his readers enjoyed the wry device of Watson's "stories-yet-to-be-told." It was a clever method of injecting humor into the often grim tales: tease the readers with promises of outlandish-sounding stories not yet written up by Watson.

For instance, there was the adventure of the Grice-Pattersons in the Isle of Uffa (wherever that was!) or the Repulsive Tale of the Red Leech, or—among the most outrageous—the strange case of Isadora Persano, the well-known duelist, who was found stark staring mad with a matchbox in front of him which contained a remarkable worm said to be unknown to science...

But this name now: J. Adrian Fillmore. It didn't have quite the properly quaint tone he was seeking. It was a trifle stuffy and stolid. Perhaps it was the middle name...try eliminating it. And what might the initial stand for? John? James? (He chortled as he thought of the printer's error that caused Watson's wife to call him James by mistake. What a tizzy of pseudo-scholastic comment that had provoked!)

James it would be then, he decided finally. And perhaps an older and quainter spelling of the surname...

And Arthur Conan Doyle wrote:

"...the incredible mystery of Mr. James Phillimore, who, stepping back into his own house to get his umbrella, was never more seen in this world..."

PART III

CHAPTER ONE

Mr. James Phillimore sat in an overstaffed chair at 221B Baker Street and grumbled to himself about the hyperbolized attractions of High Romance.

"Odd," he groused, "to be bored to death thirty-seven years before one's birth."

Watson's ship's-clock ticked away the tedium. The scholar was alone. In one hand he held a strong whisky-and-soda. His other hand smoothed the latest copy of a London daily across his knees.

He was looking for a job.

"Damn and double-damn! They all want references!"

Without capital, Doyle's London was no great delight. Holmes was away, Watson didn't know he existed and Mrs. Hudson had a great plenty of prattle with little admixture of matter therein. Phillimore was bored and broke. So long as he stayed at 221B, he was welcome to share the landlady's larder, since Mycroft Holmes kept up his brother's rent at Sherlock's own devisement. However, a protracted stay at Holmes's digs was decidedly inadvisable, the professor knew.

Everything had gone awry. Originally, Phillimore was to purchase false papers and fashion a new identity, but Holmes, never the most organized of men when he wasn't on a case, kept forgetting to make the necessary arrangements. Then the grand plan to accompany the detective on his Tibetan perambulations was scotched in an odd manner.

It seems that Holmes's cousin, Professor George Edward Challenger, was about to sail to South America to search for traces of sentient prehistoric life on that continent. Holmes was asked to come along. Delighted at the prospect; he was yet afraid to let it be known he was still alive for fear the Moriarty survivors would wreak vengeance on the entire expedition. So instead of assuming the false identity of Sigerson, Holmes made special arrangements to impersonate a genuine world explorer, Lord John Roxton, an individual whose presence in the Challenger team would hardly excite suspicion. [Further details are available in Chapter Five of the author's *The Histrionic Holmes* (Luther Norris, 1971)]

The detective extended an invitation to Phillimore to come along as well, but the scholar, having read Doyle's *The Lost World*, decided he would prefer estivating in London to possibly furnishing himself as an hors d' oeuvre for a teratosaurus. Against Holmes's better judgment, Phillimore remained behind.

"But do not tarry long in Baker Street," the detective said before starting out. "Moran saw you upon the Reichenbach ledge. He won't forget you. I have sources which tell me he is temporarily out of London, but I also have ascertained he will return by the end of the month."

This allowed the scholar a scant week to assiduously search the dailies for employment opportunities...but to no avail. He had no past, therefore there was no way to satisfy the strict scruples of the Victorian educational system.

Time was running out. So was his money. Without his umbrella, he felt trapped.

A low tap sounded at the door. Phillimore bade the tapper enter. The gray-haired landlady walked in bearing a silver tray on which rested an envelope embossed with an official-looking crest.

"It was brought a moment ago," she said, proffering the tray. Silently marveling at the London postal system which guaranteed upwards of ten deliveries a day, the professor picked up the envelope and saw his name neatly inscribed on it.

"Strange," he murmured. "Who else knows of my existence?"

The landlady shrugged, unable to advance a viable theory.

He withdrew a single folded sheet of cream-colored paper, smoothed it out and read the terse message thereupon...

IT IS IMPERATIVE THAT WE DISCUSS THE UMBREL-
LA. PLEASE CALL AT MY CLUB THIS EVENING.

M.H.

The address was inked beneath the initials.

"Hmm," Phillimore mused, "perhaps the game's afoot..."

CHAPTER TWO

As he stepped out upon Baker Street, the professor debated whether to walk or hail a Hansom. Since it was a warm, pleasant evening, he decided to apply shank's-mare toward Pall Mall.

As he strode briskly along, Phillimore mused on the import of the note. What was there to discuss? The umbrella was gone for good, borne off by the death grip of Moriarty, lying at the base of the Reichenbach torrent.

"Well, as Holmes would say, it's foolish to speculate with insufficient data. When I reach the club, I'll find out." The opportunity was too good to miss, in any event: a meeting with the one person even more brilliant than Sherlock Holmes.

Approaching his destination from the St. James's end, he stopped at a door some little distance from the Carlton. Upon stepping through the portal, Phillimore entered a club that was reputed to be the oddest in London. He followed a short hall to a glass panel through which he observed a large, luxurious chamber in which a great many men sat reading periodicals, determinedly preserving an elaborate communal silence.

A melancholy retainer accepted his card and bade the teacher wait in the visitors's room, just off the hall. It was a carpeted chamber with the suffused light of a fireplace to offset the gloom. Phillimore sank into a comfortable overstuffed chair and awaited his summoner.

That individual was not tardy in coming. Before very long, a heavy footfall announced the arrival of a large, florid newcomer. The man was positively obese, but his face, though massive, still reflected keen intelligence. Yet the peculiarly watery-gray eyes held a far-off look, the expression of a dreamer.

He extended a broad flipper and shook Phillimore's hand, saying, "I am pleased to meet you, sir. Sherlock has related your incredible adventures to me."

"And I take it that you are able to countenance the possibility of an engine which transfers the user to other dimensions?"

"Oh, I should say so," the large man wheezed. "I have bethought myself of such a device for quite some time. However, I am the most indolent individual in England and I never bothered to follow the notion to its practical conclusion. It should have meant wearisome computations, hypotheses, trails and trials, mistrials and counter-trials. But had I inherited Sherlock's penchant for induction, I would have postulated the likelihood of Moriarty conceiving and following through the identical concept."

The melancholy retainer reappeared and accepted their preferences in libation. After he left, Phillimore placed his fingers against one another, steeple-fashion and spoke.

"I take it then that you are capable of explaining precisely how the umbrella works. It appears to modulate to the brain-pattern of each user, that much I have understood."

"Well, I haven't examined the Moriarty model, but I doubt it could vary greatly. The engine draws on cosmic power sources through the attuning of the individual's mental patterns. When a destination is decided on, the thoughts affix the frequency the device must seek out."

Phillimore held up his hand. "But if it is completely governed by the operator's mental patterns, why have I not been taken precisely where I wish every time I use it? And why must I finish a sequence? And how could it allow me to become subsumed in—"

"Now, now," the other rumbled, "*festina lente*, my good man: one point at a time. In order to fully control the umbrella, you must first totally manage your own thoughts. Self-control is a rare commodity, sir; can you truly profess that you were in charge of your faculties when the engine whisked you to that place you label a 'draft-world'? Were you not distracted by the imminence of the over-amorous Ruth?"

"Indeed I was."

"You see, then? You feared you would not escape her and, at the same time, you pressed the umbrella-catch, hoping to visit the world of Sherlock Holmes and myself. The umbrella, by a sort of law of universal economy, always aims to consume the least quantity of energy possible.

When it sensed your muddled thoughts, it interpreted them by a destination which must have drawn on less energy than this world. The result: you were taken to a place on which reside analogous individuals to Ruth and Sherlock."

"And I had a devil of a time getting off again."

"That," the large man said, waving a flipper, "is another matter. There is no reason why a sequence, as you call it, must be completed. True, the engine is unlikely to work after usage until certain energy sources are redistributed and equalized, but within a day or two, at most, I should think—"

"No, I tell you I tried it repeatedly! The umbrella only operated for me in that draft-world when it seemed my life was over there, not before..."

A moment of silence. The big man sat and pondered, his lips working in and out. Then his eyebrows raised and he uttered a surprised, "Ahh!"

Before Phillimore could divine his host's latter thought, the retainer reappeared with a whisky-and-soda for him and a decanter of Tokay for the large man. They pledged one another's health and sipped in silence.

At length, the big man rumbled, "Your Achilles's heel would seem to be your sense of structure."

"I don't follow your meaning."

"You are a literary professor, a scholar of artificial worlds. Where but in fiction may one find an ordering of events such as pale existence cannot hope to imitate?"

"You are saying that my artistic sense dictated my adventures?"

"Precisely! The recharged umbrella read your inner thoughts and saw you were attuned to 'completing a sequence.' My dear Phillimore, this is totally consistent with the device's adaptation to the user's mental patterns."

The professor stroked his chin thoughtfully. "Subsumption, therefore, would appear to be similarly explicable."

"Indeed so. You could have traveled by umbrella any time you wished, if you had been aware of these factors. But self-ordering is no simple business, you know."

Nodding, Phillimore downed his drink and gestured to the passing retainer for a refill. "What a shame," he sighed, "to learn all this when it is of no practical use. The umbrella is gone for good."

"*I have my doubts.*"

Phillimore glanced up sharply. "What do you mean?"

I ask you to cast your mind back to the struggle upon the ledge. Describe for me, the precise physical attitude of Moriarty as he plunged into the torrent." Mystified, Phillimore complied, sketching the verbal picture as best he could recall: the flailing limbs, the scream of terror, Moriarty toppling backwards into the boiling cascade, snatching desperately at the umbrella...

"*Oh, no!*"

"I fear the same, sir! If Moriarty invented the umbrella, is it not probable that he would have activated it to save his life?"

"Then somewhere, on some outpost world, he may, even now, be constructing his evil schemes."

"It is quite conceivable," the large man agreed. "Who knows what alien powers he may be marshalling preparatory to re-invading his native London?"

"Dreadful," Phillimore shuddered. "But what may we do about it?"

"Sherlock was too exhilarated over the demise of his arch-foe to consider any alternative possibilities. Thus he is not in England and I fear it shall be some time before he returns. So it is up to us. But my girth ill suits me for strenuous physical activity...so it devolves upon you to execute a plan of my devisement."

"Which is?"

"To pursue Moriarty and reclaim your umbrella."

The professor sputtered. "That's impossible."

The large man ignored him. "At the very least, loss of the umbrella will delay Moriarty, hopefully until Sherlock can take a hand in this. At best, he might be on some unyielding world where a paucity of certain natural resources would render it impossible for him to build a new umbrella-engine."

Phillimore was on his feet, glass in hand. "But see here, your theories are fine, but how the deuce may they be acted upon? First of all, I have no umbrella. Secondly, if I did, how would I have any idea where to seek in a multiplicity of cosmoses?"

Setting his glass on a tray, the large man sat back and cradled his paunch in clasped hands. His lips worked in and out for a few seconds, then he fixed Phillimore with a keen gaze. "I will address your first point: the absence of an umbrella. Observe my hands." He stretched them out so they were side by side, palms upward. "Let us consider my left hand to be *this* world, the one of the original Moriarty and Sherlock Holmes. Let us also conceive my right hand to be the so-called 'draft-world' you visited, a place where you found that villainous Persano and heard of one Sherrinford Holmes. On this 'draft-world'"—here he waggled his right hand for emphasis—"there also lived a Professor Moriarty, according to Persano's report. Call him the Ür-Moriarty, if you will. Now it appears as if the umbrella you lost was originally stolen from the Ür-Moriarty. If such is true..."

"Of course!" Phillimore exclaimed. "Then *our* Moriarty, the one who went over Reichenbach, is likely to have his own umbrella!"

"Precisely! If by good fortune he had not yet invented one, then he is, in truth, a corpse at the base of the torrent. But if he did create a dimensional transfer-engine, then it is likely to be hidden in his now-vacant headquarters. Seek it there, Phillimore, by all means, seek it there!"

The scholar quaffed the last of his whisky-and-soda, then set the glass down. "I suppose there is no harm in doing that much at least. It would be reassuring to possess a means of egress from this particular island earth. But as to seeking Moriarty elsewhere...I still do not see how it is possible. I suppose I could affix my thoughts on the evil professor, but that might merely fetch me to some place where the Ur-Moriarty has gone. For that matter, there could be dozens of Moriartys on a myriad of quasi-earths!"

The large man rose and put one broad paw around Phillimore's shoulders. "Have no doubts upon this latter consideration. I have an excellent theory as to how you may determine the 'real' Moriarty's whereabouts...

The time would come when Phillimore recalled these words of assurance with some little pique.

CHAPTER THREE

Far off, a clock tolled midnight. The pale moon, partially obscured by black clouds, shed a sickly glare that glimmered on the surface of the nearby Thames.

Creeping around the side of the gloomy mansion, Phillimore stepped carefully, wishing he could have found a dark-lantern amongst the clutter of Holmes's untidy catchall closet of implementa, old files and disguise components. He yearned for the familiarity of a compact, comprehensible flashlight; instead he was saddled with a battered, rusty lantern with broken shuttering. Because of the latter liability, he did not dare employ the thing till he was inside Moriarty's lair.

Rounding a corner, he walked toward the rear entrance, testing each window along the way. But everything was shut up tight.

It was a vast, ugly pile without concession to aesthetic ornamentation. At the squat, solid-looking back door, Phillimore removed certain tools and began worrying at the lock. Before setting out, he'd studied one of Holmes's myriad monographs, a slim manuscript concerned with the intricacies of lock-picking. This knowledge, bolstered by the teacher's rusty conjuring lore, enabled him to make reasonably short work of the back portal. He was a bit surprised how relatively easy the job was, but

Moriarty probably never expected anyone to be so foolhardy as to burglarize his unsanctuary.

Having achieved ingress, Phillimore lit the lantern and looked around. The interior contradicted the baleful aspect of the outside: the flickering light hinted at expensive furnishings, thick carpeting, paintings, tapestries and armorial artifacts. Luxuriance everywhere, even to the point of decadence.

He listened intently. Nothing. Not a sound. The big house was chilly and still. The only noise was the suspiration of his rapid breathing which he could not control.

The size of Moriarty's mansion daunted him. Where in all its shadowy eyries was he to seek out another umbrella, whose existence, anyway, was purely hypothetical?

On the latter point, he soon was to be reassured, but for the moment he confined himself to trying to locate the library.

His conspirator had reasoned thus: as Phillimore's own dimensional adventures depended on the literature with which he was most familiar, it was conceivable that when Moriarty plunged over the falls, he chose a place to fly via umbrella that derived from his own leisure reading. Theoretically, then, Phillimore might trace the evil professor just by studying his bookshelves.

He stepped forward, a few inches at a time, playing the light across the floor to see where it was safe to put his feet, occasionally lofting the lantern to study the direction in which he was headed. Soon, his perambulations brought him to a wide, peaked archway through which he spied a globe so enormous he could not hope to encircle its girth with outstretched arms.

Reasoning a globe would be kept in a study/library, he entered, shining the lantern about the chamber. He saw tables butted against the walls, surfaces strewn with charts and sheets of jottings. The walls themselves held graphs and maps, some of the latter depicting London, with black stickpins thrust through at various locations. At the far side of the room stood a polished teak desk that bore a neat array of papers, ledgers, writing instruments and miscellaneous calculatory paraphernalia. An ample decantered sideboard completed the roll-call of movable furniture. Behind it, set into the wall, rose a tall, moderately wide bookshelf.

Phillimore stepped across the room, rested the lantern atop the sideboard and scanned the volumes jamming the shelves.

"Hmmph. As I expected...mainly scientific works. Some philosophy. Nietzsche—no small testament to Moriarty's percipience, few enough sold in the original German editions. *Tertium Organum*. Kant. Schopenhauer. Paracelsus. *De Rerum Natura*. Kepler. Albertus Magnus. *Principia Mathematica*. Al-hazred. *The Discoverie of*—"

The murmured soliloquy ceased. His eye backtracked to the Russell-Whitehead tomes. "Just a moment! *Principia Mathematica*...they didn't see that in print till about 1910 and even then it was only the initial volume!"

It was clearly an anachronism. Suddenly, Phillimore no longer regarded the notion as remote that Moriarty might have an umbrella stashed somewhere in the house. He scanned the books with renewed fervor: Rimbaud, Baudelaire, Villon in French jostled for space with great piles of political tracts and mouldering esoterica on every subject from thaumaturgy, kheft and culling...

There! On a shelf just above eye-level he found a scant collection of fiction. The fat Burton translation of *The Arabian Nights* stood beside and dwarfed Abbott's amusing tale of life in a two-dimensional universe, *Flatland*. Here were both 1818 and 1831 editions of *Frankenstein*, as well as the endless, lurid *Newgate Calendar*, appropriately accompanied by *The Beggars Opera* libretto and Fielding's exercise in sustained irony, *Jonathan Wild*. The only other thing on the shelf was a thick pile of sheets laboriously handwritten in German. On the top page, Phillimore noticed a vaguely familiar place name, the Rue d'Auseil. But it was no time for idle browsing.

"Must jot down the titles," he said to himself, rummaging through his pockets for paper and—

"*May I be of assistance?*"

He whirled, stunned. A shadowy figure, nearly six feet tall, stood in the doorway.

It was bad enough to be surprised in a master criminal's home at midnight during an act of burglary, but the fact that he recognized the newcomer made it all quite a bit worse. There was no mistaking the hard, lean jawline; the unblinking eyes, the mouth set in a grin that might easily be assessed as cruel. Lofting the lantern, he saw, sure enough, the deep lateral slice that creased the bridge of the man's nose.

"Perhaps you might like to tell me what you are doing here," suggested A. I. Persano mildly.

The scholar's thoughts raced. *Enough light to see, but he doesn't recognize me, I'm sure of it! Why not?*

The answer immediately struck him. He'd met Persano, Moriarty's lieutenant, in the "draft-world" and left him in a world of horror from which there could be no escape. *Then that must have been an Ür-Persano and this one is the genuine article!*

"It is, you must admit, a peculiar hour to pay a social call, let alone browse through a library." Like the other Persano, the dangerous gentleman spoke politely, never flaunting his puissance in vulgar display.

Phillimore cleared his throat. *Think fast!* "I trust you are Mr. Persano?"

The others eyes narrowed. "Perhaps. Why do you ask?"

"Well, the—ah, the fact is—"

"One of our ablest dramatists," Persano interrupted, "has stated that the phrase, 'the fact is—,' invariably signifies the imminent commission of a spectacular lie. However, do not let me stay your story."

Phillimore resolved to fabricate a history not totally removed from the truth. "Professor Moriarty told me to seek you out."

"In the middle of the night?"

"He suggested you would be able to bring me his special umbrella."

Persano smiled. "It must be quite special to do him any good at the base of Reichenbach."

"He did not fall to his death. By a strange rent in the fabric of time, he was propelled to the world which I have been inhabiting until recently. There he had me create another umbrella and sent me here to bring the original, which he says is a far superior model."

"An interesting story," Persano remarked. "Why did he not return for it himself?"

Phillimore silently cudgeled his brains. *The story's full of holes. What do I tell him?*

"You see," he improvised, "when I met him, he was in prison; I was just about to be released. He dictated the plans for making an umbrella; I made one and arrived just outside the house. But it was a flimsy affair; it didn't survive the trip. I threw it in the Thames." *There! Fast and fancy!*

Persano nodded sagely. "Ah, yes, I see...very plausible." He smiled pleasantly. "You wait right here, I'll fetch the Professor's original umbrella." Before Phillimore could say another word, Persano retreated through the archway, closing the double doors and locking them.

"Damn! He doesn't believe me," the teacher said to himself, casting about for some means of escape. But the study was an interior chamber lacking windows. His mind clicked off alternatives, saw only one possibility. "I've got to get hold of the umbrella, press its button and quit this world. But where should I go?"

He spun around to the bookshelf and desperately studied the choices. "Where would Moriarty be likely to choose? *Let's see...*"

Persano's footsteps sounded overhead. Evidently the need for silence no longer concerned him, a fact which subtly disconcerted Phillimore. He studied the book titles intently, weighing possibilities.

"Surely Moriarty would go someplace that offered the opportunity for criminous expansion. In which case—"

The footsteps started downstairs as he flipped through the pages of *The Newgate Calendar*, found what he wanted and replaced the tome. "Yes. He even has the chapter heading underlined: 'Jonathan Wild, The Prince of Robbers.' Doyle drew the obvious analogy; Wild was a sixteenth-century Moriarty. He banded all burglars and highwaymen under a common government, his own...

The lock clicked.

"But would Moriarty choose to horn in on Wild or would he hit upon one of the fictional characters based on Wild? What advantage would there be in each?"

He terminated his mutterings as the doors opened and Persano stepped through carrying two objects, a large black umbrella devoid of decorative device and an ebony cane which dismayed Phillimore.

Setting the umbrella against the wall, Persano asked if it was what the other had come to obtain.

"Indeed it is." Though he tried to sound casual, Phillimore stepped too hastily toward the umbrella. Immediately, Persano interposed himself between object and subject, simultaneously grasping his cane with both hands. A long metallic whoosh—and the weapon in the ebony sheath pointed naked at Phillimore's breast.

Persano did not appear the least bit ruffled or perturbed. In his customary even, well-modulated voice, he suggested that Phillimore might do well to offer some plausible explanation as to what he was doing in Moriarty's house.

"But I told you everything. Put that dreadful thing away!"

The other clucked disapprovingly. "I perceive a mere exhortation that you practice candor is of no weight. Very well; let me simply note that, according to your tale, you just arrived here from an alien world."

"That's what I said."

"Then it seems a trifle unlikely that you would be aware that the river which flows nearby is named the Thames."

Phillimore winced. *Reconcile it quickly, or—*

"I beg you spare me the fruits of hurried mental revision of your original tale. I have spoken ere this with Colonel Moran and he told me of a chap who fits your description showing up out of nowhere on the ledge at Reichenbach. He also said you had an umbrella which the Professor bore away with him.

"It has occurred to me and the Colonel that if that umbrella were of similar design to the one here beside me, our chief may have activated it. Your presence tonight tends to confirm that supposition."

Phillimore's resolve plummeted. Casting about for some desperate mode of aid, he returned to the sideboard where the lantern still flickered its lurid glare over walls and furnishings. "Well, I suppose I must admit you have me at a disadvantage. What next?"

"Kindly keep away from that lantern," Persano sharply warned, making a tiny circle in the air in its direction with the tip of his sword. "Eschew heroics and hear me. We may be of use to one another."

"Impossible!"

"Tut, gratuitous rudeness suggests ill breeding. There is a clear advantage for both of us to grasp."

Phillimore shrugged. "I fail to see it."

"You can help me bring the Professor back, I don't doubt."

"How do you deduce that?"

"Just before I heard you thumping around down here, I was upstairs mulling over the problem of locating him. It suddenly occurred to me the key might be in that bookshelf. When I walked in, you were inspecting it, an action that confirmed my belief."

"I still don't see what benefit that provides me," Phillimore argued.

"Simple. You tell me your deductions. In exchange, I tender you your life." It was beneath Persano to make the alternative explicit, but the still-lofted sword was eloquent enough.

Phillimore mulled over his predicament. In no way did he trust Persano to keep his word. The only hope he had to twist the situation in his favor was to get hold of the umbrella.

"I appear to have no choice but to accept your proposition."

Persano shrugged. "I certainly see no other way."

"Well, as a matter of fact," Phillimore lied, "I had just conclusively ascertained where Professor Moriarty went when you walked in."

"And where is that?"

The scholar waggled his finger in the fashion of a pedagogue admonishing the class wag. "No, no, I should be a veritable dunce to inform you of my secret. Give me the umbrella and I'll prove I'm right by going on and fetching him back to this world."

Persano chuckled. "All collective bargaining begins, does it not, with impossible demands which neither party expects to obtain, n'est-ce pas? Now that we have both insulted one another's intelligences, let us come up with a reasonable compromise. You work the umbrella so that it takes you where you have in mind, thus keeping your secret. I will make the flight with you."

"And skewer me, I suppose, upon arrival!"

With one palm upward in a gesture of bonhomie, Persano demurred. "My word as a gentleman to the contrary. If we cannot trust one another, we shall never get on with this." As a token of his earnest, the villain replaced his sword within its scabbard. Picking up the umbrella, he bade Phillimore take hold of it.

Well, might as well try what may. The question was which source to select—the *Newgate Calendar*, Fielding or John Gay's *The Beggar s Opera*. Fielding, he decided instantly, was incorrect; in that book, Jonathan Wild was little better than a cutpurse highwayman. Surely Moriarty would be more eager to consort with a criminal who organized London's greatest network of crime during the early 1700s. On the other hand, there might be practical value to dealing with Gay's Peachum, a character modeled on Wild. Peachum might easily rid Phillimore of the dangerous Persano; a word in his ear and the pious double-dealer would "peach" on Persano to the authorities and—

"Come, come!" Persano snapped. "Enough woolgathering! Activate this thing instantly, or I shall think twice about our arrangement."

Phillimore sighed. Just once he wished he might take his time and work the umbrella properly. *However...*

He pushed the button, which was in practically the same spot as the one on his own model..

The universe reversed itself and did its giddy tarantella. Phillimore, who was somewhat used to umbrella-flight by that time, did his best to joggle Persano loose, but the other merely clutched his cane tighter and paid no attention.

The flight was brief. The umbrella, automatically closing itself, deposited them on a hard floor. The air was close, cold, clammy.

They were in total darkness.

Thrashing about with his free hand, Phillimore tried to locate something solid, a wall, anything. He did not succeed. The blackness was absolute.

"Where in hell have you taken us?" Persano demanded.

At the sound of his speech, there came a sudden chorus of raucous voices. A tinder scratched, a torch flared. Snarls and imprecations. Then sudden laying-on of hands. Phillimore flailed in terror; Persano began to withdraw his sword.

Two bright objects flashed and fell and the pair, groaning, sank to the stone floor, unconscious.

CHAPTER FOUR

As it is necessary that all great and surprising events, the designs of which are laid, conducted and brought to perfection by the utmost force of human invention and art, should be elucidated to the satisfaction of the startled peruser of this modest history, it is therefore essential to explain that the hapless Phillimore and his nemesis, Persano, were brought by the device of Moriarty's umbrella to the very stronghold-cellar of that same Jonathan Wild who kept the minions of crime in London, circa 1716, under his ruthless guidance and instruction by the simple system of turning all obstreperous objectors directly over to the governmental authorities, a method which ironically caused the common press to greatly value the public services of the same Mr. Wild. But irony was one of Wild's favorite devices and he was frequently wont to state in moments of well-concealed candor that he should far prefer to stand upon the summit of a dunghill in Hell than at the bottom of a mountain in Paradise.

Irony, indeed, presided over the appearance of our protagonist in Mr. Wild's cellar that particular evening. For some time, the duplicitous Wild was troubled by the unruly exploits of a young burglar by name of Jack Sheppard, a gentleman whose derring-do excited the honest London citizenry as much as his bravura attitude towards the Prince of Robbers awoke unexpressed sympathy amongst Wild's necessarily loyal underlings. If the reader will permit yet another anachronism, Sheppard was a veritable eighteenth-century Houdini, having escaped repeatedly from confinement. When informed he must contribute a percentage of his criminous gains to the Wild organization, Sheppard sneered that "the fat rogue may seethe in his own gallows-grease ere that come to pass!" Whereupon, the same being reported to Wild, he bespoke himself to a certain corrupt official and shortly thereafter, Sheppard was apprehended and remanded to prison. The next morning, the bird was flown the coop and word circulated amongst the tapsters of the underworld that Sheppard vowed to avenge himself upon Wild by burglarizing his very establishment within a fortnight.

When Phillimore and Persano awoke, they found themselves bound with stout rope and secured to great iron rings high above the cellar floor so that they must perforce dangle, feet scant inches from the stone surface below. The ache was intolerable in their limbs, but the spectacle presented to their dismayed view took their minds a little off their physical discomfort.

It was a large cellar, stacked with wine-casks, arched here and there with portals to further recesses where all manner of rich costumery and pelf lay in tagged orderliness, the merchandise which Wild was wont to take in trade from his henchmen, thence to be "sought out amongst the lower classes and returned, sans questions," to the anxious original owners, though never for a fee other than what the good hearts of the grateful victims served by Wild might choose to disburse upon his "poor honest efforts on their behalves."

A small company of unwholesome-looking brigands stood in a band, observing Persano and Phillimore. One particularly nasty giant (whose oft-scarred countenance was distinguished by skin tinged an unhealthy blue tint) held Persano's sword-cane, the weapon partially withdrawn; the ghoulish villain leered with pleasure upon the thing, which he evidently considered to be his own fairly-gained property. Phillimore glanced anxiously about, saw the black umbrella negligently laid in a corner, an object apparently of no worth to his captors.

The group of thieves and murderers, for so they were, parted to allow their chief to descend to the middle of the cellar. This illustrious personage, none other than Mr. Jonathan Wild himself, was tall and uncommonly portly; his complexion, though fair, was mottled and pocked and his lips protruded in a parody of a judge's opprobrious pout. His raiment was of the finest cut, but the topknot which adorned his skull might have been better for a washing. He carried his hands behind his figured waistcoat and clasped them in the mode of a stem headmaster; his head turned constantly in a curiously reptilian motion as if he were seeking out the pranks of a mischievous urchin who only chose to dally when his principal's back was turned. Wild, as he passed the rogue with the blue skin, paused to observe the fine woodwork of the ebony sword-cane.

"What doth this signify, rascal?" he growled. "I flatter myself this is booty justly earned for the betterment of the establishment at large, of which you and all your fellows are pleased to benefit! Restore it at once!"

He held his hand out expectantly and there was some hesitation on Blueskin's part before he set the stick in Wild's hand. "Take it, if tha's a mind," the henchman grumbled, "but take care it do not turn about and do ye damage."

Wild glowered at the man. A more perceptive observer than his underlings would have fairly heard the fatal computation clicking in his skull to do over Blueskin to the authorities come next quarter. Having silently damned the luckless scoundrel, Wild turned and regarded the two hanging captives. Setting his weight pompously upon Persano's cane, he swaggered to a place a few feet before them, far enough back so neither could aim a kick at him.

"Well, lads," he chuckled oilily, "Sheppard fee'd ye to a bitter purpose. I wondered how he dared to brag of this venture and hope to 'scape incarceration."

"Let us down," Persano demanded. "We know nothing of this Sheppard. Free us and we will satisfy you of the strange, but innocent reason for our appearing thus."

"By addressing you," Wild admonished, "I did not mean to instance you toward debate. You will maintain silence, base fellow! It is unseemly such unprincipled rascals, garbed like lunatics, should befoul the ears of an honest citizen with the foul billingsgate to which you are accustomed in your element." He turned to one of his gang. "Fetch Mr. Brown hither with his men and deliver over these rogues to justice." Wild again studied his captives, this time with an air of perplexity. "How you managed to enter without disturbing the locks, I cannot hope to perceive, yet your master, Sheppard, has witch-power with the instruments of security and I venture to suppose he has played for his immortal part when he spirited the pair of you within mine honest walls!"

Shaking his head, Wild continued his discourse in song, much to Persano's amazement. The villains by the stairs crooned softly in harmony and Phillimore winced and murmured, "Not again!"

(AIR to the tune of *An Old Woman Clothed in Grey*)

WILD.

Through all the employment of life,
*   Each neighbor abuses his brother;*
Jack Sheppard, persistent in strife,
*   Doth cause me interminable pother!*
The thief calls the robber a cheat,
*   While poor honest Jonathan Wild*
Is slandered, although I'm as sweet
*   As an unsullied innocent child!*

The song ended, he observed, "A lawyer is as honest as I. We both act in double capacity, against rogues and for 'em! And so, gentlemen—" he winked wickedly at the dangling duo "—and so, good-night!" Turning, Wild ascended the stairs, followed by his ghastly crew.

The sound of a heavy door clanging shut resounded through the cellar; immediately ensuing was the noise of bolts being shoved into place. All the torches having been borne away, Phillimore and Persano again found themselves in the dark.

"You wretched fool!" Persano grumbled. "In what nonsensical world have you enmired us?"

Phillimore, by now a veteran of abortive umbrella-flights, hung relatively unperturbed. "It is obvious what went wrong. Had you not hurried my choice, we would have fetched the world of Jonathan Wild. But because of your precipitancy, I would venture to guess we are on a bastard earth composed of equal elements of the *Newgate Calendar*, Henry Fielding and assuredly John Gay."

"How do you make that out?"

"Wild is pretty much as history paints him, yet he speaks in a florid style suggestive of Fielding—"

"And the song obviously reflects *The Beggar's Opera*?"

"Precisely."

"But why," Persano raged, "would you pick *any* of those places?"

"Because I postulate that Wild's iron-fisted grip on the London underworld would appeal to Professor Moriarty. Here would be a network of crime ready to hand...all he need do is arrange some compromise in exchange for his unique talents. Or perhaps, he might choose to wrest power away from Wild and—"

"And stuff and abominable nonsense! My leader would not be fool enough to attempt to bargain with the most unprincipled rogue in the annals of illegality. And as for taking over, why run the dreadful risk? It would be as foolhardy as Wild attempting to oust the Professor: there are too many loyal lieutenants who would carry the intelligence to the proper source and work to quash him. No, no, he never would have come here, or anyplace like it!" Persano glowered at Phillimore, but it was dark and the expression served no purpose. "And you told me you knew precisely where he'd gone..."

Phillimore said nothing. As usual, Persano lived by the code of proper conduct. One might slit a throat or two in the course of everyday business, but deliberate prevarication was rather ungentlemanly, ergo, shocking.

"Well," the scholar sighed "never mind where we are. The question is, how do we get away?"

"As for that," Persano grunted, "I have been swinging my feet in hopes of clamping hold of the umbrella. They...left it...within reach. Except—"

"Except what?"

"I can only approximately recall its position. This blasted darkness...!"

"Well, you might as well spare the effort. It won't do us much good; the thing needs to be recharged and it takes quite some time."

"Not this model. It's quite efficient. Half-an-hour is all it requires to rebuild its energy and we have surely been here close to that, perhaps longer, it's hard to say how long we were unconscious...There!...No, not quite...but now I know where it is...and..."

Phillimore heard Persano grunt. There was the sound of his feet striking the stone wall; a clatter followed, then Persano cursed.

"What happened?"

"I'm afraid I knocked the umbrella out of reach. And I thought—"

"SHHH!"

Persano, always lightning-rapid in his reactions, immediately hushed, no questions asked.

The two hung, arms aching, breaths stilled. In the darkness, they heard the stealthy rasp of metal against metal. The most subtle of scrapings repeated twice...thrice...and then a muffled *click*.

A cold breeze suddenly flooded the cellar. The gloom dispelled slightly; Phillimore was able to see the glimmer of his own scuffed black shoes, though nothing else.

A lengthy silence, then to their strained ears came the gentlest susurration, an all-but-inaudible scuffle which indicated that someone stealthily trod the stone flagging of Wild's basement.

After an interminable period, during which no other sound was heard, the newcomer, apparently satisfied the place was temporarily safe and secure, lit a small flambeaux. Phillimore strained his neck to one side to perceive the aspect of the person who stood, unbidden, in the cellar of the Prince of Thieves.

It was a young man, scarcely past his teens, he judged. A handsome, regularly-featured face contained black, glinting eyes and was surmounted by a shock of pitch-black glossy hair. The mouth had broad, generous lips that surely were no stranger to mirth.

The intruder shone his torch around the cellar. Suddenly spying the two suspended occupants thereof, he emitted a startled hiss, immediately quelling it as he assessed their helpless situation. Laying a finger perpendicular to his mouth to caution them not to say anything, the youth approached Phillimore, the nearer of the two and brought his lips as close to the captive's ears as the awkward updrawn position would permit.

"I daresay ye've run aground of that foul and fearsome bloodsucker, Wild," he whispered.

"Aye," Phillimore confirmed. "Can ye cut us loose?" He would have feared to adopt the accent of the place, save for those assurances he had been given at the Diogenes Club as to the purely subjective nature of subsumption. Phillimore knew perfectly well this newcomer must be Jack Sheppard arrived to make good his boast, but for once kept his seerish knowledge to himself, lest the other grow suspicious.

"Any man who is enemy to Wild is my friend," the young man said, withdrawing a knife to sever the bonds. "I do not know who ye may be, attired in ludicrous gallimaufry as you are, but I will number ye evermore my fast friend, so ye do likewise. But do ye ken thy benefactor?"

"Oh, ay, right enough," Phillimore replied. "Only Jack Sheppard himself could work such wizardry with that devil Wild's locks!" As he spoke, the rope parted and he slumped to the floor with a stifled groan, rubbing his chafed wrists.

Sheppard, flattered at his renown, bowed, grinned a crooked grin, then, *sotto voce*, began to sing. Phillimore sighed; he knew from Gilbert-and-Sullivan-land that the etiquette of place dictated waiting the damned verses out.

(AIR to the tune of *A Soldier and a Sailor*)

SHEPP.

A fox may steal your hens, Sir,
A scrivener all your pens, Sir,
But all the rest you own, Sir,
With Sheppard's surely flown, Sir,
   No bar is lock or gate!
For every stay I'm picking;
And omnes: pens, hens, chickling,
Shall ever be my fee, Sir,
And if I do but see, Sir,
   I'll also—

"Will you have done with that untimely caterwauling?!" Persano interrupted in as loud a snarl as he deemed advisable.

Stopping the song at once, Sheppard turned an affronted countenance upon his aural intruder.

"Who is that ill-mannered bumpkin?" he demanded. "Never in this short life have I met one so confoundedly low-bred as to cut in on one's musical peroration! That goes beyond every runagate knave, even Mr. Wild!"

Persano, stung by the aspersions cast on his breeding, haughtily demanded that he be cut free upon the instant.

"The devil I will!" Sheppard snapped. "If your companion finds aught to pleasure him in such surly company, let him set ye at liberty, for I'll have none of it!"

Phillimore looked sharply at Persano, expecting him to speak. But that quick mind instantly assessed his personal predicament and knew better than to petition aid from the one quarter where he was certain it would not come.

Suddenly, from above: a babble of voices. The three cast apprehensive glances in the direction of the stair.

"Hurry," Phillimore whispered. "Wild has sent for the authorities to take us to prison. Mr. Sheppard, you must quit this place on the instant, otherwise you will be in great danger!"

The other pressed the scholar's arm reassuringly, cast about for some valuable to spirit away, found a large, ornate pearl-inlaid jewel-box. He gave Phillimore a broad wink. "The fat jackanapes will miss this right enough!" Then, without another word he sped from the cellar into the night.

Phillimore cursed his own stupidity. Sheppard, having taken his flambeaux, left him no light to find the umbrella. Dropping on his hands and knees, he fumbled frantically about the cold, grimy floor. Above, the voices neared.

"To my left," Persano whispered. "Judge the spot from my voice!"

Phillimore practically threw himself into the indicated corner, scrabbling every which way, arms flailing. His sleeves brushed something. He slapped his hands palm-flat upon the flagging and located the umbrella.

"I've got it!"

"I'm delighted to hear it," Persano said unenthusiastically.

Phillimore bit his lip. His conscience could not accept the responsibility of leaving Persano—arch-villain though he was—to the savage ministrations of eighteenth-century British justice.

"Well, I *would* get you down if I could, but Sheppard took away his dagger."

"I have one strapped to the inside of my left leg." Shuddering at Persano's resourcefulness, Phillimore felt for the weapon, a six-inch blade honed to razor-keenness. Withdrawing it, he slashed at Persano's bindings. The voices upstairs approached the cellar door.

"May I remind you," Phillimore grunted, sawing at the thick rope, "it was your impatience that served to keep you in this predicament."

"As for that," the other rejoined, "it was you who first chose this wretchedly inauspicious world."

Phillimore heard Wild's rumbling voice above. The keys began to turn in the lock as someone shot back the bolts. Just then the long dagger severed the rope. Persano, though his limbs must have ached bitterly, landed on his feet. He instantly snatched at the dagger, but Phillimore leapt backwards even as he grasped the umbrella securely. He tossed the dagger into a far corner so it was too distant for Persano to risk fetching in the scant time available.

"Now—*where* should we go?" Phillimore demanded, placing his thumb on the umbrella.

"I'll do that!" Persano argued, quickly grabbing at the instrument with both hands. "Don't you see, the Professor would choose a world where some important resource indigenous solely to it would be at hand. Think what a formidable tool he might fashion if he could but commandeer the—"

"Magic!" Phillimore exclaimed, cutting off the other.

"No! I was going to say—"

The cellar door flew open with a bang, interrupting Persano a second time. Torches flared, feet clattered downstairs. Wild, at the rear of the group, spied the unshackled unprisoners and roared in anger and dismay.

"Apprehend them! They are surely devils!"

"QUICK!" Persano shouted. "Move your hand!"

He and Phillimore simultaneously scrabbled to press the button of the umbrella. Both forefingers hit it at once.

Just before the first of the thugs threw their arms about the two of them, the umbrella sprang open and the quarry quickly faded from view.

"By God," Blueskin whispered, horrified, "Sheppard is indeed in league with Satan!"

"That's as may be," Wild growled, "but what is more to the point, the fiends hath swiped my second-best jewel-box!"

CHAPTER FIVE

Dimensional riptides battered them. Phillimore's stomach flip-flopped; he clutched the leather curved handpiece with a strength born of colossal panic. Cosmic cross-winds shrieked, buffeting the umbrella so ferociously that the fabric fluctuated with a violent flapping that the scholar feared would soon tear the material to shreds.

"Persano, tune out!" he screamed. "It isn't made to receive two frequencies of thought at once!"

The other did not hear him in the wild cacophony of universal protestation. Persano clung desperately to the metal shaft, though it was growing uncomfortably hot.

What if it uses too much energy? Phillimore worried. *Can't let it burn out!*

There was only one thing to do. Phillimore silently commanded it to compromise with the other signal. *Hope it can figure out what I mean!*

The umbrella emitted a high-pitched whine. Persano howled in pain. The shaft glowed red.

Compromise, damn it! Compromise!

In response, the umbrella suddenly nosed downwards, yanking Phillimore head-under-heels into a star-shot darkness. Below, though the teacher could not see, Persano had to let loose of the fiery pole; he snatched desperately at the cloth-folds. All Phillimore knew was that there was a sudden lightening of the drag. Before he could sort out his thoughts, the umbrella swerved the other way and he came rightside-up, feet glancingly scraping ground.

A wind of demoniac fury...peals of thunder...an awful yell...

Another weight depended downward from the umbrella, but the pull was enormous, easily three times that of Persano's. The umbrella soared straight up and the renewed velocity, even with its heavier burden, swiftly cooled the shaft. In the midst of all the brouhaha and wrenching alteration of motion, Phillimore fancied hearing a half-human snarl close by, while, in the distance, Persano's dismayed wail dwindled to nothingness.

The flight was surer now, swifter. Phillimore was so giddy he had to shut his eyes against the cartoon constellations gyrating in his head. He squeezed the leather handpiece, afraid that in his faintness he might lose his grip and fall.

Abruptly, all sense of motion ceased. The noise of flight dwindled to the hushed whisper of breakers on a nameless beach; the stars winked out and left him in pitch darkness. His feet touched down on the soft-hard shifting surface that was a great stretch of sand.

Nearby he thought he heard the dull plop of some ponderous weight sprawling flat. He was too weary to think about it.

Phillimore's numb fingers released the now-shut umbrella. He pitched headfirst onto the sand, sighed thankfully for the cool breeze soothing his face and sank into an exhausted slumber.

CHAPTER SIX

He woke when the first gentle plash of incoming tide slid a clamshell under his nose. Sputtering at the salt-taste wetting his lips, Phillimore sat up and blinked at the bright morning sun glimmering on the cresting ocean. The dissonant cries of a flock of circling seabirds filled the air and a mild breeze fluttered the umbrella where it lay, but there were no other sounds or signs of animation.

A second incursion of the surf hurried him to his feet and back a few steps to dry sand.

Facing inland, umbrella in hand, Phillimore studied the coastline. The broad sweep of beach curved gently and steadily backwards about a mile on either side, suggesting he might be on an island. Following the contour of the seafront at a distance of fifty or sixty feet was a thick tangle of palm, coconut and less familiar trees and brush. Further inland, the tops of lofty rock-faces were just barely discernible. Some distance away to the left, a narrow gap broke the barrier of greenery; through it flowed a thin sparkling twist of fresh water, a small stream seeking the sea.

He turned right and saw the footprints.

They began alongside a great irregular indentation in the sand close to the spot where he lay all night. They stretched in a crooked line to the trees and disappeared there.

Phillimore approached the prints, noted their size and felt vaguely uneasy. He walked beside them to their terminus at the jungle's edge. At that point, he spied a twisted, trampled alley through the brake that something must have torn open in its passage.

The scholar felt thirsty, anyway, so he saw no reason to enter the thick woods just there. Turning, he stepped along the beach in the direction of the stream, nervously darting glances into the trees as he strode the skirts of the sand.

"At least I've lost Persano. Wonder if I got where I wanted to go? How in hell am I to find out?"

At the streamside, Phillimore slaked his thirst. He opened his collar and removed his jacket, for the morning sun already felt bake-oven hot. As he pondered the best course of action to embark on, a curious sound drew his attention to the jungle. He could not be certain, but it seemed as if someone was sobbing.

Taking a final gulp of water, Phillimore put down his jacket, shifted his umbrella so he might, if necessary, employ it as a club and stepped off in the direction of the whimpering. He followed the creek-bank into the shelter of the trees.

The shade of leaves far above his head made the heat more bearable; he filled his lungs with air heavied by the sour-sweet odor of decaying matter. Carefully, Phillimore walked along the bend of stream that, like a crooked finger, beckoned him toward the source of the misery.

A few yards further and the trees parted to reveal a small, lush glade. In its middle, seated on a low, flat stone, a small man of advanced years huddled with his head in his hands. His shoulders heaved with elaborately melodramatic sighs and eloquent sobs. Phillimore noted with satisfaction the man's outlandish garb: red balloon-leg pantaloons cinched by a broad yellow silken cummerbund; blue sandals with up-pointed toes and a matching turban blotched with sweat, tattered from years of neglect. The bare-chested stranger was short, portly and white-bearded. When he lowered his hands from his puffy jowls and wrinkled brow, he displayed a pair of woe-filled eyes that flowed copious streams of sorrow.

"Almighty Allah!" he wailed, hands stretched above his head. "Is the unspeakable sin of Abu Hassan never to be forgotten? Must I endure the whips of public opprobrium even here where I had thought to shun the scornful faces of my fellow-men forever? Is not my name sufficiently blackened? Cannot the divine mercy of Blessed Allah expunge from memory the loathsome crime of Abu Hassan?" He beat his breast and plucked out a patch of chest-hair in wild grief.

"Here, here," Phillimore exclaimed, taking pity at such protracted and deep-seated suffering. Entering the glade, he asked, "Is there anything, poor fellow, that can be done to relieve you?"

Abu Hassan turned a mournful countenance upon the newcomer. "Sir, leave me to my remorse and do not mock me. Must I be shamed even here on this deserted isle where I betook myself in voluntary exile in order that I might never more see the leering eyes and pointing fingers of those who judge and condemn me? Is there no balm in Gilead? No nepenthe of my griefs?"

"But look here, I don't know what you're talking about! I never heard of you before. I only thought I might be able to help somehow."

Abu Hassan stared for a long time at Phillimore, an expression of mingled wonder and joy flitting coquettishly about the edges of his hang-dog face. Rising from his rock, the tubby little penitent took a tottering step toward the scholar, then paused fearfully. "Stranger," he said pleadingly, "do not be crueler than mine own conscience! Is it possible that never to your ears came the report of Abu Hassan's dreadful and name-less deed? Can there be a single soul who has not listened maliciously to the shame and fall of one of the most opulent merchants of the City Kaukaban of Al-Yaman?"

"I tell you, I don't know anything about it. I shall not despise you for what is long past and gone." In truth, Phillimore was beginning to recollect some vague detail of the tale of Abu Hassan, but its principal essence still escaped definition. But the important thing was he recalled it was a story from *The Arabian Nights* and that proved the umbrella had eventually listened to him. He reasoned that Moriarty, who owned the Burton translation of the famous anthology of Oriental anecdota, might well decide to fly to a world where magic was an operant part of the underlying plan. *Think what a tool he might make from Aladdin's Lamp*! Phillimore mused, unconsciously paraphrasing Persano as he last saw him in Jonathan Wild's cellar.

Meanwhile, Abu Hassan still harangued the teacher for assurance that he was indeed a perfect stranger and might embrace his company without shame.

"Believe me, I do not know you," Phillimore asserted, only partly lying. *But I'd better pretend total ignorance if I'm to get anything out of the old wind-bag*!

It took many minutes to satisfy the distrustful Abu Hassan, but at length Phillimore succeeded in turning the conversation to other topics.

"You said we are on an isle. But on what part of the globe are we quartered?" That was the trouble with the umbrella: it had no especial discrimination in the places it chose to deposit the user. If Moriarty were somewhere about, it might be thousands of miles from where Phillimore landed. *How to find him*?

"This is an uncharted isle," Abu Hassan stated, "somewhere in the southern tropics to the west of the Sea of Indus."

"And are we the only living things upon it?"

The other broke into a delighted grin, the first truly light-hearted expression he had been able to don since the arrival of Phillimore. "Ah, no, sir! You are indeed fortunate to make the acquaintance of Abu Hassan at this propitious time! For one of the most wondrous spectacles in the entire vastness of this world is about to take place upon the crags of yonder peak! Ah! how grateful I am at the limitless compassion of Mighty Allah that at length my prayers are answered...for lo! these many years have I, in my most secret heart, forlornly (so I thought) yearned for a companion ignorant of my foul transgression. For such a one, I vowed, would I ope the scintillant spectacle of this magical clime. The isle is full of noises, good friend, ay and sights beyond dream! And but this time of year, for a little while only, the fabled great creatures of the air woo the earth and bring forth their young!"

Phillimore wearily expressed polite interest. It was apparent that Abu Hassan would be no ready font of data, at least not without enduring a mighty spate of tedium intermixed. With resignation, he suggested that the other bring him to witness the marvelous thing he hinted of.

"Hush then, stranger!" cautioned Abu Hassan. "Hush and follow me, for we must go some little distance and the journey is not without peril." With that, he turned and began to pick his way through the underbrush, signaling Phillimore to follow.

Peril? A cold prickle hopskipped up and down his spine as some of the less pleasant details of the stories of Scheherazade occurred to him. There was magic in *The Arabian Nights*, sure enough, but also fabulous monsters and frights.

He followed reluctantly, realizing he had no choice if he wanted to question Abu Hassan on possible modes of escape from the island. Phillimore's stomach rumbled hungrily. Abu Hassan turned and motioned for utter silence; whether his expression denoted fear or simple disapproval Phillimore could not tell.

Their path lay steadily, inexorably uphill. As the hike grew increasingly strenuous, Phillimore paused ever more often, winded. The climb was difficult enough, but he was also encumbered by the awkward size and considerable weight of the black umbrella.

The greenery grew sparser the higher they mounted. They scrambled over steep expanses treacherous with small stones underfoot. One such place, the scholar's foot slipped; he sprawled on his face to save himself from pitching down the slope. This action precipitated a small hailstorm of pebbles clattering down the rock-side. Abu Hassan, whirling, hissed for quiet, his face white with fear rather than anger.

"There is now great danger," he whispered, pointing across to a ledge many feet higher and to the right. "The purple troll's lair!"

He insisted on remaining perfectly still for some minutes. While they waited, he strained to hear anything which portended menace.

"I thought you said there were no living things save us and the birds on the isle," Phillimore murmured directly in Abu Hassan's ear.

"That is Allah's own truth, sire," the other replied softly. "There are no other *living* things..."

Phillimore swallowed with considerable difficulty.

After a long motionless time, during which neither breathed more than necessity required, a subtle whirr, low and distant, came to Phillimore's ears. As he listened, the sound drew nearer, greatly increasing in pitch and volume. A moment more and he identified it as a colossal clamor of bird-cry and wing-flapping, louder, more terrible than any such mundane noises had any right to be. The tops of the trees beneath them began to sway and bend in the wind and they felt a sudden draft, fetid and powerful as a hurricane. The sky grew dark.

"Quickly!" Abu Hassan exclaimed in the deafening din. "This flight covers our movements!" He sprang up and scuttled diagonally across the slanted plane of rock, moving away from the direction of the troll's eyrie. Phillimore hastened to follow.

It was long past midday. The sun's burning rays beat fiercely upon them. Phillimore was so thirsty he temporarily forgot his hunger. Up and up they climbed, the wind propelling them with double speed. They had to fight to keep from being swept off the precipice as they worm-inched around a sharp spine that divided the different-facing mountainsides. Phillimore clung to the umbrella with difficulty, averting his eyes from the Cineramic riot of island, forest and sea below.

On the other side of the spine, the cliff mercifully leveled out somewhat; their feet found relatively horizontal terrain to tread upon. The wind died down and in the sudden disquieting hush, Phillimore heard the sound of the great birds more clearly than before. The noise proceeded from a point not far above.

The slope was gentle now. Abu Hassan swiftly made his way up till he gained the apex of the slanted path. Attaining it, he waved his hand warningly at Phillimore, then, lying flat on his stomach, cautiously beckoned the professor to come and join him.

Phillimore crept up the final distance and, emulating his guide, stretched out prone. Carefully he raised his head till his eyes saw beyond the latter extremity of the path.

What he beheld was a wide mesa far below the overhanging lip of rock which comprised the latter end of the slope they'd climbed. Devoid of vegetation, the vast plateau was cupped by the ridges and shelves of the confining precipice. In the middle of the tableland was a spectacle that bulged his eyes.

A stupendous white dome shone in the dwindling rays of the sun; next to it lay the rubble of an identical globe: two gargantuan hemispheres seamed, splintered and fragmented by some colossal force. Phillimore had no doubt concerning the source of the dome's demolition since, next to it, there stood a black-feathered bird as big as a brownstone in College Heights. The avian monstrosity calmly balanced first on one mammoth foot, then the other. It lifted its head up expectantly.

"It's just hatched," Abu Hassan whispered. "It's only a baby."

"I presume it's a roc?"

"Yes. See...the mother came to see if it was hatched. Now it's gone again to get junior some food."

They waited while the baby announced its hunger in periodic cries so loud Phillimore had to stick his fingers in his ears. After seven or eight minutes, the rapid approach of the mother-bird was prefigured by the same raucous whirr of wings heard before, as well as similar wind and the inevitable blotting-out of the sun.

GRAAK!!

The baby bird signaled its joy at its mother's return in a cry so mighty it nearly knocked Phillimore off the cliff. Abu Hassan pointed up at the mother roc, a bird bigger than Mallin Hall at Parker College. A creature far surpassing the hyperbole of nightmare, the roc carried an elephant in its bill, a tidbit which it delivered to its baby.

"And now," Abu Hassan chortled with suppressed glee, "you shall hear a thing that even a Caliph could not command for his pleasure!"

The pachyderm being disposed of, a mere high-tea snack, the baby roc waddled to its mother, nestled in her wings and started to croon as softly as an express train late for dinner. The mother bird joined in and the combined nerve-shattering sound made the mountain quiver.

Phillimore, fingers in ears, was about to suggest a rapid return journey when Abu Hassan nudged him to look across the plateau to a ledge some seventy or eighty yards distant.

On it squatted a purple quasi-human thing with protrusive toad-eyes, pimpled hairy tongue and thin arms terminating in sabre-curved talons. The entity mildly contemplated the cooing birds below for several seconds, then, opening its fang-filled mouth wide, began to howl and squawk in a manner calculated to bring bad dreams unto the sleeping dead. Phillimore felt the hair rise on his forearms as multitudes of goosebumps declared their presence.

"Every year," Abu Hassan confided to him sotto voce, "when the newborn chicks hatch out, the purple troll blends its voice with the bird-song. A rich thing, I declare, that so fell a beast can be thus moved by the beauty of nature's birthing music!"

"Yes, yes," Phillimore agreed wearily, shuddering at the aspect of the purple troll, "but see here, I'm ready to climb down. If I don't eat something soon, I won't have the strength to descend."

"But nay!" Abu Hassan protested. "It is too soon to return. This opportunity doth come but once a year and it is my habit to hear all the melody that they care to produce."

"In that case," the scholar groaned, "you'll excuse me. I'm going."

He started down the slope. Behind him, Abu Hassan sadly shook his head, convinced that his new companion was a tone-deaf lout. Yet in defense of our protagonist it must be declared that the very opposite was true: Phillimore's ears were too sophisticated for the grating primal musicale taking place on the mountain. For, after all, a man whose ears are accustomed to the subtly chiseled harmonies of a Dowland or Purcell, a man who revels in the ascetic tonal architecture of a Bach can hardly be expected to stay still and tolerate the primitive dynamic crudities of a roc and troll concert.

CHAPTER SEVEN

By the time he reached the jungle floor, it was nearly dark. Exhausted, ravenously hungry, Phillimore also was hopelessly lost. He had no idea in which direction lay the stream.

"Well, one thing at a time," he chided himself. "Better look for something nourishing before all the light is gone."

Not adept at natural science, Phillimore dimly guessed he was more likely to turn up edible seafood at dawn than dusk and anyway, he didn't want to waste the twilight wandering aimlessly through the woods. Aware of his shortcomings as a botanical expert, he avoided berries he did not recognize and settled for a handful of nuts and a pair of coconuts recently fallen to the ground. These latter proved an immense problem to open and he only did so by desperate measures which cost him most of the milk within one of the nuts.

Choosing an adjacent glade to consume his meager fare, he sat down and rested his back against a palm tree. Supper was soon over. Phillimore made a feeble effort to rise, but his stiff, aching limbs protested and he did not budge.

"Ought to look for Abu Hassan," he mumbled thickly, as he fell asleep.

Phillimore slumbered for hours. A pale crescent moon rose and in the forest, night-things snuffled and rooted for forage. A sea-breeze stole into the jungle, eradicating the noontide heat. He shivered, partly from the chill air, partly because of the malevolent creatures romping through his over-stimulated subconscious.

Shortly past midnight, the breeze died down. Phillimore woke abruptly, vaguely aware that something was horribly wrong. Still tired, he could not immediately single out the disturbing circumstance, but at length he gathered his wits sufficiently to isolate the thing that made him rouse from troubled sleep.

It was too quiet. The dell lay in an unnatural silence that was curiously ominous, impending. He heard nothing of the myriad sounds that small animals produce among the thick maze of boles and bramble that constitute a forest; no sound, not even the stridulation of a lone insect.

A black cloud concealed the moon. He could barely see two feet in front of his nose. And yet—

By the foot of the mountain, etched hazily against the slightly less gloomy background of the night sky, a great bulky shape loomed. Motionless it stood, possibly nothing more sinister than a slanting stand of fern. Yet Phillimore conceived the nasty notion that the thing was watching him.

Thinking over his predicament, he decided the first thing on the agenda was to get hold of the umbrella, though he was uncertain whether to use it as a weapon or as a mode of escape. Still, if he should decide the most prudent course was to indulge in a nocturnal run, he would have to take it with him, anyway...so...slowly, very slowly, he edged his fingers through the moist grass toward the place where he remembered laying the instrument.

But no sooner did he commence to move his hand, snail-slow, than the menacing patch detached itself from the surrounding murk and headed in his direction. Suddenly, the hush was shattered by a diabolic snarl/ shriek that turned his blood to frost.

As the thing hurtled at him, Phillimore rolled over, grabbed the umbrella, whirled and shot to his feet, thrusting forth the up-pointed umbrella so its tip was aimed in the general direction of the onslaught. The fiendish howl rose in pitch as it neared...and then he felt a bone-jarring impact that almost made him sit down again. He staggered backward from the blow and the umbrella instantly was wrenched from his grip.

Just then, the cloud sailed past and let the moon shine upon the glade once more, bleeding a wan light that revealed dimly Phillimore's awful adversary.

It was the purple troll. Close up, the dead thing was even worse than he'd imagined possible. Well over six feet, it stank with the odor of rot-ted blood. Glowing amber eyes shone malevolently down on him; he was sure the thing could see perfectly in the darkness. Protruding from its middle was Moriarty's umbrella, half of its great length puncturing the vile creature. And yet, though it was deeply impaled, the troll showed no sign of discomfort, or even of *noticing*.

Rooted with fear, Phillimore nearly succumbed to the hypnotic glare of the beast's eyes. But as the wicked talons whooshed towards his neck, self-preservation surged and he jumped aside with a frightened yelp, al-most braining himself against the palm tree. The troll pivoted, reared back and bared its lethal claws for a second try.

At the last possible instant, Phillimore ducked behind the tree. The troll slammed smack into the trunk, driving the umbrella further within its innards. Slavering horrendously, it slashed out at Phillimore around the curve of the bole, but only succeeded in sinking its long claws into the bark. It yanked, but they would not come out.

Panting from exertion and terror, the frightened mortal backed away and watched, ready at any moment to run if the troll showed a sign of freeing itself. But after a full minute of growling and gnashing of its teeth, it still was stuck. Phillimore approached with trepidation, knees knocking, teeth chattering, heart pounding.

But he knew he had to pull out the umbrella.

First he tried to stretch forth his hand and grab the curved grip, but the troll snapped at him so ferociously that he almost lost a finger. He leaped back five feet before timorously resolving to try again.

This time, he crouched low so its fangs couldn't reach. Ignoring the noisome breath as best he could as it ranted, he carefully stretched up his hand, grabbed the shaft and yanked. It gave slightly, then stopped. Kneeling on both knees, he leaned as close as he dared, grasped the umbrella-handle with both hands and extracted another inch of the over-sized parasol, but then it was impossible to budge it further.

One at a time, he wiped his sweating hands against his trousers and tried a new purchase on the grip. The troll howled with frustrated fury and vainly tugged to free its sharp nails from the bark of the tree.

Phillimore gained another inch of umbrella from the troll's blood-less innards and then a remarkable thing occurred. The beast suddenly stopped howling and champing its jaws. The professor, startled by the dramatic silence, looked up to see the creature gawking at something behind and above Phillimore. The troll's saucer eyes goggled so wide the scholar thought they would pop out. All at once, the purple troll began to thrash and shake with renewed vigor, mewling and whimpering as it did. Phillimore, glued to the umbrella, was knocked this way and that, but with each toss, more of the shaft came loose.

At last, with a supreme effort and a bloodcurdling ululation, the troll twisted its wrists so hard that its hands snapped off and remained nail-embedded in the tree-trunk. Not even pausing to notice the latter inconvenience, it clambered off the way it came, dragging Phillimore with it. The professor doggedly hung on, though the blundering flight bounced and jounced his posterior cruelly. But at length the umbrella twisted free and he and it tumbled once, twice, three times before sprawling in a heap at the base of a coconut-palm.

Unencumbered now, the troll lumbered swiftly off through the underbrush, burbling and gibbering. Reaching the cliffside, it scrambled its way upward toward the safety of its own lair.

Below, Phillimore lay too winded to move, a mass of bruises. Panting for breath, he had enough of his senses left to comprehend that somewhere close by lurked a hobgoblin so terrible that it even frightened away the sufficiently ghoulish purple troll.

His curiosity did not have long to wait for satisfaction. Heavy footsteps smashed through the jungle. The ground trembled with the coming. Wincing, Phillimore rose to his feet to see what new surprise ironic fate had up its sleeve.

He beheld the figure of an enormous being, fully seven feet tall, glowering down upon him in the twilight. The stranger's hair was a lustrous black and its teeth shone white in the feeble rays of the moon, but these luxuriances only formed a more horrid contrast with its watery, disdainful eyes, its shriveled complexion and straight black lips. The creature's unearthly ugliness rendered it almost too loathsome for human eyes to behold.

"Devil!" it exclaimed. "Vile insect! How didst thou dare wrest me from mine creator's island upon the very eve of the day when I was to be joined forever with my mate? I thought to see thee perish at the shore of this accursed isle, but behold! Thou hast survived that I may wreak vengeance on your treachery—which, I have some little fear, was engineered by He from whose hands I ought to have expected and deserved the most!" Here the monster gnashed its teeth and wrung its hands, wailing hideously. It was a frightful spectacle and yet some doit of pity stirred in Phillimore's breast.

Everything came clear to him in an instant. This was the great weight that was exchanged for Persano's when Phillimore willed the umbrella to compromise with its two passengers's orders. Thus he arrived in the world of *The Arabian Nights* in the company of the "tool" that Persano thought Moriarty might be eager to commandeer.

Frankenstein's monster.

CHAPTER EIGHT

Fortunately, Phillimore had once written a term paper about Mary Shelley's bizarre tragedy and therefore was quite familiar with the lineaments of its plot. More to the point, in that minithesis he maintained that the true villain of the tale was not the monster, but rather Frankenstein himself: spoiled, selfish, unable to love or even pity his innocent creation. Thus the monster's latter cruelties were but the logical consequences of a child denied its parent's affection.

Like many perfectly sound closet theories, it was difficult to derive courage from it in actuality, especially with the creature hulking over him with murder in its mind. But Phillimore resolved to put aside his natural aversion to the fearful aspect of the monster and try to deal with it humanely.

"See here," he said in a voice he hoped was steady, "you've got it all wrong! I didn't come to kidnap you, but rather to rescue you. I have your best interest at heart, which is more than I can say for the wretch who infused life into your limbs!"

The monster growled. "Speak no ill of mine illustrious father!"

Oh, damn! Family loyalty in monsters?

"But see here," Phillimore demurred, "I grant you that Victor Frankenstein is a scientist of extraordinary capacity, but what did he ever do for you besides bring you into existence? He abandoned you immediately thereafter!"

The monster moaned. "Yet he promised to make me a bride that I might go elsewhere and fill out mine days in mildness and peace."

"Rubbish! He never meant to keep his word. At the end of the experiment, he tore your intended to shreds."

The creature glowered so malignantly that Phillimore began to nervously finger the umbrella-catch. But then a puzzled expression crossed its face and it sat down on the grass and eyed Phillimore oddly.

"See here," it demanded, "how is it that you know so intimately the secrets of my past and future?"

It was no time for casual flippancy. He needed a colossal lie. "Well, the—uh—the fact is, I am something of a scientist myself. Or you might call me a magician."

"Magic?" the monster beamed. "I love magic! Do me a trick!"

"Later," Phillimore promised, realizing the monster indeed possessed a great child-brain.

"Now! Now!" the other grunted, clapping its big hands eagerly.

Oh, Good Gad! "All right, all right, calm down!" Phillimore proceeded to pretend to remove his thumb, stretch his middle finger and clap his hands without taking them apart, much to the delight of the monster.

"Teach me how to do that!" it growled delightedly.

"Only if you promise to behave and be good!"

It vigorously nodded its head, so Phillimore went through the arcane secrets of his digital conjurations. At last, when he'd regained the creature's attention with some little difficulty, he explained he chose to spirit him away from Victor Frankenstein in order to bestow eventual happiness upon him.

"How?" it demanded. "And shall I call thee master?"

How, indeed? "That won't be necessary," Phillimore replied, blushing. "When my mission is done, I will take you to a world where people won't shun you, a place where you may live happily ever after." The scholar kept his fingers crossed. *But there just might be such a place, after all. Perhaps—*

The thought was choked off, along with his breath, by the sudden seizing of the scholar by the Frankenstein monster. His first terrified thought was that the fiendish being doubted Phillimore's campaign-promise, but then he realized the bruising embrace was a thing of sheer gratitude.

"O unexpected angel!" the monster proclaimed joyously, hugging him with bone-crushing enthusiasm. "How beneficent thou art! To think I shall be delivered from the affrighted malice of the small men who would not comprehend the love I have within mine nature, could it but be unleashed! O, grant me this and I shall follow you faithfully, doing your every bidding!"

"For starters," Phillimore gasped, "how about letting me go?"

"You have but to command!"

The professor coughed and wheezed for several minutes, ruefully fingering his aching ribs and tender neck. But it occurred to him he could do worse than confront Professor Moriarty with the monster in tow.

"I suppose," he said at length, "that if we are to work together, you ought to have a name. Mine, by the way, is Phillimore."

"Mighty Phillimore, I greet thee. Though my creator failed to christen me, I am proud to take the family name of Him who endowed me with life. Call me Frankenstein."

Phillimore nodded. *Might as well, that's how most people refer to the monster, anyway.* He suggested that he might want to use "Frank" for short, but the monster thought this a sign of disrespect to his father.

"Since you, Mighty Phillimore, hath adopted me, it is meet that you select a first name for me to carry."

"Very well." The only name that came to his mind was Boris. Fortunately, the monster liked it immensely.

"It begins with the same letter as 'beautiful,'" he crowed happily.

"And now, Boris, let us return to the subject of my mission."

The monster nodded its head eagerly. "Tell me the story, Mighty Phillimore, O tell me!"

So Phillimore spun out the history of his adventures, translating certain parts for more ready accessibility to Boris's frame of reference. Thus Moriarty was transformed into a powerful evil magician and his umbrella became a stolen magic wand.

"Now, Boris, the question is how do we get off this miserable island? And once off it, where do we seek for the nefarious Moriarty?"

"As for that," Boris said, "I should think the powers of Mighty Phillimore would be sufficient to effect both ends."

"Unfortunately, I don't seem to possess the kind of magic tool necessary. An umbrella-wand is all very well and good, but it's no Aladdin's—!" Phillimore broke off, leaped to his feet. "Of course! Aladdin's Lamp! That's what we need!"

Boris had a vague recollection of such a story when he taught himself to read by browsing through a set of books in another forest of another world. "Was not this lamp the property of a great wizard who dwelled in the land of China?"

"Yes! Now all we need is a ship to take us off this island and—" He paused, wondering why the monster suddenly got to its feet and stretched its hands above its head.

"What in hell are you doing?"

"Look at the sky!" Boris crooned raucously. "So beautiful, the sky above the island, the sky..."

A thought started to surface in Phillimore's mind, an important thought, but he couldn't quite catch hold. Looking up to see what thrilled the monster, he beheld the pale tints of morning streaking the night sky.

Sky! Hold onto that word! Sky! What else? The sky above the island...
SKY ISLAND!

"*I have it!*"

"Have what?" Boris asked.

"The way to get off this island! The way to go wherever we want to go...at least I think so."

The monster shrugged. "I did not doubt that Mighty Phillimore could work the spell, if he so chose."

"Thanks for the vote of confidence," the scholar replied, wishing he could get Boris to stop calling him Mighty Phillimore. But perhaps there was wisdom in letting the other adulate him...

"Something you said," Phillimore explained, "reminded me of a book I read a long time ago: Sky Island. It's all about this boy who travels all the way from Philadelphia to the Pacific Ocean just by finding a magic umbrella."

"And so?" In truth, the monster had no idea what the other was talking about, never having heard of Philadelphia. Yet, Watson-like, he sensed that what Mighty Phillimore needed was a sounding-board, so he urged his putative benefactor to continue.

"You see, Boris, up to now I've only used umbrellas for interdimensional travel. But if it really responds to the coordinates dictated by the user, why shouldn't it be capable of a simple overland hop in the same world?"

Boris gestured, palms-up, in a what-can-I-tell-you? fashion. He didn't know what to tell Phillimore.

But the scholar needed no further prompting. His mind made up, he immediately set their plans in motion. First of all, they went to the beach where he retrieved his jacket and scooped up fresh clams. The two sat and breakfasted off shellfish and coconuts. Boris experienced no difficulty opening the latter, though the clams were something of a trial.

Slaking their thirst at the stream, Phillimore instructed Boris to wait while he went to get Abu Hassan. (He thought the little man would do better being told about the monster before setting eyes on Boris.) But Abu Hassan refused to come with Phillimore.

"If you have decided to leave the isle as mysteriously as you came, that is your business, sire. Abu Hassan remains exiled in his eternal shame. I ask only that you do not tell a soul of my whereabouts. Let my memory die when I am perished!"

Promising he would keep his secret, Phillimore bade Abu Hassan farewell and walked away, still wondering what heinous deed the little stinker once committed.

Back at the beach, he instructed Boris to grab hold of the umbrella-shaft. "If you keep your mind blank, I don't think it will heat up." Actually, he had no idea what the thing would do, but the worst that could happen, he told himself, was that Boris would fall off and Phillimore was still undecided whether the monster's presence was an asset or a liability...

"All right, Boris, you ready?"

"Yes, O Mighty Phillimore!"

"*Then here we go!*"

Affixing the idea in his mind of Aladdin's Lamp and, secondarily, the general direction of China, Phillimore brushed the catch with his thumb and pressed down.

Instantly the umbrella rose in the air. Boris whooped with delight, but Phillimore squinted his eyes shut at the dizzy panorama of surf that suddenly yawned beneath him.

Up, up they went, higher than the clouds. *Easy*! *A little lower*! Philli-more ordered in panic, gasping for breath. The umbrella gently descend-ed until he was able to adequately fill his lungs. *That's fine. Now—let's go!*

And it did. They zipped across the sky at a speed that terrified the professor, though the monster thought it all great fun. After several min-utes of daredevil flying, Phillimore ventured to open one eye, only to shut it immediately when he beheld the ocean far beneath his dangling feet.

He had no idea how long they flew; it seemed an eternity. But even-tually, Phillimore sensed the umbrella both decelerating and losing alti-tude. Daring to look down once more, he beheld a picturesque landscape not so very far below. Close by and coming up fast was a tall, intricately-sculpted pavilion with peaked spires and rosy-tinted minarets.

The umbrella floated closer, closer to the pavilion that shone gold in the setting sun. Leveling with one of the upper windows, a glassless casement that revealed within a mandarin-red bedchamber, the umbrella hovered undecided for an instant, then swooped through and set the ad-venturers gently onto the thickly-carpeted floor. The hood closed auto-matically and the flight-button popped back out with a click.

The monster sucked in a sharp, startled breath, let it out again in a deep, contented sigh.

"O Mighty Phillimore!" Boris breathed. "O benevolent master! *O, wow*!"

CHAPTER NINE

Billowing in the honey-laden breeze, the scarlet tapestries shyly hid from view the maiden secrets of nook and niche and ceiling. The floor—clad in costly rugs blazoned with dragons and sailing vessels worked in gold wire—bore but two articles of furniture. The first was a lofty wood-en cabinet hand-carved with a riot of heroes, handmaidens and holy men; its top was festooned with garlands of sun-bright blossoms in crystal bowls, jade-girdled hookahs, decanters of strange-colored liqueurs made from violet and hibiscus. The other furnishing was the great bed itself, a downy field of luxurious pillowing held by a sturdy frame of gold inlaid with silver, studded with star sapphires, opals, rubies, opulent amethyst, giant pearls, chrysoberyl and bloodstone. The gleaming corner posts supported an ornate canopy of cinnabar from which depended gossamer veneers of silk tied back by gold-rope that, released, would whisper into place the diaphanous stuff so it might shield from untutored eyes those arcane rites practiced by the initiates of that alluring inner sanctum.

Expensive joint, thought Phillimore, *but over-decorated. Rather tacky.*

Jasmine scent heavied the air. From someplace far below, the reedy piping of a seductive melismatic melody wafted upward. Taken altogether, the richly-appointed chamber, the perfumed breeze, the distant sinuous music combined to create a delicious redolence that lulled the senses and hinted at ecstasies bordering on dreams.

But what of that she who dwelled therein? For surely it was none of the rare pleasantries of the place that so transported the newly-arrived monster, but rather the incomparably alluring inhabitant of the vermilion bedchamber who introduced within Boris's innocent breast the unfamiliar condition of transcendent rapture.

It was a damsel slender of form and dazzlingly beautiful, as she were the effulgent sun itself. Clad in translucent veils of delicate pastels, she languished upon the yielding textures of the bed and there recalled the words of the poet Oubralz:

> *She shines forth in the night and all our thoughts arise*
> *To seek the nutless meat of her swell almond eyes;*
> *And all men yearn to spread their honey-praise so sweet*
> *Upon the well-bred turn of her well-bathèd feet;*
> *When she unveils and all her hidden charms appear,*
> *I shall not crave aught else, unless it be a beer.*

Oping her doe-like eyes upon espying the two strangers alight upon the thick pile of carpeting near her bedside, the ineffably lovely damsel parted the curved grace of her coral lips and spake unto them thus: "Suffering Sinbad, who in the howling hot halls of Eblis are *you*?'

Boris began to speak, but Phillimore cut him off.

"We're sorry to—uh—drop in unexpectedly, but we're looking for Aladdin's magic lamp."

"Ooh, that bum!" she exclaimed, slipping out of bed so she could stamp her tiny foot upon the floor in petulance. "That's all he cares about, is it? I'll give him from lamps!"

"Who are you talking about?" Phillimore asked, confused.

"Aladdin, that's who! That bum, that no-good, I should only get my hands on him! Sending somebody else to pick up the lamp, he couldn't come in person! Me, I should have my head examined; I must have a hole where the brains used to be. Husbands! Did my mother tell me to wait, don't grab the first klutz that comes along? But no, I think I'm so smart! So I get a real jerk, some prize my hubby is...without that damned lamp, he'd still be the son of a peasant and maybe I'd be married to a Prince instead of a bum!"

The tirade continued in a similar vein and Phillimore waited impatiently for it to run down. He was uneasy, suspecting that he and Boris had landed in the latter portion of the Aladdin tale, the part in which an evil magician gained possession of the lamp and bade the genie carry the pavilion and its inhabitants to a remote clime where he, the mage, might at leisure enjoy the uses of the lamp, the palace and also the Princess.

Which means the wizard must be close by...

The Princess finally stopped vilifying Aladdin long enough for Phillimore to explain that he and Boris had nothing to do with her husband, though it wouldn't be long before Aladdin saved her from the loathsome advances of the sorcerer.

"Actually, if he'd wash his turban once in a while, he wouldn't be so bad," the Princess yawned. "What'd you say your cute friend's name was?"

He introduced her to Boris, but oddly enough, the creature's ardor for the Princess had noticeably cooled. Inscrutably peculiar are the ways of monsters.

"And now," Phillimore insisted, "do you think I might have the loan of your husband's lamp?"

She shrugged disgustedly. "You imagine that if I could get at it, I'd still be here? That old smelly-headed clown of a wizard has it locked up."

"Where?"

"Right there." She waved her hand off-handedly at the carven cabinet. "It's inside."

"All right," said the teacher. "Boris—*fetch*!"

"Yes, O Mighty Phillimore!"

The monster lurched over to the cabinet, flung his arms about its midpoint and hoisted it into the air until he was able to shift the balance and raise it over his head.

"Watch out!" Phillimore warned as Boris dashed the cabinet onto the floor. He and the Princess skipped back a few steps while Boris hefted it a second time and again pounded it against the carpeting. On the third try, its doors sprang open.

"I'm afraid the noise will summon the sorcerer!" the Princess exclaimed, dashing forward to scrabble amongst the splinters for the lamp. "Hurry up and help me find it!"

Phillimore joined her. The cabinet was filled with bolts of costly cloth, jeweled bowls, goblets and less-recognizable omamentalia, but nowhere could either of them see a lamp.

"Look, master!" said the monster, pointing across the floor to a drawer which must have flown out of the cabinet during one of the impacts. Phillimore and the Princess scrambled over and peered within. The drawer contained a single smooth box, polished and painted to depict a Shinto temple by a placid lagoon. It had no crack or keyhole, but when the Princess shook it, something inside rattled.

"The lamp!" she exclaimed. "Quick! Open it!"

"I'm trying to!" the professor grunted, running his fingers around the corners and edges, seeking a panel to push. "Must be a puzzle box. I used to have one..."

"Hurry!" the Princess nagged. "Before the wizard arrives!"

Someone chuckled. "*Too late. I am here.*"

The unctuously menacing voice sent shivery pizzicati down Phillimore's vertebrae. Turning, he saw, looming gaunt and terrible in the doorway, a cadaverous old man with knife-edge features, tangled beard and rock-hard vulpine eyes. The mage wore a wine-red robe embroidered with cabalistic hieroglyphs; on his head there was a wrapped white turban so dingy as to verily cry for an ammonia bath. In one gnarled hand the sorcerer carried a long ebony stick tipped with silver that glowed with an unnatural light.

Phillimore, for once, was at a loss for words. An excuse that he merely wanted to borrow the lamp, though strictly accurate, would seem barely plausible in the face of the destruction which had been wrought upon the locked cabinet. His thoughts raced, but to no purpose, while simultaneously his fingers skittered frantically back and forth along the edge of the box, trying to find a section to jog or shift or slide.

"Foolish intruder," the magician gloated, "thou hast displayed uncommon courage and a great want of wit coming here to take possession of mine most valuable treasure. But didst thou truly imagine I would be such a dullard as to flaunt yon puissant artifact wholly unfettered? Bah!"

Saying so, he waved his wand and the wooden box slid out of Phillimore's grip and began to flop end over end towards the wizard. The Princess threw herself upon it to stop its progress, but the wizard just laughed and waggled his wand. The box responded by shooting up into the air; he aimed the wand higher, higher, until the object hovered just beneath the silken-sheathed ceiling.

Now this maneuver was the undoing of the miracle-worker. Standing in the doorway, he could not see the corner of the room where Boris stood. The monster, in turn, had not yet set eyes on the magician, but he commanded a perfect view of the middle of the chamber. Thus the animation of the box riveted him with boundless wonder and when the thing soared high in the air, Boris could no longer contain his enthusiasm.

"MAGIC! MAGIC!" he crowed, hopping up and down in his excitement and clapping his huge hands. "I LOVE MAGIC!"

The room shook with the monster's jouncing delight. The startled sorcerer took an uncertain step into the room, then turned to discover the cause of the ruckus.

His jaw flapped south. The towering fiend outdid in ugliness the most malevolent afreet that had ever gibbered at him during his most dire evil spells. With a great effort of will, the magician forced his paralyzed vocal cords to work overtime at a scream.

Boris's feelings were deeply hurt. Pounding his hands together in a fit of anguish, he howled, "Curses! Scorned again!" and as he did, his watery eyes rolled in his head and his black lips twisted wide, displaying his great white teeth.

The spectacle was too much for the magico. His knees buckled and sagged and he slumped onto the carpet in a dead faint. The magic wand slipped from his numb fingers and nestled in the deep pile of the scarlet rug.

As soon as the wand left the wizard's grip, the puzzle box smashed straight down, missing Phillimore by a scant fraction of an inch. The impact splintered one edge and incidentally caused its secret drawer to spring open.

With a delighted utterance, Phillimore swooped up the burnished brass oil-lamp that lay within. He fished a handkerchief from his pocket and swiped it in long polishing strokes across the convex sides.

Great purple billows of smoke filled the room. The Princess coughed. Boris sneezed.

"*Gesundheit!*" a deep voice pronounced with exceeding distinctness and deliberation.

The smoke cleared. An enormous grinning entity squatted on the floor wheezing asthmatically and picking its teeth. Fat, dusky, jolly-looking, it had a great bare belly on which was tattooed the likeness of a brown-and-white-striped rabbit. It blinked mildly at the company and scratched its tummy, acknowledging Phillimore with a deferential bow, dismissing Boris with a "Hi, junior!" and a casual hand-wave and wink. It gave the Princess a more protracted scrutiny, but she haughtily deigned not to notice.

More for something to say than out of a need to establish credentials, Phillimore inquired, "Are you the genie of the lamp?"

Nodding, the genie pointed at the picture on his stomach. "Sure. Ain't you ever heard of the genie with the white-brown hare?" He preened proudly. "Actually I just work the lamp nights."

"What?"

"I've got the night shift."

"I don't understand," said Phillimore, surprised. "I thought genies were eternal slaves to the lamps and rings and bottles they live in...one genie apiece."

The genie waved a deprecating mitt. "That stuff went out with button-down togas! No more of that getting stuck in a bottle for three hundred years, then getting your cork popped by some rumbum sailor who keeps you hopping day and night digging up undressed dames. Phooey!"

"So how have things changed?"

"We formed G.A.G.S."

"Huh?'

"Genies, Afreets and Giaours Society. It's an international union. From now on: eight-hour days, five-day weeks, two weeks off each year. Whaddaya think, the genie game's a picnic?"

"If it's that bad," Phillimore asked, "why do you do it?"

The genie shrugged philosophically. "It's a living." The amenities aside, the Princess attempted to get control of the genie, claiming royal privileges. But the genie showed her an iron-clad, four-point-high clause in the standard contract which all lamp-sprites carry to the effect that no other master than the "rubbee" might be served at one time.

"But stick around, Toots and we'll work something out while I'm off-duty." He winked at her, then turned to Phillimore. "Okay, what's your pleasure? Pleasure?"

The scholar shook his head. "First of all, take care of *him*"—he indicated the wizard, who was just waking up—"before he makes a nuisance of himself."

The spirit stashed the sorcerer in a cellar in Zanzibar, then returned to hear the rest of Phillimore's instructions.

"On another world," said the scholar, "an arch-criminal named Professor Moriarty fell into a cataract, the Reichenbach Falls. I was there. So was a detective, Sherlock Holmes."

(He included all the information so the genie would be able to pinpoint the proper planet.)

"Now," Phillimore continued, "I have reason to suspect that Moriarty didn't die but instead traveled magically to another world, probably this one. Your mission is to find out whether he still lives and if he does, where he is."

The genie clopped a hand to his forehead. "Hoo-boy! Is that a toughie!"

The professor was surprised. "I thought nothing is too hard for a genie."

"Did I say I couldn't do it?" the other rejoined, somewhat stung. "I just can't give you the usual whisk-zap-your-wish-is-my-instant-command crap. This is gonna take time! First off, I have to find—"

"Never mind all that," Phillimore interrupted, afraid the explanation would take longer than the execution. Doubtfully he asked, "But you think you can do it?"

The genie, pride deeply wounded, said stiffly, "I don't *think* I can do it. I *know* I can; willya just gimme some time?"

"How long?"

"Maybe fifteen minutes."

"Oh, that's all right," said Phillimore, relieved that it wasn't a matter of days or weeks. "We can certainly wait that long."

"Damn decent of you," the genie grumped, dematerializing in a disgruntled huff. Thirteen-and-a-quarter minutes later, he returned, task completed, feeling a bit guilty at the surly way he'd spoken to his new master. Afraid he may have discredited the noble profession to which he belonged, he resolved to respond promptly and respectfully to any other demand that might be made of him.

Which explains what happened next.

"I found him!" the spirit eagerly informed Phillimore.

"On this world?"

"Nope. In a place you wouldn't *believe!*"

"Well, in that case," the scholar said, "I have one last task for you to carry out." He nodded in Boris's direction. "He and I must travel to that world."

"Yessir!" the genie exclaimed and instantly gesticulated at the pair.

"HOLD IT!" Phillimore yelled. "WE'RE NOT QUITE REA—"

Neither the genie nor the Princess heard the rest of the sentence. Both James Phillimore and Boris Frankenstein were gone.

Without the umbrella.

* * * *

Turning end over end, Phillimore aimlessly wobbled and at the same time, purposefully sped on towards Moriarty's world. He felt like a hurtling knuckle-ball in a cosmic cricket match.

Flying via genie was decidedly worse than umbrella travel. Without the comforting reality of the leather handle to grip, he had no means of orientation; every direction was simultaneously up and down. His stomach protested. He squeezed his eyes tight to shut out some of the carnival-ride dizziness.

He heard Boris howling from some place either far above or below. "O Mighty Phillimore! Why dost thou visit this punishment upon me? Canst thou truly conceive that I, who was born unwillingly, am so vile as to deserve this?" The monster moaned piteously, but the sound of his despairing voice soon dwindled and was borne away by the rushing waves of space-time and Boris was lost in darkness and distance.

Behind his eyelids, the twinkling chaos of the shifting dimensions still danced, but gradually the penetrating glow dimmed and at length, winked out altogether. Suddenly, freefall ceased...his feet touched something solid...his body jostled against three, four, five beings...

A wild chorus of shrieks assailed his ears.

Phillimore opened his eyes.

Onto madness.

CHAPTER TEN

Phillimore's first thought was that a wire in his brain must have fizzled out with the result that he was nine-tenths blind and ten-tenths loony.

All he could see were lines. Lines and dots. Darting lines, gleaming lines, pulsating lines, bright dots, dots that were nearly invisible, yet more lines and dots and lines and lines and dots and — —• — — —• —•— •

Dimness. Brightness. Some kind of fog disclosed — — —— • and concealed other — • —— — — and everywhere he turned all he saw were bright — and dim —— and occasionally a • or two.

Immensity of space. Fluttering. Breeze? Yes—outdoors.

He heard many screams and shouts in an unintelligible tongue and also, from many directions at once, a strange, high ululation.

Well, he told himself, *this is it, I have gone one hundred per cent stark raving bibblebibble bonkers!*

But as a matter of fact, the scholar had lost neither his eyesight nor his marbles. Still, it was a minor wonder that the ensuing events did not serve to place him permanently in a parlor for the perpetually puzzled.

A great multitude of lines surrounded him on all sides. They produced a complicated din to which Phillimore did his best to respond by spreading out his hands in a *non-comprendez* gesture.

And he noticed he had no hands.

Also no shoulders. No legs. No feet.

His body was totally askew, it didn't make anatomic sense. He felt its thickness, its length and with a little experimentation, realized he could move forwards, backwards, sideways...but on what, with what he had no idea. He could hear and he could see, though the latter faculty was reduced to perception of a uniformly thin margin of distance stretching to infinity. Within that expanse, dots and lines shimmered and scuttled everywhere while other, duller lines remained stationary. The mobile configurations appeared to alter somewhat as they hypothetically turned and surely there was fog to aid his eyes in distinguishing shapes.

The noise that the lines made continued. It suggested a simple test to Phillimore. He waggled the place where his jaw used to be. *Yes, I think it's there*...Though he couldn't touch it, he was sure he had a mouth. Someplace not far from where he was able to see there seemed to be an opening. He made it gape wide, willed sound to emerge.

"HEY! WHAT IN ALL GOOD HELL IS HAPPENING?!"

He got no answer, but at least he knew he could still converse in English.

Fat lot of good that does!

Just then, the noisy conglomeration of geometric oddities parted and a much larger shining line approached through the space they quitted. The indecipherable chatter ceased and there was a hush Phillimore could have sworn was nothing short of deferential.

The large line stopped. The teacher stared at it, instinctually certain that it was engaged reciprocally. After a brief silence, the thing rumbled. A pause, then it repeated the sound.

It's trying to talk to me!

"Look, I'm sorry," Phillimore apologized, "if you can't speak English or French or German, I'm afraid I-"

He stopped. The shining line was retreating. Sliding smoothly to one side, it rumbled a new series of sounds. Instantly, a quantity of smaller lines, short and rather shady, moved forward, closer, closer, closer to Phillimore. They hedged him in on all sides.

They stopped quite close to the professor and as they did, Phillimore noted their dimensionality, inferred their *shape*. They were not lines after all, but rather a great array of narrow triangles, probably isosceles and they all had their deadly points aimed at him. They only appeared as lines because he was eye-level with their perimeters. If he could rise straight up and hover over them, he would be able to view them as the triangles they must certainly be from above...

Except that in this world, there was no up, no above. The only thing Phillimore could see was edge and even the concept of height was a trifle confusing to him at the moment. He knew it existed, but it was difficult to picture it in this two-dimensional place.

Now Phillimore knew precisely where he was.

Flatland.

"Imagine a vast sheet of paper on which straight Lines, Triangles, Squares, Pentagons, Hexagons and other figures, instead of remaining fixed in their places, move freely about, on or in the surface, but without the power of rising above or sinking below it, very much like shadows—only hard and with luminous edges—"

He remembered quite well the satirical masterpiece by one Edwin A. Abbott, a Shakespearean scholar who turned his avocational delight in higher mathematics into one of the first important works of speculative fantasy, *Flatland*: a world of only two dimensions, length and width; where neither buildings nor people have any perceptible height; where it is so difficult to recognize the shape (and hence, social station) of one's neighbors that the greater portion of university training is devoted to the science of inferring shape.

Though Phillimore saw the thin book on Moriarty's shelf, he never considered it as a possibility. Flatland was no picnic to live in. The angles and points of lower-class citizens were perpetual dangers and an accidental trip against a square might mean impalement. What was worse, Flatland had an extremely repressive social system, complete with elitist government, castes, police-state authoritarianism and state-engineered executions of undesirables (who were primarily those unfortunate enough to be born with slightly irregular sides).

Now why on all the earths would Moriarty pick this lousy spot to come to? Surely, it has no magic, no great instruments of power to—

His perplexed pondering was interrupted by the prodding of one of the isosceles triangles. Because of their narrow angles, these Flatlanders had commensurately tiny brains and thus served as the country's soldiers. Their pointed angles functioned much the same as bayonets; there was no arguing with their insistent nudging. Clearly, they wanted Phillimore to start moving, so he did so.

Where? Why do I rate a military escort?

As they traveled, he noted the land maintained its featureless, heightless character. Every once in a while, he heard the strange ululation he'd noted before and realized it must be some woman's peace-cry. Flatlander women were straight lines, which meant that turned sideways, they presented a near-invisible dot which might skewer a careless citizen who ran upon it. Thus, by law, women in public had to keep up a constant unnerving whine. *Like a belled cat. Or a leper.*

During the journey, Phillimore considered his predicament. Translation to Flatland included adaptation of one's body to the structural logic of that world. He worried lest the return journey fail to restore him to his customary form. Then a thought kicked him: *What return journey?* Moriarty might be two feet away and he wouldn't recognize him and how on earth could he possibly find his umbrella when he didn't even know what shape it was presently in?

Suddenly, a great gray motionless line loomed up, stretching as far as he could see to left and right. The soldiers in front paced away and stopped, leaving an opening through which the scholar moved. He entered a dim space, bounded by distant gray lines. It was evidently indoors.

Based on his propensity to incarceration while on his cosmic adventures, Phillimore guessed he was in a Flatland prison. A large angular figure approached and gently nudged him along till he entered a place consisting solely of gray lines.

There was a clang. Phillimore turned and saw he was alone.

"Prison, sure enough," he grumbled, more to keep up his courage than in expectation of receiving a reply. He moved around the confining quarters and observed the omnipresent grayness. Dull lines. Surely the inside of a cell.

Partway along one line a series of thin openings permitted him to look into another space bordered by a more distant dull line. He induced he was staring through bars into another chamber.

"Anyone there?" he asked, wishing someone could answer in English. He'd never before realized the wonderful property of Moriarty's umbrella to eradicate language barriers for the traveler. Now that he could not communicate to anyone, the—

"Is it possible?" a voice asked, eagerly. "Have I the privilege of addressing a noble Spacelander?"

Phillimore almost dashed himself against the wall, so anxious was he to see who, in the other cell, spoke. As he peered through the bars, a bright shape that might be anything from a triangle through a polyhedron drifted into view.

"You can talk in English!" the professor exclaimed. "Are you a Flatlander or—"

"I am indeed a Flatlander," said the other, dashing Phillimore's ill-defined birthing hopes. "I doubt not it is wonderful to you that I am able to converse in the tongue of civilized Spaceland, but perhaps you are aware of the modest treatise I caused to be circulated in your glorious world?"

Yes. When Abbott first had his book published, he pseudonymously signed it as if it were written by a native Flatlander visiting, for the first time, the world of three dimensions:

FLATLAND
A Romance of Many Dimensions
With Illustrations by the Author, A SQUARE

"Indeed," said the Square, "I am that same lawyer-square who happily, sadly was permitted to spend some time in your astonishing world. Many times have I tried to convince my fellow countrymen that there is a dimension called height, but you see what contempt they hold me and my theory in!"

"Why?" Phillimore asked, a sudden chill numbing the place where he supposed a heart must be. "Where are we? In prison?"

"No," said the Square, "in a mental institution."

CHAPTER ELEVEN

Trapped!

No umbrella. No way to communicate with his captors. No way out. Phillimore flung himself against the padded lines that comprised the walls of his cell and found they were quite as efficient as any in a three-dimensional asylum. He was caught, transfixed. *Trapped*!

Gossip traveled quickly among the inmates. Soon the Square, his neighbor, was able to explain exactly why Phillimore had been brought to a ward for the insane.

"If you could speak our language," said the Square, "you would be a national hero, rather than a patient here."

"What? *How*?'

"Flatland, you see, is frequently beset by riots and insurrections that never quite come off. Our lower classes, the isosceles triangles who opt for a life of trade rather than military service, are a disgruntled lot. Together with an occasional irregular Flatlander who has somehow escaped execution—these latter are our criminal element—the dreadfully-pointed isosceles often demonstrate against the hierarchy of the polygons and circles, for you must know that the more regular sides a Flatlander possesses, the higher he stands in the social scale. (Our high priest, by common courtesy, is assumed to have at least ten thousand sides, though it would be absolutely impossible for anyone to count that many. While this ruling luminary is called a circle, only God is believed to be a perfect Circle.)

"Now nature has so admirably disposed our world's order that the less sides an individual possesses, the fewer angles he has and the less angles, the less space for brains. By the time we descend to the common isosceles, we are dealing with a remarkably stupid lot. As for women—" Here the Square disdainfully sniffed and did not see fit to comment further.

"Because the isosceles are so witless," he continued, "their insurrections have always been an easy matter to put down. They simply do not have any leaders to organize their rebellions effectively. But recently, a grave thing happened here."

"Yes?" Phillimore asked, interested in the story in spite of the fact that he was sure the Square had rambled away from the subject of his own incarceration.

"A Flatlander of mysterious origin suddenly came to the fore some months ago. Though I have not seen him, I hear he presents the aspect of a nearly-perfect circle. This fact, in itself, is highly threatening to our present government. But what is worse, this stranger whom nobody seems able to identify has taken it into his head to preach civil rights for women and the isosceles class. He wants the ancient practice of painting revived. He demands passage of the Universal Color Bill—"

"I read your book some time ago," Phillimore interrupted, "and do not clearly recall these latter things."

"Long ago in Flatland," the Square explained, "pigmentation was discovered. People began making up in all sorts of bright hues and it suddenly became infinitely easier to recognize one another. This seemed to be a good thing at first, but soon the university arts of sight recognition and shape inference fell into disuse. Irregular figures camouflaged their abnormalities and attempted to marry into the best families! At the height of the horror, a particularly crafty irregular tried to pass the Universal Color Bill to require everyone, even priests, to paint. The purpose was to totally demoralize our hierarchy and create a virtual state of—democracy." (Here the Square shuddered.) "It was a terrible time in our history, but eventually the rebellion was quashed and the art of chromatism lost. Today it is a crime punishable by instant puncturing to color in any way!"

The Square huffed indignantly at the memory of the trials of yesteryear. Phillimore suddenly was struck with curiosity.

"I say, what kind of figure do I represent to your vision?"

"Oh, you are a hexagon," the Square stated deferentially. "It is the lowest class of our nobility. That, plus your praiseworthy action in the center of town, should have made you a national hero but for—"

"Yes, yes," Phillimore prompted impatiently, "but what *did* I do?"

"The tale circulating is that you effectively ended the new rebellion."

"What? How did I do *that*?"

"The mysterious polygon of whom I spoke was holding his penultimate demonstration for all the things inimical to our government which he organized the lower classes to obtain. There were isosceles by the thousands parading before our National Capitol, all demanding their rights—and incidentally the setting-up of this divisive polygon as our new high priest, or Chief Circle. (I doubt not this is his real reason for stirring up so much trouble.)

"In the midst of this terrifying rally, just when our state enemy seemed assured of winning, you abruptly and inexplicably descended!

Evidently you landed on a number of isosceles, knocking them by accident into other of their brethren, causing puncturing and maiming in great profusion. (Indeed, you were lucky to escape accidental impalement.) Since the isosceles class is thoroughly brainless, the disturbance grew into a full-fledged brawl, abetted by the sudden, purposeful appearance of the loyal militia. Within less than five minutes, so I understand, the ranks of the opposition were totally decimated. Only their leader, the polygon, escaped alive!"

The Square paused. Phillimore had a notion he was being regarded with pity by the other. "How ironic," his neighbor murmured after a time, "how very ironic that you had bestowed upon you such an honor and yet were unable to appreciate it."

"What honor?"

"You, a lowly polygon, were vouchsafed an audience, right there on the street, with the Chief Circle himself! But when he heard you babbling that which appeared to be nonsense, he had no choice, sad as it must have made him, but to commit you to this institution."

Just then, Phillimore heard the click of a cell-door not far away. He turned expectantly, but the Square cautioned him not to maintain any false hope of instant liberation. "That sound is but the delivery of dinner by one of the women who tend us." Again he colored the word "women" with off-handed contempt.

"Perhaps," Phillimore mused, "I could learn the Flatlander language from you. Then I could explain my situation to the Chief Circle and—"

"And you would remain here the rest of your life," the Square interrupted. "I who am a native of this land but visited your dimension and was foolish enough to tell of my discovery of *height*...and here I languish. You who indeed hail from Spaceland would fare no better and perhaps worse."

"Then I could fabricate a story to get me sprung from this place! Will you teach me the tongue?"

"I should be honored. But there is ample time. The Chief Circle only visits us once a year."

Phillimore's hypothetic heart sank into his nonexistent boots. A *year*! By then, Moriarty could mount a new campaign—for he had no doubt that the Professor was the mysterious polygon—or return to his native world and start up his old criminal organization.

The question was: if Moriarty came to Flatland (for what purpose Phillimore still could not imagine), why hadn't he used the umbrella ere this to escape?

The cell-door of the Square clanked open and someone entered. Phillimore smelled a pleasant food odor.

"Let me advise you," said the Square, "to stay out of reach of this domestic. Women are not generally required to utter their peace-cry indoors, but these cells are more roomy than many interior chambers and she could damage you if she were to carelessly bump against you!"

Phillimore was momentarily embarrassed that the Square would speak so disparagingly of the serving-woman in her presence, but then he remembered that she could not understand English and probably thought the other was merely indulging in lunatic ravings.

The Square's cell-door clicked shut and after a few seconds, Phillimore heard a key grind in his own lock. He turned and saw a portion of one gray line slide to one side, revealing another gray line further off. In the intervening space shimmered the straight line of the serving-woman. She turned sideways to pick up the dish of food and he noticed how she dwindled into a point that was almost invisible.

The woman approached with the serving-dish and Phillimore, following his neighbor's advice, moved away to give her ample turning space. But in spite of this maneuver, she kept coming closer, closer than necessary to give him his supper.

"Here, back off," the scholar commanded, "that's close enough." But she drew nearer, so much nearer that he began to worry that the Chief Circle might have decided it would be cheaper just to finish him off...

"I said back off!" Then he remembered the language barrier. Hurrying over to the bars that divided the cells, he was about to call the Square to interpret to the menacing female when suddenly in his ear there sounded a surprisingly familiar, wonderfully reassuring voice.

"*Shhh!*" the "woman" whispered. "*Come, James, come! The game is afoot!*"

CHAPTER TWELVE

"Holmes!" Phillimore exclaimed. "Is it possible? Can it be you?"

"Shhh!" the other cautioned. "We are not yet out of danger." Turning sideways, he began rubbing against Phillimore with a steady, purposeful stroking.

"What are you doing?" the scholar wondered.

"Applying makeup," Holmes whispered. "Without hands, it's a difficult business. Women in Flatland can travel about with little notice paid them. That is why I have disguised myself thus and propose to do the same to you if you will hold still so I can get the shading even. It's all a matter of refraction of light and a hexagon may easily appear to be a straight line with a—"

"Yes, I know all about that," Phillimore murmured, following the detective's example and keeping his voice low. "But using makeup is a crime punishable by death."

"Dire instances require dire methods. Your timely arrival broke Moriarty's strength. Now we have but to pursue him to his lair. The Flatland aristocracy has vainly attempted to assassinate him in his home-quarters, but could not locate where he secrets himself. But it was a simple matter of comprehending the rationale of architecture. Putting my theory to a test, I shadowed the Professor and ascertained his location. Unfortunately, he was well protected in his fortress and till now, I could not move against him. *Turn around, let me do your other sides.*"

Phillimore obliged. "Then you have been here for some time?"

"I have. This was the logical place to look."

"But how did you get here sans umbrella?"

Holmes continued to apply makeup as he explained. "When I returned from South America, my brother told me of your quest..."

"I've been gone *that* long?"

The linear equivalent of a shrug. "Who knows what amounts of time pass during umbrella flight? At any rate, I made to examine Moriarty's bookshelf as well and reach the sole possible conclusion concerning his whereabouts. Destination decided, I quickly engineered a new umbrella, drawing on my brother's theoretical expertise."

"You have a *new* umbrella?" Phillimore exclaimed. "Where?"

"I took the precaution of strapping it to my body before employing it. Thus, though I cannot see it, I am aware by feel that it is still tied to what ought to be my arm."

A clamor from some of the cells further along caused Holmes to quicken his rubbing of makeup on Phillimore. "They are beginning to wonder where the woman is with their food...another few strokes and then we must dare the guards and make good your escape." More rubbing, then Holmes asked Phillimore why it took him so long to come to Flatland.

"I did not reach the same conclusions concerning Moriarty's decision at the time he pressed my umbrella's catch at Reichenbach. I assumed he would fly to a world where there was some magic tool handy for the betterment of his nefarious schemes."

"Too studied," Holmes objected. "A man in imminent danger of plunging to his death would hardly mull over the comparative advantage of one or another safety-zone. The destination would surely be a thing of chance, dependent on the random thoughts racing through his brain at that dire instant."

"And what," Phillimore asked, "do you suppose Moriarty was thinking of?"

"Elementary, my friend. It was surely something in the nature of this: "If I should *land*, I shall be crushed *flat*! The umbrella merely interpreted as literally as it was able."

Phillimore started to laugh, but Holmes shushed him.

"I've done you as best as the circumstances allow. Quick, James, you must emulate a needle, for that is how you shall appear to the guards...the din grows great, we must hurry!"

Holmes hastened through the gap in the gray line and Phillimore followed. He stayed on the detective's heels (?) as Holmes led him down one corridor and up another. There were no stairs, nothing but length, width and more length and width. Occasionally, a shining line moved past them on some errand or another, but Phillimore noted with relief that they were always afforded considerable space to pass. Women, though scorned in Flatland, were evidently much feared.

At length they reached the outdoors. An isosceles on duty at the opening grunted something and Holmes addressed him in the peculiar jargon of the country. Phillimore marveled at his companion's ability to so quickly take on the customs of so alien an environment.

Once outside, Holmes quickened their pace. "We must hurry if we are to catch Moriarty. He is holed up in a fortress out of town. The place is an abandoned weapons-house, which is why no-one thought to search it for the disruptive polygon."

"I don't understand."

"Houses in Flatland, by law, must be built with at least five sides to prevent accidents from colliding with too sharp-pointed an angle. But in the old days, weapons repositories were deliberately fashioned with many points and angles to prevent Flatlanders from approaching too close."

"I see," Phillimore said, "rather like barbed wire surrounding a U.S. Army base."

Holmes, instead of replying, suddenly let out an awful high-pitched screech. Phillimore thought he'd run on a triangle, but then realized there were polygons approaching. The scholar also produced the weird sound that was the peace cry of female Flatlanders.

They proceeded over the countryside, sometimes shrilling the unpleasant sound, sometimes hurrying on in silence. The trip seemed longer than it really was, due to the absence of distinguishing features for the eye to fix upon.

After a time, Holmes cautioned Phillimore to slow his movement.

"We are drawing near. See that confusing line in the distance?"

Phillimore said yes. The line glimmered in odd places and was shaded in others. "An irregular figure, I presume?"

"Indeed. There is a second such wall within this first. I warn you to proceed very carefully, very slowly. Bumping against interior or exterior of either might prove fatal..."

They crept along, Holmes in the lead. After a time, he indicated a narrow gap in the boundary. "We slip through there." With extreme care, Holmes edged his way up to the aperture and passed through it, stopping while Phillimore did the same and joined him.

"You see," Holmes said in a low voice, "the inner wall does not permit entrance at the same point. We must work our way round till the other door is found. By no means should you go any nearer either wall than we are now."

They started forward again and this time Phillimore rested lightly against Holmes, turning as he turned, stopping where he paused. They went at a snail's-pace and more than once, Holmes had to carefully negotiate around some linear obstruction which Moriarty evidently placed in the path to impale anyone foolish enough to speed around the space between the two fortress-lines that were walls.

"Here, now," whispered Holmes, "here it is. The door."

"No need to whisper, my good Holmes," a dry, unpleasant voice said from within. "Come in, come in, I have been expecting you."

The line that was the detective turned to look at Phillimore. "Surely," said Holmes, "he is indulging in braggadocio. Our makeup is indistinguishable from the aspect of women."

A large line emerged from the interior of the fortress and waited some distance away. The thing chuckled nastily. "Excellent acoustics here, my dear Holmes, I have heard your whispered colloquy. However, let me assure you that my identification is no matter of guesswork. Who but my most illustrious enemy could penetrate to my hideaway and decipher my own disguise?" He moved perhaps an inch closer. "I assume the companion by your side is the good Dr. Watson?"

"Do not answer," Holmes warned Phillimore.

"Come, come, there is no reason why we cannot be open with one another," Moriarty said sweetly. "Your time is almost come and there is some salve in discharging all one's secrets at the last."

Holmes said nothing.

"Well, well, keep your counsel if you must. The silence of kings and beggars, the silence of the grave."

"I had not known you to indulge ere this in idle threats."

"My dear Holmes, surely you know by now that nothing I promise is empty sabre-rattling!" The great line that was the evil arch-criminal suddenly called out and out of the aperture which was the door to his's inner fortress there emerged a half-dozen isosceles triangles, points directed towards Phillimore and Holmes.

"Farewell, dear nemesis," Moriarty said condolently, "I shall miss our war of wits."

The triangles began their slow, purposeful approach.

"What do we do?" Phillimore asked urgently. "Run? Fight?"

"I am afraid," said Holmes grimly, "that neither course will do us much good. Flight will certainly impale us on one of those near-invisible obstructions or else the treacherous walls will pierce us. As for combating a squad of isosceles—"

Moriarty laughed unpleasantly. "I doubt that your expertise with singlestick or baritsu will be of much aid, my soon-to-be-late friend."

"Maybe you can out-talk the Professor?" Phillimore urged. "Persuade these triangles that—"

"Save your breath," the villainous master-line stated. 'These are my hand-picked guard. They are all deaf."

The points were perhaps twenty inches away and the triangles—as cautious about the fortress walls as Holmes had been—drew steadily, slowly closer and closer.

"What about the umbrella?" Phillimore shouted. "Wouldn't you like to go back to London?"

"I shall, never fear, I shall. For a good while, I couldn't find the thing, but now I know exactly where it is. As soon as I re-arouse this rebellion that you temporarily quelled and as soon as this world pays me my due tribute, I shall move on...just as my soldiers are doing..."

Moriarty, dismissing them as lost causes, turned to reenter the fortification.

His soldiers were a mere nine inches away.

"Soon they will charge," said the detective. "There is nothing we can do but meet death stoically."

Phillimore, far from being frightened, was extremely annoyed. *All that effort outwitting Persano, escaping from Jonathan Wild, fighting the troll and so on and on...and it all ends like this!? High adventure—Bah!*

The triangles stopped when they were only six inches off. They quivered for the charge, ready to dash forward and stab Moriarty's enemies...

One of them uttered a warlike cry. Their signal.

But before they could charge, another sound drowned out the noise of the officer-triangle.

A deafening smashing, ripping noise behind Phillimore and Holmes stopped the execution in its tracks.

The scholar whirled about to see what was happening.

The exterior wall of the fortress quivered and shook and as they watched the line splintered into fragments that skittered forward and sideways. Something on the other side of the wall punched it again and again, enlarging the hole.

Moriarty turned to see what intruder dared his wrath.

Through the gap in the battered remnant of a wall emerged a gigantic line glowing in peculiar places, dim in others. When the isosceles triangles saw it, they screamed and began to run in three directions: left, right, backwards, anywhere but forward where the newcomer stalked.

Two of the triangles collided harmlessly, but before they could part, a third skewered both during its flight; the impaler, in trying to free its point, snapped it off and also died. The fourth and fifth isosceles tried to run around the side of the central building. Each crashed into one of the protrusions of the inner wall, thrashed and was still.

As for the last triangle...

"HELP!" Moriarty screamed. "GO BACK!"

But the terrified triangle rammed directly into the Professor and turned him into a bisected line on the instant. Moriarty choked a single word of hatred at Holmes and with his dying convulsion broke his murdering triangle in two.

Silence. Holmes and Phillimore regarded their savior. It was an enormous line, but the random way in which the light played and fell on its facets suggested it must be an extremely irregular polyhedron.

And then the stillness was shattered by the grievous wail of the thing that saved them.

"*Curses*!" Boris howled. "*Scorned again*!"

CHAPTER THIRTEEN

They entered the weapons-house to seek Phillimore's original umbrella and as they did, all three carefully circumvented the dotted line that was Moriarty's corpse. As they passed it by, Holmes pointed out the presence of makeup on one length.

"He had to make up because he was an irregular polyhedron, although the abnormality was comparatively slight. But it would have been enough to make the lower classes distrust him if the Chief Circle had found out about it."

Phillimore suddenly stopped, horrified. "I've just remembered something!"

"What?" asked Holmes.

"There is an Ür-Moriarty floating about with an umbrella, victimizing other worlds. Shouldn't he also be stopped?"

The Great Detective sighed. "I see it shall be some time ere I will be able to take up again the fairly mundane business of sleuthing in Baker

Street." Again he sighed. "Yet the more I consider the fact that there may be countless worlds on which the circumstances of Victorian England are reproduced, the more probable becomes the conclusion that there shall always be a Moriarty..."

Phillimore concurred. Then he asked Holmes how he proposed to find his original umbrella, the one Moriarty snatched from his grip at Reichenbach.

"Elementary. I have ascertained that Moriarty landed in this very fortress. Now he was assuredly extremely disoriented when he arrived and no doubt relinquished his hold on the umbrella and then could not find it again. In a land of lines and dots, what clue is there to the translated shape of a three-dimensional umbrella?"

"I have thought about it," said the scholar, "and I wonder whether it is possible to track it down at all! It seems unlikely."

"Not in the least," the sleuth demurred. "Moriarty himself hit upon it—probably when our disguises turned his attention anew to the art of painting."

"I don't follow."

"My dear fellow, this is a world in which color is outlawed! All we must needs do is seek the one touch of tint in this gloomy gray pile!"

It took them perhaps an hour of rummaging about to spy the still-startling trace of pastel hues that indicated the two-dimensional presence of Phillimore's incredible umbrella. He nudged it against a wall, not without affection and managed to grasp the bright line in his mouth, his only means of holding it.

It took them another hour to figure out how to push the button.

EPILOGUE

SCENE—An Arcadian Landscape. A river runs around the back of the glade. A rustic bridge crosses the river.

A troupe of Fairies enter, dancing and singing. Suddenly in their midst, two men appear. One is short and rather stocky. The other is a giant, with black hair, extremely white teeth and black lips. The Fairies admire the latter personage enormously, though one or two cast curious glances at the impractically-large, gaudily-dyed umbrella the smaller man totes.

Phillimore looked about for the Fairy Queen. Spying a large woman with wings, a Disney-esque wand and a diadem that twinkled in her hair, he brought Boris meekly along to meet her.

"Welcome," she said before Phillimore could speak. "I see that you wish to find a home for this poor, injured gentleman, a place where he will be loved and not scorned, for this is what you promised him if he performed services on your behalf. I perceive that you regard our world, a world you seem to equate with one of our sisters, Iolanthe, as a gilbertandsullivan place, whatever *that* is. But you maintain that in a gilbertandsullivan world, the comely and fair are frequently villainous, while the homely are generally decent folk whose eventual rewards are great. Am I not correct?"

"Why, yes..." Phillimore stammered, "but—"

"Your friend is certainly welcome to stay with us," the Fairy Queen interrupted, "for we find him most attractive in a rather baroque manner—" (here Boris shyly blushed) "—and I also note that having kept your word to him, you intend to travel to other worlds. Am I not correct?"

"Yes! Absolutely!" Phillimore said in mighty wonder. "But how do you know all that about me?"

The Fairy Queen's eyes sparkled as bright as her diamond tiara. "Bit of a fey quality, I fancy," she remarked.

The End of
The Incredible Umbrella.

ANNOTATIONS

While I was writing *The Amorous Umbrella,* I said to my Doubleday editor Pat LoBrutto that in some future edition, I ought to include annotations for all of the many literary and related allusions in both books; Pat thought that would be a good idea. So after a delay of years, here are my notes for all four stories set out in order below. They appear in the place that they do in each story.

The first two parts of this book originally appeared in issues of Fantastic and were bought by its editor Ted White.

I briefly considered naming it *The Incredible Unbrella,* but decided that (1) it was just too cutesy and (2) it would be annoying to remember the odd spelling each time that the word had to be typed. To my surprise, when the Dell paperback edition was released, that's the way the title appeared on the inside cover page, though they got it right on the front cover and the book's spine.

DEDICATIONS

Richard L. Wexelblat and I became friends in 1949 while we were in sixth grade at the Bryant Public School in West Philadelphia. He instilled a lifelong love in me for Walt Kelly's Pogo. At that time, I only knew Gilbert & Sullivan through a ten-inch vinyl album of patter songs sung by Nelson Eddy. Dick had many of the old D'Oyly Carte Opera Company's 12-inch vinyl recordings of many of the operettas. (Later in life, Dick wrote what is said to be the definite text on programming languages.)

William B. R. Reiss was, at that time, my literary agent. He made a suggestion that I ought to write a Sherlock Holmes novel based on one of Dr. Watson's stories not yet told, which I did in *The Incredible Umbrella.*

Ted White, then editor of *Fantastic* magazine, was the first to publish Umbrella stories, the first and second parts of the initial volume.

I regret to say that over the years I've lost touch with Sol Cohen and don't remember what role he played in publishing the Umbrella stories.

Pat LoBrutto is my dear friend and erstwhile poker-playing buddy, now removed to Maryland. While an editor at Doubleday, he took over editing *The Masters of Solitude*, which I wrote in collaboration with the late Parke Godwin. The day that Pat and I met, he said that the first book he wanted to buy was *The Incredible Umbrella* provided that I add what is now Part Three. He also asked me to do a sequel, which I had no intention of writing. But since I didn't want to turn down a sale, I did *The Amorous Umbrella* and I'm glad I did because it's my favorite of all four stories. It still makes me laugh and wonder how I came up with some of its ideas.

PART 1

EPILOGUE

"We've a first-rate assortment of magic …"—is a line from John Wellington Well's introductory song in the Gilbert & Sullivan operetta *The Sorcerer*.

Parker College is really The Pennsylvania State University in University Park, Pennsylvania. It is where I took my B. A. and M. A. in theatre and English literature.

Rosencrantz …This refers to a short (although in three acts) play that was included in W. S. Gilbert's collection, *Foggerty's Fairy and Other Tales*. Its original title: *Rosencrantz and Guildenstern*. In it, its title characters are invited to the castle by the queen in hopes that they can cheer up Prince Hamlet and also stop him from soliloquizing.

CHAPTER ONE

The Yeomen of the Guard is the ninth Gilbert and Sullivan operetta and is my personal favorite of all fourteen.

The Boar's Head Tavern in London's Eastcheap district is where Sir John Falstaff liked to hang out in William Shakespeare's *Henry IV Part One*.

Old Main is proof that Parker College is really Penn State. It is the main administration building and it dominates the central part of the great grassy campus. I had to take two years of ROTC as part of my undergraduate training.

Rose is Rose Maybud, the feminine leading role of Gilbert & Sullivan's operetta *Ruddigore*.

CHAPTER THREE

The woman is Ruth from G&S's *The Pirates of Penzance*.

"The man who would a pirate be ..." is roughly set to the tune of "I am a pirate king" from G&S's operetta *The Pirates of Penzance*.

CHAPTER FIVE

Sir Joseph Porter, K. C. B is the main comic role in G&S's *H. M. S. Pinafore*.

Ralph Rackstraw's name is pronounced "Rafe."

CHAPTER SIX

"Good fellow, I'll assist you in your leaving" is to the melody of *Pinafore's* Act Two duet, "Kind Captain, I've important information,"

"DEADEYE: This very night" is derived from *Pinafore's* Act I finale.

CHAPTER SEVEN

In this chapter, I wanted to reference all of the operetta that don't figure in the action. So Castle Adamant refers to *Princess Ida*, the Tower of London—*The Yeomen of the Guard*, the statutory duel is *The Grand Duke*, Utopia refers to *Utopia, Ltd.*, Mount Olympus is *Thespis* and Castle Bunthorne is *Patience*.

"I once was a thoroughly wicked young Bart" echoes the opening second act duet in *Ruddigore*.

CHAPTER EIGHT

Knightsbridge—there was a Japanese exhibition in that section of London, which Gilbert visited and according to an apocryphal story, bought a sword that he hung up at home. When the sword allegedly fell, it gave Gilbert the idea to write a Japanese operetta. In *The Mikado*, when asked where the minstrel Nanki-Poo, really the Mikado's son, moved to, Knightsbridge is named. This, of course, is an in-joke.

"My life at court" is part of a patter trio in Act I of *The Mikado*.

CHAPTER TEN

Cellier was the name of Sir Arthur Sullivan's assistant conductor. Cellier wrote some of the overtures based on the order of melodies that Sullivan gave him.

"Hark the hour of ten is sounding:" with slightly altered lyrics is *Trial by Jury's* first chorus.

"When Fred'ric tùrned twenty-and-one" with different lyrics is the Judge's song, "When I good friends was called to the bar." The remainder of songs in this chapter are based on parts of *Trial by Jury*.

John Wellington Wells, the titular sorcerer of that operetta, may be seen in an excellent performance by the estimable Clive Revill in a DVD of *The Sorcerer*.

PROLOGUE

"The old ladies in love" is the title of my Penn State master's thesis.

PART TWO

CHAPTER ONE

The opening paragraph of PART TWO paraphrases one of Doctor Watson's stories about Sherlock Holmes. The second paragraph employs images from the opening chapter of Charles Dickens's *Bleak House*.

Newman Street is one that I made up. But when I first visited London and looked it up in my A to Z street directory I found that not only does it exist, but is even just about where I put it!

The George and Vulture is a tavern where the Pickwickians convene in Charles Dicken's first and delightful novel *The Pickwick Papers*.

Snodgrass is one of the friends of Mr. Pickwick, who appears later.

Note that 221 Baker Street is the correct street address for Sherlock Holmes and Dr. Watson. The "B" refers to their apartment on the second floor.

Sherrinford Holmes and (soon to be mentioned) Ormond Sacker were the original names that Arthur Conan Doyle was going to give his lead characters.

Mrs. Bardell is Mr. Pickwick's landlady.

In one story, Watson indeed names the landlady as Mrs. Warren. Though this has been justified more than once by other authors and scholars, it is believed that Doyle simply had a memory lapse.

CHAPTER THREE

Persano is a character named by Conan Doyle in an untold story. What happens to him is the basis of the idea that made me write *The Incredible Umbrella*.

Dodson and Fogg are the shyster attorneys who represent Martha Bardell in *The Pickwick Papers*.

CHAPTER FOUR

The accidents that happen to Fillmore in this chapter echo those that almost kill Holmes in his final confrontation with Professor Moriarty.

Fredric Brown was a splendid fantasy, mystery and science fiction writer. The novel referred to is the wonderful *What Mad Universe*.

"*It's an air rifle!*" is what Moriarty's chief lieutenant Colonel Moran uses to try to kill Sherlock Holmes in "The Adventure of the Empty House."

CHAPTER SIX

Mrs. Raddle is Bob Sawyer's shrewish landlady in a very funny chapter of *The Pickwick Papers*.

E. F. Benson's "The Room in the Tower" is one of horror literature's best and very frightening ghost (seemingly) stories. His brother Robert Hugh Benson, a Catholic priest, wrote at least two superb books of hard-to-find ghost stories, *The Mirror of Shallot* and *The Light Invisible*.

Cloisterham, the scene of Dickens's *The Mystery of Edwin Drood*, is really Rochester, England, where Dickens was born and eventually died.

CHAPTER SEVEN

Wolves baying and blue ghost-lights come from the opening chapter of Bram Stoker's *Dracula*.

Dracula's first speech is an exact duplicate of his words to Jonathan Harker, as is his remark about the "children of the night."

"Bit of a fey quality, I fancy," was meant to be a one-time jest, but it keeps cropping up in these tales.

Persano's experience at the fountain is based on E. F. Benson's horrific story "Caterpillars."

CHAPTER NINE

The Cataract of Lodore is a fine poetic example of onomatopoeia by Robert Southey.

CHAPTER TEN

The closing Holmesian excerpt is the idea that started me on this book.

PART THREE

CHAPTER ONE

Holmes is the cousin of both Professor Challenger in Doyle's *The Lost World* and Brigadier Gerard in a series of amusing French tales set in the Napoleonic era. This idea was proposed by William S. Baring-Gould in *The Annotated Sherlock Holmes*.

Holmes accompanying Challenger to South America is my own idea from my first book *The Histrionic Holmes*. Holmes disguises himself as the explorer Sir John Roxton.

CHAPTER THREE

The able dramatist who Persano refers to is Oscar Wilde and the phrase "the fact is" occurs in Wilde's comedy *The Importance of Being Earnest*.

CHAPTER FOUR

This chapter is a pastiche of the style of Jonathan Fielding in his novel *Jonathan Wild*. Wild was a notorious and hypocritical stolen goods fence and "thief-catcher" which means that he would hand over to the authorities any henchman who tried to cheat him. Wild served as the model for both Sir Arthur Conan Doyle's and Rex Stout's criminal masterminds Professor James Moriarty and Arnold Zeck.

Blueskin was one of Wild's thieves and he really had a bluish tinge to his skin. He tried to kill Wild and was turned over to Tiger Brown, soon mentioned, who was a fierce lawman who worked hand in hand with Wild.

Jack Sheppard was the Houdini of his time. He did break into Wild's stronghold. When he was put into a prison that was considered escape-proof, he actually managed to get away. His two songs are based on the folk-operetta written by John Gay, *The Beggar's Opera*, in which Wild also appears. His second song, which ends with "I'll also—" would have ended with "steal your mate."

CHAPTER SIX

Abu Hassan appears in *The Arabian Nights*. His "loathesome crime," not mentioned here is that while visiting his ruling lord, Abu broke wind—a detail that a careful reading of this chapter will reveal a few inside jokes.

The pun that ends this chapter is the first in this book and is the best (to those who agree that puns may be so described). I was very pleased when a friend told me that when she read it, she threw the book across the room. A year later, she read it a second time, but had forgotten about it, so she had to throw the book across the room a second time!

When I wrote *The Passion of Frankenstein*, my sequel to Mary Shelley's novel, I grew to care so much for "Boris" that I could no longer call him a monster, so I substituted the term creature, instead.

CHAPTER EIGHT

Sky Island is one of L. Frank Baum's non-Oz books, though its main character is Button Bright, who appeared earlier in *The Road to Oz*. It comes right after *The Sea Fairies*, which tells of a little girl named Trot and her friend Cap'n Bill. Both also appear in *Sky Island* and then Trot and Cap'n Bill go to Oz in *The Scarecrow of Oz*.

CHAPTER NINE

Oubralz—At Penn State, my roommate and friend Dave Ossar and I came up with two pretend scholars. One of them is D. Oubralz, which really stands for *Deutschland Über Alles* (which neither us supports!)

CHAPTER TEN

This chapter—the hardest one to write in the entire book—is set in Flatland, the name of a wonderful mathematic fantasy and political satire by Shakespearean scholar Edwin A. Abbot.

THE INCREDIBLE UMBRELLA IN OZ

To the memories of
L. Frank Baum, Jack Snow & Captain William Bligh,
who deserves to be remembered for his virtues.

ACKNOWLEDGMENTS

Of those who assisted with anecdota, literary permissions, plot ideas and research, those below rank foremost:

Jim Demes, Henry Holman and Marc Lewis of what used to be called the Gryphon Bookshop for loaning numerous scarce books and other printed matter.

The late L. Sprague de Camp for liking the umbrella stories and permitting his own enchanter Harold Shea to make a guest appearance.

The late Daniel Mannix, fellow author and friend, for advice, information and an autographed copy of his father's book, *The Old Navy,* which Dan edited.

David Ossar, long-time friend and erstwhile college roommate at Penn State, for first thinking up "the Ship" and for co-developing Vacillia.

Peter Shaffer, justly renowned author and playwright, for permission to fashion Vacillia from dialogue derived from his superb drama, *Five Finger Exercise.*

Dan and Lynn Smith for telling me about their ancestor, Captain Hanson Crockett Gregory and thanks to Legrand Henderson for his charming book about Captain Jason Dow.

And especially my very earliest (and still) friend Richard Wexelblat for introducing me to Gilbert & Sullivan, the land of Oz and a certain cantankerous alligator who (sic) "look good in *any*thing he throw on!"

—Marvin Kaye

New York City, 2013

ENLISTMENT PAPERS

The reader of this document signs on of her or his own volition for voyages in foreign waters as shipmate of J. Adrian Fillmore (Gad! what a name!) aka James Phillimore.

The (assistant) professor's escapades were initially logged in *The Incredible Umbrella.* The exploits revealed in these pages occur shortly after the conclusion of that composition, but prior to the adventures chronicled in *The Amorous Umbrella.*

Those who have already shipped with the pedagogue may pocket their sovereign and stow their gear below. But midshippers, virgins and other newbies had best acquaint themselves with the following Articles of Engagement.

ARTICLES OF ENGAGEMENT

The Incredible Umbrella introduced J. Adrian Fillmore (!), an assistant professor of English Literature at Parker College in central Pennsylvania, where he taught American drama, English literature and Shakespeare.

A dour, undersized teacher on the cloudy side of thirty-five, Fillmore derived little pleasure from the stuffy embroilments of his academic career. He craved adventure, high, low, or anywhere in between. His cravings were unexpectedly fulfilled when he visited a curio shop and bought "a long, heavy pole that ended in a large flounce of silky material emblazoned with orange-and-yellow stripes on which various cabalistic symbols seemed to dance in pastel figurations. It was clearly an umbrella, but its size was impractical: too large for everyday use, too small for beach-basking ..."

A few days later, a cloudburst prompted the professor to try the contraption as a rainshield, but swiftly discovered that it was actually a dimensional-transfer engine that whisked him away to a succession of "literary" worlds peopled by characters familiar to him: Count Dracula, Mr. Pickwick, Professor Moriarty and the assembled Gilbert & Sullivan *dramatis personae*. However, these folk knew nothing of the authors with whom Fillmore naturally associated them. Yet their behaviors always stayed close to the style, conventions and plots of literature he knew so well.

Eventually, Sherlock Holmes figured out how the umbrella works.

Pressing its button would take the teacher to whatever place he was thinking about at that moment. Since he taught literature, it always landed him on worlds that, in the infinity of possibilities in the cosmos, most nearly resembled the places in his imagination. If his thoughts were jumbled, though, as sometimes they were when he activated the umbrella, it would take him to whichever place most closely approximated his mind's tangled coordinates. Which is why at one point he landed in an incomplete early draft of the first Sherlock Holmes novel.

Said Holmes: "These worlds do not exist because they were written about on your native planet. Instead, the fiction with which you are most familiar must consist of notions and conceptions telepathically communicated across dimensional barriers. Your artists, perhaps when they sleep, or when attuned to their Muses, unwittingly tap the logical premisses of parallel worlds."

So it appeared that Fillmore/Phillimore could employ the parasol to visit anywhere he'd ever read about. But there was a catch. Once there, he could not leave, even in the face of imminent danger, until he "completed a sequence" comparable to the plotting of the authorial style the place most closely resembled.

Another danger he discovered is that there is a fine line between cautious participation in the events of a world being visited and total acceptance of that plane's underlying tenets. Which means he would always run the risk of becoming "subsumed," i.e., permanently stuck there.

During his travels, the professor befriended the Frankenstein monster, whom he named Boris. The creature, grateful to be liberated from that bleak destiny awaiting him in Mary Shelley's novel, gladly became Fillmore's sidekick and a loyal and useful companion he often was. At length the grateful teacher repaid him by taking him to the one world Fillmore was sure Boris would be welcome in, for Gilbert & Sullivan's England is a place where, in typical topsy-turvy fashion, the ugly are honest, moral, mellow and ultimately well-rewarded. Boris instantly won the hearts (& C., as the G&S libretti often puts it) of the Fairy Queen and her enchanted distaff brood from *Iolanthe*.

But it was not a good spot for the professor. His earlier adventures there were far from pleasant and though the fairy ring where he and Boris now stayed was restful, its gossamer attractions were beginning to get on his nerves. It would be dreary to find himself subsumed therein, so he knew it was time for him to seek out new experiences.

This constitutes our Articles of Engagement. You have no choice but to accept them because while you were reading this, the Captain weighed anchor and set sail for unknown waters.
Ye've been shanghaied, matey—so get down below!

PART ONE

On the Nonestic Ocean

CHAPTER ONE

Nautical Thoughts

On a grassy promontory by the sea, a dour gentleman in his early middle years sat gazing out somewhere over the rainbow. As he pondered his destiny's perilous paradoxes, he was lightly sprinkled by a summer shower, yet the garishly bright umbrella by his side remained unopened.

J. Adrian Fillmore (Gad! what a name!), aka James Phillimore, stared moodily over the Great Waters lapping the coast of an England peopled with folk corresponding to the collective personae of the Gilbert & Sullivan operettas. "What a strange place to be stuck in," he grumbled. "Still, it's better than life at Parker College—or at least more colourful." (He preferred British spelling, even when thinking.)

The professor (more accurately, Assistant Professor of English Literature) was a stocky fellow slightly less than medium height (except in Wales). He wore a three-piece grey (*not* gray; UK style, *please!*) flannel suit. But eschewing the drab dull necktie his ensemble would have required had he still been wedged, as it were, into Academe's wooden grooves, his neck was spared a tight collar by his choice to sport, instead, a bright blue ascot. His tousled hair was the same hue as his deep-set brown eyes and his strongly moulded features were drawn down into a concurrency of frown lines.

"Odd to be bored after the raft of strange adventures I've been through," he soliloquized. "But when you're life's at stake, at least you know you're alive."

His train of thought was derailed by the appearance upon the hilltop of a great ungainly monster, whose arrival coincided with the cessation of the drizzle. Sunlight sparkled through the clouds and highlighted the giant's pale watery eyes and cracked black lips as he addressed his friend.

"O puissant Professor—" *He never pronounces that right!*

"The feast stays thy coming," said Boris Frankenstein (his own personal name choice). "Eftsoons shalt be sumptuous fare."

"Great Gad, you've been reading Coleridge again."

The monster grinned. "You always seem to know."

"I recognize the style." The Ancient Mariner passage about a frightful fiend treading close behind appealed to Boris.

"You've kept the Fairy Queen a-wait. I fear she is a bit pissèd at you."

Fillmore sighed; even when he tried the vernacular, Boris tended to favour iambs. "Send her my regrets. I don't have much appetite today."

His companion gently laid his hemstitched hand on the professor's shoulder. "Dear Friend, I sense that you are troubled. Why?"

"Walk with me a bit and I'll tell you."

So the pair threaded their way down the hill and paced beside the sea-wall; the professor right-shouldered his ponderous bumbershoot. Overhead, the cries of seagulls pierced the twilight.

"This umbrella," Fillmore said, "has taken me to some mighty peculiar places, sometimes by myself, sometimes with you and Sherlock Holmes. But now Holmes is off chasing Moriarty throughout the multiverse and you've found this world's enchanted glade, where the Fairy Queen and her adorable cohorts coddle and pamper you. But there's nothing here for me."

"Where, then? What seekst thou?"

The professor shrugged. "If I knew the answer to that, I wouldn't be me. My umbrella could fly me anywhere I want, but what do I want? I've already visited places patterned on the works of Charles Dickens, the Arabian Nights, Henry Fielding, Bram Stoker's *Dracula,* even Edwin Abbott's *Flatland*—" (Both of them shuddered.)

"There were pressing reasons for those trips and I was glad to be quit of them as soon as I could escape."

"But here, at least," the monster observed, "there is a dearth of risk."

"True, but there's nothing to do, either, not for me. Maybe you're content to sit around all day wining and dining …"

"I have other duties."

"Let's not go there. The point is, I have to move on. But there's something daunting about unlimited options. Do you know what I'm trying to say?"

Boris nodded sagely. "Self determination sucks."

"On the button. So—any advice?"

"I will bethink me."

The sun's crimson rim dipped into the water; they paused to admire the twilight. Then, after a few bethinkful moments, Boris spoke. "O'er the course of our exploits, it hath been impressèd upon me that a multiplicity of worlds and their governing logics are stored within thine mind. Wilt not, then, select a destination matching someplace that in days gone by whetted thine appetite for wonder?"

"Maybe. But the prospect isn't as appealing as it used to be."

"Experience hath been a harsh tutor."

"You've got it, Boris. Picaresque fantasies are all well and good, but the imagination doesn't consider the risks involved."

"Then 'tis adventure, that for which you seek?"

"Not per se. I'd just like to go someplace where I'd fit in."

"Before you brought me here, I should have said no place existed where *I'd* be welcome. I should think your quest would be easier."

"You'd think."

"Is there nowhere that comes readily to mind?"

"As a matter of fact, there are several places, but they're all plenty dangerous."

At that moment they heard a soprano voice, mellifluous, yet shrill, calling out their names.

"Oops," said the professor. "The Fairy Queen does sound—"

"That's what I tried to say before, my Friend. We'd best make haste and join them in the glade," Boris iambed. "Yet summat later on this very night, I prithee take thou counsel with me before thou maketh too hasty an exit."

"I'll definitely talk it over with you, Boris, before I do anything." (Hindsight allocated that utterance to the category of "Famous Last Words.") With a shake of his friend's huge mitt, Fillmore turned his steps toward the clearing in the woods where Iolanthe and her sisters, cousins and aunts prepared yet another in what, to the professor, seemed an interminable succession of feasts.

The Fairy Queen's pique over their tardiness was swiftly mollified by the giant's tender ministrations. They sat down on the sward and dined elegantly, if a trifle insubstantially. The professor didn't object to mistcakes and moon-milk, but had he been able to choose the fare, he might have opted, instead, for a Philly cheesesteak and a flagon or two of Brooklyn lager.

After the meal, Frankenstein and his harem shifted their venue to a bonfire that one of the fey band conjured up for them. For entertainment, the women sang music hall songs accompanied, as always, by an unseen orchestra. (In the professor's Gilbert and Sullivan world, invisible music is a natural phenomenon, referred to by the natives as Holy Tone.) When they paused between numbers, Boris told them hugely hyperbolic stories that generally culminated (appropriately enough, the professor supposed) in monstrous puns.

Fillmore lounged against an elm and digested his meal and Boris's advice.

He's right, he told himself. *I'd better think it over carefully before I press the umbrella's button again. Everywhere I've gone so far, I've had all sorts of trouble. I've been thrown into jail, into the brig of the H. M. S. Pinafore, into prison, even an insane asylum. I've been shot at, almost brained with a brick, close to strangled and nearly turned into a vampire by one of Dracula's mistresses. Wherever I go, the umbrella lands me in hot water ..."* His thoughts were interrupted by a chorus of feminine groans.

"O, that's the worst one yet!" proclaimed the Fairy Queen. "Have you told it to your friend?"

"Told me what??"

(Apropos of nothing, lately Boris developed a penchant for self-mockery—

Q: How does a monster change a light-bulb?

A: He doesn't. He punches a hole in the ceiling.

Or—

Q: What do you buy a monster for his birthday?

A: Anything he wants—*NOW!!)*

"But nay," Boris replied. "I related a tale about an exceedingly wicked old man who left his estate to two maiden sisters. They refused to accept anything from their profligate sibling, but before the mansion was put up for sale, they thought of the fortune their brother amassed during his wicked life. Banknotes and jewelry were somewhere on the property, so whilst they would not visit it themselves, they engaged their dim-witted nephew to search the grounds. Everywhere he looked proved unfruitful, but at length he summonèd the courage to examine the old man's burial site. Indeed, that is where the deceased's riches were concealèd, but the boy did not know his uncle had set a curse upon anyone who ransacked his resting place and when he cracked open the coffin, the great grey gravestone above toppled over on the lad and knocked him senseless. The next day, the local newspaper ran this headline—*Dowagers shy a house and crimes; the grave butts dunce."*

The professor's appreciative groan segued to a yawn. His day of seaside self-examination, plus the feast, albeit evanescent, tired him; he felt too restless, though, to turn in, so, begging off further festivity, Fillmore strolled to the edge of the green where he could contemplate the calm night-sea in the distance.

What world, he wondered, could he go to where he'd be—what *was* that phrase?—*Master of my Fate, Captain of my Soul?*

—No, that's the one everyone quotes. James Benjamin Kenyon, that's the one I want … *Be the proud Captain of thine own Fate.*

– OK, but where?

The quote brought another to mind: "A rude and boisterous Captain of the Sea." Clearly the professor's thoughts were steered into a decidedly nautical direction. *Well,* he admitted, *I do love books about ships and sailors.* It could hardly be happenstance that he'd spent his day of inner communion near the ocean's edge.

If only life were four times as long, one could follow all the heart's choices. If I hadn't pursued the literary muse, maybe I would have joined the Merchant Marine or possibly the Coast Guard—they have such a great song, "Semper Paratus!"

Not quite ready for sleeping, yet nearer Morpheus's embrace than he knew, the professor let his imagination play with the nautical notion. He poled a raft upon the Mississippi, no, no, it was a catboat skimming the Okefenokee swamp. And now he was at the helm of a clipper ship, which swiftly became a longboat setting off from the side of a squat whaler, but in a trice he studied the seas above, eye pressed to the lens of the periscope as the mighty engine surged *ta-pocketa-pocketa-pocketa-pocketa!*

He'd already had nautical adventures, some aboard the *Pinafore,* some on the Cornish coast with the pirates of Penzance, but what about all those other fascinating men of the sea? Billy Budd, Mr. Midshipman Easy, Captains (in alphabetical order) Ahab, Bligh, Kidd, Nemo, Queeg! *Who else? Not Claggert, that's for sure and certainly not Wolf Larsen! The Sea Wolf's ship would be like a one-way ticket to Hell!*

In the clearing a little way off, he could still hear Boris, who was telling a shaggy dog story that included multiple puns upon the word "pun" itself. The professor sighed. Though he was quite fond of Frankenstein, he knew it was time to put some distance between the two of them, at least for a while.

But where should I go? Treasure Island? Too dangerous. Mysterious Island? Worse.

Boris came to the end of his long drawn-out story, which the fairies seemed to appreciate considerably more than Fillmore. *Listen to them encourage him … all those 'oohs's and 'ahs.'*

And suddenly he knew where he wanted to go more than anywhere else.

In the glade, more fairy songs lulled the professor into shutting his eyes. But Boris's hoarse voice was hard to tune out; Fillmore's mind teetered on the filigreed edge of sleep.

"Once," said Boris, "the mighty Poseidon sired Ondine, a mermaid princess. On her twenty-first birthday, her progenitor ascended the heavens to capture the flying horse Pegasus as her birthday present. Poseidon meant to transform the horse into an amphibian that she might ride across the ocean floor. But Pegasus was too buoyant and though he rocked comfortably atop the waves, the sea-god with all his power could not force the horse to submerge. Which proveth the axiom—*"You may cede a horse to daughter, but you can't make him sink."*

A chorus of distaff lamentation did not disturb the professor as his subconscious mind continued to mull over the question of selecting a safe destination for his next umbrella flight. Soon he was deep asleep. His slumbers were tormented by bloodthirsty buccaneers, tentacled Krakens, tyrannical Captains, typhoons, naval battles, phantom ships, sea serpents, mutineers—

And suddenly his nightmare got worse! A stupendous tidal wave washed him overboard; he clutched the nearest jetsam he could lay his hands upon—a shaft of driftwood that glowed with cabalistic symbols. The sleeper's thumb brushed a button at its base.

And the incredible umbrella opened.

CHAPTER TWO

Spindrift

SPLASH!!!

Without transition, the world was wet, wild and tumultuous.

Phillimore, suddenly awake and still clutching his umbrella, found himself rudely adrift in the depths of a storm-swept sea. He kicked off his shoes and managed to get his head above the waves long enough to sputter salt water out of his mouth and gulp a little air into his lungs before going back down. In spite of imminent crisis, it didn't take long for him to figure out what was wrong...his thumb still rested on the umbrella's catch.

Well, for once, he mused sourly, *the blasted thing hasn't landed me in hot water.* Mainly because the ocean was ice-cold.

And in a total uproar! *Must be a typhoon.*

No time to wonder what kind of place he'd landed in by accident. His immediate task was trying not to drown. If he could manage that, he realized, he'd still probably die of exposure, *but first things first!* He wasn't much of a swimmer, but he remembered he was better at froglegs than scissor-kicking, so he lumbered sluggishly upward for another great gulp of breath.

As his head broke the surface, the professor was startled to hear a high-pitched voice shouting something incomprehensible into the wind. He yelped for help.

"There's someone in danger!" a second voice shouted.

With preternatural swiftness, the winds died down and the great whitecaps dwindled and became gently-rolling foam. Fillmore treaded water; he stuck the sodden umbrella above his head and vigorously twirled it to shake off moisture.

A little way off, a great flat craft was heading towards him. The odd way it skimmed above the water gave it the appearance of a motorized vessel, but the fact that one of its occupants dissipated the storm suggested it was not powered by fossil fuel but some mode of nonpollutant sorcery.

Two personages rode upon it: a slim delicately-featured youth with dark hair and bright friendly eyes and a short rotund old man who wore a scowl as craggy as the boy's smile was sweet.

"Don't you see him?" the young man asked his elder. "Over there, a few points starboard...he's in trouble!"

"I'm not blind!" the other growled. "I only calmed the waters to speed my quest, not to lug floundering flotsam aboard. He'll slow us down."

"Well, if you won't save him, at least you don't have to run into him. That might damage the raft."

Fillmore suddenly realized that the large raft was on a direct trajectory and could well plough into him with considerable force.

"You've got a point, lad," the old man conceded. He muttered a few words and the vessel aimed a little to the left of the professor.

"But slow down! You'll swamp him."

"Tough nuggets if I do!" the sorcerer retorted, but just then he got a better glimpse of the contraption with cabalistic symbols that the stranger was twirling about. A curious change played over his broad squat features. He spoke to the raft; first it slowed and then it maneuvered itself into a mild drift-and-bob a few yards away from the man in the water.

Fillmore frog-kicked himself the intervening distance. The slim young man reached a hand out to him and pulled him onto the raft.

"Be careful," the other cautioned. "Don't let him lose hold of that interesting-looking umbrella."

Uh-oh, the professor thought, drying himself with a large thirsty towel the youth handed him. *That sounds like trouble...*

* * * *

A low orange sun heralded the arrival of twilight. Fillmore sat down with his back against the wooden side of a cabin erected at the far end of their flatboat. Everything was made from some sort of timber, but his forest lore was too rudimentary to know what kind of boards composed the raft's floor and cabin walls.

He contemplated his companions. The man had spiky grey hair that hung over bushy eyebrows. He wore a broad brown vest over a ruffled brown shirt and matching trousers with an unusual number of pockets in them. His gold boots had toes that curled up and around like a conch-shell.

The boy was more colorfully attired in blue and white blouse and pantaloons. His shoes were plain cloth of a silvery hue and he carried a green knapsack. His dark hair, cut short, fringed a high pale forehead. His eyes were merry, though at the moment he looked irritated.

"Dry him off! It won't cost you anything."

"All right, all right." The old man growled a few words and gestured at the sodden professor.

Suddenly Fillmore felt warm and dry. He thanked them both and asked what their names might be, but before the youth could reply, the old man muzzled him with a hand over his mouth.

"Tell us yours first!" He sounded like a box of shaken gravel.

"Call me Jim. Don't worry, I don't know any name-magic."

A snorted retort. "You shouldn't even know it exists!"

"I'm not a wizard, but I've read about them. You're one."

A grunt, but he took his hand away from the boy's mouth. "Talk to him if ye've a mind."

The boy clasped his hand in a friendly shake. "You can call him Rug, I'm Pit."

"Pit? Rug?! What sort of names are they?"

"You don't like 'em? Swim, then!"

"Sorry ... that was rude of me. Still, they *are* unusual."

"Rug's for short. The lad doesn't remember his name, so I call him Pit."

"Why?"

"Short for Pitiful."

The young man laughed. "It's all right, I don't mind."

Fillmore nodded. "OK, but how about if I call you Pete?"

"Close enough."

The old man did not object.

It was time to exchange stories. Fillmore went first, figuring that he'd better appease Rug's keen interest in what he evidently took for an instrument of magic. When he was done, the old man crossed his arms and squinted at him suspiciously.

"So it only works for you, eh?" He held out a pudgy paw. "Let's see if you're telling the truth. Hand it over."

"I don't trust you."

To his surprise, that fetched a hearty laugh. "That makes us even. I like your honesty, Jim."

"OK, then." The professor held out the umbrella. "Go ahead, give it a try. It won't work."

"Why not?"

"Because it's never worked for anyone but me. And I just used it. It takes time to cool off."

"It was doused in cold water," the gravel box rattled.

"True … but once it takes me somewhere, it won't work again till I've finished a sequence."

"Meaning what?"

"I have to work out the functional basis of the world I'm on before I can leave it. It's a little complicated."

"You think I'm too dumb to understand?" he barked.

"No, but there's one thing I think I've figured out."

"Yeah?"

"Your name."

The old man sneered. "Well, it ain't Rumpelstiltskin."

"No, it's Ruggedo."

This time the eyes and mouth that gaped belonged to the erstwhile nemesis of the Wonderful Land of Oz, none other than the Nome King. Before that fiery-tempered monarch could recover from the shock, suddenly the sea air was troubled by a chorus of sharp quacks. Fillmore looked astern and saw a peculiar flock of birds (or were they mammals?) swimming in a double line. They had huge eyes and each wore spectacles perched on bills as wide and orange as Donald Duck's. As they swam past, they chattered rhyming observations at the professor. They drowned each other out, but he managed to catch a few of their remarks—"You're always the wettest before you're dry!"

"You can't try again until you try!"

"But we've got bigger fish to fry!"

"What on earth are they?" Fillmore asked.

"Aah, don't pay them any mind," said Ruggedo. "Just a bunch of duck-billed platitudes."

The professor winced. He figured he'd landed in a world patterned on the jumbled seafaring dreams he was having when he activated the umbrella in his sleep. *Which should be enough, thank you, but no! this goofy place also includes Boris's blasted puns!*

Meanwhile, Ruggedo was holding the umbrella and was waiting for instructions. The professor told him what to do. The old man shut his eyes, obviously thinking of a destination, muttered under his breath and then pushed the button.

The professor's jaw dropped. Ruggedo and the umbrella both vanished.

Pete said, "I thought it only works for you!"

"So did I!!!" Some heavy thinking was in order. First of all, what was Ruggedo doing on the Nonestic Ocean? (Well, that's where this must be). What was the Nome up to? He was probably in exile plotting some way to oust his former servant Kaliko and retake the reins of his subterranean monarchy and if he did that, his next step would probably be to try to conquer the land of Oz.

Which makes it quite likely that he told the umbrella to take him somewhere in the neighborhood of his old caverns.

But what about Pete? How does he figure in all of this? He could ask him, anyway, so he did, but the youth didn't have very much to say.

"Whatever brought me onto this flatboat," Pete said, "I have no idea. I'd only been with Ruggedo a little while. Before that, I have no memory."

"Did he tell you, at least, where he wanted to go?"

"He said this is the Nonestic Ocean and we have to cross it. There's a big island continent covered with all sorts of kingdoms and countries."

"Did he mention any of them?"

"A few. One is called the Happy Valley, though he said it's also called something else."

"Mo?"

"That's it! Then there's a place called Merryland and somewhere I'm sure I wouldn't like because it's underground. But the land whose name he most often mentioned—or rather, growled—is Oz."

"Mm-hmm. Rug's got a checkered history with Oz." Fillmore said, "As a matter of fact, that's where I was thinking of heading when the umbrella dropped me into the Nonestic."

The professor had a vague memory of the Australia-like map of the island that had Oz in its middle, surrounded by the Deadly Desert. "Pete," he asked, "did Rug give you any idea how long a trip it was going to be?"

"He told me we were almost there. He expected to reach land by tomorrow." Pete suddenly frowned. Shading his eyes with the back of his hand he said, "Looks like we're not alone."

Fillmore stared off to starboard and saw a large sailing ship lurch-ing—yes, *lurching* across the sea in their direction.

CHAPTER THREE

Aboard Ship—1st Shift

The shape of the ship was—well, stupid! There was a succession of oars that dipped down and up, down and up, into the waters of the Nonestic. But there was a decidedly snub bow and three masts festooned with multi-hued garlands, as well as ropes and sails. With some alarm, the professor noticed how very much the vessel trembled.

They could not hope to outrun the ship, so they waited till they were tossed ropes up which both Fillmore and Pete scrambled up onto the rocking deck. Fortunately, thanks to his time served on the H. M. S. Pin-afore, the pedagogue had gained his sea-legs and Pete seemed altogether at ease.

They faced a number of sailors in varying manner of garb. The crew regarded them with mild curiosity. And then they all heard approaching footsteps: thump! thump! thump!

A wooden leg! Fillmore thought, knowing there were two likely pos-sibilities rattling round his mind. He hoped it would be Captain Ahab and it was.

"What have we here?" the grey-haired officer asked. "Strange flot-sam, indeed."

"W-we f-found them r-r-riding on that," a young seaman uttered, pointing to their flatboat.

"Thank you, Midshipman Budd," the captain said. He regarded the newcomers with frank amazement. "You actually had the nerve to at-tempt to brave the ocean on *that?!*"

"Actually, no," Fillmore replied. "Neither of us had a choice and we're glad to be off the thing."

"I should think so."

"May we take berth on your ship, Captain Ahab?"

A shocked gasp.

"Who told you my name?"

"Nobody."

"Then how did you know it?"

The professor shrugged. "Bit of a fey quality, I fancy."

A wintry smile on Ahab's lips. "I'll accept that for now, fellow. But who are you and what can you do to earn passage on my ship?"

"I'm James Phillimore, also called Fillmore and this young man is

Pete. I don't know his last name."

"Neither do I," Pete stated.

"As for what we could do," he continued, "we'll endeavour to perform whatever chores you deem necessary."

"Well said, sir." The captain patted him on the back. "I welcome you to my shift."

Shift, not ship? What does he mean by "my shift"?

"We'll find you work and it will not be over-taxing. Now tell me how you knew my name."

"Could anyone faintly maritime not know, or at least have heard of the famous Captain Ahab?"

Ahab chuckled. "You appeal to my vanity, sir. Of which commodity I have very little. But I do have another question for you, sir." He beckoned him to stand beside him and when he did, the captain said, in an undertone, "Your companion … Peter, is it?"

"Pete."

"Don't you find him a trifle effeminate?"

"Never occurred to me, actually."

"All the better, then. Now it's time to be under weigh. Claggart!" he called. A somber man of fair height came forward. "Mr. Claggart is my First Mate. He'll find more suitable work garments for you both and after that, work of some sort."

"Captain?" Fillmore ventured. "May I ask one question of you?"

"Aye."

"Why is this ship not a whaler?"

Ahab's mood visibly darkened. "When the need arises, lad, be sure that *it will be!"*

CHAPTER FOUR

Aboard Ship—2nd Shift

Though Ahab promised them chores that would not overtax them, the pair found themselves quite tired by the time they were done and when they were finally invited to share the mess, they were ever so grateful, even though the food certainly deserved to be called just that.

Back on deck they chanced sitting down with their backs against a bulkhead, but they swiftly got to their feet when a short sharply-uniformed naval officer appeared and fixed them with a puzzled frown. He demanded to know who they might be.

"This is my friend Pete," the professor replied, "and I'm J. (for James) Adrian Fillmore."

"Gad!" the officer choked. "What a name! What are you doing on this vessel?"

"We were brought aboard by Captain Ahab."

A frosty smile. "Kay. Which means I'm stuck with you." He took a pair of silvery marbles out of his pocket and began rolling them around in his left hand. "So what can you do to earn your keep?"

Fillmore told him how they'd been employed for the past few hours: swabbing decks, picking oakum, doing the ship's laundry.

"The captain's mood brightened. "Kay. You *have* been busy. In that case, welcome to my shift." He saluted them smartly. "Lieutenant Commander Philip F. Queeg, RN. Where were you headed when you came across my ship?"

"We're trying to find the land of Oz."

"Ahs?" His eyebrows beetled. "Now why does that sound familiar?"

Midshipman Budd spoke up. "Th-that's where the p-p-prisoner said he wanted to g-go."

"Oh, yes. That crusty dwarf! Bring him to me."

Budd went below deck and returned shortly afterward leading a very red-faced, scowling and swearing Ruggedo. Fillmore was relieved to see that he still had the umbrella.

"Give that back to me," he said, snatching it out of his hand.

"Take it and welcome!" the Nome King growled.

"Kay," said the skipper. "A stowaway *and* a thief."

"No, actually I loaned it to him. Ruggedo, how on earth did you end up here?"

"Damned thing almost smashed me on some rocks! I didn't know how to steer it."

"But I told you how it works."

"You also claimed it wouldn't work for me!" Ruggedo snapped.

Fillmore nodded. "I really didn't think it would. It must be this world we're on. Magic always works here, I guess."

"Well, anyway, it took me by surprise. The only thing I could think to do was tell it to set me down somewhere safe." The Nome King shuddered. "Magic or not—never again!"

Good, Fillmore thought. *One less thing to worry about.*

Pete said, "Welcome back, Rug."

"Oh, shut up," he shot back.

The professor turned to the captain. "So why is he under arrest?"

"Because he can't keep a civil tongue in his head."

"You hear him, Ruggedo. Think you could modify your temper?"

"It's not my nature," he sputtered.

"Give it a try!"

"All right, I will. Captain Queeg, I apologize for whatever I called you—I forget what it was."

"Oh, I remember." The silvery balls click-clicked. "Kay. Show me some respect and you can have a berth aboard." He swiveled round abruptly. "What the hell is *that?!*"

"That" was a jolting brassy noise coming from a ship that suddenly appeared on the horizon. It was a four-masted British topsail schooner and on it a company of naval officers, midshipmen and ready hands were all blowing a large array of musical instruments: bugles, cornets, English horns, flugelhorns, trombones, trumpets and tubas.

Everyone gaped at them and some stuck their fingers in their ears. With a groan, the professor figured out what they represented.

"Do you know what they are?" the captain asked.

"I think I do—a kind of visual pun."

"Tell it."

"It won't mean much to anybody who is not familiar with the nautical stories of C. S. Forester."

"I've read them, the Horatio—" The skipper suddenly slapped his forehead with his free hand. "I don't believe it!"

"Oh, yes," Fillmore nodded. "They're a book collector's delight, a complete set of hornblowers."

CHAPTER FIVE

Aboard Ship—3rd Shift

The professor concluded that there must be two shifts on this ship. His reason: he heard the thump! thump! thump! which, he was sure, announced the arrival of Captain Ahab. He was, however, quite seriously wrong, for when he turned round he saw coming toward him a rough-looking piratical thug with a red bandanna tied about his forehead, a large gold ring dangling from his right earlobe, a wooden pegleg and the worst case Fillmore had ever seen of ten o'clock shadow.

"Aaarrrr," he growled in classic buccaneering style. "Who be these landlubbers?" He pointed at the two with the business end of a dirk.

First Mate Claggart introduced them. "They do work hard, Captain."

"Do they now? Well, in that case, I'll put off the pleasure of keel-hauling them." He squinted at them. "Welcome to this ship's third shift. You've probably heard tell o' me—" Fillmore nodded. "You must be Long John Silver."

"What tar bandies about my name?" he bellowed.

"No one did," he hastened to reassure him. "But your name and reputation are quite famous, you know."

"Are they now?" Long John grinned. "I'm gettin' t' like you, landlubber. But I do prefer 'infamous.'"

"I'll remember that."

"That would be wise, my friend." He raised his voice. "I'm talkin' to everybody now."

A chorus of assent.

"We're not far offshore. Today we're going to do some backbreaking work, lads—we're going to dig up Captain Flint's treasure."

Vociferous cheers!

"And when we do—" He stopped. "What in all good hell is *that?!*"

The professor would have thought it was a repeat performance by the hornblowers but this noise was very different. He looked off to starboard and saw a little way off an outcropping of rocks. On it sat a solitary man in sporran and kilt and he was doing his utmost to play something similar to a melody on the bagpipes.

He groaned.

"What is it?" Pete asked.

"Another pun, but it won't mean anything to you, at least I don't think so. It's the visual equivalent of 'scotch on the rocks.'"

The captain poked his chest. "That's one, landlubber. And there ain't no two."

Just then there came a shout from the crow's nest.

"Land ho!"

Happy noise all around as the crew stared in all directions until they spotted in the distance a beach. Long John snapped a series of orders and they began to sail straight toward land.

The professor began to make plans for escape, though where was an unsolved part of the equation. His revery ended when he suddenly realized that the ship was aiming for the now much closer beach with alarming rapidity.

"Captain, sir," he said.

"Aye?"

"Aren't we running too fast? Won't we crash?"

Silver laughed. "Oh, laddie, we're in no danger. Y' don't know what this vessel be capable of. Watch and learn!"

Seagulls began to shriek as the ship swiftly invaded their domain. The beach was practically upon them, or vice versa. And then they were on it ... ... and the ship was actually walking, as it were, on the sand!

They shivered to a stop and rope ladders were slung over the side. Sailors began to clamber down them.

"Now how d'ye like that, eh?" Long John exclaimed, slapping Fillmore so heartily that he flopped onto his knees.

"Now get on down, landlubber. You, too, young 'un. It's time for shore leave!"

PART TWO

On the Way to Oz

CHAPTER SIX

Dangerous Wheels

They'd forgotten all about Ruggedo and that was his intention. If nobody saw him, they couldn't make him work. But now he grabbed a rope as fast as he could and scrambled down to the beach. He saw the professor and Pete and hurried to join them, not that he liked them all that much, but they were safer company than the sailors.

"We're on our own now," he told them. "Let's skedaddle."

"No argument with that," Fillmore agreed, "but where?"

"That way," the Nome King pointed toward an outcropping of rocks. "Let's see what's on the other side."

First they checked to see whether any of the ship's crew was watching them, but no one paid them any mind, so they hurried in the direction Ruggedo indicated and found on the other side of the rocks a quiet stretch of sand.

"Uh-oh," Ruggedo clucked, "wheel tracks."

"What's that mean?" Pete asked.

"It's not good."

The Nome splashed into the water, bent down and fished up a double handful of clams. He took out a knife and began to pry them open. "Want one?" he asked the professor with scant enthusiasm.

"Thank you," he answered and was given exactly one.

None were offered to the boy, but he showed no enthusiasm for the idea of downing one.

Ruggedo finished his makeshift meal and began to think about what to do next when they heard the ominous sound of wheels coming their way.

Six strange men approached them. They wheeled onto the beach, for instead of feet their legs ended in large unicycle wheels. They formed a semicircle around the trio and sneered.

"Trespassers!"

"They're Wheelers," the Nome murmured. "Nasty critters, but they're also cowards. I'll handle them." He stepped forward, his knife outstretched in his right fist. "So which of you wants to get cut first? Come on now, speak up. You, maybe?" He stomped over to the leftmost Wheeler and brandished his blade.

"Not me, not me!" the Wheeler caterwauled and vamoosed.

"The rest of you won't join him? Not a good choice."

"There are still five of us," one of them said. "We're going to gang up on you, Nome."

"Nome?" he roared. "You dare call me that? I'm Ruggedo, the Nome King!"

Former King, Fillmore thought, but kept it to himself.

When they heard the pronouncement, four of the Wheelers swiveled round and left as fast as they could. But the sole remaining one was made of sterner stuff.

"You are obviously unaware, churl, that Wheelers have excellent hearing. I heard you call us cowards. But I am Whirligig, Prince of the Wheelers and I say it's you who are a coward, for I am unarmed, whereas you've got a knife. Throw it away and face me in a fair fight!"

Ruggedo handed his knife to the professor. "I expect that back."

"Shall I write a pawn ticket?"

"Oh—shut up!" Ruggedo faced Whirligig. "I admit that I was wrong. You, at least, are brave. Now I ask you, Whirly, what harm are we doing here?"

"Fair question," he conceded. "You're trespassing."

"Can you show me a deed that proves you own this beach?"

"Are you deliberately trying to provoke me?"

"Am I? Well, let me do some more. Provoke, provoke, provoke." He sounded like a crow.

Whirligig lost his temper. He wheeled directly at Ruggedo at great speed, but the Nome King stepped aside with the deftness of a bullfighter and as the Wheeler went past, he snatched as high into the air as his short arms would allow. He was about to toss him into the ocean when Whirligig cried out, "No! Don't! My wheels will rust! Let me go and I promise to leave you alone."

"Rust?" Pete said, perplexed.

"How do I know I can trust you?" Ruggedo asked.

"As one monarch to another."

He set him down with surprising gentleness. "Sir, you are a worthy opponent."

"And so are you." The Wheeler Prince saluted him and Ruggedo returned it. Whirligig then went away.

* * * *

Fillmore was enthusiastic in his admiration of the Nome.

"Thanks," Ruggedo replied.

The professor smiled and as he returned the knife to Ruggedo, said, "So which way do we go now?"

"Depends on where we want to go. As for me—" But Pete interrupted. "We're going to Oz."

Ruggedo scowled. "My least favorite place. But if that's where you're headed, you've got to go inland."

"And then we have to stop," said Fillmore, "because of the Deadly Desert."

"One problem at a time, lad. Let's start you off in the right direction and see what-all happens next."

So that's what they did.

CHAPTER SEVEN

The Worst Wolf

But before they got under way, a ship suddenly rounded the curve of the beach and began to dock.

"We'd better hide," the professor said.

In a short while the ship was moored and out of it came the most desperate-looking crew the three companions could imagine. Soon their captain joined them. He was a solid man of middle height and his countenance displayed concentrated malice.

Fillmore heard one of the sailors address him. *Oh, no! It's Wolf Larsen—Jack London's Sea Wolf!* Larsen had a brilliant mind, but he also had a huge streak of utter cruelty.

Three men in chains were dragged before him. Two were two common sailors, both terrified. The third, though, was an officer and he regarded the captain with contempt.

Captain Larsen confronted the first prisoner and without a word cut his throat.

When he saw what was about to happen, Fillmore whispered to Pete, "Don't look!" The boy put his hand over his eyes.

Larsen did the same with the second prisoner, but when he stood before the third man, he wiped his sword and sheathed it.

"Well, well," he crooned, "if it's not my beloved brother Wolf."

Fillmore realized, horrified, that he had been mistaken. The captain was not Wolf Larsen, after all, but his ominously-named brother Death Larsen—the only man Wolf ever feared, though at the moment that emotion had been replaced with pure anger.

"Get it over with, you bastard," Wolf growled. "I'll be grateful."

"Oh, you'd like that, wouldn't you? Well, brace yourself, my fellow bastard. I'm commuting your sentence. You're free and will be returned to your own ship. How our mother will rejoice!"

"Your cruelty ever outstrips mine," the other said.

"Compliments won't change my mind. Let me offer you an aphorism appropriate to your position. You won't find it in your beloved Nietzsche. 'Life sucks and then you—live.'"

Wolf cursed his brother with noteworthy thoroughness. Then they all set off and soon were sailing again.

The three travelers came out of hiding. Even the Nome King looked upset.

"I used to think that I was a rotter, but compared to that pair, I'm some kind of chivalrous hero."

PART THREE

Somewhere Over the Etc.

CHAPTER EIGHT

In the Land of the Gillikins

They trudged wearily on for hours. They weren't thirsty, at least, because they encountered a clear stream, but they were all beginning to feel hunger pangs. Once in a while, they found berries, which Ruggedo refused to eat.

Just as the sun began to set, they came upon the Deadly Desert.

"How do we know this is the desert you're worried about?" Pete wondered.

"It's right where I expected it to be. Careful, now, don't even take one step on it, that's how bad it is."

"That's for sure," Ruggedo said. "Anyone who puts his feet on it withers away into dust."

"All right," Pete nodded, "so what do we do now?"

No sooner had he spoken than a sudden thunderstorm started up. Before they could even take cover, it was just as quickly gone and after the brief rainfall they were delighted to see the rainbow that spread across the sky. To their utter surprise, they saw a lovely young woman clad in multicolored diaphanous garments dancing down the rainbow's descending curve.

"It's Polychrome!" Pete declared.

The maiden approached them with delighted curiosity. "Yes, that *is* me—Polychrome, the rainbow's daughter. But who are you, young man? I don't think we've ever met, have we?"

Pete looked thoroughly nonplussed. "Somehow I know you, but I have no idea why."

"Well, at any rate, I'm pleased to meet you. All of you." She turned to Ruggedo. "You I know, or at least know about, but I've no quarrel with you."

"Likewise," he grunted.

"So what are you all doing here? Trying to cross the sands?"

"That's right," Pete replied. "We want to get to Oz."

She laughed. "Well, that's ever so easy. But touch my robes and you shall be upheld through more than this."

Pete and Fillmore, who, of course, recognized the Dickension allusion, did as she said. Ruggedo held back. She laughed again. "Roquat!" she addressed him, using his old name. "Don't be shy, now. Take hold of my robe and we'll all go to Oz."

"I suppose I have to," he grumbled, doing as he was told.

Their flight was swift and breathtaking. Polychrome set them down in a landscape covered with purple flowers. "Oh, my!" she said. "I've flown you further north than I meant to. This is the country of—"

"The Gillikins!" Pete exclaimed.

"That's right. You've been here before?"

"I must have, but I don't remember a thing."

"Well, you're very close to a village that's populated by some large women. They're a bit bossy, perhaps, but they love visitors and they've got good generous hearts. Go to them and let them lavish ever so much affection on you." With that, she sprang up onto the rainbow and was lost in a burst of glory.

CHAPTER NINE

The Aunt Hill

Their way led them up a steep hill. At the top, they passed through open gates and gawked at a village full of very large houses. Its inhabitants, who were busily shopping or gossiping were on an average nine feet tall, though three of them were closer to twelve. This trio saw Fillmore, Pete and Ruggedo and hurried over to them, cooing happily.

"Look how cute they are!" said the one with dark brown hair.

"They look like children!" the blonde said.

The redhead added, "I want to hug them all!" And with that she snatched up Ruggedo and squeezed him to her breast. He struggled and kicked and finally got out: "Can't ... breathe!" So she set him down.

"Welcome to our little town," said the blonde. "I'm Aunt Edith and these are my sisters."

Little town?! Fillmore gaped.

The brunette told them her name is Aunt Harriet and the redhead identified herself as Aunt Mildred. Then she asked them if they were hungry.

"Yes!" chorused in triplicate.

So Aunt Mildred again seized Ruggedo, Aunt Harriet chose Pete and the blonde got the professor, who said, "We *can* walk, you know."

"We wouldn't think of it," said Aunt Edith. "You're our guests."

A while later, after a hearty meal with many plates of meat, vegetables and fruit and lemonade—they positively refused to serve the Nome beer. "It'll stunt your growth," Aunt Mildred warned him—they told the women about their adventures and how they got to Oz. Then Fillmore explained that it was important that they reach the Emerald City as soon as possible. He was afraid that the aunts wouldn't allow them to leave, but the sisters, along with other villagers who peeked in to see "the children" all agreed somewhat sadly to help them continue their journey.

"But," Mildred declared, "we've got a present that you must take with you."

Aunt E (for Edith) carried in three baskets stuffed with food and jugs of water. The baskets were allocated from their daughters's doll houses, but to the travelers they were quite hefty.

They thanked their hostesses for the much-appreciated gifts. Rug-gedo outdid himself with decidedly un-Nomish behavior, blowing them all many kisses.

"When will you be going?" Aunt Harriet asked.

"Right now," Fillmore answered. "Can you tell us how to find the yellow brick road?"

She shook her head. "Never set eyes on it. But we know someone who can help you." She sketched a map and handed it to them. "It's not very far off. We're close to the border of the Winkie country. This is the path to take to find the castle of their ruler."

Pete lit up. "Nick Chopper!"

"Well, yes, that is his name."

Another round of thanks, then they said goodbye and set out towards the yellow land of the Winkies. Fillmore muttered, "Well, that wasn't bad at all."

"What wasn't?" Pete asked.

"Being captured by giant aunts."

* * * *

Once they were on the road, Ruggedo shook his head and said, "Old Nick C is not going to be pleased to see me. I'll have to wait for you outside."

"Suit yourself," said Fillmore.

"In that case," the Nome replied, "I've got another direction that I need to go in."

"Where?"

"I want to return to my kingdom."

"Uh … I hate to mention this, but you're no longer its king. Kaliko is its ruler."

"That jumped-up steward!" Ruggedo groused. "I'll take care of him!"

"How?"

"Come with me and you'll see for yourself."

Fillmore shook his head. "You're not thinking this through, Rug. What you're proposing means we'd have to cross the Deadly Desert—twice!"

"I know it's asking a lot, lad, but—"

"But there's nothing you can say … I'm going to be stuck in the land of the Nomes. How will I make it back?"

Ruggedo shrugged. "I don't have a clue." He sighed. "Of course it's asking too much. I'll do it on my own."

"And how are you going to get there?"

"I haven't worked that out yet."

Fillmore cursed under his breath. "I know I'm going to regret this. But I know how to get us there. It'll be difficult, though, with three of us—"

Pete interrupted. "Two. I'm not going."

"Why not?"

"Because, Mr. Fillmore, I want to visit the Tin Woodman. I'll wait for you there."

"As you wish." The professor turned to Ruggedo. "OK, are you ready?"

"Ready for what?"

Fillmore held up the umbrella.

The Nome King turned white. "I'd rather die!"

"In that case, try walking on the desert."

"How do you know it'll work?"

"I don't, not for sure, but it's been a while since I used it, so I think maybe it'll work. Now climb up on my shoulders." He stooped down.

Ruggedo grimly shook his head. "I'm going to regret this." He grabbed the other round the neck and circled his legs round his waist.

"Easy there, don't choke me!" Fillmore stood up, said goodbye to Pete and pressed the umbrella's catch.

PART FOUR

The Return of the King

CHAPTER TEN

The Glorious Revolution

They landed with a soft plop on a rocky trail that ended in a great stone archway.

"That's the way in," Ruggedo said.

"You first," Fillmore suggested.

They descended into the Nome Kingdom and after a deal of walking they were challenged by a pair of sentries, but when Ruggedo told them who he was, they quailed and bowed low. Ruggedo strode past. The guards tried to stop the professor, but stood aside when their monarch said, "Leave him alone. He's with me."

At last they came to the throne room. On it sat a lean angular Nome wearing a crown that was obviously too heavy for his head. As soon as he saw Ruggedo, he hopped off the throne, removed his crown and held it out. "Take it, I'm sick of it!"

"Take it, *who*?"

"Take it, Your Majesty!"

"Well, that wasn't hard," Ruggedo said, putting the crown on his head and thus retaking his place as the Rightful Ruler of the Nomes.

"Please, sir, may I become your steward again?"

Ruggedo shrugged. "The job's open."

Kaliko started out gleefully, only to be called back. "Your first duty is to assemble my people."

"Yes, Your Majesty." Kaliko turned round and the monarch kicked him.

Once he was gone, the professor said, "How do you feel your people will feel about having you as their king again?"

"We'll soon find out. Here they come."

From the deepest bowels of the earth marched a great quantity of Nomes. When they saw Ruggedo seated above them, there was a long tense moment, but then he challenged them. "You arrant scurvy knaves, why aren't you on your knees?!" They did so immediately. "That's better. I'm your *real* king and don't you ever forget it! All right now, stand up and get ready for a feast."

The Nomes rose and cheered.

"That's enough noise. Now clear out ... I'm sick of looking at you."

They double-timed it out of every available door.

"This is more like it," Ruggedo said with a smile.

"It's like they say, I suppose."

"What? What do they say?"

"That there's no place like Nome," the professor replied.

The Nome King glared at him. "It's about time for you to get going, ain't it?"

"I suppose so, only how am I going to cross the Deadly Desert?"

"Dam'f I know. But you *will* need this." Ruggedo fumbled in the pockets of his jacket and produced a key, which he gave to Fillmore.

"How do I use it?"

"Come on! You know how a key works! You'll need it fairly soon. The key's an extra, so I don't need it back."

Fillmore thanked him and began to leave, but then a thought that had been in the back of his mind made him halt. "Uh, Your Majesty?"

"Yeah? What?"

"Have you ever thought—now hear me out—that it might be good policy to enter into a friendly accord with the land of Oz?"

The Nome King scowled. "Not only is your idea utter idiocy, but so is your use of the word 'friendly.' By now you ought to know that's not in a Nome's nature."

"So call it a cordial pact. But why is it so dumb? Think of the benefits of having them as an ally."

"And vice versa. All right, it might not be such a bad idea, after all. But after all I've tried to do to them, what makes you think they'd go for it?"

Fillmore grinned. "For this reason—they're by nature ever so friendly."

"I'd forgotten. Very well, then, laddie. I hereby appoint you the very first ambassador for the Nome Kingdom. Now don't screw it up."

"I'll do my best not to."

With a bow, the professor left the "palace."

CHAPTER ELEVEN

Hammering it Home

Fillmore took the only trail that there was. As he walked along, he thought about his adventures so far and to come, especially the latter. The first thing, of course, was to return to Oz and join up with Pete. After that, they would travel to the Emerald City, where he meant to broach his plan for an Ozzy-Nomish alliance.

The countryside he was passing through was all grey or brown rocks and pebbles. Nowhere was there any water, trees or flowers, but at least the path was clean and clear.

And then he not only heard, but felt, a mighty noise.

CRASH-CRASH-CRASH!

This could not be good. As he stepped along, he felt the trembling earth beneath his feet and the further along he went, the greater were the tremors.

At last he saw the reason for the noise and the seismic activity. A colossal metal man, gleaming in the sun, stood astride the trail that he was on and pounded it with a huge hammer.

CRASH-CRASH-CRASH!

Well, now what?

CRASH-CRASH-CRASH!

What did the Nome King tell him? That he'd need something fairly soon. This must somehow be what Ruggedo was referring to.

The professor only could see one way that he might pass the danger; he would have to wait till the hammer was up in the air and then scoot on past before it hit the earth again.

It's just a matter of timing.

He began to time the crashes. Yes, there was certainly enough time between each impact.

Sure about that?

CRASH-CRASH-CRASH!

Wait! The key! Why did Ruggedo give him a key? He took it out and looked at the giant hammer-wielder.

Maybe this turns him off? But where do I insert it?

He saw nothing remotely resembling a keyhole in the giant's head, shoulders, arms, back, trunk or legs.

You're not thinking like a Nome!

Fillmore squinted and scanned the hammerer's ankles and feet.

Yes, there it is!

The keyhole was set in the middle of the automaton's right heel. He hurried forward, stuck in the key and turned it. The giant shuddered to a stop, its hammer poised high in the air. The professor sighed with relief.

* * * *

He continued on his journey. After about half an hour, he came upon the edge of the Deadly Desert, which sent noxious yellow fumes curling up into the sky.

"And now—how do I get across?"

PART FIVE

In Limbo

CHAPTER TWELVE

An Incompleat Encounter

"Well," the professor said, "I could always try the umbrella. But it's been used too recently, it probably won't work. On the other hand, it's been doing some weird things lately. Why is that, I wonder? Probably because this is a place where magic works, so the usual rules don't apply. Well, let's see what happens."

He pressed the umbrella's catch and it did indeed open, but after that he got totally unexpected results. It deposited him on a flat plane that ran featurelessly to the distant horizon. There was no sun, but the sky was full of light.

"Where in hell am I?" Fillmore exclaimed. "What's this supposed to represent? It's sure not the land of Oz!"

No answer came to him and the empty space around him supplied no clue to what or where it might be. But then he saw something vertical in the distance and it was moving toward him. It turned out to be a man dressed jauntily with an ascot round his neck and a cap on his head. He came up to him and held out his hand.

"I'm Harold Shea. And you are?"

Taking his hand and shaking it, he said, "J. Adrian Fillmore."

"What a nice name!"

Fillmore decided to like him.

"Well, J. A., what *is* this place?"

"I have no idea. I just found myself here, all of a sudden." He showed him his umbrella and explained how it worked.

"So," said Shea, "it brought you here. Something like that happened to me, too. I was just using my—"

"Syllogismobile."

He laughed at that. "Now how could you possibly know that word?"

"Bit of a fey quality, I fancy."

"You look about as fey as a tank. Now, come on, how did you know there's such a thing as a syllogismobile?"

"I've read about you."

"So I've been written up? I ought to get royalties."

"Well, anyway, I'm not so concerned about where or why we're here, I'm more concerned about how to get out of here."

"Right. Me, too. So I guess we're someplace between the worlds."

"That could be."

"Call it, for want of a better name, Limbo."

"Limbo it is," the professor nodded.

"I've done a lot of world-hopping—"

"So have I."

"And there's always a blurry spot somewhere in between. Looks like we got stuck in one of them."

"Looks like."

"Excuse me," said Shea, "but I'm going to hazard a guess that you are, or were, involved in Academia."

"I was. I am a professor. And you were also a college teacher, weren't you?"

"Sure was. Mathematics was—is—my bailiwick. What's yours?"

"English literature. American drama. Et cetera."

"Lot of good that does when you're world-hopping, right?"

"Oh, you'd be surprised. Knowing the underlying premises of the places I visit helps me survive them."

The other nodded. "Well, that's true of where I've gone as well."

"But to get back to what I was saying—how do we get out of here?" He clicked the umbrella-button, but nothing happened. "It takes time to cool down after it's been used."

"Maybe I should teach you the formula for my syllogismobile."

"Wouldn't hurt."

"All right. Pay attention." He took him through it three times. "Just keep saying that out loud."

"But it could take me anywhere!"

"That's true."

"Maybe if I concentrate on where I want to go, it'll act like the umbrella."

"You know, that could work! Why didn't I ever think of trying that?"

"But this will still leave you stuck here."

"Would you consider loaning me your umbrella?"

"How would I get it back?"

"I think I could manage that."

"Well, maybe you can," the professor said doubtfully.

"May I ask where you were headed when you landed here?"

"To the land of Oz. And where were you?"

"Having a complicated adventure on Mars. Edgar Rice Burroughs's Mars."

"That couldn't have been much fun."

"It sure wasn't!"

"You know," said Fillmore, "it's very lucky we showed up here at the same time. Maybe it wasn't an accident."

"Maybe not. We do seem to have interconnections. Anyway, I've got to get back. My wife Belphebe is expecting. She needs me home. I'll use your idea and umbrella and see if it takes me there."

"Here's hoping. And here's the umbrella. I hope you can get it back to me."

"I'm sure I can." He smiled. "It does seem a logical conclusion. I'll just recite my formula and while I do, I'll think of the proper destination."

Harold Shea stuck out his hand. "Pleased to meet you, J. A."

"Likewise." They shook hands. "Bon voyage."

"Au revoir." And he pressed the catch of the umbrella and vanished.

Look at that! Works for someone else! Again!

The professor concentrated on the formula for the syllogismobile. He started saying it out loud. With the third repetition, he left Limbo.

* * * *

"It's Oz!" he said, relieved. There was a plop at his feet and when he looked down, he saw it was the umbrella. "Wonder how he did that?"

Fillmore looked at the countryside and saw that it was mostly red.

"OK! I'm in the land of the Quadlings."

PART SIX

In the Lands of the Quadlings and the Munchkins

CHAPTER THIRTEEN

Glinda the Good Witch

"I'm in Quadling country, for sure," he said aloud. "But why? Ah—I get it. The syllogismobile is like the umbrella. If you think exactly where you want to go, it picks the shortest route. Well, let's take a look around."

Everywhere he saw flowers and grass in all the shades of red. Close by, he spotted a lofty ruby-colored palace and knew what it must be: the palace of Glinda, the Good Witch of the South.

Fillmore headed there and in a little while he faced Glinda on her throne. She was stunningly lovely and wore the sweetest kindest smile he'd ever set his eyes upon.

"Welcome to the land of the Quadlings, J. Adrian Fillmore," she said and did not say (but thought), "Gad, what a name!"

"Pleased to meet you, Glinda. Do you have a title I ought to use?"

She laughed. "I never stand on such ceremony. I'm glad you managed to come to me. I've been expecting you."

"Really? How? Oh, wait, I know—it's your book!"

He'd learned from reading L. Frank Baum's Oz stories that Glinda had a book that inscribed every single event in the land of Oz that ever happened.

"So you know about it?"

"Yes and I've always wondered how you manage to keep current. How can you possibly read it all every day?"

"It takes a deal of effort," she admitted, "but I'm a speed reader."

"That explains it, then." Which he thought it did not. "So you know exactly why I'm here?"

"I do," said Glinda. "It's your friend Pete. You don't know this, but he's been enchanted by a witch."

"Which explains why he has no memory. But he must come from Oz because he kept remembering little things about it. Where can I find this witch?"

"She lives in the land of the Munchkins."

"Could you disenchant my friend?"

"I probably could, but I don't know what spell was used on him.

Which means unforeseen damage could be done. No, you're going to have to go to her and ask her to remove the spell of her own volition."

"What if she doesn't want to?"

"Think positive!"

"Very well, I will. But how do I get there?"

Glinda gestured. "Like this."

CHAPTER FOURTEEN

So Very Undecided

Munchkin country, without a doubt. Everything's blue.

Right up ahead, he saw a quaint city consisting of small houses and one moderately large castle. A young man in riding clothes was sauntering down the road. When he saw the newcomer he paused and greeted him.

"Hello," Fillmore said. "Where am I?"

"Why, right here!"

"I mean, what is this place."

"Oh! This is Vacilia … I think."

"You think? Don't you know?"

"I'm not too certain."

"Well, what is Vacilia?"

"It's the home of the oldest dynasty in this land."

"What dynasty is that."

He screwed up his forehead and thought. "I think, if I remember correctly, though I usually don't, but I think it's the family that they call the most uncertain dynasty in the world."

"Uncertain?"

"Well, they never do anything because they never can make up their mind."

"Well, who are some of your kings?"

"Let's see now … I'm on surer ground here. There's Vladimir the Vacillator and then there's Ulrich the Uncertain and of course Dorothea the Downright."

"Dorothea the Downright? She doesn't sound at all unsure of herself."

"She was the black sheep of the family."

"What do these rulers call themselves?"

"They are the Perhapsburgs."

The professor groaned to himself. "And yet another pun!"

"Now that I think of it," the young man said, "there was another of our kings who was sure of himself...Louis the Three-Hundred and Forty-fifth."

"The three hundred and forty-fifth?"

"Yes."

"What was he famous for?"

"Boozing and sleeping around. When he died they buried him beneath Mount Ludwigshalter. He said that if the country ever needed him, he'd be sure to come back. That's why we hold our annual ritual."

"Which is?"

"All of the elders of Vacilia march around Mount Ludwigshalter and chant, 'The country's fine! The country's fine!'"

Fillmore had to laugh at that. He said goodbye and went on his way.

Soon he found himself standing in front of a thatched cottage. He wanted to knock or ring a bell, but neither action seemed possible, so he gathered up his courage, of which he was not supplied with an overabundance and knocked on the front door.

A leering crone cracked it open and looked at him mistrustfully. "What? Why? State!"

"You put a spell on my friend."

"I do that a lot. How am I supposed to know who you mean?"

"His name is Pete and he has no memory."

"Hm. Well, that means I used two spells on him. I do remember the lad." Her face contorted into a crafty grin. "I suppose you want me to reverse the magic?"

"That would be very nice, yes."

She poked his chest with a crooked bony finger. "Queezenok don't do nice. Queezenok don't ever do nothing for nothing."

"Well, what's your price?"

"I thought you'd never ask. There's only one thing I need. A black sunflower."

A black sunflower? Where have I read about them? Oh, yes—I remember!

"You want to become young again," Fillmore said.

"What are you, a reporter?"

"No, no."

"So shut up and get me one and if you do, I'll take the spell away from your pal."

"Do you have any idea where I might find a black sunflower? I hope it doesn't mean a long journey."

"Naahh, you'll find a clump of them close by."

"How do I get there? And get back?"

"I'll send you there in a jiffy, but you gotta understand something. The sunflowers are in a cave guarded by a dragon."

"Oh, terrific! Is it a friendly dragon, at least?"

Queezenok laughed, sounding like a rusty grate. "Dragons don't come in friendly and they don't come in vanilla. But this one is reasonable, that much I can tell you. He'll be curious to know how you had the guts to come anywhere near him."

"So you're saying I won't be in danger?"

"Not if he's already eaten."

"All right, so let's say he decides to let me take a sunflower. How do I get it back to you?"

She muttered what he thought must be a spell. "Here's what you do—you say my name three times. Don't do it till you're ready to return."

"OK," he nodded. "Can you send me there?"

"Bon voyage." She waved her hand and he zoomed off.

CHAPTER FIFTEEN

Riddle Me This

It certainly was a dragon and a big one at that. His scales were purple.

Fillmore introduced himself, waited for the usual reaction to his name and in the meantime hoped he would be spared the pains of being devoured.

"My name," said the dragon in a surprisingly melodious voice, "is Tandelus. Lucky for you I don't have a taste for scrawny men."

"I'll say it's lucky! Didn't you used to live in the land of Mo?"

"No, that was my brother Dandelus. They stretched him thin." He yawned. "I've been meaning to get them for that. Maybe tomorrow. Or next week. Now just what do you want?"

"I need a black sunflower. The witch Queezenok says that you have some."

"They're not for sale."

"Well, I guess that's that."

"Now hold on, youngster. I'll give you one if you're willing to hand over a nice tender maiden."

"I'm fresh out."

"Hm. Well, I have been feeling a little bored. Do you know any riddles?"

"I can probably think of some."

"Well, do it, then. We'll play us a riddle game."

Fillmore asked for particulars and learned that they would ask three riddles apiece. Tandelus said that he would go first.

"Listen up, now. Here's my first. What's young and pretty and delicious to eat?"

It was the wrong time to ask it. Fillmore knew the answer right away. "A maiden."

"That's right," the dragon said, actually looking somewhat pleased. "Now it's your turn."

The professor thought and thought. This was the same riddle game that Bilbo Baggins played against Gollum in the fifth chapter of J. R. R. Tolkien's *The Hobbit*. But he couldn't remember any of the tricky posers they'd asked each other. A riddle finally came to him.

"What doesn't know a thing about Who, What, Where or How, but is definitely the one you should consult if you need to ask When?"

"An historian!"

Fillmore was startled that the dragon was grammatically correct. "Very good, only that's not the answer."

Tandelus brooded for a while, but then said, "It's a clock."

"Right you are. End of the first round and we're tied."

"Now brace yourself for a tougher one. What can't you find unless you go outside and sometimes it'll brush against you, but you can never catch it?"

This one was indeed harder. Fillmore pondered it for over a minute. The dragon became impatient. But just then a breeze ruffled the professor's hair.

"It's the wind."

"That's it. I have to give you credit. Nobody has ever won two rounds off me. All right, now. Ask me the next one."

Fillmore held up his hand and thought. The sea and the ship he was on came to mind and that gave him what he was seeking. *But how do I phrase it? Oh, yes—I've got it!*

He smiled at Tandelus. "What's yellow and is good to eat and only costs a dollar, but is thoroughly piratical?"

The dragon frowned. "That's much too easy. Yellow? And you can it? Corn, of course."

"Yes ... but no."

"Then I must have left something out. Oh, right—it only costs a dollar. Meaning what? Is there another word for a dollar? Peso? Pound? Franc? Deutschemark? Oh, wait! It's also piratical."

Fillmore wondered how a strictly Ozzy dragon could know anything about European currency.

"I've got it!" Tandelus exulted. "A buccaneer!"

"That's it," the professor admitted, a bit ashamed at committing another pun. "Two rounds and still tied."

"Final round. Here's a good one—What never stops running, but while it does, you can't catch it and there's nothing else that you can do except grow older."

But Fillmore knew the answer immediately, for this was a variation on one of the riddles that Gollum asked Bilbo.

"The answer is Time."

"Well done! You won, boy and you're the very first who ever did. Now step into my cave and take what you came for. Snap it off as close to the ground as you can. But mind you, don't take more than one."

"One is all I need, I promise." Fillmore walked inside, saw the sunflower and picked it as he'd been instructed. He put into a bag that Queezenok supplied. When he stepped out of the cave, he saw that the dragon was kneeling.

"Climb up on my shoulders and I'll fly you wherever you need to go."

"That's very kind of you, but there's no need. Queezenok, Queezenok, Queezenok." And he evaporated.

"What on earth did he say? Was that some kind of a sneeze? Maybe that was his way of saying goodbye?"

CHAPTER SIXTEEN

A Change of Cast

Queezenok took it from him without a word of thanks. "Well," she said, "it'll be a long time before I need another sunflower. But how did you get the dragon to give you this one?"

"I tied him playing a riddle game."

"Wow! Who'd have ever thought?! Do you remember the riddles?"

"I think so."

"Then write them down for me."

"All right." He did so. "Now what about changing Pete back?"

"It's as good as done," said Queezenok. She read the riddles. "The next time I have to send someone to get me another black sunflower, he'll have an advantage with this information." She then made a cabalistic gesture and suddenly Peter was there, sound asleep on the witch's cot. A few magic words were muttered, there was a flash and there, instead of Pete, lay—a girl!

She opened her eyes. "Where am I? What am I doing here?"

"You're in my house," the witch told her. "This is Munchkin-land."

"Oh, my!" She stood. She was dressed in a blue and white pinafore. "I'm awfully hungry."

"Well, I'm not feeding you," Queezenok said.

But luckily the professor still had the basketful of auntly provisions and it was still quite full.

"Take it outside!" the witch yapped. "I don't want no crumbs."

Outside they went, but not before Fillmore said, "After we eat, we've got to go to the Emerald City. Can you send us there?"

"What'll you give me if I do?"

"I already wrote down five riddles."

"Well, that's true," she said sourly. "All right, I'll send you there."

He and the girl sat down on the blue grass and began to eat. The professor snacked, but she had a good meal. While they ate, he told her about the enchantment that the witch had just removed.

"So that's why I couldn't remember anything!"

"Yes—and I venture to guess that you are the Princess Dorothy?"

"Yes, I am!" she dimpled at him.

Just then a Munchkin farmer ambled past and surprised Fillmore by singing about making it big in Nashville.

"How did he ever hear of Nashville, I wonder? It must have something to do with the pun part of this world. Nashville, indeed and here we are in Munchkin-land. But I get it. After all, this is bluegrass country."

Dorothy looked at him, perplexed, but was too busy with the food to bother to ask.

He asked her what she remembered of Oz.

"Everything!" Dorothy happily declared. "It's the most wonderful place ever, even when it's dangerous … do you know anything about it?"

"Yes, I do. I've read all of the Royal Historian's accounts of your adventures and of others."

Her eyes grew misty. "The Royal Historian! What a dear old man he was. I know he passed on, which never happens in Oz. I wish he'd come and stayed here."

"His spirit's here, that I'm sure of," the professor said. "Have you read his books? They're wonderful."

"Oh, yes, I've read all fourteen, plus the short stories."

"Which was your favorite?"

"All of them!" She dimpled. "I know they're supposed to be histories, but I reread them just for fun. Plus I've read his others about the lands of Mo and Yew and Ix and others. I've read them all."

By now they were done eating, so Fillmore called, "Queezenok, we're ready to go."

She emerged from the hut and it was obvious that she'd already used the black sunflower.

"Queezenok!" the professor exclaimed, "you're absolutely beautiful!"

"Well, thank you," she smiled and promptly kissed him on the lips. He almost fainted. She not only kissed him, she patted his cheek and not the one just below his forehead. "Come back and see me sometime," she invited. "And now—to the Emerald City."

Fillmore gathered his basket and umbrella and wondered if he'd ever come back this way, but was sure he wouldn't.

The witch waved her hands at them. "Take them to the Emerald City and mind you set them down gently just outside the gate."

CHAPTER SEVENTEEN

Just in Time for the Party

The magic of Oz is perfect. Before they could collect their thoughts, they were catapulted into the air and touched down in front of the gate to the Emerald City.

The professor pulled the bell and a little green man looked out of a round window and before he could say it, the ringer himself said, "Who rang that bell?"

"Well, yes! Who are you and what do you want?"

"This is Princess Dorothy, who I'm sure you know and I'm J. Adrian Fillmore."

"Gad!" said the gatekeeper.

"What a name," Fillmore added. "Yes, I know."

"Well, come on in," the other said and opened the gate for them.

"I was hoping to ride the horse of a different color," the prof said.

"What in Oz are you talking about?" the gatekeeper asked.

"Hush," said Dorothy. "That's only in the movie."

"Then you've seen it! How did you like it?"

"Loved it! The songs are wonderful. I especially like 'Over the Rainbow.'" But the movie didn't have an awful lot to do with what really happened to us."

They entered the Emerald City. Fillmore's eyes grew wide with wonder. They were shown into the throne room, which was thronged and Ozma herself greeted them. Everywhere he looked, the professor saw Oz's many luminaries: the Cowardly Lion and the Hungry Tiger, the Scarecrow, Rinkitink, Tik-Tok, the Patchwork Girl, the sawhorse, Professor H. M. Wogglebug, T. E. (H. M. = highly magnified; the Wogglebug used to be ordinary sized, but then he got caught by a teacher who projected him, enlarged, onto a screen. When the room suddenly cleared of pedagogue and pupils, the wogglebug stepped down and stayed that size from then on. T. E. = thoroughly educated.), the Wizard of course and there was Glinda and standing next to her was the Tin Woodman.

"Dorothy!" the Tin Woodman shouted. "Where have you been? We'll all been worried about you!"

"Dear Nick," she replied, "I was under a spell, but I'm all right now. But you met Pete and that was me."

"Ah," the woodman said. "That's why he seemed to know me! But shush—we're about to start."

The Wizard of Oz cleared his throat. "Citizens of Oz, let us celebrate our beloved Princess's birthday!" He shot a glance at the professor and said, "It's a party, son!" He gestured and suddenly Fillmore was dressed in pantaloons cinched at the waist with a green silk sash. He had on a buttonless leather vest and about his forehead was tied a bright red bandanna. He looked like a pirate.

Everyone willingly agreed. The Wizard then delivered a few remarks that were mercifully brief and then it was time for a chorus to step forward and sing several of Oz's national songs.

The Wogglebug then delivered his prepared speech, which was not mercifully brief. Once he was done, Fillmore understood that the ceremony was concluded.

"But before we go to the dining room," said Ozma, "I notice that we have a visitor."

By now, Dorothy had taken her place by her side. She said, "That's my friend J. Adrian Fillmore."

To their credit, no one, not even the Wogglebug, said a thing.

"Your Majesty," the professor stated, "I come here with a mission."

"We will be pleased to hear it. Who is it from?"

"The Nome King."

The party mood suddenly evaporated.

"Oh," said Ozma, "you mean Kaliko."

"I'm afraid not, Princess. He's back to being steward. Ruggedo has become king of the Nomes again."

Gasps. Muttering. Imprecations.

"Now everyone be still," Ozma commanded. "How did this come about?"

He recounted how Ruggedo regained the throne. "And now I should tell you that he appointed me special ambassador to the Nomes."

"Quite amazing, sir. Well, what's the nature of your ambassadorship?"

"Before I tell you, I should explain that he has really changed. He's still surly, of course, but now he actually has agreed to the idea I proposed."

"Which is?"

"To form an alliance with the land of Oz."

That got many laughs, but Ozma shushed her people. "Bring Ruggedo here. I will talk with him."

"He's ready when you are."

A flash and a crash and there stood Ruggedo.

"What in tarnation is going on?" he yowled, but then spotted Fillmore. "Good going, lad! They're actually going to do it?"

"I'm not sure, but Princess Ozma is at least willing to talk with you."

Ruggedo, not without effort, bowed courteously to the Princess.

"Ruggedo—I should say King Ruggedo—I am willing to entertain your idea," Ozma said. "What are the terms?"

"Just that we stay friendly and out of each other's way."

"When have we ever bothered you, other than the times that you tried to attack us?"

"Yeah, yeah," the Nome nodded. "Sorry about that. Won't happen again."

"How do I know I can trust you?"

"I'm giving you a King's word, one monarch to another."

She sighed. "I suppose that will have to do. She gestured and a scroll appeared, which she signed and then passed on to Ruggedo.

He read it, then said, "You sure drew this up fast."

"Magic did it."

"Oh, yeah, well, sure." He signed it and gave it back to her.

"Just one moment." Another gesture and a second scroll appeared, which she also signed and handed to him. "We both ought to have copies."

"Good thinking!" he agreed and signed the second scroll.

"Now if that's all, are you ready to return to your kingdom and your people?"

"That I am. Ta-ta." He waved with decidedly un-Nomish good cheer. And he vanished.

"Mr. Fillmore," Ozma said, "you've been a good friend to the peoples of Oz. How may I help you? Whatever you desire, provided that it's wholesome, I promise to grant you."

He bowed to her on one knee. "I just want to go home again. No, wait! Not yet! I have to say goodbye." He stepped over to Dorothy and they hugged each other. "If you were only older, I'd want to marry you."

"Who knows?" she dimpled. "I might just say yes. But don't wait till

I'm all grown up because that will never happen in Oz."

"Yes, I know. Well, all right, I'm ready now."

And Princess Ozma sent him on his way.

EPILOGUE

"Where *have* you been?! And what have you been up to?" the Fairy Queen demanded to know.

"I'll be glad to tell you," the professor said, "but it's going to take me a little while."

"Very well. After supper."

He sat down and poured some sunflower ambrosia. Boris Frankenstein came up to him and said, "I am ever so glad to see you again, dear puissant professor."

He's never going to get that word right.

"Will you stay here now with me or will you be off again?"

"I need a rest, so I'll spend some time here, but sooner or later I'll get going somewhere."

"Where? What will you be looking for this time?"

"Romance. I've never found a woman I could spend the rest of my life with … well, I almost did just a little while ago, but she's way too young."

"So that is what you intend to look for next?" Boris looked skeptical.

"Yes. Why?"

Boris shook his head. "I don't want to be a nay-sayer, friend Fillmore, but I just don't think you're going to find her."

"Why not? Maybe I will. There are a lot of beautiful unwed princesses, for instance, if I go to a world based on fairy tales."

"True, but there are also many dangers."

"Yes, well I never seem to stay out of trouble."

"I still don't think it's going to work. I'm sure it won't happen for you. I just have this feeling …"

"But how do you know this?"

Boris shrugged. "Bit of a fey quality, I fancy."

The End of
The Incredible Umbrella in Oz.

ANNOTATIONS

This book was originally going to be called *The Nautical Umbrella*. Though it is second chronologically, it was written third.

PART ONE

On the Nonestic Ocean – the Nonestic surrounds the continent with the land of Oz at its center.

CHAPTER ONE

Dowagers shy a house and crimes; the grave butts dunce" is an elaborate pun on a sentiment fabricated from words of Shakespeare and Oscar Wilde: "Cowards die a thousand times; the brave but once."

CHAPTER TWO

Rug is the former Nome King from the Oz books. Originally his name was King Roquat the Red, but after he lost his memory in *The Emerald City of Oz*, he became Ruggedo.

The amphibian ship is another joint idea by me and my college roommate Dave Ossar.

CHAPTER SEVEN

In Jack London's novel *The Sea Wolf*, the formidable Captain Wolf Larsen only fears one man, his brother Captain Death (Deeth?) Larsen.

PART FOUR

CHAPTER ELEVEN

The giant with the hammer indeed appears in Ruggedo's kingdom.

PART FIVE

This is where Professor Harold Shea appears. He is in several books and stories by L. Sprague de Camp and Fletcher Pratt. I was fortunate to become friendly with Sprague, as he preferred to be called. He liked my Umbrella stories and said he wished that he and Pratt had done a Harold Shea story in the world of Gilbert & Sullivan. He generously gave me permission to use Shea in this book, though he wanted to read that section first. But he died before that was possible.

PART SIX

CHAPTER FIFTEEN

Vacilia is a mythical country that my college roommate Dave Ossar and I made up. We based it on a few lines from Peter Shaffer's play *Five Finger Exercise*. Shaffer generously gave me permission to refer to or quote from that source.

CHAPTER SIXTEEN

The original purple dragon appears in L. Frank Baum's *The Magical Monarch of Mo*.

THE AMOROUS UMBRELLA

This one is for my delightful in-laws, NANCY AND WAYNE PORT and their children AMY AND LOUIS—may they always be happy under the umbrella of their love for one another.

ACKNOWLEDGMENTS

An hosanna and a couple of hallelujahs for those fine fellows, onlie begetters and mavens of impeccable taste, Moshe Feder and Lou Stathis, for early brandishing the "umbrella." My seals and shibboleths art thine to command, sires!

A pair of farandoles and a tarantella for Jim Frenkel, who set the measure for the professor to tread beneath the Dell banner and three gigues for Dan Steffan's amusing illustrations in that edition.

Two art songs, a watercolor and a schottische for faithful reader Ross Clements's gadfly request for more Boris, granted herein.

A Grand Waltz is set aside on my dance card for that fresh insight into the psychology of fairy princesses and soap opera villains granted me by Ms. Louise Shaffer, a fey friend from the parallel world of "Ryan's Hope."

Lastly, but not in the least leastly, at least half a dozen tons of brotherly love and a low mass for Pat LoBrutto, who proves it's still possible for an editor to be a member of the family.

EXEGESIS

Publishers of sequential volumes (such as this) are wont to proclaim that readers need not peruse the precedent tomes to understand and (hopefully) enjoy the latest installment. It is a claim that generally is as valid as walking in during the shower murder of *Psycho*, then staying in the theatre long enough to catch up on the part of the film that was missed.

Despite this caveat, it *is* possible to embark on the amatory pursuits of Professor James Phillimore without reference to his virgin voyages in *The Incredible Umbrella*. The data requisite to comprehending the present narrative is included in the Prolegomenon, but those already acquainted with the professor and his bumbershoot may skip directly to the first part However, repeat students will be held responsible for all material included in this text.

—Marvin Kaye
Manhattan, 1979-80

PROLEGOMENON

J. Adrian Fillmore (Gad, what a name!) recently taught English literature, American drama and Shakespeare at Parker College in central Pennsylvania. He was a dour, thirtyish professor, his chief frustrations being his own name, a profound disparity of opinion with his department superior and thesis advisor and an inability to relate to the opposite sex in a manner to which he wanted to become accustomed.

One fateful day, the teacher purchased a strange object in a curio shop, "a long, heavy pole that ended in a large flounce of some silky material emblazoned with orange-and-yellow stripes on which various cabalistic symbols seemed to dance in pastel figurations. It was clearly an umbrella, but its size was rather impractical: too large for everyday use, too small for beach-basking..."

He soon learned it was really a dimensional-transfer engine. It whisked Fillmore away from his mundane academic life to a succession of "literary" worlds peopled by such colorful figures as Count Dracula, Mr. Pickwick, Sherlock Holmes and the assembled dramatis personae of nearly all the Gilbert and Sullivan operettas.

Oddly, none of the denizens of these strange worlds ever heard of the authors with whom Phillimore naturally associated them...and yet their customs hewed closely to the styles and conventions of the Writers the professor knew so well—e.g., without any awareness of Gilbert or Sullivan as aesthetic influences, the G&S world's people often broke into song that either matched or closely parodied melodies and lyrics of existing Savoyard choruses and arias. There was an unseen universal accompaniment—"Holy Tone" according to one inhabitant—and all thought Fillmore odd for *refusing* to sing.

Eventually, Fillmore learned the rationale of the umbrella's operation: it took the user to the place determined in his mind. Since Fillmore taught literature, it was inevitable he'd be deposited on alternate worlds that, in the infinity of possibilities that comprise the cosmos, happened to resemble recognizable patterns of human literary endeavor.

Sherlock Holmes himself stressed the professor's error: "Those worlds do not exist because they were written about on your original earth. Instead, the fiction with which you are familiar must consist of notions and conceptions telepathically borrowed across the barriers of the dimensions. Your artists may unwittingly tap the logical premises of parallel worlds..."

In effect, J. Adrian Fillmore (Gad!) could employ the parasol to visit virtually any place he'd ever read about. But there was a trap. His mind, professionally and professorially attuned to literary structure, found it hard to force the umbrella to transport him out of a world where danger lowered...for he had a pedantic subconscious compulsion to "finish sequences." His adventures tended to follow the shape of the plots he'd read in those literary analogues of the places he visited.

Even worse, his pre-umbrella life was reclusive and emotionally deprived. The infinitely alluring worlds of his imagination, even when dangerous, held the possibility of "subsuming" him into the base logic of that planet. He learned there was a fine line between calculated participation and total acceptance of a parallel earth's underlying tenets; the latter could permanently immure him in that world and the umbrella would not function.

Only greater self-knowledge and repeated use of the umbrella might enable Fillmore to master the device and successfully steer past the shoals of interdimensional exploration. Yet the first thing he did in his altered life-plan was to attempt to negate certain aspects of his spiritual upbringing; this Gyntian aversion from Self was characterized by the professor's changing his name to an older spelling, so that he clept himself James Phillimore.

His new persona did not alter his root personality, however and soon he became enmeshed in yet new interdimensional dangers partially brought about by his inescapable pedantry.

* * * *

During his latter flights, Phillimore met and befriended the Fran-

kenstein monster, whom he appropriately named Boris. The monster—
grateful to be rescued from the bleak fate awaiting him in Shelley's
novel—proved a loyal and useful companion. As eventual repayment
for the creature's assistance, the professor flew Boris to the Gilbert and
Sullivan world where, in typical Gilbertian fashion, the comely are often
shallow and selfish, while the ugly generally are honest, moral, mellow
and ultimately well-rewarded.

Having bestowed Boris Frankenstein (the monster insisted on adopting his father's surname) in G&S-land, James Phillimore resolved to
seek new adventures on other as-yet-unvisited planets.

PART I

Once upon a time, an adoring bevy of immortal women danced about
an enchanted glade feeding sweetmeats to a large, ungainly gentleman
named Boris. As they busied themselves in this adulatory pursuit, the
gorgeous troupe of fairies, for so they were, caroled forth sweetly...

> *Tripping hither, tripping thither,*
> *Nobody knows why or whither;*
> *We must dance and we must sing*
> *Round about our fairy ring!*

The Frankenstein monster, for that was the identity of the man they
fussed over, neither marked nor minded their lyric. All in all, he preferred
their ministrations to foraging for food amongst the less-than-friendly
Germanic peoples of his homeland; yet the discerning eye might note the
merest trace of surfeited appetite in the monster's mien, an attitude not
wholly traceable to the fairies's Arcadian fare.

On the fairies's part, there was still enormous Baroque fascination
with Boris's uncompromisingly frightful aspect and they loved him for
it, one and all.

All four-and-twenty.

* * * *

Not far from the glade an oddly-encumbered personage suddenly
appeared. It was James Phillimore, late professor of Parker College. He
was a trifle weary, but not with the exhausting adventures he'd recently
concluded; rather, his spirit bent under the burden of ennui.

"Probably just lonely," he told himself, turning his steps toward the
fairy forest where his old friend, Boris Frankenstein, made his home.
In the distance, he thought he saw the creature lolling languidly in the

middle of a circle of the sisters of Iolanthe, the fay for whom W. S. Gilbert named one of his most popular operettas.

As he drew near, he heard the pattering chorus and grumbled to himself, *Don't they ever sing anything else?*

The damsels skipped delicately about the rustic landscape, which was graced in the distance by a gentle river spanned by a rude wooden bridge. Their mincing dance eternally revolved about the reclining giant whose shriveled skin, lustrous black hair and lips of the same tone immediately proclaimed his identity to the approaching professor.

"Boris!" he called. "How are you?"

The monster looked up, recognized Phillimore and leaped happily to his feet. He ran forward and hugged the other in an embrace that nearly broke the teacher's ribs.

"Kindly modify your rapture!" he gasped. The monster released him immediately, grabbed a nosegay from the nearest naiad and proffered it to the scholar, who promptly sneezed and pushed it away. "Hay fever," he groaned, wiping his eyes and nose.

Boris beamed benignly before his benefactor.

"O peerless friend! O Mighty Phillimore, it hath been all too long sith I beheld thee in these parts. What marvels hath since passed? I perceive thou'rt not the same staid sorcerer that last I looked on!" (The monster attributed the powers of the umbrella to necromancy on the professor's part, a notion that Phillimore encouraged on the grounds that it was sound business to keep a seven-foot giant a bit in awe of one, even if the emotion was founded on sham. *Wizard-of-Oz ploy No. 1*, he thought.)

The scholar settled himself on the ground and leaned against a tree-trunk. "I suppose, Boris, that I *have* changed a little since the last time we saw one another."

"You hath said it!" saith the monster.

Phillimore's customary dull academic garb was nowhere in evidence. Instead, he wore scarlet pantaloons cinched about the waist by a green silk sash. Save for a buttonless leather vest, his hirsute chest was bare. A multicolored bandanna circled his brow. His sole remaining accoutrements were an unwieldy curved snickersnee thrust into the sash and, of course, his transdimensional parasol (whose garish hues seemed less startling at that moment, viewed as they were against the professor's new raiment).

Boris joined him on the ground. They breathed the perfumed air and Iolanthe's fey sisters flitted from one to the other, fitting nuts in their mouths, pouring drafts of nectar, offering them ambrosia in abundance, as well as pignuts, gossamer pastries and moonlight melon.

Phillimore longed for a cheesesteak loaded with onions, peppers and hot sauce and a flagon of Foster's to wash it down.

* * * *

Boris eventually asked what his friend had been doing since last he saw him.

"Ah," Phillimore sighed, filled with *acedia*, "I've been wandering the worlds and sailing up and down on them."

"From thine numerous scars, I surmise thou hadst a devil of a time." The other nodded. "Had quite a job just staying afloat" He shrugged. "I've always loved the sea and ships and thought if I had the time to pursue a nautical career, rather than an academic one, I'd be happy." He shook his head. "Oh, boy, was I wrong!"

Boris waved away a shellful of sugared raisins and airily told Leila and Fleta to flit off. Then he begged the professor to narrate the particulars of his recent adventures. "Perhaps," he reasoned, "I might detect some vital missing element which, once discovered, might enable thee to conquer thy present apathy."

Phillimore shrugged again. "Don't see what, but all right. First of all, though, do you think you could order me something a little less colorful to wear?"

Boris said a word to Iolanthe; the peri waved her wand and magically altered Phillimore's clothing to his customary gray vested suit and ascot. The professor thanked the fairy, acknowledged Boris's courtesy and began to tell his story.

* * * *

It took several hours. By the time he finished, the forest was bathed in moonlight and the weary fairies sat curled upon the sward, heads daintily cradled on their forearms like ballerinas miming sleeping swans.

Nodding sagely, Boris yawned, stretched his joints and rose, all seven feet of him. A grin widened his big lips. "O Puissant Professor," said he (unaware how Phillimore detested this particular encomium, possibly because Boris's pronunciation was shaky), "at last I can repay some doit of that boundless kindness thou hast still shown me!"

"You can?" Phillimore asked, puzzled, as he creakily got to his feet, bracing his weight against the umbrella-shaft "How?"

In reply, the monster flung his arms wide apart Phillimore flinched, afraid that Boris meant to subject him to another painfully untrammeled display of affection. But the creature merely turned and indicated with outstretched hands their rustic surroundings.

"Observe," he grunted, "the many wonders of this magical forest. Yet we have but to consider the travails of our past lives to realize that the evanescent glories of this wood are as dust without the solace of companionship."

"True," Phillimore agreed, "I *have* been too much a loner. Maybe I should have asked you along on my nautical adventures, except—"

"But nay!" Boris interrupted, amused that, for once, he was more knowing than his illustrious mentor. "Thou hast mistaken mine meaning, Noble Friend! To me, 'tis apparent that thou lackest, not friendship, but rather, distaff affiliation."

Conceding the delicate distinction, the professor pensively twisted his lips. "True, true," he murmured, "I've always been unhappy about my shyness with women."

"Then you need ask no more, Mighty Benefactor!" Boris patronizingly patted his friend's head. "But take thee another glance about this glade, Master..."

The professor regarded the voluptuous sleeping damsels with new interest. In typical Gilberdan fashion, each maiden—though a mythical sprite who mainly dined on low-cal dewdrops and polyunsaturated starlight—yet boasted the alluring proportions of a West End music hall chorine.

Phillimore carefully mulled over Boris's offer, but at last, thanking him for the generous impulse that prompted him to make it, nevertheless demurred. "I must admit, Boris, I *am* tempted...these immortal waifs are knockouts. But after all, you are virtually their husband—their sultan, anyway, so to speak. I can't intrude upon your sylvan existence, I'd be nothing more than an interloper."

"O say not so!" the creature wailed wearily. "'Tis true I am possessed of preternatural stamina, but there are limits, even for a monster! I am but one and they are four-and-twenty, not counting the Fairy Queen who, at present, mercifully is on a buying trip at the J. W. Wells supply house, London!"

Sinking onto the grass, Boris turned his watery eyes full upon the professor and beseeched him to reconsider.

"O Mighty Phillimore," he wheedled as he rested his great head on sandwiched hands, preparatory to sleep, "taketh my waifs...*please*!"

* * * *

But joy incessant palls the sense and after a few idyllically inactive weeks in Gilbertian Arcady, the professor began to feel a bit like Harold Shea stuck in Xanadu. The mild-climed glade, the caroling sprites, the insubstantial fare surfeited his jaded palate.

But the deciding circumstance was that the airy fairies treated Phillimore with the utmost respect and that was the only treat he enjoyed of them. He wondered whether they avoided him because his own mind (which always dictated the tenor of his adventures in spite of his conscious wishes) perceived Gilbertian morals in the Victorian stage tradition in which the operettas were rooted. Or maybe it was just a simple function of the world's topsy-turvy nature: to reward the unhandsome Boris and not the much handsomer (so the professor thought!) James Phillimore.

Whatever the reason, he was an honored guest, nothing more. And it didn't suit him one bit. In a kind of proud desperation, he told himself he didn't really fancy any of them, anyway. All looks, no brains! But a mocking inner voice contradicted, made him turn the matter over in his mind more than his ego wished.

The truth is, he admitted, *women never pay me much attention. I'm always thirteenth at table, Cyrano in the gloom of Roxane's garden, Sganarelle outside the bedroom-door, Lazarus at the feast.* It's easy to insist on brains, but in his heart, Phillimore knew physical comeliness was important to him. The fair that toil not, that are the product of lavish nature, not their own industry, were so agonizingly out of reach that they naturally fascinated the professor mightily.

Beyond that, though he was essentially a soured romantic, deep within he considered the Quest for the Eternal Feminine perversely appealing. He longed for Goethe's *das ewig-weibliche* with as little comprehension of the term as Peer Gynt, but still Phillimore craved Her nearly as much as he longed for a mint edition of *Dark Carnival*.

He told Boris, "I'm going, that's for sure and it has to be another world than this. The Gilbertian scheme inescapably matches physical comeliness with shallowness of character."

Boris didn't understand most of what he said, but dutifully inquired where Phillimore planned to go.

"I don't know, Boris. Some world where I can find a woman that embodies all I desire in a mate."

The monster paused to quaff some mead. "The possibilities are endless," he murmured in his cup.

"You're telling me?" Butting his back against a bole, Phillimore tapped his forefinger against his forehead. "It's all in here, Boris! Every desirable woman I've ever read about...Shakespeare's Cleopatra, Grimm's princesses, Trollope's high society coquettes...Glencora and Guinevere and Galadriel and Queen Mab (as if I didn't have enough of woodland sprites!). Don Juan might envy me, Casanova turn green with jealousy!"

"Yes, yes," said Boris, "but where will you try first?"

The professor shrugged. "I think I'll just trust to luck. Whatever is in my subconscious is what I'll go with. I'll think of The Perfect Mate and press the umbrella-catch!"

The great creature rolled his watery eyes. "It sounds rather risky to me, O Professorial Phillimore!" He glanced about the glade. "Cannot aught here stay you? The Fairy Queen, you know, has just returned from London. She has ample charms."

"Quite ample," Phillimore murmured. "No, thanks. I may crave, indeed, a fairy princess, but these ladies are a bit too ground-treading. Every time they trip about the glade, I swear they hike up their garters."

"But they don't wear any," the monster innocently confided.

Which information only further confirmed the professor in the opinion that he didn't belong in G&S-land.

* * * *

Next morning, after a brief farewell and a promise to come back and introduce Boris to his future betrothed, Phillimore betook himself to another part of the forest, where he attuned his mind to tender thoughts and delicate emotions. Then he pressed the catch of the umbrella.

It opened. A mighty wind plucked him off the ground.

Flying beyond the tinted heartwall of the pulsing universe, night screaming in his ears, the scholar did his best to concentrate solely on visions of distaff loveliness, wonder and delight...

* * * *

Without warning, the umbrella snapped shut. Phillimore dropped heavily, sprawling on a patch of grass pale in the cloaking shadow of tall, twisted trees.

clump clump clump

A sinister music filled the air, an ominous melody he recognized from *Pictures at an Exhibition,*

clump clump clump

The ground shook with the pounding tread of approaching feet. Gigantic feet...

What's wrong? He rolled over, sat up, stared into the dark forest...and gawked at a monstrous *thing* drawing steadily nearer.

Clump Clump Clump

Phillimore scrambled to his feet, horrified. He stood in a thick, wild-looking wood in which unfriendly animal eyes peeped out all about, watching him. The brush was so tangled and tall that it choked out most of the afternoon sunlight. Somewhere nearby, angry bees droned. A hoarse raven croaked from the direction of the coming catastrophe.

CLUMP CLUMP CLUMP

No use using the umbrella, it won't work till it's cooled off! He tried to move his feet, attempted to run away from the *thing* that was now hardly twenty yards distant, but his legs were transfixed by a powerful spell of staymagic.

CLUMP CLUMP CLUMP

The nightmare hurrying toward him was a great thatched hut girded round with a fence of grinning skulls. Instead of resting on the earth, the frightful little house grew out of two mighty *living* fowl-legs that resembled the clawed feet of a giant turkey or rooster.

It was these bird-feet that produced the clumping sound as they carried the bizarre hut straight towards him.

It's going to trample me to death!

But suddenly the fowl-legs halted, scant inches away from him. Out of one of the hut's windows suddenly was thrust the face of a woman with shriveled skin, baleful eyes, a big pimple-ornamented nose, few teeth, many warts and filthy gray hair combed in an untidy sweep secured by a coil of chicken-wire. She wore a frayed gray fragment of fichu around her gnarly shoulders.

Phillimore roundly cursed the umbrella. *This is what it gives me when I specify womanly beauty*?

As if in answer to his mental grumble, the crone cackled and addressed him in a raspy voice.

"Yoohoo, sonnyevitch! Have I got a girl for you!"

* * * *

Phillimore sat in a comfortable, if slightly mildewy armchair in the old woman's parlor and tried to get a word in edgewise.

It wasn't easy. She rattled on, fussing over the professor as if he were the Prodigal Hen come home to roost. Below and beneath the floorboards, the hut's fowl-feet stomped through the woods, making the tiny house pitch and tremble. But compared with the last voyage he'd taken, he was scarcely troubled by the motion.

The professor knew enough about Russian folklore to identify the witch. Her name was Baba Yaga and she was a Slavic variant of the British bogeyman or the American foolkiller; she existed chiefly to frighten willful children into better behavior. There was another detail connected with her, too, but he couldn't recall it. The thing that convinced him of her identity was the famous hut on fowl's legs itself. An essential part of the Baba Yaga legend, the strange dwelling, circled by victims's grinning skulls, constantly stalked the woods, seeking bad youngsters for the witch to capture and devour.

But I hardly fit the classification, he mused wryly. *Then why am I here*?

"Nu, sonnyevitch, put down your umbrella, it ain't raining inside! Take off your shoes, get comfortable! Maybe you're cold? I'll get you a nice *glayzala tay*..." As she spoke, she patted and prodded him fondly with bony fingers. But a sly light glinted from her one green eye.

And yet, even though he distrusted her, Phillimore rather liked the old woman: she reminded him vaguely of someone dear, he couldn't remember exactly who.

As she pottered about getting the tea ready, he scanned the surroundings with interest. It was a small single-chamber hut, with two chairs, a kitchen table and a cot comprising the principal furniture. A large iron cauldron hung over a stone fireplace, next to which was curled a chubby gray cat with yellow eyes. The animal regarded the newcomer with sour amusement. Baba Yaga stirred the cauldron once or twice, then ladled out an amber mixture which Phillimore presumed must be the tea. As he watched her tender ministrations, he suddenly realized who she reminded him of.

Can't do enough for me, wants to fix me up with a woman. Won't let me get a word in edgewise!

Wistfully, he thought about his late foster mother.

* * * *

"You know, you're different from what I would have expected," Phillimore remarked.

"How could you expect?"

"Well, you're Baba Yaga, right?"

For some reason, the witch clapped both her hands over her mouth. She waited a moment before uncovering so she could speak. "How would you know my name?" she asked somewhat nervously, but nothing happened and she exhaled with apparent relief.

*What's wrong with her? Something to do with...*But Phillimore couldn't bring it to mind.

"I said, how do you know who I am?"

"Sometimes," he said, "I'm a bit fey. Anyway, I've heard stories about Baba Yaga. All about how you eat up wicked children."

"Ho-boy!" she snorted, with a disgusted sweep of her hand. "I knew I never should have accepted that retainer!"

"I don't understand."

"Whole bunch local peasants commission me to keep the brats in line. I ride around the forest scaring the crap out of the little darlingskis."

"Then you don't actually eat them?"

Again she startled Phillimore by clapping both her hands over her mouth. Then, finger by finger, she pried them away and replied circumlocutiously, "I'm not saying I eat kids, I'm not saying I don't, sonny-evitch—all I'm saying is there's a lot of PR connected with this kid-scaring sideline I've got and if you want to believe one way or the other, how can I say the opposite?" But she slapped one hand against her cheek and rocked her head and moaned, half to herself, "Oy vey! The things a old lady's gotta put up with!" She gave him an affronted squinty glare and waggled a thin finger at him. "I'm not saying what I do or don't do, mine little guestnik, but this I'll say: eating kids is feh! Take my word for it or don't!"

With that, she dismissed the subject and poured the tea into a somewhat chipped crystal tumbler. She handed it to Phillimore. He raised it to his lips, feeling the warmth of the brew through the glass. But before taking a sip, he stopped and stared at the fat feline in the corner.

Its mouth turned down in disgusted disapproval and it slowly and emphatically shook its shaggy head.

Baba Yaga caught the movement from the side of her eye. She swiveled around angrily and shouted at the cat "Don't be a buttinski, Rimski! Go catch mice!"

"Hmph," the cat sniffed disparagingly, "if *you* don't eat kiddies, Babaleh, then I don't eat mice." He yawned, then licked his paws in lordly fashion.

The witch made an indignant appeal to the professor.

"I ask you, where today is it possible to find good help?"

Phillimore's eyes goggled from his head. "But the cat talked!"

"Such a miracle?" she sneered. "It would be more amazing, sonny-evitch, if only he knew when to shut up!"

Rimski shrugged. "So, all right, I'm bothering you. So I'll go out." And the cat vanished.

* * * *

The teacher recovered his wits with difficulty. His trembling hands spilled some tea as he set down the tumbler. A drop or two splashed on the floor and killed a pair of amorous cockroaches.

"You're nervous, dollink?" Baba Yaga inquired solicitously. "Sip a little tay, it'll put you to sleep."

"I'll *bet* it will."

"Maybe you think I'm from poisoning guests? *Feh*! In such business is no profit, take my word from it!"

"You're telling me this is just a sleeping potion?"

"Would I give you something that wouldn't be good for you?" Baba Yaga asked, carefully countering his question with a question.

Some detail of the Baba Yaga legend kept niggling at Phillimore's mind. A little more concentration and he'd have it. *Something to do with questions...*

"All I wanted is to make my little guesteleh nice and comfy, so I figured you'd be happy if you could gaien shlafen for a while and—"

"And then," interrupted Rimski's bored voice from midair, "she'd zap you with a geas."

"Hoo-boy, am I gonna give it to you, cat!" she shrilled, leaping to her feet. "If I ever catch you, I'll turn you into a tax collector!"

The awful threat didn't faze the invisible Rimski. "In that case," he meowed, "I'll make sure you don't catch me."

Turning back to Phillimore, the old biddy flashed him a sycophantically ingratiating smile, but he was on his feet, umbrella in hand, ready to push the catch and escape. His thumb joggled against the button as the hut on fowl legs clumped over some particularly rocky terrain below.

"So that's what you're up to," the professor accused. "Magic spells so I'd have to do whatever you will me to perform!"

"We-e-ell," she wheedled, "I was going to ask you a little favor, but I have to be careful, see? Anytime—"

"Why fool around with magic when you could just ask?"

"NO QUESTIONS!" she yelled, startling Phillimore. "DON'T ASK ME QUESTIONS!"

"Look," he snapped, "I've had about enough of this mystification. Why don't you tell me what you want?"

Baba Yaga's face went white. A fearful curse escaped her lips and she began stumping around the room and venting her temper on the scant furnishings. She kicked over a rush-broom, pounded the table and smashed a sugar bowl, whirled three times on her left toe and spat in the teakettle.

Wonder how often she does that? He was doubly glad he didn't drink any.

"OOOHHH!" Baba Yaga howled, wringing her wrinkled hands, "now you've *done* it!"

"Done *what*?"

His second question provoked an even louder yowl. She bashed her head against the fireplace in frustration, then, in a paroxysm of rage, ripped a bag of dried bear-snouts out of an herb-box and scattered them wildly about the room. "STOP WITH THE QUESTIONS!" she screamed, then suddenly threw herself into a cane-bottom chair and began to sob.

Feeling sorry for her without knowing why, he patted her shoulder and asked what was wrong. But that made her shriek again and knock his hand away.

"Now it's three *unavoidable* questions! Idiot! SHUT UP!" She tore her hair in rage and despair. "A year a question! Now I'll lose three years because you can't stop with the *dumke* questions...and *that's* what's wrong, Shlubya!"

No sooner were the words out of her mouth than she began shaking so violently that she flopped off her chair and banged her pimply proboscis on the unplaned planks of the rustic flooring. As she flailed about, Phillimore remembered the missing piece of the Baba Yaga myth.

After quite some time, she quieted and feebly crept back to her seat. The furrows in her forehead were etched deeper than before and the sparkle in her single blue eye had perceptibly dimmed.

"Nu," she wheezed, "ain't you gonna wish me happy birthday?"

He did.

"That," the witch gasped, "is what happens when I have to answer a question. I age twelve months in a minute...and *that's* what you've done, shmendrick!"

As soon as she said it, she was seized by another convulsion, exactly like the first. It tossed her about for precisely sixty seconds and so enfeebled her that, when it was over, Phillimore had to help her hobble over to the bug-infested pallet by the far wall of the hut.

"A picnic it ain't," she complained. "Whenever I get a visitor, sooner or later some question pops out that I can't avoid answering and then *wham-bam*!" She exhaled shakily. "*Gevalt*, I ain't as young as I used to be!"

He nodded. "Then I assume that's why you were going to knock me out and fix a quest-spell on me. That way I'd go do your bidding without asking questions."

"Is that"—she glared suspiciously—"another question?"

"No, it's an assumption."

"Good," she murmured, plopping her head on her pillow, "assume all you want, sonnyevitch."

She lay still for quite a while. Finally, the professor suggested it was about time she explained what she wanted him to do.

"Not now," she demurred, "that would answer your third question and I ain't up yet to another four seasons. Let me rest a while. Instead, you should tell me about yourself. Like how come a big *boytchik* like yourself walks in the forest with an umbrella but no galoshes?"

To pass the time, he spoke about his adventures in various worlds and told Baba Yaga all he knew of his umbrella's peculiar properties. She looked so feeble lying there he could see no harm in being totally honest.

It was a serious tactical error.

* * * *

The hut stood motionless in the middle of a moonlit clearing. Every so often, one or the other of its bird-feet lifted to scratch an itch on the opposite leg. Trotting around the side of the shack, Baba Yaga stuck two shriveled fingers in the corners of her mouth and vented an ear-splitting whistle.

"That," she cackled, "will fetch Walter, right enough. Wait, sonny-evitch, he'll be here in a couple minutes."

Out of deference to her penchant for instant chronology, Phillimore refrained from asking who or what Walter might be. *Just hope it's nothing too gruesome.*

The professor was ready to start out on the witch's quest, or at least to make a great show of doing so for her sake. He was tired of her company and especially of the sour chicken-fat odor of her hut. But his main reason for wanting to get away from her (and any spells she might have the power to cast should he seem recalcitrant to her wishes) was that he intended to escape her world entirely. *The umbrella can do better than Russian fairy-tales!* Other than Baba Yaga, he knew practically nothing of Slavic myth; the only reason her tale was vaguely familiar to the professor was because of his lifelong interest in fantasy-horror literature.

* * * *

Earlier, after Baba Yaga somewhat recovered from two years of on-the-spot aging, she offered him supper and a blanket for the night. Fearing the first (though perhaps not so much as the second), Phillimore politely declined. To spare her feelings (on the grounds that it was poor policy to wound a witch's vanity), he expressed a keen desire to set out right away on her errand.

"How come suddenly you got *shpilkes*?" she wondered, squinting at him suspiciously. "I ain't even said yet what my favor is."

"I'm in a generous mood. I can't refuse you anything."

"You just did." She sighed. "However, health comes foremost and I can't wait too much longer to drink the magic elixir. Another year or two could kill me!"

He began to ask what she meant by a magic elixir, but hardly were his lips open than she angrily gestured for silence. "Clamp a lid on it, blabbermouth! I'm *telling*, I'm *telling*!"

"Sorry, I forgot. But it's hard to restrain curiosity."

"Oh, is it?" she asked sweetly. "Would it help if I turned you into a tarantula?"

"That's all right," he gulped, "very kind of you, but I think I can manage from now on."

"Go-oo-ood, sonnyevitch, go-oo-ood," Baba Yaga crooned, "now give a listen—there ain't no way I can stop myself from growing a year older when I answer questions, that's in my original contract. However, my agent managed a kind of escape clause so's I can backtrack and get young again. I have to whomp up a drink made outta falernum, pig-sweat, slivovitz and black sunflower, put in a blender and run ten seconds at Mix—*yah, yah, I see you dying to ask, I got blenders, I'm a witch, ain't I?*—and serve stirred, not shaken, on the rocks. After I swig it down, I drop couple hundred years maybe and believe me, is that a *machaiya!*"

"I suppose," said Phillimore, "it's impossible to home-grow these black sunflowers."

"Was that a question?" she yelped, reaching for a book with the ominous title, *Wells's Magic and Spells: Blessings, Curses, Ever-Fitted Purses, Prophecies, Witches, Knells.*

"A supposition, only a supposition!"

"It better be, buster!" she snarled, replacing the tome. "Now *the* black sunflower grows on a certain enchanted island. One at a time, see? It gets picked and then another grows a long, long time later." She paused fearfully, but evidently Phillimore's last remark was credited as a mere supposition, so nothing happened to the witch. Heartened by her escape, she continued with greater enthusiasm.

"Okay, sonnyevitch, now pay attention 'cause soon is coming the part you're gonna like! On this enchanted island lives the prettiest, sweetest, purest, most innocent young lady you'd ever want to meet! A real *zoftich maidele* and *stacked* like you wouldn't believe! Over there is a magazine, pick it up and flip, you'll see!"

Phillimore plucked a tattered copy of *Necromantic Age* out of a small pile of tidily-arranged soot. It was evidently a trade magazine for sorcerers, warlocks, witches and other magical practitioners. The issue evidently had been bent back many times to a certain page, for when he picked it up, it fell open to a colorful spread of photos and text that told about an unusual spell of staymagic holding a young woman (simply identified as the Beautiful Child) on an unnamed verdant isle, latitude and longitude unknown. He noted with vague disquiet that certain passages of the article's text had been blacked over so they were totally illegible. And at the bottom right of the right-hand page he saw a picture had been torn out of the periodical. *No point asking her about it, she'll get mad and won't tell me, anyway.*

"Nu, sonnyevitch," she grinned, "some knockers, hah? If Mama Yaga was just telling, you wouldn't be believing, but there you are, the magazine is showing, so now get ready to go fetch me that black sunflower and when you bring it back, the broad should come, too, and

I'll fix it up permanent between the two of you! Now excuse me for one minute, I just answered your remaining question and—HOO—BOYYYYYYYYYYYYYYYYYYYYYYYYYY!!!"

While she quivered and quaked, Phillimore tried to decide what was niggling away at the back of his brain that made him so uneasy about the enchanted island. The thought would not come, *but it doesn't really matter, anyhow, because I'm not going in the first place.*

At least, having seen the picture of the damsel on the isle, he had to admit the umbrella *had* been trying to do its job right, after all.

* * * *

The witch, having gotten back her breath, told the professor she had a friend named Walter who'd be of immense help on his journey. Before he could protest that he preferred traveling alone, Phillimore suddenly was hurtled across the room where he landed head-downwards in a barrelful of rancid pickle-brine. This circumstance was the direct result of the crone's abruptly ordering her hut to come to a screeching halt.

Phillimore extricated himself with considerable spluttering from the gherkin-juice. Before he could recover his wits, Baba Yaga whirled him merrily around by both hands in a grotesque peasant dance, then yanked him outside the door, down the steps and into the summery gloom of the deep woods.

* * * *

She whistled a second time. From somewhere in the midst of the trees, not too far away, came a cross bass voice.

"I'm coming as fast I can, you old bone-sack! Contain your urine! I'm not a bagpipe!"

Recognizing the Shakespearean allusion, Phillimore strained his eyes to see the speaker, but the moonlight did not illuminate the depth of the forest. He did not have to wait long, though. Soon, to his ears there came the muted *clip clop* of hooves. Out of the night suddenly cantered the most remarkable creature the professor had seen in quite some time.

It was a lean, sinewy stallion with mournful red eyes and a dour expression that twisted its large muzzle sideways, giving it the appearance of one about to spit in disgust. The most unusual thing about the riderless creature was its coat; it glowed bright pink in the rays of the waxing moon.

"Walter," said the witch, "I want you should meet a friend of mine."

"Pfui," Walter rumbled in his raspy, deep voice, "any friend of yours is bound to be a real *zhlub*." He regarded Phillimore darkly. "What're you gawking at, shorty?"

"You're pink!"

Curling his lip contemptuously, Walter complimented the professor on his perspicacity. "If pink is good enough for elephants, then how come you object to the way I look?"

"I don't object," the man soothed the animal. "I just never saw such a hue on a horse before."

"Damn right I'm hoarse," Walter growled and lapsed into contemplative silence.

* * * *

"Walter here will be your noble charger," Baba Yaga informed the professor. "He can read road-maps good and on his back, you'll make better time, too."

Walter snorted at the last notion, but said nothing.

"But I don't need to ride," Phillimore reasoned, "I can fly wherever I want to go with my umbrella." He started towards the hut "I'll be just a minute, I left it inside."

He didn't notice the witch make a certain hand-signal behind his back, but he immediately observed that as soon as he approached the hut, its two clawed legs began to hobble towards the forest. Phillimore stopped. The hut stopped. He sprinted forward three steps. It trotted backwards the same distance. He sidled sideways. It edged laterally, but in the opposite direction.

Disgusted, he turned to the witch. "Ask your skittish house to stand still!"

Smiling a broad, unpleasant grin, she apologized for the hut's recalcitrance. "What can an old lady do with a dumke chicken without a head? I'll he lucky to get back in it myself!"

"But I have to get my umbrella!"

"Not with Walter handy." She bowed and ducked her head in conciliatory fashion. "Nu, you shouldn't worry, sonnyevitch, Mama Yaga will take good care of your umbrella *till you come back with the black sunflower.*"

Phillimore got the point. He sighed, defeated. "It won't work for you, you know. It's imprinted with my brain-set and won't operate for anyone else."

She looked positively scandalized. "Are you accusing that I would touch your crummy umbrella? Since when have I given you cause to make such nasty thinkings?"

"Two questions," the teacher snapped. "Why don't you answer them yourself!?" He turned away, thoroughly disgruntled with his own stupidity, with the witch's duplicity, with Boris's original suggestion that he seek The Perfect Mate and finally, as always, with the unpredictable caprices of the umbrella itself. "Come on, Walter," he glumly grumbled, "let's go."

"Okay," the stallion snorted, "but if you climb up on me, I'll dump you in a cesspool!"

Oh, boy, Phillimore mused silently, *some quest this is going to be*! With a resigned shrug, he followed Walter out of the clearing.

Immediately, the hut pranced over to Baba Yaga, paused while its mistress entered, then resumed its customary sylvan perambulations.

* * * *

Man and beast trudged along a broad path that cut, with few twists, through the forest. The foliage was thick, too tangled to permit much light to penetrate, yet here and there a pallid patch shone with surprising distinctness in the irregular illumination of the wistful moon.

Walter knew the trail well, but Phillimore often stumbled over unexpected stumps and stones. The horse did his best to endure it patiently, but when the other tripped and landed rather heavily against his flank, Walter neighed nastily, "Pick up your feet, klutz!"

"Sorry. I lost my footing."

"*Do* tell!" the animal grumped in his gravelly bass. "If I'd known how clumsy you are, I would've borrowed Baba's firebird so you could see where you put your feet."

"I'll attempt to be more careful," Phillimore said rather stiffly.

Walter disdainfully shook his mane. "Thanks for trying, shorty, but you'll probably break your neck long before you reach the island." Beneath his breath, the horse mumbled, "Which'll probably be more pleasant, anyhow."

Phillimore caught it. *Uh-oh.* A too-familiar chill tickled an arpeggio along the length of his backbone, an unwelcome sensation frequently experienced on umbrella-jaunts. "Suddenly," he addressed the horse, "I have a feeling this errand isn't quite as easy as Baba described it." Lustily clearing his hoarse throat, Walter tried to change the subject. "You commented on my scratchy voice before. Wanna know how I got this way?"

"Not particularly."

"Cigar-smoking."

"You smoke cigars?!"

"Naw, a toad I once knew, when I used to hang around the swamp, was always puffing away. Said he was a congersman."

"The word is *congressman*," Phillimore punctiliously emended, but with little real interest. "And would you like a ladder to get down off this story?"

"It's true," said the horse. "And that's the way *he* pronounced the word. Anyway, he was always blowing cheap smoke in my face. Y'see, sometimes I used to let 'im ride on my neck and I think that's when I developed this chronic hoarseness. I must've been allergic to his stinking stogies."

"Serves you right for not taking care of the frog on your throat," the professor replied. "Now stop avoiding my question. You won't discourage me about this quest...I *have* to get back my umbrella! But at least you might prepare me for what I'm going to run into on that rotten island."

"How should I know? I never set hoof there."

"You haven't?"

"Nope. I only take you as far as the final boat. I'll hang around on the shore for a few days and if you don't come back, I'll tell Baba you screwed up, too."

"*Too?*"

"You bet your borscht-belt. Whaddaya think, you're the first sap she's suckered on this gig? In the old days, there was nothing to it, I'd escort her errand-boys or girls back and forth, but ever since the island got magicked, it's been strictly a one-way trip for them." He licked his great lips with a light-pink tongue. "Sorry, but you wanted the truth."

"Thanks," Phillimore glumly replied. "Now I know the worst."

"That all depends," said Walter, "on how you feel about Hessians."

"*What?*" Phillimore shook his head, thinking he'd heard incorrectly. "Did you say *Hessians?*"

"You repeat like a radish," the horse replied dourly. "Actually, it's just one Hessian, but he's behind us. You'd better get a move on." Phillimore looked around to see what Walter was talking about. There on the trail several yards further back but slowly approaching was a coal-black charger on which was mounted a tall, dark-caped figure with a vaguely military air about him. The professor thought he spied the glint of dress-uniform brass buttons and braid, but he couldn't be positive, it was too dark.

"Who *is* he, Walter? Why's he following us?"

"Not us, buster, just you. He occasionally shows up on this road around this time of night. He'll disappear once he reaches the bridge a little way ahead."

The mention of the bridge caused an unpleasant thought to pop into Phillimore's mind. Glancing back again, he studied the rider more closely. The Hessian plodded along at an easy gait, but though his horse paced unhurriedly, still it steadily diminished the distance between mounted horseman and horse and man on foot. Suddenly the soldier cantered into a sickly pool of moonlight and in that instant Phillimore got his first clear glimpse of his pursuer.

Just as he'd feared, the gigantic, cloak-muffled man had no head above the stiff, high circle of his collar. But on his saddle-pommel he balanced a grisly object that the professor did not care to inspect too carefully.

Walter confided, "He's got an incurable hankering for other people's craniums. I don't know if he's looking for his own head, or just one that fits."

"He has a head already," Phillimore whispered weakly.

"Yeah, but as soon as he gets a new one, he'll throw the old model away."

The professor swallowed with difficulty. "Uh, how far ahead is that bridge?"

"From here? Maybe eight hundred meters."

"That far?" Calculating quickly, he groaned, "That's almost half-a-mile!"

The horse nodded. "Better shake a leg, shorty."

"Uh...I don't suppose you'd change your mind about letting me ride on you, just for a little while?"

The pink steed snorted, refusing to dignify the question with any further reply.

"I didn't think so," Phillimore sighed, then, taking a deep breath, started off at a sprint. He called over his shoulder to Walter, "See you at the bridge!"

"If you make it," the horse observed darkly.

As soon as the professor began to run, the ghostly horseman lightly touched spurs to his charger and his midnight stallion quickened its pace.

* * * *

While Phillimore scrambled and stumbled along the path, he wondered what the hell the Headless Horseman was doing in Russia. *Sleepy Hollow is in upstate New York! Maybe—*

But there wasn't time to calmly contemplate the implication. He jogged on as fast as he could safely manage without tripping over roots, rocks or other impedimenta.

He shot a brief glance backwards. The spectral horse trotted along silently, little by little closing the gap. *Perhaps he's a sportsman*, Phillimore thought, noticing that the Hessian had not yet urged his steed to its swiftest gait. Beneath the professor's speeding feet, the dry leaves crackled, the only sound in the deep woods.

Or is it?

Maybe it was the strangeness of the surroundings, or the ghastly nature of his pursuer, but Phillimore began to imagine he heard the soft subtle sound of something running alongside him on the forest trail. He couldn't be sure; it was only a faint rustle, yet it seemed slightly out of phase with his own hurrying footsteps.

"Dammit!" he gasped. "IS there something running beside me?' He muttered sourly, "My luck, it's The Damned Thing!"

"I *beg* your pardon!" said an affronted voice practically beneath his feet. It so startled the professor that he broke stride, stubbed his toe, yelped and sprawled flat on his face.

"Hmph," a voice he'd heard before sniffed. "Better get up before the dummy grabs you."

Shoving himself quickly to his knees, Phillimore stared fearfully back down the path. The horseman was now only some fifty feet distant. As he watched, he saw him draw a long saber that glinted dangerously in a vagrant shaft of lunar light.

"Get *up*, goofball!" the voice urged. "Follow me!"

"Are you kidding?" the professor protested, rising. "I can't even see you."

"Oh, yeah, I forgot...sorry!" With that, Baba Yaga's large gray cat, Rimski, instantly materialized. "Now stay close behind." He padded across the road and ducked through a gap between two distressingly conspicuous maple trees.

However, inasmuch as the Headless Horseman was by now a scant thirty feet away and (b) it was Rimski who stopped the professor from swigging the witch's hypnotic and (3) he could see no other hope for escape, anyway, Phillimore decided to trust the feline. He ran between the maples and hurried over to the place where the cat's eyes glinted in the gloom.

"Let him ride past," the cat whispered. "He will."

Phillimore was skeptical, but he did his best to hold his breath, which wasn't easy, since he'd been running. Still, he forced himself to avoid twitching a single muscle. Soon, to his astonishment, the phantom reached the place where he'd left the road, but neither slackened pace nor even glanced in the direction of the unmistakable lofty maples.

"How'd you know he wouldn't—" Phillimore began, but the cat hissed for silence.

"He's dumb, but not deaf," Rimski whispered.

They waited a good two or three minutes before the cat spoke again. "That'll take care of him for the night. Pretty soon he'll be at the bridge."

"How'd you know he'd do that?"

"He's as dim-witted as a rhino. By the time he got to the spot, he forgot you even existed. No brains at all."

"You mean because he doesn't have a head?"

"I mean because he's a Hessian." The cat stretched and yawned. "I hope you don't mind that I've been following you and Walter all this time."

"I'm glad you did!" said Phillimore. "Would you mind, though, if I asked you a few questions?"

"Not at all," Rimski meowed importantly.

"First off, how'd you learn to disappear like that?"

"Pretty flashy, huh?" The cat was obviously proud of his talent.

"Did Baba Yaga bestow the power on you?"

"Hmph!" Rimski grunted. "From that old biddy I don't get bupkis! Naah, I picked up the trick a couple years back from an English cat I met on vacation."

"An *English* cat?" Phillimore smiled. "Was he, by any chance, from Cheshire?"

"As a matter of fact, he was. You know him?"

"No, but I've heard of him. He vanishes and just leaves his smile behind, right?"

"Yeah," Rimski drawled disapprovingly, "he pulls that sometimes. Cheap trick, if you ask me."

Sour grapes, perhaps? Phillimore tried wheedling the cat. "I've always wondered about it, though. I mean, how can one see a grin without also seeing at least part of the cat behind it?"

"Wonder away, professor, you'll never catch me doing it."

"Why not?"

"Around here," Rimski said scornfully, "what's there to smile about? *Next question*?"

* * * *

Sitting down to rest, Phillimore asked the cat how it had been possible for the Headless Horseman to see him in the first place. "Does he use the eyes of the head he carries?"

"I doubt that," the cat said, after mulling it over for a moment. "Allowing for the possible piecemeal survival of the victim's spirit and assuming that same geist, so to speak, chooses to hang around its separated head, still it's very unlikely it would allow its appropriated orbs to do service to the predator who stole the head in the first place. No, no," the cat meowed mellowly, "I would postulate that the horseman sees with astral optics."

"You appear to be something of a philosopher," the professor remarked, impressed.

"Thanks for noticing," said Rimski, gratefully rubbing himself against the man's legs. "That's what I once was."

"I don't follow."

"You see before you the transmogrification of a fledgling philosopher. But though my thoughts pursue their arcane windings as before, I cannot write them down since Baba klopped me with a spell."

"You mean she changed you into a cat?"

"Precisely. Which is how I can speculate with authority on the behavior of victims of the supernormal."

"What did you do to provoke her?"

"It's what I *didn't* do," the cat purred.

"Namely?"

"I wouldn't go fetch her a sunflower."

"If that's so," Phillimore asked, "why are you here with me? Change your mind?"

"Hardly. It's just that it's safer than hanging around the hut. Baba threatened she'd change me back into a tax collector."

"*Back* into? I thought you said you were a philosopher!"

"Avocationally. Who can make with the venns and zens and earn a living?"

"Well," Phillimore mused, "in the world I originally came from, there was sometimes a lot of money to be made playing guru or pragmatic philosopher. There was even a foreign businessman who made a fortune by persuading teenagers to attain inner peace by relinquishing all their personal property to him."

The cat chortled. "And I thought *this* place is loony!"

"I'm still confused, though, Rimski. If you used to be a tax collector until Baba Yaga turned you into a cat, then why would you run away now that she wants to remove the spell?"

"Because," the animal sighed, "*she* knows and I know that, compared with collecting taxes, it's not *so* bad being a cat."

"Why do you emphasize *so*?"

Rimski shrugged. "Catting has its drawbacks, like any other line."

"Such as?"

"The worst part," he replied, grimacing, "is trying to acquire a taste for mice."

Despite the unappetizing lead-in, Phillimore realized that he hadn't eaten in several hours. He mentioned it to the cat. "Okay, I know a house where you can mooch some dinner," Rimski said. "It's a little out of the way, but eventually we'll get back to the bridge. Are you game?"

"Yes."

"Then follow me." The cat started over a nearby knoll. It led to a narrow path that paralleled the road, but with frequent detours and round-abouts. The professor did his best to keep Rimski in view, but it was dark and he often lost sight of him. However, the considerate feline soon sensed the other's confusion and made sure to turn around every so often so Phillimore could catch the yellow glimmer of his eyes.

They wove a twisted circuit for perhaps a quarter of an hour. Then, spying a tiny cottage a little way off nestling snugly in a dim dingle, Phillimore hailed the cat. Rimski loped over to him. "Better not stick around here," he warned. "This is a very popular neck of the woods for all sorts of mischief."

"But that house over there...I thought that might be where you were taking me."

"Normally I would," the cat said, "but tonight, it's bad timing. The place we want is right next to the road, three rises from now."

"What do you mean by bad timing?"

The cat flicked his tail in the direction of the cottage. "The owner's kind of grumpy, he just got burgled this morning. It's not a good time to ask him for charity."

"Burgled?" The professor repeated the word, surprised; somehow he always associated that crime with city dwellers on the idyllically distorted assumption that the country is the last outpost of a more innocent civilization.

"It's no big deal," the cat explained with a yawn. "While the family was out, some snotty kid busted in, broke some furniture, ate up their kid's food, then, to top it off, clumps all over the bedspreads with muddy boots yet. Now I *ask* you—what's happening to good old respect for private property?" He paused for an answer but Phillimore, to Rimski's surprise and annoyance, just stood there, eyes wide and mouth half-agape. "Professor," he mewed with some pique, "haven't you been listening to me at all?"

"What? Oh, *yes*! Yes, I have—I'm sorry! It's just that while you were talking, an idea I've been chasing around in my head for almost an hour finally surfaced. Your tale made it happen."

"It *did*?" Rimski stared suspiciously at his nether member.

"Listen, were you still in the room when I told the witch about my umbrella?"

"Yes. Invisible and listening."

"Did you believe what I said?" Phillimore asked.

"Once you've tasted Baba's cooking, anything is possible," he replied with a shudder.

"All right, Rimski. Now since you're a philosopher, I doubt that you'll have any difficulty countenancing the preternatural implications of what I'm about to explain—" But before the professor could utter another word, the cat emitted a hair-raising shriek.

Phillimore shrugged, somewhat nonplussed. "Well, of course, if metaphysics upsets you, I wouldn't think—"

"*Noodnick!*" the cat snapped, leaping up. "Somebody just stepped on my tail!"

Jumping to his feet, the professor looked around, but all he could see was the night-shadowed forest...then, without preamble or permission requested, countless dainty hands suddenly reached out of the darkness and seized him.

Drums rumbled. Trumpets blared. A brilliant burst of light sprang up all around, dazzling the professor's eyes and totally confusing him. The woods rang with merry laughter, sparkling but heartless.

* * * *

The music rollicked and swelled. Phillimore was swirled about so swiftly that he was powerless to resist. Coronets shined and flashing diadems twinkled past while he was delicately compelled to quickstep all about the green. In the midst of the melee, he thought he caught the hilarious roar and spoor of a wild good-humored beast cavorting nearby, but could not possibly stop to study the source.

When the tempo accelerated, something quite remarkable happened. Perhaps it was the kinesthetic consequence of his exertions and exploits of the past few hours, but suddenly the professor no longer required the press of soft, insistent fingers to speed him along; Terpsichore possessed him and he gave himself over to the fury of the dance.

Whirling and leaping, Phillimore spun in madcap pirouettes that decidedly out-dervished the surrounding stately mincing that his captors affected. As for those other dancers, they paused, two at a time, to mark the unexpected prodigy until, at length, only one reveler remained beside the professor to tread the measure. Sensing one another's proximity, the pair logically veered into each other's arms—and Phillimore found himself swaying cheek to jowl with a great sharp-toothed grinning lion.

And yet the frantic music carried him beyond logic; clutching the beast's golden mane and accepting its proffered upheld paw, off he stepped with redoubled vigor, dipping, dodging and delving a two-step up and down the sward. Now here, now there, the odd carousers swung with the spirit of the mirthful melody and all the world was a meld of verdant scenery whose hues bled one into another while merry watching eyes glinted and laughter mocked a counterpoint unminded by man and beast as the two, panting and sweating, scampered the precipice of a *prestissimo tutti* that blurred them to a wash of tawny tweed.

But then, too soon it seemed, the hidden consort of tympani and brass trembled on the brink of the penultimate tonic, quavered a last reluctant ritard before plunging, dead, into the gleeful final ejaculation of the crashing dominant chord that concluded the dithyrambic dance.

Tottering for an instant on the tips of his toes, the breathless professor toppled in temporary collapse beside the crumpled lion on the turf.

* * * *

"*Bravo!*" shouted a single enthusiastic voice. The rest of the assemblage mingled polite condescending comments with a smattering of indifferent applause, then lost interest in the winded professor and his tired feline companion.

At length, Phillimore sat up groggily and surveyed his surroundings. He was surprised to find he sat just within the mouth of an immense cavern, the nature of which he'd never seen before, although he was a moderately enthusiastic amateur spelunker. Though above his head there loomed a great overhang of rock that served as the outer lip of the subterranean landscape, the ground resembled no cave he'd ever known. Instead of stone, he rested on a rolling short-cropped lea dotted with leafy orchards bearing gold and silver fruit. Nearby, a castle sported pastel pennants above the meadow; from it had proceeded the martial din and blare of the kettles and horns. A river running beside the grassy lawn spilled from the cave into the exterior wood where deep night still held sway.

Looking out into the forest, Phillimore saw an old bridge that spanned the stream. He presumed it was the one mentioned by Walter the hoarse, but there was no pale-scarlet stallion standing there waiting for the professor.

Rats! the professor grumbled to himself, glancing about in vain for his philosophic friend, Rimski, *the cat vanished and now I'm also damn well minus pink Walter!*

Musing on Rimski reminded Phillimore that he still shared a potentially imprudent proximity with another kind of cat. He began to rise, but the lion, emitting a deep bass purr, put a paw on his shoulder and effectively restrained the professor from getting up.

"All right, all right," Phillimore nervously soothed the beast, "don't worry, I'm not going anywhere!"

The lion's cold, wet nose nuzzled him. It was not a delicious tactile sensation, but the professor did his best to tolerate it He had no desire to hurt the lion's feelings. *Wouldn't want it to be mutual.*

Just then, a man approached, the same who shouted so enthusiastically in favor of their recent choreographic display. Though Phillimore guessed him to be in his middle years, his boyish smile made him appear younger. He was of medium height with curly dark abundant hair and wore nothing but a gray toga draped loosely about his spare body and flung carelessly over one arm. His feet were bare.

Patting the big beast's head, the newcomer reassured the professor that the lion would not injure him. "He's usually harmless."

"*Usually?*"

"He doesn't hurt those he likes...and he seems to have taken quite a fancy to you." He lowered his voice. "That may prove beneficial, considering the circumstances..."

"What do you mean?" the professor asked, alarmed. "*What* circumstances?" He sprang smartly to his feet, a feat accomplishable by virtue of the fact that the lion was temporarily transferring his affection to the second man.

"I am alluding to our hosts," said the man in the toga, indicating the other dancers, who, between sets, milled about tables laden with provender, pastries and pale punch. "They have rather a peculiar attitude toward strangers."

"Their attitude is certainly peremptory," Phillimore sourly stated, eying the company distastefully.

The group was composed of a dozen dazzling damsels dressed in pastel tutus, flesh-colored tights and slippers studded with gems, as well as a like number of sleek-haired young men in burnished military garb replete with gold braid and brass buttons. Both sexes sported jeweled circlets on their brows, indicative of their noble caste.

Hmph! Phillimore sniffed silently. *Looks like a stranded touring ballet troupe and a second-string male chorus from* The Student Prince *about to team up and perform* The Black Crook *to earn fare home*!

While Phillimore watched the fairy princes and princesses, they in turn cast covert glances in his direction. He sensed their sly disapproval. *Far from friendly.*

"While you remain here," said the lion's confidant, "I don't think you're in any immediate danger."

"Well," the professor replied, "at the moment I have no intention of going anywhere till I satisfy my appetite. Or does their hostility extend to denying me access to their table?"

"Oh, they'll let you eat. Will you join me?"

"With pleasure. By the way, my name's Phillimore. Professor James Phillimore."

"Delighted to meet you," said the man in the toga, taking Phillimore by the arm and steering him to the banquet "You may call me Andy. Come along now, best stay close to me."

The lion arose, stretched and yawned so that his powerful teeth and claws were prominently displayed. Then he ambled after his cherished human companions.

* * * *

They sat down on the sward, Phillimore balancing an exquisitely-fashioned china plate and a crystal goblet of punch. Andy contented himself with a single silver chalice of ruby-red wine and the lion gobbled down a succession of raw steaks.

"He is rather a remarkable beast," the professor said. "Other than in certain forms of Oriental theatre, I've never before encountered a dancing lion."

Andy nodded proudly. "I taught him all the graces. Once, he roamed the wild like any predator. But then, after we met under singular circumstances, we became fast friends and he decided to remain with me and adopt the ways of civilization. He's since grown especially fond of diversions such as feasts and masquerades and balls. As a matter of fact, he's become much sought-after as a desirable guest by many aspiring hostesses."

"I imagine he *would* provide a certain novelty at soirees."

"Indeed, yes!" Andy averred. "During the *season*, he's a regular party lion and, don't you know, he's *always* busy." He paused to quaff some wine.

Swallowing a morsel of mutton, Phillimore brought the conversation back to the topic of his personal predicament "You said I'd be running no risk if I remained here, but unfortunately, I must soon be going."

"They won't let you."

"Why not?"

"They're afraid you'll try to tell their father, the king, where they've been."

So *that's it*! Phillimore nodded vigorously. "I believe I know all about it! The princes are under an enchantment, right?"

Andy nodded. "The exact nature of the spell has long been forgotten, but according to rumor, the curse will wind down eventually, so long as these maidens keep them company for an indefinite number of nights."

"And while they do, they dance their shoes to ruins!"

"Correct. The cobblers clamor for payment constantly and the cash drain is driving the king to distraction. He's offered substantial rewards (including marriage to any one of the young women) to whoever reveals where they go each night." Andy tossed off the rest of the wine, wiped his lips and stared sorrowfully at Phillimore. "So, you see, they'll never permit you to escape to claim the reward."

"Except that's *not* what I intend!" the professor protested. "Anyway, what can they do, after all, to prevent me from leaving?"

"Around here," Andy said, "they consider cutting off one's head a remarkably effective deterrent." Just as he spoke, the professor swallowed a sip of punch. The lion solicitously pounded his back till he stopped coughing.

"Are you, too, in danger?" Phillimore asked, wiping his eyes.

"Not at all. They know I'm already married."

"You are? Where's your wife?"

"She moved out when the lion moved in."

"I can understand that," the professor said, then, smiling at the lion, quickly added, "No offense intended."

"None has been taken." Andy laughed, clapping the professor upon the shoulder. "No, no, dear fellow, I was quite aware that my spouse *might* prefer some other vicinity to that in which this lovely beast dwells." He cuddled the animal's head affectionately. "*Good* boy, *goo-oo-ood* boy!"

* * * *

"Do you think he'd stand them off if I decided to leave?" Phillimore asked, indicating the animal.

"Oh, undoubtedly he would, he's a loyal, loving lion. But the princes are trained hunters and there are arms in the castle. I doubt if you could get very far. Even a lordly beast is not impervious to musket and ball."

The professor nodded. "True. And I wouldn't want to risk any lives, anyway. But see here, I am under obligation to complete a quest for a crone who won't return my property till I do. I simply must get going!"

"Well, you might try taking it up with the eldest princess. She pretty much decides things around here."

"Which one is she?"

"The brunette with the baggy eyes."

"I didn't notice. Baggy eyes?'

"Certainly. What can she expect? She's turning thirty, but never gets any sleep (what with all this dancing) unless she naps in the daytime—and if she does, it's not enough. She's always cranky."

"*Is that so?*" a new voice exclaimed.

* * * *

They whirled about. There, hovering a few steps away, was a tall dark-haired princess with thin, stern lips, a straight patrician nose and, in truth, rather baggy eyes.

Certainly the plainest of the lot, thought Phillimore.

"How dare you speak so of me, churl?" she sneered at Andy. "If you were not of such low birth as to render your effrontery of no great significance, I should see your curly head separated this instant from your shoulders!"

The lion curled the side of his mouth back from his great teeth and began to snarl.

"On the other hand," the princess said, "I am of generous nature and see no real injury in remarks which, perhaps, have the seeds of truth in them, after all."

The lion sniffed disdainfully and closed his mouth and eyes. In his social set, such jumped-up nobility were hardly worth a yawn.

* * * *

"You, sir," the princess addressed Phillimore, "claim to be bound upon a quest that has nothing to do with our nightly revels."

"That's true," said the professor, rising respectfully. "I have an errand to perform for the witch Baba Yaga."

"Never heard of her," the princess yawned, failing to cover her mouth as she did. "If this be true, then why did we discover you skulking about the woods near this enchanted spot? Was it not to learn our secret and discover it to the king, my father?"

"Not at all!" He vigorously shook his head. "I was taking a shortcut through the forest, that was all. I didn't even see you and wouldn't have, if you hadn't kidnapped me!"

The princess frowned thoughtfully. "You may, of course, be telling the truth—in which case, it is unfortunate enough. But I'm afraid however it happened, we cannot now permit you to leave."

"But I have no interest in wedding a princess!"

One eyebrow raised and she pursed her lips. "And why," she demanded, "should you be different from any other commoner?"

Commoner! Phillimore's temper began to boil. "I'll have you know, first off, that I am the native of a country where royalty was ousted centuries before in favor of a republic."

"Do you speak of Rome?" Andy asked eagerly.

"No. Not quite." The professor faced the princess with elaborate dignity and hauteur. "As for marrying one of your vile lot, it is true I came to this world to seek a female companion, but I should never elect to settle for spoiled brats who have so little regard for human life as to condemn to execution all who'd strive for your frivolous selves!"

"I *see*" she said idly. "And now, speaking of the latter subject, you will permit me to retire and arrange your own imminent demise."

Swiveling sharply on one slipper, she stormed off, snapping her fingers at the first prince whose eye she caught.

"Uh-oh," Andy murmured mournfully, "*now* you've done it!"

"Yes, I'm afraid so," Phillimore concurred. "However, here's my plan..."

* * * *

Phillimore, Andy and the lion sat down and waited by the side of the river, near a dock where twelve bright blue boats bounced on the billows. Andy said the princes rowed upstream each evening to pick up the twelve dancing princesses and paddle them to the vicinity of the subterranean castle.

"They *ought* to be paddled," Phillimore grumbled. "What a grim lot." Nearby, the sisters wrangled over the best way to terminate him. Some were in favor of drowning, some preferred simple strangulation, one foolishly suggested feeding Phillimore to the lion.

Eventually, however, Drusilla (the eldest) had her way and traditional decapitation was agreed upon.

* * * *

A company of musicians in the castle struck up a solemn march. Lackeys emerged carrying the appurtenances of a public beheading. One bore a plush cushion on which rested a gleaming sword. Another carried towels. A third's arms encircled a large, sinister wicker basket. In the rear, the professor noticed two servants dangling between them a big black net. *Probably to throw over the lion during the ceremony.*

He stood up as the procession halted a little ways off. The thumping and blaring of the music ceased. Drusilla stepped forward.

"Are you prepared to die, stranger?" she asked haughtily.

Exchanging a look with his two friends, Phillimore addressed the eldest princess in a tone as challengingly chilly as her own. "And do you mean to tell me," he sneered, "that yours is a country barbarous enough to send off a man with so little ceremony?"

Her brows contracted and her lips turned down. "It lacks an hour of dawn, stranger; we have no time for elaborate charades. What would you have? You've already partaken of your final meal!"

"In the civilized world, from which I hail," he replied with a touch of pride, "a condemned prisoner is always granted one last simple request."

She shrugged. "Time is scant. We must return to our father's castle. You'll set no special favors unless your demand is easily and speedily fulfillable."

"It is."

"Then *name* it!"

"I crave a chance of treading a final measure with this noble beast."

The lion grinned appreciatively.

* * * *

Drusilla talked it over with her siblings. Though inclined to be suspicious, none of them could raise any tangible objection to the odd request, so they reluctantly agreed to permit the pair one last dance together.

"What tempo? A fast one?" Drusilla demanded.

"No, this time I should prefer a slow, measured rhythm—a ponderous quadrille, if the musicians can manage it."

"Executions are certainly becoming a bother," Drusilla sighed. "However, I'll see what they can do for you."

She strode up the hill and spoke to the conductor. He gave one knowing nod and, whispering to his players, signaled the downbeat.

They managed it nicely. As the band struck up a four-square strain, repetitive and compelling in its simple melody, the professor bowed to the lion. He stood on his hind legs. Phillimore put an arm about the beast's waist and the animal propped a paw about his. They stood side by side.

"What kind of dance position is *that*?" one of the younger sisters wondered.

"It comes from Greece," Phillimore replied. "It's known as a chain dance."

"A *chain* dance?"

"Yes. That's because more than two at a time may take part. It's possible to form a veritable chain of dancers."

The youngest princess, a somewhat unsure little auburn-haired lass, clapped her hands enthusiastically. "Ooh, that sounds like fun!" She looked for approval to Drusilla, did not find it forthcoming, yet did not altogether subside.

The professor said the Grecian chain dance was one of the world's great communal cultural artifacts and was quite simple to learn. With that, he and the lion stepped off deliberately with their right feet, described a large circle with their left, took a few sideways crossovers that placed them in a position to step out rightwards again, circle to the left, step-step-step, outward and circle and step-step-step and...

Andy got into position beside the dancers, placed his hand on the lion's other hip and joined the chain.

Step-step-step, outward and circle and step-step-step.

The court musicians played the slow, stately, monotonous music, repeating again and again an air that never modulated nor changed, but sang itself into the time-tapping feet of the princes and princesses who watched.

Step and step and step and outward step and circle, step and step and step and as they passed near the youngest princess, Phillimore reached out one hand invitingly toward her waist and she pranced obediently into place and stepped and stepped and stepped and took one outward step and circled with one foot and then she curved her tiny hand about the waist of her admiring opposite youngest prince and together the five danced and danced and soon it was six and then seven who stepped and stepped and stepped and took that one deliberate outward step and circled and the company grew and grew until only the frowning eldest sister, Drusilla, momentarily refused to lilt with the impelling mind-deadening refrain, but at length even she—for she was, after all, one of the renowned twelve dancing princesses—even she encircled the end prince's waist and led off into that outer step that was almost a foot-stamp and completed with her left foot the circle that riveted the mind to the life-bestowing earth beneath fifty-four compulsive dancing feet, stepping and stepping and stepping, over and again and over and yet again.

The mesmerizing *perpetuum mobile* communicated itself to the players of the music; enrapt, they repeated the principal subject of the piece, eyes closed, abstracted, on a plane whose pleasures are primarily known by musicians. As they tootled, keened and thumped out the swelling steady accents of the composition, the evening hours waned.

And now the central links of the chain—Phillimore, Andy and the lion—shifted their weights subtly and introduced an undulation into the great curve of dancers, a snaking ripple that billowed gently out to the furthermost ends of the line. The three repeated the maneuver a bit more forcefully, a trifle wider; again the caravan of flesh heaved to the motion.

Andy, the professor and the lion stepped wider and continued to ply the human ribbon with slowly increasing insistence. The rapt nobles coiled and contracted and dilated in fluctuating arcs that, by imperceptible degrees, carried them to the edge of the river. Their feet strutted upon the down-sloping bank and the drag and thrust of more than two dozen bodies aided the work of gravity as they footed it faster to avoid stumbling or losing the time.

Suddenly, the trio leaned into the cordon of flesh with all their weight and the professor nodded. With one mighty effort, they *snapped* the chain as hard as they could.

An unexpected melee: shouts and bewildered exclamations; twenty-four waking princesses and escorts, knotted together in a complicated tangle of intertwined limbs, falling and jostling and rolling in the same direction...

"*Release!*"

When Phillimore shouted, he and his friends yanked their hands away from the crowd and gave mighty shoves to anyone they could reach, thus creating an effective riptide that added to the confusion. The furthest tottering royal representatives had begun to regain a little of their equilibrium but the professor's new tactic conquered whatever momentum they had started to reestablish.

With a mighty splash, half of the dazed and dizzy dancers plunged simultaneously into the river. The others either collapsed breathless by the shore or followed the bulk of the company into the water.

"*Now! Hurry!*" the professor yelled, but Andy and the lion were already speeding toward the dock and Phillimore matched them in a race to throw off as many mooring ropes as they could manage while the beached nobles were still too vertiginous to collect wits and combat them.

They managed to loose most of the punts before one of the princes groggily drew his sword and started uncertainly in their direction. Andy nudged the professor, who turned and saw the approaching adversary. With a confirmatory nod, Phillimore and his companions scrambled into one of the two remaining boats, cast off the rope and furiously started to paddle away from the dock into the middle of the river.

The lion roared delightedly as the men rowed with all their might. Andy nodded at the beast. "Yes, yes, I totally agree."

"What did he say?" asked Phillimore.

"That it was the best damn party in years!" He chuckled. "That was quite a dance at the end. How did you know it would work so well?"

"I didn't for sure. It was a chance I had to take. The Greek chain dance was supposed to be a public ritual in which, say, the populace of an entire town might hypnotize themselves into dancing off a cliff rather than surrender to marauders." Phillimore craned his neck around. "Look and tell me whether we're being pursued, Andy; I can't see well enough."

Andy looked. Back on the dock, the prince who'd given token chase stood in doubt for a moment as to whether to jump in the one remaining boat or hurry down to the beach and help rescue some of his floundering kinfolk. At last, with a disgusted wave of his arm, he dismissed the professor and stumbled off to yank Drusilla out of the drink.

"Row on," said Andy merrily, matching Phillimore stroke for stroke. "We're in the clear."

* * * *

Overhead, the sky paled with the approaching dawn. The punt rode the river out of the cave and into the forest, through which the great flood twisted.

"The bridge is one more bend downstream," said Andy. "Are you making for it?"

The professor shook his head. "I was supposed to meet Walter, my guide, there, but that was hours ago and by now, he's probably gone home, figuring I was killed on the road." He yawned. "I sure got myself stuck in one hell of a world."

"I beg your pardon?"

"Never mind, it's too complicated." He yawned again. "I'm exhausted. Just a few seconds ago, I saw a cottage over on the near shore, a little ways into the woods. I believe I'll beg a bed for a few hours before continuing my quest. Will you join me?"

"I'm afraid not," Andy replied, rowing toward the indicated riverbank. "We're on our way to town to a cotillion the lion promised to dance at."

"Do you want to use the punt?"

"No, it's not that far by foot. You keep to the river. It'll be faster for you and possibly safer than the woods."

* * * *

At the bank, they stepped into the shallows and hauled the small boat onto dry land. The lion gave Phillimore a farewell hug and Andy shook hands with his new friend. Then the amiable Roman and his peculiar companion ambled down the trail and were soon lost to view...

"*It's about time* you got rid of that monster!"

The professor yelped. Jerking his head in the direction from which the unexpected voice proceeded, he saw, sitting in a clump of weeds, the half-invisible philosopher cat.

"*Rimski!*"

"Nu," the cat yawned disdainfully, "you were expecting maybe Puss in Boots?"

"Some friend you are! Where've you *been* all night?"

"As close as I could safely come without getting trampled by those klutzes with ferryboats for feet! And as far away as I could stay from that overgrown alleycat's teeth!"

"You mean Andy's lion? He's harmless."

"To you, maybe." The feline padded out of the woods and deigned to rematerialize completely. "As for me, I didn't have any too sure an idea that he wouldn't've regarded me as an hors d'oeuvre." Rimski rubbed appreciatively against Phillimore's legs. "Anyhow, it's good you got away safe. I'm glad to see you again."

"Likewise," said the professor, wondering whether it was proper manners to pet a former tax collector.

* * * *

Rimski guided Phillimore underneath the trees to a small clearing lit by early morning sun. A neat small lawn with flagstones set in its midst beckoned the way to the tiny cottage the professor had seen from the river.

"Wait here," the cat suggested. "The men of the house will be leaving for work soon. Then you can ask for a place to lie down for a while and when you wake, the girl will fix you a good meal before we start again. By the way, before you snooze, maybe you could sneak me a saucer cream? I couldn't get near the food in the cave."

"Why can't you ask for it yourself?"

"I'll be invisible in the house."

"How come?"

"In these parts," Rimski whispered, crouching behind a berry bush, "it's *tsooris* traveling with a cat. You'll be suspected of being a warlock and me, your familiar."

"Hmm." Phillimore mused. "And something else falls into place."

"What?"

"Is it possible that seven men live in there? Seven *small* men?"

The cat's eyes widened. "How'd you know that?"

"Bit of a fey quality, I fancy."

"Fey-shmay!" the animal scoffed. "To a philosopher you shouldn't talk *kasha*!"

"We-ell, if you *really* want to know—"

But the cat, shushing Phillimore, closed his eyes for a moment and cogitated. His small whiskery lips pushed in and out thoughtfully. At length, he inclined his head knowingly and opened his eyes. "Of *course...*"

"Of course?"

"Yes," he mewed, "I think I see. Given an umbrella that whisks you to other dimensions by attunement with your thoughts, it is logical to postulate that it might take you to places that correspond in some mysterious metaphysical fashion with your own mental expectations of your destinations."

"Well reasoned, Rimski," Phillimore said, impressed, "and generally correct. When I pushed the umbrella's release this time, I didn't have any clear definition of the best place to go, but I was thinking along the lines of what our world sometimes calls 'fairy tales.' However, I seem to have gotten more than I bargained for."

"Namely?"

The professor ticked them off on his fingers. "Baba Yaga, the Headless Horseman, Goldilocks, the Twelve Dancing Princesses, the Seven

Dwarfs, Andy and his lion… and I suspect the island I am bound for is none other than one I know of in a story entitled Beauty and the Beast."

"Sounds accurate, from what I've, heard around Baba's place," the cat purred reflectively.

"In other words," said Phillimore, "I seem to have landed in a world of Faërie, one that may include any legend, folktale or invented myth in my head." He groaned. "The only thing I considered at the time was fairy-tale princesses; I forgot about the witches and monsters I might meet in such a place!"

"Yes," the cat agreed, "and you didn't do so hot in the princess department, either." He ambled over to the professor and nudged him gently with his head. "Look, doc, you're a nice fellow, but you shouldn't get all kinds of hopes up, *f'shtay*?"

"What do you mean?"

"You've got extra data in your head from your own preconceptions of this world, so maybe you'll actually get Baba her black sunflower. But don't trust witches! They all have this insatiable desire for objects of power. The day you get old Baba to let go your umbrella is going to be some special morning!"

"But it won't work for her. It's set on *my* mental frequency."

The cat eyed him gravely. "Even if you're dead?"

"You have a point, Rimski. But look, if she doesn't give it back, she won't get her sunflower."

"All the same, I'd be very careful, if I were you," the cat warned. "And another thing—you should be glad you got rid of that zhlub Walter. He-"

But just then, the door to the cottage swung wide.

"He what?" Phillimore demanded. "What about Walter?"

"Shh! Not now...here come the dwarfs!"

They waited silently while a baker's half-dozen of diminutive miners issued from the cot and trudged down the forest-path, pickaxes slung over their shoulders. Risking a peek, the professor saw the last of them stomping off. They all sang a hearty hiking song as they strode away.

"Funny," Rimski ruminated, "I never heard them sing before." He waved his tail in rhythm. "Catchy little thing..."

But Phillimore did not hear him—or, for that matter, the song. He spied a blithe raven-haired maiden framed in the doorway, smiling and waving at her seven protectors. She was scarce twenty, simple and unspoiled. Though her shoulders had a regal pride to their set, she emanated gentleness and good humor. Her clear skin displayed no trace of time's encroachment, but about her parted rose-pink lips were a few laugh lines, exquisite parentheses to the dainty perfection of her small, perfectly-shaped mouth.

"Come on," Rimski said, "let's go before she closes the door. What's the matter with you?"

"I think," said the professor in a faint voice, "I just fell in love!"

The chubby gray cat made a derisive sound like a razzberry and disgustedly disappeared.

* * * *

Sailing into the graceful harbor, Phillimore steered just north of windward, dipped his oar and impelled the punt toward the doming crest that was the nearest shore.

It was a beach of spun-sugar sand that rolled gently back and upward to a small hill but lightly downed with early spring grasses. The island itself put out two peninsular projections to either side of the bay, tame curvets of land that circled so far around the water they nearly enclosed the flood and made it a lagoon. But not quite; the waters opened to the sea and Phillimore, having negotiated the narrow gap, drove steadily onward till the punt scraped lightly on the rising floor of the bay. He got out and pulled the craft upon the beach, shipped the oar, then trotted off toward the neighboring hillside.

All was silent, all was calm. The perfumed breeze bore a hint of lush tropic vegetation, but mostly the air was thin and fresh as the world's primal morning. Somewhere overhead caroled a lark of paradise.

Phillimore's feet printed their trail in the pristine sand. At length he left the beach and trod lightly on the dewy ground out of which sparse blades of grass thrust up here and there. The hill was close now and he quickened his pace to reach it. As he did, he cast about for some trail cresting the rise, but could find none.

Then he saw, a little ways up from the level of the ground, a darkness in the hummock of earth. Approaching, he identified it as a cave, not very large, sunk into the hill. Memories of the lair of the purple troll, a dreadful creature in one of his earlier adventures, flooded into his mind; he tarried his pace, reluctant now to proceed further...

But he had no choice. Without warning, the gentle clime darkened and the wind quickened to howling gale force. All, all was sham and the seeming-pleasant harbor was an evil lure. Lightning flickered in the lowering sky, the lark changed to a bird of night, croaking dire instances of death. He tried to turn and make good his escape, but the bare earth suddenly sprouted noisome growths everywhere, stinking twines and vines that corded about his ankles and rooted him fast.

The ground tilted; the creepers released his legs and he slid, slowly at first, then with nightmare acceleration, directly toward the hill that now was a twisted, malevolent mountain. The cave's edges shivered and altered and its perimeter was a jagged saw-toothed mouth that dilated to a wide cavern, then irised tight, a puckered channel of death. Phillimore flailed his arms to wrest free of the danger, but his efforts were useless. Doom hurtled closer; the world gaped and devoured him and he screamed as he felt the prickling of a million teeth and he woke on the floor in the middle of a rug whose harsh weave scratched him all over.

He sat up and blinked at the brightness of late afternoon sunlight. Memory returned: he was in the home of the seven dwarfs. The elfin maiden had treated him kindly, preparing him breakfast, putting him to rest in her own bedroom, where he'd suffered the nightmare and tumbled out of bed in the process. But as he thought of her, the terror fled and his heart fluttered with the flame of his infatuation.

Phillimore noticed a movement in the corner of the room. Turning, he saw the cat, Rimski, seated in front of a mirror, half-invisible. As he watched, the animal faded repeatedly in and out of sight "What are you doing?" the professor asked, getting to his feet.

Rimski abruptly zapped into focus. "Well, it's about time you woke!" he purred. "You've been asleep all day."

"I needed the rest," said the professor. "What were you doing just now?"

"Doing?" the cat echoed, somewhat embarrassed.

"Appearing, disappearing, coming back and vanishing again." Suddenly the man grinned. "I know what you were trying to accomplish!"

"What?" Rimski asked surlily.

"You were attempting to fade out of sight while leaving your grin behind!"

"Nonsense," the cat grumped, looking deeply wounded. "Why would I do anything so meretricious?"

But before Phillimore could reply, an anguished shriek froze them both.

* * * *

The professor's face went white. "It's her! She's in trouble!"

"Brilliant deduction," the cat yowled, darting toward the door. "Stop jawing and *move*! Needing no second hint, Phillimore shot out of the bedroom and clomped toward the stairway that led down to the rustic ground-floor kitchen, nearly stepping on Rimski's tail as he did.

The kitchen was a large cheery place bedecked with flowers and lacy curtains. In the middle stood a great iron stove, at the side of which hung a big pot of heating water, suspended over an enormous hearth. Snow White had evidently just begun dinner preparations.

Thundering downstairs, Phillimore missed his footing and tumble-shot the landing. He skidded into the kitchen, Rimski right behind. Fortunately for the professor's seat, the kitchen floor was stone, unlike the thick-grain lumber in the rest of the house.

Snow White was at the far end of the room, near the vestibule to the outer door. Her dainty hands clutched at her throat and breast and as they watched, dismayed, she sank into a swoon. Phillimore managed to hurl himself forward and catch her before her head hit the flagging.

Rimski sniffed nervously at her. "I think she's dead. Let's get out of here before the dwarfs return!"

"No!" Phillimore snapped. "Control yourself. It's something she ate. I can save her!" He lofted her in his arms, fumbled the constraints at her waist loose and quickly untied the ribbon circling her slender neck. Then, joggling the maiden into the proper first-aid attitude, he jounced her till a morsel of poisoned fruit dislodged itself and fell from her lips.

No sooner did it escape than her eyelids fluttered. "What happened?" she asked faintly as Phillimore eased her to a sitting position.

"What happened," the cat said, "is that my friend just saved your life." Rimski turned to the professor. "I presume you knew why she was choking in the usual manner?"

Fetching a napkin to clean away the expelled foodstuff, Snow White wondered what other way there was to choke. Rimski attempted to explain he was referring to the professor's "fey" faculties, but soon gave it up; she was unable to comprehend the subject.

However, Snow White fully understood Phillimore's heroism. Demurely stepping up to him, she said, "If thou wouldst treasure one such as I, but say so and I am yours."

Pleased as he could be, the professor embraced the young woman and would have spoken his love in rapturous phrases, but for Rimski's insistence that she relate what fell thing felled her.

"A decrepit peddler woman," she said, "came to the door and gifted me with a fresh piece of fruit. I bit into it and the world spun about.

"My throat closed in, my pulse pounded...and naught else do I recall till this gentleman restored me to life."

Rimski shook his head. "Peddler woman? Sounds uncomfortably like a typical trick of the witch-queen."

At the instant he said it, the door blew open.

"*Correct, cat!*" a horrible voice shrilled. Rimski disappeared.

The crone was whisker-lipped, with dry-straw hair and fierce yellow-amber eyes. Cloaked all in black, with a basket upon her arm, she was unmistakably the peddler-witch of Snow White's recent peril and Phillimore's hallowed memories.

The witch was not in a good mood.

"Swine prince of toads!" she hissed, pointing a bony finger at the professor. "How *dare* you interfere in the purposes of a queen?"

Phillimore shrugged offhandedly. "Probably because I'm a Democrat" He eyed the kettle in the corner speculatively. Meanwhile, Snow White, trembling like a frightened hind, snuggled against her protector.

"Mortal, you do not even display proper obeisance. I shall make you suffer!"

"Possibly," he replied, tenderly extricating himself from the girl's grasp, "but at the moment, I suspect I have you at a bit of a disadvantage." He took three rapid strides toward the hearth, grabbed a pair of pot-shields and hefted the full kettle from the flames. *Wonder whether Baum's remedy works on* all *witches*?

The horrible crone blanched when she saw the vessel of water. Skipping back as fast as possible, she waved an imperious hand at the front door, which gaped wide at her magical command. On the threshold she paused long enough to warn Phillimore in dire tones to stay out of her way—if he could.

"Just try!" she cackled. "But I'll get you..." She glowered at Snow White. "You, too, my pretty!" The witch stared at an empty spot in the living-room. "And that goes for your little cat, too!"

The invisible Rimski meowed miserably.

A loud burst of thunder shook the cottage, though the day was bright and sunny. In the midst of the hurly-burly, the witch vanished, leaving behind a noxious yellow cloud of billowing sulphur.

"My hero!" Snow White cried, flinging herself into Phillimore's arms. Wheezing from the sorcerous pollution, he hugged her with avuncular affection, surprised that such unaccustomed feminine propinquity stirred so little libidinous personal response.

Must be the stress of the moment, he reasoned silently, gazing fondly down at her lovely visage.

* * * *

"Let's get the hell out of here—*fast!*" the cat advised. "The first thing we should do is put distance between us and this cottage. Make her chase after us. Here we're easy game!"

"But you must not abandon me!" Snow White begged, clutching the professor's lapels.

"I meant all of us!" the animal yelped.

"But how can I leave my dear friends, the dwarfs, without even saying goodbye to them?"

"They'll be safer, I suspect," said Phillimore, "without our presence.

Best leave them a note."

"Make it a short one!" Rimski pleaded.

"Yes, yes," the man reassured the animal, "we'd all better move our tails."

The idiom greatly puzzled the cat.

* * * *

After she jotted a terse missive to her diminutive friends, Snow White packed a basket of food, threw a shawl over her slender shoulders, affixed the letter to the front door and shut it fast Though she longed to hear the particulars of her new protector's history—and especially how he happened to travel with a sometimes-invisible cat—the maiden spared them her curiosity and hurried with Phillimore and Rimski to the water's edge.

"Using the punt," said Phillimore, "we can cover a great deal of distance yet before it grows dark." But their escape plans were foiled. A great cleft in the small boat had somehow materialized since last he'd ridden in it. The gap was so wide, the punt was nearly shorn in two.

"How did this happen?" Phillimore mused.

"The witch must've done it," Rimski mewed. "You sure made one powerful enemy, *tovarich*."

The professor shrugged hopelessly. "If I had my umbrella, I could save us all, but there's no chance of that now. Two witches to worry about...one I can't satisfy unless I complete her damned quests while the other may get me while I try. If only I'd met Walter when I was supposed to!"

"As for him," said Rimski, "put Walter out of your mind. He doesn't deserve trust."

"Why not?"

"Baba Yaga has him under an enchantment. He's wholly devoted to doing her will. He's a mathologic animal."

Phillimore blinked. "I beg your pardon?"

"I said he's mathologic."

"Don't you mean mythologic?"

"Nope. Mathologic. You can't count on him."

Snow White, impatiently enduring the conversation, decided to get things back to more immediate practicalities. "What are we supposed to do now? How shall you save me, mighty champion?"

"Well," Phillimore drawled, shifting uncomfortably from one foot to the other, "I suppose we have no choice now but to hoof it."

Snow White opened her sparkling eyes wide. "In sooth, do you expect me to destroy my dainty feet hiking?"

Rimski interrupted. "Let's hide in the woods tonight. There's a ferry due six miles upstream, but it won't come till tomorrow morning. I know a fairy ring where we'll be safe this evening."

"Okay," answered the professor. "We'll catch up on some needed sleep."

"Hmmf," the cat sniffed, "you've been snoozing all day."

"And I'm sure I'll need a lot more rest before this adventure's done." They started off for the enchanted clearing and reached it soon after dark. The professor bundled his jacket for Snow White to rest her head on.

The night passed without incident, but Phillimore didn't get much sleep, after all. Snow White kept him awake for hours asking him questions.

* * * *

Rising early in the morning, the three companions made a hasty breakfast from Snow White's basket of goodies, then briskly proceeded along the water's edge to the spot where Rimski claimed the ferry would moor.

Arriving at a rude wooden dock, the cat and the man sat upon the blanched sand to await the vessel. Meanwhile, Snow White, trilling merrily like some bird of the morning, scouted the perimeter of the woods for berries.

The shingle sparkled in the morning light. Phillimore was pleased to see an absence of civilization's litter in the cool dawning vista. Scanning the opposite shore, he noted a cluster of cottages. Rimski explained they were close to the capital and the tiny houses marked the edge of the suburbs.

No sound but the breeze's breath ruffled them. Snow White gamboled hide-and-seek around the boles and branches of the forest until Phillimore tired of following her blithe form dancing midst bush and bramble. The morning lulled him; all danger seemed remote, all travail transient; he wondered on the arbitrariness of Meaning...

"Excuse me, is this where the ferry docks?"

The lilting voice at his elbow startled him, half-asleep as he was. He turned, surprised, having heard no footsteps—and there before him stood the most serenely beautiful blonde he'd ever been privileged to view. Tall she was, regal in bearing without any trace of hauteur; wide blue orbs twinkled mischievously in an oval heart-face whose creamy skin was draped and caressed by long gold tresses. The woman was clad in gossamer green and carried a sparkling emerald diadem in one hand. Upon her feet she wore an exquisitely-fashioned pair of pure crystal slippers.

"I said, is this where I catch the ferry?" The damsel spoke in a mellow, throaty tone that tingled Phillimore's spine.

"Yes, it is," he replied. "Will you sit and wait with us?"

"In a minute," she promised, striding off to inspect the horizon where the river kissed the sky. But she barely took two steps when she tottered. Uttering a startlingly earthly imprecation, she hobbled to the dock, leaned against a piling and yanked off one of her slippers. "Damn," she grumbled, massaging her foot, "these things are sure hell on the arches!"

"Women," Rimski observed, "will kill themselves in the name of Fashion."

"It's not *my* fault," she retorted. "Designers never consider how our feet feel when they come up with their torture devices." She held the shoe up to the light and squinted. "Of course, this is rather a fetching number." She inverted the slipper, dumped a quantity of sand out, then put it back on and repeated the business with the other.

"I presume," said the professor, "that you are none other than Cinderella?"

"And what if I am?" she demanded, glancing at him suspiciously. "Are you one of the prince's spies?"

"Hardly. I'm just curious. I associate glass slippers with Cinderella."

"Who doesn't?" the blonde sighed. "Ever since I crashed that lousy Grand Ball, glass slippers have been *the* thing. You can't buy a simple pair of sensible shlumpfing-around-in shoes anyplace!"

"So," Rimski purred, regarding her with mild interest, "you're the famous Princess?"

"Not any more, catnik! I've had it with that royal bum!" Her mouth described a disgusted moue. Wetting her lips, she looked out for the ferry but, failing to see it, left the dock and sat down by the professor's side.

Phillimore, shocked, asked, "Are you saying that you left the prince?"

"You bet your bird I did!"

He winced at her colorful argot, but realized he must make allowances for the fact that, after all, she had started as a chimney-sweep. It dismayed him, though, that one of his favorite childhood stories had somewhat not managed to end happily ever after. He expressed his feelings in so many words and urged Cinderella to confide in him.

"Don't call me Cinderella," she said, placing a hand on his. "Only my stepmother and her lousy daughters like to tack on the 'tinder' part. I'm *Ella*, but you can call me Ellie." With that, she smiled at Phillimore with that vague unspoken promise which is the natural province of only the most innocent or the most flirtatious of women.

The press of her hand on his caused Phillimore's pulse to heat in rapid syncopation that, paradoxically, lulled his critical faculties to sleep.

"Why *did* you leave the prince?" he asked, holding her dainty hand.

"He's not the man I married." She sighed. "Godmother knows, I should've seen the signs sooner, it was obvious enough. But I was too infatuated."

"Nu?" the cat impatiently prompted, but the professor gestured for him to be silent.

Ella leaned her head conspiratorially close. "It was the slipper business. I lost one of them at the Grand Ball."

"Yes, I've heard about that" Phillimore nodded. "In order to find you, the prince said he'd have the slipper tried on the feet of all the eligible maidens in the land and he sent out a messenger to—"

"Messenger, hell!" Ella interrupted. "He went himself!"

"I beg your pardon?"

"The prince *personally* tried the glass slipper on all the eligible women of the land. That should have clued me in!"

"To what?"

"He's got a foot fetish."

* * * *

"ALL'BOARD!"

The handsome young skipper called out lustily as the last of the arriving passengers disembarked. The ferry was a paddle-wheeler gaily bedecked with bunting, reminiscent of a Nineteenth Century Mississippi riverboat, except for a single modification. Attached to the roof was a long medicinal dropper with a rubber bulb on top. When the professor asked what purpose it served, Mike Fink said, "It's for protection in case we get into waters too deep for our draft. If that happens, I'd go up there and shove the end of it into the water, then squeeze the bulb for all its worth, then I'd swing it out over the shore and empty it, then repeat the process till the water's a workable depth." He grinned. "So how do you like my ferry with the syringe on top?" The scholar groaned.

Phillimore, Ella, Rimski and Snow White were the only embarking passengers at the quay. Ella walked a bit ahead, hiking up her gossamer gown so it would not trail in the splashes or get caught on the splinters of the ramp. She deliberately held herself aloof, shoulders high and proud. The cause of her chilly attitude was Snow White's seemingly innocent query, upon being introduced to the ex-princess, as to "what mode of alchemy accomplished the striking paleness of yon cornsilk tresses?"

Rimski trotted after Ella. Phillimore brought up the rear, his arm firmly linked to Snow White's own and securely held there by her delicate little fist. As they stepped on the gang, he looked up and saw Ella at the top rearranging her skirts in such fashion as to reveal one immodest, fleeting glimpse of tapered thigh.

"Ah, sweet champion," Snow White sweetly suggested through clenched teeth, "pay heed to thine own legs lest they unwittingly deposit thee in yon river..."

To underscore her loving advice, she gently punctuated her caveat with an educational hip-nudge that instructionally introduced Phillimore's breadbasket to the handrail of the gangway.

Though his sole monosyllabic utterance hardly shed light on his views of Snow White's pedagogic pretensions, mentally he observed that her rustic lack of breeding *ought* to be taken into account Also, he noted his ego *ought* to be flattered by what might be construed as jealousy on her part. Yet these silent considerations held little persuasive force compared with his need to negotiate the remaining segment of gangway in a posture reminiscent of a Groucho Marx sidle.

* * * *

They all sat down together, Ella on a bench just opposite James Phillimore.

The lines wore loosed, the ferry slipped into the current and soon the captain left the pilothouse to greet his passengers.

The skipper was a sun-bronzed youth of perhaps twenty-two or three. Sinewy and skinny, he was all angles; his ruggedly good-looking face included a lantern-jaw and enormous handlebar mustache and when he grinned, he flashed a gold incisor. His eyes were steely blue that matched a uniform studded with brass buttons. On his head perched a visored cap. To the professor, he resembled the sort of riverboat pilot one reads about in Twain or Ferber, so Phillimore was not surprised to hear him speak in a recognizably southern U.S. drawl.

"Ah'm Cap'n Mike," he introduced himself. "Jes's make yourselves comft'ble and tell me what we can do t' make yer ride *fun*." He grinned; his tooth glinted. "And what's yer name, lil lady?"

Snow White blushed, curtsied and told him. Ella complied with a similar request, but with no personal confusion and without getting up. The professor introduced Cap'n Mike to Rimski and gave his own name. As soon as he spoke, the seaman squinted curiously and asked whether he might hail from the "Yewnited States."

When Phillimore avowed that he did, the captain pounded him on the back so heartily that the professor dropped Snow White's basket "Ah'll be hawg-tied and double-damned! Yer the fust Yankee I set eyes on in a coon's age!" With that, he pumped Phillimore's hand so hard he might have been priming for oil. "That's the sperret, son! Put 'er there! What brings you all th' way over t' here?"

Phillimore started to explain, but Rimski pressed his lips together and gave a frowning shake of the head. He stemmed his tale in midtide.

"Got a secret, huh?" Mike asked with a sage nod. "I's okay, son! You won't find a closer ear for a fellow countryman, even if ye do be a Yankee!" He grinned again, but the professor demurred from closer discussion. The sailor shrugged. "It's yer hand, Jimmy-boy; if you wanna play close t' the vest, that's your privilege, but if yer running from trouble, feel free t' change yer mind."

With that, he bowed deeply to Snow White and invited her to accompany him to the wheelhouse where he would allow her to steer the ferry. She demurely dimpled and said she would join him presently.

Phillimore frowned.

* * * *

"Rimski," the professor said, once Cap'n Mike was gone, "why did you shake your head before? What harm would there be in telling the captain our troubles?"

The feline preened as he spoke, pleased that the professor took his word as sterling. "He *may* be harmless, but...he's a bit nosy for my taste. And he volunteered his assistance a little too quickly, don't you think?"

Before Phillimore could reply, Snow White interrupted huffily. "How canst thou suspicion such an one? To scan his visage is to know his mind!"

Rimski grunted. "I'm sure your opinion counts, Snow-baby. But remember, the queen has spies everywhere!"

"Nonsense, cat! She could never suborn such a specimen! He hath sparkling blue eyes! How canst *not* trust him?"

The professor's own orbs sought the heavens in unspoken exasperation. Then he turned to Ella. "What was *your* opinion of the skipper?"

Brushing a wayward strand of blonde hair into place, Ella made a *who-knows?* gesture with one hand and smiled at Phillimore. "I believe he's too straightforward to worry about," she said. "Of course, if he were in the employ of our neighborly witch-queen, he might well affect that bluff, hearty manner. But we must take into account what this raven-haired maiden has brought in evidence."

Snow White was delighted to have her views apparently confirmed from a quarter where she least expected an ally. She smiled at Ella and asked, "Then you agree that our skipper is too divine to be in any way suspect?"

"Dear child," the other sweetly answered, "you completely mistake my meaning. I meant to call notice to the fact that he paid you a good deal of attention. Now if he's *that* undiscerning, how can anyone credit him with sufficient brains to be duplicitous?"

Snow White jumped to her feet, fury blazing scarlet in her cheeks. She glowered at Phillimore. "Dost thou sufferest this low person to address me—thine own beloved—*thus*?"

"Uh..." the professor stammered, "let's...let's not have a scene, ladies..."

The angry girl began to frame a scathing reply, but then waved Phillimore away with one disgusted gesture and confronted the blonde, instead.

"I warn thee, strumpet, from now on thou'd best keep a civil tongue in thy head."

Ella rose slowly, pushing back her sleeves. "You better watch how you talk to an ex-princess, junior!"

"Ex-princess?" Snow White laughed. "*You*? Your origins proclaim you, plain enough! Ignoble scullery wench!"

"Now that's enough!" Phillimore begged. "Both of you, calm down!" But his suggestion was not acknowledged. The disputants, incensed beyond words, threw themselves at one another, pinching, slapping, yanking hair, squealing and caterwauling sufficient to make the professor cringe and the cat wince.

"Let's step aside," Rimski suggested, scuttling out of the path of one of Ella's slippers, which scudded across the deck to smash to bits against a recumbent anchor. "The true philosopher finds it prudent to observe all such phenomena from an objective distance."

Phillimore joined him by a bulkhead, pausing only to dodge a wild roundhouse that went wide of Ella's midriff. "And what moral precepts are you able to derive from a study of the present phenomenon?"

"That I'd rather be a cat than married," Rimski replied fervently.

* * * *

The brouhaha brought the captain on deck.

"What in tarnation is—?" He stopped, cognizant all of a sudden of the source of the ruckus.

"A minor difference of opinion," meowed the cat as Snow White tugged a quantity of hair from her opponent's skull and uttered a triumphant exclamation: "Dark roots! What did I tell you?"

Ella neatly rebutted her opponent's argumentation by butting her. The tactic did not daunt the younger woman, though; she smartly advanced the issue of balled fist against jutting chin. Ella switched techniques at that stage and shredded Snow White's logic with a systematic tattering of her outer garments.

Cap'n Mike joined Phillimore by the bulkhead.

"I suppose we should do something," the professor remarked.

"I dunno," said the sailor, obviously enjoying the pyrotechnics of distaff debate.

"But oughtn't we try to part them?"

"Are you itchin' to step in between them hellcats?"

"Well," Phillimore sighed, "I guess they'll wear each other out eventually."

"Or kill themselves," Rimski yawned.

* * * *

But the tussle ended sooner than any of the observers anticipated and in an unexpected manner.

The men were facing starboard, so did not immediately see the reason for the sudden diplomatic détente. The women, during a brief pause to catch breath, happened to glance out off the port rail.

Their combined screech set the cat's hair on end.

"What in hell's wrong?" Mike swore. By way of reply, the women pointed to the river portside. The men and Rimski followed their trembling fingers and spied, at a distance of perhaps forty yards, a huge and surprisingly unappealing serpent churning up the surface in a pell-mell rush towards the ship.

"Aww, grape-shot and gopher-guts!" the captain grumped. "It's gonna be one o' them kind-a days!"

With that, he rushed into the wheel-house.

* * * *

Rimski mewed miserably. "Either the skipper's a coward, or he set this all up." He huddled against Phillimore's pants-leg.

The women hunkered down under one of the benches; in spite of their recent enmity, they clasped one another tightly.

"Ah, dear champion," said Snow White to the professor, "wilt thou protect me 'gainst yon fell beast?"

"D-ditto with n-n-nuts on top!" Ella stammered.

"Quit nagging," Phillimore replied. "Rimski, what is that thing?"

"Looks like Nessie."

"*Nessie*? From Scotland?!"

"The same."

"But what's he doing *here*?"

"I imagine," the cat answered, "that the witch-queen sent him."

The man gave a low whistle. "She *does* play rough."

As if to punctuate the sentiment, the creature uncoiled itself until its head was perhaps twenty feet above the surface of the water and roared like an iron foundry at rush-hour.

"*Chuttarachmaunos!*" Rimski wailed, blanching beneath his shaggy gray coat. "We're doomed!"

"Buck up," Phillimore said. "I'll reason with him."

The cat looked at him as if he'd gone mad.

* * * *

Phillimore didn't feel especially courageous, but someone had to refuse to give in to panic. *Maybe I can stall for time?*

Actually, the monster wasn't quite as dreadful as the purple troll. Phillimore hoped that the serpent's vast bulk was not commensurate with a like quantity of intelligence.

As the water-worm hove into view some fifteen yards from the ship's rail, Phillimore held up one hand like a traffic cop and said in a stem voice, "HOLD IT, NESSIE! LET'S SEE YOUR LICENSE!"

The beast stopped short, raised its head another few feet above the surface and fixed Phillimore frostily with an immense yellow eye.

"Lee-cense?" Nessie growled in a deep fortissimo *burr*. "I ken nae lee-cense! Wha' dostha jabber about, mon?"

"I asked for your lee—for your license!" The professor employed his sternest *where-is-your-term-paper?* tone and snapped his fingers impatiently. "Come, come, produce your license at once, Nessie! If you don't have it, prepare to tread water all the way back to Scotland!"

The threat was so unexpected that Nessie actually retreated an inch, eyes wide at the cool air of authority projected by the insignificant mite. But then the serpent remembered he was on queen's business. Bringing more coils out of the water, he used the additional yardage to crane his head down level with the professor's.

"Lee-cense?" he repeated, fixing the man with a baleful glare. "I say I ken nae lee-cense! Lee-cense for who?"

Phillimore crossed his arms and insolently returned Nessie's glower. *Look for a bare spot!* he thought, remembering that dragons and serpents often have a single unprotected patch where they can be assailed. Not that Phillimore had any weapon handy. *Doesn't matter, anyhow*, he told himself, examining the body of the monster in vain for a place without a protective layer of scales. His neck was covered with scarlet wedges like overgrown armadillo-plate; his breast was similarly protected, though there the shingles were a dull amber in hue.

"*Lee-cense for wha'?*" Nessie demanded once more.

"Attack and despoilment!" Phillimore replied. "You can't wreck ferries out of season without the proper papers!"

"*Really?*" Nessie asked, nonplussed. "Truly, lad," he grumbled, lofting another fourteen feet of his gargantuan body from the river-bottom, "I dinna ken tha local customs!"

"Oh, ay," the professor nodded sagely, "ask anyone, you'll discover I'm telling the truth..."

"And I'll jus's do tha' richt na, I weel," the monster replied, suddenly diving below the surface—but not before Phillimore glimpsed a tiny spot near the belly that was bereft of scaly protection.

* * * *

As soon as Nessie disappeared, Cap'n Mike popped his head out of the wheelhouse and cursed roundly.

"Dawg-bone double-damn!" he shouted. "Ah had 'im in mah sights! Whyntchoo keep 'im talkin' another couple seconds?"

The professor shot a dirty look at the tar, but before he could frame an appropriate rejoinder, a perfect geyser of water boiled up from the river not five feet away from the port railing. Phillimore gestured toward the disturbance. "Well, as for that, skipper, I believe you're about to get a second chance."

The captain immediately ducked back into the wheelhouse.

Out of the water stormed a livid Nessie, the pale yellow glow of his enormous eyes now flecked with a dangerous shade of scarlet "Varlet!" he roared. "How dast tha trifle wi' me? There's no sich thing as thy lee-cense!"

"Says who?"

"Says all th' denizens below! I consulted with a school o' eminent sturgeons and nane e'er heerd a' sich a ridiculous thing!"

"Bosh!" Phillimore bluffed. "How can you take their word for it? What do *they* know about topside regulations? Are you trying to defy authority with this fishy tale?"

"Och, I've had weel enow!" the monster bellowed. "Tha queen hast commanded me t' wreck this vessel, an' wreck it I shall, lee-cense or no lee-cense! If there be aught i' the way o' a fine, the dame hersel' can richt wed assume th' debt!"

Further parlay was useless. Nessie rose as far out of the water as was serpently possible, emitting an ear-splitting screech in the process. Phillimore hurled himself beneath the bench where the ladies still quavered with fright.

"Maybe we'd do better overboard!" he yelled at them, but the monster's mighty bellow drowned him out.

Rearing back with his massive skull, Nessie gave the ferry a powerful ram that set the ship rocking sickeningly—though it managed not to founder. With a playful snort, the serpent butted the side of the vessel a second time, obviously toying with it before its final onslaught.

Phillimore clung desperately to the bench, which, fortunately, was solidly fastened to the deck planking. With one hand, he cushioned Rimski against his side. The cat nervously flexed his claws to the detriment of the professor's epidermis.

The; two women's mouths were open, but it was impossible to hear them scream. The river crashed over all the passengers as the ferry rocked from port to starboard to port, righting itself only to yaw in a decidedly alarming fashion.

In the midst of the turmoil and artificial tempest, Phillimore cast one desperate glance aft. To his surprise, the captain, whom he'd written off as a hopeless craven, straddled the port rail with his long legs and aimed a rifle at the rampaging Nessie.

Not a chance, thought Phillimore, deciding that the very desperation of their plight must have lent Cap'n Mike the courage of a raging berserker. But with the pitching ship threatening to broach to any second and with the lake monster vulnerable only in one minute patch and with the target in violent motion, it was clear that the skipper hadn't the slimmest chance of—

CRACK!

* * * *

When the boiling whirlpool swallowed up the dead fresh-water serpent and the captain maneuvered the ferry out of danger of being sucked down with the creature and only when the deck-surface returned to a reasonable facsimile of an horizontal plane, Rimski agreed to stop burrowing his whiskers in the professor's belly.

"What happened?" the cat mewed, still terrified.

Phillimore petted him to reassure Rimski he was no longer in danger. (He still felt peculiar about lavishing affection on a onetime tax collector. Somehow, it seemed a trifle *gauche*).

"What happened," said Snow White with adulation in her every syllable, "is that yon brave seaman hath rid us of the dastardly demon!"

"Shucks," said Cap'n Mike, "'twarn't nothin' ma'am."

"Well," the blonde ex-princess Ella admitted, "it *was* a lucky shot. But the greatest bravery was shown, I ween, when this dear man"—Here she put her arm in Phillimore's "—when this dear man, I say, faced the creature and gave the skipper the opportunity of locating Nessie's one weak point, which, by happy fortune, he managed to penetrate with a single bullet."

"Fortune?" the captain fumed. "Chance? Gol' dang it, ma'am! Don't yew know crack marksmanship when y' sees it? *Luck* mah Aunt Nellie's aspadistra!"

Something at that moment clicked in Phillimore's memory. Pointing to the skipper, he blurted out in a positive voice: "Fink!"

The captain squinted suspiciously. "Who y' callin' a fink?"

"Aren't you *Mike Fink*?"

The other displayed his gold tooth in a broad grin. "Y' mean ya heard o' me, chum?"

"I should say I have! The best sharpshooter on the Mississippi river! One of the greatest folk heroes of the American Midwest!"

Mike Fink turned scarlet to the tips of his hair. "Aw, shucks, y' shouldn't oughtta say them things."

"But they're true."

"Waal, *shore* they are! But they still put th' flush on a man's face, right 'nough..."

* * * *

Now that the captain's identity was firmly affixed, Phillimore was able to assure Rimski that they couldn't hope for a better ally. The cat was still skeptical, but considering the accuracy of the skipper's shooting, decided to accept the new companion for the time being. As for Snow White, she literally clung to the tall man's sleeve. There was no doubt she'd totally switched allegiance to a new champion.

"Never mind," Ella whispered to Phillimore, "*you* don't need a schoolgirl! *You* deserve a maturer mate..."

The professor shrugged. *Some gentlemen do prefer blondes, I suppose.*

They quickly described to Fink their plight in reference to the witch-queen and Phillimore also outlined his quest for Baba Yaga's black sunflower. When he was finished, the captain clapped him on the back.

"*Two* witches!" the stringy sailor exclaimed. "You are sure one Yank with more troubles than a possum in a kettle o' pot likker! Well, we just gonna hafta cancel th' ol' ferry run for a time an' see you-all get hold of that li'l ol' sunflower safely."

"Thanks," the professor said, heartily shaking his hand, "that'll be an enormous help, if you can pilot me to the enchanted island." He turned to Rimski. "Can you tell the captain how to get there?"

The cat shook his head. "No and neither could Walter, if he were here."

"But Walter said he guided other searchers there."

"He did. But that wouldn't make any difference."

"Why not?"

"The island is enchanted, remember?" the cat explained. "It moves around."

"Oh, terrific!" Phillimore groaned. "How do we catch up with it?"

"By consulting a magic atlas."

"And where do we get one of them?"

"In a magic library, shmendrick!" Rimski yelped, his patience at an end.

Cap'n Mike broke in. "There's a castle just upstream that I hear tell has a bookroom like what y' need. I often shuttle visiting sorcerers over thataway."

"Sounds like the right kind of place," Phillimore nodded.

"Only one thing," the skipper said. "It ain't the safest place, I hear, t' fetch a visit on."

The professor sighed deeply.

"I'm delighted to hear that," he murmured. "I was so afraid life might begin to grow dull..."

* * * *

Brambles everywhere.

Brambles crackling underfoot, brambles choking progress along the faint footway. Brambles twined with brake and branch, brambles twisted around tree-trunks. Brambles tearing sleeves and catching trouser-legs. Brambles forbidding access to the ancient castle, brambles screening the way and brambles blocking it. The only edge-tools the two men had were boat-hooks. The going, therefore, was tortuously slow. While the women waited with Rimski back on the docked ferry, James Phillimore and Mike Fink grimly hacked a passage through the barrier of thorns.

"How long have these damned things been sprouting?" the professor growled, taking a vicious sideswipe at one bristly bush.

"Accordin' t' local stories," Fink said, "these here stickers've bin shootin' up well over a hunderd yar."

"I *thought* so, but let me make sure...What, precisely, is the nature of the danger to those who enter the castle?"

"I heerd if y' stay too long, y'drop off t' sleep and don' wake up."

Just what I thought! Phillimore paused in his labors to wipe sweat from his forehead with the back of his hand. "All right, Mike, now listen to me—when we finally chop our way through these damnable weeds, you go straight to the castle library and search for the map that'll show us where the enchanted isle is."

"But how 'bout you?"

"Trust me. I have a plan to gain time for us..."

* * * *

The main reason Phillimore sought the tower, Phillimore told himself, was to save the two of them from falling into a magical slumber. Yet the task did not totally repel him, either. After all, what *had* he come to Faërie for in the first place?

He put all thoughts of Snow White and Ella temporarily out of his mind.

It was not easy to locate the legendary tower room. When the young princess called Sleeping Beauty first climbed up to that fatal hideaway, it was to a part of the castle unknown or forgotten by her royal family. (In the Disney film, the professor recalled, the garret-room was concealed by a secret entranceway. He wasn't sure which version his subconscious might conjure up in the world-set he was in.)

He had no recourse but to trust to luck. Up and up he went, traversing dusty, drafty corridors, poking his way through venerable cobwebs, timidly testing the treads on rotted wooden staircases, clambering like a goat up stone steps chewed and pocked by time's devouring teeth.

The air grew increasingly stuffy. He found it harder and harder to breathe.

Wonder how Fink's doing down in the library?

Phillimore stopped to catch his breath. He leaned against a tapestry-covered wall.

It was so quiet he could hear the pounding of his heart laboring for oxygen. Dim sunlight filtered through dust-caked casements. It was as close as an attic packed with curios.

Phillimore yawned.

* * * *

In the library, Mike Fink cracked open a huge Atlas. Its title was *Necromantic Age: Cartographic Supplement, Annual Sites & Plots*.

He turned the great pages, one at a time. The book was so big it was a tiring effort just to turn the leaves. The repetitive action drained and lulled him; his glazed eyes found it difficult to focus properly.

A familiar contour roused him, a curve of river in one blue-dominated chart. Squinting, he moved close to the page and discerned the very waters on which they navigated...and here was the spot he'd tied up to less than two hours before. Beyond, the stream swept past town and harbor and out to sea...

And there—perhaps twenty-five leagues from shore and concealed by a chain of coral islets—was a single green hummock of land. The legend beneath noted it as the approximate location that season of the enchanted domain of the Beast. Instructions for plotting its precise position were offered in a footnote whose letters were so tiny that Fink had to slit his eyes to read them.

Bit by bit, he deciphered the cabalistic formula. Then, flopping flat on the tabletop, scattering maps and books right and left, he fell fast asleep.

* * * *

"What's keeping them?" Rimski mewed for the tenth time, anxiously pacing the deck.

"Mayhap they've fallen afoul of the witch again," Snow White worried, chewing her lip. "Perhaps it were good that we absent ourselves from the vicinity?"

"A splendid idea," Ella cheerily concurred. "Why don't you leave first?"

"Giving you a free hand with my champions? Never!"

"*Your* champions?" The blonde laughed. "They don't need a girl, there's a lady aboard!"

"True? *I* see her not..."

"Please," Rimski begged, "don't quarrel. We've got enough *tsooris* without another free-for-all."

"Odd that you quote this maiden's going rate," Ella remarked with a toss of her golden locks. Snow White's cheeks flushed angrily, but before she could reply, the blonde walked to the exit ramp and declared her intention to go to the men's assistance. "Coming, Snowy?"

"I'll wait here, thank you," she replied frostily.

"Really?" Ella inquisitively cocked an eyebrow. "Aren't you concerned I'll steal away your champions?"

"Only common women traipse after men," Snow White declared airily, arranging the pleats of her peasant skirt.

"I suppose you'd be the one to know." Turning away from her, Ella bent down and affectionately patted the shaggy cat. "Better stay here and protect Snowy's putative honor."

"What's that supposed to mean?" hissed Snowy.

"A charitable fiction, child." Ella smiled blithely and stepped onto the gangway.

* * * *

Somehow managing to rouse himself, the professor forced his heavy feet to work, one shuffling step at a time.

Don't fall asleep...don't fall asleep...asleep...fall asleep...sleep...

He shook his head vigorously, alarmed at the way his thoughts conspired to lull him. He fell to cursing Baba Yaga for taking his umbrella, but the imprecation assumed the quality of ritual, repeating itself and repeating itself, so he tried to think of other things.

Hope Mike's found the map. Hope he's not asleep...asleep...asleep...

Once more, Phillimore wrenched himself back from the abyss of unnatural slumber. He concentrated on his catly companion, Rimski, philosopher-feline, but soon monotonous mewed syllogisms reiterated propositions in his skull...

Just then, he noticed a subtle sound, a drone. Save for his own footsteps, it was the first thing he'd heard since leaving Fink on the ground floor. The muted buzz woke him a little.

He blinked. Up ahead he spied a narrow, winding staircase that led yet higher to a shadowy eyrie at the very apex of the castle. *Must be it*! Step by sluggish step, he staggered up and up and up. Three-fourths somnolent, he negotiated the latter portion of the stairs on hands and knees. He pinched himself to stay awake. At last he crawled onto a small stone landing, thick with dust. His hands and knees were coated with grime.

There was a tall oaken door giving off the landing. He padded to it on all fours.

Got to rest a second...

Phillimore leaned his head against the door. It swung inward, depositing him with a smart smack on the flagging. *OW*! The pain woke him up.

Scrabbling at the portal, he hauled himself to his feet and took a tottering step across the threshold.

Here the buzzing was louder. It was a lofty garret, oval-shaped and fashioned entirely from green stones. The close atmosphere which choked the whole castle evidently emanated from the attic he was in, for nowhere else was the thick air so concentrated, dense and still. A new wave of ennui washed over him.

And then he saw Sleeping Beauty.

* * * *

In a far curve of the cell, beneath a thin, dusty window, there stretched a long pallet. The only other objects in the room were a mirror hung on one wall and an antique spindle at the head of the bed. On the cot lay the princess.

Tall she was, well over six feet, a veritable Amazon. *Never liked rangy girls*! Her flaming scarlet tresses were complemented by a bright red mustache and chin-whiskers of the same startling hue.

Good Gad, Phillimore winced, *her hair's been growing all the time she's been asleep!* He closed his eyes.

The buzzing now was so loud it jangled every synapse he owned. The sound came from the dreaming princess—no less a phenomenon than her regal snores.

Gorblimey! the professor shuddered, *do I really have to kiss that*?

In spite of the sleeper's lumber-camp suspirations, he felt tired once more. The spell fought to subdue him. *Really no choice, I have to break the enchantment.*

He tottered to the foot of the bed and climbed onto the cot next to her. Eyelids drooping, brain whirling into night, he began to add his own snores to those of the princess. But as he flopped beside her, he managed to aim his lips accurately at hers.

* * * *

Downstairs, Ella took a welcome breath and got up from the floor where she'd fallen. She continued her search, soon found the library door, peeked inside and saw Cap'n Mike stretching his arms and yawning with wide-open mouth.

"B'gosh," he muttered thickly, "that *were* a refreshin' forty winks!" He rubbed the sleep from his eyes and saw her. "Hey, gal, good news! I found Jim-boy's map!"

"Wonderful...but where is he?"

"Upstairs someplace."

"Come on, then—he may need our help." She took his hand and pulled him along. Now peering here, now there, they mounted steps, peeked into bedrooms and pantries. Nobles and slaveys alike sat up, trying to recollect the business of a life long laid aside. All were too disoriented to pay much note to the pair of strangers prying into every niche of the waking castle.

"Look," Ella suddenly exclaimed, pointing to a line of footprints in the deep dust of a remote hallway.

"He must've come this way, Ellie!"

They dashed along, following the trail.

It eventually led them to the narrow stone staircase. Climbing to the top, they heard sounds of a struggle within.

Ella burst through the door first. She saw a furious professor vainly trying to free himself from the ardent embrace of a giant red-haired maiden.

"Let me go, will you!"

"Nay, wee champion, nay!" the Amazon crooned. "Ye've roused me from a wicked fairy's spell and now tha'll reap the reward of thine brave action!"

Mike Fink, observing her mustache and chin-whiskers, silently agreed such a rescue was, indeed, brave—if not downright foolhardy.

"What in hell is going on here?" Ella demanded, arms folded, foot tapping impatiently. She squinted at the princess in decidedly unneighborly fashion.

"This cute wee morsel," said the red-haired woman, "woke me from a sorcerous sleep with the salute of his lips. I know my rights—who rescueth me, marries me!"

"*Marry you*?" Phillimore spluttered. "If I could've woken you up some other way, I wouldn't even have kissed you!"

"Ah, well," Unsleeping Beauty philosophically observed, "ye'll grow accustomed to me in time."

"I'll *never* grow accustomed to your face."

She frowned. "What's wrong with my face? I was always rated comely."

"But have you looked at yourself recently?"

Hefting Phillimore under one arm, the princess tramped to the suspended looking-glass and studied her reflection. After a few seconds, she grinned broadly and emitted a delighted giggle. "O wondrous rare! And my stuffy father once boasteth that only a man can be thus resplendently ornamented."

Marvelous, Phillimore groaned to himself, *an incipient libber*. He stared at Fink and Ella and coldly asked whether they might stop laughing long enough to help him get away from the redhead.

"Sure," Ella said, doing her best to straighten up. "Come, Captain, let's take care of yon crimson pirate."

But the skipper was too busy holding his sides together to be of much assistance. Undaunted, Ella strode smartly up to the princess and, without pause or preamble, briskly belted her in the brisket. Quoth the princess: "Oof!"

Releasing her hold on Phillimore, she staggered backward, clutching her tummy. Her bent position presented a generous target to the waiting point of the potent spindle.

Quoth the princess: "Owoo!"

Plucking the offending object from her seat, the redhead glared at it, exasperated, then sank down upon the couch.

Quoth the princess: "Here we go again..."

And she recommenced to snore.

* * * *

"Quick," said the professor, "we have to get out of the castle before the spell puts us all to sleep!" He punctuated the comment with a great yawn.

Fink grasped Phillimore's arm with one hand and Ella's with the other. They plunged out the chamber-door and tumbled downstairs, flailing end over end.

At the bottom, the professor wobbled to his knees, but immediately began to sway rhythmically, eyes closing.

"Help me stand him up," Ella said, extricating herself with difficulty from the tangle of intermingled limbs.

* * * *

Somehow the trio managed to descend to the ground floor. But by then, the professor, who'd been in the higher reaches of the castle longer than the others, was deep asleep and could in no way be shaken out of it. Mike and Ella lugged him by the arms toward the front door, but it was still a long way off.

Ella's legs rubbered beneath her. "I...I don't think I...can...make... it..."

"Lie down, then, honey-puss," the captain told her. He was strangely alert.

"Naaw, Ellie-gal, let ol' Jim go, I c'n manage 'im th' rest o' th' way. Once we's outside, he'll wake up 'n' we c'n both hightail it back here 'n' carry you out." Nodding gratefully, Ella slumped onto the cold floor and slept. Fink, though not altogether unaffected by the enchantment, managed to keep his word and jostle Phillimore to the entrance portal and through it. The professor immediately woke. After a few grateful breaths of fresh air, he was sufficiently revitalized to reenter with the skipper and rescue the sleeping blonde.

At last, all three stood in the forest. Ella's fluttering eyelashes flickered at the sailor.

"Dear Captain Fink," she cooed, "how on earth *did* you manage to resist that sleep-spell so long?"

"Waal, Ellie, it were either that or g'wan back and *personally* smooch Ol' Daddy's Mustache!"

Phillimore heartily slapped Fink on the back. "Good work, Mike! You got the map, I see!"

"Yep, but shucks, I on'y did part o' th' job." He tipped his hat as he helped a frankly-admiring Ella to her feet. If Phillimore noticed any look pass between them, he said nothing about it.

* * * *

They began to walk toward the path the men hacked earlier through the forest. "At least," Phillimore remarked, "we've earned a brief—"

As if in ironic punctuation to the sentiment, an ominous growl rose from a spot not far off and to their left, screened from view by the thick tangle of brambles that networked the woods.

The men stared uneasily at one another.

"Probably just a wild animal," the professor suggested.

"NOT...WILD...ANIMAL!" a throaty growl objected.

Ella whimpered. "What *is* it?"

"Whatever it is, I tell ye what," Fink whispered. "You draw the critter round th' other side o' th' castle, then have it chase y' to th' ferry."

"And what will *you* be doing?" Phillimore demanded with some asperity.

"This!" said Fink, running like hell up the forest path.

* * * *

"Whenever it gets the least bit dicey," the professor grumbled, "that Fink manages to duck out." Ella came to the skipper's defense. "That's not fair! When the serpent attacked, Mike only went to his cabin to get his rifle."

"Maybe," Phillimore grumpily conceded, "but *this* time—"

"THIS TIME YOU GET EAT!" the as-yet-unseen thing growled. It was much closer; they could hear it scuffling and stomping through the undergrowth.

Grabbing Ella's arm, Phillimore sprinted around the side of the castle, stopping at the corner to see what manner of danger stalked them.

A tremendous crash. Suddenly a great flailing bludgeon flashed into view, flattening a section of thorny interposing branches. From the woody ruins emerged a single-eyed ogre that looked something like a fourteen-foot-tall goat standing on its hind legs.

"Uh-oh," gulped Phillimore. "Wonder if the witch-queen sent him?"

"Who cares?" Ella yelped. "Let's move our butts!"

But the monster heard the professor's question. It grinned nastily. "*NOT* FREELANCE!" came the throaty reply.

* * * *

So they led the beast a chase about the castle. It could not see well out of its one centrally-located eye, but the shag-legged thing had an excellent sense of smell. Though they ducked behind buttresses and dropped beneath eaves and hid within porticos, it but paused each time long enough to sniff once or twice before licking its protrusive canines in anticipatory pleasure and prancing in their precise direction.

"Come on," panted Phillimore, "that's enough eaves-dropping. Let's run!"

He had observed that the ogre was incapable of speed and therefore decided a protracted sprint was the best plan. It was true that the thing's gait was hampered by a peculiar dragging hunch of its haunches—but in partial compensation, it took large steps. Another factor militating against the wisdom of the professor's scheme was that both he and Ella were physically exhausted from their foray in the enchanted castle.

Still, now that the initial shock upon first seeing the monster had worn off, the two experienced a brief surge of adrenalin that carried them around to the castle-front.

"Hurry, Ella! To the forest!"

They dashed across the clearing to the narrow path hewn earlier by the two men. Stopping at its edge, Phillimore stooped and retrieved the two boathooks they'd employed. He passed one to Ella.

"Try to hit it in the eye!"

The ogre thumped menacingly into view.

"Wait till it's closer..." said the professor. "All right...NOW!"

They both threw the boathooks. One stuck in the beast's leg. The other, thrown by Phillimore, came close to its forehead, but the ogre managed to catch it in midair. In a leisurely fashion, it brought the iron point up to its mouth, bit off the entire hook and began to chew it methodically.

"AHH!" the creature belched. "IRON GOOD IN DIET!"

The sight appalled the professor and his companion. But worse was a sudden crash from a point some thirty yards off to their right.

A new voice—loud, deep and gravelly-textured—rang out in the woods. "SAVE ME ONE, MANNY!"

The ogre waved a claw in acknowledgment and yanked Ella's boathook from its leg. "APPETIZER WAITING, JACK!" it roared in reply.

"Oh, Good Lord!" Phillimore complained. "Now there's two of them!"

"USED TO BE THREE!" said Manny. "BUT DRAGON ATE BROTHER. WE AIN'T GOT NO MOE!"

* * * *

Weariness was taking its toll of the two mortals, but they started through the woods, nevertheless, forcing their legs to carry them as fast as they were still capable.

The day was near its end. The trail between the trees was narrow and gloomy and brambles conspired to snag their garments. More than once, they tripped, bumping elbows or knees.

The diversion of the boathooks gained them a few precious minutes, but now the hunt was up again. The second ogre swung its club from side to side, wantonly smashing branches as it gave chase.

SMASH! SMASH! SMASH!

The twin horrors drew inexorably nearer.

Phillimore and Ella broke through to the beach, but the ferry was another fifty feet along the shoreline.

"We *have* to make it!" Phillimore insisted, half-shoving, half-carrying Ella.

"I can't do it!"

SMASH! SMASH!

Out of the forest emerged the ogres. Grinning evilly, they spread out to right and left. One of them cut off their passage to the ferry, the other circled round their flank.

"What can we do?" the blonde cried. "We're trapped!"

"Keep moving, Ella! Fake them out! Run zigzag!"

"I *can't*! My ankle hurts!" She sank to the sand.

"Get up!" he yelped, tugging at her sleeve. The material ripped.

SMASH!

The second ogre swung its club against the bole of a cherry tree and broke it in half. Then it stamped further into the sand, nearing its prey.

On the other side, the first ogre marched steadily onward, slavering and chomping its teeth. It was close enough for them to smell its fetid breath.

"*Jim-boy*!"

Phillimore whirled, sudden hope flaring. He anxiously scanned the seascape but could not see the skipper.

"Over *here*!" Fink shouted, waving his arm. The professor spotted him at the edge of the forest, rifle in hand, standing ankle-deep in a small stream.

"Quick!" Phillimore yelled. "Plug 'em!"

"Not yet!"

"Huh? What do you *mean*?"

"I mean, *not yet*, mate! Make 'em chase y' a while."

"*What*?"

"Get 'em t' chase after y', Jimbo!"

Before Phillimore could protest the two ogres turned in his direction, grinning.

"HO-KAY BY US!" roared Manny.

"YOU BET!" Jack agreed.

And they both converged on the professor.

* * * *

Phillimore dodged and twisted and scampered along the beach in a desperate effort to escape becoming an ogre's entrée.

Little by little, the great beasts closed in on him. All the while, Fink lounged patiently, feet in the water, rifle trailing negligently by his side.

"How long do I have to keep this up?" Phillimore croaked. "I've been dodging them for five minutes!"

"IT OKAY TO STOP," Manny said considerately.

"*WE* DON'T MIND!" Jack echoed.

"Just a little longer," Fink called. "Make 'em come t' you, then drop down on the sand!"

"Are you *crazy*?"

"*Just do like I say!*"

"YEAH! DO LIKE HE SAY!" Manny advised.

"SOUND LIKE GOOD PLAN TO ME!" Jack opined.

Now they were only a few feet away. Phillimore spun and tried to run to the water, but Manny interposed himself between the professor and the sea. Pivoting, Phillimore dodged the other ogre's reaching arm and attempted to run between its legs, but it closed them.

"That's *perfect*!" Fink shouted. "Now hit th' sand!"

Phillimore collapsed in a heap upon the beach, resigned to the inevitability of his destiny as a nutriment. Behind him, Manny rasped hot breath on his neck. In front, Jack hobbled up hungrily.

Mike Fink hefted his rifle and squeezed off a shot.

Crack!

Both monsters howled in rage and pain, clutching the remains of their eyes.

Manny emitted a bellow, crumpled to the sand and died.

The other ogre blindly reached out one talon, raking the air in an attempt to rend Phillimore to bits. But then it, too, folded over, dead, and landed smack on top of the professor.

* * * *

"*See*?" Ella exclaimed while Fink shoved the ogre off his friend. "Mike saved us both! Now aren't you ashamed you spoke so ill of him before?"

Rising painfully to his feet, Phillimore ignored her and demanded why Fink made him wait so long before shooting the ogres.

"Shucks, son," he replied, "I on'y had one bullet left: had t' wait till they got in a straight line so's I could hit 'em both."

With that, Phillimore rather abruptly stretched out again upon the beach.

* * * *

Once they were all back on board, Fink instructed his crew to set off and sail as long as the moon shone bright. He hoped to make town by morning, stopping just long enough to replenish supplies—cartridges in particular.

Once he found a liniment for the professor to massage on his stiff spots and after he'd prepared a cold pack for Ella's ankle, the ferryman sat down with his friends. Rimski happily snuggled on the professor's lap, glad Phillimore was safe.

"Is it true, Rimski," the professor asked, "that Puss in Boots once swallowed an ogre?"

"Hmpf. I wouldn't be surprised. That cat has one *big* mouth."

Ella, gritting her teeth against the ache in her *tarsus*, remarked upon Snow White's absence. The maiden was nowhere upon the boat.

"Well, after you left, Ella," said Rimski, ruffling his whiskers, "the whole *shmegeggle* of dwarfs showed up. They've been looking for Snowy ever since we all ran out of her cottage with the witch after us. Anyway, she thought maybe she better stick with her original protectors."

Ella nodded. "Naturally. After all, there's *seven* of them." She yawned. "Tedious topic. Is there any food aboard?"

Rimski said, "Oh, I forgot to mention: she left her picnic basket behind. Said there's an apple in it for Ella."

The blonde dug into the folds of the basket, found an empty thermos and a single pome with tooth-marks and a missing chunk.

"Don't eat that," Phillimore warned.

"I know better," said Ella, tossing the apple over the rail. Where it splashed, a sudden foam of bubbles gurgled in the moonlight.

"Poisonous little bitch," Ella cursed. "What *did* you ever see in her, Jim?"

Phillimore had no answer.

"Waal, never mind, thar's plenty o' grub in th' cabin."

Ella beamed. "And would *you* serve me sup?"

"Why, shorely, ma'am!" Fink rose, touching his cap in salute to the blonde.

The professor and the cat exchanged a knowing glance.

"*La donna è mobile*," Rimski mewed beneath his breath.

* * * *

The night air was mild and there was a pleasant breeze. They decided they all would sleep beneath the stars on the top-deck. Fink provided bedrolls for the humans and a warm blanket for the animal. Phillimore worried the accommodations might offend Rimski, but the cat dismissed the notion with an off-tailed gesture.

"When I was a tax collector, believe you me, I *shlaffed* in a lot worse beds!" Abruptly vanishing, he padded invisibly to the blanket, snuggled down and reappeared a little at a time.

* * * *

Long after Rimski and Ella fell asleep, Phillimore and Mike Fink sat and talked. The lanky riverman, looking rather uncomfortable, chewed thoughtfully at a tobacco-plug.

"Waal, I know why y' might uv bin ticked off when I hotfooted it back t' th' ferry, but mah rifle was the best bet, doncha see?"

"Perhaps. But why couldn't you take it along in the first place?"

"Aww, son, don't ask me that..."

"But I *am* asking."

"I'd druther not tell ya. It's kind-a personal." Expectorating the tobacco-chaw, Fink shamefully lowered his head. "I'll say this much, Jimmy: if'n I had brought muh rifle 'long, it wouldn't of done *no* good and that's a fact!"

Just then, an odd bit of data concerning the Mike Fink legend dislodged itself from Phillimore's memory. "Of course!" he exclaimed, snapping his fingers. "You're only a crack shot when you fire *across water*! We were too far inland. On land, you can't hit the side of a dead dragon!"

Swiveling so he faced the professor, Fink stared at him in amazement, not altogether friendly. "Now how the deuce," he demanded, "did Y know that? It's m' closest kep' secret."

Phillimore shrugged. "Bit of a fey quality, I fancy."

"Fey, my granny's nanny!"

So Phillimore explained about interworldly travel and the marvels of owning a thought-controlled dimensional transfer engine in the form of an umbrella.

"Man, *man*," Fink murmured when the other was through. "An' I thought I heerd tall tales before!" Still, he was at a loss to find any better explanation.

Suddenly, the ferryman pulled a long face. "You ain't gonna go tell Ella about this, are y' Jim?"

Phillimore sighed. "No, I suppose not."

"Yer a real pal!"

Hmph, the professor thought sourly, but could find nothing specific to complain about in Fink's behavior to the blonde, so he held his tongue.

"Funny how I cain't hit nothin' on land," Fink mused. "Mebbe it's 'cause I growed up on th' river and got used to a deck beneath mah feet."

"Hold on," Phillimore said, suddenly puzzled. "When you shot the ogres, you were on the beach."

"Yeah...but I had m' tootsies in a brook. Long as I got water near mah feet, I c'n hit the left earlobe of a moth at fifty yards! I gotta shoot across water to make it count."

Phillimore screwed up his face in deep concentration. "Pardon the pun, Mike, but you just triggered something."

"Like what?"

"A way for you to shoot well on land."

"*Real*? What *is* it?"

"I can't remember it yet. But give me time, I'll bring it to mind."

"We're both pretty tuckered," Fink said, patting Phillimore gently on the arm. "Let's turn in now and talk some more t'morrah. We gotta get up early if'n we wants t' see the magic isle by mid-afternoon."

Fink crawled into his bedroll and said good night, but Phillimore sat up a while longer, deep in thought.

He reflected sourly on his many troubles: on Baba Yaga's highhanded appropriation of his escape-route *y clept* umbrella (which Rimski believed was gone for good); on the crone's geas to locate her blasted youth-restoring black sunflower; on the unflagging malice of the queen-witch and her menacing minions—ogres and serpents *and who-knows-what's-coming-next*? Not to mention the miscellaneous perils of Hessians, horses and headsmen...

So far, Phillimore grumbled, *this trip has not been a picnic*! As for his original amatory reason in coming, it was not only unfulfilled, but Phillimore now had grave doubts that he'd even come to the best of all possible worlds for his purposes. Most of the women he'd met were extremely unappealing, Snow White being a particularly insidious bit of poor judgment on his heart's part. How easily he might have succumbed to her superficial charms, how tardy *might* have been his disillusionment!

Even Ella was no prize, he told himself (not totally successfully). He had to admit she was refreshingly down-to-earth and, in her own feisty fashion, quite loyal. But still, the blonde was no intellectual giant and, *anyway, she's just as fickle as Snow White*! And that *was* what mattered, ultimately, wasn't it?

But on the other hand, what if Phillimore's ill luck in distaff quarters were really his own fault? *Do I expect too much*? *Do I invite women at first, but finally drive them off*?

It was an impenetrable maze. At fast thought, he could think of nothing specific he'd done or said to justify the unexpected personal speculation. But at root, the professor knew he regarded life too often from a distance, weighing it and finding it not up to his personal standards. He admitted being guilty of a particularly unbending formality that might initially intrigue a woman, but ultimately bore her.

But the ego always expects to meet its equal, even though the privilege is rarely warranted! And what, then, were the perquisites of the Phillimorean Perfect Mate? The professor ticked off the necessities on the fingers of one hand:

1. *Beauty*—though he blushed to admit the shallow truth, the fact was, he couldn't imagine himself taken with any but the comely.

2. *Intellect*—he noted the difference between mere intelligence (*a kenning for homely common sense*) and the quality he craved: a recondite command of the secreted treasures of the mind, a rarified joy in the subtle play and tang of words in profuse gradations of subtlety.

3. *Good humor*—a sweet temper was a soothing commodity, much to be valued...but more important to Phillimore was the capacity to see every situation in its most ridiculous light and laugh at it despite any gods that might deem the matter sacrosanct. (Sad to relate, Phillimore, in his pre-umbrella days, was thought to be totally devoid of humor by his Parker College colleagues. But he stoutly maintained that his risibility was of so dry a character as to be perceptible solely by discerning sympathetic souls...an exclusive company that naturally *would* include his ardently-craved Hypothetical Heart-of-Hearts.)

To the professor, then, *das ewig-weibliche* must be invested with the above commodities, cunningly intermingled with a lusty interest in practicing (or rather, *rehearsing*) for the production of progeny.

But where, O where, is she to be found? his spirit apostrophized.

No place, buster! his mocking mind answered. *She doesn't exist—and even if she did, you wouldn't deserve her!*

He wondered why he was always prepared to believe the worst of himself. But even as he considered it, Phillimore lay down to sleep, resolving to give up his foolish search for *la belle dame sans pareil* and confine himself, instead, to recovering his umbrella. *Then I'll go home. Wherever that might be.*

* * * *

By late afternoon, they reached the magic isle.

The morning was spent resupplying the ferry. Captain Fink pointed out the chart he'd studied indicated there was no fresh-water source on the island, so, since the professor had no idea how long it might take to discover the whereabouts of the sunflower, it was deemed wise to stock up on sweet water and jugs to carry it in. Fink himself took to carrying the thermos left behind by Snow White.

There was one other commodity that the skipper scoured the town for: silver bullets. It almost delayed them past sailing, but he insisted on waiting till a smith fashioned a few, "jest in case th' witch sends somethin' wuss at us!"

Despite the late departure, they reached their destination while the sun still shone on the face of the waters.

"Thar 'tis, Jimmy!" Mike Fink declared, pointing to the verdant mound lying low in the sea. "It's 'zackly where I figgered it. Wanna set out for't now? Or wait till mornin'?"

"I'd just as soon go immediately," Phillimore said.

"Okay, I'll stow gear in th' jollyboat an' we'll—"

"Hold on, Mike," the professor interrupted. "There's no we this time. I'm going alone."

"Aww, now, don' start playin' hero, Jim-boy! Tain't safe t' go an'—' Phillimore forestalled him with an upraised palm. "The last thing I feel is heroic! But this started out my quest and it's likely to be dangerous on the island."

"All the more reason I better go with ya'!"

"All the more reason I *cannot* permit my friends to come along! I've appreciated your protection, Mike, but the understanding was you'd help me reach the island, not come along with me. I don't think at this stage fancy shooting would be of much use...and besides, your marksmanship deteriorates dramatically on dry land."

Mike Fink argued with the professor, but the scholar proved adamant. At the last, he reluctantly agreed to permit Rimski to come along on the venture, but only if the cat promised to stay invisible, a stipulation to which Rimsky gladly agreed.

The professor's courage momentarily turned Ella's head. At the last instant, she tried to bull her way into the boat. Phillimore, shaking his head, gave her a friendly kiss on the cheek, a salute that was totally without passion. Then he turned away and clutched the oars.

Just before he faded from view, Rimski nuzzled his shaggy head against his friend's arm. The look on the cat's face was decidedly grim.

"You don't seem sanguine about the outcome of this foray," Phillimore remarked. "Are you sure you won't wait on the ferry?"

"Sure I'd like to, *zhlub*!" the unseen cat replied with unaccustomed severity. "But I got you out of trouble with Baba in the first place, so I better stick with you now her quest is near the end!"

"Thanks, Rimski." With that, the professor hastily turned his face toward the island where dwelt Beauty and the fabulous Beast.

It looked peaceful enough from far off.

* * * *

Sailing into a graceful harbor, Phillimore rowed toward the doming crest that was the nearest shore.

He and the invisible cat stepped onto a beach of spun-sugar sand that rolled gently back and upward to a small hill lightly downed with early spring grasses.

On either side of the bay, the island extended peninsular projections, tame curvets of land that circled so far around the water they nearly cut off the sea and made the place a placid lagoon.

All was silent. The perfumed breeze bore a hint of lush tropic vegetation, but the air was mainly thin and fresh as the earliest dawn in Eden. Somewhere above, a lark trilled.

"I don't like this," Rimski grumbled, printing a line of feline footpads along the sand.

"Why?"

"Can't say, *tovarich*...but there's something infernal in it."

"Nonsense," Phillimore scoffed, "it's a veritable paradise." But he didn't believe it. Something disturbed him about the beach, he couldn't define what it was.

They trod lightly on the moist ground from which sparse grassblades stuck up. They were closer to the hill. The professor quickened his pace. Rimski hung back.

"There must be a trail to get over that rise," said Phillimore.

And then he saw the mansion.

* * * *

A little way above the level of the ground, he noted a darkness in the hillock. As he peered into the cave's dimness, the professor discerned— glinting in a wayward shaft of late afternoon sun—the marble columns and ornamentations of a great hidden building, wide doors invitingly agape.

"I'm not going in there," Rimski whined.

"Of course not. Wait for me."

The feline did his best to dissuade Phillimore, but to no avail.

* * * *

Although the entire place was below the surface of the earth, a resplendent glow softly lit it. All was gleaming pink and white: vaulting ceilings bedecked with rococo friezes; glimmering flooring cunningly worked with tiled designs swirling and shimmering; winking dimples of mother-of-pearl sparkling in the iridescent blush of coral walls; scintillating chandeliers that shed crystal drops of light.

Gently Phillimore stepped along, afraid lest one heavy footfall dispel the delicate magic and leave him lorn upon the lonely shingle. And so he passed the outer chambers, following the curving tiles that swept him toward the promised mysteries of the house's innermost recesses.

* * * *

At the heart of the abode was a bedroom buffered with folds of satin and rich velvet. In the middle of the room, on an oval bed, reclined a smiling woman with skin so fair it seemed too soft to touch with aught harsher than a feather.

Young she was and so beautiful that, beside her, Snow White would have appeared an unweaned infant; Ella would but reflect femininity like a muddy pond feebly returning the glory of the dawning sun.

Her body was slim and perfectly proportioned. Her arms were graceful without being either too thin or fleshy and they ended in long, artistic fingers that traced the blue gossamer of her gown and decorously draped it over a thigh sculpted, he was sure, by the Muse herself. Her sparkling eyes—merry with the irrepressible spirit of good humor—shone blue as her diaphanous chamber-wear; her long hair was so light in color as to be nearly white; its glorious sheen thrilled with silver highlights as she turned her bewitching smile full upon the professor.

Her graceful pink lips parted to reveal even white teeth, small and exquisitely shaped like the buds of new-picked early corn. Her eyes found his and held them in a long, searching look that was almost an embrace. And then, at last she spoke.

"My Love," quoth she, "is of a birth as rare
As 'tis for object strange and high..."

Emotion surged in Phillimore's breast. Fervently he replied, "My love is begotten by Despair—"

"Upon impossibility," she breathed in perfect unison with the professor.

Marvelous! thought Phillimore.

* * * *

How long he rested with her he did not know. It might have been a moment or the better part of an hour, he could not keep track of the enchanted seconds that elapsed as they spoke of things little known and long forgotten. He found her as clever as she was wise, as brilliant as she was beautiful and withal, possessed of a wit so nimble that he had much to do to scamper to comprehend its capering subtleties. All *he* knew, she knew...and more. Every transient mood and whim and dread he'd ever pondered laboriously upon in his solitude *she* danced lightly over, understanding all and dismissing the old terrors with conquering laughter.

At length, they held each other close and kissed and James Philli-more found the shape and terms of love.

* * * *

"So you must pluck *the* black sunflower in my keeper's garden," Beauty said sometime later.

"It's all I need to repossess my umbrella. Then I can take you away from all this."

"Yes," she sighed, "I *am* weary of this castaway life. The Beast is kindly to me, but I find his thought shackled and his manners coarse. I can never love him...certainly not now that I have sampled perfection."

The professor beamed and pressed his lips to her fingertips.

"And will you return for me when the flower is in your possession? Shall we flee together?"

"Yes!" he fervently replied.

"Then I will tell you where to find it." Uncertainty appeared briefly in her azure eyes. "You *will* return? You haven't simply used me to dis-cover—"

"Hush," breathed the professor. "I love you!"

At that, she smiled and traced the contour of his cheek and chin with the nails of one hand. Where her fingers touched his skin, they left thin red lines.

* * * *

Outside, he walked where she'd instructed, oblivious to all but the promptings of his heart. He thought he still heard Beauty calling his name, but so ensorcelled was he that Rimski had to repeat himself thrice before he could get the professor's attention.

"Oh, Rimski, it's only you. I thought—"

"*Only* me?" the cat grumbled. "You were expecting maybe the Bre-men Town Musicians? I'd just about given you up! What took you so long?"

"Ah, Rimski, I just met the most magnificent lady in my entire life!"

"Is *that* what you've been doing? *Shmutzing* around when you're supposed to be looking for that *f'shimmelte* sunflower?!"

"You don't understand! I'm in love!"

The animal snorted in disgust. "Again?"

"No, for the *first* time."

"May I remind you," Rimski yawned, "of your great passion for Snow White and your unarticulated, but woefully obvious hankering for Ella?"

"I didn't know better then. They were infatuations—this is the real thing!"

"Excuse me for being skeptical."

The professor tolerated his companion with the pity of the truly enlightened. "I don't blame you for not understanding, Rimski. A love like
this comes along seldom."

"For which, much thanks," the cat replied. "When it comes to Great
Romance, I'd rather have a gall bladder attack!"

"How would *you* know? You're only a cat."

"Let me remind you I was once a tax collector," Rimski huffed. "And
I chased plenty of women in those days, even landed a few. I suffered lots
of grand passions and I even got married once. For all I know, I still am."

"Really? What happened? Did you leave her?"

"Just the opposite. She took up with that damned English cat you're
so inordinately fond of! Love! Feh! At least gas stays with you all your
life."

* * * *

They entered the garden that covered the innermost acres of the isle.
All was lushly planted, all was neatly arranged. The evening air was
heavy with the perfume of the myriad blooms and the last gleams of the
westering sun shone along the stalks and cups and blossoms.

"You could search for years and never find that *f'shlugginah* flower!"

"Don't worry," Phillimore reassured him. "I've got inside information. It ought to be just on the other side of that dell to the left..."

They stepped along, careful not to trample the flowers. Beauty had
specifically warned the professor about that, but he would have avoided
spoiling anything so lovingly tended, anyway.

Ducking around the low-hanging branches of a slanting willow,
Phillimore saw the shallow bowl of a peaceful glade before him. The
trees to one side thinned out and the full glory of the dying sun illumi-
nated the spot. There, in the very center of a close-cropped circle of turf,
grew a tall sunflower, ebony in shade.

Unique, Phillimore thought. But he approached the single flower;
reluctantly he reached out a hand to grasp its slim stem...

* * * *

"Come now, sir," a thick voice grated near his ear. "You look too
decent a sort to be a common poacher."

Stifling a yelp, Rimski (forgetting he was invisible) put distance between himself and the newcomer.

Phillimore turned, hand still extended toward the black sunflower.
And there was the Beast.

* * * *

Neatly attired in Edwardian frock coat with tweed vest, cravat and silk handkerchief tucked into the breast pocket, the Beast had tangled wild hair, a wet snout, great fangs and glowing green eyes, one of which was shielded by a monocle on a cord. His hairy paws emerged from spanking-white sleeves that were affixed by diamond cufflinks; a matching ring bedecked the appropriate talon of his left claw, which clutched an ebony walking stick with silver handle.

Looks like Edward Hyde!

"I say, old chap," growled the Beast, "you *weren't* actually attempting to divest me of my prize helianthus, were you?"

"It's needful," Phillimore replied.

"Best let me judge, sir. Come, sit you down in my arboreal retreat a few steps away and explain all."

He led him across the clearing, through a screen of ferns and onto a flagged terrace where several chairs and a table were set with the appurtenances of teatime, or rather the remnants of that afternoon's repast.

"I do believe the pot is still warm enough," the Beast observed, gingerly testing its sides. "May I offer some tea to you, sir? Unfermented brew, decidedly delicious, transcendentally heady..."

"By any chance, is it pinhead gunpowder?"

"The precise brew!"

"My favorite!"

"Egad!" exclaimed the Beast "For a flowerly filcher, you have uncommonly civilized tastes! Sit you down! I've not had company on these shores for at least three years."

The professor chose a chair and reclined in it, relieved that the Beast was decidedly unlike the fairy tale original, or for that matter, the Cocteau version. His initial impression that the creature resembled cinematic depictions of Stevenson's Mr. Hyde was soon affirmed in the course of a delightful chat, during which Phillimore discovered that the Beast's sole recreation, other than tending the flowers, was to watch fictional entertainments on a dimensional receptor once sold him by an enterprising sorcerer named John Wellington Wells on one of his sales trips via umbrella. (Phillimore's own umbrella was manufactured by Wells's firm. See *The Incredible Umbrella*). Thus the resemblance to Hyde was deliberate.

"I may be doomed to wear this hirsute embodification," the Beast remarked between sips, "but don't you know, it is not one's appearance that counts, but rather the style with which one chooses to live out one's life. I may be stranded on this backwater, but at least I can conduct my few activities with dash and verve. I daresay no beast of land or air or sea can boast as much!"

"You are certainly urbane," the professor concurred. "But I had construed your existence here as pleasant to your apperceptions. After all, these flowers—"

"An engrossing hobby, right enough and one I should miss, were I finally to leave this isle. But," he continued with a sigh, "I really appear fated to suffer the absence of any social nicety, so I make the best of my confinement. I cannot leave the isle in any shape but this unless the maiden who dwells here commits herself to loving me." A rueful smile flickered on his whiskery lips. "There's a small mercy, at least. I frighten her. Indeed, I make it a point to do so. There's little chance she shall grow fond enough to rescue me from the spell."

Phillimore blinked. "What are you saying? That you prefer remaining a beast? I don't follow."

"Oh, I should like to be a man, once more. But the curse is that she who speaks love to me shall not only loose the spell, but also will marry me."

The professor's head spun. There was some slip in the logic of the Beauty and the Beast tale as he knew it. *Well, it's happened before.* But if there were some variation, what might it be? A sudden thought struck him and he delicately voiced it. The Beast shook his mane disdainfully. "Not a bit of it, sirrah! I am fond enough of distaff company, but this Beauty creature now—she's so awfully dull, don't y'know? A regular empty-headed lass. One might bed such an one, but never would I wish to wed her!"

Phillimore was totally confused. Could they be thinking of the same woman? He questioned the Beast further, but there was no mistake. The magnificent lass he'd met in the subterranean palace, a damsel upon whom his entire heart and mind were irretrievably fixed, filled the Beast with boredom and contempt.

"She prates of naught but clothes, the shallow slip! I'd rather wed a bearded lady from the circus than be tied down to such a vacuous filly!"

Shaking his head positively, the Beast was unaware of how his declarations offended his guest. But before the professor could argue, the creature brought the topic of conversation back to the thwarted theft of the black sunflower.

Happy to change the subject, Phillimore discussed his plight in some detail. Fortunately, the Beast knew all about the Wellsian umbrella device, so some of the usual expressed incredulity and detailed explication demanded by other auditors was eclipsed. He outlined to the Beast his original purpose in flying to the world of Faërie and how it had been diverted from full-time consideration by Baba Yaga's enforced quest.

(At mention of her name, the Beast displayed a panoply of pointed teeth. Phillimore, after all, was but the latest in a long line of mostly unsuccessful emissaries from the Russian witch. The monster did not supply details as to his predecessors's fates and Phillimore did not press for it—though he did learn that he was one of the few to be stopped *before* picking the sunflower...a fortuity for which the Beast said he ought to be grateful.)

Quickly, the professor sketched in the latter events of his search. One portion of it vastly interested his host and Phillimore had to repeat it.

At length, the Beast put down his empty cup and leaned back, contemplating. The sun had long since gone down and the only feature Phillimore could see was the twin glint of his host's baleful green eyes.

"I believe," said the Beast, after a long silence, "we have the rudiments of an arrangement that might benefit me mightily, as well as you... although there is one circumstance I cannot easily recommend to your thoughtful consideration. So, all in all, I suppose I *dare* not hope..."

"I pray you, try me!" Phillimore urged. "I might be thoroughly amenable to your plan."

"Well," the other said doubtfully, "you require from me a blossom that grows slowly and would take years to replace. Normally, I would never permit such a liberty. But I should consider sacrificing *any* of my blooms if it meant I might escape my fate!"

"And how have I created such a possibility?"

The Beast thoughtfully ruffled the hairs of his chin. "I should not object to remaining in my present form if I could but find a mate suitable to my aspect and station...and your narrative suggests one, indeed!"

"It does? Whom?"

"The maiden with the scarlet tresses."

"*Sleeping Beauty*?!"

"I believe that is what you called her."

"But she—" The professor stopped himself.

The Beast was not offended. "Precisely," he said. "Her appearance would match mine sufficiently to pair us in the public eye. I would not object to her red mustache or whiskers if she were in other ways gracious. As for me, I suspect she would automatically accept me, such is the stuff of spell-breaking."

"Then you propose to seek her out and kiss her?"

"Ay, sir, if I could but rid myself of *this* lass with whom I am inextricably conjoined. The curse has it that I must be her mate...unless some other claim her, in which case I continue as the creature you see before you."

"I'll be happy to take her off your hands," Phillimore assured the other. "I love her deeply!"

Rising, the Beast stared into the other's eyes with genuine concern. "Lad," he said huskily, "I would not ask you to do this unless you are willing. I was sure that could not be! Do not be hasty, you have not met her yet."

"Ah, but I have!"

"You *have*!"

"Yes! And I adore her!"

The Beast shook his head. "You are, I perceive, a man of considerable intelligence and somewhat ratified taste. How can you be content with this vapid mannequin?"

"Sir," said Phillimore stiffly, "you are speaking of the woman I love!"

"Well, well," sighed the Beast, "*de gustibus, chacun à son* and all that. If you've a mind for her, my good man, then it's settled. No doubt dimensional travel has loosened your wits, but *I* shall hardly be the one to suffer from the circumstance. Pick my sunflower, do and be good as your word."

"I shall, never fear!" Then, because it was too dark to see, he was led by the Beast to the stalk of the bloom. He reached out his hand...

"Stop!" the Beast begged. "Even though our pact is set, I cannot bear to witness the sad despoilment. Permit me to retire before you pluck the plant."

Phillimore waited till the Beast was gone from the glade. Then he drew the black sunflower from the ground and folded it tenderly within his inner jacket pocket. "My quest is completed!" he said. "Now to claim Beauty for my own!"

* * * *

The garden was too dark to find a path, but luckily for the professor, Rimski—now that the Beast was no longer in the dell—rejoined his comrade. The cat shimmered into view and Phillimore recognized him by the sparkle of his feline orbs.

"Nu, it's turned out easier than I expected," the animal admitted. "You're still alive and now we can get out of this place before something happens."

"If I recall, you can see in the dark, can't you, Rimski?"

"I'd be some kind of dopey cat if I couldn't, now wouldn't I?"

"Then take me back to the underground mansion."

"*What*?" the shaggy gray cat squawked. "Are you totally *meshugah*? Let's move off here while the getting's good!"

"Not until I fetch the woman I love!"

The cat uttered a rude sound.

"Spare me your anti-romantic demonstrations. It's part of the pact I made to secure the sunflower from the Beast."

Rimski rolled his eyes skyward. "It *was* going too easily..."

* * * *

Gladstone bag in hand, the Beast rowed to the ferry, accompanied by Rimski to prevent Mike Fink from blowing the fearsome apparition out of the water. When all was explained, the cat returned with the skipper.

"What's up?" Fink asked the professor, hopping out of the jolly-boat. "I'm going to fetch Beauty. As soon as I do, we all can go."

"Be glad t'come 'long, Jim-boy," Fink grinned.

"Never you mind! This lady is *very* special to me."

"Attaboy! Go get 'er!" He slapped Phillimore playfully on the back. "Well, Rimski, do you want to come with me or wait here?"

"Feh," the cat uttered in disgust, "I don't like either choice. If this gal is so hotsy-totsy, why doesn't the Beast want her? He knows her far better than you. Don't—"

"I refuse to discuss it," the professor stated with great precision. "Coming or not?"

"Lead on," Rimski replied, "but 'this cannot come to good.'"

* * * *

They quickened their pace. Phillimore saw the trail a little above ground level, a darkness in the deeper black of the hillside. Pallid moonlight limned their way.

"The trail moved," Rimski stated worriedly.

"What?"

The animal lowered his voice. "I'm saying there's something weird. The trail moved."

"Nonsense. You're just disoriented in the darkness. It's the night-shadows."

"It is not! We'd better get out of here, there's something wrong, I can *feel* it like I was ready to put my paw in a mouse trap."

"You're just trying to get me to leave Beauty behind. If you were a woman, I'd think you were jealous!"

"Don't give me such *kasha*, Rimski growled in a sullen *sotto voce*. "Cats have well-developed sixth senses and mine is tingling like a bolt of lightning!"

"All right, all *right*! So you wait here for me, like you did this afternoon."

"And let you walk into danger? I'll *plotz* first!"

The professor bent down and petted his friend's shaggy back. "Look,

Rimski, you're upset. Maybe it's better you *do* wait. If you're wrong, no harm is done. But if you're right—and I'm not admitting you are—well, you could make a dash for the beach and fetch Mike."

The cat saw the sense of the plan. Reluctantly, he agreed to wait just below the trail for Phillimore's return.

The professor stepped upon the narrow footway. Truthfully, he was beginning to feel a trifle uneasy. *Bah! I'm just letting Rimski's warnings affect my nerves*...and yet, why did the moonlit scene seem so tantalizingly, forebodingly *familiar*?

But danger or no, he was fully determined to keep his promise to his own true love and return. The exquisite Beauty was the apotheosis of those desires which initially prompted him to undertake yet another umbrella-flight. Head high, heart bravely striving to be light, Phillimore purposefully tread the path to the underground palace.

Now the shadowy portal was near, the cave-mouth opening into the hill. Memories of the lair of the purple troll flooded his mind...and he briefly paused, suddenly reluctant, in spite of his romantic resolve, to proceed further. He looked over his shoulder and saw, a good way off, the shine of Rimski's eyes in the darkness. *Wish he was here to help me make my way in the gloom. I can't see a thing up ahead*!

But suddenly, the blackness was dispelled by a blinding burst of light from within the hill. Phillimore turned in amazement, but the glare instantly died and it was night once more. Yet in that instant of unnatural illumination, Rimski's vague fears washed over the professor a thousandfold, augmented by his own burgeoning terror. He turned to depart the sinister neighborhood.

But now he had no choice. His feet stuck fast in the footway that suddenly was stickily undulant. Somewhere, ominous organ music rolled and the clouds skimmed swiftly across the sky, blotting out the moon. The wind quickened to the force of a shrieking gale. Lightning flickered under and over hill and a bird of night shrilled above the profundo fluctuation of the swelling organ-tone. He felt creepers twist about his ankles, rooting him even faster in the roiling earth—and then the trail tilted and began to hustle him towards the cave in the hill.

Wrenching his head around, he yelled to Rimski to get help. He couldn't see the cat, but thought he heard the thin whine of his voice.

Whether Rimski was reassuring him that he was speeding for reinforcements, or whether he was also caught in some deadly trap, Phillimore had no way of knowing.

And now the cave's edges altered and shivered as a glare of sickly yellow light pulsed from the malevolent mountain. Phillimore flailed his arms to wrest free, but icy laughter mocked him as he plunged within the portal and smashed with bone-jarring force upon the marble flooring of the mansion.

* * * *

"Won't you wake, my pretty?"

He cracked open one eye. The voice sounded like Beauty, but there was a cold mirth in it that was thoroughly unfamiliar. Tilting his head, he saw her a little way off, arms outstretched to enfold him.

"Here I am, lover!" she laughed, white teeth gleaming like the fangs of a serpent. "Your dream awaits! Come, claim me, you precious—*meddler*!" Her voice rose to a hideous shriek. The lovely lineaments of her face and body melted and ran together like pustulant liquors.

"Who *are* you?" Phillimore gasped.

"Tis Beauty!" she mocked. "Your precious Beauty!"

"Impossible!"

"Not at all, vain champion! The Beauty that dwelt on this isle is properly disposed of, but what care you for *her*? You never met her."

"Yes, I did!"

"No, 'twas *me* you encountered.—the embodiment of every attribute your puerile mind conceives as the perfect match: someone as uselessly pedantic as yourself. Twas *me* you met, in the guise of the one thing you most desire, a womanly version of your own tedious self! You met *me*... ME!"

And as her thick laughter rumbled, the flesh of her face and form reshaped itself and there, towering before him, thinner and taller than the first time he saw her, was his dreaded, enemy, the witch-queen.

* * * *

Being a traditionalist, the witch whistled for her broomstick. It scudded obligingly between her legs. She swooped up her prey and shouted directions. The broom shot into the air so swiftly that the air was knocked out of the professor's lungs. By the time he regained his breath, they were soaring out of the underground castle into the night.

"Where are we going?" Phillimore demanded.

"It's *Walpurgisnacht*, my quixotic buffoon! I've arranged a little ceremony on your behalf." She uttered an unctuous chuckle and said no more. But she'd told him enough. He was pretty sure of their destination.

They flew over the isle. Clouds no longer obscured the moon and as Phillimore glanced desperately down, he could see, far below, the silhouette of Mike Fink waiting on the palely-glowing beach.

"HELP!" the captive howled. "UP HERE!"

Fink looked and saw the shadow of witch and broom and pedagogue etched against the moon.

"What'r y' doin' up *thar*?" he called.

"TRYING TO STAY ON!" Phillimore replied. "HELP ME! USE ONE OF THE BULLETS! SHE'S TAKING ME TO THE HARZ MOUNTAINS!"

"Cry out all you want," the witch mocked; "he can do nothing to aid you. Naught but a silver bullet or cold iron slayeth creatures of darkness."

"He *has* silver bullets!"

"In that case," the witch said, addressing her broom, "Fleet! Get *moving*!"

The broom accelerated, but Phillimore, looking down, knew the sorceress stood in no danger, anyway. There was nothing but air between the rifleman and the witch.

Maybe that's why he's hightailing it for the ferry?

Indeed, Mike Fink was speeding across the beach to the jolly-boat.

By the time he stepped into it, Rimski close behind, the witch-queen and the professor were lost in the shrouding depths of the night-sky.

* * * *

Phillimore wondered how far from the island the Harz chain was situated on this particular world. (Because the witch had specified they were headed for *Walpurgisnacht* rites, he never doubted there was a Harz range somewhere.) After several minutes of soul-freezing flight in the upper atmosphere, he heard a weird familiar strain of music float up from the earth. The ghostly melody, though far-off, steadily grew louder. Phillimore recognized it now: *Night on Bald Mountain*! He wished he were a better geography student, he couldn't recall where that haunted peak was, *probably in Russia*? But since his subconscious linked it with the Harz region, maybe that fact would dictate proximity of the crags, not that he hoped for much from Mike Fink. *Even if he does know where to find me, he'll never get here in time and anyway, how many silver bullets can one man fire? There's bound to be witches galore where we're going!*

There were.

* * * *

There were also several dragons, fourteen warlocks, three wizards, nine generals, four hundred-and-eighteen statesmen, innumerable will-o'-the-wisps, three parvenu-witches, a like number of huckster-demons, Mephistopheles, Lilith (looking decidedly out of place but determined to see the dreary business through), five hundred-and-eleven members of the stagehands's union and a single apoplectic proktophantasmist ranged along the niches and ascending trails of the mountain.

Somewhere in the middle of the witchly crowd, an incredibly ancient crone bobbed up and down, trying to catch Phillimore's eye. She shrilled out a greeting: "YOOHOO! SONNYEVITCH! DID YOU GET IT FOR BABALEH? I'M NOT GETTING NO YOUNGER, Y'KNOW!"

A wild surge of hope swelled up in Phillimore's breast! Baba Yaga was there! Perhaps he could arrange to trade off the black sunflower— still in his jacket pocket—for his umbrella! Once he had his marvelous bumbershoot back, he could instantly escape.

But the witch-queen had other plans for him. Her strong, long fingernails stabbed into his shoulder as she dragged him to the top of the mount, just below the swirling wings of the king-demon who beckoned spirits of evil from all points to join in the grisly revels below.

As for those unhallowed delights, Phillimore took a single look into the heart of the roiling throng and saw too much; afterwards, he kept his eyes closed or, if he had to study the path ahead, turned as much skyward as was commensurate without breaking his neck *en route*.

* * * *

"This," snickered his witchly nemesis, "is a bit of poetic justice derived from the muddy depths of your own subconscious."

With a sweep of her gnarled hand, she indicated a colossal amphitheatre that took up one large sector of the mountain-top. Its edges shimmered hazily and Phillimore suspected it was created solely by demonic magic. In form, it resembled a Roman gladiatorial arena, surmounted as it was by tier after tier of marble benches, on which squatted obscene spirits-in-the-making, jeering and braying and committing miscellaneous noxious social errors.

The detail that distinguished it from any depicted replica of the Circus Maximus in Phillimore's memory was the presence of two doors, side by side, at ground level on the far side of the amphitheatre.

"Once you set foot on the sand," said the witch, "there will be no turning back. A barrier will form. You must open either of the doors at the further end."

The professor groaned inwardly: *The Lady or the Tiger*!

"Since you sought this world for amorous companionship," quoth the mind-reading sorceress, "I shall permit you to seek it here. The lady whom you *thought* you adored awaits you. You have but to summon her out of her proper portal. But take heed—" (and here the witch smiled bloodthirstily) "—that you do not select the incorrect door, for behind it lurks a beast of savage ferocity."

Phillimore started to say something, but the witch gestured impatiently and a sudden energy-field plucked him high, depositing him unceremoniously onto the sand of the arena.

The salamanders, swine and toad-things in the bleachers snortled and snuffled with glee at his discomfort and in a special reserved box above the double doors, a fleshly journalist scribbled up an account of the event for the early evening edition of the *Bloksberg Post.*

Phillimore whirled and tried to escape, but as the witch said, he was hemmed in. An iridescent veil covering the open end of the arena flickered with a fluctuant radiance that spoke of enormous untapped powers. The professor did not try to defy the energy-membrane, he had a fair idea of what might happen if he did.

His mind raced, ticking off options. He'd flown too far. Even if Mike Fink sped at top speed to assist him, he could not arrive in time. As for Baba Yaga, she obviously was outranked by the queen-witch and never could force her way through the energy barrier to rescue him. It occurred to Phillimore that *Walpurgisnacht* was a diabolic ceremony delimited by the approach of the sun. How long might he stall? But he doubted the witch's great wrath at his thwarting of the apple-death of Snow White would allow him to escape disaster merely by adopting a dilatory tactic.

No, there's no other option, he gloomily decided. *Might as well try the doors.*

Absurdly, selfishly, even as his reluctant feet stepped slowly in the direction of the paired portals, Phillimore wished Rimski was with him. The dour cat had shared so many of his tight spots, had indeed helped him out of at least one of them, that he yearned for his companionship at this moment of ultimate danger.

But he's not here, so...press on!

He pressed on.

The ghouls and hobgoblins and trolls in the stands yowled and grunted mocking, conflicting advice to him:

—*Open the left door*—

—*She's behind the right door!*

—*Open both and take your pick!*

—*Open either! Then climb up it*—

(This last was particularly malevolent. The surfaces of the doors were studded with sharp spikes.)

Shutting out the shrill cacophony as best he could, Phillimore stepped midway between both doors and attempted to recall the original Frank R. Stockton story, "The Lady or the Tiger?" In it, the enigma was not which door the prisoner opened, the professor told himself, but what came out...

Got it! Stockton's prisoner was beloved of the king's daughter, but she'd lost him. With great difficulty, she found out the secret of her father's doors that fateful day. If one were opened by her lover, a fierce tiger would bound out and rend him to pieces. But behind the other portal waited the princess's most hated rival, a woman of the court to whom the prisoner would immediately be married if he chose her door. Either way, the princess lost him. Which was worse, to see him torn apart and go to another plane, there to await her when she herself died? Or watch him wed her detested rival and live, enjoying another's secret delights? The princess agonized over her decision for days, but gave her lover an answer in an instant when he entered the arena and sought her eyes with a question he *knew* she'd have the key to...and (in Stockton's own words), "without the slightest hesitation, she had moved her hand to the right."

The right!

That ironic phrase, "without the slightest hesitation," had always hinted to the professor of the true answer to the riddle. That, plus the fact that Stockton spent a mere half-dozen lines depicting the princess's mental agonies at imagining her lover devoured by the tiger, while the suffering she would feel if he selected the lady took a good score of print-rows for the author to describe—in a telling paragraph that began with the extremely suggestive omniscient third-person declaration, "*But how much oftener* had she seen him at the other door!"

I'm sure of it! thought Phillimore. *The tiger was actually behind the right-hand door indicated by the princess!*

And since the witch-queen freely admitted she'd derived the notion of the amphitheatre with the two ominous portals from Phillimore's own subconscious, it was extremely likely that the placement of the lady and tiger would correspond with *his* own opinions of what Frank Stockton originally intended, so if the tiger *was* behind the right-hand door, as Phillimore hypothesized, the door he must open *has to be the left one*!

Doesn't it?

He paused, hand grasping the left doorknob.

But what if the witch is depending on me to follow my own theory? She may have read that, too, when she peeked into my mind...

Phillimore removed his hand from the knob and stepped back.

Which? Which door would the witch expect me to choose? Perhaps she guessed he'd avoid his natural inclination because he'd figure she was depending on that, therefore she might hide the tiger behind the door he wouldn't normally pick. But, on the other hand, knowing *that*, he might revert to his original selection and, shrewdly judging his behavior, the witch-queen then would...

Or would she?

Or wouldn't she?

Or...or...or...

* * * *

At that moment, a broad-shouldered apparition stepped onto the sands of the arena and approached the professor. Clad in vaguely Arabian garments, he was of cheery disposition and carried, hilt in his right hand, broad blade resting on his broad arm, an enormous scimitar, the upturned edge of which was keen and bright as any razor.

Phillimore shuddered. He had a pretty good idea who the smilingly threatening personage was.

"I," said the big man with a courteous grin, "am the Discourager of Hesitancy. My mistress, the queen, grown weary of your dallying, hath dispatched me to persuade you to pursue your course more speedily." Lowering the blade from its cradle, the Discourager plucked a hair from his head and dropped it on the sword, neatly splitting the single strand. "You may choose between me and the doors."

* * * *

Now the point is: which door did the professor pick? The question cannot be glibly answered, involving, as it does, such niceties of reasoning as might be expected to revolve within James Phillimore's pedagogic brain. His own course would have been to avoid the door indicated by Stockton's fictional princess, but the fact that the witch had looked into his thoughts turned the problem into one of Talmudic complexity.

Hardly could I, dear reader, presume myself the sole authority capable of solving this dilemma, so I leave the question with you: *which door did he choose? And why?*

* * * *

And what emerged from within?

The tiger? The lady?

Or...or...?

As the portal swung wide, the professor heard a deep growl emerge from within. In horror, he took a step back, but the point of the Discourager's scimitar prodded his posterior.

That was no lady! Phillimore groaned inwardly, *But that was his knife!*

And now, out of the open door, bounded the great beast that was intended to devour the professor. Stepping back a few paces, the witch's broad-shouldered lackey regarded the scene with a soapy grin, awaiting the impending bloodshed with keen professional interest.

The animal roared lustily. It sounded delighted.

Phillimore blinked, hardly able to believe his eyes. "Hey!" he exclaimed, glancing at the Discourager. "That's not a tiger!"

"So, sue us," the Stocktonian slayer yawned. "Her Majesty couldn't find one at short notice, not even by conjuration. This critter was ambling around the neighborhood, so we snatched the opportunity...*and* him. Don't worry! I'm sure he's hungry enough to take you to heart!"

In a fashion, the Discourager was correct, but not in the way he'd intended. The wild feline that pounced through the door was a tawny lion of immense girth and stature. When he recognized the professor, Andy's lion roared in bright delight, stood on his hind legs and hugged Phillimore with wonder and great affection.

The professor automatically grasped the animal's outstretched paw and they stepped off smartly, providing their own off-key accompaniment to the animated dance they did on the sands of the witch's arena. As they whirled dizzily about, the slimy creatures of evil attending as spectators howled in bafflement and disgust.

The Discourager of Hesitancy rubbed his eyes, unable to believe the merry spectacle taking place before them.

From someplace beyond the circumscribed perimeter of the amphitheatre, the witch-queen shrieked, lividly horrified at the profanation of fouldom with the professor's decidedly un-*Walpurgisnachtian* display of genuine affection and terpsichorean pleasure.

Far above the witch, His Satanic Hostship smirked at her discomfiture—anything that reminded the damned of the quintessential joylessness of their Being was not without use...

* * * *

Below, James Phillimore whispered something to the lion. They separated, caroling and winding and waving celebratory limbs aloft. The Discourager tried to watch them both, could not, swiveled and turned to keep them each within view. He nervously fingered his sword, but was at a loss on whom to use it; his instructions had not covered the present contingency.

And now the professor minced and danced and dived this way and now the lion crooned a throaty musical *purr* and trotted in concentric circles, irregular, yet always fixing the Discourager of Hesitancy as their center-point. The Discourager howled at them to stop, but his adjuration only succeeded in making them swirl about at a greatly accelerated tempo, the lion roaring in mocking melody, the professor confusing the Discourager with *prestissimo* renditions of Gilbert and Sullivan patter-songs.

"MAKE THEM STOP!" howled the witch from her lofty vantage

point "KILL THEM BOTH!"

The Discourager heaved a sigh of relief. Now he had orders! Now he knew how to think! Taking a firm grasp on the hilt of the scimitar, he advanced toward Phillimore. But his legs were wobbly and his head swam from watching the dizzy dance so long and before he could reach his prey, the professor was gone and the lion was there and the Discourager hefted his weapon, but had to swing to the left to follow the beast and wasn't fast enough because now the lion was all the way on the other side, but here again was Phillimore, loping into view. With a frightful yell, the Discourager sliced the air in a wide swath, but the professor nimbly ducked and pranced *en pointe* to a position 180 degrees away, but up danced the lion, instead; again the witch's savant swept high his blade, preparing to part the animal's head from his shoulders. But suddenly the lion feinted, passing under his impotent sword-cut and there the creature was! Inside his guard! Towering above him on hind-legs! No longer did the lion grin, but with a devastating roar of anger, he bared his great glistening fangs, bathing the Discourager with hot, fetid breath.

The Discourager screamed with fright and backed away—only to trip over James Phillimore, cunningly crouching behind him. Head over heels he tumbled, flopping to the sand with a mighty expulsion of breath. His scimitar flew from his grasp and stuck, some distance away, in the ground.

The professor hopped up, gave the lion a satisfied nod and sped over to the sword. Grabbing it, he called an order to the friendly beast: "Run over to the other of the two doors! All fours! You'll have to save us both!"

Even as he shouted, the animal was on his way. Phillimore also ran to the closed portal, yanked it wide, shouted to the occupant of the chamber on its other side, "Come on! Hurry! I'll save you!"

Overhead, the trolls and gnomes and toad-things gibbered and grunted furiously, champing teeth and hurling enraged curses at their enemies below. Some of the fouler fiends scrambled over the engirdling parapets and dropped heavily onto the floor of the arena, snuffling as they came.

Beauty walked into the harsh light and blinked in confusion at the obscene things squirming their way in her direction. She smiled uncertainly at the professor, on whom she obviously had never set eyes in her life.

Understandable. I only met the witch disguised as Beauty, Phillimore told himself, noting briefly the transcendental loveliness of the woman who stood before him now. She outshone her sorcerous replica as the sun might shame a glowing stick of punk. But there was no time to admire her, the first of the infernal revengers was almost on them.

"Quick! Hop on the lion! I'll explain later."

"But 'tis not seemly!" she balked. "Such a position wouldst revealeth too generous a quantity of mine maidenly flesh!" Hushing demurely, she averted her eyes.

Oh, hell!

A slug-like cacodemon extended its sucker-arms toward them. Phillimore sliced at the tentacles, at the same time grabbing the squealing Beauty and unceremoniously dumping her onto the lion's back. "Someday you'll thank me for this!" the professor assured her as he leaped onto the beast's shoulders and grabbed a handful of mane.

Roaring so loud that the front rank of ghoulies halted one single precious second, the lion bunched mighty haunches and sprang over their startled semi-heads. Another bound and he cleared the first parapet and landed with his passengers in the bleachers.

He scampered along the first row, ducking over the massed monsters when he could, snapping with powerful jaws when he had no alternative, spitting out the repulsive goblin parts his sharp teeth could not help biting off every so often.

Scrambling to a higher row of the arena, the lion broke clear of the hellish pursuers and put distance between them. The fading growls and snorts and grunts and mutterings made Beauty break into uncontrollable sobs and even the professor shivered at the ghastly malevolence of the damned.

"Make for that arch!" Phillimore advised the lion, pointing to a gap between a pair of supportive columns through which he could see a portion of the night sky. Baleful forks of lightning split the dark.

The lion galloped through the space between the towering columns and skittered to a stop on the marble shelf beyond. Beauty shrieked. Phillimore paled.

Beyond the outer lip of the polished stone flooring was nothing but mocking night, alive with fiery forms and chaotic colors.

The professor dismounted and helped Beauty off the lion's back. They stood forlornly on the marble paving and stared out into nothingness. Behind them, the pursuit, still faint, grew steadily nearer, louder.

"Prithee tell me where we are," Beauty whimpered.

"On the edge of illusion," Phillimore grimly replied. "This bogus arena is fashioned out of magic on the very brink of Bald Mountain."

It was true. Stepping gingerly to the edge of the ledge, Phillimore saw below the steep slopes of the precipice and far, much further down, the floor of a broad, tree-covered plain enclosed by other lesser peaks. And then, a horrid sound made him look up.

Hovering in mid-air, grinning balefully, the witch-queen straddled her broomstick and laughed heartlessly at their plight.

"Soon, soon, my troublesome friend, I shall rollick with joy as my minions mince your bones!" She swooped whistling down on them. "But I shall have the pleasure, first, of plucking out your eyes, one by one!"

Her laughter rang shrill in the chill mountain air. Phillimore wondered how near it was to dawn, but no sooner had he thought it than the witch, landing upon the ledge, bared her teeth in malevolent mirth. She waggled a crooked finger at him.

"Don't delude yourself, there is fully an hour of darkness before us, during which I shall prolong my vengeful delights!" She suddenly whirled and stuck a gnarled forefinger in the direction of the lion, poised to spring. He paused, suddenly transfixed.

Beauty moaned and cowered in a corner.

Now the sound of the legions of Hell was quite loud. The witch strode across the terrace and held up an admonishing hand.

"Later, my pets!" she laughed cruelly. "The initial bloodletting is mine!" With that, she advanced toward Phillimore.

He gave back a step and hefted the sword of the Discourager in a feeble effort at self-protection.

The witch chuckled as she gestured at the scimitar. It trembled and shimmered and turned into a nosegay of poison ivy. Phillimore flung it at her in disgust, but it vanished in mid-air before a single envenomed branch touched her shriveled skin.

And now she strode forward, unchecked, and the professor stood his ground, smartly planting his feet in the middle of the lofty ledge. *No point in running, there's no place to go! Maybe I can grapple with her, pitch her over the edge?*

But as soon as he thought it, he knew she'd caught the thought. The leering light of her baleful eyes told him he had no hope of surprising her.

And now her long-nailed claws reached forth and raked the air in front of the professor's bulging eyes.

Fitting justice, he chastised himself. *I've been blind enough in the pursuit of a mate!*

Reading the thought, the crone cackled. Then she caught Phillimore's head in a steely grasp and bent it upwards so the last thing he might see was her suddenly-transfigured visage, which she'd shaped once more to resemble his illusory beloved Beauty.

Phillimore flinched, as much from the irony as the proximity of the witch's talons. But now there was a spell upon his eyelids and he could not lower them to avoid the spectacle of the lewd travesty of his Immortal Beloved getting ready to tear out his organs of sight.

Her nails grazed his gaping eyelids.

Crack!

In an instant, Beauty's second visage melted into the startled glare of the witch's own face. No sound but a whistled intake of breath escaped her lips, but her nails, gone wide of their intended mark, suddenly ripped smartly along the professor s cheeks, tracing thin red lines.

And then, all around, the hosts of Hell howled in anger and dismay. The marble beneath Phillimore's feet tottered and started to crumble.

But in the same second, the staymagic seeped away and his head was no longer fixed. Andy's lion roared and sprang to Phillimore's aid, tossing him onto his back. His paws skidded over the deteriorating marble, but the beast managed at length to similarly rescue the genuine Beauty, who stood in abject fright at a far corner of the swiftly-disappearing terrace.

The lion turned his head toward the twin columns from which they'd first emerged. The entranceway was clogged with spectres and sin-spawn, chittering and shaking amorphous menacing appendages in their direction.

Just then, a mighty shout resounded through the valley. So impossibly loud was it that Phillimore could not hear for many seconds after. With the sound the terrace totally surrendered, disintegrating in a massive terminal shiver, plunging the dead body of the witch-queen into the valley below.

At that very instant, the lion leaped over the heads of the demons (now too concerned with their own immediate salvation to pay further heed to the professor's squad). The lion aimed for the place between the columns, but the amphitheatre was breaking up. The beast landed in slippery grass, fouled with the effluents of the night's rites.

"What in Hell is happening?" Phillimore exclaimed. A mighty din resounded around and upon the mountain, bellows and shouts and the keen whine of bullets.

The cavalry got here in time!

It was still night, though the moon was down. Warlocks and crones and council-members swarmed shrieking over the mountainside. Leathery wings fluttered overhead, but most plunged earthward as silver bullets pierced their owners's vital organs.

Dashing down a narrow side-path, the lion entered a small dale through which dithered frightened elementals hurriedly heading back to the security of their native elements. Here Phillimore and Beauty dismounted and allowed the panting beast to catch its breath.

"What hath transpired?" the trembling woman asked.

"Not sure," the professor panted. "We seem to be rescued, but how, or by whom, I don't know. How *he* could have gotten here so fast, I have no idea!"

"He? Who?"

Phillimore held up one hand, restraining her questions. "Just a minute, I thought I heard—"

"*What*?"

"Shhh!"

Into the dim seclusion of the tiny valley rode a stranger, dressed all in black. Riding up to the professor, he touched the brim of his hat with solemn respect. A pearly six-shooter shone at his side.

"You Jim Phillimore?"

"I am."

Turning in his saddle, the stranger called over his shoulder. "I found him, Fink!"

The familiar voice of the skipper sounded a little ways off in the wood. "Who you calling a fink?"

Mike Fink trotted into the glade on horseback. Curled about his shoulders was a gray shaggy cat with yellow eyes that gleamed happily as they saw the unharmed professor.

"Rimski! Mike!" Phillimore shouted gleefully.

* * * *

All but Beauty squatted on the grass. Rimski was still timid when it came to meeting the lion, but when he heard how the animal had repeatedly helped the professor, he warmed up considerably to him, though he still preferred to sit some distance away.

Beauty stood to one side, shyly darting glances at the three men, each in turn. Mike Fink grinned openly at her, but the stranger in black didn't seem to notice she was there; his eyes, brooding with too much knowledge, turned inward on the private griefs that the man carried with dignity and quiet grace.

When Phillimore brought his story up to the moment when the witch was about to tear out his eyes, Fink took over and explained how he'd "rounded up a posse to he'p out!"

"But how did you get here so fast?" Phillimore wondered. "And was that *you* who shot the witch?"

"Nope," Fink shook his head sheepishly, "not a lake or river in the hull dawgoned valley! M' pal here snapped off that shot, all th' way from th' bottom o' th' mountain."

The professor thanked the stranger and took the thermos-cap full of Tennessee whiskey that Fink passed to him. "That was mighty fancy shooting, sir."

"Nothing to be proud of," the stranger replied. It was not, coming from him, an admonishment, but rather the observation of one who'd shot too many wrongdoers in his day and found that, maybe, deep down, he really liked to kill.

They all sipped whiskey in silence.

* * * *

"We stocked up, quick-like, on silver bullets," Fink resumed. "Lucky I bought some in town."

"Yes," the stranger added, "and it's a good thing that masked man agreed to come along, too. Never saw so much silver in my life outside a bank!"

"Where's Ella?" Phillimore asked abruptly.

"Back in the ferry," Mike said. "Didn't want her t' get hurt!"

"Who is Ella?" Beauty suddenly interrupted.

The captain shrugged. "Guess y' might describe her as th' lady I'm sorta sweet on."

"Oh," said Beauty, "I see," and turned her attention to the stranger in black. "And art thou perchance affianced?"

The stranger's brow knitted. "Only loved one woman and I no way could have her." He rose swiftly to his feet. "You'll pardon me. There's work yet to be done." Without another word, he swung into his saddle and cantered off, headed up the path.

Mike Fink rose to his feet, too. "He's got a point, Jim-boy. There's a lot o' moppin' up t' be done yet." He sighed. "Wisht we was on th' water, so's I could assist."

"Well, there's not much that Rimski or I can do, either," Phillimore stated, "and I think Andy's lion here has worked hard enough for one night. But I *am* curious as to what's happening on the mountaintop."

"Okay," Fink agreed, "let's take a look." He rubbed his hands briskly and led them back in the direction of the peak.

* * * *

They paused at the edge of the woods and watched the battle. The forces of darkness were taking a terrific beating. Everywhere Phillimore looked he saw silver swords and silver bullets destroying the fouler denizens of the world of Faërie.

The professor whistled. "Wow! Where'd you manage to enlist such a large army so fast?"

"Got a friend who spread th' word round real quick!"

"But there's hundreds of champions in the field!" the professor marveled.

"Yep!"

"Who could possibly gather them so swiftly?"

"Hold off with th' questions, Jimbo, I don' wanna miss th' best part!" Before them, a great host of heroes rallied and flanked and charged and attacked. Phillimore recognized some of them instantly: Snow White's dwarfs, stout axes in hand, heartily hewed down demons, singing a catchy tune as they did. Elsewhere a company of archers clad in Lincoln-green fired silver-tipped arrows into the heart of the diabolic throng. A company of knights dashed mail against the armor of flame-breathing dragons, while, on another part of the mountain, a rather dim-witted lout in a Scotch kilt laid about him with a Billy club, cracking unhallowed skulls. He was aided by a large, ferocious monkey, whose teeth and long claws tore the hides of hobgoblins.

Pointing to the dolt and the ape, Phillimore asked who they might be.

"A strange pair," Rimski observed. "Doomed to live their lives over and over again condemned to the shapes you see. Once both were evil, but evidence of nobler hearts persuaded the gods to commute their fates and now they live forever and battle the forces of chaos."

"What's their names?"

"Oh, the lummox is known as The Eternal Chump; Ian, though, is his given name. And that's The Eternal Chimp with him."

"I see." Casting his eyes again over the battlefield, Phillimore found much more to marvel at: a quartet of caped swordsmen, silver ferrules on the tips of their foils, skewered satanic slaves. Close by, a solitary fencer with an enormous proboscis outshone even the pyrotechnic fighting of the foursome. Elsewhere, a young cowboy with a woman by his side whooped and yowped like a desert-dog. They both swirled lassos that cinched their enemies, hoisted and hurled them to the moon.

"That's m' buddies," Mike Fink grinned, his gold tooth bright in the flash of sorcerous light that glinted off sword and shaft "Pecos Bill 'n' his saddle-pal, Sluefoot Sue!"

"And the *peasant* in boxing trunks?"

"Aww," said Fink, "he got t' fight from now to doomsday. That's The Eternal Champ-peon."

Turning aside from the noisy fray, the professor asked Fink once more how he was so quickly able to summon up such a vast array of heroes and arrive in time.

"Another thing! You say the man in black shot the witch-queen from the bottom of the mountain..."

"Yep, Jimbo, that's right."

"If that's so, then how did he get to the top of the hill almost immediately?"

"Easy!" Fink replied. "I *tol'* ya I got a special pal."

But before he could elaborate, a hurtling figure sped out of the midst of the great battle and flew straight towards Phillimore.

"*Hang on, sonnyevitch!*" Baba Yaga yelled. "I'll save you!" And with that, she plucked the professor off the ground and shot into the air, the witch on her broomstick, the man dangling in the feeble grasp of the incredibly ancient harridan.

"Don't shoot!" Phillimore called to whoever might be listening. "She'll drop me!"

Mike slapped his palm against his forehead. "Sufferin' catfish! Do we gotta rescue him *again*?"

* * * *

The Russian witch carried the professor to another mountain some ten miles distant. They alighted on a steep slope.

The old woman, much more wrinkled than the last time he'd seen her, wheezed and panted for breath. Phillimore was once more reminded of his late foster mother.

But the sly leer in her eye was anything but maternal. "Nu, sonnyevitch?" she inquired. "Did you find my black sunflower? I've been keeping tabs on you...I know you reached the island!"

How'd she find that out? "Yes," he said, "I made a bargain for the flower."

"Then you *got* it?" Ha eagerness was uncontainable. "Hand it over! Hand it over!"

"Not so fast," he demurred. "I want my umbrella."

She cast a fretful glance at the lightening sky. "Hurry up, soon it'll be dawn and my broomstick won't work!"

"The umbrella! I *insist* upon it!"

Baba grinned innocently. "Would I keep you from your precious property, dearie?" She twirled the umbrella by the handle. "*You* hand me the sunflower, I'll give you the umbrella in the same movement."

"Sounds fair," said the professor, digging in his jacket for the folded flower. He drew it forth, smoothing out the curled stem as he did.

When she saw it, the witch's eyes glittered. A trace of saliva foamed at the corner of her wrinkled mouth.

Phillimore held out the flower, simultaneously striving to get hold of his umbrella...

And at that instant, without warning, the sunflower was snatched from his grasp. A blur, some great pale thing passed before his eyes and the witch crowed in triumphant delight.

Her pink horse-servant, Walter, had dashed up behind, grabbed the flower in his mouth and trotted it over to Baba Yaga.

"HEY!" Phillimore shouted. "What's the big idea? Give me my umbrella!"

"Sorry," Walter rasped in his deep voice, "but orders is orders, pal!"

* * * *

And now the witch, clutching the sunflower and the umbrella, laughed spitefully. "Did you *really* think, sonnyevitch, that Mama Baba was gonna give you back your sweet little parasol?"

"*You* can't use it! I told you! It's imprinted with my brain-pattern and—"

"And what happens," she crooned, "if your brain don't function no more, bhubbaleh?"

The professor mentally swallowed his Adam's-apple.

"Maybe I'm some kind of greenhorn?" the witch sneered. "Possession of magic is my game, shtupid! Soon's I heard about your little toy, I knew all I had to do was tell Walter to kick out your *fshimmelte* brains and the umbrella would work for me!" She turned to the horse. "And now that the thought occurs to me, Walter-baby..."

"But how did you know I reached the island?" Phillimore hastily interrupted, trying to play for time. The first dim streaks of twilight were faintly washing the sky and while Baba apparently did not lose anything but her powers in the daytime, it *might* be impossible for her to command Walter after sunrise. Anyway, it was worth trying—*what else is there for me to do?*

Somewhere, a long way off, thunder shook the air.

Baba preened herself. She patted Walter's mane. "Tell 'im, mine Waltaleh, tell how clever Baba is!"

Walter shrugged sourly. "When you didn't show up at the bridge, I figured either the Headless Horseman got you or you were hiding in the woods. I snooped around and got on your trail as fast as I could, but when I found you, you were traveling with a lion, so I kept my distance. Then, just when I thought we'd join up, *plop!* You go and get in dutch with the Chief Honcho among the local witches! So I trotted back to Baba and *she* got in touch with the queen and they made tentative plans to let you get to the enchanted isle—"

"Not without a few obstacles along the way," the professor grimly observed.

"They didn't want to make it too easy for you." The horse shook his mane in disgust. "I hope you remember I'm just a messenger in all this. I don't have much choice, it's either do what she says or—"

"*Shah!*" snapped the witch. "Just tell the story!"

The thunder was nearer now. Phillimore felt its rumble shake the—

"So," Walter resumed, "I was sent off to spy out the water-route and when I saw you in the ferry heading out to sea, I let Baba know and she let the queen in on it...and all that remained was for her to capture you and whisk you off on *Walpurgisnacht*."

"Which is why, I suppose," said Phillimore, "she didn't grab me the first time I saw her on the island."

"That," the horse confirmed, "and also because she'd agreed to let you find the sunflower for Baba."

"So it was all a trap."

The thunder was so loud the mountain shivered. "What in the name of blighted blintzes is *that*?" Baba Yaga suddenly exclaimed. "Something's wrong! Enough with the talk—"

But Phillimore persisted. "Then there really was no chance of your returning my umbrella, was there? Rimski warned me not to trust you!"

"That buttinski!" Baba howled, her voice thin in the din.

"So you never meant to give my umbrella back. Is that right?" Phillimore pestered.

With a self-satisfied self-righteous nod, Baba Yaga confirmed the accuracy of what he had just asked...and then the color drained from her ancient face.

"OY-OY-OY!" she howled. "YOU NO-GOODNIK! YOU TRICKED ME INTO ANSWERING A QUESTION!"

A mighty convulsion seized the witch just as a mighty hand seized the top of the mountain and ripped it off.

A thunderous voice rattled the professor's eardrums. *"HO-HO! FINK! WE FOUND THEM!"*

A vast face beamed benignly down on the professor, the startled steed and the violently-shaking witch. Straightening, the colossal figure stretched forth one palm, opened it and out of its center tumbled Rimski and Mike Fink.

"Y' okay, son?" the sailor asked, worried.

"I'm fine!" Phillimore replied, grabbing his umbrella and pointing at the positively stupendous man in overalls who looked down smilingly as the morning sun basked the company in birthing radiance. "Who is *that*?"

"Ah told y'" Fink said proudly, "a special friend he'ped us out tonight, Jim-boy! Lemme innerduce Mistah Paul Bunyan, o' Kennebunkport, Maine!"

The megagiant bowed politely to Phillimore. The motion started up a breeze that wafted over the face of Faërie, waving and fluttering six flags as far-off as that world's equivalent of Texas.

Baba Yaga was in her death-throes.

"I won't survive this one!" she told Walter. "My l-l-l-l-l-last order is t-t-t-t-t-to KILL HIM!"

The stallion dutifully raised his hooves to dash in Phillimore's skull, but Paul Bunyan chuckled and picked up the horse between thumb and forefinger.

"*I T'INK I KEEP HIM!*" Paul declared. "*HE GO GOOD IN MY TOY SOLDIER COLLECTION!*"

* * * *

Next morning, nearly all the champions sat down at a table hastily fashioned and laden in the midst of the ruins of the witches's festival. They ate a breakfast of ambrosia, leosylla-cakes and mellofern-ale, toasting to fortune with clear, sparkling drafts of a heady wine drawn from a nearby stream where (Mike Fink said) it flowed unceasing. The company was served by a sultry, smiling beauty in Egyptian headdress and scanty surplice. According to Rimski, she once danced attendance on none other than great Queen Cleopatra, but now the woman was pleased to wait upon the mighty who labored virtuously throughout the ages, battling the spirits of chaos. Phillimore gratefully accepted a cup of eternal champagne from The Eternal Charmian.

Only Paul Bunyan and Andy's lion refused to stay for the victory feast. The animal had a pressing social engagement and the Brobdingnagian lumberjack explained he had to go home and feed his blue ox, Babe. Besides, he preferred his own usual light morning meal, consisting of a jeroboam of cranberry juice, forty tons of flapjacks floating in enough maple syrup to turn the Grand Canyon into a public beach, a billion bacon slabs, three thousand gross of fried eggs (ostrich, if possible) and fifty water-towers-worth of coffee.

Bunyan stooped and sought the pink stallion, Walter, but could not find where he'd put him. Phillimore looked anxiously around the spot where the giant had tethered the horse, but the rope was chewed through.

"*NO MATTER!*" Bunyan bellowed jovially. "*I ALWAYS BE MISPLACING MY TOYS!*" With a flick of his comb (an uprooted pine tree), he tossed one unruly cowlick the size of a cornfield into place, waved goodbye and started off, calling a good-luck wish to Phillimore over his shoulder as he went.

The professor sat down with a melancholy sigh, Rimski to his right, Beauty on his left hand. The morning meal was pleasant enough, but he knew he was still in a mess. There was always the option, of course, of employing the umbrella to take him elsewhere, but the last time he tried that, he discovered, to his dismay, that a kind of law of universal economy interfered with his choice of destination and landed him in a world where a similar problem to the one he'd fled still confronted him. (For details, see Part II of *The Incredible Umbrella*).

Nope, I made a bad bargain—and now I'm stuck!

"Hey, give a look!" Rimski suddenly exclaimed. "Company's coming!"

Phillimore turned in the indicated direction and saw, riding along the road, the Beast of the enchanted isle. He was clad in a new morning-coat with matching top-hat. His monocle shone in the early sun. Mounted at his side was a tall woman clad in wedding-dress, sporting flaming red hair and matching whiskers.

"Well," the professor sighed, "I've been expecting them, sooner or later."

* * * *

The Beast walked back and forth, teacup in one hand, pinky tilted daintily skyward. Phillimore fell into step beside him as the other paced the meadow at the foot of the mountain.

"It's too bad, don't y' know," the Beast commiserated, "but there's no going back, old chap, is there? And didn't I warn you that Beauty is a vapid little bit of fluff?"

"You did. You did. But you see, I was laboring under the delusion that she was entirely different from what you described."

The Beast nodded sagely. "At that time, I could not comprehend, but now you've elucidated. You are the hapless victim of an evil prank. The witch-queen's malice lives after her."

The professor eagerly agreed with the Beast's assessment of the case. "Then you concede that I do not deserve to have to marry Beauty?"

"Certainly!"

"Ah," Phillimore sighed gratefully, "you are uncommonly civilized. You know, in my travels in this world, I have learned a bit of a lesson concerning beauty as a marital determinant. It only took me a moment to recognize Beauty's unworthiness of deep affection."

The Beast sipped his tea. "True enough, my good sir. But of course you must marry her, nevertheless."

Phillimore stopped dead. "What?"

"I have already made arrangements for the ceremony. It shall take place within the hour on this very green."

"B-but, I thought y-you said I don't have t-t-to wed her!"

The Beast shook his head sadly. "I said you don't *deserve* to be saddled with such a light lass. But unfortunately, the laws governing this world do not permit the shunting aside of bargains, especially when they are pacts that involve spells and ensorcellments."

Phillimore's face grew long. "Then there is no hope?"

"Not unless you find someone else to take her off *your* hands. Otherwise, you are forced to keep your word...and recall, you *did* pick the sunflower and you *did* retrieve your umbrella."

"Much good it will do me," Phillimore replied bitterly. "Wonder whether I can talk Mike Fink into throwing over Ella for Beauty?"

But he couldn't.

* * * *

The ceremony was not elaborately arranged. Mike Fink himself, it seemed, had the authority to conduct the nuptials, due to his position as the captain of a vessel. Phillimore tried to argue that skippers only could marry people on the high seas, but Rimski pointed out that there were different legal traditions on the world of Faërie.

The groom and his intended stood before the ferryman, attended by Rimski, the Beast, a rather aloof Unsleeping Beauty (still a bit insulted by Phillimore's cavalier behavior toward her some days before) and divers champions, heroes and trusty talking steeds. Neither principal had bothered to change into ceremonial garb; neither had much to say to one another. Phillimore sulked and Beauty clearly was displeased. She clutched her bouquet with nails white with pressure.

Mike Fink began the ceremony.

"We-all is gathered here t'day t' join t'gether these pore sons-a-guns. Does anybody got somethin' t' say agin it?" He shook his head. "I mean, besides *you*, Jim-boy!"

"Well, well," the professor grumbled, "get on with it."

"La, the way you talk," Beauty moodily murmured, "thou mightst be suffering the extraction of thine appendix!"

Rimski softly meowed something sarcastic about gaining a useless part, rather than etc. The animal felt immensely sorry for his friend, the professor.

"Okay naow," Fink drawled, "who-all gives away this here filly?"

"Oh, I do, *believe me!*" the Beast exclaimed with a profoundly satisfied sigh.

"Now d' you take this professor-type for yer intended hubby?"

"Do I *have* to?" the maiden wailed.

The Beast's redheaded fiancée remarked that if she didn't say yes, she might sustain a sudden bodily injury.

Beauty said yes.

"'N'how 'bout you, Jimbo?"

"Well, if there's no way out of it, I suppose I must."

"Uh-*oh*!" Rimski abruptly said. "I got an all-of-a-sudden that maybe there is a way out of this, professor!"

"There *is*?"

"Don't get excited," the cat warned, "but if you don't turn around quick, you'll never make it to the honeymoon!"

Phillimore swiveled and saw, to his dismay, the pink horse Walter thundering across the meadow on a collision course with himself.

The wedding guests scattered left and right. Rimski scooted up a slender tree some yards away.

The professor ran in the same direction, Walter in hot pursuit. "Hey!" Phillimore yelled over his shoulder, umbrella flailing, "Baba's dead! Leave me alone!"

"Can't!" Walter rasped, steadily gaining on his quarry. "She told me to kill you and I've got to do it! Nothing personal."

"Help!" the professor howled, dashing toward the same tree Rimski was nestled in. "Fink! Do something!"

The captain's voice sounded far off. "Who you callin' a fink?" Roundly cursing him, Phillimore leaped for a low-hanging branch, grabbed hold and started to clamber up.

Walter, now directly behind, reared on his hind legs and aimed a powerful kick at the professor, narrowly grazing his down-hanging posterior.

Phillimore yelled and jumped higher, clutching the branch with all arms and legs. It sagged noticeably under his weight; he couldn't manage to climb to the more solid center of the tree.

"Rimski! Help!"

"What on earth can I do?" the fat cat mewed. "He's forty times my size!"

"Jump on him! Scratch him!"

The cat nodded at the plan, but somehow could not manage to pry his trembling paws free of the tree trunk to carry it out.

Below, Walter whinnied and slammed his hooves against the bole. The tree shook and Phillimore's branch curved dangerously, just out of reach of the stallion.

Crack!

Mike Fink fired a round at Walter, but the shell went wide, ricocheted off a stone and neatly drilled a hole in four calling birds, three French hens, two turtledoves and a professor in a pear tree.

"Watch it!" Phillimore screamed. "You just punctured my pants!"

"Are you hurt?" asked Rimski.

"No. My wallet stopped the bullet."

"Dawgone it!" Fink swore from a distance. "I hastes t' waste them silver bullets! Only got two left!"

Crack!

"Aww, hell! I cain't hit *nothin'* ifn I don't shoot over water!"

Fink wasn't quite correct. His second bullet *had* managed to strike the limb on which Phillimore was suspended. The wood split and cracked, but did not break through totally. But the branch hung lower than before.

"Cut it out!" the professor pleaded. "You're just making matters worse!"

The first shot startled the horse enough to make him trot away from the tree, but upon observing Mike Fink's poor marksmanship on dry land, Walter regained his courage and again drew near to the dangling, helpless professor.

The branch creaked and lowered Phillimore another inch.

"Just about in range now," Walter said, backing up to align himself.

Rimski, regaining some of his nerve, padded along the tree trunk to a spot as close as he could manage to the horse. But now the angle was not as good as before. Still...

The cat leaped, vanishing on the way down. He landed several feet short of the horse, looked up, saw the great size of the creature, almost lost his nerve, finally jumped as high as he could, hoping to land on the horse's back. But he was too fat to manage the elevation. Instead, Rimski clumped against Walter's flank, instinctively uncurling his claws to hold on.

Walter neighed in unexpected pain, shook himself and flopped to the ground, rolling onto the side that hurt.

Overhead, the professor heard a high whine of fear.

"*Rimski!*"

Without thinking, he dropped to the ground to run to the feline's aid.

"I'm all right," Rimski yelped. "Get back in the tree!"

Too late!

Walter cantered swiftly, interposing himself between the tree and the professor. The horse exhaled noisily.

"Do you *mind* letting me get this over with?" he protested. "You're wearing me out."

"Good!"

"Don't you see, Baba gave me no alternative? I'm under a spell. I have to do her dying command."

Out of the corner of his eye, Phillimore saw Mike Fink circling slowly around to the other side of the tree, hoping to get a better vantage before firing his final silver bullet.

Uh-uh, he'll kill me before Walter does! *If only he could shoot ac-*

curately—

And just then James Phillimore at last remembered a vitally important detail.

"Mike!" he yelled. "Do you still have Snow White's thermos?"

"Why, shore," came the puzzled reply. "Right by m' side."

"Is it filled?"

"With hunnerd proof akwee vitee. But why in th'—"

"Unscrew the cap!" Phillimore interrupted, eyes on Walter.

The horse pawed the earth.

"Okay!" the perplexed captain hollered. "Now what?"

"Fill it!"

Walter lowered his head.

"Y' think m' aim'll be better if'n ah'm drunk?"

"No! Put the filled cap on the ground in front of you!"

With a mighty whinny, Walter bounded for the professor. Phillimore dashed to one side. The animal screeched to a halt, turned and chased his prey.

Phillimore sped to the tree, Walter two yards behind. As the professor ran beneath the dangling branch, it snapped and dropped straight down, smacking Phillimore's skull so hard that his knees crumpled. He fell to the ground, insensible.

The stallion, seeing the accident, checked his pace and stepped up to the recumbent figure. Walter prepared to smash down with all his might. But Fink suddenly realized what Phillimore had been trying to communicate. Swinging his rifle into position, he aimed over the thermos-cap.

Crack!

Walter roared and toppled over backwards.

True to his legend, Mike Fink was a sharpshooter only when he fired across water.

* * * *

The professor woke just in time to see the pink stallion close his eyes and expire.

What happened next surprised everyone.

As life left the great body, the horse-form trembled and dimmed and faded from view. Where Walter had been, there now lay a tall, handsome youth with graceful features but newly attained to manhood. He was dressed in the fine clothes of a nobleman.

As Fink and Phillimore gazed upon him in awe, his eyelids twitched and opened. His blue eyes filled with tears of gratitude and joy.

"O dear friends," he addressed the professor and the skipper in a voice gentle and manly, "I thankst thou for freeing me with a silver bullet from the witch's powerful enchantment."

"Why, who are you?" Phillimore asked, amazed.

"My name is Florizel. I am a prince whose homeland lies at some distance. Being the youngest of three brothers, I determined to seek my fortune in lands unknown. But on my very first foray into wilderland, I fell victim to the dangerous potions of the witch, Baba Yaga. Yet was my nature noble enough, I thank the fates, that I would not do her bidding to fetch the fabled black sunflower and prolong her evil existence on this globe!

"Such was the nature of the potent magic in which she raveled me that, so long as I bore the form of an animal, I must do her bidding. Because I refused her in the one favor she could not wrest from me, I was sternly commanded to enact her will in all else.

"But your bravery hath brought disaster to that wicked witch and now I am free to undo the awful work she made me perform...or if I cannot right all the evil my baser form perpetrated, at least may I hope to repent."

Rising then from the dewy grass, the prince resolved to begin his good works with a special favor on behalf of his liberator, James Phillimore.

The professor was overjoyed when he heard the proposal. Swiftly he sought out Beauty and the Beast and put it before them.

Beauty had only to take one look at the elegant Florizel to lose her heart to him.

The Beast shook the newcomer's hand and affirmed that his offer to marry Beauty would quite adequately satisfy the conditions of the curse he'd passed on to Phillimore. To the professor, the Beast merely said, "Congratulations, old man! What fortuity, eh? A convenient prince, charming solution, don't you think?"

* * * *

The two couples, once wed, said farewell. The champions departed, leaving Mike Fink and the professor alone in the field. Together they searched for the missing philosopher-cat, last unseen near the tree. They had to comb the grass gently for some time before Rimski could be discovered.

With a shaky *purr*, he popped into view. "I must have passed out," he apologized. "That big lummox almost squashed me when he rolled over. I just managed to wiggle free."

"Then he *did* land on you?" Phillimore asked, worried.

"A *bissele*."

Upon examination, they saw that Rimski had sustained a broken leg, the pain of which was responsible for his fainting.

Phillimore fussed over him, binding up the injured limb carefully. Fink administered a small quantity of akwee vitee to deaden the ache in the cat's paw.

* * * *

"Waal, what's the plan, Jim-bo? Wanna come 'long 'n' see me 'n' Ella tie th' knot?"

"No, I'd rather not," the professor candidly admitted, cradling his wounded friend in one arm. "I think it's time I moved along. This is a lively world, but it didn't work out too well for me, not at all according to plan."

The ferryman shuffled his feet, feeling rather sheepish. "Aww, Jim-boy, ah hope y' don't hold it 'gainst me 'bout Ella. I reckon you was a bit sweet on her y'self."

"Maybe a little," the professor admitted, shielding his face from the glare of the noonday sun. The brightness made his eyes sting, or so he told himself. "But we weren't really suited for one another. A good person, though, in her own—ah—colorful way."

Fink shook the professor's hand heartily. "Waal, ifn you say so, Jim, then no hard feelin's, right?"

"Right."

"Cmon back this way sometime 'n' set a spell."

Phillimore shivered. "Don't say 'spell'! I never want to hear that word again!"

Fink uttered a hearty laugh, then ruffled Rimski's fur. "Wanna come long with me 'n' Ella, ol man?"

"No"—the cat shook his head—"I'll be all right. Have a good trip home."

The ferryman said a final farewell, then started off on his journey, rifle in hand, filled thermos ever after at his side.

* * * *

Phillimore frowned at the cat.

"Why didn't you go with him?"

"I didn't want to, that's why. Such a genius you have to be to figure?"

"But damn it, you *know* I'm leaving."

"I know." The cat yawned and licked his paw.

"Well, damn it, I can't leave you behind with a busted leg!"

"I know," Rimski said smugly.

"But I may *never* come back!"

"I know, I *know*...what's so great here, anyhow? So long as you don't fly me someplace where there's no milk, everything is okay by me."

The professor shrugged. "In that case..."

He pressed the release button on the umbrella and the vast folds of the hood unfurled, blotting out the world of Faërie from their view.

As they disappeared (smile lattermost in Rimski's case), the cat wondered whether his friend really had no regrets about leaving.

"You loved Snow White, Ella, Beauty, or at least you thought so," Rimski meowed. "Do you wish you could've—"

"The only thing I wish," Phillimore yelled to make his voice heard over the roar of the cosmic winds, "is that they all live happily ever after!"

And they did.

PART II

"It's my turn!" Leila declared.

"I *beg* your pardon!" Fleta contradicted, stamping her dainty foot "It's *my* turn, sis!"

"No, it's not!"

"Yes, it is!"

"Not, not, *not!*"

"Too, *too*, TOO!"

Boris Frankenstein stifled a yawn. The great creature sat beneath an alder, weary beyond recounting. Maybe it was the rarified fare of the fairy forest that depleted his reserves of energy; truly he felt enormously anemic. On the other hand, perhaps it was *not* the food.

"I say 'tis *my* day to serve this quaint gent," Leila insisted.

"Greedy pig!" Fleta spat spitefully. "You served him these three days hence!"

"You say me false!"

"True!"

"False!"

"*True!*"

Into the glade tripped the Fairy Queen, petulantly swishing her magic wand. "Here, here, what manner of disharmony have we, ladies? This behavior 'tain't seemly, it smacks of mortal fray."

The two fey sisters spoke simultaneously, advancing each her particular claim upon the pitiable monster slumped against the trunk of the alder-tree.

The queen signaled impatiently for silence. "If you do not reconcile yourselves to our customary condition of gentle unanimity of viewpoint and voice, I shall dispossess ye both of service for the nonce and take up the slack myself!" Boris groaned at the idea.

Leila and Fleta, who knew their sovereign would use any excuse to steal more time with Boris, smiled sheepishly at one another. As the universal accompaniment sweetly stole over the scene, they warbled and trilled a thoroughly Gilbertian duet of unanimous assent to the will of the queen, characteristically adding a *sotto voce* chorus depicting their cleverness at thwarting the will of their queen.

Halfway through the second verse, Boris sneaked off to catch some sleep. He had a favorite hiding-place within a hollow log, a secret spot he resorted to with increasing frequency as the long summer nights crept by.

* * * *

Morning. The trilling of a bird. Boris stirred. With a mighty yawn, he stealthily poked his head out of the log.

The first thing he saw was a pair of yellow unblinking eyes staring curiously into his own watery orbs.

"*Vayzmir, boss!*" said a grumbly, somewhat thickly-accented voice. "*This must be him! What I call creatively ugly!*"

With a growl, Boris clambered forth...and saw none other than his old friend James Phillimore smiling at him with outstretched arms.

The professor endured a bone-crunching hug of affection.

"Am I *glad* to see you!" Boris happily howled. He did not exaggerate. The last time the professor visited him, the fairies left him alone for several blissful days. "O Mighty Phillimore, regale me with thine latest ventures, *do!*"

"Well, Boris," said the dimensional traveler, "it's rather a *long* story..."

"Thou wert ever the bearer of happy tidings!" Boris exclaimed, tears of relief welling in his eyes.

Before he allowed the professor to begin, the monster hosted him to the central glade, making sure to bring the presence of his friend to the attention of the Fairy Queen. Then he ordered breakfast for all.

Phillimore introduced everyone to his feline companion, Rimski. Then as soon as milk and melon were set before the company, he began his story.

* * * *

It took all day to tell. Boris languished languidly and listened, hanging on every syllable. Often he stopped the professor to question a point and once or twice, so enrapt was he with the narrative, that he asked some part to be told again.

But by the onset of evening, the tale was finally unfolded to the last turn. So unusual did the fairies find it that they, too, sat in the circle, taking in the details of Phillimore's amorous quest in the world of Faërie.

During the telling, many of the sprightly sisters vied for the opportunity to pet the shaggy cat, Rimski. They made a considerable fuss over his injured paw and the queen herself bathed it with healing fey lotions. The animal purred happily, relishing the attention lavished on him that afternoon.

When night fell, Iolanthe rose and hustled up some of the customary delicate grub that Phillimore knew he must tolerate in Arcadia. *Mist-cakes are hardly gut-stuffers*, he silently grumped, but considering the enormous spell of talking that he'd subjected his throat to, their blandly moist texture was not without reward.

But they'll never replace a pint of Watney's.

* * * *

After supper, the professor said he was tired. So he and Rimski stretched out beside Boris (who insisted on their proximity) and the three friends almost instantly fell into the slumber of the virtuous, the innocent, the blameless, the blessed, the redeemed and those that are just plain pooped.

* * * *

As the world turns, so does the G&S planet likewise eke out the days of our lives in its own petty pace and thus did James Phillimore rest for a time, temporarily soured on amatory quests. Meanwhile, Rimski's limb mended slowly and the professor vainly sought assistance of all the doctors of the neighborhood, but none were acquainted intimately with feline anatomy, so at last the professor decided it was necessary to dispatch his friend to a general hospital for animals in London.

The night before they were to go to the city, the guiding light of inspiration again visited Phillimore. Being young and restless, he could not endure the thought of eternal celibacy and from a sense of duty to a hypothetical posterity, the professor at last hit upon another world where he thought he might discover the perfect mate.

So he called his friends to him and spoke thus of the promptings of his spirit: "As I have but one life to live and since I have a great love of life, I must set out once more on my connubial search. All my children that yet might be demand it of me!"

Cocking his head, the cat looked quizzically and skeptically at him. "You didn't fare so well looking for her in the world of myth. Have you a better place in mind?"

"Yes, Rimski. My earlier mistake was picking a place solely because of the availability of comely women."

"Beauty ain't everything," Boris grunted.

"True," said Phillimore, "willingness counts for a great deal. Now there is a kind of fairy-tale place popular in my own world that includes both distaff physical attractiveness and a mature attitude towards love and sex upon the part of at least some of its women. In the infinity of worlds that the umbrella may take me to, I assume this fabled spot must also exist."

"And what is this marvelous place?" Rimski asked.

"A world based on what is known in my native country as 'daytime drama.'"

Neither of his comrades had ever heard of such an institution, so the professor briefly explained:

"They're also known as soap operas...ongoing stories that chiefly deal with male-female relationships. These programs employ some of the loveliest, yet most palpably *real* women on all of television!"

The latter term was also totally foreign to his friends, so Phillimore described to them the mysteries and intricacies of kinescopes and icono-scopes, networks, sweeps, counterprogramming, ratings wars and also commercials.

At first the others attended with wonder and fascination, but slowly their eyes glazed and their heads drooped and when the professor was done, Rimski sighed and squeezed his lids shut tight; Boris stared stonily into space.

"Once, Mighty Phillimore," the monster muttered, "thou saidst that I hail from a world based on the horrors of thine own globe." His lips compressed. "Thou hast always been faithful to me, yet how may I countenance this thing you call television? I never encountered it on mine native planet..."

* * * *

The professor wanted to delay his umbrella flight till Rimski was all healed, but the cat would not permit his injury to delay the successful conclusion of his friend's quest. At last it was agreed that Boris would accompany the animal to London (the monster was eager to quit the glade, now that he had a satisfactory excuse to offer the powerful Fairy Queen).

"If you return here," said Boris, "I can be your Best Man!"

"Of course I'll return!" said the professor. "I want you and Rimski to be present at the festivities. And we'll go get Mike Fink, too!"

"He may prefer to be Best Man," the cat observed.

"Well, we ran quibble about it later," Phillimore answered, privately wondering whether Boris's feelings would be hurt if he asked him to serve as Best Monster.

Rimski pouted. "And what about me?"

The monster patted his shaggy head. "You can be Best Cat."

"Hmpf. We'll see about that," he purred sulkily, but would not elaborate on his meaning.

* * * *

Boris suggested Phillimore might want to set out at once, but he shook his head. "It's too dark. I don't care to fly by night. Besides, I want to see you and Rimski start on your journey before I employ the umbrella. I can certainly delay my search for tomorrow's necessary business. And now, I think I'd like to wash up before going to sleep." Boris stood and brushed the grass-stains from the palms of his meaty paws. "O Dearest Benefactor, shall we not toast this night the success of our respective ventures?"

Phillimore grimaced. "Sure...if you can persuade the Fairy Queen to conjure up something huskier than that insipid Nectar!" Winking, the monster said he'd do what he could. A few minutes later, beaming proudly, he returned with a bottle of rye and soap for the professor's bath.

The three friends drank one another's health, Rimski lapping booze from a saucer.

* * * *

They finished the bottle and snoozed the better part of the day. Thus it was late afternoon before Boris gently picked Rimski up in his enormous hands and started on his journey to the big city. The professor, despite his unwillingness to travel after dark, could not manage to clear his head and press the button of the umbrella till it was practically the edge of night.

* * * *

Foggy, stormy evening. Not a wise time to negotiate the hairpin curves of Skyline Drive, but Myra left him no choice. After the things she said, the accusations she made, there was no way they could stay together and so Brett packed his bags and threw them in the trunk of the station wagon, rain streaming down his face, lightning illuminating the countryside that sheltered the little lake house in the folds of a rise of oaks and maples and all the while Myra stood by the door, shouting, screaming her anger which, he knew, was not a product of her best nature, but the excrescence of poison that Louisa Stone insidiously whispered to poor confused Myra, at a loss to know where she stood with Brett who could *not* tell her, no, that he *dared* not declare his desire to wed her now that she carried his child...

A swirl of remembrance. Old Doctor Tom waggling his finger and head. A thin recollection of sound echoing and reechoing in Brett's tired, taxed brain.

DR. TOM

...can't recommend it, lad. You may go into remission, but if not, what then? Should you saddle Myra with a husband who'll rot before her eyes like an over-ripe fruit?

BRETT

And...and what about the baby? (ECHO: *the baby, the baby, the baby, the baby...*)

DR. TOM

(*SIGHING*) There's no danger. It's not hereditary. But do you want Brett Jr. to grow up with an old man who's a decaying fruit? (*ECHO: fruitfruitfruitfruit.*)

BRETT

No, I guess not.

The last bag in place, the trunk closed and latched, Brett turned to Myra, beautiful Myra, noticing yet again how desirable she was, especially when she was angry.

"If you walk out now, Brett, it's goodbye! And it's still goodbye if you don't tell me the truth."

"Whose truth?" he snapped. "Mine? Or Louisa Stone's?"

She only hoped that Louisa was wrong, but if she was, then now was the time for Brett to take her in his arms at last. But would he?

Will he?

"Goodbye, Myra."

"I mean it, Brett! If you leave now, I never want to see you again!"

As he drove off, he heard the word *never* repeatedly slashing him with its awful finality. *I'll never see Myra again. Never...*

It was the noblest thing. *But damn Louisa Stone!*

He pressed on the fuel, savagely wishing it was Louisa's lovely, spiteful face. The rain slanted across the windshield in sheets so thick he could not see anything but the white line of the road a few feet ahead of the front wheels.

Shouldn't be driving this fast. Dangerous.

Brett laughed a bitter laugh.

What do I care? Maybe I'll go off the road, maybe the car will burn and I'll die! What difference—

"OH, MY GOD!"

Brett twisted the wheel, shouting.

* * * *

Myra was inclined to ignore the ringing of the bell, the pounding of the door. But he wouldn't stop, so at last she threw wide the portal.

"I told you never to come back, Brett!" She tried to bar the way, but he pushed her aside.

"I have to use your phone," he declared, his face white and tense. "I just ran over a man. And, my God, my God, I swear he appeared out of *nowhere!*"

* * * *

Dark clouds swirling behind his closed eyelids confused him. He tried to will them away, but they had their own thoughts on the subject and would not accommodate him—Him?

Who is "him"? he wondered, wincing from the pain of unaccustomed concentration. He could not manage the resolution of the question, so he returned his attention to the clouds. After what seemed like hours, he found the strength to open his eyes.

The first thing he saw was a poignantly beautiful blue-eyed blonde in nurse's white uniform and cap bending over him. When she saw him open his eyes, she smiled so happily that his heart skipped an entire cadence.

"Can you hear me?" she asked.

His throat was dry, he couldn't make it work, but at least he could nod his head slightly, enough to reply affirmatively.

"That's wonderful!" the nurse exclaimed. "Now you just rest up, I'm going to fetch Dr. Tom immediately!"

She hurried from his limited angle of vision, but in a few moments returned and told him he was under the care of the senior surgeon, Dr. Tom. Her head disappeared again and a kindly, aging male face hove into view.

Dr. Tom was a florid elderly physician with a habit of squinting nervously every few seconds. His features ware doubtless once handsome, but age etched a veritable roadmap of secondary highways upon his face. He smiled down, asked a few polite questions, squinted, checked vital signs, then sat down at the side of the bed and patted his patient's hand.

"I realize you are still quite enervated, so I'd rather you don't exhaust yourself asking questions just yet. You had a close call, but we pulled you through the accident. You're in Regatta Heights Infirmary."

With great difficulty, moistening his lips, he managed to ask the physician what accident he was talking about. "You were hit by a car."

"Ah."

"Though I really insist on your resting, before I leave you to do that, perhaps I should ask whether you have any relatives you want us to call. There've been no inquiries and I'm afraid someone may be worried at your absence."

The patient wrinkled his forehead. "I...I'm afraid," he whispered, "that I can't remember."

Eyes narrowed, Dr. Tom frowned. "Can't remember what?"

"*Any*thing. I don't even know my own name!"

* * * *

The physician turned to the nurse and whispered a few words to her. She nodded, then went to a closet and rummaged through the pockets of the trousers the patient was wearing when he was first brought into Emergency. She returned with a billfold and handed it to her superior.

The doctor examined the wallet and found a neat white identificatory pasteboard. Withdrawing it, he held it beneath the invalid's nose.

"I assume this is your name, lad."

The patient's eyes focused with difficulty. He read the card.

J. ADRIAN FILLMORE

38 C Pugh Street
College Hills, Penna.
377-0725

"Sound familiar?" the physician inquired.

"Not really, Dr. Tom."

The older man smiled. "Oh, you doesn't have to call me Tom. You may use my first name."

"I thought I *was*. What is your first name?"

"Thomas."

Fillmore regarded him doubtfully as he left the room.

* * * *

Resting back against the pillow, the patient yawned through a shielding hand, managed a wan smile in the nurse's direction and closed his eyes.

J. Adrian Fillmore, he repeated to himself. *Nice name. Dignified. I like it...*

And, repeating it over and over to himself, he fell asleep.

* * * *

She sidled into the room, glancing back to see whether she'd been followed. Satisfied no-one noticed her arrival, she shut the door and turned to her superior officer.

The government agent nodded at her and she sat.

"Have you learned anything new?" he asked.

"Yes." She reached into her purse and withdrew Fillmore's calling-card. "This was in his wallet. I really think he's lost his memory."

The agent glanced at the card, then turned it over and over in his fingers, eyes studying a spot on the wall some feet above the blonde's head. "Hmm," he mused, "a man materializes from nowhere. A car hits him and he loses his memory. His name appears to be that of a prominent literature professor. I wonder..." Suddenly he swiveled to his telephone, picked it up, dialed.

While he waited on Hold for his field researcher to run down the information, he turned back to the blonde. "How long did you say this 'Fillmore' was in a coma?"

"Five months."

"Hmm." Just then a voice sounded through the wire and he gave his attention to it. After a short time, he hung up.

"Well?" she asked.

"J. Adrian Fillmore is at this moment teaching a class in Shakespeare. Your patient is indeed an impostor."

"Then...?"

"Then either the United States has a new weapon, or we have our first genuine space-traveler in our reach, *tovarich*!" A transitory doubt shadowed his brow. "Unless your source is mistaken..."

The blonde smiled idly. "Brett has never told me a lie."

"Very well," the agent replied, "then we must carefully investigate the scene of the accident in case—"

The lithe woman interrupted by getting to her feet and opening her long coat. "I already have. I found *this* in the bushes..."

She placed a large, garishly-colored umbrella on his desk.

His face fell. "An *umbrella?*'

"That's all I found. Shall I try again?"

"No, no, your thoroughness is a byword in the service. There's nothing else to do except see that the fellow is brought around gradually to remember who he is. And as the clouds of amnesia disperse, you must be there to glimpse through the rifts."

She frowned. "That will be difficult. Dr. Ryan has been assigned to his case."

"Not *Myra* Ryan?"

"The same. Ever since Brett Richards recovered, things have gone downhill with the friendship I deliberately built up with Myra. They're engaged now and I no longer have her confidence."

"Well," her boss drawled, "I've never known you to be stumped by such a minor obstacle. After all, this bogus Fillmore is in your care. Surely you can think of something."

Louisa Stone licked her lips, the ghost of a smile twitching at their corners. "Something might occur." She rose, smoothed down her dress. "Shall I give him back his umbrella?"

"Not yet. There may be something about it we're missing, a secret message compartment, perhaps. I believe I'd better study it..."

* * * *

Several days later, when Louisa telephoned the agent to report her progress, she did not get an answer. Worried, she hurried to his office.

It was empty. He was gone.

She checked to see whether he'd been recalled, but the central office could not enlighten her.

It was as if he'd vanished into thin air.

* * * *

Bells pealed. As the groom lifted the Bridal veil and saluted his mate's lips, a soprano of Wagnerian girth cut off the carillon with an imposing slice of her hand that made the balcony on which she stood tremble. Her gesture was a signal for the organist; he played the introductory chords of "Oh Promise Me" and the large woman made an heroic effort to bellow on key.

Below, the couple strode up the aisle, he looking perplexed, she triumphant. Behind them walked Dr. Thomas Tom who, since neither had relatives or friends in town, had consented to give away the bride who, after all, *was* one of his nurses, all of whom he thought of as daughters.

At least Myra and Brett Richards had arrived at the last minute, their teenage son in tow. (Brett, Jr., their sole offspring only recently had returned from school abroad.) The Richardses were not there because of any consideration for the bride, but each cared about the groom for different reasons. He was, after all, Myra's patient and she wanted desperately for him to regain his memory; never before had she encountered such a complete case of amnesia and her compassion for her subject was intermingled with personal fears of inadequacy because so far she'd had no success effecting his cure. Brett, on the other hand, still felt enormous guilt because he'd hit the groom with his car, thus causing his loss of memory in the first place. He blamed himself, too, for what he regarded as a disastrous nuptial event.

* * * *

Louisa attempted to hug Brett, but he pulled away, bestowed a limp handshake upon her and drew her husband to one side.

"I hope you'll be happy," he said without much conviction. "I still think you might've waited, though."

"What for?" Fillmore wondered, pumping Brett's hand.

"Don't you feel it dangerous to marry without knowing who you are? It'd be damned awkward to wake up one morning and recall you have a wife already stowed elsewhere."

"Louisa was worried about that, too, but I'm positive I'm single." Overhearing the remark, Myra joined the two men. "What's this? Have you finally recalled some detail of your past?"

"Not really," said Fillmore, running his finger around the inside of his uncomfortably tight formal collar. "I just have a feeling that I never met anyone in my life like Louisa. And I'm *so* worried about saddling her with my problems, Myra! I'm still not well. Time is *so peculiar* for me." He passed a hand across his forehead; his eyes wore a dazed expression. "Ever since I came out of that coma, I've been disoriented. I black out frequently, each time for precisely two minutes. Some days, moments stretch out until, before I know it, the sun is down and I never noticed. Other times, things move so swiftly that though I see the results of some action I performed, I cannot recall ever having done the thing. But the weekends are worst of all!"

"What happens then?" Brett asked.

"Fridays are my most normal days, everything tends to function in real time (always excepting the blackouts). Then all of a sudden, it's Monday! I know I've been asleep all weekend, yet I can't remember ever having gone to bed. And whatever the last thing was that I did on Friday still seems to be taking place. All over again! And yet the calendar has been torn off and it's Monday!" He pressed Myra's palm with fond fervency. "What does it all mean, Myra, what does it all mean?"

"It's a product of your accident," she said, without much conviction. "Eventually it'll stabilize and you'll have your memory back." She restrained herself from adding "I hope." Myra then changed the subject, contributed briefly to the small talk, then, excusing herself, pulled Louisa aside.

"I hope you're aware that Adrian is still recuperating?"

"Yes, Myra. Why?"

"He adores you. I don't want you to hurt him."

A flash of pique tightened the blonde's features, but quickly disappeared. "Myra, I admit you have some reason to think ill of me. So I'm going to confess that when I first paid attention to Adrian, it was for a selfish motive. But it's gone now."

"Are you sure?"

"Ah, yes. Shall we say it, uh...*vanished*?" the blonde uttered, a faint smile-line curling her cheek "And now I am deeply, unselfishly in love for the first time in my life!"

Noting the sparkle of the bride's eyes and the radiance flaming on her cheeks, the psychiatrist said, "Louisa, maybe I'm a damn-fool romantic, but I'm disposed to believe you!"

"Do, please!" Louisa impulsively pressed the other's hand. *"I've never been so happy in my life..."*

* * * *

Overhead, the Wagnerian soprano leaned against the balcony rail. It groaned rustily and dislodged a great chunk of stone from the side of the mezzanine.

The singer attained G above high C as the big block hurtled downward towards Louisa.

* * * *

Dr. Brett Richards Jr., staff psychiatrist at Regatta Heights Hospital, doubtfully eyed the bushy-haired gentleman in gray seated in the swivel chair on the other side of his desk.

"The individual you're inquiring about," the doctor explained, "is one of my outpatients. I cannot reveal any of his personal—"

"Please, please," the other interrupted, nervously fingering the straggly whiskers bristling beneath his squat nose, "I wouldn't want you should violate your professional ethics. All I'm asking is for the public facts."

Dr. Richards exchanged a suspicious, furtive glance with the sad-eyed nurse standing behind the gray-haired visitor. Her lips compressed when she heard his foreign intonation of English.

"Could you tell me his name again, doctor?" the man asked.

"J. Adrian Fillmore."

"Hmm," the stranger mused, the ghost of a dour smile shivering his upper lip. "Very good. Now please share the public facts with me."

"Very well," Dr. Richards replied, casting a concerned glance at his nurse. She was biting a knuckle in considerable agitation. "It's a long story. Years ago, my late father hit Fillmore with his car. Dad always claimed he popped out of nowhere. Fillmore was badly hurt, but he recovered. However, the accident caused almost total amnesia. He was in the old Regatta Heights Infirmary, on the ground of which this hospital is built. He and his nurse, Louisa Stone, fell in love and were married. But on their wedding day, she was dreadfully injured by a loose stone block that fell from a balcony. After six months in intensive care, Louisa seemed to die and—"

The man in gray, looking rather distressed, held up a hand to halt the flow of words. "What do you mean she '*seemed* to die'?"

"A sad story. She's a cataleptic. They were going to cremate her. But at the last instant, an attendant noticed the perspiration and knew she was not dead. Eventually she totally recovered."

The other nodded. "Then she's Fillmore's wife."

The physician shook his head. "No, for shortly after Louisa was admitted to the hospital, my father died of an obscure disease that he supposedly had been cured of. That was just before old Dr. Tom was disbarred and went into politics. Now poor Fillmore was so upset at Louisa's accident, he talked over his grief with his psychiatrist, my mother, Myra Ryan Richards. But when my father died, my mother was so grief-stricken that she talked it all out with J. Adrian Fillmore, who'd studied psychiatry in his spare time while he waited for Louisa to recuperate. Well, by the time Louisa appeared to drop dead, Fillmore and my mother were deeply in love and they immediately married when they learned Louisa was supposedly no more."

"Rather hasty behavior, wouldn't you say?" the chubby stranger commented.

"Well," said the doctor, "considering my mother was several months pregnant, it was not totally reprehensible."

"Then she and Fillmore are the parents of your half-sibling?"

"No. My mother miscarried. That occurred when she learned of Louisa's resurrection. It was a complicated legal tangle, but Louisa finally permitted a divorce and now Fillmore is my patient and...well, I can't talk about that."

The man in gray mopped his brow. "Perhaps that's just as well. All this *angst* is too much for me to handle, let alone the time factor—"

"Time factor? What do you mean?"

The other waved the point away. "No more. My head feels like it's filled with two-cents-plain! But tell me, where is this Fillmore now?"

"Out of town. I prescribed a vacation for him and my mother. It's connected with the difficulties he's seeing me about."

"When do they return?"

"Soon. I'm not sure which day, though."

"Mm-hmm. And Louisa Stone? How may I locate her?"

"Search me," said the physician. "She left town years ago."

Sighing, the curious stranger rose. "Oh, one last thing," he remarked, hand on the door-handle. "When Fillmore was admitted to the infirmary for the auto accident involving your father, do you know whether he had any—ah—*unusual* object in his possession?"

"You're asking me about an event that took place before I was born," Dr. Richards replied stiffly.

With a dismayed lift of his shoulders, the man left. As soon as he was gone, the thin, sad-eyed blonde nurse collapsed into a chair. The psychiatrist circled round his desk and placed his hands comfortingly on her shoulders.

"It's all right, Louisa, he's gone. But surely you're not going to tell me he's connected with your old secret-agent fantasy?"

"Damn it, Brett, it's not a fantasy! Why won't you believe me?"

"I'm not supposed to," he replied simply. "I'm your psychiatrist."

She pulled away from his touch and spoke aloud to herself. "I always was afraid that sooner or later someone would show up from headquarters investigating my boss's disappearance. Now this man arrives, asking questions about whether Adrian has any odd possessions. That means my superior must have transmitted his suspicions about that weird umbrella to HQ before he fiddled with the contraption and vanished."

"Are you afraid, Louisa? Do you feel you are in danger?"

"Not me, you fool! I'm worried about Adrian."

"Fillmore? You still have feelings for him?" Brett sighed.

She exhaled noisily. "Goddamnit, don't you ever pay attention when I'm talking on the couch? What kind of bargain-basement shrink—"

But she was cut off by the sudden opening of the door. In walked an agitated old ex-Dr. Tom clad in pinstripe suit covered with campaign buttons. An unlit cigar dangled from his lips; his face was pale, his jaw set in a stem line.

Brett asked, "What's the matter, old ex-Dr. Tom?"

"I have terrible tidings," he said, squinting fiercely. "Brace yourself, lad...your mother is dead."

The psychiatrist promptly collapsed.

"Confound it," old ex-Dr. Tom grumbled, "I *told* him to brace himself."

Louisa grasped his arm. "Then Myra is gone?" He gravely inclined his head. "And what about Adrian? Is he—"

"We-e-e-ell," he interrupted, "I have both good and bad news about our old friend Fillmore."

Louisa sucked in air to control her impatience. *"Well?"*

"The good news is that he got in a fight and nearly had his block knocked off—"

"That's the *good* news?"

"Let me finish. The blow to his skull brought back his memory. Now the bad news: his fight was with a man the police assume was Myra's lover. The authorities think Fillmore shot them both."

At which point, Louisa collapsed, too.

Old ex-Dr. Tom squinted, squared his shoulders, stuck his stogie in an ashtray on Brett's desk, muttered, "Aww, what the hell," and also fell on the floor.

* * * *

On the opening day of J. Adrian Fillmore's murder trial, the new judge stood in front of the mirror in his chambers, primping. The son of an impoverished linotype operator, the elderly magistrate was proud of finally achieving a lofty civic position.

Not that I haven't worked hard for it! Refusing to learn his father's trade, he'd scrimped and slaved and saved until he could afford to enter college and study medicine. After graduation, he rose slowly but steadily to the exalted post of senior surgical resident at Regatta Heights Infirmary, later becoming chief surgeon at the hospital of the same name. And then...a meteoric rise in the political sphere, which he'd entered after his "retirement." His services with the county election machine led to nomination to a slot on the revenue review board which, in turn, paved the way for his honorary law degree. After that, it was a simple matter of high legislative redaction to clear the statutory path toward attaining the state Supreme Court judgeship.

He chuckled to himself. *Pretty neat accomplishment for old Tom Tom, the typer's son*!

Adjusting his black robes, he stepped into the corridor with his sternest no-nonsense squint to show he was an arbiter to be reckoned with; nodding at the bailiff, he strode into court and seated himself at the Bench.

In the front row sat Louisa Stone, looking worried and sad. He bestowed a slight nod and subtle wink in her direction.

* * * *

Damn, thought Louisa, *the wages of sin and all that stuff*! But she knew she had to go through with it, for after all, she was not proud of the evil, spiteful things she once did in her youth and now that Adrian was in danger, no course lay before her but to sacrifice herself for his salvation.

Well, she mused bitterly, *I always said security counted more than love...*

Just then, out of the corner o£ her eye she caught a glimpse of gray. Turning anxiously, she saw, there in the first row of the spectators's section on the opposite side of the central aisle, the chubby foreigner in the old-fashioned Mad. Ave suit. Perhaps sensing her scrutiny, he hunched back on the long bench so he was hidden by a bald, bearded tall man to his right. As she continued to stare, the nearer individual turned and smiled rakishly at Louisa.

She looked away, having seen enough. She knew what the man in gray had been staring at intently before he realized she was watching him.

He'd had his eyes riveted on an object resting on the prosecutor's table...a large, garishly-colored umbrella too big for street use, yet too small for beach employment as a sunshade.

The thing was clearly labeled STATE EXHIBIT A.

* * * *

(THE COURTROOM. THE ASSISTANT PROSECUTOR IS IN THE MIDDLE OF HIS OPENING REMARKS).

ASST D.A.

And the State concedes that this must have been the unpremeditated act of an irrational man, the crazed consequence of both physical and psychological shocks to the psyche of a person whose mental health has not been stable since he arrived in—

FILLMORE

(OUTRAGED, HE JUMPS TO HIS FEET) I object! The competency of the defendant has not been proven or disproved at this stage.

THE JUDGE

Don't act like a nut, lad. You know you've been out of your gourd for years.

FILLMORE

May we approach the Bench, Your Honor?

THE JUDGE

(SIGHING) If you *have* to.

(FILLMORE AND THE ASSISTANT D.A. SPEAK TO THE JUDGE IN WHISPERED COLLOQUY).

THE JUDGE

Why make such a fuss, lad? The best way to let you off light is to prove you're a Hoo-Hah Loony!

FILLMORE

But I didn't murder him!

THE JUDGE

Well, maybe Jack here can cool it for the time being?

ASST D.A.

I'll outline the facts of the case as we see them, then I'll be finished.

THE JUDGE

Good. I've got a lunch date I want to spruce up for.

(FILLMORE EYES THE UMBRELLA ON THE PROSECU-TOR'S TABLE).

FILLMORE

(SLYLY) if you'd just allow me to examine the umbrella in your chambers, Your Honor, I could clear this whole thing up one-two-three.

THE JUDGE

Nothing doing! This is my first big case!

ASST D.A.

No soap. That's State's evidence. I can't permit you to put your hands on the bumbershoot.

(FILLMORE, LOOKING EXASPERATED, RETURNS TO THE DEFENSE TABLE. THE JUDGE NODS HIS HEAD AND THE PROSECUTOR AGAIN ADDRESSES THE JURY).

ASST D.A.

What apparently occurred that evening is that the defendant went out to buy some food at a local diner. He and his wife, the dead woman, intended to have dinner in their motel room. When Mr. Fillmore returned, what he evidently discovered was his wife in the arms of another man.

There was a struggle, during which the defendant freely admits he was bashed over the head with an umbrella. He claims to have lost consciousness and says that when he revived, he found both his wife and his assailant dead. The State contends that what really happened is that the defendant shot and killed both Myra Ryan Richards Fillmore and the as-yet-unidentified second man during what he has termed a "blackout." The State means to show that the defendant has a history of such psychologically peculiar incidents and that during one, J. Adrian Fillmore was capable of and indeed did murder two persons.

(THE PROSECUTOR SITS DOWN).

THE JUDGE

The Defense may present its opening argument (HE GESTURES FOR THE ATTORNEYS TO APPROACH THE BENCH). Are you sure you don't want me to appoint an attorney for you, lad?

FILLMORE

No, dammit! If you would allow me to show you a peculiarity of that umbrella.

ASST D.A.

I already told you—no tampering with State's evidence!

THE JUDGE

Well, lad? Shall I get you a competent lawyer? (FILLMORE SHAKES HIS HEAD) Very well. But you're a pigheaded fool. (TO COURT STENOGRAPHER) Don't put that in the record, stupid!

THE CLERK

How do you spell "stupid"? One P or two?

(THE JUDGE SIGHS AND DISMISSES THEM. THE CLERK AND THE PROSECUTOR SIT. FILLMORE GLANCES AT THE JURY, GRIMACING WITH DISGUST).

FILLMORE

Look, the only mental problem I've had is years of amnesia. That night, when I came back with food for my poor late wife, Myra, I found a strange man holding her at gunpoint. He swung around. I ducked. Maybe he didn't want to fire in a motel room where the shot could be heard. Instead he swung an umbrella at me, knocking me on the head. I passed out. When I came to, I finally remembered who I am. And I knew the umbrella I'd been hit with belongs to me. I opened my eyes, but the stranger was sprawled across the bed, dead. So was my wife. I searched for the umbrella, saw it underneath the bed. Just as I was reaching for it, the door burst open and police entered and arrested me. That's all I know.

(FILLMORE SITS DOWN).

THE JUDGE

The State may call its first witness.
(SHAKES HEAD: VOICE-OVER OF HIS THOUGHTS) Worst excuse for an opening argument...the lad's doomed...

* * * *

During the testimony of the police witness, J. Adrian Fillmore slouched low in his chair and silently groused.

Well, here's another fine mess I've gotten myself into! He'd been so intent on securing for himself la dame juste that he'd neglected to analyze the probable dangers of a world that operated on the underlying plot devices and traditions of TV soap operas. *Such as a high percentage of melodramatic misfortunes: accidents, rare diseases, amnesia, & c.—as they say in D'Oyly Carte libretti...*

ASST D.A.

And then what happened, Officer Horton?

POLICEMAN

I read the suspect his rights and affixed handcuffs to his wrists.

And what about the time factor? the professor worried. There's nothing constant on soaps, except when they mention something will happen on Friday and then it's sure to coincide, just to "cliffhang' the viewers till the weekend's over. Otherwise, soap opera time is illogical and unpredictable, the whim of the writers. Kids go away at age five and return three years later as college sophomores...

ASST D.A.

And is that suspect in this courtroom?

POLICEMAN

I see him there.

THE JUDGE

Let the record indicate that the witness pointed to the defendant.

ASST D.A.

No further questions, Your Honor.

THE JUDGE

Lad?

FILLMORE

No questions at this time, Your Honor. The Defense will recall the witness.

THE JUDGE

(STARTLED) What the hell for?

FILLMORE

I'd rather not go into that now...

(SUDDENLY, HIS HEAD SLUMPS ONTO THE DEFENSE TABLE).

Two minutes later, after Fillmore came to, the prosecutor called his second witness, the motel clerk. While that individual went through the business of identifying the suspect as the man who signed his register that night and also recounted the sounds of struggle and gunshots from that room unit, the professor drummed his fingers impatiently and thought about the subsumption problem. *According to Holmes, there oughtn't to be one...*

The Great Detective once theorized to Fillmore that his incredible umbrella responded to the thoughts of its user and therefore ought to do whatever was expected of it. Certain principles of energy conservation governed its employment, so that one could not ply it again immediately after it made an universal hop, but Holmes contended there was absolutely no logical reason why the professor should have to "finish a sequence" before escaping any given world. Nor should it be possible to become "subsumed," a concept which the sorcerer who manufactured the parasol once defined as the wholehearted mental acceptance of the axioms and tenets on which any given planet was formulated. Subsumption meant that if Fillmore participated too heartily in the soap-opera world, he might find himself permanency stuck there—a prospect that was extremely unappealing, considering...but he couldn't even-bring himself to think about *that* problem at the moment.

The monkey-wrench, he supposed, was his own sense of literary form. Something within was extremely reluctant to allow him to escape the world he was on without somehow rounding out his adventures in a manner befitting the style of the place as he induced it. Of course, the fact that he immediately lost his umbrella upon arrival on the soap-opera planet precluded his putting his suspicions to the test, but the fact that he blacked out frequently—*right where the commercials would be liable to come*— profoundly disquieted him; it strongly suggested he might be so deeply enmired as to be incapable of extricating himself.

I'm just lucky the umbrella popped up again. How the stranger holding Myra at gunpoint managed to have it in his possession, Fillmore did not know, but he theorized that he was some kind of villain who, by chance, happened on the device and learned something of its usage. If he was aware it once belonged to the amnesia victim at Regatta Heights Infirmary, he might well wish to interrogate him about its properties and origins. *But why'd he wait so long? Did he use it and get stuck on another world? That would fit. And there'd be two factors that might well make him show up right in our motel room: his own mentally communicated desires and also the preponderance of coincidence in soap opera plots...*

ASST D.A.

No more questions, Your Honor.

THE JUDGE

Does Defense wish to question the motel clerk?

FILLMORE

No, thanks. I'll probably recall the witness later.

THE JUDGE

Will Counsel approach the Bench?

(THEY DO SO).

Are you trying to get off, lad, by acting like a nut?

FILLMORE

(STIFFLY) I beg your pardon?

THE JUDGE

(WEARILY) Oh, never mind. Let's get on with this. I've got a lunch date.

The thing to do, Fillmore mused as he sat again, *is find the fine line between participation and subsumption and never stray over it. Now that I know the world I'm in, I can manipulate its premises and get myself acquitted. But—will the umbrella still work for me?*

He glanced over his shoulder at the spectators, wondering why one of them looked vaguely familiar. *Well, if I'm permanently stuck here, at least there's Louisa...funny how she reminds me of Cinderella!*

But there was still his problem, the one he was going to Brett Jr. about. Could he solve it? Could he ask Louisa to countenance such an humiliating thing? Was it fair?

Damn it, there I go again! Too much participation!

* * * *

Louisa saw Fillmore look at her and she smiled wanly. *I* have *to save him!*

She leaned forward and casually checked up on the man in gray. Again he hunched back in his seat and the big bald man with the beard hid him from her view. Again the tall, hirsute stranger flashed a disquieting smile in her direction...

The assistant district attorney cleared his throat and called his final witness.

Louisa's brows knit. She turned to see whether it was a surprise to Fillmore as well.

It was. The professor blacked out again.

* * * *

THE JUDGE

(SOURLY) If the defendant is awake...?

FILLMORE

(NERVOUSLY) I'm not asleep.

THE JUDGE

Goo-oo-ood! (TO PROSECUTOR) Your witness.

ASST D.A.

State your name and profession.

BRETT JR.

Brett Richards Jr., chief psychiatrist, Regatta Heights Hospital.

ASST D.A.

Are you acquainted with the defendant?

BRETT JR.

(NODS) He's my patient.

ASST D.A.

What precisely are his problems?

FILLMORE

(LEAPING TO HIS FEET) I object!

THE JUDGE

Overruled.

FILLMORE

(FURIOUS) Why?

THE JUDGE

I don't have to tell you.

FILLMORE

May we approach the Bench?

THE JUDGE

There's nothing to discuss. Request denied.

FILLMORE

The witness cannot he permitted to answer.

BRETT JR.

I don't mind.

THE JUDGE

Look, lad, I'm in a hurry. Sit down and let's get this turkey done with.

FILLMORE

But he's asking him to violate a professional code of privileged information. (TO BRETT JR.) You *know* you should refuse to reply.

BRETT JR.

(SHRUGS) So sue me.

THE JUDGE

Defendant will kindly sit down, or I'll hold you in contempt.

FILLMORE

The feeling's mutual. I move for a mistrial.

THE JUDGE

Petition denied.

FILLMORE

(SITTING) If I lose, I'm appealing.

THE JUDGE

Win or lose, you're repulsive. (TO CLERK) Read the question to the witness.

THE CLERK

"What precisely are his problems?"

BRETT JR.

He's an amnesiac. Or was. He blacks out for precisely two minutes at a time.

ASST D.A.

As has been observed in this very courtroom, Your Honor.

THE JUDGE

I saw, I saw.

ASST D.A.

Are there any other psychological problems, Dr. Richards?

BRETT JR.

Oh, yes. The main one he came to me for in the first place.

ASST D.A.

Its nature?

BRETT JR.

Sexual.

ASST D.A.

Describe it.

FILLMORE

(SCREAMING) *I object!!!*

THE JUDGE

Overruled. (TO WITNESS) Go ahead, lad, get to the hot stuff.

BRETT JR.

Mr. Fillmore has a strange sexual problem. Whenever he attempts to engage in romantic endeavor, he blacks out.

ASST D.A.

You mean the way we witnessed earlier?

BRETT JR.

No. This is an entirely different kind of blackout.

ASST D.A.

Please describe it.

FILLMORE

(HOARSELY) I object.

> (NOT DEIGNING TO REPLY, THE JUDGE
> NODS AT THE WITNESS)

BRETT JR.

His two-minute blackouts are true bouts of fainting. When those spells occur, Mr. Fillmore loses all consciousness and his body falls into a sleep mode. But the blackouts he undergoes at intimate moments are sheerly a mental phenomenon. Bodily, he apparently functions as expected. But his mind blanks. It's like a curtain was drawn between him and the scene in progress. (PUZZLED) It's very odd. It's almost as if he felt he had to censor himself from seeing what takes place.

> (A BLONDE IN THE FRONT ROW GASPS).

ASST D.A.

I see. Now, doctor, answer this next question very carefully, after giving it proper weight and consideration.

BRETT JR.

I'll do my best.

ASST D.A.

Is it conceivable that, under extreme stress, this "sexual" type of blackout might occur to the defendant in a nonromantic moment? That he might see something so shocking that his mind quits while his body still performs some action or other?

BRETT JR.

Oh, yes, it's possible. If he saw, say, another man making love to the woman he himself—

FILLMORE

I object to this entire line of questioning!

ASST D.A.

Your Honor, the State has been attempting to prove the defendant might have shot the two victims during one of these mental hiatuses...

THE JUDGE

(NODS) sounds plausible. You may proceed.

ASST D.A.

I have no further questions.

THE JUDGE

Well, lad? Do you intend to recall this witness as well?

FILLMORE

(RISING) no. I have two questions I want to ask him.

THE JUDGE

Go ahead.

FILLMORE

Dr. Richards...are you in love with Louisa Stone?

(ANOTHER GASP FROM THE
BLONDE IN THE FIRST ROW).

BRETT JR.

Your Honor, am I required to answer?

THE JUDGE

(TESTILY) Yes, damn you!

BRETT JR.

Very well. The answer is—yes.

(GENERAL CONSTERNATION.
THE JUDGE RAPS FOR ORDER).

FILLMORE

In that case, haven't you broken your professional code by revealing aspects of my personal life merely to make Louisa think twice about marrying me again?

BRETT JR.

(SOFTLY) Yes.

FILLMORE

Therefore your testimony concerning my condition is extremely suspect.

BRETT JR.

But my mother's files verify you've had the same problem for years!

(HUBBUB. THE JUDGE RAPS HIS GAVEL).

FILLMORE

(BLUSHING) no further questions.

ASST D.A.

No questions, Your Honor.

THE JUDGE

The witness may step down.

(BRETT JR. LEAVES THE COURTROOM).

ASST D.A.

That concludes the case for the Prosecution.

THE JUDGE

There will be a two-minute recess. When the defendant wakes up, we'll hear the case for the Defense.

* * * *

Well, this is it, Fillmore thought. *Friday afternoon in soap opera land and it's my turn. "A crisis now affairs are coming to!"*

He rose and approached the Bench. The prosecutor, looking rather curious, joined him.

"*Now* what?" Judge Tom rasped. "You haven't done anything yet, how can you have a question?"

"I want permission," said Fillmore, "to call more than one witness at a time."

"And what do you intend to do with more than one witness on the stand?" Hizzoner inquired sarcastically. "Elicit antiphonal responses? Or stage an orgy?"

Inhaling slowly to maintain his equilibrium, the professor answered, "I'll be done sooner if you'll just say yes."

"Okay by you?" the judge asked the prosecuting attorney. That worthy shrugged eloquently. "In that case, lad, you go right ahead and make a fool of yourself."

Fillmore turned to the bailiff and told him to recall the police officer and the motel clerk. A moment later, the pair stood in the witness box, jostling each other for space.

Said the professor: "Gentlemen, earlier you positively swore that I am the man you met on the night of the tragedy. Do you still maintain that position?"

THE CLERK

Of course.

POLICEMAN

Absolutely.

FILLMORE

You couldn't possibly be mistaken?

THE CLERK

Positively not.

POLICEMAN

Impossible.

(*Whoops. Don't participate so freely, straddle the fine line!* In an attempt to back away from the subsumption threat, the professor paused and sipped some water. Then he told the bailiff to summon the sole remaining witness for the Defense.)

THE JUDGE

Another witness?

POLICEMAN

There's no more room in here!

Fillmore tried to ignore the impulse to play the melodrama for all it was worth. Just then, the new witness walked into court. The buzz from the spectators waxed to a loud drone and the judge had to pound for silence.

The witness was slightly below medium height, wore academic garb but sported a colorful ascot about his full neck. Fillmore instructed him to state his name and occupation.

"J. Adrian Fillmore, literature professor, Parker College, Pennsylvania."

(A GREAT HUBBUB. THE JUDGE RAPS
HIS GAVEL FURIOUSLY).

FILLMORE

(POINTS HISTRIONICALLY AT THE CLERK AND THE PO-
LICEMAN) And now...can either of you swear which one of us you actually saw that night?

THE CLERK

(AFTER A BRIEF SILENCE) I can't tell the two of you apart.

FILLMORE

And you, sir?

(THE POLICEMAN EXAMINES EACH FACE
FOR A LONG TIME BEFORE SPEAKING).

POLICEMAN

No way I can distinguish between the pair.

FILLMORE

Defense is prepared to submit documentation attesting to the truth of the witness's identity. Also we are prepared to undergo fingerprinting to show we both possess the identical patterns. If the State does not so insist, I have no further questions.

But the prosecution did so insist and the business proceeded for several minutes more until the judge ascertained that there were, in fact, two identical J. Adrian Fillmores bearing no relationship to one another.

THE JUDGE

The case for the Defense being completed, I will instruct the jury to—

ASST D.A.

Excuse me, Your Honor, but the State has not cross-examined the witness for the Defense.

THE JUDGE

(LIVID) Will it take long?

ASST D.A.

Only one question. (TO FILLMORE II) Do you suffer blackouts while making love?

FILLMORE II

(OUTRAGED) I certainly do *not*!

ASST D.A.

No further questions.

Well, the professor groaned, *that's that! The fancy footwork failed. I'm doomed. Unless...*

Unless he could grab the umbrella. IF it would work.

He prepared to lunge towards the State exhibit table. But just at that moment, Louisa Stone stood up and spoke in a ringing voice that all could hear.

LOUISA

Stop the trial! This man is innocent!

(GENERAL CONFUSION. BROUHAHA).

THE JUDGE

(PEERING AT HER IN ASTONISHMENT) Louisa?

LOUISA

Yes, Tom. I know this is irregular, but I have important information that will—that MUST—affect the outcome of this trial!

Gazing fondly on his former wife, Fillmore totally forgot to resist participating in the soap opera world-set. *Gad, she's beautiful Just like Cinderella!*

Neither attorney objected to hearing her testimony, so the judge permitted Louisa to enter the witness-box and take the oath.

LOUISA

As soon as the newspapers ran the photograph of the dead man, I recognized him. He was a Russian spy. I know because I once worked for him.

(ENORMOUS REACTION IN THE GALLERY).

I still have documents hidden in my room to prove what I say is true. I've brought a few here. (SHE OPENS PURSE) You'll see that one of them is a photo showing the deceased and myself at a party rally. (LOOKING SORROWFULLY AT FILLMORE) I hate to say this, but I have no choice...the deceased was my husband.

FILLMORE

No!

THE JUDGE

Louisa!

LOUISA

(CRYING) It's true! It's true! But it was inconvenient for us to appear as man and wife, he needed me to use my...oh, I can't say it! He was a beast!

Louisa broke into uncontrollable sobbing that lasted precisely the 120 seconds that Fillmore suddenly napped. After he woke and she gained control of her emotions, she told about her late spouse's speculations concerning the umbrella.

The judge eyed Fillmore with considerable curiosity and suspicion.

LOUISA

I believe my husband accidentally activated the mechanism and it took him somewhere from which he could not manage to return for several years. When he finally found a way back, he traced Adrian, arrived while he was out, tried to elicit information at gunpoint from Myra, then, when Adrian returned, they struggled and that's when he hit Adrian with the umbrella.

THE JUDGE

But he wouldn't go shoot himself and Myra while Fillmore was unconscious!

LOUISA

No, but *another* enemy agent would! My husband was a loner, he was always being reprimanded by headquarters for keeping things to himself till he could be sure of garnering all the credit. It's my contention that a spy from the central office entered the motel room while Adrian was out cold. They argued and who knows what took place? Perhaps shooting Myra was accidental. But I'm sure—

THE JUDGE

Now, now, Louisa, this is all quite ingenious of you, but after all, you're merely speculating there might be another secret agent. You don't know it for a fact.

LOUISA

Oh, yes I do! I know because that very person, that spy, that MURDERER is sitting here right in this courtroom! (RISING TO HER FEET, LOUISA POINTS DRAMATICALLY AT A SMALL, CHUBBY, BE-WHISKERED INDIVIDUAL IN GRAY IN THE FRONT ROW OF THE SPECTATOR GALLERY) *That's Him*!

The crisis happened swiftly and unexpectedly.
As soon as Louisa pointed, up leaped the tall, bald, bearded stranger next to the little man in gray. Screaming a Russian imprecation, the tall man withdrew a pistol and fired at Louisa.
She screamed, clutched her side and slumped to the floor.

FILLMORE

Louisa!

THE JUDGE

Darling!

The spectators, shrieking, scrambled to their feet and pushed and shoved to clear the courtroom. The clerk ducked. The bailiff yanked out his gun. But he lowered it without firing.

The bald assassin was flailing about blindly, yowling in pain. On his back, the man in gray clung with arms and legs and raked his long fingernails along the cheeks and temples of his prey.

Bounding over the railing, Fillmore seized the spy's gun hand and prized the weapon free. As soon as he did, several spectators turned about and tackled the big man, bringing him to the floor. The bailiff hurried over to his side and rapped his skull with a nightstick.

During the confusion, the little man in gray dashed to the exhibit table, snatched up the umbrella and disappeared through the first open door he could find.

* * * *

In the judge's chambers, Louisa sat up groggily.

"Luckily," proclaimed His Honor old ex-Dr. Tom, "it was only a flesh wound." He lowered his voice and, anxiously squinting, said to Fillmore, "Don't let the A.M.A. find out I treated her without a license..."

Fillmore regarded him with an expression of numb, hurt bewilderment.

"You called her 'darling.'"

"Yes, lad. Louisa and I are betrothed."

"Is that *true*, Louisa?" Fillmore searched her face anxiously.

"I'm afraid so," she replied wanly. "He took advantage of me several months ago. I'm carrying his child."

The professor squeezed his eyes shut tight.

"Well, I hope you'll be very happy together."

"Thanks, lad," the judge beamed. "I suppose you're free to go now. Sorry your umbrella was stolen."

Fillmore nodded without replying, shook the proffered hand, kissed Louisa lightly on the cheek and left.

* * * *

Outside, on the courthouse steps, J. Adrian Fillmore sighed sadly and considered his options.

No choice. I'm stuck here now. I suppose eventually the umbrella might cross my path again. For that matter, if I wait long enough, perhaps Louisa will be free once more and I can marry her.

"But what about the baby?" he asked himself suddenly, aloud. The vaulting edifice behind him picked up the sound and made it reverberate in the wind...*the baby, the baby, the baby...*

In a soap opera world, the child would probably be full-grown in five or six years. He might resent Fillmore taking his father's place. There'd be friction in the household. Louisa and the kid would become estranged from the professor, the rotten brat would play them off against one another and *who knows? He might even try to kill me!*

No, all in all, it was a lousy world to be trapped in. Fillmore swore to himself that if ever he got free, he'd be much more careful about where he'd travel next. But he was too honest with himself to really buy his own assertion. *Man can engender what he is himself. Nothing more.* He twisted his lips in a self-mocking smile. *There I go, quoting literature again, even when I'm thinking! Miserable, asocial pedant, that's what I—*

Just then, someone plucked at his sleeve. Turning, he was astounded to see standing just below him on the courthouse steps the small round man in gray.

"I figured you'd be missing this," he said, handing the umbrella to Fillmore. "I only grabbed it because I was afraid the State might latch onto it and refuse to let it go after that blonde dish described it so accurately."

"Much obliged," said Fillmore, narrowing his eyes, "but how do you know she was correct? Who *are* you?"

The other grinned. "Some difference, huh? You really don't recognize me?"

"Should I?"

"I'll give you a hint." With that the man in the gray suit slowly faded from sight, his smile the last thing to hover in the air. Then he popped back into view. "How's that, boss?"

"*Rimski!*" the professor yelped in delight, hugging his friend the former cat.

* * * *

Rimski unlatched the door and ushered the professor into his living room. "I rented this place, boss, while I was trying to track you down. It's not the fanciest neighborhood in Regatta Heights, but I didn't figure to stay forever. Anyway, once you've been a cat, you get used to sleeping practically anywhere. Can I get you a beer?"

"By all means," said Fillmore, easing himself into an overstuffed armchair, "and please proceed with your tale."

His friend, looking puzzled, glanced behind himself, then grinned sheepishly. "Force of habit," he murmured and went into the kitchen for a bottle of Carlsberg Elephant and an iced milk for his own palate.

"So," said Rimski once he was ensconced upon a couch (he curled up on it in a decidedly feline fashion, the teacher noted with some amusement), "after I got my busted paw fixed in London, me and Boris went to the shop of this sorcerer you mentioned."

"John Wellington Wells. He manufactures interdimensional umbrellas just like mine."

"Not quite," Rimski grinned, "he's worked up some fancy new improvements."

"Such as?"

"I'll come to that. But the first time I visited his shop, it was to ask him to remove the witch's spell that once transformed me into a cat."

"I thought you preferred that shape to being a tax collector."

The chubby man lapped at his milk, prior to replying. "In my native world, sure, I had no choice but to go back to my old job. Employment's scarce there. I really wanted to be a bum, but the I.I.I. has that field all sewed up, so—"

"The triple I? What's that?"

"A union. Itinerants & Idlers's Internationale. Anyway, on the G&S world, I could see lots of advantages to shifting to mortal shape. Boris pointed them out to me."

The professor's mouth twisted in a sardonic smile. "I'll *bet* he did. So then what happened?"

"Wells took off the spell and I became the way I am now. Me and Boris returned to the fairy glade and a lot of time passed..." Rimski sighed pleasantly. "But eventually we wondered where you were, why you hadn't come back yet with a fiancée."

The professor frowned worriedly. "How *long* before you began to worry? I've lost all track of the time I've spent on this crazy world."

The ex-cat calculated on his fingers. "Lets see...maybe six or seven months before we started getting anxious. Another three or four months while we tried to tell ourselves we needn't be concerned, that you could take care of yourself. Boris would suggest something, I'd nix it. I'd come up with a plan to find you, he'd agree but the Fairy Queen would pick holes in it...All in all, a little over a year before I actually set out to track you down. I went back to London and bought an umbrella from Wells. There it is, over in that corner."

Fillmore rose and walked to the instrument. He picked it up and examined it carefully. "What's this subsidiary shaft and button?"

"One of those improvements I mentioned. It's a kind of searchlight."

"You mean a *flashlight*?"

"Nope. A searchlight. It helped me search for you throughout the cosmos. After all, I couldn't program my umbrella too accurately with a description of the world you were on. I had to give it a rundown of *you*, boss...and even then, I had a lot of parallel Philli-Fillmores to sift through before I ended up here."

"A searchlight," Fillmore mused. "Sounds familiar."

"Wells claims he got the idea from some wizard he once met." Rimski eyed his friend curiously. "Nu, so are you ready to go?"

"You bet I am, Rimski." The professor got to his feet and handed the newfangled bumbershoot to his friend, then readied for his own umbrella.

"By the way, boss, what do I call you from now on? Fillmore? Philli-more? And how come you changed your name in the first place?"

"It was my original name. While I had amnesia, Louisa found an old Fillmore name card in my wallet. The funny thing is I like 'Fillmore' now, but I used to hate it."

"Meaning?"

The professor shrugged. "Beats me. Maybe it's because I got used to hearing Louisa say it with a special kind of caress in her voice. That was in the early days before she started calling me Adrian." He winced. "Well, I think I still prefer 'James's or 'Jim,' but I've decided to go with the name I derived from my father: 'Fillmore.'"

"Okay, Jimmy," Rimski purred affectionately, "so now let's go visit Boris and let him know you're all right."

They positioned their thumbs on the release catches and prepared to press them. But suddenly the professor stopped.

"What's the matter?"

"Better let me push my umbrella's flight-button first. I'm worried it might not work."

"Why not?" the chubby man in gray asked anxiously. "You think it's busted?"

"It's more complicated than that. I'll explain later." Fillmore pressed the catch.

It did not open.

"I'm stuck here," he groaned. "Subsumed."

And then he passed out right on schedule.

* * * *

"*Vayzmir*, boss!" Rimski wailed once the professor woke up and detailed his plight. "What are we going to do?"

Fillmore shrugged. "There's not much that can be done. You're free to go. I have to stay."

"Maybe if we exchanged umbrellas?"

"I doubt it. They tend to become imprinted with the owner's brain-patterns and can't be operated by someone else. Still, I suppose we can try."

They handed one another their umbrellas, but again Fillmore cautioned Rimski to allow him to go first. "If you vanish, Rimski, it'd be a long time before you could return. It takes a while for the umbrella to cool off after any flight."

He depressed the button on Rimski's umbrella, but nothing happened.

"You see?" Fillmore remarked gloomily. "I'm stuck."

Rimski sadly shook his head. "All that *tsooris* for nothing. What I call ironic."

Fillmore nodded. "Yes, I might as well have remained at Parker College on my native Earth for all the—"

Abruptly, he stopped talking. His eyes widened. His jaw dropped.

Rimski clutched his arm. "You're maybe thinking something good?"

"Yes! *Yes!* You just told me how I can escape this world!"

"I did?" Rimski asked, puzzled.

"Absolutely! Listen: every world has its own peculiar governing principles. Once I was on a planet derived from popular horror literature. Finishing a sequence there, I was morbidly certain, would mean my death. I tried to get away by umbrella, but the damn thing wouldn't open. It *knew.*"

"So what did you do?"

"I jumped out a window."

"*What!*"

"There was no way I could survive the defenestration. It was an immense drop and I was as good as dead, anyhow, so the umbrella finally opened and took me away."

"Whew! But how does it apply here? Are you going to hop off a cliff, maybe?"

Fillmore shuddered. "Hardly. On a soap opera world, a physical suicide attempt might result in some lingering horror...brain damage, coma, hospitalization encased entirely in bandages, all bones broken. No, there's only one surefire way out of a soap that I've ever witnessed."

"And that is?"

"Give you an example. Once, on a show called 'Days of Our Lives,' this sweet redhead, Maggie, said words to the effect that it was the happiest moment of her life. Practically immediately afterward, Mike—her husband Mickey's son by a former marriage—got pinned under a wagon. He lost so much blood he needed a transfusion. Which is when Mickey learned, to his horror, that neither he nor his former wife had Mike's blood type. Mike was the offspring of Mickey's brother, Bill. Mickey went dotty, shot Bill, had to be stuck in an asylum. Later, Maggie became an alcoholic, had her adopted daughter taken away from her by the courts and one day invited her friend, Julie, to her farm; the stove blew up, burned Julie hideously. Julie finally lost her husband because of the accident...and Maggie blamed herself for Julie's troubles. All because poor Maggie tempted the Fates by saying how happy she was. Get it?"

"Mmm-hmmm," Rimski mused, fingering his whiskers, "soap operas operate on a system of melodramatic irony."

"Precisely. When you used the word 'ironic,' I realized immediately what I must do to ensure the termination of my role on this planet." Hefting the umbrella, he placed his thumb against the catch. "And now, Rimski, do me a favor?"

"You name it, boss!"

"Ask me how I feel."

The ex-cat grinned. "Nu, Jimmy, so how's by you?"

FILLMORE

(BEAMING) Old buddy, *I never felt better in my life...*

With a sudden, violent, phthisic cough, J. Adrian Fillmore pressed the button and the umbrella snapped open with a profoundly satisfying click.

FADE OUT

PART III

"Brightly dawns the wedding day," trilled the Fairy Queen, smartly rapping the men's feet with her magic wand. "Wake up, you three! Our troupe must bless a multiple nuptial and there's many a mile to go ere we reach our destination." She placed her hands on her ample hips and, with compressed lips, shook her head. "If you weren't so stubborn, I could induct you into our immortal band, then you'd all grow wings and we wouldn't have to rush. We could all fly to Castle Bunthorne."

The professor, first to rouse, demurred. "The prospect of life without foreseeable cessation is not without attraction, but I should prefer not to flit through it."

The Fairy Queen shrugged tolerantly. "Well, I shan't force you. There's nothing so dismaying as an unwilling fairy, they do not contribute cheerfully to the communal gaiety. Well, do as you will, but get your lazy companions ready to leave directly after breakfast." She fluttered off to the central sylvan glade to supervise her people's preparations.

J. Adrian Fillmore rubbed the sleep from his eyes and poked gently at a chubby little man in a gray suit curled up by the foot of a maple. His friend Rimski opened his eyes, yawned, stretched in a decidedly feline fashion, then trotted off on all fours to wash himself in a nearby creek. Fillmore smiled to himself. Rimski once was under a witch's spell and spent several years in the guise of a cat. *And he hasn't quite got it all out of his system as yet.*

He really hated to disturb his other friend, Boris, the Frankenstein monster. The hapless favorite of all four-and-twenty adorable members of the Fairy Queen's fey company, the hulking creature simply could not cope with the unceasing demands upon his affections. In the year-and-many-months since Fillmore last set eyes on his huge friend, Boris's Shelleyesque appearance had grown more pronounced, even alarmingly so. His watery eyes were as baleful as ever, his black lips neither more nor less shriveled, but there was no doubt that he was thinner, gaunter and his sickly yellow skin faded to a wan ivory hue.

Fillmore could do little for him. The sprightly sisters frankly regarded Boris as their personal property. They treated the professor with considerable respect, but that was the full extent of their treats. Only the diminutive Rimski was able to compete for their attentions and he positively basked in the glow of their distaff delight in him. *Good thing we got back when we did! I fear for Boris's health...*

Gently, Fillmore nudged the monster's shoulder. "Time to travel, Boris. The weddings, remember?"

One watery eye trembled open, then the other. Boris sighed deeply. "I have blessed this day already. A moment more and I shall rouse me sufficient to perform mine ablutions."

"The Fairy Queen says to get up now. Sorry."

Groaning, the monster lumbered to his feet.

* * * *

They arrived in time to witness the last in a series of unexpected, typically-Gilbertian reversals in marital status of the principals of the rites in question. The invitation had specified Reginald Bunthorne, lord of the adjacent castle and a fleshly poet of vast pretensions, would wed a village milkmaid, Patience, but by the arrival of the nuptial morn, Bunthorne's fortunes twisted and dipped until he had no prospective mate left to marry but a stout cellist by the name of Lady Jane.

But no sooner did the skinny, black-velvet-clad poet proffer his hand to the large woman than a blare of trumpets silenced him. A splendidly-garbed nobleman, the Duke of Dunstable, strode forth on the greensward and himself proposed to the same massive damsel.

Lady Jane dropped her cello on Bunthorne's foot, threw wide her arms (incidentally bashing the poet in the face) and thundered over to the Duke, whom she accepted with simpering glee.

"Fickle frump, ain't she?" whispered Rimski to Boris and the professor, all three of whom stood a little to one side in a grape arbor watching the goings-on of the assembled cast of Gilbert and Sullivan's operetta, *Patience.*

"Don't be too swift to judge," Fillmore cautioned. "Actually, Lady Jane's doing the right thing. Bunthorne is an aesthetic *poseur*. He goes around pretending that his only passion is for the pure, chaste form of a piece of aspidistra or perhaps a poppy...and all the while, out of the corner of his eye, he studies the ladies's legs. No, to Bunthorne, women are playthings at best, at worst the necessary reflectors of his own sterling worth. He's vain, conceited, cantankerous, egotistical, self-centered and enormously selfish. He's taken Lady Jane for granted for quite some time. No, no, she definitely deserves a better husband than him!"

Boris regarded him in amazement "But how dost thou know aught of either of these strangers?"

With a sour smirk, Rimski spoke before his friend could say it. "Bit of a fey quality, he fancies."

Boris nodded sagely. "I had forgot! Mighty Philli—" He corrected himself. "Mighty Fillmore's puissant practices!"

The professor emitted a sigh of long-suffering acceptance of the minor, uncorrectable fault. *Won't Boris ever learn to pronounce that word?*

* * * *

The universal accompaniment struck up and the Duke of Dunstable joyfully proclaimed his marital intentions in song.

Duke.

After much debate internal,
I on Lady Jane decide...

Pointing toward two other couples awaiting the notary's official administrations, the Duke completed his quatrain:

Saphir now may take the Colonel,
Angy be the Major's bride!

The drearily-dressed poet sneered, then, clutching to his bosom a demure representative of the vegetable kingdom, Bunthorne echoed the Duke's melodious statement.

Bun.

In that case unprecedented,
Single I must live and die—
I shall have to be contented
  With a tulip or lily!

"That," said Fillmore to Rimski (who had a better grasp of the principle of parallel worlds than Boris did), "is a thoroughly Gilbertian rhyme-joke. What's more, there's a delicious irony to an operetta subtitled *Bunthorne's Bride* which ends with everyone *but* Bunthorne hitched to one another!"

"Aww, who cares?" Rimski yawned. "When do we eat?"

Just then, the company of maidens and dragoons chanted a finale to the stanzas of the Duke and Bunthorne.

All.

Greatly pleased with one another,
  To get married we decide.
Each of us will wed the other,
  Nobody be Bunthorne's Bride!

At that, everyone broke into a decidedly dithyrambic celebration and even the professor joined in the dance.

* * * *

"First solid meal I've had in weeks," Fillmore said to himself, putting down the beef-bone to refill his beer-mug. He wiggled his bare toes in the grass and inhaled the sweet air of summer. Though he knew it was, at best, a transitory state brought on by the food and brew, he could not help but feel at peace with the worlds.

Nearby, Rimski reclined by the side of a coquettish redhead, Daphne, a member of the Fairy Queen's immortal ring. The two indulged in light amatory games; Fillmore saw them and sighed.

And there goes my contentment, he told himself, feeling like Lazarus at the Feast, observing everywhere romantic companionships and the tang of dalliance without, however, being able to partake of the tiniest morsel.

An immense shadow suddenly interposed itself between Fillmore and the sun. Looking up, he spied the homely but honest countenance of Boris Frankenstein. Quaffing deeply from a flagon of mead, the monster wiped his mouth with the back of one great hand, burped, observed of the drink that it was "Good stuff!" and plopped heavily onto the grass beside the professor.

"Thou hast about thee, Dear Benefactor, an air of indescribable melancholia."

"Foolish, isn't it?" Fillmore mourned. "This is supposed to be an occasion of mirth and pleasure."

"Yet," said Boris with a sage wag of his head, "as a great poet once remarked, ''tis agony to recall joy in adversity,' and, in like manner, I perceive it pains thee to perceive plenty when thou art wracked by privation."

"You're marvelously percipient, my friend," Fillmore replied, draining his mug and mentally admiring the creature's self-taught literacy.

"O well," Boris said, patting the professor's hand, "he who suffers is sensitive to the symptoms in others."

"True. You did have a hard life where you came from."

"Aye. Yet I bethink me it be grand irony that I suffer now from a surfeit of the very commodity whose absence I once sorely lamented."

"Yes, Boris," said the professor, feeling cosmic (a mood in him that was concomitant with slight tipsiness), "there is always danger when one attains one's dreams." He refilled his beer-mug. "Take, for example, '*das ewig-weibliche*' that I have sought in other climes. The Eternal Womanly is as chimerical as her opposite, which I certainly do not embody. Yet, though I grant myself unworthy, still I seek, even though I know it's a quest impossible of fulfillment."

"And yet," countered Boris, "I see a restlessness that waxeth in thee of late and Rimski hath confirmed mine observation with the witness of his own orbs."

The professor shrugged. "I have little enough here to entice me to stay. Perhaps I do dally with the notion of having another go at seeking a mate. Yet I'm almost disposed to believe nothing will come of it if I do."

The monster leaned forward, intensely interested. He lowered his voice to a whisper, afraid the Fairy Queen might overhear. "And hast thou selected a new world to conquer, O Professor of Probity?"

Fillmore smiled at Boris's hyperbolized esteem. "A notion has occurred to me, as a matter of fact. And yet, I don't know."

"A world, perhaps, of great risk?"

"One might say, 'who chooseth it must give and hazard all he hath.'"

Boris's brows contracted; he shut his eyes and rocked in fierce concentration. "Certain I am that once I heard or read that phrase—or one with a similar ring." Suddenly, his eyelids opened wide. He regarded his friend with mingled respect and doubt. "Friend Fillmore, I believe I perceive your plan."

"At this stage, it's hardly a plan. Only a notion."

"An heroic one! A planet of high adventure, colossal danger—"

"And potential reward," Fillmore added. "Think of the *women*!"

Boris inclined his enormous head. "So you consider a flight unto a land populated by the characters of The Bard?"

"To the world of Shakespeare, yes."

* * * *

Standing, the monster grasped the professor by an elbow and helped him to his feet. "Come, Benevolent Leader, let us turn our steps toward yon inviting wood and, as we ramble, bethink us of the virtues and perils which your scheme portendeth to us twain."

"To us?" Fillmore echoed, slipping on his shoes. "You mean you'd like to come along with—?"

"*SHHH*!" Frankenstein interrupted, darting fearful glances all about lest their counsel be heard. But he noted the Fairy Queen at some distance flirting outrageously with Reginald Bunthorne. The poet did his best to keep his attentions centered on the limp *flora* in his limp hand.

Boris steered the teacher to a small copse, then, casting frequent glances about to ensure their privacy from the jealous ears of the fey sisters, he reopened the discussion.

"Forgive me, O Sire, for dwelling on that which is doubtless painful to remember, but save for the friending of Rimski, thine earlier amorous searches were fraught with disappointment and dire event."

"You're telling *me*?" the professor agreed, reflectively running his finger along the garish folds of the umbrella-hood. "I didn't even get close to marrying the woman I wanted in Faërie and as for the daytime-drama planet, I found someone I cared for dearly, only to lose her."

"You refer to the ineffable Louisa?"

Fillmore sighed. "Yep. Angelic features. And I guess I've got a thing for blondes. But—" Another sigh. "*But* there are some women, I guess, that are never meant for anything other than my distant admiration." His mouth quirked sideways. "Funny how she resembled Cinderella." Silence. Recollection drained the professor of the wish to converse further on the subject and Boris seemed lost in thought. But after several still moments, the monster began to muse aloud.

"Long and long ago," he said in a low voice, more to himself than his companion, "I haply found a set of Shakespeare's plays. How I reveled in their heady verse, the sweep of heightened prose. Even when

I read the appendices and learned he'd borrowed his plots from other sources, still I thrilled at his vasty projects and reversals, marveling how his genius wrought sea-changes on the crudest of stories." Boris sighed, he could not tell why. Then a comical expression suddenly lit his face. He prodded Fillmore with one long, bony finger. "Those were early days when my soul might have inclined this way or that, but for your beneficence. Twas then I had an odd notion. Wouldst hear?"

"Of course. Something concerning Shakespeare?"

"Aye. I perceived what I thought to be a sole flaw in his tales."

"And that was?"

A scowl appeared on the monster's countenance, a look so concentrate with murderous fury that the professor started and involuntarily drew back. He'd been friends with Boris for so long, he'd almost forgotten the towering, menacing rage that once grew within that manufactured breast. "Thou must recall, O Professor, how I was, in those incunabular days of mine birthing spirit, a creature shunned and stoned where'er I roamed. How should I not wish the worst to creatures of the light of day when I seemed doomed to haunt the night with ghouls, predators and murtherers?"

"Yes, yes," Fillmore nervously agreed, attempting to soothe the other's sudden anger, "but what has this to do with Shakespeare?"

The mood passed and Boris smiled once more. The professor exhaled. "I but mentioned mine early state," said the giant, "to show why I might peruse the plays of the Immortal Will and wish the villains all success."

Fillmore laughed, more in relief than appreciation. "You mean, you wanted the Claudiuses and Iagos and Aarons to win?"

"Aye," Boris chortled, "and for a time I had a scheme to re-pen the plays myself, redistributing the villains so they'd stand a better chance elsewhere."

"Huh?"

"Take, for instance, that Cassius, he of the lean and hungry look! Couldst not, Sage Pedagogue, perceive him working his wiles on Laertes, Polonius and the like, just as he did when he plied honest Brutus to join the assassins of Caesar?"

The professor smiled. "You have a cute idea there, Boris. Cassius might well have brought it off, where Claudius ultimately failed to snuff out Hamlet soon enough." He frowned. "But this idle talk isn't helping me make up my mind. How do you think I should proceed, Boris? Ought I risk the world of Shakespeare? The women, I admit, are tempting, indeed: Cleopatra and Juliet, Portia and French Kate..."

"Apace, apace!" Boris cautioned, holding up a forestalling palm.

"Forgive me my boldness, Dear Professor, but wouldst thou truly court treacherous Egypt or seek out Capulet, green in years?"

Fillmore sighed, but nodded his head somewhat vigorously. "You're absolutely right. I always set out too quickly before I think things through." He rummaged in his pockets for a pencil and a small notepad. "I'll make a list..."

"Another thing," Boris said warningly, "did I not read that the women of Shakespeare's plays actually were portrayed in those times by young boys of the company?"

"Yes, but that is *not* a factor to worry about, Boris. These worlds I visit are presumably the places from which authors with which I'm familiar derive their root-notions. Shakespeare may have had to employ boys to play his distaff roles, it was the custom of the time. But in his imagination, he *surely* saw real women when he created his great female characters...The professor's face darkened. "Still, I wish you hadn't brought that up."

"Why not?"

"There's a kind of universal economy that functions when I use the umbrella. Call it energy conservation, if you will. The umbrella mechanism, responsive as it is to my thoughts, appears to fetch out every subconscious fact relating to the proposed destination. If it's possible to fly to a world which matches the general mental specs, but also embodies the irrelevant facts—and if *that* world's easier to reach than the planet that doesn't include the unwanted extras—the damned umbrella always seems to travel the route that costs the least energy." He shook his head. "Well, never mind, it's too late now. When I go, I'll just have to concentrate as carefully as I can on the proper coordinates."

"Then you are determined that you *will* go?" Boris asked eagerly. "And may I accompany thee?"

"Sure you can!"

The monster leaped up, crowing with happiness. He threw his arms about the professor and nearly choked the life out of him in his enthusiasm. "O Convenient Saviour, thou hast always been mine guardian angel! Thou protectest me like a father!"

"Fine," Fillmore wheezed, "just don't call me Daddy."

Boris gave him another affectionate squeeze before releasing him. When he did, he was astonished to see Fillmore collapse in a heap. The monster, immediately contrite, dropped to his knees and anxiously prodded his friend.

"I'm all right," the teacher groaned, "but if you don't control your elation, you're going to tip off the Fairy Queen."

A look of pure terror passed over Boris's face. Helping Fillmore to his feet, he murmured, "Shall we not depart on the instant, ere she discovers our intent?"

"No, we ought to say goodbye to Rimski. Besides, he might want to join us. And I need more time to think. I'll fly tomorrow."

* * * *

The next morning, just before dawn, the three friends crept to the copse by separate routes. Meeting in the central glade, they exchanged farewells in whispers.

"Sure you won't come, Rimski?"

"Naah, boss, I like it here fine. But you watch out for yourself, hear?"

"Don't worry," the professor said. "This time I've thought things out quite carefully."

Boris and Rimski exchanged a significant glance, but said nothing.

Fillmore consulted a bit of paper scrawled with various notations. "I've gone over the entire Shakespearean catalogue painstakingly. There are only a handful of women in his plays that I perceive might be fitting companions for my future."

"For example?" Boris prompted.

"The ones with the best minds and wit, the women who refuse to sit back and play passive pawn-roles in their male-dominated society."

Boris interrupted. "Well, I, on the other hand, would have imagined the fair, innocent Miranda just the sort of lass thou wouldst elect to pursue."

Fillmore shrugged. "Well, I considered her. But I had an unpleasant experience with another sweet young thing. Remember Snow White, Rimski?"

The chubby man winced.

"No, no," the professor expounded, "those whom I most admire in Shakespeare are his Portias and Rosalinds, Violas and Isabellas. They are more than a match for their Bassanios, Orlandos and Prince Hals, you name them. Actually, the one woman in all the plays whom I suspect might be the most interesting of all is—don't laugh!—none other than—"

"The Fairy Queen!" Boris howled.

"Huh?" Fillmore blinked foggily. "Titania? Hardly. No, the character I meant—"

"*I* meant," yelped Frankenstein, "that the Fairy Queen is coming! And she seemeth passing fierce!"

Fillmore looked up and saw the magical monarch swooping down upon them, her diaphanous wings buzzing angrily. The professor grabbed Boris's hand, wrapped it tight round the haft of the umbrella, then stabbed the flight button, leaving Rimski behind to tender their regrets.

* * * *

ACT I.

SCENE.—SCOTLAND.

SCENE I.—An open place. Thunder and Lightning.

Enter two Witches.

1 Witch.

What work's afoot? What's to be done?
I fear our battle's lost and won.

2 Witch.

Our sister Hazel's set her lure,
The Duke shall perish by the Moor!
                    Enter third Witch.

3 Witch.

Our prey hath 'scaped! Pursue we must!
That stupid Moor's a foolish bust!
Be quick, make haste, we'll track 'im down
Before he hides in yonder town!

1 Witch.

Bestir thee, Hilda! Wake! Ne'er mope!
Come shake a stick, thou arrant dope!

2 Witch.

Have done, thou drab, with apish jibes!
Dost thou not sense peculiar vibes?

Ye Witch sniffeth.

1 Witch.

I'sooth, 'tis true! Och, what's amiss?
Disturbance in the ether, sis?

2 Witch.

A mage?

1 Witch.

An imp?

2 Witch.

A sprite?

1 Witch.

A wight?

2 Witch.

Some ghoulish flotsam of the night?

Ye 3 Witch peereth

3 Witch.

I see a fiend a ghoul might fear!
He's pierced the veil, he's flying here—
His dreadful face gives *me* a wrench!
And with him hies a dour *mentsch*...

2 Witch.

What doth this mean?

3 Witch.

I do not know.

1 Witch.

It matters not! Bestir! Let's go!
Our prey escapes! We must not gab!
The Duke, the Duke's the one to nab!

3 Witch.

She's right; we must forget this pair
That ply the worlds and filthy air...

[Witches *vanish*.]

SCENE II.—a blasted heath. Thunder.

Enter FILLMORE & BORIS from above.

The rain swept in sheets upon the moonless plain. Boris and the professor floated gently downward, but as their feet touched the ground and Fillmore's eyes opened, the umbrella snapped shut and the torrent instantly soaked them to the skin.

The teacher uttered a terse, terrible curse for the umbrella's special behest, but the thunder raged and the wind snatched the words from his mouth, so neither Boris nor the bumbershoot heard.

Being a good foot taller, the monster commanded a better vantage of the dreary countryside. Peering every which way for shelter, he squinted in the direction of a low hummock in the middle distance. A livid talon of lightning split the sky, limning the small hill against the firmament. Thinking he spied a deeper shadow in the slope, Boris tucked the professor under the crook of his arm and slogged toward the mound, shivering in the icy wind and driving rain.

An occasional flicker of heavenly fire gave Boris his bearings, but in between flashes, he could not accurately gauge the distance in the dark, which is why the hill loomed up faster than anticipated and he came to a stop when his friend's pate smartly smacked the side of the slope.

"Dammit, you lummox, do you think I'm a battering ram?" The professor's shrill voice sounded loud beneath the overhanging rocks that somewhat hushed the fury of the tempest. *"Put me down, you big jerk!"* he snapped with uncustomary pique.

Feelings somewhat injured, the monster instantly obeyed, depositing the teacher in the middle of a mammoth mud-puddle. "Methinks," mused Frankenstein, "this adventure hath not got off to an auspicious start."

"*Do* tell," Fillmore growled, poling himself to dry land with the aid of the umbrella and squelching to his feet. He glowered at Boris, but said nothing further, busying himself instead with the futile task of trying to wring the excess moisture from his trouser-legs.

* * * *

They stood beneath a low stone outcropping sheltered from the rain, though not from the wind's stiletto-edge. The professor trembled in the wet and cold and cursed the capriciousness of his infernal umbrella.

"Where, O where," Boris groaned, "didst thou command it to deliver us? What portion of the globe that's patterned on The Bard? What clime?"

"Certainly not here," the professor rumbled. "I expected to alight in

Italy, probably Padua."

"Padua?" Boris echoed, amazed. "*Really?*"

"Sure." The professor shrugged. "There's a maiden there with a quick wit."

"Aye," the monster agreed, "and a quick left to the gut if any male is witless enow to tackle her."

"Bah, the only reason Kate's so unruly is that she's a woman of intelligence trapped in a society that circumscribes woman's role." Fillmore spoke in his stiffest classroom manner. "I considered Beatrice for a time, there's some similarity in her talent for repartee."

"Aye, but Beatrice is a winsome lass, whereas—"

"Whereas Kate is, by the very title of the play in which she appears, a shrew. Which is probably because she knows she has a lot to offer a man, if only there were one worthy of her mettle."

Boris put a hand to his forehead and rocked from side to side, but said no more to contradict his benefactor. "Well, then," he asked at last, "is't your intention to tame the virago? For sure she will not lightly list to protestations of ardor."

"Well, I don't plan to rush into it quite so fast, Boris. I'd like to cultivate her acquaintance, turn aside her rapier-wit with the gentleness of true understanding."

Boris sighed. "And if you can't manage it?"

"Why, then, I'd just move on to another Avonian maiden." He waved it away, the corners of his mouth down turned as if he smelt a spoiled egg. "Anyway, what's the use discussing it? As usual, the umbrella fouled up. We're nowhere near Italy."

"Where thinkst thou we've been untimely ripped?"

"My guess," said the professor, disapprovingly eying the terrain, "is that we're either plump in the middle o£ Lear's storm, or else we've fetched ourselves Scotland."

Boris grimaced horribly. "*Macbeth*, you mean?"

"Sure looks it."

They huddled against the damp earth, shivering from the wind's slicing sting. Neither spoke for a time. Each was preoccupied with thoughts of murder, diabolism and bloody vengeance, the plot appurtenances of Shakespeare's starkest tragedy.

"Ah, well," Fillmore sighed, breaking the silence, "maybe being in *Macbeth's* better than trying to teach it to a lumpish collection of unwilling sophomores..."

"Doubtless these sentiments intendeth comfort," quoth Boris, "yet I have nothing with this answer. These words are not mine."

"No, nor mine now," Fillmore replied melancholically.

* * * *

Time passed, but the storm did not slacken.

Suddenly, Boris remembered that he thought he'd seen a cave in the hillside when he regarded it from a distance. He communicated this new bit of data to the professor and asked, "Thinkst thou that we should search for it and seek shelter within its recesses?"

"I don't know, Boris. It might be the lair of some wild animal. Or worse, considering where we are. Which way does it lie?"

"To the left, I do thinkst."

"Well, we might as well have a look at it But be on the alert It might prove dangerous."

"There's little I fear, Mine Friend." Boris smiled grimly. "Come on, I'll go first."

"Want to borrow my umbrella?"

"What for?" the Frankenstein monster asked, mystified.

"You can wield it like a club."

"Nay, keep it for thine own protection. But I spy up ahead a pile of kindling. There will I select me a spruce stock."

"Okay, Boris, let's go. But step softly."

"Aye; and I shall carry a big stick."

Cautiously, they approached the mouth of the lightless cave.

SCENE III.—A cavern, within. Total darkness.

BORIS *thrashes with stick.*

Fil.

Good Gad, it must be big. But I can't see.

Bor.

Nor I. But sure, this cave's a vasty thing,
Fit to harbor Death's fell brood, a throng
Whose lightest thought's enough to make a corse
Of him who, hapless, hears such filth unclasped
Unto the skinless air. But list, O list,
Good Sire, my cudgel flaileth wide and near
And far and yet nor roof nor wall I hear.

Fil.

The portal's here, but then the sides give way.
I feel a wall and now I'll pace it out.

Bor.

Hast done?

Fil.

Some forty feet from side to side.

Bor.

Now mark me: though I stand so wondrous huge,
That in the catalogue of men—of which
Tis said I am a very catalogue
Of men—am assessed quite monstrous tall,
Yet cannot I, with twig outstretched above,
Effect to tap this cavern's lofty top!

[Thrashing.]

Fil.

Rest, rest, perturbed spirit—Let's sit
Upon the ground and tell dull tales so dry
That we might shake this all-pervasive wet

[They sit.]

Bor.

Hsst! Methinks that I did hear a stealthy sound.

Fil.

Relax, relax. The cave is surely full
Of mice. We'll hide in here till all our clothes
Be dry and then, when the firmament shuts up,
Perhaps we can fly away from here.

Bor.

How's *that*?
And can it be?

Fil.

It can. Not likely, no,
That we could leave this world behind yet,
But, Boris, do you not recall one time
When you and I flew *overland* by virtue
Of this same umbrella?

Bor.

Aye, I do. But hush!
Again I hear a susurration like
The sibilance of richly Eastern silk...

[They listen.]

Fil.

It's just an echo, sure. These caves possess
Such eerie tricks. There's no one here but us.

Bor.

And yet—

Fil.

AUGGHH!

Bor.

What? I did not catch—

Fil.

AUGGHH!

Bor.

Master, *what is 't?*

A Voice.

Budge not, or else he's dead!

A struggle, quickly cut short. A light is struck, BORIS, on his feet, has cudgel ready to strike, FILLMORE, on ground, is held by a small youth encloaked and hooded. This nameless figure has one arm round the professor's neck and a dagger bladed at his throat but nearly drops it when the light first reveals BORIS. Holding the lantern and a little way off is he who spake: a richly-dressed patrician of early middle years, tall, sinewy, brawn-bearded. He is VINCENTIO, Duke of Vienna and he, too, starts upon beholding BORIS. BORIS lowers stick.

Duke.

O'ername thyself, fiend, before my lad dispatch him.

Bor.

How dast thou threaten? Who are you that demand aught of those who've done no harm to thee or thine?

Fil.

Boris, don't argue!

Duke.

Good words and well pronounced. Do not make me ask again. His life's forfeit if I do.

Bor.

I'm Boris Frankenstein, you know me not. I'm new to these parts.

Duke.

And he?

Bor.

I shall not say.

Fil.

Boris!

Bor.

Master, I dare not reveal thy true name. The Mage who does, 'tis said, forfeiteth the greater part of's power.

Fil.

[*Groans.*]

Duke.

'Tis as I guessed. A sorcerer, doubtless leagued with those fearful hags that chase me. Though the Thane's plan miscarried and I 'scaped, I'm followed by wights and frights. I'll tend to thee, at least and when you're despatched, sure that beast-with-the-club-who-must-be-your-Familiar will vanish, too, into the pits of Hell.

Fil.

But damn it, you've got it all wrong. Tell him to take away his knife for a moment and I'll tell you who I am. Not only don't I wish you any harm, but I might be able to help. Who knows?

Duke.

You'd coin me counterfeit to credit thee guiltless. Have done, I am no jade, no gull. Lad, what thinkst thou?

Youth.

[*Shrugs.*] He *may* be harmless.

Duke.

Well, well, I wish none injustice. I'll hear thee ere I judge. Retire to a further recess of this tunnel and there my man shall watch that you conjure not further infernal aid.

Fil.

Prejudging a bit, aren't you?

Duke.

Thy thing must not come with's.

Fil.

All right, all right! Boris—*stay!*

Duke.

Each dog shall howl, each spy shall have his say.

[*Exeunt;* BORIS *manet.*]

SCENE IV.—another part of the cave.

Enter FILLMORE, DUKE, YOUTH, DUKE sets down lantern.

Fil.

So. Now have I satisfied you?

Duke.

A wilder tale mine ears hath never heard.

Youth.

Sire, if what he says is true, he'd be
Great use in thy escape!

Duke.

'Tis true. But can
You really speak me sooth? My Fate?

Fil.

More or less. Like I said, I know you from a play penned in
my home-world. It's called (the play, not the planet) *Measure
for Measure*. In it, you, Duke of Vienna, announce you mean to
spend some time in travel and study. So you appoint a deputy to
govern in your absence.

Duke.

Quite true.

Fil.

But the truth is that you've grown worried that your country's morals are slipping and that the law has not been properly
upheld. So instead of leaving the country, you disguise yourself
as a poor friar and sniff around, especially checking up on how
your appointed deputy's running Vienna. He begins well, but
soon is lured into corruption by the paradoxical chaste offices of
a woman, Isabella—

Duke.

Pause, friend. To a point, what you said's true, but now your
tale hath veered from mine.

Fil.

I was afraid it might. In what particulars?

Duke.

Give ear to mine history:
Be absolute in the firstlings of your tale:
I did intend, at first, to pry and peer
When everyone did think I was not here
But shipped abroad to visit kingly friends,
To mark the springs and styles that fellow dukes,
Or kings, or thanes, or earls, or other chiefs

Employ to wind the clockwork State and see
It tick those tunes that are the hour-tithes
That rulers seek to shape whene'er they rule
The shape of Time. But hear me now, what happed:
This deputy I appoint me somehow learns of my real plan.
He seeks me out and says: "Vincentio,
Your scheme is mere corruption, you wrong
Your people and your State to make of me
A puppet-surrogate, a bastard-Duke,
A jester deputy who, sceptreless,
Shall be but mock and butt when all the facts
Are known, as e'er such tricksy deeds shall out."
Well, well, I heeded his counsel and spake I should
Truly go abroad. My deputy, wily,
Suggests I sail to see the newly-crown'd
King of Scotland. But unbeknownst to me,
This false deputy sends forth secret notes
Unto that fledgling king, a man who stole
His throne, I hear. "The Duke, Vincentio,
Approacheth thy shore," so runs the traitor's
Letters. "Immure him in deepest dungeon,
Or have his head at once and thou hast won
Vienna's favor, Vienna's lasting debt!"

Fil.

What in hell? Your deputy, Angelo, pulled that old Rosen-crantz-and-Guildenstern number?

Duke.

I beg thy pardon?

Fil.

Never mind, I've got the picture. Angelo—

Duke.

The second time you've said that name? But who's he?

Fil.

He? Who?

Duke.

Angelo.

Fil.

Your deputy!

Duke.

Nay. I know no such man.

Fil.

Uh-oh...

Duke.

Pale, art thou? But nay, the deputy of whom I spake is a native of Britain, an expatriate noble of the Plantagenet line. Now to the latter turnings of my history: shortly before I set sail for Scotland, this lad here puts into Court, beseeching me a place. His nature's sweet, his need's desperate, I sensed he fled some secret of's past (Nay, blush not, lad, I'll ne'er inquire what 'tis.) So I took him on and the two of us come to Scotland. The Moorish king all too readily doth my foul deputy's bidding, shuts me up—but look you, thou'rt ghastly pale, indeed!

Fil.

What do you mean by "Moorish king"? Isn't the Scottish usurper a native named Macbeth?

Duke.

Thourt befuddled still. Macbeth's in Rome, third member of the triumvirate. The Scot's ruler's Aaron the Moor.

Fil.

[*Aside.*] Why in all good hell did I discuss things with Boris? Macbeth in Rome! Aaron at Dunsinane!

Duke.

You've heard, then, of the Moor?

Fil.

Have I! He's one of Shakespeare's bloodiest, most treacherous villains. From *Titus Andronicus*.

Duke.

These names portendeth naught to me. But aye,
This Aaron is a fiend. He chained me up

And meant to stock his larder-store against
The coming cold by slicing off from me
Each day a single filament of flesh.
But this, my servant-lad, hid him away
And steals me the key to Aaron's charnel-vault.
But for his grace, I'd grace this night or morn
That ogre's festive board. Scarce three hours since,
We fled, though Hell itself sent hounds to chase
Us down. We refuged in this chilly cave,
Pursued by awful sprites and hags of Doom
Who wouldst enforce their compact with the Moor.

Bor.

[*Within*.] O Mighty Fillmore!

Duke.

What's this, what's this? Your man (if man he be)
Hath broke his word, which was to leave thee
Unattended here. He comes.

Fil.

Will you calm down? Boris won't hurt either of you. Relax.

Enter BORIS.

Bor.

I thought you'd wish to know, outside hath come
A nasty band of nasty things; they seem
To do the will and bid of biddies three,
Three crones that hath a mean and hungry look.

Duke.

They've found us out, Aaron's vile mentors!
[*Drawing sword*.] Defend us, if thou truly hast
Good will to mine estate. If not, the, foe!

Fil.

Cool it, Duke. Are you forgetting my plan? Boris, c'mere a minute... [He whispers to BORIS.]

Duke.

How may I know whether they plotteth aught

Against us now?

Youth.

O Sire, I *think* they're true.

Fil.

All right, Duke, now listen. Here's my plan...

Whilst they converse apart, the YOUTH *cowers in a corner waving a dagger in* BORIS'S *general direction,* BORIS *deigns to smile benignantly at the frightened aide...an unsettling spectacle.*

Bor.

Nay, lad, ye've naught to fear from me this night,
And I will rout these things without, or fight.

[Tableau.]

SCENE V.—outside the cave. Thunder and Lightning.

Enter three Witches.

The storm split the paling sky. The First Witch, suspiciously sniffing, said, "I tell thee, Hazel, I don't like it."

"Bah," scoffed Hazel, studying the East. "No time for vague portents. Rather, perform your requisites. See not how the dawn marcheth swift out o' th' East? If we don't capture this Duke straightway, he'll win a full day's flight."

"So what?" the First Witch countered. "From dawn to dusk he may flee and not reach the border (beyond which our power's much weakened, save for certain delimited places further south). But I tell thee, sis, there still be something ill within. I like it not. I smell a kind of death that's yet won'drous quick."

Hilda, the Second Witch, cackled, "But if we send our *leetle* pet inside, he'll roust all out quick enow."

"A good idea," Hazel agreed, ignoring the First Witch, who still shook her head skeptically. She signed to Hilda, who stomped into the mud and pushed her way through the massed pack of miscellaneous hounds, beasties and diabolic vermin that the weird sisters had brought with them. She returned a moment later accompanied by a slavering, vile-smelling cacodemon principally distinguished from others of its foul breed by a bright green horn growing from its forehead. It smiled crookedly and perched on its hindmost limbs, croaking, "Eat? Eat?"

"Aye, Rover," Hazel nodded, indicating the cave. "In there."

Even the Witches stopped their ears at the hideous sounds which soon emerged from the dark gaping mouth of the cavern. After several minutes, all within was silent. Smiling at one another, the Three Witches agreed the whole affair had been handled admirably.

"Well," said Hazel, "let's go in and collect a few relicts for our pains."

With a jaunty shrug of her gnarly shoulders, she started to enter, Hilda right behind. Their sibling was not so quick to follow. Which was just as well for her since she would have been trampled by the others suddenly spinning on their heels and running out of the cave, shrieking at the top of their wizened lungs.

* * * *

From the Stygian blackness that was the mouth of the subterranean channel emerged an enormous man in a heavy cloak and hood that for the moment hid his features. In his arms he carried the broken remnants of what was once the horn-skulled cacodemon.

Scornfully, he dropped the twisted thing, brushed off his hands, then, throwing back his hood, grinned malignantly at the Witches.

"Keep your pets to yourselves," Boris warned, then, turning toward the rest of the Hell-pack, uttered a triumphant howl so malignant that the entire demon-band, yelping hideously, instantly fled away across the heath, committing innumerable nuisances in the process.

Frankenstein faced the hags who, though they seemed dismayed, had not quit the spot. Hilda and Hazel hunkered behind their bolder sister, prodding her to speak on their behalf.

But Boris did so first. "Begone, vile insects!" he commanded, pointing at the sun. "It lacks but a few moments till the dawn doth peep its round above those bleak pinnacles. Thou canst not further impede us!"

"Y'wanna bet, you warehouse retread?" the First Witch sneered. "We won't go till we bear away the Duke."

"You shall not have power of me," a new voice proclaimed ringingly.

Vincentio emerged from the cave, Fillmore close behind, umbrella in hand. The youth who'd loaned Boris the cloak kept to the rearward shadows. "Bid thee tell the Moor that the Duke, his better, hath 'scaped the stays of shackles, bolt and locks."

* * * *

Fillmore eyed the Duke with considerable respect. The outcome of the nefarious battle was not yet certain, but Vincentio's nobility rose above fear, it appeared. He stood tall and proud in his wine-hued tunic, jeweled fingers clasped against the hilt of his burnished sword, his silken brown beard none the worse for the pelting it took in the rain.

"I am a free spirit," the Duke retorted. "You can do nothing to stop me from leaving this cursèd Scotland."

"Maybe *I* can't, dearie," leered the First Witch, "but *he* can, I'll wager." With that, she pointed a willow-wand at the broken heap that had been the cacodemon.

Instantly, each part lurched up on end and from every section grew a new fiend identical to the first.

Boris snarled and prepared to fight them, one and all, but the professor commanded him to stop.

"She'll reanimate them," he said grimly, "and every one you tear apart will reknit. You can't fight an army of them."

"Can *try*," Boris growled.

"Enough chatter!" the First Witch shrilled. "Our time is short. Either surrender the Duke at once, or they attack!"

Fillmore tapped the nobleman's shoulder lightly. "Okay, time to work my plan. *Hop to it.*"

Before the hag could wave the cacodemons into service, Fillmore thumbed open the umbrella-catch and as the hood spread, Vincentio grasped the handle with one sinewy hand. The other he kept on his sword.

Instantly, the two arose high in the air. Below, the witches gaped stupidly at the men as they ascended far into the stratosphere.

"*Damn it all!*" Hazel muttered at last, "*if that don't beat broomsticks!*"

When the evil trio finally turned their vengeful eyes toward Boris, they were too late. The storm had stopped, the sun shone bright. In the first flush of dawn, the cacodemons melted mumpishly into the earth, leaving behind a stench that was swiftly dispelled by the cleansing breeze of morning.

Now Boris leered at the sisters and stamped his foot Howling, they bumped into one another in their haste, quickly sorted themselves out and sped off across the blasted heath, fingers in ears to avoid hearing the monster's triumphant bellowing.

When they were lost to sight, Boris stopped yowling and turned around. A worried look crossed his face. The Duke's friend had fainted dead away.

With a sigh, the monster removed the cloak he'd borrowed to mask his visage till the proper dramatic moment. Wrapping it about the youth's shoulders, he gently rocked the sleeper awake.

"Nay, wee one, fear me not. Though I be cursed with a face that only the sightless can stand before unshaken, I have no hatred in my heart for good things. Calm thyself till my Master returneth and fetch us from this inauspicious spot."

"He *will* return, then?"

"Aye. He took first the Duke, for it was he they most desired. Your principal's tall and muscle-heavy, so I was left to protect thee till Mighty Fillmore reappear. When he does, I doubt not thou mayst cling to me and all may go together to rejoin the Duke. And now, sit! We must needs endure the passage of some little time together, shall we not know one another better?"

"Aye, 'tis seemly. You may call me Baptista."

"And I am Boris. Come, let's sit in the cave where 'tis warmer and there I'll tell mine tale. Tis a strange one, I warn thee, that well might set thine youthful hair to stand up like the fretful quills of porpentine."

"I've known a mundane horror or two myself." Baptista smiled grimly. "Come, let's away."

* * * *

When the professor returned by himself an hour later, he found the pair engaged in sober conversation. No longer did the youth fear Boris. The two had become fast friends.

As Frankenstein predicted, it was easy for him to carry Baptista on his back and no great strain on the umbrella to bear all three aloft.

SCENE VI.—another part of the heath.

Enter three Witches.

2 Witch.

That cursèd pair hath robbed us all,
Hath ta'en our prey, hath dared our power.

3 Witch.

[*Peering.*] I see them now. They've crost
The country's southern edge.

2 Witch.

Then all
Is lost, we cannot chase 'em there:
Our union cards ain't good below
The border of these northern lands.
That's Local # 1984,
They don't got reciprocity.

3 Witch.

But we've got spies who'd do our bid
Even down in England, kid!

2 Witch.

That's very true. Let's think this out;
Is't worth the risk to use them 'gainst The Duke?

1 Witch.

Forget that paltry knave.
A token hurt's enough to quit
That score. But shall we brook that pair
Who interposed their will betwixt
Ourselves and our prey?

2 Witch.

Ah, nay!

3 Witch.

Ah, nay!

1 Witch.

And I say nay until I'm hoarse!
Now mark me as I map our course:
Let's lure them south unto a clime
Outside the union's temporal sway.
Wilt thou be ruled? Art game?

2 & 3 Witch.

We are!

1 Witch.

Then we must travel, near and far.

[*Exeunt severally*]

ACT II.

SCENE.—England.

SCENE I.
Eastcheap, a room in the Boar's Head Tavern.

The time is out of joint, J. Adrian Fillmore groggily told himself, studying his watch. *But how does one keep a contemporary Earthly chronometer accurate across the interstellar continuum?* He had no answer; at the moment, he wasn't even sure what properly could he called contemporary.

Never one, however, to modify his cosmic perceptions by the merely relative, the professor rallied his spirits and sat up in bed. He pushed the rough ticking off his bare legs, swung them to the floor and began to clothe himself.

Far as I can figure it's been the better part of two days. The combination of inclement Scottish weather and three long-distance hops over a huge chunk of British mainland greatly wearied him. The Duke, too, was tired from his ordeal in Aaron's dungeon and the subsequent flight across the storm-swept moors.

But before he retired, Vincentio insisted on treating the group to new garments to replace those spoiled by the rain. Boris, less tuckered than the other men, accepted a quantity of ducal ducats and went off shopping with Baptista. Together, they gathered a creditable wardrobe for all concerned and for surprisingly little expense. The merchants Boris patronized displayed an astounding lack of avarice when debating price with him.

Both Fillmore and Vincentio slept one full day and the greater portion of a second. When the teacher finally quitted his bed, extremely hungry, he found the others, the Duke included, just sitting down in an antechamber to a supper of boiled beef, partridge, fresh greens, thick slabs of brown bread and strong beer.

Looking up from the table, Boris beamed at the professor. "And have you enjoyed your rest, Master?"

"Sure did," Fillmore yawned, stretching. "That grub looks marvelous."

"Thou puttest on a good face," the Duke said, biting into a slab of beef, "but I feel keenly the lack of grandeur I should have treated you to, had we been in my native Vienna." He paused, swallowed, then raising his beer-stein, rose to his feet. "I owe thee a debt, sir, which I know not how to repay in this makeshift position which you discover me in. But wouldst permit me to toast thee in good fellowship?"

Fillmore felt his cheeks burn with pleasure and embarrassment. Though his democratic origins did not permit him to evidence obeisance toward those of rank and tide, yet in the presence of the Duke's easy courtesy, the professor felt inclined to duck his head.

"You honor me too much, sir. To aid a fellow in distress is a duty which none should use as claim to extra honors. And as for the board that's set here, I could not ask for grander fare, sharing it as I shall with one of the nicest rulers in all Shakespeare."

Vincentio changed a puzzled look with Baptista. The pair shrugged, as who should say, *well, well, these foreigners are strange, yet's plain they meaneth well...*

* * * *

Little was said during dinner. After the tapster refilled the mugs a second time, the teacher pushed back far enough to allow his stomach freedom from the table-edge. Taking another draught of the strong, sour brew—*probably unsanitary, but I sure could develop a taste for this stuff!*—Fillmore studied at a more leisurely pace the features and mien of his host. Vincentio was a tall man whose sturdy spirit belied his years; he seemed a good ten years younger than his position and probity proclaimed him to be. His ascetic features were cut fine and surmounted by a scant fringe of curly brown hair, mirrored below in a well-trimmed beard. His brown eyes, when not actually engaged in converse, had a deep-set brooding cast, as if their owner were preoccupied with the weightiest of issues (as indeed he was). Yet when they rested on another in talk, common or lofty, these same orbs shone with keen attention and sardonic wit. In clothing, the Duke's tastes ran to sober understatement. Though the cloth was costly and the style precisely tailored, he did not affect to bruit his rank in gaudy finery; his suit was quietly dignified in keeping with his characteristic manner.

Fillmore regarded the youth seated to the right of the Duke. There was something curious about Baptista, a familiarity that, till now, the professor had been too preoccupied to analyze. But now he examined the delicate mouth, the upturned nose, the corn-tasssel hair, the eyes bluer than star sapphires...and suddenly a pained expression contorted Fillmore's face.

Oh, damn! He cursed to himself, snapping his fingers at the realization, *now I've GOT it!*

Misunderstanding the professor's gesture, the tapster bustled to the table and freshened his patron's mug. Draining it in one gulp, Fillmore glared at Boris, who was obliviously engaged in idle table-talk with Baptista.

* * * *

After dinner, Vincentio sent his young companion out to procure tobacco for his pipe. While he waited for Baptista to return, the Duke took
up a spot by the great stone hearth in the corner, rubbed his hands in the
fire's glow and began to discuss his plans:

Duke.

As I no longer trust my deputy,
I can't return unarmed, 'twould folly be:
One taste of power's enough to taint
The wills of lesser men and he hath shown
A crooked bent that speaks a mind as wracked
And warped as he himself is crooked bent.

Fil.

Uh-oh...

Duke.

Didst speak?

Fil.

[Waving a hand.] No, no, go on. [FILLMORE glareth at a
blithe BORIS.]

Duke.

When I return unto mine native land,
It shall not be alone; I'll seek me here
Some band of hardy men who'll fight for pay,
And I and they shall storm the capital.
O Fillmore, friend;
O Boris Frankenstein,
I have no hold on either one of thee,
But wouldst thou think to throw thy lot with me?
Art apt to help me wrest away my throne
From he who stole the precious diadem
And put it in his pocket?

Bor.

Aye, I'd fight on thy behalf, O Gentle Duke.
But what doth Mighty Fillmore say?

Fil.

[*Sighs.*] Oh well, I guess
My plans will wait; we'll help what way we may.

Duke.

For this, much thanks. And wilt thou swear, good sir?

Fil.

Before this venture's done, I'm sure I shall.

Duke.

From this time forth, I'll count thee both a pal.

[*Exit* DUKE.]

SCENE II.
EASTCHEAP. the public room of the Boar's Head Tavern.

Enter PRESTON *and* BAPTISTA *from opposite doors.*
Bob Preston, veteran tapster at the Boar's Head for more years than
he cared to consider, shook his grizzled pate and wondered at the strange
customers on the upper floor. Nobility was not uncommon, *but the foreign Duke's friends*! The giant, doubtless a mercenary, *has the vilest visage that sure shouldst make Mother Moll drop her bairn before full time!
Good he keeps to's rooms and shows not his baleful front in here; 'twould
empty the common-room!* He chuckled to himself. *Or else our liquor
sales'd triple...*As for that other companion of the Duke, the dour-faced
fellow with the great capacity for beer, *how oddly was he suited when
they arrived! And speaks an idiom like none I've ever 'eared*!
"Mr. Preston, sirrah!"
The drawer turned. "Aye? Who hails?" He saw a slip of a youth approaching and recognized the Duke's other friend.
"Ah, what's that, laddie?" the tapster asked. "Good tobacco? Aye,
there's longbottom leaf in th' cellerage. Sit ye down and patient be; I'll
fetch a plug anon."
Preston bustled through the public room, bestowing a greeting here,
a wink of the eye there. Pausing long enough to slap the shoulder of a
wizened chap playing draughts *with that rascally Bardolph*—"Take care
the whoreson rogue don't cheat ye when tha' blinkst."—the drawer finally clumped down a flight of sturdy oak stairs leading to the basement.

* * * *

Baptista sat and watched the noisy revelry in the pub with keen interest. Suddenly, someone tapped the shoulder of the blonde-haired youth.

Turning, Baptista saw a darkly-handsome, well-muscled man of early middle years. He wore an Italian doublet and cloaked himself in honest homespun, yet appeared to be a person of some substance and character.

The stranger's face was broad, open and honest, but it wore a troubled expression as it faced Baptista. "Lad," the newcomer said in a low tone, "art thou the man o' Vincentio, Duke of Vienna?"

Baptista's brow contracted in an expression both puzzled and guarded. "I am. What's your business with me?"

The stranger sighed, seemingly relieved. "My business is but to take a vital word unto the Duke. Tis good I found thee. There's matter crucial to his peace of mind and future State."

"Then I'll convey thee to my Master at once," said Baptista, rising and taking a step toward the staircase leading to the higher reaches of the tavern.

"Nay, lad," said the stranger, shaking his head, "first I must fetch certain packets of documents that must be hand-delivered to your principal. They're cased in a chest of some considerable heft. Wouldst think to take an edge and aid me in carrying it?"

"Of course! Where is't?"

"By my horse in the stable. I hid it in the straw. Come, boy and help me bring it to the Duke."

He hastened toward the door and Baptista followed him through it and out into the night.

SCENE III.
EASTCHEAP. A room in the Boar's Head Tavern.

Boris studies FILLMORE'S face.

Bor.

Is't possible that I have done some wrong?
Thou glarest at me as if I owed thee cash.

Fil.

I *know* it's not your fault but still I'm ticked.
I never should have talked with you about
The world I planned to visit next.

Bor.

Why not?

Fil.

Because, although you could not know, that chat
I had with you about the Shakespeare plays
Stuck in my mind; and when we flew, your words,
Ensconced within my brain, got mixed up with
My thoughts about our destination.
The universal economic rule
By which the bumbershoot is ruled
Has snapped us to a place not *quite* the place
I had in mind.

Bor.

What's wrong with it?

Fil.

You're blind?
You haven't seen—but no, of course, you were
Not there. Or there.

Bor.

Not where? Or where?

Fil.

The world
Of Faërie and the world of "soaps."
In each I met a lass that I did crave:
And both resembled one another, too;
Louisa Stone was one, the other was—

Bor.

The princess Cinderella. Yes, you told me so.

Fil.

I thought there'd be a woman here,
An analogue of that complexion that I seem to love.
But you sure put the botch
On that.

Bor.

I have? And how?

Fil.

And how! You spoke
To me about the way, in Shakespeare's day,
The women's roles were played by boys.

Bor.

So what?

Fil.

So this the Duke's lad, Vincentio's aide—

Bor.

Baptista?

Fil.

[*Nods*.] Is the spit and image of Louisa Stone and Ella that
I loved.

Bor.

Oy!

Fil.

Yeah and that's not all. You also talked
About the villains in the plays and how
You'd switch them 'round about, to help them out.
And so the Moor's in Scotland and Macbeth's
In Rome. And do you know who's waiting for
The Duke at home?

Bor.

[*Nods*.] I picked that up. "A noble
Of the Plantagenet line." And one who has
A crooked frame: the Duke of Gloucester is
His name; Humpbacked Dick.

Fil.

Uh-huh. Instead
Of Angelo, the deputy that rules
Vienna's Richard the Third!

[*A knock.*]

Who's that?
Come in!

Enter PRESTON *with a packet.*

Pres.

Tis me. I bring the Duke tobacco.

Bor.

[Puzzled.] But where's the lad he sent?

Pres.

I do not know.
I bade him wait within the public-room,
But when I came again, I could nor hide
Nor hair of him espy. I thought he thought
No need to pause below and so I came
And now I press this plug into thy care
And so I've done.

> [*He waiteth for a tippe, which, when not forthcoming,*
> *causeth him to exit with some little pique.*]

Fil.

Hmm. I wonder where Baptista's got to.

Bor.

This likes not me.

Fil.

Me, neither. The kid may just have gone to take a walk and yet it's late and London after dark is not the best place to perambulate in Elizabethan times (or whatever time it is now, I can't figure all the anachronisms). Where on earth could the boy have vanished to? I'm worried that—

A stone crasheth into the room.

Bor.

> [*Howls with surprise and anger.*]

Fil.

What the hell—!!?

Enter the DUKE.

Duke.

What noise is this? Are we attacked?

Fil.

Someone threw a rock right through the window there!
See? It's in the middle of the floor.

Duke.

Some street beggar, a rascal unworthy of note.
But where's my man?

Fil.

He went for tobacco, but didn't get back. The tapster brought the
order a moment ago, but Baptista—

Bor.

HA!

Fil.

Huh?

Duke.

Hm?

Bor.

A note is tied about the stone!

Boris *unwraps the paper, readeth and frowneth.*

Duke.

Why, what's the matter?

Bor.

The matter which I read's the matter with me, Duke. But
note the matter of this note and sure thou'lt note what matter
pulls my face awry. Tis for thee, Duke, that matter you will instantly denote.

Duke *accepteth the paper and readeth therein.*

Duke.

"Vienna-laid-low, list: if thou wouldst see thy lad alive again, immediately come alone to th'alley one block south of the tavern-door; thou hast but five minutes ere the boy be dead."

Duke *throws down the paper, claps hand on's sword and strideth to the door.*

Fil.

No! It's you they want! You mustn't go!
They've set a deliberate lure.

Duke.

That's obvious as the grossest thing to sense,
And yet I have no choice except to do
Their bid. Baptista saved my life, I shall
Not pause to reckon up my State against
His tender loyalty. Have off thy hands!
Whilst we stay jawing here, his time doth lapse!

Fil.

We'll come with you then! Right, Boris?

Bor.

Yes, we will!

Duke.

Alone! The missive specifies *alone.*
By heaven, I'll make a ghost of him that lets me.
[*Drawing sword*] Corragio, lad! I follow!

[*Exit* DUKE.]

Fil.

We can't let him go alone.

Bor.

Nay, let's follow!

[Exeunt FILLMORE & BORIS.]

SCENE IV.
EASTCHEAP. a street and an alley.

Enter BAPTISTA, *bound, and* IAGO.

No moon relieved the darkness of the narrow street. Offal cluttered the walkways and in one corner just within the entry to the alley, a huge mound of some spherical stuff all but choked off pedestrian access.

Into the deserted thoroughfare came two figures, one kicking and struggling in the burlap sacking bound about the unfortunate's head, tethered with stout cord.

The other impelled the prisoner along, half-dragging, half-carrying his victim. When they reached the alley, the captor withdrew a thin, sharp dagger from his doublet and prodded the point into the place where the other's neck dwelt inside the sacking.

"I'll slice your throat in twain unless you're still," Iago hissed in Baptista's ear. "You feel my poignard?"

"Aye," the answer proceeded, muffled, from within.

"Then have done with your struggling. I shall not harm thee, you're but the bait for bigger fish. Now brace thyself, egg, for you must fall."

With that, the villain shoved the youth smartly in the midsection, tipping balance so that backwards fell Baptista into the alley, landing atop the roundish mound and headfirst flailing to the further side within the narrow passage. A deep, mournful groan arose; Iago shushed with vehemence.

"The Duke's coming, I see him. Peace, or else I'll rip thy entrails out! If thou wouldst save thy life," Iago lied, "best hold thy tongue!"

Silence, save for approaching footsteps.

* * * *

"Put up thy sword, Vincentio," Iago called, "or else the pup's dead."

Vincentio reluctantly sheathed his sword. "What do you want? I knew thee once, traitor. Art now in Gloster's employ? Or Aaron the Moor's?"

Iago grinned. "Nay, Vienna, I've fairer employment. Three comely dames I bet tha'st met in thy travels."

"The weird sisters? They pursue me here?"

"Aye," the other said, not wholly truthfully. "I'm fee'd to settle a score on their account. Wilt cross me, Duke, in dagger-play?"

"I have but the longsword you see."

"Ah, but I can loan thee a weapon." Iago reached within the folds of his jerkin and withdrew a second stiletto. Smiling, he held it, half out-ward, for the Duke to take.

Vincentio reached for it, but Iago withdrew a step toward the alley, waving the weapon just out of his foe's reach.

"Give it me, churl!"

"Come get it, Vienna," Iago laughed. He tempted Vincentio like a wayward child who steals the possession of a weaker lad and proffers it tauntingly beyond his reach.

Suddenly, Vincentio lunged at Iago, but it was what the Italian had planned. Ducking to his knees, he made a pass with his first and forward-pointed poignard (on which he'd maintained a grip since loosing it to threaten Baptista). The Duke uttered a terse cry of pain as the steel sliced deep within his thigh. Iago scuttled sideways to clear the alley and Vincentio pitched prone upon that same great mound behind which lay his friend.

Smirking wickedly at the loud groan he heard, Iago approached the Duke's helpless figure, weapon ready to plunge into his enemy's back. "Hear me, Vienna," said he, "the sisters only hired me to wound thee, but I have some wrongs of memory, methinks, which now to claim my vantage doth invite me." He raised his knife.

And then the vast thing on which the noble lay—a pile that Iago thought must be a mountain of refuse—tilted and heaved like a storm-tossed sea, gently rolling Vincentio down its further side. Rearing up like an amoeba that somehow learned to stand on end, the dreadful entity balanced on lower limbs as thick around as tree-boles. It stretched two fleshly appendages out on either side and, muttering unintelligible noises vaguely akin to civilized speech, began to shamble towards Iago.

The terrified ancient held out his dirk; the creature ran upon it, the point driving in easily enough, but apparently inflicting no pain. The huge pile still shuffled toward Iago, who strained his eyes in the darkness to make out what manner of monster it might be. He tried to free his dagger, but it seemed stuck in the beast's hide; he wrenched with all his might and it came out. Where it had stuck, there spurted forth a dark stream of strong-smelling liquid. As soon as the weapon emerged, the ponderous creature slapped flabby paws to the bleeding, hole and roared with rock-shattering force and unmistakable rage.

Iago screamed and spun upon his heel, blinking at a sudden burst of light. He ran, but only a few steps, for he was halted by the outstretched arms of Boris Frankenstein, who folded him tightly in his powerful embrace. It was more than Iago could stand; he took one look at his captor, then his eyes turned up, his knees buckled, his shoulders sagged, his knife clattered to the ground and he sank, unconscious, upon the cobblestones.

Adjusting the catch, Fillmore held the dark-lantern aloft, starting when, in its glare, he beheld the enormity that terrified Iago.

The monster, dazzled by the illumination, screwed up its massive face and bellowed anew.

"WHAT WHORESON BULL'S-PIZZLE HATH PUNCTURED MY SACK O' SACK?"

The professor saw a tall, white-bearded man of such great girth as to be a veritable Everest of avoirdupois. The man-mountain noticed Fillmore and, clutching the ruptured wineskin, whined, "O, who wouldst dash away the cup from a supplicant at Sunday reck'ning? Quick, friend, fetch me a chalice, a bowl, a soldier's brassy family protector, O! a chamberpot if there's naught else, but let me not lose one precious drop o' this divine Ichor!"

And thus (to use a worn, but enormously apt phrase) did J. Adrian Fillmore first meet Sir John Falstaff in the flesh.

SCENE V.
Eastcheap a room in the Boar's Head Tavern.

Enter PRESTON *with a flagon of sack.*

"Aye, Bob," quoth fat Jack, seated at the table, "go the rounds once, but leave the residue by my place, here where the cold fowl's bones rest uninterred. Hast aught wee morsel left in larder to stay me?"

The drawer unstopped the wine and splashed some in the waiting vessels. "There be a remnant o' beef, Sir John. And shall it be upon thy tab?"

Falstaff leaned back in his chair and both he and it wheezed at the effort "Nay, laddie," he demurred, merry eyes crinkling at the corners, "this foreign Duke's that grateful that I saved 'im, he's bade me eat and guzzle what I want here in's antechamber. All's at his expense."

Bob Preston put the container of sack next to Falstaff and headed for the door, shaking his head. "A gratitude untaught, to 'quite the saving of's life with ruination of's State. An if thou takest him at his word, why then by morn Vienna's bankrupt."

Falstaff boomed with laughter. "Thou'rt unparalleled 'mongst seers!" Draining his goblet, he called to the tapster's retreating back, "O Bob, good Bob, Bob of all Bobs, these gents within may have an hearty thirst to slake and beef that goes down dry's as vile a thing as bussing virgins in church; best bring another measure o' sack."

* * * *

The drawer soon returned with the meat and additional wine and set them on the table, leaving the gross knight alone to enjoy the repast Falstaff fell to with an appetite.

Midway through the meal, the inner door leading to Vincentio's bed-chamber opened. The physician came out and departed. Behind, Fillmore and Boris emerged and took up seats at the table with Falstaff.

"Drink up lads!" the fat man invited. "And how's our host?"

"He'll be all right," said the professor, "but it'll take a while for his leg to heal and till it does, he'll have to stay off it. It means a delay in his plans, I'm afraid. Ditto, mine."

"Plans?" the knight echoed, chewing a great morsel of gristle. "Why, what's up that may be sped?"

"It's a long story, I'm afraid," said Fillmore.

"No matter, lad," Falstaff majestically shrugged, smacking his lips, "we'll summon up more sack to moisten thy teeth and tongue and make the telling run more smooth."

* * * *

And so the professor outlined the pertinent details of both his and Vincentio's histories, pausing once only when Baptista joined them and said the Duke was sleeping peacefully from the pain-draught administered to him by the doctor.

When Fillmore's tale was finally done, the elephantine knight leaned back from the table, belched comfortably and clasped his great hands about the continent which was his belly.

Fal.

[*Wheezing.*] Well lad, there's stranger things, I see, than e'er I dreamed of in my philosophy. But touching on this Duke, why there's nothing that need stay the swift instatement of Vincentio at the helm of's State, where he ought ne'er have budged. While he heals here, we four shall go depose this crumpled deputy! I hath at my dispose a doughty crew o' picked warriors who'll sail with us in two days's time and battle do in Vienna's cause. What thinkst thou? Mayn't we sweep foul Gloster from his borrowed throne and then pen the news to this royal invalid to return triumphant to his native land?

Bap.

But I can't leave my Master here! That man
We threw in jail may only be the first
Of many wretched hirelings that might
Be fee'd to end the work the witchly crew
Hath broached: to murther the good Duke.

Bor.

Tis all
Too true: the convalescing Duke can ill
Defend himself, nor is that office apt
Alone for this small lad.

Fil.

I know, I know.
And yet, each day that Dicky Three's in charge
May swell the sufferings the citizens
Endure, might mean the loss of lives, for all
We know.

Fal.

If thou'lt be ruled by me, Fillmore,
Tomorrow morn I'll call my men and I
And they and thou shalt sail the after-dawn.
Behind we'll leave this loyal lad to soothe
His Master's malady and with him, set
This tree-trunk of a man to guard them both.

Fil.

Hm. What do you think, Boris?

Bor.

It shall be so.
Weakness in great ones must not unwatch'd go.

[*Exeunt.*]

ACT III.

SCENE.—ENGLAND and ITALY.

SCENE I.
LONDON. The stern of a docked ship.

Enter FILLMORE and FALSTAFF.

Two dawns after the Duke was wounded, J. Adrian Fillmore stood near the taffrail of the *Hamilton* and wondered whether it would survive Sir John Falstaff leaning on it. "So that's the grammarye-device of which thou toldst me?" the knight inquired, staring wide-eyed at the professor's umbrella. "And thou claimst it hath power to waft me to the very antipodes?"

"It *does* have its limitations," Fillmore admitted, dubiously eying Falstaff's paunch. "I wouldn't care to put it to that test. No offense."

"There's none ta'en," the other laughed, belly a-jiggle. The rail groaned, but held up under the strain. "Why, lad, I worked long years at my hemisphericality, as 'twere; this girth denoteth a large character; give old Jack Falstaff, fat Jack his due, though he may love tippling better than prancing in fields waving edged wands, yet is he of generous denomination, stamped with toleration of all the huggermugger earthly state that lesser men chaff at withal. I had as lief cheat the worms o' nine years's sup with preservation of this continent of cells in sack than dressing up like popinjay to tilt at arduous swiving. Say what ye will, a fat man's never hated, it is nor sin nor temp'ral breach; here's room in this plump planet for love of all the world and fat Jack, kind Jack, true Jack forgives his fellows's faults and banisheth them not, a courtesy I hope shall lovingly be returned to me."

At the latter words, Fillmore remembered Falstaff's bleak fate at the mercy of the ungenerous Henry V. He gently laid a hand on the knight's meaty shoulders. "Well, Jack, here's one friend who loves you, vices and all. But take a tip: don't put much trust in kings."

Falstaff waved away the advice. "Oh, Dick's a goodly chap, I'd trust him as much as any monarch, which says little enough, i' truth. But what with's hangers-on, I was but another member o' th' gang. Courtiers there be enow, but *not* Jack Falstaff! Truth to tell, though, I made a pallid bust o' palace life, and—"

"Hold on, I'm thoroughly confused," said Fillmore. "You just threw me a powerful curve."

"Interesting idiom," Falstaff remarked.

"I assumed Henry was king."

"Henry? There's not been a British Henry for some time."

"The hangers-on you mention...are they cronies of the king with the names of Bushy, Bagot—"

"And Green. Aye. What are they to thee?"

"Then Richard II is the ruler?"

"Well, of course he is," Falstaff replied, perplexed. "What is the trouble with ye, lad?"

"Never mind, it's too complicated to explain." The professor put a hand to his head, feeling a trifle dizzy. Of course, Shakespeare's character Falstaff made reference to being present during the court of Richard II, but he must have been a young man at the time and *here he is in his sixties, at the least. No mention at all of Henry Bolingbroke or Prince Hal—which is just as well, considering how Falstaff fares at their hands. On top of the other anachronisms, Richard of Gloucester, later Richard III, is old enough to manage the government of Vienna!* Fillmore sighed, unable to bring it all into focus. *The time IS out of joint.*

He wished they'd set sail already. The voyage south past Portugal and through the straits to the Mediterranean would consume a good deal of time. Eventually, the *Hamilton* intended to put into port at Venice, after which their journey must continue overland to Austria.

For the fortieth time, Fillmore took out the ruby ring to make sure it was still safely in his pocket. Its gold-worked seal would identify him to Vincentio's advisory council as a true and reliable emissary from the Duke. Then he'd deliver instructions to unseat Richard and imprison him pending the rightful Duke's return...

Just then, the captain of the vessel hailed Falstaff. Excusing himself, the knight joined the seaman and spoke for a few moments. When he returned to the taffrail, the fat man's normally cheery features were drawn down in worried thought.

"What's the problem?" the professor asked. "Is our departure delayed?"

Falstaff shook his huge, bearded head. "Nay, the tide waxeth and there's a breeze shall help us swiftly scud."

"Then what's eating you? You look green around the gills."

Falstaff nodded. "A pretty idiom, that and apt. Hear me, James, my news: a ship is lately put into port with news from the continent that distresseth me full sore. Tidings of the State whereat we tilt; I like them not at all."

"Specifically?"

"That crooked Richard's ambition hath swoln so that he's fitted out a company of mercenaries to do his bid and yestermonth, this force, augmented by glory-drugged private citizens, marched forth and did battle in all the neighbor-states to Vienna. They've won and all victories but greater swell his standing-army. The short of it, then, is that Richard's no more merely th' Viennese Duke-deputy, but calls himself king!"

"King? Of *what*?"

"All Austria. He's bound them to his sway; the country groans with tax and arbitrary laws and now his neighbors quake lest he try to push the borders further."

"This *is* serious!" Fillmore agreed. "Dictatorship certainly's within Dicky Third's psychological makeup. Now it's no longer a matter of you and me assailing a minor municipal official. He'll be harder to get near, much harder to depose."

"What thinkst thou we ought do, then? Return to Vincentio and help him compose's mind t'accept the drear fate o' one in exile?"

"Positively not!" Fillmore protested, surprising himself by his own vehemence. "We have to stop Richard before he grows any stronger. Let's see," he mused, "what do I know about his methods? He manipulates people with hypocritical false candor. He—"

"Lad, lad," Falstaff broke in, alarmed, "what madness is this? He's already too powerful. What may we do, who are but thee and me and a scantling o' warriors?"

"Well, as for that," the professor said, "the first thing might as well be to dismiss your men, they'll no longer be of any use. We'll have to rely, instead, on strategy, not force of arms. Incidentally, where are they? When did you tell them to show up today?"

Turning away red-faced, Falstaff looked over the taffrail and watched a dockside crew loading a barrel of pickles on a dray with uncommonly keen interest. "I asked where your men are," Fillmore repeated, suddenly suspicious.

"Ah, well, they're here already," the corpulent gent muttered.

"They've stowed their gear below deck and wait, like us, the casting-off. I'll just step around and see 'em. They'll be that sorry, but there's no help for't, I must dismiss them with but a moiety o' what was promised for this venture."

Fixing Falstaff with a frosty eye, the professor informed the knight he would come with him.

"If thou must," the other said unhappily, looking like a small boy caught with his hand in a cookie-jar.

* * * *

Just as I suspected! Fillmore pressed his lips tight and surveyed a small group of the runtiest, skinniest scarecrows that ever tottered along on breadstick legs. *Fight? They look like breathing's a conscious effort of the will*!

Calling one of Falstaff's "handpicked doughty warriors" over, the professor questioned him briefly, then, letting him go, watched while the knight paid each and sent them all on their way. When the business was completed, Fillmore sharply summoned Falstaff.

"Wilt keep me stumping about all morn, lad, on these poor o'er-worked legs?" he wheedled and whined. "Standing up's a business I have scant stomach for; that organ's more properly reserved for the full-time occupation o' stomachs..."

"Don't try to charm your way out of this," Fillmore snapped. "Hand over the rest of the Duke's money."

Sheepishly, the knight reached within the capacious folds of his doublet and took out the bag from which he'd given his crew their severance pay.

Snatching it from him, Fillmore warned, "See here, Sir John, I'm quite fond of you, but I won't tolerate any more of your nonsense or tricks on this voyage, understand?"

"Trickery?" Falstaff wheezed, a caricature of offended innocence. "What crimes dost accuse me of?"

"Of informing the Duke you needed X amount of money to pay each soldier with, then rounding up the sorriest batch of feeble factory rejects that any baby could wrestle to a fall. Of promising those shambling wrecks a fraction of what you told the Duke you'd give each man. Of intending to pocket the difference."

"Ah, well," Falstaff reflected philosophically, "no one's perfect..."

"And that's not all. I expect you planned to stay to the rear while your skeleton crew destroyed themselves attempting to manage whatever work there was to do."

"But Jim, good Jim," the other argued, eyes wide, "a good commander's ne'er found in the thick o' th' fray!"

"Hmph."

"O, that such fearful travails shouldst assail one o' my advanced years," the knight complained, emitting a windy sigh. "Probity better suiteth white hairs than mortal combat."

"I'm not buying it, Sir John," Fillmore said, though not without the hint of a smile at the corner of his mouth. He hefted the money-bag in his hand. "Just remember for the duration of this trip who's paying all your bar-bills."

Falstaff shrugged. "Ah, well, as thou prescrib'st no remedy else, there's naught but to store up sweets 'gainst the coming bitter."

A shrill whistle blasted from the foredeck. Crew members bustled about on last-minute tasks: securing of rigging, unloosing of lines, weighing of anchor.

"Well, lad," the knight inquired, bestowing a broad wink on the other, "wouldst break thy fast with an arrant blackguard?"

"I believe I will," Fillmore laughed, slapping his fat friend good-naturedly on the back. The pair stepped off toward the galley.

Neither noticed a furtive figure who had been watching them from an alley near the ship's stem move out into the middle of the dock and question one of the sailors busy with the taking up of the gangplank.

[*Exeunt.*]

SCENE II.
LONDON. A dark parlor.

Enter 1 WITCH *and* SPY

"Be brisk," the weird sister told her hired underling, "I must not stay out o' my licensed territory lang lest sair pain I maun bide. What hast?"

"The fat one and's umbrella-friend," said the bandy-legged rascal, "set sail this day aboard a ship called *Hamilton*."

"Where bound?"

"O, many ports, but this pair intends to disembark upon Venetian soil."

"That suits well," the old woman murmured. "Now hark'ee, I must thee use again. An urgent task—"

"I must tell thee, madam," he interrupted, "your business is something else than my usual. Couldst not thou employst me in my more normal custom? We're citizens of th' wide world, are we not?" He winked and ducked his head in studied servitude.

"Have done, Pandarus," she scowled, "I can conjure up those who'd put thy plaguey stable to shame."

"But-"

"Peace, bawd! I have no need for hold-doors! Now ready thee to travel faster than Phaëthon's chariot ever clipped."

"Where? To what purpose?" the crestfallen Trojan asked.

"To Austria. Warn Richard of his impending guests, describe all ye've said to me, their looks, appurtenances and all dependent matter."

"And when shouldst I depart?"

"Now," said the Witch, gesturing.

[PANDARUS vanisheth. Exit 1 Witch.]

SCENE III.
VENICE. Fillmore's cabin in the Hamilton.

Fillmore *discovered, asleep. To him,* FALSTAFF.

Fal.

Wake, lad, wake! We must depart! Awake!

[Fillmore *snoozeth still.*]

Ah, what shall we do? This Duke's safe in London, but good Jack Falstaff risketh his ponderous butt in an hopeless cause. Whew! Danger's hot work; it lacks malt to clear the palate and cool the blood! Yet here's no malt...shalt make do, then.

Falstaff hauleth out his wineskin and sitting on FILLMORE'S bed, begins to drink. But the frame gives out beneath his great weight and bed, knight and professor crasheth to ye floor. FILLMORE sitteth up and gripeth.

Fil.

Can't you find some simpler way to wake a person up?

Fal.

O hush thee, Jim, be still!
There's danger that we did not count upon:
Whilst we did slowly sail us past the Rock,
The villain-king invaded Italy
And with his brutish mercenary band
Hast torn the northern lands away from Rome.

Fil.

Oy! And how far south has Austria pushed?

Fal.

He claimeth all the land above the boot.
Venice is his and I have seen upon the docks a fell
And fiercely gang ringed up to board us when
We dock!

Fil.

You think they're after us?

Fal.

Tis best t'assume the worst
But may we 'scape, dost think?

Fil.

It sounds as if there only is one way.

Fal.

[*Swallowing hard.*] Umbrella-flight?

Fil.

Mm-hmm. But I don't know
If it can lug us both.

Fal.

[*Holding his stomach.*] I don't feel well.

Fil.

Well, there's no choice.
We'll have to try it, Jack.

[*He riseth from what was once the bed.*]

I'd better think this through.
Have you a map?

Fal.

I have one here.
What wouldst?

Fil.

Where may we fly
To hire some manner of conveyancing
Us to the capital of Austria?

Fal.

The closest possibility I see
Upon this map is Padua. Yet it
Is in the villain's gripe.

Fil.

But that's a place I meant to go. What luck!

Fal.

I prithee, jinx
Us not with talk of luck. I'll count us not
Among the lucky-born until we're quit
Of this vile mess. To Padua we fly,
And I shall pray th'umbrella bears up brave
Beneath my weight.

Fil.

Let's go on deck, come on.
We have no choice, we've got to risk it man,
And hope we each don't end up on our can!

[*Exeunt.*]

SCENE IV.
VENICE. On deck of the Hamilton.

Enter FILLMORE, FALSTAFF.

The pair peered over the rail cautiously. It was night. Below, torches flickered, lighting up stone gargoyles leering on the ledges of the surrounding buildings.

No Gorgon, though, instilled fear in Falstaff's and Fillmore's hearts like the grim company of silent sheriffs below. They were the ones who held the torches patiently till the *Hamilton* should set down its's gangway.

Fillmore plucked his friend's sleeve and led him into the shadows. "Aye?" Falstaff whispered.

"They haven't seen us yet, Sir John. Let's hope we can gain sufficient altitude to fly free before they fire at us. At least the darkness ought to ruin their aim."

The knight's knees knocked together. "I dread this thing that we must do, James. Instruct me; must I ope my eyes when we're aloft?"

"All you have to do is hold tight to the umbrella's clasp and keep your mind free of thoughts concerning direction or destination."

Falstaff frowned. "I might as well count off twenty without consider-ing armadillos!"

Fillmore winced. "I guess I should've put it some other way. Sorry!" He shrugged. "Well, too late now. Grab hold and let's see what happens."

* * * *

Wobbling alarmingly, the umbrella rose into the night-sky at a much slower rate than usual.

As soon as they saw their prey escaping, the members of Richard Gloucester's police force shouted ferociously. Their leader barked an or-der and all fitted arrows to strings and shot volley after volley.

Evasive action! Fillmore thought and the umbrella began to zigzag, much to Falstaff's discontent. He moaned piteously.

"O, this is more than flesh can withstand. No more, lad, I'll take my chances on the ground; a patch of brown furze beneath my heels!"

As if in answer, the umbrella suddenly tilted to one side and sank a few feet.

"Sir John," the professor yelled, "get hold of yourself, you're affect-ing my directional control!"

"Put me ashore, lad! I'm not a ruddy hummingbird! I'll take what Crookback Dick disheth out; can be no worse than this."

"Like hell it can't! Now *knock it off!* We're losing altitude."

"Thank'ee, Jim!"

"I'm not *trying* to, damn it!"

The umbrella plummeted toward the deck at a sickening speed. Bit-ing his lip and squeezing his eyes tightly shut, the professor furiously concentrated on willing the device to time out Falstaff and listen only to its owner. Slowly, tossing as if buffeted by a mighty wind, the umbrella righted itself and climbed once more.

But just as it changed direction, an arrow whizzed by so close to Fal-staff's bulbous nose that the man-mountain instinctively flung out both hands to protect his eyes. Instantly realizing his catastrophic mistake, Falstaff grabbed frantically for the umbrella, missed and plunged down, down, bellowing in terror.

High above the ship, Fillmore flinched as Falstaff hit the deck of the *Hamilton* with a devastating crash. Looking down, the flier could not distinguish the knight's figure, but he had no trouble at all making out how the entire vessel distinctly listed to one side.

The professor tread air and waited to see what damage Falstaff had sustained. The ring of torches reshaped into a line and the sheriffs moved up onto the craft. *The gangways down, then...*

An indeterminate wait. Fillmore's heart beat dully; he felt cold and numb. The same words throbbed in his head, a melancholy litany he could not face nor ignore: *what if he's dead?* At first, he thought it astonishing that he should have grown to care so deeply for the fleshly rogue in so short a time, but on reflection, Fillmore realized his feelings were logical enough. *Ever since I read the first part of* Henry IV, *I've loved Falstaff—and ever since I read the second part, I've pitied him.* He began to brood on the character of Henry V, but just then, the torches began to move again and all other considerations fled.

Deciding to risk a closer look, the professor dropped behind the masking architecture of a massive cathedral, then worked his way across alleys and parapets till he came to rest upon the balcony of a banking establishment on the border of the quay.

Six groaning sheriffs carried Falstaff spread-eagled off the ship, dropping him on the stone paving of the docks. Their chief came up and said something and two of them peeled off to execute some errand.

Keeping one hand clutched upon the handle of the hovering umbrella, Fillmore tried to hear what the head sheriff said, but could not. The nasty laughter of the others, though, did nothing to reassure him.

He briefly considered swooping down to rescue Falstaff, but quickly rejected the idea as hopelessly quixotic. *Too many of them, too well-armed. Besides, he told himself, Falstaff probably broke some bones in his fall. His injuries might worsen if he's moved...and what the hell could I do, anyhow? Toss him over my shoulder and fly off? He's no bag of feathers!*

* * * *

An ominous rumble.

The two sheriffs returned from the shadows, rolling with great difficulty an enormous wooden barrel which they brought to rest by the side of the wounded knight "An appropriate gallows," their chief ironically commented. "Is't full?"

"With malmsey. To the brim."

* * * *

Fillmore's eyes bulged from their sockets. He suddenly knew the hideous thing about to take place. *And there's nothing I can do to stop it! If I act like Errol Flynn, we're both dead...and the monster, Gloucester, goes unchecked!*

Josephine Tey notwithstanding, that Richard who stole Vincentio's throne was identical to Shakespeare's bloody king of that name. *And villains may change place in this world, but their methods stay the same...*

Thus, the cask of malmsey: prior to attaining the crown, Richard murdered, among others, his own brother, the Duke of Clarence, accomplishing the deed by hiring assassins who drowned Clarence in a butt of malmsey-wine.

"Grab the old man's heels!" the head sheriff raucously ordered. "Tip 'im up and pickle his suet-guts!"

The teacher watched in fascinated horror as one ruffian removed the barrel-lid and several others, puffing and heaving and straining, jack-knifed their victim into the waiting receptacle, head downward. Falstaff screamed once, then the sound was cut short; he kicked wildly, causing some of the liquid to spill over the top and stream down the sides. Hooting, laughing, swearing, cursing, jeering, the unholy crew dabbled handkerchiefs in the overflow and wrung them dry inside their mouths. One even licked the wood and caught a splinter in his tongue; the other sheriffs roared with merriment at his predicament. Meanwhile, just above their heads, the fat knight's thrashing dwindled and finally ceased.

The chief sheriff, borrowing a boot from one of his men and a boost from another, put back the lid and hammered it down, sealing Falstaff's body in the cask.

* * * *

Stifling a sob, Fillmore waited several minutes for the killers to leave, forlornly hoping he might somehow still revive Falstaff with mouth-to-mouth resuscitation. But the sheriffs showed no inclination to hurry off and realizing at length there was nothing else he could do, the professor finally allowed the umbrella to carry him away from there.

Salt tears stung his eyes, but in his breast there burned a desire for vengeance of such terrible intensity as might only be equaled in the heart of some embittered liberal of post-pubescent years.

[Exit FILLMORE, above.]

ACT IV.

SCENE.
ENGLAND; ITALY; AUSTRIA.

SCENE I.
LONDON. a street.

Enter BORIS *and* BAPTISTA.

Bor.

Thou wouldst not jest with me?

Bap.

O, no, 'tis true!
I trust thee so, I've told thee full my tale;
Then why distrust this wish I hold, most dear?

Bor.

My mind's as thine and yet I'm scored with scars.
Upon my soul; my psyche suffered them,
As I have told, when I was young—

Bap.

O, hush!
The past is dead, your pains are o'er; and though
That one who gave thee life didst spurn thee from
His company, must mind it not; no more.
Who's lost thine hand in loyal friendship's band
Is far the worse. Nepenthe, friend; O, balm
Of Gilead! Affection's everywhere,
And we who have the wit still seek it out,
And he who lacks't is damned to the unwept,
Unhonored and unsung; no minstrel-lay
Or any other kind inspireth he.
But Boris, friend o' heart, why dost still sigh?

Bor.

I think on Fillmore, fearing how he fares.

Bap.

[*Gently.*] Shall I be vex't? Must mope? Canst feel no joy?

Bor.

I cannot help but feel for him; some guilt:
I should be there and Fillmore here.

Bap.

The news,
I must admit, is ill, if tars tell true:
This Richard-villain's grown too strong.

Bor.

A word
I further rue, this news from Austria,
Tis ill. Best hurry home and tell the Duke.

Bap.

Yes, let's.

Bor.

I do not doubt 'twill make him puke.

[*Exeunt.*]

SCENE II
PADUA. A tavern.

FILLMORE discovered, drinking.

In a corner of the nearly-empty saloon, the professor squatted on a wooden bench somberly sipping sour *grappa*, a potion apologized for by his host, who said the best vintages were tribute to the new emperor. "He bleeds us dry," the bartender mourned.

Only a few patrons remained in the tavern. Each drank alone, eyes averted, lest an innocent glance offend some imperial spy.

The country's scared, Fillmore observed bitterly. *Richard's new laws are oppressive and arbitrary. The people groan.*

A morose quintet of musicians played melancholy madrigals. Some other time, the professor would have found their name (enscrolled upon the side of the percussionist's tabor) mildly amusing: Ye Fulle Fathom Fyve. But now nothing raised Fillmore's spirits.

One thing to read about tyranny, quite another to witness it firsthand.

Just then, the round little pubkeeper returned with a long, thin wrapped package. Setting it at the professor's feet, the man plumped down next to his customer on the bench and murmured in his ear.

Pub.

I've wrapped th'umbrella neat, as you did ask;
Can do ye no more handsome, but ne'er let
On that I knew this thing, I beg, or else
They'd close me up and cart me off, what's worse,
Unto the sheriff-camp, from which but few
Return and those nor whole nor hale.

Fil.

My thanks,
And never doubt my faithfulness. But have
You found a coach for me?

Pub.

I tried, good sir,
But just before I asked, a lass engaged
The lastly cabriolet available
Tonight. See her? She's over there.

Fil.

Uh-huh. The dark-haired gal in green, the one who sits like
there's a poker up her back?

Pub.

The same.

Fil.

I wonder who she is?

Pub.

A saintly lass,
A foreigner but lately come from Rome,
Although she's Viennese by birth.
Her name is Isabella and she hurries home.
Some tragedy, I'm told, impels her north
To 'seech the vile oppressor at's court.

Fil.

Y'don't say?
Isabella, hey?

Pub.

Tha'st heard of her?

Fil.

Uh-huh, I surely have.
[*Aside.*] The major female character that's in
Vincentio's play, *Measure for Measure*. Hm.
She has a brother, Claudio; I'll bet
My boots he's in a mess of trouble now.

The door of the pub crashed open. A powerfully-built youth with close-trimmed black mustache and beard staggered in.

"A portion o' your finest wine!" he roared, planting himself before the bar. "Don't make me ask again!"

"Oh, here's one I'd hoped would not trouble's again," Fillmore's host grumbled, rising and bustling to the bar. "Twilt be a short one," he warned the newcomer. "It's nearly closing-time."

"WHAT?" the young man shouted. "There's ample night yet for quaffing deep! The joint's not out of time!"

"Thou forgetst the curfew," said the barman, placing a half-measure of wine in a cup before the rowdy.

"Curfew," he growled. "I count myself a free man, to come and go as I like. Tell me not o' curfews."

"Shhh! Petruchio, hush! If they catch you out past eleven, they'll throw ye in sheriff-camp."

"O, damn the sheriffs," Petruchio raged, shaking a menacing fist. "Damn the curfew, damn all dams and *damn the emperor*!"

The publican's face went white. Of those five customers remaining, two immediately drank up and scuttled off, casting frightened glances at Petruchio as they departed. The band, too, quickly packed and left. "Lack-wit!" the host snapped. "Get out!"

"I han't done this rotgut!"

"Try me no further; two minutes, then *out*!"

Leaving the roisterer to curse in his wine-stoup, the bartender apologized to Isabella, then hurried to the professor and did the same.

"I pardon ask for this sottish blow-hard, sir. I pray he's signed none death-writ but his own with's bootless, imprudent subversions i' public. Yet word o't may draw down on us th'emperor's ghastly sheriff-gang. Best take up thy bundle and be off."

"Guess you're right," nodded Fillmore, grabbing the wrapped umbrella and getting to his feet "By the way, did you call him Petruchio?"

"Aye. A loathely lad, a braggart and a bully. Who blames his wife (though Kate, she was counted a shrew until she met her match in him), who blames her that she quits her husband's estate i' the dead o' night, runs off and leaves 'im to his brutish ways alone?"

"She skipped, huh? Good for her!"

"CHURL! REMOVE THY HANDS! LET GO!"

* * * *

Fillmore and the publican spun around and saw Isabella struggling in Petruchio's arms.

"Release me! No gentleman art thou!"

"Nor lady, thou," he laughed, planting a sloppy kiss on her lips. "Faugh!" she grimaced. "Thou'st vile breath!"

"O, monstrous!" the barman chided. "Petruchio, desist! She's done naught t'offend thee!"

"Nay, but she hath: she jigs, ambles, lisps, promiseth much, delivereth little, like all her dissembling sex. Be she a wench, she o'erpainteth her blotches, stuffing sweetmeats in her face. Winning what she'd have, contains herself all else, unless she play the shrew and have's lick her placket-hem!"

All the while he raged, he clutched the squirming woman close, assaulting her maidenly parts with gross license. At last, Isabella wrenched one hand free and raked her long nails down her assailant's face. Howling, he stuck her fingers in his mouth and bit hard. She shrieked.

"Abominable man, have done this disgraceful pother!" the barman bawled, tearing at Petruchio's arms. The youth merely smiled and shoved the older, weaker man away.

"Bewitching bitch," swore the misogynist, "unloose thyself; I'll have thee here and now." He ripped at her bodice.

"Horrible, O horrible!" she sobbed. "Wilt none deliver me from this insufferable beast?"

"How's this?" the professor asked, swinging the umbrella two-handed as hard as he could against the attacker's skull.

With a curious sigh, Petruchio let go of Isabella and folded up into a pile on the floor.

Isa.

I stand within thy debt.

Fil.

Then will you do
Me a big favor?

Isa.

And if it be within
The scope a maid may freely grant, freely
Is it ceded thee.

Fil.

I'd like a ride
To Vienna.

Isa.

Yes, that's good; thou hast it now,
And I'll the better feel to have thee handy
On the long and lonely road; there's talk about
These parts o' highwaymen and brigandry.

Oh, swell, thought Fillmore. *I look for a mate, but all I find is trouble.*
He glanced curiously at Isabella, but put the thought aside. *Too priggish.*
"The carriage comes. Bestir!" said the publican.
As they started toward the door, the professor heard Petruchio groan.
He turned and saw the young man on his knees, clutching his head and
scowling at him.
"Well, anyway, I'm glad I didn't hit him too hard."
"Hmph," Isabella sniffed disdainfully. "I'm sorry thou didst not."

[*Exeunt.*]

SCENE III.—OUTSIDE PADUA. A road.

Enter three Brigands, *bearing darkened lanterns.*

1 Brig.

But who did bid thee join with us?

3 Brig.

Big Boss.

2 Brig.

He needs not our mistrust; since he delivers
Our offices and what we have to do,
To the direction just

1 Brig.

Then stand with us.
The night yet glimmers with some beams of moon:
And anyone who trav'leth now's a goon.
Now spurs these lated passengers apace,
To gain far-off Vien; and near approaches
The subject of our watch.

3 Brig.

Hark! I hear horses.

Fil.

[*Far-off.*] Go faster, dammit!

2 Brig.

Then 'tis they: the last
O' cabs this night to pace this darksome road.
All ready?

1 Brig.

Aye. How far's these horses, say?

3 Brig.

Almost a mile; but he does usually,
From there to here, eat up that space in half
A trice.

2 Brig.

A light, a light!

1 Brig.

Tis time! Stand to't

Enter coach with FILLMORE, ISABELLA, Driver.

Driv.

Whoa there, whoa!

Fil.

What's up?

The coach halteth and the Driver *gets down.*

Driv.

Alight, alight!

2 Brig.

[*Aside.*] That's what I said.

Fil.

Hey, what's the big idea?

The Driver *withdraweth a sword and pointeth it at his passengers, motioning them to dismount. The three* Brigands *open lanterns, illuminating road.*

Driv.

Get down, I said.

Isa.

O, treachery!

Fil.

Aww, hell!

1 Brig.

A good night's work. Let's take 'em to the Boss.

Driv.

[*Nods.*] And whilst you tell how much is done, the loot I'll bring: it's in the boot.

3 Brig.

Hands up! I'll shoot!

The third Brigand *hath withdrawn an handsome pair of pistols and aimeth at the* Driver *and other* Brigands.

2 Brig.

Art daft? The Boss will be displeased.

3 Brig.

I serve
No Boss of thine, thou scurvy swine; a Boss
Who's bigger's mine.

2 Brig.

[*Sarcastically.*] "He needs not our mistrust."
O ass! O boob! O cream-faced lout! Thou dolt!

1 Brig.

[*Shrugging.*] Go know. So hit me with a thunderbolt!

The third Brigand *driveth off the horses, then addresseth* FILLMORE *and* ISABELLA.

3 Brig.

Both follow me. Collect thy gear.

Fil.

[*Groans.*] What now?

Isa.

I cannot brook delays, my brother lies
In mortal fear. I'm wroth! And thou?

Fil.

And how!

[Exeunt FILLMORE, ISABELLA, third Brigand.]

SCENE IV.
OUTSIDE PADUA. A cabin in the forest.

The third Brigand leadeth in FILLMORE, ISABELLA.

The robber set his lantern on the rough-hewn table which, except for a handful of chairs and one enormous tree-stump covered with a quantity of blankets, comprised the sole furniture in the chilly room.

"Wait here," he said, then left them all alone. They waited in worried silence for a short time, then the brigand reentered, holding the door wide.

"Here's the Big Boss," the grinning highwayman announced. "He's been expecting you."

Stepping aside, he made way for the entry of a large man. A very large man. He was so immense that he had to squeeze through the entranceway with much huffing and expenditure of effort Isabella, who'd never seen anyone so staggeringly gross waddling about on two legs, stared speechlessly, mouth agape.

The professor's jaw dropped even further. "Good Gad!" he exclaimed exultantly. "It can't be!"

"O Jim, sweet Jim, this is, indeed, the happiest o' hours!" boomed Sir John Falstaff, clasping his friend within his fleshy arms and hugging the breath out of him.

* * * *

The brigand, Peto, served cold supper and wine to the professor and his distaff companion. The fat knight sat upon the upholstered stump (the only perch available that was wide enough for his ponderous butt) and swigged seas of sack.

Fal.

And so you see, dear James, the only place
I thought to come was Padua, in hopes
I'd find thee here. By chance, I chanced upon
My sometime pal, this Peto and the times,
Consid'ring what they are, suggested we
Make shift to swell our purses how we may.

Fil.

[*Nods.*] Meaning: highway robbery.

Fal.

O, call
It rather mimic reenacting of
An hallowed English way of life; and I
Am Robin and this Richard knave's both John
And Nottingham.

Fil.

Hmph. Well, go on.

Fal.

Instructions I did give; I said to him,
"Good Peto, keep a watchful eye and ear
For any stranger who doth bear a thing
Most like a bumbershoot and yet not quite..."

Peto.

Ay; and I'm not alone, I found, in search
For thee, Sire Fillmore, for the men—

Fil.

[*Impatiently.*] I know,
I'm down on Dicky Three's Most Wanted list.
But, Sir John, you still haven't told—

Fal.

How Peto found you out?

Peto.

I lay conceal'd beside the tavern-door
And saw you there converse and brawl. The dame
Beside thee here invited thee inside
Her coach. I knew the modus operandi
O' that driver and's fellow-thieves and took
Advantage o' their ignorance.

Fil.

[*Impatiently.*] All well
And good, Sir John, but damn it, man, I saw
You drown!

Fal.

[Guffaws.] In malmsey-wine? M'lad, 'twas naught:
I simply slurped it up.

Fil.

A BARREL-full?

Peto.

Why, once he drank so deep that, for a lark,
'a piddle-gushed a pond t' grace a park!

Fal.

Tosh, bawd! Curb thy tongue's too lib'ral bent!
How dar'st this tale before this dame and gent?

Fil.

Oh, never mind, but tell the rest: how did
You get away?

Fal.

With mighty mournful moans,
With ghastly graveyard groans, I quit the cask;
The craven constables did choke and spew;
They thought me dead, that superstitious crew,
And ev'ry man o' them took to's heels!

Fil.

I hope they died of fright, those damned *shlemiels*!

Peto cleared away the supper dishes. Isabella rose, curtsied formally to the still-seated knight and addressed him thus: "I thank thee, sire, for delivering us from the clutches of the brigands, but now I must beg thee t'escort us safely to the coach and round up the team your man scattered. I am broached upon a dire business and every second I delay may mean my brother's death."

"Why, what's the matter, lass?"

"This monstrous tyrant, Richard, passed a law that states that all who flirteth, leer, or wink (Unless connubially linked), shall forthwith be beheaded."

"Monstrous!"

"The report's come to me that my brother was ta'en in amorous embrace with's fiancée. And now he languishes in jail and soon shall die unless I find a way to plead for's life!"

Falstaff smashed one great ham-sized fist upon the table. "Shall this be borne? Since when's romance a crime?"

"Well, Sir John," Fillmore interposed, "if the deputy had been Angelo, the law would have been more strictly confined to the procreative act itself, but now Richard Gloucester's king and he, you must know, fears he has nothing to attract a woman unless he play upon her gullible nature and manipulate. Such a frustrated man might well seek to make all lovers suffer for his pangs."

Isabella sighed. "And must this extend to my poor brother Claudio who fully meant to wed? What can be done? I freely own I'm proud, but if I must bend my knee to move this king to look more kindly on this purely technical infraction, then must I do't!"

Fillmore said nothing. In *Measure for Measure*, he recalled quite well, Isabella did indeed beg for her brother's life. Up till then, the deputy, Angelo, was an honest official—*though a merciless cold fish*—but meeting the chaste Isabella corrupted him; conceiving a passion for her, he tried to trade Claudio's life for her virtue, but she would not accede to the proposal. *I remember now why she's an unsympathetic character to most of the kids I taught the play to. They always think she's a lousy sister.* A passing reference to a line in Hochhuth concerning women's honor occurred to the professor, but he put it aside, the vague firstlings of a scheme to overthrow Richard having occurred to him from thinking about Shakespeare's Angelo-Isabella plot.

* * * *

Just then, a heavy knock sounded at the door. Peto, startled, took out his knife, but Falstaff waved away the weapon.

Addressing the professor, the knight said, "There's one without who may help us. He comes most carefully upon's hour. Peto, let him in."

Gapping the portal, the brigand admitted a corpulent graybeard. Richly, though soberly dressed, he wore a black skullcap on his balding pate and a lettered prayer-shawl about his broad shoulders. His heavy-lidded eyes took in everything in the room with a keen appraising glance.

Despite his girth, Falstaff rose and shook his guest's hand, though the engineering feat cost him much energy. Plopping down again, he waggled a finger at Peto and the highwayman poured some wine into a goblet and set it before the old man. A health was drunk, then Falstaff introduced Isabella and Fillmore.

Fil.

Excuse me, did he say your name's Tubal?

Tub.

[*Gravely inclines his head.*]

Fil.

Are you, by chance, Venetian?

Tub.

I am.

Fil.

What do you do?

Tub.

A moneylender, I.

Fil.

That's what I thought. You have a friend, Shylock?

TUBAL *pusheth out his thick lips in expression of pity and scorn.*

Tub.

Well, I knew Shylock many years and am
The poorer now by full a thousand ducats.

Fil.

The which he loaned a merchant of your town?
Antonio?

Tub.

Pfui! That swine! Indeed,
He writ a deed with Shylock for a sum,
A goodly part o' which derived from me.
The bigot forfeited, it came to court;
A case well-known and dire it did turn out;
How Shylock suffereth; and yet I'd said,
"Get thee t'attomey, ere thou craftst this deed."
O, if he'd but heed, but nay! so stubborn, he;
Had it been me, the phrase had run this way:
"*Approximate: one pound o' flesh and blood.*"
But Shylock would not hark. [Shrugs.] Go, give advice!

Isa.

Forgive me, must be brisk: Sir John hath said
That you may aid us in our common goal.

Tub.

He did? And who are you, lady?

Fal.

O, friend
Tubal, thou needst not peer suspiciously.
We're all friends here, united in a hope
I told thee of. Rememb'rest not?

Tub.

May be.
Forgive me, knight, that I maintain a while
A certain circumspection. We Jews
Are not accorded status in this land,
Cannot obtain our cit'zenship, cannot
Own land, so we are forced, to live, to loan
Our wealth, the which I have full-store. It needs
But small excuse t'entrap one o' my means
And leach my cash t' th'envious State.

Fil.

Okay.
I know just where you're coming from. I'll say
It first. We all would like to overthrow
This deputy that stole the throne. Sir John

And I are leagued to help restore to power
The rightful Duke. This lady's kin's in jail,
Condemned to death by Richard's rotten laws.

Tub.

Well, then: I have, perhaps, more pressing cause
Than all of thee. The tyrant's men each day
Doth grow in bold and bloody deed; and to
My clan's the danger's worst. Now what's to do?
If thou'st a plan, unhatch it here; my friends
And I shall back it to the full.

Fil.

All right.
I've got a way to work this thing, if we
Can iron all the difficulties out.

Falstaff agreed immediately, even adding a suggestion from his own past experience. Tubal, too, concurred, pledging money and means.

"Well?" Fillmore prompted, looking at Isabella. "It's up to you."

She considered it a long time before making up her mind. "Some doubts I hold concerning the propriety of the role thou'd have me enact," she said primly, "yet to rescue Claudio, I *think* I might act with greater scope than custom might otherwise dictate."

"Believe me, no shame's attached," the professor said. "Now the first time you see Richard, don't be too obvious, he's no dope. The second time, wear a low-cut dress. That's not overstepping modesty too much, is it?"

"I look quite nice in red," Isabella replied.

* * * *

It took two hours to find transportation; the robbers's carriage was gone. But Tubal pulled a few strings and secured a comfortable conveyance. Just before they left, the old man gave Fillmore many instructions for safe travel and provided him with a long list of names, together with their respective prices.

[Exeunt.]

SCENE V.
VIENNA. A room in a private house.

Enter FILLMORE and FALSTAFF.

Fal.

Art worried, lad?

Fil.

Damn right I am. What if—?

Enter LABAN, *cousin of* TUBAL.

Lab.

She's back! She's met the King!

Fil.

She's safe?

Enter ISABELLA *with flushed face.*

Isa.

O, yes,
I'm safe and could not safer be. Is't hot
In here? I feel so flushed!

Fil.

What's up? What did
He say? Is he allured? And will you meet
Again?

Isa.

We will, tomorrow morn. He let
Me see my brother's safe, though Claudio
Didst see me not [*Sighs.*]
A most unusual king,
Not what I thought he'd be.

Fal.

Indeed? You mean
He's e'en more warped than rumour paints?

Isa.

O, fie!
Should Christian knight berail a fellow man's
Infirmities? Have charity, Sir John!

Fal.

O, grant me grace to draw a breath!

Fil.

Oh, cut
It out, you two! Now, Isabella, tell
Me what you think: is Dickie handing you
Red tape, or is he really interested?

Isa.

This much I'll tell: tomorrow morn I meet
With him, not in the Hall of State, but in
Less formal rooms within the Palace.

Fal.

Haw!
Ye've hooked the fish! Now needs must reel him in!

Not deigning to reply, Isabella swept haughtily from the room, glancing coldly at the fat man as she went. "I don't like this," said the professor. He forgot how persuasive Dicky Three can be with women. He seduced his wife, Anne, literally over the dead body of her father-in-law and king, whom Richard killed."

"What art babbling?" Falstaff complained. "I beseech thee, temper thy tendency to wax fey. Plainer, sirrah!"

"Okay, here it is in a nutshell: we can't trust Isabella, Richard's playing on her."

"Impossible! That rigid ramrod in a skirt?"

"Sir John, trust me, Isabella's pride's what makes her vulnerable to Gloucester. I can just imagine how he'd work on her, molding her like putty while she thinks *she's* got the upper hand." The professor turned to Laban, still waiting in the doorway. "Is there some way to sneak me into the Palace tomorrow?"

The pale-faced youth pushed aside his skullcap and scratched his head. "Hmmm...hast ever cleaned an arras?"

"No," said the professor, "there's not much call for that sort of thing where I come from. But now's the time to learn..."

[*Exeunt* Fillmore *and* Laban.]

SCENE VI.
VIENNA. An Apartment in the Duke's Palace.

Enter FILLMORE in laborer's dress.

Fil.

It's almost time for her to meet with him.
I'd better hide.

> [FILLMORE goes behind the arras.]

Ah-CHOO! You'd think they'd dust
Some time! I hope that I don't sneeze again.
Ah-CHOO! Oh, damn! I hear him coming now.
Ah-mmmf! I'd better hold my nose...

Enter RICHARD *the usurper, soliloquizing.*

Rich.

Ere dawn doth creep astern night's murky cape,
This rebel's blood shall stain the steely blade;
And at his fall, a sister's name shall join
That dust to which the sibling's gore shall run.

Fil.

[*Aside.*] I knew we couldn't trust this louse! Ah-mmf!

Rich.

Plans have I laid, that from my falsest art
She cannot choose but fall; but soft, she's here:
Sink, thou slimèd light, below the scope of sight!

Enter ISABELLA.

Isa.

Dread lord, with fear I greet thy sober self,
To know thy mind: if thou wilt countenance
Recourse of form, of show, of stern decree?
If it be meet to search thine fearsome brow
For aught of mercy, then I scan it now.

Rich.

Nay, do not give thy graceful self the lie

With base affect of suppleness of spine,
To see an thou can shame my granite heart
To spewing forth some half-regretted "yea."
Such grov'ling whines are not thy powered art:
For I will split the gore of twice a score
O' brothers, ere I'll brook thy hollow prayers.
Thou wast not born to kneel to man, fair maid:
Thou shouldst command, proud Isabel!

Fil.

[*Aside.*] Wormwood!

Rich.

Thy head erect, thine eye ablaze doth suit
Thee best; and when thy tongue proclaims thy will,
That brooks not opposition, then sure
As death doth follow life, all else must check;
Nor writ, nor law, nor silver sceptre's swing,
Nor thoughts or words or deeds or any cloak
Of action shall dare to stir a breath
To say thee aught except that which thyself
Thine sov'reign statute stands.

Isa.

Thou flatt'rest well;
But dost thou mean that I, unfettered, free,
May freely strike the fetters from my kin?

Rich.

I mean there is a way.

Isa.

A way, I trust,
A maiden chaste may chastely tread.

Rich.

O, no.

Isa.

Why, what a wanton thing thou mak'st of me!

Rich.

Yet they who love dare much.

Isa.

I dare do all
That may become a maid; who dares do more
Is none.

Rich.

Proud Isabel—

Isa.

I'll hear no more,
Unless it be to free my Claudio;
And if—

Rich.

Nay, hear my suit!

Isa.

And if a chance
There still may be to make thee change thy mind,
Then neither shifting sand, nor rank, nor place,
Nor precedence, nor conduct o' the times
Allow me e'en a wayward word to waste!

Rich.

O Isabel, yet hear me, sweetest soul!

GLOSTER *kneeleth.*

Isa.

E'en so? Say on.

Fil.

[*Aside.*] Oh, hell! The same old trick
He used on Lady Anne in "Richard Third"
Is having like effect on Isabel...

Rich.

Then know, proud dame, that it is yet my fate
To stand and brace the sliding structure of

The law 'gainst blows and flames of fire and worms
That work within; and I must do't e'en to
This sternly crush o' good gone once astray,
Deflowering of innocence deflowered;
But see, O see what now hath hap't: there steals
Into mine all-too-mortal heart a smile
That sits in fleshly ice upon thy lips.
O, such a cross-grained join o' law and love
Can ne'er unite to form a peaceful soul.
Then tell me, maid, if aught of remedy
Thy nimbler wit espies, that lying thus
Within my grasp, I may apply.

Isa.

[*Smugly smiling.*] O, free
My brother Claudio, my most dread lord,
And, by this hand, I'll love thee well.

Rich.

The law
In mighty majesty proclaims: "This man,
This Claudio, must die"; and yet my most,
My very secret self doth say, in whisper'd
Colloquy: "O, show a front o' mildness,
On him bestow the tender touch o' life,
But not so much for thine own soul's content;
Let this proceed, despite decree, for his
Sweet sister's self." And thus thou seest me now:
A man to double bus'ness bound; I stand
In pause where I shall first begin and both
Neglect. What if I choose to fell the axe
That like the hurricane shouldst sweep, swoopstake,
Thy brother's head, his very life away?
But then the fear of thine concentrate
And time-enduring hate must give me pause.
Tis well, he gains his years. And yet, now see
What now proceeds: that tiger, Duty, shall
Bare his reeking teeth and if the breach
The light o' day e'er view, O still
The bitter gall o' conscience set awry
Shouldst raven me with rank and rav'nous claws!

Isa.

What tongue, what voice, may sway thee for his life?
If thou dost care for me, as now thou spak'st,
Then shall my tongue, my voice command him free!

Rich.

I fear thee, dame, I fear that this demand,
Giant-like in thy affections,
Shall spur thee on to use thy powers, charms,
Thy wits and arts, to wheedle me, to force
Mine all-too-spineless resolution
To cast away my sober caution;
Thus, profiting from my weakness, thus to damn me
To commit that which cool reflection shuns,
Only, upon gaining thy keen desire, to laugh
And toss aside and scorn my panting love.

Fil.

[*Aside.*] Oh, bull! She can't be buying this, can she?

Isa.

Try me, sweet lord, but grant this boon, I pray,
And all thy ardent hopes shall come to pass.

Rich.

I tremble, I sway, I fear I'll be undone.

Fil.

[*Aside.*] A ham, a ham, a very palpable ham.

Isa.

If thou profess to love so well, then list:
Thou'lt promise not what you are loath to give;
Deliver Claudio to safety's shore,
Then live; our love, my love, forevermore.

Rich.

Beloved star! thou soar sublimest songs
Unto mine ear, they grace the fragile shell.
But mark you well, some risk attends unto
This breach of mine own solemn law, to which
We needs must both together brave the lets

That I've imposed; to pardon Claudio
Undoes the many goods my law hath wrought
O'er vice in this fair land. Then needs we seek
To hide thy kin, as if he 'scaped from bars,
From bolts, from shackles, chains and cells and locks.

Isa.

I'm yours t'instruct.

Rich.

Then meet me, dame, tonight,
Beyond the prison walls, where, presently,
At thine abode, my man shall lead thee thence
To me.

Isa.

And whither shall we go from there?

Rich.

I have a private home where, safe from spies,
Our plans we'll shrewdly lay.

Fil.

[*Aside.*] I'll bet!

Isa.

I'll go.
Then, till thy messenger, by mercy sent,
Shall teach me where to roam, farewell, sweet gent

[*Exit* ISABELLA.]

Fil.

[*Aside.*] Whew! I wonder who has got the best
Of whom? I'll bet that each must think the other
Lost that round.

RICHARD *laughs nastily to himself.*

See? That's what I thought

Rich.

[*Solus.*] Thus well my crafty ruse doth go. Ere dawn

Shall peek its golden round above the rim,
This wench I'll rudely force unto my will;
Her brother soon soars high or plunges deep,
And sure, her lily lips shall greet his shade.
To glut my soul with foulest lies I choose,
That she, to conquer, stoops and yet shall lose.

[*Exit* RICHARD.]

Fil.

Ah-CHOO! Oh, boy, we're in a pretty pickle!
    Move fast! or Claudio's life's not worth a nickel!

[Exit FILLMORE, running.]

SCENE VII.—VIENNA. A room in a private house.

Enter FILLMORE, ISABELLA, FALSTAFF.

Isa.

I tell thee, churl, I've got that crookback'd king
Enwrapt about my thumb! He'll do my bid!

Fil.

Like hell he will! If we don't act right now,
Your brother's dead and you can say goodbye—

Fal.

Unto thy maidenhead!

Isa.

O, bawd! O, fat
And foul-mouthed bawd!

Fil.

Oh, well, he's right. Now, look,
This thing has got beyond you, Isabel.
You're staying home. Sir John—

Isa.

I take command
From none else but the dictates of my heart!

How dar'st thou think that I'm not in control?
And wast thou there?

Fil.

You're goddam right I was.
Behind the arras.

Isa.

O! And heareth all?

Fil.

You bet I did.

Isa.

O, lowly-crawling knave!
O, shame!

Fal.

O, peace!

Fil.

Oh, crap. We're wasting time.

[*A rapping within.*]

Fal.

Hark! Who's there?

Laban. [*Outside the door.*]

It's me. The king has sent
His messenger. He waits for Isabel.

Isa.

I come!

Fil.

Oh, no you don't! Let's grab her, Jack!
Sorry, kid, we have no choice.

Isa.

LET GO!

FILLMORE and FALSTAFF struggle with ISABELLA, eventually subduing her. FILLMORE gags her, ties her arms and signals FALSTAFF who hauls her, still kicking, into her bedroom.

Fil.

[*Calling to* FALSTAFF.] Grab some of her clothes.

Fal.

[*Off.*] OOF! I'd best secure her feet, she kicks fierce.
What said'st thou, lad?

Fil.

I said, take some clothes from her!

Fal.

There's time
For that?

Fil.

No! I mean some things that she's
Not wearing now.

FALSTAFF *reenters with an assortment of* ISABELLA'S *garments.*

Fal.

What next?

Fil.

A change of plans.
We have to separate. Now listen well:
There's not much time. Here's what I have to tell...

[*They whisper together.*]

SCENE VIII.—VIENNA. A room in the prison.

CLAUDIO *discovered.*

When the rusty lock rasped, the condemned man turned to see who turned the key. He prayed the time of his execution had not arrived. The first thing that entered the room was an enormous laundry-cart.

"O, I see it's only you, Solomon. What make ye here? I'll little usage have o'clean linen if the rumor's true that I'm to die this day."

A strange voice answered him. "Solomon is feeling poorly tonight.

I'm his cousin, Laban, taking his place."

The speaker pushed the cart further into the cell and appeared to Claudio. The youth's eyes popped. He'd never seen anyone so fat as the clothes-washer, Laban.

"Funny," said Claudio, "you don't look Jewish..."

"*Shh*," the other whispered, "I'm not. There's little time! A friend am I o' thy sister."

"Isabella! Where is she? Here in Vienna?"

"Aye. But rather tied up at present. Hark: we must work fast to save thee. Hop in th' laundry cart and pull th' linens o'er thy head." Falstaff chuckled. "A trick I learned once in Windsor."

Claudio did as he was told. Falstaff pulled the cart back through the cell-door, locked it and did his best to make haste slowly, lest his anxiety to scoot attract the suspicion of the prison guards.

[*Exeunt.*]

SCENE IX.
VIENNA. The Bedroom of RICHARD'S private home.

Enter RICHARD.

When the messenger stepped in and told him the maiden had arrived and was bestowed in the sleeping-chamber, Richard permitted himself a tight grin. He sent his man away and spent ten minutes soliloquizing before scuttling upstairs.

"I'll play this game a trifle longer still," he muttered, tapping on the closed door.

"O, is't you, my lord? I'm here within," the high voice giggled.

"How strange she sounds," he said, pushing the portal wide. "She must feel nervous, shy."

The room was dark, save for the pale moonbeams streaming through the wide french windows. He barely was able to make out her dim form seated on the edge of the bed. Richard began to light a taper, but a forestalling hand fell upon his wrist "I'm bashful, Dick. Let's keep it dark."

The king plumped onto the bed, scowling. "I see. Thou canst not bear to see this beastly shape I bear."

"Not it at all," the other whispered, falsetto.

"You sure sound diff'rent."

"I caught a cold."

"Well, let's to work." Richard tried to put one arm about his companion, but "she" slid away, wily-shy.

"Not yet" the high voice piped. "Come see the view!"

"Games she plays?" the king grumbled, watching her silhouette as she stood in pale blue relief, framed in the windows. "I thought her taller!"

"O, come, admire the night!"

"O, hell!" Richard got up and stumped over to her side. "I hope this . won't take long."

"Not long at all. Wouldst do me a favor, pray?"

"What?"

"Nay, thou'lt be angry..."

"I'll be angry, wench, if thou dost not say. *Swiftly*!"

She tittered nervously. "Wouldst turn and let me rub thy hump for luck?"

Richard counted ten, considered ripping off her dress and having her without further preamble, decided he'd rather have her cooperate, at least at first. "O, go ahead," he snapped, turning his back to her.

"Thanks, Dick!" a deeper voice sounded at his shoulder. An arm circled his neck and tightened. The other held the point of a knife an inch or two away from his left eye. "*One move, one word and you're dead*!"

Richard did not flinch, nor move a muscle.

The arm about his throat lowered as far as his waist and clutched him tight about his middle.

"*Bend, damn you, bend*!"

Richard leaned forward; the arm about his midriff lifted him up. And up—*and up*.

"Zounds!" he gasped. "How tall *art* thou?"

But his captor made no reply. Gloucester gaped as he watched the floor move still further away, followed by the retreating window-frame, succeeded by the receding balcony.

"O, STOP!" the king screamed, but to no avail. As he ascended into the night-sky, he saw the ground gleaming dimly far below. And then he fainted.

"That's better," the professor remarked. "It's harder to fly while you're struggling."

[Exeunt FILLMORE & RICHARD, above.]

SCENE X.—Vienna. A street before the palace.

Enter FILLMORE, FALSTAFF, ISABELLA, CLAUDIO, LABAN; also Citizens & Soldiers.

Lab.

The villain's safely stashed away, ne'er fear;
And safe he's hid until the Duke returns.

Fil.

That's good. Vincentio but waits our word,
And he'll return. Until that time, I vouch
For Claudio. Will you be ruled by him?

All.

We will!

Clau.

[*To Soldiers*.] Then call those cut-throat sheriffs home;
I'll deal with them in manner kinder than
Those swine deserve. Then I'll return all lands
They stole to Rome. But thou, Fillmore and thou,
Good knight, wouldst care to serve my steward-court?

Fil.

No, thanks.

Fal.

The Duke awaits.

Fil.

Let's cut this short.

[Exeunt FILLMORE & FALSTAFF.]

* * * *

The professor and the knight returned to Venice. By what appeared to be a remarkable stroke of luck, they found a ship ready to sail to England, nonstop. The Captain was unavailable, so they arranged passage through the First Mate and soon were under way.

They suffered a slight delay when the *Pembroke* made an unscheduled detour north around the boot and into the Ligurian Sea. Fillmore thought it odd that they put into Genoa at midnight and only stayed an hour, but at least since then, the ship made good time.

"We've passed the Straits," the professor said one afternoon, lounging in a deck-chair, feet resting on the starboard rail. "I figure any time now we'll tack about to northward and head along the Portuguese coast."

"Mff," Sir John Falstaff nodded, mouth full of hardtack. He squatted comfortably on deck, stuffing himself and washing down the dry crackerfood with draughts from his omnipresent wineskin.

"Y'know," said Fillmore, "it's odd, but ever since we stopped at Genoa, I've been hearing funny noises below deck."

"Such as?"

"Subdued sobbing, soon hushed. Like a whimpering child."

"I doubt not 'tis but an animal or bird."

"Maybe," he said dubiously, "but another strange thing, Sir John: how come we've never met the Captain? He keeps to his cabin."

"O, he may be shy."

"Hmph. If I was in another world, I'd guess we were on a ship of Ahab's."

"A-*who*?"

"Never mind."

"Well," said the knight, munching and sipping, "whate'er be his reasons, he's welcome to'm. But what of thee, lad? Hast plans? Seek ye still a mate?"

"Still?" Fillmore repeated with irony. "I never even began. But to tell the truth, I've lost heart for that quest. Maybe I've grown some. The more I think about my amatory adventures, the more convinced I've become that attempting to corner an ideal is sheer illusion. They always seem to turn out smaller than expected. And even if I could find 'das ewig-weibliche,' what hubris has led me to think that I, being flawed, have any right to aspire toward perfection?"

"Ah, well," Falstaff shrugged, "Venus wed Vulcan. But then what *will* you do, friend Fillmore? Quit this world?"

"Not quite yet."

"O, dost'a fear that thing you spake to me about t'other day?"

"'Subsumption'? No; I've given it some thought and I believe I may have been conceiving things falsely. A man I know once tried to tell me subsumption is a myth, that the umbrella obeys my subconscious desires, that's all. Still, I keep getting this weird feeling, which makes me think I may be stuck in some particular planetary milieu."

"Weird feeling? Canst describe't?"

"Like I was fixed, condensed, notated on a two-dimensional plane... as if some artist on my native world was dreaming about me and fashioning a fiction from my experiences."

"That's not occurred to thee here, though."

"Oh, yes, it has, off and on. But for the first time, I realized there may well be an alternative reason why it sometimes appears as if I've become permanently immured in a world, why the umbrella refuses to open up and fly me through the cosmic planes."

"Aye?"

"Perhaps the umbrella only works for dimensional flight when I know, subconsciously, that the sequence is totally resolved—and in a manner appropriate to the derived literature with which I'm familiar."

"Hmmm." Falstaff wiped crumbs of hardtack from his lips and the fringes of his white beard. "If this be true," he meditated, "then thinkst thou it but remains for you to bring the good news to the Duke, collect Boris and resolution shall've been achieved?"

Uh-oh. Fillmore's face paled. *Too anticlimactic for Shakespeare.* He screwed up his face in fierce concentration and held up one finger at a time.

"What *art* thou doing, James?"

"Trying to see if my exploits here follow the developing-and-falling shape of an Elizabethan drama. I usually think of Shakespeare's plays in five acts, though that was a later scholarly imposition. Still...exposition, complication, crisis, resolution, let's see: Scotland's certainly Act I; London, II; Italy must've been III; Austria—*oh, damn!*"

"Dost not work out?" Falstaff asked.

"Worse than that," said the professor, jumping to his feet "Take a look out there. What do you see?"

The knight squinted over the rail and saw, quite some distance to starboard and behind the stem of the ship, a huge curvature of beach and greenery that formed the eastern extremity of the European mainland.

"Why, James, is't not Portugal?"

"You're damn right it is. Why aren't we steering north and following its coastline? We're still headed west, straight into the Atlantic."

"What ill portendeth?"

"I don't know, Jack, but I'm about to find out." The professor rose and stripped the brown paper from his umbrella. "We'd better be ready for a fast getaway."

Falstaff trembled. "O, no! Not that!"

"Might be necessary. Come along," Fillmore commanded, stumping towards the hatchway, "let's find out what the hell's going on!"

* * * *

Falstaff waited on the last rung of the companionway and watched the professor pound on the closed door of the Captain's cabin.

"*Yo,* open up! What's happening here?"

With a click, the door swung wide. On the threshold stood a powerfully-built youth with a close-trimmed black mustache and beard. He grinned malevolently at the gaping professor.

"Holy cripes!" Fillmore exclaimed. "*You're* the captain?"

"Aye," said Petruchio. "And now you and I hath a score t'even up..."
He swung a fist at Fillmore, who ducked.

"Back on deck, Jack!" the professor yelled over his shoulder. "*Fast!*"

Petruchio lunged; Fillmore swiftly interposed the umbrella and
shoved hard, knocking the other off-balance. Before he could regain his
footing, the sailor sustained another blow on the head from the same
instrument that felled him in Padua. Again he collapsed.

Fillmore spun around and dashed up the ladder, shoving the laboring
Falstaff ahead of him. Bursting onto the deck, they ran sternward, where
there was more room to take off from.

"Where d'ye think he was going t' take us?" Falstaff panted.

"My guess would be Bermuda," the professor replied, lofting the
umbrella. "Okay, Sir John, hold tight! We're going to fly straight to England."

The knight moaned, but though thoroughly miserable, he bravely put
both hands around the umbrella-handle.

"To London!" Fillmore yelled, thumbing the catch. "Boar's Head
Tavern, Eastcheap!"

The hood opened. The umbrella began to rise, straining to lift both
at once.

Neither saw the seaman who stole up behind Fillmore with a belay-
ing-pin in his hand. With a powerful leap, he cracked the hardwood instrument against the professor's skull. Uttering a muffled groan, Fillmore
fell heavily to the deck.

Relieved of some of its burden, the umbrella ascended a few feet
higher and floated beyond the ship's rail and out to sea. Falstaff stared in
horror at the receding vessel, where his companion still was.

"O, how to control this demon device?" the knight wailed to no avail.

The seaman who felled the professor shouted down the companionway, "O, Captain, my Captain, the prisoners hath tried t'escape."

Petruchio, clutching his forehead, emerged from below, squinting to
make his eyes come back in focus.

"O Captain, my Captain," the sailor mourned, "Fatguts hath 'scaped!"

"No matter, Bosun, thou'st done a good piece 0' work," Petruchio reassured him, slapping the crewman appreciatively on the shoulder. "The
tub o' lard may drown, for all I care. You saved us th'important one."

Fillmore sat up groggily. The skipper stamped over to him, glowering. He growled, "As for you, count thyself lucky, swine, for if twere not
for my commission to deliver thee intact to those more powerful than
me, I swear tha'd be dead this instant."

* * * *

ACT V.

SCENE.—The Sea, with a Ship: afterwards an uninhabited Island.

SCENE I.
on a Ship at Sea.—A Storm with Thunder and Lightning.

Enter PETRUCHIO *and a* Boatswain.

Pet.

Boatswain,—

Boats.

O Captain! my Captain! our fearful trip is done.
This ship can't weather evry rack—

Pet.

Pace, pace: thou dost assist the storm!
Speak to the mariners: fall to't yarely, or we run ourselves aground; bestir, bestir!

[*Exit* PETRUCHIO.]

Enter Mariners.

Boats.

Heigh, my hearts; cheerly, cheerly, my hearts; yare, yare: take in the top-sail; 'Tend to the master's whistle.—Blow till thou burst thy wind, if room enough!

Enter PROSPERO, *the rightful Duke of Milan.*

Pros.

Good Boatswain, have care. Where's thy master? He promised me safe passage when we did's ship at Genoa!

Boats.

I pray now, keep below.

Pros.

Where is thy master, Boatswain?

Boats.

Do ye not hear me? You mar our labour; keep your cabin; why, you assist the storm!

Pros.

Nay, good, be patient.

Boats.

When the sea is. Hence! What care these roarers for the name of Duke? To cabin: silence: trouble us not.

Pros.

Yet remember who thou hast aboard. My little girl, whom I doth love—

Boats.

None that I more love than myself. You are a Duke that's dispossessed: if you can dispossess these elements, if you have pow'r to still the still-vex'd. Bermoothes, why do't, we'll not handle ropes; use your authority. If you cannot, give thanks you have lived so long, make yourself ready in your cabin for the mischance of the hour, ift so hap.

—Out of our way, I say!

[*Exit* PROSPERO.]

An mighty Wave crasheth on the Deck, sweeping half the Mariners *into the Sea.*

Boats.

Down with the top-mast; yare; lower, lower; bring her to try with main-course!

Re-enter PETRUCHIO.

Pet.

A plague upon this sorcery! no natural storm's this; a witchly concoction, rather: the three weird dames intend t' murther the prisoner and cheat me o' reward, but fie! they'll not play wi' me! Thy worst! I—

A bolt of Lightning striketh the top-mast, which splits and falls on PETRUCHIO.

Boats.

Woe! ah, woe! The *Pembroke's* broke!
My Master! Is't some dream that on the deck
You've fallen cold and dead?

Pet.

O yet assist me, friend; I am but hurt!

Boats.

What's to be done?

Pet.

Go below; release the prisoner. Give him his fair chance t'
escape.

Boats.

It shall be done.

[*Exit* Boatswain, *below.*]

Another Wave, which maketh the rest of the Mariners, *save
only* PETRUCHIO, *to fall in the Sea.*
Re-enter PROSPERO *with* MIRANDA, *his six-year-old daughter.*

Mir.

O, what's this noise? O, Father, hast put these waters in this
pitch and made the very waves to howl?

Pros.

Nay, child, they drown, wailing as the waters take 'em all.
O, what a sorry sight is here: the Master o' th' ship's felled and
pinned by a fragment o' the mast! Must be dead; there's blood.
Nay, Miranda, look not on't, but hasten thy steps. There's two
lifeboats and I already stowed the one, some days ago, with wa-
terproofed packets: food, my cape, my books. To't, then.

PROSPERO *and* MIRANDA *climb into the lifeboat. He works the
lines and lowers it into the sea.*

[*Exeunt.*]

Re-enter Boatswain with FILLMORE.

Fil.

Thanks again. Where's Petruchio?

Boats.

There!

Fil.

Petruchio! Are you still alive?

Pet.

But little life's left. Yet I would give a thousand furlongs of sea for an acre of barren ground; long heath, brown furze, any thing: a handful o' sod, a few leaves o' grass!

Fil.

Let's get this wooden shrapnel off his chest, at least.

FILLMORE and the Boatswain remove the splintered mast from PETRUCHIO.

Boats.

The ship splits! To the boat!

Fil.

Help me carry the skipper.

They load PETRUCHIO into the second lifeboat and FILLMORE follows. The Boatswain makes to enter, but the ship pitches and he falls into the Sea, screaming.

Boats.

I'm lost! O, I beseech—

Pet.

[*Weakly.*] He's dead, but I would fain the a dry death upon a beach...

[Exeunt, FILLMORE rowing.]

SCENE II.
The Island: a beach.

Enter FILLMORE, *dragging* PETRUCHIO.

Beaching the dory, the professor gently lifted the dying seaman and carried him to the shore. Fillmore was not as tired as he thought he'd be; the hardest part of the row was getting away from the pull of the sinking ship and the tempest. "Funny how calm the weather became all of a sudden," he mused aloud. "The storm only seemed to rage a little distance around the *Pembroke*."

"No accident, that," Petruchio gasped, "it was an ill wind, blowing no good."

"Shh," the professor cautioned; "save your strength."

"O, do not hope for me, I know I have but little breath left. Sit you down, here upon the sand and let me give you warning while I've still a moiety o' life."

Fillmore obeyed. "Is there anything you want? A drink of water?"

"Nay, too much o' that element." Petruchio coughed, then spoke again, so soft the professor had to put his ear close to hear. "A trio of witch-hags hired me to haul thee hence; I repent me o't and bitterly I've paid for my crimes. Revenge, if thou canst, but have an eye o' them, they're somewhere on th'isle."

"What place is this, Petruchio? Bermuda?"

"It hath no name. 'Tis uncharted. O, I die; forgive me; but should thou 'scape, wouldst seek my wife? Kate, daughter o' Padua's Baptista; tell her I repent me that I dealt her harsh; say for all my faults, I—" But he died without finishing the message.

* * * *

Well, that's probably another loose end for me to tie up if I ever want to leave this world, the professor sighed, digging a shallow grave with one of the lifeboat's paddles. *And that's not the only if:*

If the witches don't catch me.

If I ever get off the island alive.

If Falstaff ever finds me.

That's the toughest IF *of all!* The time sequence was so mixed up on Fillmore's Avonian world, he couldn't be sure the fat knight had any idea where or what Bermuda might be. Though the island actually was discovered in 1503 by the Spaniards, its existence did not become common knowledge until sometime after 1609, when a nautical expedition led by Sir George Somers landed there to avoid destruction in an Atlantic storm, the very tempest that inspired Shakespeare's next-to-final play. *He killed off Falstaff years before writing* The Tempest *in 1611 or '12, but on the other hand, Falstaff was supposed to be alive during the War of the Roses, which took place when? Oh, hell, there's no way of figuring it out!*

Burying Petruchio, the professor hauled the lifeboat over the pink sands and into a concealing clump of semitropical vegetation. Though he didn't expect to brave the Atlantic again in it, the fact that it might be his sole; mode of transportation made the professor exercise extra caution.

He began to push inland. Some fifty yards from the beach he found a brook. As he slaked his thirst, he again pondered whether or not Falstaff was likely to bring help.

Petruchio didn't know the island, but maybe Jack does. If so, I just have to hole out someplace and hope the hags don't find me. The professor shivered. But if he's never heard of Bermuda—well...

[Exit FILLMORE, worried.]

SCENE III.
At Sea.

Enter FALSTAFF, *above.*

Scudding dangerously close to the surface of the water, Sir John Falstaff regarded the churning ocean crests beneath his feet and groaned, utterly wretched.

"O James, good James," he lamented, clutching the umbrella-handle, "shall I survive this fearsome flight? And if I do, how may I rescue thee? Why, what's Bermuda? Where is't? What Never-land o' thy fey imagining?"

[*Exit* Falstaff, *above.*]

SCENE IV.
Another part of the Island.

Enter three Witches.

1 Witch.

The ship, the ship hath broke!

2 Witch.

O, sister, sure, you do not joke?

3 Witch.

Didst not thou feel't? I saw it sink.

1 Witch.

I smelt a storm and it did stink.

No earthly tempest toss'd that bark;
I smell a power passing dark.

2 Witch.

But did he drown, that Fillmore vile?

1 Witch.

O, no!

3 Witch.

He's somewhere on this isle.

2 Witch.

Let's catch 'im then, since he's our prey.

3 Witch.

O, no! Our wrath for him must stay
Until we learn who else is here!
What magic brew'd that storm? I fear
Some evil thing doth rule this strand,
And we may find a war's on hand.

All.

We'll give 'em double, double trouble;
And when we're through, they'll be but rubble.

[Exeunt.]

SCENE V.
another part of the Island: a cave nearby.

Enter FILLMORE.

Uh-oh, thought the professor, *that looks like a footstep in the mud. I'd better go the other way*, He turned off before reaching the cave-clearing, afraid he'd run into one of the weird sisters. *Who else's footprint could it be?*

Enter MIRANDA, *from cave.*

Mir.

O, Father, didst not hear a noise? Methinks
Some creature scuff'leth not too far from here.

Enter PROSPERO, *from cave.*

Pros.

Most like.
That tempest was a Hell-born storm.
Now do I need those books still in the boat;
The food is stored, I wear my magic cloak,
But if we are to thrive upon this plot,
We must rely upon my sorc'rous art
Rest thee, love, I'll fetch my lore-packed books.

Mir.

Oh, I'm afraid! Don't leave me, dad!

Pros.

[*Gesturing.*] Now sleep;
Enchanted rest hang on thy lids and whilst
In slumber wrapt, no harm shall come to thee.

PROSPERO *draweth a circle in the air with his finger and* MIRAN-
DA *falleth asleep within it.*

In all ill luck's a grain o' good; had we
Not got away the night we did, we'd been
Bestowed in rotten ship by my false kin,
And sure had sunk or ere we spied this isle.
O, here the sky is clear, the air is fair;
Polluted Milan's stench cannot compare...

[*Exit* PROSPERO.]

SCENE VI.
The Island: a wild place near a Mountain.

Enter three Witches *and* SYCORAX.

Sycorax was a malevolent crone so ancient and bent with malice and
envy that her fingers touched the tips of her toes and her back curved so
extremely that, from a distance, she resembled a living hoop. But though
she far surpassed the three weird sisters in spite, yet their mastery of the
forces of evil much outstripped hers.

Thus it was, then, that the sibling trio dragged Sycorax into a gloomy
glade just beneath a bear-haunted peak at the center of the midmost

stretch of the elongated isle.

Two of the hags clutched her twitching fingers, preventing her from working further necromantic mischief.

"Tell's now why thou loos'd that superfluous storm!" the Third Witch demanded, gnarled hands on bony hips. "Didst not know that we were here? Might you not ha' guessed to sink that ship might thwart our plans?"

Sycorax first cackled toothlessly, then curled her lip in derision. "From Argier I came, condemned for working spells. I had been burned, except I carried child, contrived while I waited i' th' cell. For that reason, those scurvy innocents cast me here, instead, marooning me. Here I've held sway for lo! these twenty decades. None other witch here reigns; you scabs invade my land; *begone*! no wetbacks need apply!"

The Third Witch's saffron pupils shone with an unholy light as she glared balefully. "Then thou refuseth cousin-witches courtesy befitting a sov'reign t' extend to visitors?"

Sycorax scornfully spat. "Kin thou'rt not; I've kin enow. Tis my desire, drab, that nevermore shall I set eyes on thee or thine!"

The sisters exchanged a meaningful glance.

"As you wish," shrugged the Third Witch, taking Sycorax literally.

[Exeunt.]

SCENE VII.
The Island: a grove.

Enter PROSPERO, *carrying books.*

A Voice. *[Groans.]*

Pros.

This isle is full o' noise; I thought I heard
A mournful sigh and as I fetched from out
Our beached craft, methinks I also heard
A doleful song. Where should this music be
That sweetly, sadly crept by me upon
And o'er the waters; where, O where this plaint?

A Voice.

O, hark! I shall not leave thee in the dark:

[The Voice sings.]

Come unto this broken tree.
And then help me:
Syc'rax lock'd me in its wood.
(And it ain't good).
Foot it featly over here;
And please lift this burden drear.
Hark, hark!
Blech, god-dam,
I hate this pine:
The one that's split—
Hark, hark!—
Is mine!

Pros.

I see thy plight. But what's thy name?

Ariel. [Within the cloven pine-tree.]

Ariel.
The foul witch, Sycorax, imprisoned me
A long, long time ago; I am a sprite
O' upper air and if thou hast the spell
To free me from this place, I'll serve thee well!

Pros.

I'll help; must get my cloak; please wait a while.

[*Exit* PROSPERO.]

Ariel.

"Please wait"? A genius he ain't, that shmoe!
Just where the hell's he think I'm gonna go?

[*Manet* ARIEL.]

SCENE VIII.
The Island: a wild place near a mountain.

Enter FILLMORE.
"Well, it *is* a big enough place to hide in, anyway," the professor observed, stepping along stealthily, peering every which way. "There ought to be someplace I can conceal myself for the night, maybe at the foot of that mountain; it's wild enough."

It was not a very lofty peak, more of a super-sized hill, rounded with age. An animal snuffled somewhere from above. *Could there be bears on Bermuda?* Fillmore craned his neck to see what shape seemed to be moving in the brush halfway up the rise, but it was too shadowy in the midst of the thicket to see clearly. *Maybe if I climb a tree?*

Physical labor was not one of his strong points, but adventuring via umbrella inevitably firmed up some muscles, especially those employed in running. He found one reasonably tall tree with enough rifts and branches to make scaling it fairly simple. Taking hold of its lowest branches, he swung himself up and climbed to the top.

Just in the nick of time.

* * * *

He'd barely time to ascertain the actual existence of a few brown bears upon the nearby peak when he heard some large creature crashing through the forest below. The sound stopped, only to be replaced by the most ferocious howl the professor had ever been unfortunate enough to hear. So terrible it was, he nearly lost his hold on the supporting branch and had to throw both arms around it and hug tight, lest he fall out of the tree. Fillmore prayed the noise he made passed unnoticed below. When he was sure there was no alteration in the tone or direction of the infernal caterwauling, he ventured a peek downward.

A little ways off in the thicket, he saw two things, neither of which reassured him one bit A great twisted monstrosity hunkered on its haunches and wailed over the strangest skeleton Fillmore ever saw: a set of bones curved so unnaturally that he almost doubted it once belonged to a human being—except the skull, surmounted by a long tangle of white hair, was unmistakably that of some long-dead individual.

"Mother, O mother," the misshapen giant raged, gnashing snaggly teeth, "who did this foul deed? Who'd strength to cast down thy colossal wickedness? O, reveal't!" The jaws of the death's-head opened. The professor thought he'd faint when it spoke.

"*Revenge, son*, REVENGE!" the dead witch shrieked.

Leaping to its fish-webbed feet, the thing below swore a vile oath, then asked the ghost where to find the culprit "On the isle, not far from here..." it replied, but its voice faded swiftly and the sentence was never completed.

* * * *

After the monster set aside the skull and lumbered off into the jungle, Fillmore let himself down from the tree with considerable difficulty, his legs and hands shaking.

So that's Caliban, he shivered. *Spawn of Sycorax and the Devil. Half-man, half-beast*. Caliban was the rebellious servant of Prospero in *The Tempest*, trusted by the magician until the deformed entity attempted to rape his daughter, Miranda. *But how come he's so big? I always thought of Caliban as a runt, something like Lon Chaney playing Quasimodo.*

Fillmore's first impulse, naturally, was to put as much distance as possible between himself and the savage. Yet the notion that the monster and he might later accidentally meet was remarkably unappealing. *He might accuse me of murdering his mother!*

Deciding it was better to keep track of Caliban's whereabouts, Fillmore reluctantly decided to follow at a discreet distance.

[Exit FILLMORE.]

SCENE IX.
The Island: Prospero's cave

MIRANDA *still slee'peth; enter* **PROSPERO** *with books.*

Pros.

My precious child still slumbereth. O, if
A witch doth dwell yet on this isle, as poor
Ariel saith, 'twere best to strength the spell
That keeps Miranda safe while in this round.

Setting down the books in the cave, PROSPERO *maketh a large circle with his finger about* MIRANDA.

Peace, the charm is firm and good. My cape;
'Tis meet I put it on.

> *He donneth his magic cloak.*
> *Enter* CALIBAN, *rampaging.*

Cal.

Thou filth! O, piece
O' dung! I'll rip thy entrails out!

Pros.

Why, what
A bestial knave art thou? To burst on me
And mine, who've hurt not thee and threat to kill?
Who'rt thou, clay? Thy proper name pronounce,
I conjure thee—

Cal.

By all that's vile!

Pros.

[*Gesturing.*] Thy name!

Cal.

'Ban, 'Ban, Ca—Caliban!

Pros.

Too long;
I'll call thee Caliban: why rail on me?

Cal.

I saw thee making magic whirlings in
The air; 'tis thou that killed my dam!

Pros.

You lie!

Cal.

Have at you, then!

Mir.

[*Wakes.*] O, father, ha! What is't?

CALIBAN *sees her and stops, fascinated,* PROSPERO *takes advantage of the distraction to gesture toward* CALIBAN. *The creature screameth and becomes twisted, bent and small.*

Cal.

By cock, give back my shape, thou stoup o' stale!

PROSPERO *gestureth again at* CALIBAN.

Pros.

Thou'lt keep thy shape, slime-tongue. Be dumb! Begone!

CALIBAN *discovereth he can no longer speak.*

[*Exit* CALIBAN, mewling and gibbering.]

MIRANDA *flieth, frightened, to her father's side.*

Pros.

O, be not fear'd, my child; the beast is gone.

Mir.

O, grave new world that hath such creatures in't!

Pros.

New neighborhoods are always strange.

Mir. [Still fearful.]

But who's
That lurking yet within the woods?

Pros. [Peers suspiciously.]

Hm, who,
Indeed? Thou skulker, show thyself or taste
My wrath.

Enter FILLMORE, sheepishly.

Fil.

Excuse me, Duke, I wasn't sure
If it was safe to show my face.

Pros.

If thou
Be true and good, there's naught to fear from me.
But what's thy name?

Fil.

[*Smiles.*]
To conjure with? Fillmore.

Pros.

A name to conjure with, indeed! Then you
Survived?

Fil.

The shipwreck? Yes, I did. But how—

Pros.

Thy name's well-known in Italy: the man

Who freed us from the tyrant Austria!
And even I, though foolishly enwrapt
In books o' grammarye, could not escape
The talk of how one man, Fillmore, deposed
Vienna's deputy; but where's that thing
You stole him with?

Fil.

My friend, Falstaff, took off
To summon aid. We sailed, you know, upon—

Pros.

The very vessel where I was. I heard,
Yet saw thee not.

Fil.

I was a prisoner.

Pros.

Then evil work's afoot!

Fil.

You're telling me?

Pros.

That beastly Caliban—

Fil.

He's not the worst.
I think there's witches, two or three, somewhere
Upon the isle.

Pros.

Tis like they kill'd his dam.

Fil.

Uh-huh. What should we do?

Pros.

Stay here. I'll go
Enlist some supernatural aid. But guard my child.

Fil.

Of course I will.

Pros.

I'll be right back.

[*Exit* PROSPERO.]

FILLMORE sighs.

Fil.

So you're Miranda, huh?

Mir.

That's me. I like
Your smile.

Fil.

[*Nonplussed.*]
Uh...thanks.

Mir.

And yet it seems you frown
Much more than you do smile.
How come?

Fil.

[*Shrugs.*]
I guess I don't have much to smile about.

Mir.

O, sad!
Yet if I kiss thee, sir, perhaps thy life
Will grow more glad, for all the fairy tales
That I have heard doth stipulate that lips
O' one who rues thy fate, saluting, sets
Thee free; then, may I make thee ever glad?

MIRANDA kisseth FILLMORE'S cheek. He stares at her, speech-less for a second, then, laughing, gives her a big hug.

Fil.

You are a doll! Your father's fortunate
To have a daughter nice as you. [*Aside.*] It's just

My luck: the sweetest female character
That Shakespeare ever wrote, I have to go
And meet when she is much too young for me.

Mir.

Ah, did th'enchantment work?

Fil.

[*Smiling for her benefit.*]
You bet it did!
Now how 'bout you? I'd like to do something
To make you happy, too.

Mir.

Wouldst play a game?

Fil.

Why, sure.

Mir.

[*Claps hands in glee.*]
O, goody-good!
But do you know
A game called Hide-and-Seek?

Fil.

[*Laughs; Aside.*]
I'm glad to find
Some things don't change from world to world.—Do I
Know Hide-and-Seek? Why, that's my favorite game.
Miranda, hon, I'll bet that I'm the best
Darned Hide-and-Seeker that you'll ever meet!

Mir.

Why, if that's true, thou must be fair with me,
And in that case, thou must be firstly It.

Fil.

You've got it, kid.

Mir.

So you must hide your eyes

And count to ten times ten, nor never speak.

Fil.

[*Hides eyes.*]

Here goes: *a*-ONE, *a*-TWO, *a*-THREE, *a*-FOUR-

MIRANDA silently runs about, looking for some place to hide while FILLMORE continueth to count.

Fil.

A-FOURTEEN, FIFTEEN, SIXTEEN, SEVENTEEN-

After a time, MIRANDA chooseth a Tree a little way within the Forest. She hideth behind it, but peereth out at the still-counting Professor.

Fil.

A-THIRTY-NINE, *a*-FORTY, FORTY-ONE-

Out of the Woods creepeth CALIBAN*, an evil leer on his ugly face. He sneaketh up behind* MIRANDA *and clappeth one distorted claw over her mouth. She struggleth.*

Fil.

A-SIXTY-SIX, *a*-SIXTY-SEVEN, 'EIGHT—

CALIBAN *lifteth the kicking child and steeleth off silently into the Forest.*

Fil.

—TY-NINE, *a*-HUNDRED! There! Ready or not, Miranda, here I come!

FILLMORE puts down his hands, looks about, amused.

[*Calls.*] I'll bet I know
Just where you are: you're either over here...
Or over there...right by the cave, or near—

[*A scream, off.*]

Miranda, hey! What happened, hon?

Mir.

[*Off.*]

O, help!

FILLMORE runs in the direction of her voice and peereth.

Fil.

Oh, cripes, it's Caliban! He's kidnapped her!

He begins to follow them, but stops abruptly.

Aww, hell, I'd better leave a note to let
Her father know what's wrong—

Mir.

[*Further away.*]

O, help me, friend!

Fil.

No time; can't wait, must chase—he'll run too far
Away and I won't know just where they are!

[Exit FILLMORE, running.]

SCENE X.
The Island: on CALIBAN'S mountain.

Enter eight Bears, *frolicking.*

Halfway up the mountainside, Caliban stopped and set Miranda down upon a narrow ledge. Behind them, some of the hillside was scooped out, forming a recess too small to classify as a cave, but ample enough for the web-footed mooncalf to keep a stock of noxious food and a few trinkets his mother, Sycorax, once gave him as souvenirs of her native Argier.

"Please let me go," Miranda pleaded, shrinking back from both Caliban and the bruins cavorting near her, "I ne'er harmed thee."

The monster gestured to his mouth and, growling, shook a fist at her. His guttural grunts frightened the bears; yelping in terror, they scampered off hastily.

"O," Miranda lamented, "I forgot my father rendered thee dumb!" Nodding angrily, he hopped from foot to foot, gesticulating wildly. Though Prospero's spell both robbed him of stature and speech, it had no effect on the creature's strength and as his fury mounted, Caliban pounded the rearward slope with his fists, knocking off great chunks of stone that tumble-crashed down the side of the mountain to the forest-floor.

His rage terrified Miranda so much that she began to cry. But as soon as she did, the sound and spectacle of tears checked his choler. Cocking his head, perplexed, Caliban squatted beside the cringing girl and, with a gentleness foreign to his nature, tentatively touched her on the shoulder with the tips of his fingers.

* * * *

Fillmore watched them from below. When he saw Caliban calm down and try to comfort Miranda, the professor felt great relief. *Shakespeare hinted at a rudimentary capacity for higher feelings in Caliban. Now if I can just think of some way to appeal to his better nature...*

But when he pictured the way Caliban treated the rocky mountainside, Fillmore hesitated; he decided to mull over more carefully the wisdom of stepping boldly forth to parlay with the brute.

Some hours later, when darkness fell, he was still busy mulling.

[*Tableau.*]

SCENE XI.
The Island: PROSPERO'S cave.

Enter PROSPERO *and* ARIEL.

Pros.

Why, what is wrong? Why, where's my child? Did I
Do wrong to trust that stranger so?

Ariel.

O, no,
O master mine: here's work that I do sense
Doth stem from nothing mortal; no; the tang
O' witchcraft warreth here.

Pros.

But not the hag
Who locked thee in that tree; she's dead.

Ariel.

She had
A son, a thing called Caliban.

Pros.

I know
That beast! I shrank him down and made him dumb.

Ariel.

He's ta'en revenge! Best follow me!

Pros.

I come!

[*Exeunt.*]

SCENE XII.
The Island: by CALIBAN'S mountain.

FILLMORE, CALIBAN, MIRANDA, as before.

The professor hardly was able to keep his eyes open. Miranda had stopped crying long before and Caliban did not bother her, but neither moved from the spot they'd been hours ago. Once, the beast withdrew some food from the recess and offered a little to the child, but she turned up her nose at the rank stuff, so Caliban dined alone.

The moon came out early. No one budged.

Shades of King Kong, Delia and Prince Albert, thought Fillmore. If only he'd fall asleep so I could make a run for it with Miranda. Wonder if she's smart enough to know I'm here? He smiled. *I'm sure she is.*

For the first time in his life the professor pondered the putative pleasures of parenthood.

Which is why he missed the first evidence of help arriving from an unexpected source.

* * * *

Caliban caught it before the professor. His squat nose suddenly twitched. He growled deep in his throat and cast suspicious glances everywhere, but mostly towards the top of the mountain.

Fillmore rubbed his eyes in disbelief when he looked up where Caliban's head was turned.

It's not possible...is it? So soon?

Almost afraid to hope, the professor intently watched the stupendous shadow float down past the peak towards the forest-floor.

It must be him! the professor reasoned. *Who else in all the worlds could be so fat?*

Perhaps ten feet above the ground-line, the elephantine silhouette came to rest upon the slope, startling another group of growling grizzlies.

Fillmore was positive it was Falstaff. *But I never expected to see the knight on Bear Mountain!*

He hurried in his direction.

[Exit FILLMORE.]

SCENE XIII.
The Island: on CALIBAN'S mountain.

CALIBAN discovered; *MIRANDA* sleeping.

Dumb show: CALIBAN *peers at* MIRANDA, *satisfies himself she really is asleep, then steps silently away to investigate the strange shadow he just saw go past. But when he reaches the extreme edge of the ledge, he freezes in horror, looking outward and upward* CALIBAN *faints. Enter, from above,* BORIS *and* BAPTISTA, *clinging to the professor's umbrella. They stop on the ledge; the hood folds up.* BORIS *regards* CALIBAN *for a moment before speaking.*

Bor.

O curses! Scorned again!

Bap.

Ah, see: a child,
And she is beautiful beyond compare;
What doth she here in this forbidding, cold
And lonely spot?

Bor.

I cannot tell. Wait here.
I'll go and seek the knight and good Fillmore.

Bap.

And leave us here alone? What if that weird
Thing wakeneth?

Bor.

You know that looks deceive:
Despite his form, he may be mild.

Bap.

[Agitated.] Or wild!
Protect me, please! Protect this helpless child!

Bor.

[Sighs.] I will; calm down; relax and don't get riled!

[*Exit* BORIS, *carrying* CALIBAN.]

SCENE XIV.
The Island: at the foot of the mountain.

Enter FALSTAFF *with new umbrella.*

"I am accursed to fly in that pair's company," the enormous knight groused, stumping along and thrashing with his new, extra-strength umbrella to prevent himself from bumping into trees. "Why the devil could they not stay close, as I requested? Bah! I doubt not but to the a fair death for all this—"

"*Pssst*! Sir John! Over *here*!"

"Ha! Who's't?"

"*Me*! Don't make so much noise! Walk *this way*!"

"*O, any way* is equal torture," Falstaff lamented, "eight yards of uneven ground is threescore and ten miles afoot with me!"

But, despite his discomfort, the fat man stumbled in the direction of the whispering and soon he and the professor were reunited.

* * * *

"I was afraid you might not be familiar with Bermuda," Fillmore said.

"I wasn't, Jim, but Boris claimeth to have knowledge o' this Shakespeare, too, and he flew swift to some other place, came back with this sturdier umbrella (purchased, saith he, of a merchant named Wells) and led us here."

"Us?"

"The lad Baptista clung to Boris's bumbershoot."

"And Vincentio?"

"Returned to Vienna. His crown called him back, as well as a desire to meet that dame, Isabella."

"Yes, they'll probably marry. They do in—"

"Shakespeare, I know, I *know*." The knight waved it aside. "Th' Duke o' Vienna's rewarded thee well. I have a bag o' gold that—"

"Never mind that now, Jack. Where's Boris?"

"*Here, O Puissant Professor*!"

The voice at his elbow was so unexpected, the professor jumped a good inch into the air. It would have been higher if he'd seen who the Frankenstein monster had slung over his back like a potato-sack. But it was too dark to discern anything but the dim silhouette of the giant's great bulk.

"Boris! How long have you been here?"

"I just arrived a moment ago. But why do we whisper?"

Fillmore swiftly outlined events for his two friends, but partway through, Boris interrupted, chuckling.

"O, fear that fish-thing no further, Friend, I hath him o'er mine back."

"*What*?" the professor exclaimed. "Let me see!"

Frankenstein obligingly moved a few paces to the left, where a pale patch of moonlight showed him and his burden more clearly. He let Caliban down, but kept a restraining hand on his shoulder. The creature was awake now, eyes bulging with fright.

"Caliban," said Fillmore, "did you hear everything I just told them?" Still unable to speak, Caliban nodded his head jerkily.

"Then you understand it was not Prospero who killed your mother, but probably the witches who've been making it hot for me?"

Another nod.

"All right," the professor continued, putting into practice his theory that the beast had a better nature, "since you realize we're all faultless, how about releasing Miranda?"

"No need," Boris began, but Fillmore shushed him.

"It's important for him to answer, anyway."

The mooncalf growled. Boris gave him a warning shake.

"*Well*?" the professor insisted. "Will you promise not to harm her, but willingly give her back to her father?"

Caliban struggled with the problem for a long time, but at last, grimacing horribly, gave one more curt nod to Fillmore.

"That's a *good* Caliban," the teacher reassured him. "Now I know Miranda will be safe from all—" He stopped in mid-sentence.

Two terrified shrieks sounded a second time from above.

They all spun round to see what was the matter—but just then, the moon passed behind a cloud. The mountainside went dark.

"*It's Miranda*!" Fillmore exclaimed. "Come *on*!"

He sprinted toward the slope, ignoring the lash of twigs and nettle-stings. Boris and Caliban hurried after the professor.

"O, 'twill catch our deaths bumblefutzing around i' th' darkness," Falstaff complained, lagging pitifully behind, yet making a valiant effort to catch up.

[*Exeunt.*]

SCENE XV.
The Island: CALIBAN'S ledge, now empty.

Enter FILLMORE, then BORIS & CALIBAN.

Fil.

Miranda! Hey! Baptista! Hey!

Bor.

[*Lamenting.*]
    O, gone!
    'Tis all my fault! I never should have left
    Them all alone!

Fil.

You didn't know. You're not
To blame.

Bor.

But that's not all: they bore away
With them th'umbrella that belongs to you.

Fil.

Oh, damn! It's all your fault! You never should
Have left them all alone!

CALIBAN *gesticulates to catch their attention.*

Oh, what do you
Want now?

Bor.

See where he points? A note!

Fil.

A note?

Bor.

Aye; note it not?
O, note the note!

Turning, FILLMORE sees and picks up a scrap of paper.

Fil.

[*Reads.*]
    High-and-mighty,—Come alone at once to the peak's peak,
or thy two friends perish.

Bor.

O, Fillmore, do not go!

Fil.

I have no choice.

Bor.

A trap! You seek your death.

Fil.

Maybe. Stay here.

[Exit FILLMORE, upward.]

Bor.

O, what am I to do? They need my help!
[*Lamenting.*] I'll never see my friend again! O, woe!

CALIBAN *impatiently plucks him by the sleeve,* BORIS *looks at him, begins to speak, but* CALIBAN, *putting a finger to his lips, gestures for* BORIS *to follow him. The mooncalf disappears behind a crevice in the stone,* BORIS *peers within.*

Bor.

A secret way? And it ascends? I'll try
It then, for what more, then, is there to lose?

[*Exeunt.*]

Enter FALSTAFF, *wheezing and puffing.*

Fal.

'Sblood, I'll not bear mine own flesh so far afoot again for
all the coin Vincentio gave th' professor.

He lieth on his back, his belly resembling a beachèd whale.

Fal.

Unless someone hath levers hereabout,
'Tis here I'll lie and die, I do not doubt.

[FALSTAFF *manet.*]

SCENE XVI.
The Island: at the top of the mountain.

Enter FILLMORE.

Just before he reached the top, he saw the flicker of some unwholesome green fire. He climbed over the last rise and stared at the five figures motionless by the central cauldron.

The moon shone; no further clouds interposed themselves. By firelight and moonlight, the professor examined the terrible tableau.

Two of the weird sisters clutched Miranda and Baptista, crooked-bladed knives at the throat of each. The third crone stood nearer to the place he occupied; in her hand was his umbrella.

"At last we meet again," the Third Witch said triumphantly.

"It's a pleasure I could easily have relinquished," Fillmore replied dourly. "Now what?"

"Come closer."

He did not move.

"I said, *come closer*!"

"Not until you release my friends."

Though the night was clear, an ominous rumble of thunder sounded far-off. Yet the sky held few clouds and the moon was still as bright "Let my people go," the professor repeated.

The Third Witch's eyes glared with an evil yellow glow. "Thou'rt in no position, Fillmore, to dictate terms. Approach, or else my sisters shear their throats in twain."

Miranda whimpered, but, remembering that she was the daughter of a Duke, forced herself to stop.

Reluctantly, Fillmore walked slowly toward the witch.

"All right," he snapped, "I'm close enough. What do you want?"

* * * *

Overhead, summer sheet-lightning suddenly flickered. Thunder rolled again, somewhat closer.

"Damn you all," the professor swore, "I asked you what you want!" The sisters snickered.

"O, patience," cautioned the Third Witch, "we've waited long and long to face you once more—this time without your ghastly friend."

"I suppose you plan revenge because I helped save Vincentio. All right. You've got me now. But let *them* go, they've had no hand in it."

The crone smiled toothily. "O, that's true, we know, dearie, we know. But small bus'ness did th' Duke's lackey discharge, the child no thing at all."

"Then you *won't* harm them? *Please*."

"Ah, tha' crav'st a favor of us, whom thou crossed repeatedly? And what's it worth?"

"My life," Fillmore murmured.

The witch spat. "Why, what good's that to us?"

* * * *

A strong wind sprang up out of nowhere, whipping the white whiskers of the witch wildly.

Storm coming up—and fast, the professor thought, irrelevantly.

And then he saw something that made his heart flip-flop. He didn't know whether to be angry or glad. *Depends on how it turns out...*

Fillmore looked the Third Witch squarely in the eye. "Okay, lady," he grumbled, "if it's not my life you're after, then what in hell *do* you want from me?"

Keep her talking...keep her talking...

* * * *

"O, we had entertained mortal thoughts on your behalf," she replied, "but chance hath changed our minds." She held up the umbrella. "Instruct us in the usage of this thing, show us how to fashion others like it and we'll put aside revenge."

Yeah, sure you will.

She jerked her thumb at the prisoners. "Refuse and they die first and won't be swift despatched."

Lightning struck, close by.

"And how do I know you'll keep your promise? *Keep her talking... just a few more seconds...*

"Well, thou must trust us," she leered wickedly.

Uh-huh. As far as I'd trust a constipated cobra.

"No more delay!" she shrilled. "Reply: wilt tell?"

Judging the time was right, the professor shouted an answer so staggeringly unprintable it actually shocked the witches. For one vital second, they glared, open-mouthed, at him, simultaneously chagrined and respectful...

And then all hell cut loose.

* * * *

Happily, the storm picked that precise instant to break forth in towering force. Deafening thunder. A wall of water sloshed down and drowned the witch-fire. Skeletal talons of lightning ripped and cracked, totally confusing the sisters...

And Boris and Caliban leaped upon the First and Second Witches, grasping their knife-hands in bone-crushing grips. The Third Witch spun around, astonished at the instant alteration of Fortune. Cascades of water slashed at her, but she shot out a bony hand and started to cast a spell.

Fillmore threw a flying tackle at her legs. He brought her down, twisted the umbrella from her grip and bopped her smartly on the forehead. She dropped back heavily on the turf, wrinkled mouth wide open.

Good, thought the professor, *maybe she'll drown*. He ran to Miranda's side, hugged and comforted her. Baptista joined the pair and huddled over the child to shield her a little from the rain and also prevent her from witnessing the ferocious fight raging on either side.

* * * *

Boris wrestled with the surprisingly-strong Second Witch. They tottered close to the edge of the mountain. Fillmore shouted to warn Frankenstein, but could not be heard above the violence of the elements.

Caliban, exhilarated to have one of his mother's murderers in his grasp, was more than a match for the First Witch. Slowly, he forced the twisted blade still clutched in her hand towards her own stringy throat.

A scream. Boris staggered back from the Second Witch, blood streaming down his face. Laughing demoniacally, she rushed upon him, knife poised for a mortal blow.

Roaring, Fillmore dashed to his friend's aid, all too well aware he'd never make it in time.

But suddenly, a thing like some enormous toad sprang up and leaped upon the Second Witch, smashing her to the ground. Caliban, finished with his other opponent, grasped the hag's head and, with a savage yank, actually tore it off—a gratuitous gesture, since she'd already landed on her own rune-cursed knife.

Dripping wet and sneezing, the professor continued toward Boris, who still teetered dangerously close to the brink of the precipice. But before he was able to reach him, Fillmore was horrified to see Boris suddenly lurch, pitch, and, with a frightened scream, plunge backward over the side and into the abyss below.

Fillmore froze, rooted to the spot, listening to Boris's fading cry of terror. It did not go on for long, nor could his ears discern any sound of impact, but the groan of agony that ensued was unmistakable.

"*O, no!*" someone wailed behind him. "*O, Boris!*"

And then the professor heard another sound, a profoundly chilling one. The Third Witch was laughing.

* * * *

The storm stopped as abruptly as it started. The clouds cleared, the moon shone again—and Fillmore saw the Third Witch rise up out of the grass close to the place where Boris fell.

"You pushed him!" Fillmore screamed, brandishing his umbrella like a club. But the witch pointed a finger at him and his muscles stiffened and joints locked. He could not take a step.

Behind her, Caliban crouched, fingers flexed in anticipation...

Without even turning, the hag etched a glowing sign in the air, said a few words...and Caliban's brain broke down. He forgot his name, his past, all memory of language. She watched him scurry off through the grass like some timid animal. Then, stepping up to Fillmore, she took away his umbrella a second time.

"I've punished your friends," she said, snapping her fingers and dissipating the rigidity in his limbs. "Now let's get back to business. My offer still holds."

He told her what she could do with it. "Very well. Perhaps you'll change your mind in time to save your other companion."

With that, the witch beckoned toward Miranda and the child, as if in a trance, pulled out of Baptista's arms and started toward the crone.

"Miranda, no!" Fillmore shouted, running to stop her. But he bumped into an invisible barrier which the sorceress casually waved into existence.

The girl took one faltering step after another, bringing herself closer and closer to the malevolent hag who awaited her with claws outstretched to encircle Miranda's pale throat. "Help!" the professor screamed. "Someone, something—HELP!"

* * * *

An answering growl sounded. Out of the forest lumbered a great brown bear. Miranda stopped walking.

The witch cackled. "Hast pow'r, Fillmore, o'er all dumb beasts? He'll harm thee ere he'll touch a hair o' me. No mortal thing may pass the magic shield."

The bear did. Her white eyebrows shot up. "What airy phantom is this? Thou hast no hold on me, we serve the selfsame master!"

The bear bared his teeth and stalked toward the old woman.

"Desist!" she warned. "T th' name o' Beelzebub, I charge thee, leave this place!"

The bear came closer, rearing up on its hind legs.

"*Go away*!" the witch screeched, pointing her knife at the animal.

The bear began to grow. As he did, he waved a paw in her direction and a bolt of blue flame shot out and crackled along the blade of her dagger. She howled in pain and dropped it; it was nothing more than a hilt by the time it hit the ground.

And now the shape of the bear shimmered and the entity turned into a colossal Harpy with hair of flame. Swooping down upon the screaming witch, the fell thing clutched her tight and, rising on leathery wings, flew away with her to sea.

* * * *

"*Daddy!*"

Sobbing with fright, relief and happiness, Miranda ran to her father's arms.

Fillmore walked across the mountaintop to Prospero. "Good work, sir. I imagine the Harpy was really Ariel?"

"Indeed, 'twas," said the Duke of Milan, Miranda's father. "I freed him from arboreal imprisonment and he, in gratitude, hath pledged to serve me true so long as I shall desire't."

"He sure saved our necks. Wish he could've made it here a little sooner, though," Fillmore said sorrowfully. "I lost my good friend, Boris."

"O, that's not true," Prospero smiled. "I cast a spell and slowed his fall. He may be bent a bit—I'd little time to spend in his behalf—and yet I think you'll find—" Fillmore didn't listen to the end of it. He and Baptista rushed over to the edge. They stared down as the first streaks of dawn painted the sky pink.

Some distance below, they saw Boris standing on Caliban's ledge waving up at them.

"Are you all right?" the professor called.

"Aye! I landed on a soft pillow!" Boris answered.

And then Fillmore heard the voice of Falstaff rumbling furiously.

"Pillow, lout? I'll give thee pillow! How dast thou bellyflop like that? O, what a beastly stomach-ache I've got!"

Laughing in relief, the professor followed Prospero, Miranda and Baptista down the descending path.

[*Exeunt.*]

SCENE XVII.
The Island: a beach.

Enter FILLMORE & PROSPERO.

Fil.

I can't persuade you, then, to leave the isle?

Pros.

[*Smiling.*]
I can't persuade you, then, to stay?

Fil.

No way.

Pros.

I like this clime; the air is clean and pure;
And we are nowhere near a high-rent zone.
If what you say is true, for twelve sweet years,
I'll see my daughter grow and then a ship
Shall bring a mate to her and sweet revenge
To me.

Fil.

That's right. But don't forget to keep
An eye on Caliban.

Pros.

I will. He's pleased
To serve me true. I've lifted off the spell
That binds his tongue, but can't restore his brain.
Miranda says she wants to teach him speech.

Fil.

She will. But don't forget to watch him close.

Pros.

I swear I shall.

Fil.

[*Sighs.*]
A shame she's started out
With such bad memories. She might have lots
Of nightmares for a while.

Pros.

O, no. I've sent

Miranda deep into enchanted sleep.
She'll wake refreshed, but won't recall a thing.

Fil.

I guess it's for the best. But does that mean
She won't remember me?

Pros.

The spell will blot
Out all that happed until we both took ship.

Fil.

Well, kiss her for me every night and tell
Her all about me some fine day. [*Smiles.*] At least,
She won't remember what I told the witch!

Enter FALSTAFF, with *umbrella*.

Fal.

Art ready to depart?

Fil.

I am.
Where shall
We drop you off?

Fal.

If it's all right with you,
Why, lad, I'd like to fly along with thee.

Fil.

[*Surprised.*]
Across the void? But why?

Fal.

O, Boris told
Me much about that fairy glade where he
Hath ruled a veritable Paradise
O' fairy dames! Sounds very good to me!

Fil.

Free eats and all the wine that you can drink?

I guess that you might like it fine. Let's see:
There's two umbrellas, so we'll have to make
Two trips.

Pros.

No need; my ever-potent spells shall send
The extra traveler where'er you wish.

Fil.

That's great. Okay, that's that. Where's Boris now?

Pros.

He's on his way and hath a great surprise
For you.

Fil.

[*Aside.*]
Uh-oh...surprises still? I thought
This sequence almost over, but what new
Shakespearean reversal's now in store?

Enter BORIS *and* KATHARINA, *richly dressed.*

Fil.

Now who the hell is *that*?

Kate.

You knew me in
Disguise; Baptista was I called.

Fil.

Good Gad!

Kate.

A husband horrid have I had; so bad
Was he I stole away and played a boy.

Bor.

Wouldst ever guess they once proclaimed her shrew?

Fil.

(The last loose-end!) Oh, Kate, I've searched for you

Both near and far! Your husband's dead and you
Are free; he died upon this beach and begged
For me to find you out to tell, at last,
He did repent the way he treated you.
I think he also meant to say, for all
His faults, he loved you still.

Kate.

Then I am free
To wed again?

Fil.

[*Startled*]
Well, yes, but don't let's rush!
I'd like to get to know—

Kate.

Ah, Boris, mine!

Bor.

O, Kate, canst love me true? I'm scratched anew.

Kate.

And if thy face yet bore an hundred-score
O' witchly scars, I could not love thee more!

BORIS *and* KATHARINA *embrace passionately.*

Fil.

[*Aside.*]
Oh, curses! Spurned again!

Pros.

All's fair, my friend,
In matters of the heart
And now, good speed,
For we must part I'll send thee off in style,
And if we ever meet again, we'll smile.

[*Exeunt.*]

EPITHALAMIUM

Wedding-day in Arcady. Boris and Kate clasped hands and prepared to join in nuptial bands. Falstaff took the arm of the Fairy Queen, a lithe damsel in his eyes. Rimski grinned, flickering in and out of view in his happiness, for, despite mortal law, there was no fairy statute to prevent him from marrying all the other sprightly sisters. Which was precisely what he intended to do.

As for J. Adrian Fillmore...

* * * *

"Oh, well," he sighed, "at least I solved the Best Man wrangle by being *every*body's Best Man."

If the professor learned anything from his amatory pursuits, he refused to talk about it with his friends, but at least he responded to one direct question of Rimski's.

"Do you intend," asked the ex-cat, "to make any other cosmic hops in search of *la belle dame avec merci?*"

"No way. I have higher things in mind."

"Like?"

Fillmore shook his head, refusing to elaborate on the cryptic statement.

The wedding march struck up. All began to sing.

Bor.

After much debate delightful,
I on Katy dear decide,
Falstaff now may take the Sovereign,
Omnes be our Rimski's brides!

Fil.

In that case unprecedented,
Single I must live and die—
I shall have to be contented
With a quest that's rather high.
Or he'll have to be contented
With our heartfelt sympathy!
Greatly pleased with one another,
To get married we decide,
Each of us will wed the other,
Nobody be Fillmore's Bride.

DANCE

CURTAIN

The End of
The Amorous Umbrella.

ANNOTATIONS

PART I

"snickersee" is the sword mentioned by Ko-Ko in Gilbert & Sullivan's *The Mikado*.

Harold Shea is the "incompleat enchanter" in the novel of that name by L. Sprague de Camp and Fletcher Pratt. He makes a guest appearance in one section of *The Incredible Umbrella in Oz,* whose annotations appear next.

"*das ewig-weibliche*" comes from the second part of Goethe's *Faust.* It means The Eternal Feminine.

"But joy incessant palls the sense" is from the Defendant's song in G&S's operetta *Trial by Jury.*

Sganarelle is a character who appears many times in Moliere's comedic plays.

Dark Carnival is the first scarce collection of dark fantasies by Ray Bradbury.

The walking hut on fowl's legs belongs to the Russian witch Baba Yaga, who soon appears.

I didn't plan to make much use of the cat, whom we learn is called Rimski, but I found him so enjoyable to write that he became a major character in this book.

The cigar-smoking toad is a congersman (sic) from Walt Kelly's *Pogo.*

This section is based on the fairy tale "The Twelve Dancing Princesses."

"*I'm also damn well minus pink Walter*" is a pun on the name of the great American children's and YA comic (mostly) author and cartoonist Daniel Manus Pinkwater, with whom I've corresponded.

The Black Crook was, I believe, American theatre's earliest musical.

Andy is, of course, the lion from Bernard Shaw's play *Androcles and the Lion*.

I learned to do the Greek chain dance at Penn State. It is indeed hypnotic and our professor told us that when a village was attacked, they'd ward off rape and pillage by doing the dance at the edge of a cliff and thus collectively commit suicide.

"Rising early in the morning" is a second act song from Gilbert & Sullivan's operetta *The Gondoliers*.

Cinderella – Ella, as she prefers to be called – is based on my friend, a beautiful blonde who played an important role on the late lamented ABC daytime drama *Ryan's Hope*, mentioned in *Part II* of this book.

Mike Fink is a great American riverboat (not ferry boat) hero who is an expert sharpshooter as long as he is on a moving vessel firing over water – as we will soon see.

Nessie, of course, is the Loch Ness Monster.

"a school o' eminent sturgeons" is a pun by my late lamented friend Dick Mazza, who went to high school and Penn State with me. The last time I met him in Manhattan, he told he was going to Hollywood for a lucrative job because he'd read and recommended the proposal for a film that turned out to be *Dirty Dancing*. But he died a week or two later.

Manny and Moe are, of course, part of the famous retailing firm Manny, Moe and Jack.

The graceful harbor is based on an obscure erotic story called *Merryland*.

The beast does not really look like Robert Louis Stevenson's Mr. Hyde. He is based on the way my old Penn State friend Bill Kotzwinkle used to dress. Bill went to become an award-winning writer.

The list of people attending *Walpurgisnicht* in the Harz Mountains appear in slightly different form is Goethe's first part of *Faust*.

The proktophantasmist, one of Goethe's characters, utters a wonderfully funny complaint (not rendered here word for word): " I have conclusively proven that ghosts have no legs, so – *stop dancing*!"

The Discourager is from "The Discourager of Hesitancy" a sequel to "The Lady or the Tiger?" by Frank R. Stockton.

The stranger is Jack Schaefer's Shane.

The Eternal Champion – mercilessly punned on here – is an ongoing hero in many, many, *many* novels by the British fantasist Michael Moorcock. Though quite a few of them are easy to forget, they are all enjoyable to read and reread.

PART II

(*Second section*)

This chapter names all of the daytime dramas on American TV at the time it was written. The hardest to fit in was *Ryan's Hope*. See if you can spot where it is punnishly worked in near the end of the chapter.

(*Third section*)

Dr. Tom is modeled on *Days of Our Lives*'s "tentpole" character, played by Macdonald Carey.

Like Cinderella, Louisa Stone is patterned on Louise Shaffer, whom it may be apparent, I've always had a crush on.

(*Tenth section*)

Fillmore's blackouts correspond to TV's two-minute commercial breaks back then.

PART III

"Brightly dawns the Wedding Day" varies "Brightly dawns our wedding day" from Act Two of *The Mikado*.

ACT I

"…untimely ripped" is from the last act of Shakespeare's Scottish play.

ACT IV, SCENE III

This is a parody of the famous Third Murderer scene from the Scottish play. It appears as the third scene of the third act there, too. The riddle of the third murderer's identity has puzzled scholars for nearly four hundred years and some of the proposed solutions are preposterous. At Penn State my late wife Saralee came up with a spectacular answer that I used in my third Hilary Quayle mystery novel *Bullets for Macbeth*. I was happy to learn that our answer was used in a production at the Stratford, Canada, Shakespeare Festival.

Tubal's complaint about Shylock's short-sightedness had more details in the original manuscript. He said that to escape the burden of becoming Christian, Shylock and his daughter Jessica migrated to what is now Miami, Florida, where Shylock became a shrewd land developer.

This scene sets up the next, based on events in Shakespeare's *Measure for Measure*.

The scene between Richard III and Isabella is, in the play, between her and Angelo, but by now I had the idea that it would be fun to substitute villains from one play to another. I did this twice. This is the first one. The second time brought Cassius from *Julius Caesar* to *Hamlet*.

ACT V

This act clearly is based on Shakespeare's final play *The Tempest*.

SCENE I

"O Captain! My Captain!" is a well-known Walt Whitman poem about the death of Abraham Lincoln.

SCENE TWO

"What place is this, Petruchio?" A shipwreck off the coast of Bermuda was Shakespeare's inspiration for *The Tempest*.

SCENE NINE

"'Ban, 'Ban, Ca – Caliban!" is part of the lyric for a song based on the text.

SCENE TEN

"Eight Bears, frolicking." is a stage direction from Scott Joplin's opera *Treemonisha*.

SCENE TWELVE

King Kong, Delia refers to a much-criticized episode on the soap opera *Ryan's Hope* in which Delia Reed Ryan Ryan Coleridge, marvelously played by the adorable Ilene Kristen, is captured in a tower in Central Park by a large ape.

" ... *the knight on Bear Mountain!*" is, of course, an atrocious pun on Moussorgski's tone poem *Night on Bare Mountain*, which plays near the end of Walt Disney's *Fantasia*.

EPITHALAMIUM

"No way. I have higher things in my mind." refers to Fillmore's final adventure *The Cosmic Umbrella*.

THE COSMIC UMBRELLA

PROLOGUE

Professor J. Adrian Fillmore (Gad! What a name!) sat upon a bluff overlooking the sea and thought about Cinderella. *God!* he thought. *She is so beautiful! If only—*

Well, his life was full of if onlys, lots of them. It amused him, at least, that he'd just thought of the name of the alleged deity as a figure of speech.

A vestigial habit. But what if—?

He'd been thinking about that for quite a while. He clutched his transdimensional umbrella and tried to figure out where to go to begin his new quest, but he had not yet worked out that detail.

"Oh, Pwee-sant Professor!" Boris Frankenstein declared, joining him and sitting down. "See? You didn't think I'd ever learn how to pronounce that word."

"Good job!" Fillmore admitted. "So how's it going?"

"As usual—bitters and mistcakes and rather too many fairy maidens."

The professor sighed. "Don't remind me."

A flock of geese flew overhead.

"How wonderful," Boris said, "to be able to fly. But of course, you have your own method of doing that."

"True, I do."

"And that reminds me—I've been thinking that it's about time for you to get ready to go off on another chapter of your cosmic adventures."

"I expect so."

"Where do you intend to go this time? Maybe I'll come along."

"You're very welcome, but of course you know that. But here's the thing—I can't seem to decide where to tell the bumbershoot to take me to—even though I do know what I'm going to look for. Or maybe I should say who."

"Do please fill me in!"

"I want to see whether God exists."

"Really?! I thought you didn't believe."

"I don't, but what if I'm wrong?"'

"So you want to find God. Then what?"

"I haven't thought it through that far."

The creature laughed. "Well, it does sound like a case of hubris."

"Yes, I'm afraid so."

Time passed. The sun shone down on them indifferently.

"When," Boris asked, "will you be going?"

"As soon as I figure out where to go. I have thought of a few places. Such as the Graeco-Roman Empire since its jam-packed with deities, the same ones with different names."

"So why not?"

"It's just too violent. I also thought about the so-called Twilight of the Gods, but that's way too cold!"

Boris thought about it for a while and then held up his hand. "From what I understand, a lot of people think of Heaven as a place in the clouds. I don't know how, since clouds are so insubstantial, but I suppose that's no problem if you're a spirit."

"Hm." The professor considered it. "You may have something there."

"As they say, let luck go with you. Unfortunately, I won't. It's just not my thing."

"I can't blame you, Boris." Fillmore rose and held up his umbrella.

"What? Right now?"

"As good a time as any. Goodbye, dear friend."

CASTING CALL

What amazed him is that these were clouds he could walk on. And since clouds are really condensed water, like fog, this was quite some achievement. But it's where the umbrella took him. Straight ahead he saw a large building, which he wondered whether it was built or decreed into existence. He walked up to its front door and passed through, entering a large open space with a big sign posted on the wall—

TALENT

Sign in and wait your turn

What on earth? Or Heaven, I should say. Think. He saw a second sign affixed to the main double-door entry.

Pick a God, any God.

He walked into a large room containing curved rows of tables, two sloping aisles and an oval-shaped central area. A bearded man with frameless glasses sat at a table with pencil and clipboard in front of him. A little way further along, a long-haired blonde, also holding pencil and clipboard, stood and smiled as she saw the man who'd just entered.

"Splendid!" she proclaimed. "Our third judge!" She went over to

Fillmore and shook his hand. "Oh, you'll need—" and she gave him a clipboard and pencil. "There's a sharpener on the wall if you need it."

"Thanks, but what's this about my being a judge?"

"Well, I thought that's who you must be. Anyone else isn't permitted in here."

The professor shrugged. "I can be a judge, I guess. A judge of what?"

"This sector," said the bearded man, "needs a new deity. We have to pick one from the applicants."

"There's eight of them," the woman said. "By the way, my name's Messalina."

"As in the Roman empress?"

"I *am* the Roman empress!"

"Pleased to meet you."

"So you've obviously heard of me. All good, I expect."

"Oh, yes, definitely!" He'd heard of her, all right. She'd been married to Claudius, later Caesar and she was supposed to have slept with every man, woman and child in Rome.

"And what, may I ask, is your name?"

He said what it was and got the usual gaddish reaction. The man just coughed.

"Fillmore said, "I haven't been introduced yet to this gentleman."

"I'm Friedrich Nietzsche," the man answered. "I'm a philosopher."

"Oh, yes," the professor said. "I've read many of your books." He quoted an aphorism, 'What is done out of love is beyond good and evil.' I've always loved that!"

Nietzsche did something he seldom did. He smiled.

"Well, gentlemen, if you're both ready, shall we see the first applicant?"

They both said yes. Messalina pushed a button on the table before him and the door opened.

And Laurel and Hardy entered, complete with jackets, long neckties and bowler hats. They bowed to the judges in the most courtly manner possible and then they produced a long cloth scroll with writing on it. They stretched it out between them, but it was upside down. When they realized that, they stepped closer to each other and fiddled with the sign for a few seconds and then they stretched it out again...only this time the lettering was facing the wall and not the judges. Another confused moment and then they finally got it right. The sign said:

They gathered up the sign and put it away, then went off to the (actor's) right. Music began to play and it was Mendelssohn's Scherzo from *A Midsummer Night's Dream.* Stanley began to enter, but Ollie held him back. He then walked in first looking ever so important—until he tripped and fell flat on his face. He got up and gestured impatiently for Stan to join him. They looked upstage and suddenly there stood a large apple tree. Laurel pointed to one of the apples and pantomimed eating it. Hardy nodded and waved at him to go to the tree and get one.

Laurel and Hardy in the Garden of Eden

Laurel did so, but of course when he got there he couldn't reach, it was way too high. He tried climbing the tree, but he couldn't manage to find any place to lodge his foot, so next he went back to the right edge of the playing area and then ran toward the tree and at the last moment he jumped and soared straight up so that he was directly opposite a branch filled with apples. He started to reach for one, but stopped when Ollie whistled at him. Stan looked down, saw that his position was untenable and promptly fell to the floor, landing on his head, which smooshed his bowler over his eyes. He sat up, pried it off and put it back on properly.

Fillmore chuckled, Messalina smiled and even Nietzsche looked amused.

Laurel thought about it for a moment and then called Ollie to come over. He mimed what to do, so Hardy braced himself against the tree trunk and Laurel scrambled up onto his shoulders. He managed to stand up and when he reached for an apple, he succeeded and got one, at which point he and Ollie and the apple all hit the ground...and so did the tree.

The three judges all laughed.

Stanley scrambled to his feet and took a bite of the apple. He smiled, obviously enjoying it. Then he offered the unbitten side of it to Ollie, who tried it and also smiled, rubbing his tummy appreciatively.

But just then God, who was actually played by Jimmy Finlayson, entered left. He saw the condition of his tree, scowled and then marched up to the boys, shaking his finger at them. They promptly set things right, upending the tree so that when it steadied itself as it had been before, its trunk landed squarely on Ollie's foot. He yanked it out, took off his shoe and began massaging his toes.

Meanwhile, God gestured somewhere off left and Lilith (Mae Busch) entered. God whispered something to her and she nodded, then sidled over to Ollie. She threw her arms around him and gave him such a passionate kiss that steam rose up from his head and his hat flew off. When she was done, he plopped onto the ground, panting and waving his hand at himself to cool off.

Stanley watched this with great interest and when his partner hit the ground, he walked past him, grabbed Lilith and kissed her just as passionately as she'd did done. This time smoke rose from *her* forehead. When he released her, she also slumped onto the floor, fanning herself as well.

God snapped his fingers, pointed off left and Lilith went out with God following behind.

Now that they were alone again, Ollie got to his feet, found the apple and took another bite of it before passing it back to Stanley. The latter also bit it, but then he held up a finger, made sure he had his friend's attention and then said, "I've got an idea!"

"Do tell!"

"I think," said Laurel, "that we should leave this place and go somewhere east of Eden. We could find us a house and move in and make it into a very cozy home that we can both live in. And every morning for breakfast we can have orange juice and pancakes with maple syrup and coffee and ... and we'll live happily ever after!"

Ollie tried to follow this, but became confused. "Tell me that again," he said.

Stanley nodded. "We ought to move east of a house and get us another Eden (my, that makes sense!) and we can have maple juice every morning for breakfast. And we can also eat orange pancakes and coffee and ... and we'll live happily ever after!"

Babe (his friends's nickname for Hardy) beamed like the midday sun. "That's a good idea! Let's do it right away!"

"All right, let's!"

Mr. Laurel began to exit left, but Mr. Hardy stopped him and then went first, which resulted in his tripping again and landing on his belly. Stan, not noticing, walked right over him.

"Hey!" Ollie bellowed.

"Hey what?!"

"Aren't you going to do something?"

"What?"

"Do something to help me!"

Mr. Laurel smiled, tipped his hat and helped the other to his feet. They then walked off, Mendelssohn's music playing till it ended.

The three judges applauded. "That was very entertaining," Messalina said.

The two men came back onto the playing area. "Thank you," Hardy smiled. "We put in a lot of work to bring it off."

"I imagine you did. There's just one thing—"

"Yes?"

"You already had a God in your scene."

"True, but so?"

"So you didn't do anything godlike."

Stan spoke up. "But we *can* do that, you know."

Fillmore noticed that when they weren't in character, both of the boys spoke with intelligence and discernment. He said, "All right, then. Tell us how you'd run the world we're trying to find a god for."

Hardy nodded. "First thing we'd do, we'd make sure all of our people had enough food and had jobs that they enjoy doing. We'd clean up the water and we'd make the work week just five days long."

"And we'd sing all the babies to sleep every night," Stanley added.

"Will you give us a moment?" Messalina asked.

"Certainly," they both replied.

She went into a huddle with the men. "I really like them!"

"Me, too," the professor agreed.

"They're surprisingly amiable," Nietzsche concurred. "But what's wrong with them? I can see there's something troubling you both."

"Afraid there is," said Fillmore. "What if they've played clumsy idiots for so long that they can't break the habit? The outcome could be disastrous."

"But funny," Nietzsche pointed out.

"Look at them now, though," the empress suggested. "They're quite competent."

"Yes, I see that," the professor agreed. "But how can we be sure?"

"So you don't think we should take the chance."

"No, Your Majesty, I don't."

She sighed. "Oh, very well." Raising her voice, she said, "Gentlemen, we all love your act … but I'm afraid you're just not what we're looking for."

"That's all right," said Hardy. "We don't mind."

"However," she continued, "we would like to appoint you both as our professional understudies. It does pay."

Two broad smiles ensued. "That sounds great!" Laurel exclaimed.

"Leave us your card," she said, "so we'll know how to get in touch with you. By the way, where do you live?"

"Just where we said," Laurel replied. "East of Eden. And we do have orange juice and pancakes and coffee every morning for breakfast."

"It sounds like you've both got very nice lives."

"Yes, we do," Laurel agreed.

"So why," she wondered, "would you want to take on the responsibilities of being a god?"

"Now that you mention it," Hardy said, "we don't."

"In that case," the empress suggested, "why don't you just go on home and enjoy your rich existence?"

"That's just what we'll do!" Laurel said, but frowned. "Does that mean we don't get paid?"

"Oh, no," she said. "You'll still be sent your salaries."

"In that case," said Hardy, twiddling his tie, "toodle-oo!"

And they left the room, though on the way out, Hardy once more tripped and fell flat on his face.

* * * *

Messalina pushed the call button and the next auditioner walked in. He was a lanky hayseed wearing overalls. He had a guitar on a strap round his shoulders. Without a word of introduction or explanation, he strummed a chord and then began to sing:

> Now there's an office in the sky
> Where the angels zip on by
> And this memo on the desk is from the Lord:
> "If the Devil phones so bold
> You just put his call on hold.
> He ain't got diddly-squat to say that I ain't heard!"
> Now that's the memo of the Lord,
> With his terrible swift sword,
> But it don't apply to you and not to me.
> Call him any night or day,
> He'll say "Howdy" right away—
> He's a good boss. His line is always free.
> He's on call from sun to sun,
> 'cause his work day's never done—
> And he don't do lunch, he don't take coffee breaks.

Like a good ol' country Doc,
He's on duty round the clock,
And you oughta see the prophets that He makes!
There's Isaiah, Zeke an' Joe,
Obadiah and you know
That the words they wrote are meant for you and me.
And the gist of what they say
Is love your neighbour every day
'Taint Revelation—just our comp'ny policy.
So here's a memo from the Lord:
"If you're feeling sad and bored,
Take a look around and see what you can do—
Help the poor who've never smiled,
Feed the hungry, hug a child!
While you're at it, clean my air and water, too!"
That's the memo from the Lord
And his terrible swift sword
He has beat into this gilded office plaque:

DO GOOD DEEDS AND YOU WILL FIND
PEACE OF HEART AND PEACE OF MIND
AND THIS GOLDEN RULE WILL NEVER GET THE SACK!

"Now what the hell was that?" the empress asked.

"Ma'am," said the bumpkin, "y' really oughta not use words like that."

"Noted. But what does your song have to do with your trying out to become a god?"

"Shucks," he grinned, shuffling a foot, "I weren't doin' that, ma'am."

"Then why are you here?"

"Jes's wanted to put in a good word for the Great Good God above."

"I see. All right, then, it's been put." She turned to the other judges. "Any questions?"

"No," the professor said. Nietzsche just shook his head.

"In that case," Messalina said, "Mr.—?"

"Jes's call me Lem."

"Very well, Lem—now how do I put this?"

"I think I can say it right," the philosopher put in.

"Please do, Friedrich."

He nodded, then addressed the hayseed. "Don't call us, we'll call you."

* * * *

"Now brace yourself, gents," she said. "This is going to be a big one." She pressed the call button.

Through the door strode a large group of deities. There was Jupiter a/k/a Zeus and there was Hermes/Mercury. Venus alias Aphrodite did her best to enchant them, whereas Hephaestus/Vulcan ignored them while he honed the edge of a battleaxe. More of them filled the playing area, but none of them did anything.

"Well?" Nietzsche asked. "What are you all going to do? Sing? Dance? Do card tricks?"

"We will rule you!" Zeus/Jupiter proclaimed.

"Ah, I see!" the Roman empress said. "*Next!*"

* * * *

Well, the next group were the gods out of Valhalla, but they made so much noise and wouldn't stop singing and fighting that the three judges had to put their fingers in their ears. They tried to get through to them, but couldn't penetrate the wall of noise. The gods decided for themselves that this wasn't the place for them and so they clamorously exited, but not before they took a few encores.

All three heaved sighs of exhaustion and relief.

"I'm not quite ready to see anybody else," Messalina complained. "Could we just spend a little time in small talk?"

"I don't do small talk," Nietzsche demurred as he began to jot down whatever he felt he had to write.

"I like a bit of conversation," the professor said. "Name the subject."

No hesitation whatsoever. "By all means, sex."

Fillmore blushed. "I barely remember that."

"Well, we could kill a little time having some fun. I don't mind if he watches."

"I'd be too embarrassed!"

"Pity. Oh, well, I suppose we'd better call in the next loser." A button prod. "Next!"

The door opened, but what entered was not a person, it was an amorphous pink shape.

"What on earth *are* you?" Messalina asked it.

"The spirit of love," it told them, which made Nietzsche make a rude noise as he did a double-take.

"And you think you could become a god?" she asked.

"Love is everything!" it asserted.

"No, I think not. That'll be all."

"Wait, lovely lady! Let me at least embrace you."

"Phone it in. *Next!*"

It dissipated without leaving the room.

There was an unaccountable pause and then the air grew unaccountably colder.

"What's happening?" the professor worried.

"Whatever it is," Messalina said, "I don't think it's good."

Nietzsche excused himself and left the room.

An insubstantial entity drifted into their space. Fillmore was suddenly frightened.

"Calm down," Messalina said. "This is just the ghost of an idea."

"What does it call itself?"

"Dianetics. It's pestered me before."

"But dianetics," Fillmore said, "is long dead!"

"That's why I'm a ghost!" the entity replied and then vanished.

* * * *

A sudden cacophony of clacking. The door entered and Nietzsche slipped back in.

"What's that dreadful noise?" he asked.

Neither of his colleagues had the slightest idea.

A large group of men entered. They wore shirts and had armbands on their sleeves and they also wore eye-shades. Each one of them had an old typewriter which they proceeded to set down and then began pounding at, stopping every now and then to check ledgers set beside them.

The judges all were totally puzzled.

"What are they doing?" Fillmore asked. "Who are they working for?"

"For US!" The door slammed open and a number of men marched in. They all were dressed in Brooks Brothers suits and ties and they all seemed ever so satisfied with themselves.

"Who are you?" Messalina wanted to know. "And why the accountants?"

A portly gentleman with white hair and a red rose in his lapel stepped forward. "The accountants work for us. They mustn't stop, for our empires keep on growing exponentially, you see."

"That's all very well," Nietzsche protested, "but why are you at an audition for the sector's latest god? Are you applying en masse? Deity by committee?"

The portly man smiled. "Oh, my dear man—"

"I am *not* your dear man!"

"In answer to your question, we are already gods ... or at least what we worship is the true God."

"And what do you worship?"

"Why, money, of course! You see, in America—"

"America?" Nietzsche echoed. "Never heard of it."

"It's in the New World!"

That irritated Messalina. "Isn't the old world good enough?!"

The portly man just shook his head, but he continued. "In America, we represent the best hope for survival of that God-blessed land."

"Yes? But who are you?"

"We are the G. O. P."

"And what is that?" Nietzsche asked.

Fillmore answered. "It means the Grand Old Party. Also known as Republicans."

"Oh, I get it," the empress said. "We're talking politics."

"Yes," the professor groused. "Bad politics."

The portly man at last introduced himself as William Jennings Harrison the third. "Money, I repeat, is the true God. We Republicans serve it. And that's how we will govern this sector, which, by the way, we've already bought."

Messalina smiled sourly. "That sounds to me suspiciously like corruption. *Next!*"

The Republicans and their accountants retired huffily.

"What pompous asses!" Nietzsche declared.

"Don't let their utter ridiculousness fool you," Fillmore warned. "They can be dangerous."

"Not to us," the philosopher scoffed. "Though they do remind me of certain German nationalists."

"Well, at least they're gone," Messalina said. "And now we've got another applicant, or rather applicants, waiting for us to pay them some attention."

Ecstatic music! In danced a company of fairies—not the tiny, airy variety, but full-grown and dressed in various shades of forest green. They were succeeded by their ruler, King Oberon and his wife Queen Titania.

"Please identify yourself," said Messalina.

"I am King Oberon, ruler of the Fairy Kingdom."

"I'm Queen Titania. And these are our people."

Lots of dancing ensued.

The empress said, "Now I hope you are here because we have to choose a god for this sector."

Oberon smiled. "No, not at all! We merely crave an audience. Sit back and let us entertain you." And with a wave of his hand, he set the fairies in motion. They danced and sang and told delightful stories and when they were done they offered the judges all kinds of delectable food and drink.

Nietzsche declined to try anything, while Messalina said she had to watch her figure. Fillmore reached out for some kind of brandy, but then remembered that fey food might very well put him into an extended sleep, so he reluctantly said no.

"And now," Oberon began, but suffered a rib-nudge from his wife.

"It's time that I be heard. These two men and this woman have been a fine audience, although—" Her brow darkened. "—none of you will eat anything we tried to give you. Still, I'm feeling generous—kindly, even—so you are all forgiven."

"Thank you, my beloved," Oberon said when he was sure that she had nothing further to say. And I so appreciate the way you enjoyed our little show that I feel quite generous toward you. Thus I promise that none of the fey folk will ever do you any kind of mischief."

The queen muttered, "For a while, anyway."

With quite a quantity of sparkling fairy dust, they all danced out, singing as they went.

"I rather enjoyed that," said Messalina.

"Definitely diverting," said the philosopher.

"I'm only sorry I didn't eat anything," Fillmore mourned.

"Yes, well if you had," said Messalina, "you'd probably be sleeping for a decade or so."

"Is there anyone else?" Nietzsche asked.

"One more."

"Well, bring her or him or whatever in," said Nietzsche.

"Coming up." She pressed the call button.

A tall man entered. He wore a tuxedo and top hat, which he doffed. He drew a red silk handkerchief out of his breast pocket and it suddenly turned into a long cane. He bowed to them and said, "Lady! Gentlemen! Let me entertain you!" And with that, he launched into a chorus of the song by that name. The judges endured it graciously. Next the tall man produced showers of coins and cards and then made seemingly solid large rings link with one another without making a sound, as well as many other wonders.

When he was done, Fillmore said, "Deftly done, sir, but what does it have to do with you becoming a god?"

The other grinned. "I'm so glad you asked me that! But first, allow me to introduce myself. I am the Great Razzledini! You may have heard of me?"

"Afraid not," the professor said. "Maybe my colleagues have?"

Messalina and Nietzsche both shook her heads.

"Well, never mind," Fillmore said. "Mr. Razzledini—"

"Mr. GREAT Razzledini!"

"Yes. You were about to say?"

"What I just showed you," the G. Razzledini replied, "was only a warm-up. Now watch this!" Flowers shot from his fingertips and then the heavens loomed above them and they were full of incident—explosions, comets and planetary collisions.

"Yes, very impressive," Nietzsche judged, "but I'm more concerned with this sector, not cosmic interplay. Do you have anything in your bag of tricks—"

"Illusions, please!"

"Illusions, then. Do you have anything, for instance, that would be able to end hunger or pollution?"

"A mere bagatelle! Lo and behold!" And he showed them his solutions and they were excellent.

Nietzsche called a conference. "I've got to admit," he said to the others, "this guy is good."

"He does seem to have the right stuff," Messalina agreed. "I think he may be our man." She turned to the professor. "But you're not saying anything. What gives?"

"I'm just not convinced."

"Why not?" she asked.

"I myself could probably come up with a five-year plan—no, I'm not a communist!—that could make things the way they should be."

"Possibly," said Nietzsche, "but you're not an applicant. So what's your point?"

"My point is this—there's something about this Great Razzledini that I don't trust."

"Could you be specific?" Messalina asked.

"I'm working on it. Let me have a minute." And then Fillmore suddenly noticed the off-colored hue of the magician's skin and the way the skin was stretched around his eyes. He reached out and flicked at his temple and it all fell off like a mask, which of course it was and instead of the Great Razzledini there stood instead none other than—

Satan!

"Well, you've found me out," His Infernal Nibs admitted, "but what does it matter? I *can* do the things I showed you. I can also vanquish death and cut down on the population without resorting to pestilence or anything unpleasant and I can cure the sector—for that matter, I can cure each and every populated planet of pollution! So what do you say? Am I your man? I mean, your God?"

"You've been after this job for quite some time," the professor observed.

"Yes, I have."

"But he's got a good argument," Nietzsche admitted.

"He's the Devil incarnate!" Fillmore shrilled. "It doesn't matter what he tells us! He's the Prince of Lies and proud of it!"

"So what?" Nietzsche said. "I think we should give him a chance. We can let him have a three-month trial."

"He wouldn't need more than three minutes to do endless mischief," the professor groaned. "Messalina, what do you think?"

"I admit that I'm worried. I don't think that we can trust him."

"Exactly!"

"So, it's two to one against," she said. "I'm afraid, Mr. Great Razzle-dini, that we can't use you."

"You will live to regret this!" the conjurer growled and then disappeared in a shower of sparks and thunderclaps.

"Curious smell of sulphur," Messalina declared, fanning the air. "Well, we're almost done. There's just one more. He just showed up."

They brought him in – a middle-aged man in a flowing white Greek robe. He introduced himself. "I am Socrates. You may have heard of me."

All the judges nodded.

"I did not come to audition," the philosopher said, "but when I heard that one of you is Nietzsche, I had to come, in hopes of discussing our field of endeavour."

"But how," Nietzsche asked, "could you know about me? They killed you long before my time on Earth."

"True, but I always kept up with what has been happening in philosophy. I've even read some of the religious ones, despite my dislike of all things churchly-dogmatic. I found Joseph Butler interesting and certainly David Hume, though he *was* a bit wordy. I've read Kierkegaard and Bertrand Russell and very much liked him and also Jean-Paul Sartre and Albert Camus – "

"Yes," Nietzsche cut in, "but what do you wish to discuss with me?"

Socrates nodded his head somberly. "I wonder whether you agree with me that he who inflicts harm is more miserable than those he hurts."

"Absolutely!" The German scowled. "My dreadful sister actually told one of those abominable Nazis that Hitler was the model for my *übermensch*. Bah! That evil mad mass murderer was the ultimate *under-man*!"

Socrates smiled, which the judges did not realize was a rare thing for him. "I was especially interested in your essay on the genealogy of morals."

"Why?"

"Because of your interpretation of the Bible's two testaments."

A vigorous head nod. "Yes! In the older of the two, there is good and bad, but the newer set of gospels disemploys badness and refers, instead, to evil, which is why so much vileness has been committed by the various churches throughout the ages.

"Yes," Nietzsche exclaimed, "We're all better off without gods."

"Amen," said Socrates. "And yes, I meant that ironically." He nodded to the trio and left.

"So now what do we do?" Fillmore asked. "We didn't find anyone. Should we schedule another set of callbacks?"

"Why don't we just give it?" Nietzsche replied. "What do you think, Messalina?"

But she was sound asleep and had been ever since Socrates began talking.

"Don't wake her," said Nietzsche as he shook Fillmore's hand and said, "I must thank you again for liking my aphorism about love."

"It was a real pleasure to meet you."

"You are in a very select company. Well, I must go. God be with you!"

The professor looked shocked.

"It was a joke! Goodbye! Though that also presumes there is a deity." And he departed.

"Well, that's that." Fillmore pressed the umbrella's catch. For want of any better idea, he returned to Limbo.

AND IN THE BEGINNING …

He looked around disapprovingly. "It wouldn't be so bad here if there was anything to look at. Such as grass or a carpet."

Both things instantly appeared. The grass was green, the carpet red.

"Whoa! How did that happen?!" He couldn't imagine his expressed wish brought it about, but he thought he'd try something else and see if that worked, too. "How about some clouds in the sky?"

And there they were.

"Well, I guess it's true, then. My wish is my command."

The possibilities were endless. He thought and thought and finally said, "Let this world no longer be flat, but let it roll and dip and undulate, but very gently."

And the landscape took on a delightful character.

"Some trees and flowers and some water would also be nice."

Trees sprang up everywhere and the grass became festooned with roses and hollyhocks, lilies, tulips and forget-me-nots, as well as daisies and other species. A sparkling stream started to flow a little way off.

"Now we need some houses—nothing too big or fancy, mind you, but cozy and self-heated with non-pollutant fuel."

Cottages appeared everywhere.

"No, that's too many. Reduce it by about a quarter."

It happened as he said.

"And finally we need people to live in them. Let there be men and women and children—babies, too—and in that case, let there be diapers and harmless detergents and laundries (make them free) and let the people consist of men and women of all races and colors and let them be friendly and helpful and have no prejudices or stupid ideas like the G. O. P. and let them all have loving hearts."

A happy hubbub suddenly sprang up and folks of all sorts came over and introduced themselves and shook his hand. This took quite a while. Then Fillmore realized he'd left something important out.

"Let there be twenty-four days a month and let there be nights of equal proportion and let there be sun, moon and stars."

And it came to pass.

He looked appreciatively at his handiwork. "So this is what feels like to be a god. Not bad. This is a very nice world I've made. Good job, professor! But I'm sure I've left something out—what? He slapped his forehead. "Of course! Literature! Let there be novels and poems, plays, films and short stories and let there be riddles and nonfiction and puzzles of all sorts and let this all include everything I've ever read or wanted to read!" He snapped his fingers. "And let there be music of all kinds, classical and popular, opera and chorales, folk songs and oratorios, all that I've ever heard or wanted to hear and don't forget painting and sculpture!"

There suddenly sprang up a large museum with a library next to it, while on its other side stood an art gallery.

"But what else am I forgetting? This is a full-time job! Oh, yes, let there be hobbies and food and totally-safe-to-drive whiskey/whisky and all others goodthings to drink and let there be clothing of every kind." He took a deep breath. "This is going to take some time. I'll have to take a break soon. But I know I've left out something very important. What?"

It came to him then and he decreed into existence a large number of artists and philosophers, cooks and mechanics and even some janitors.

And on this still-unnamed place that used to be Limbo came, at Fillmore's call, Charles Dickens and Wilkie Collins, all of the Benson clan, Henry and M. R. James, L. Frank Baum, William M. Thackeray, Henry Fielding, Oscar Wilde, Bram Stoker, Jane Austen and all of the Brontes. And here was Robinson Crusoe and Captain Bligh, to whom Fillmore said an appreciative word or two. And he also rubbed shoulders with

Scrooge and Marley and the Swiss Family Robinson, as well as Citizen Kane and Shane and Hondo and even Donald and Daffy Duck, who still complained that he couldn't understand anything Donald said.

And suddenly of their own volition, terraces appeared with table and chairs and waiters serving coffee and tea and things like scotch and other hard liquors and nowhere did Fillmore see money exchange hands because he hadn't willed it into existence, nor did he mean to. He helped himself to a scotch on the rocks—decreeing that hangovers would never happen—and he looked everywhere at a great variety of marvels.

Here at a table sipping coffee were Sherlock Holmes and Professor Moriarty and they were pondering a mathematical problem together. At the table next to them, Count Dracula was having a blood transfusion. Standing near Holmes was Dr (British usage) Watson, who was flirting with one of the waitresses. In another place, Captain Bligh and Fletcher Christian were hugging each other, Captain Philip Francis Queeg (who looked a lot like Humphrey Bogart) was shaking hands with Lieutenant Maryk (Van Johnson). Best of all, Prince Hal was giving fat old Falstaff a big hug, which greatly affected the professor. He had to dry his eyes.

"I think that's as much as I can do for now," he told himself. "I'll do some more stuff later ... *wait!* How could I forget?! Two more things! Let there be Scotland!"

And it appeared in the distance and was so beautiful it brought tears to his eyes.

"Finally," he declared, Let there be—"

But he didn't have to finish, for as soon as the thought came to mind, it came about. A beautiful woman who looked exactly like Mary Tyler Moore when she was younger and before she'd contracted diabetes or been savaged by Edward Albee hurried across the room to Fillmore and hugged him for all she was worth.

"Jimmy!" she exclaimed. "My adorable Jimmy! When will you marry me?"

"At once! I'll arrange it as soon as I can!"

"Good! Let me have a taste of that." She sipped the scotch. "That's Glen Turret—but you know you shouldn't pour a single malt over ice!"

A taste for scotch and the knowledge to go with it! Now I know what to call this place!

"Why, what are you thinking?" she asked.

"I just decided on what to name this planet."

"Yes."

"From this moment on, this place shall be known as Paradise!"

She kissed his cheek. "It already is."

"Please don't be offended, but what's your name?"

"Why, what else? Laura Petrie!"

"Of course. But I thought you were married."

"Don't be silly, Jimmy! I've been saving myself for you."

So J. Adrian Fillmore (waive all future Gads!) and his wife-to-be Laura and all of the people whom he created or recreated—and he was pleased to see Nietzsche, who waved at him, but he was now clean-shaven and did not wear glasses—and all the people, to repeat and the professor and Laura—well, they all lived happily ever after.

And high in the sky, he heard Boris declare, "Amen!"

The End of
The Cosmic Umbrella.

ANNOTATIONS

CASTING CALL

Messalina was the wife of the emperor Claudius, surely Rome's best Caesar, though he often was made fun of.

Friedrich Nietzsche was the greatest German philosopher and still is and NO!!! he was *not* a Nazi sympathizer. He hated German naturalism. It was indeed his sister who rewrote some of his work after he was put into an asylum, insane. She *was* involved with a Nazi officer and had the nerve to tell Hitler that he was her brother's "Superman."

Jimmy Finlayson ("Fin") was the comic villain of many Laurel & Hardy movies, though sometimes he was just an innocent victim who ran afoul of their idiotic attempts to make money.

Fillmore barely remembering sex echoes a time when I took my sister Evelyn (Evey) and brother-in-law Paul, who were visiting Manhattan from Philadelphia, to a performance of the improv troupe Chicago City Limits (CCL). At the first half of the show, the audience was asked to call out fantasies that the actors might use for a sketch after the intermission. Paul, on my left, immediately shouted, "Having sex!" Evey, on my right, then called, "*Enjoying* sex!" Then I made the suggestion that CCL used:

"Remembering sex … "

Mae Busch appeared in many L&H movies. One of her best is "Them Thar Hills" and its sequel "Tit for Tat."

Fillmore's opinions about Republicans are, of course, my own.

The Great Razzledini is based on one of my best friends R. J. Lewis, a professional magician who appeared in the Broadway musical *Barnum*, both onstage and as the lobby magician. Star of several excellent short films, he is a superb chef, an excellent writer whose stories I have bought and a converted Jew who probably knows more about the religion than Moses.

Socrates needs no introduction. One of his most interesting dialogues (i. e., Plato's) is *Gorgias*, which has true dramatic power as one of its characters and Socrates become impassioned in arguing for and against the philosopher's contention that wrongdoers suffer more than their victims. It has been suggested that this unpopular doctrine contributed to Socrates's death by hemlock and that one of the citizens who helped condemn him was Callicles, his opponent in *Gorgias*.

AND IN THE BEGINNING…

Mary Tyler Moore—I confess to having a lifelong crush on her, too, and I'm still mourning her death.

www.ingramcontent.com/pod-product-compliance
Lightning Source LLC
Chambersburg PA
CBHW030745030726
47497CB00001B/133

* 9 7 8 1 4 7 9 4 4 2 1 9 5 *